THE BEST FANTASY STORIES FROM THE MAGAZINE OF Fantasy & Science Fiction

EDITED BY EDWARD L. FERMAN

OCTOPUS BOOKS LIMITED

This edition first published in 1985
by arrangement with The Magazine of Fantasy and Science Fiction
by

Octopus Books Limited
59 Grosvenor Street
London WI

Editor: Jennifer Rhys
Art Editor: Ronnie Wilkinson
Jacket Designer: Fiona Carpenter

ISBN 0 7064 2568 5

Printed in the United States of America
by R.R. Donnelley and Sons Company

CONTENTS

FAR FROM HOME

Walter S. Tevis

The first inkling the janitor had of the miracle was the smell of it. This was a small miracle in itself: the salt smell of kelp and sea water in the Arizona morning air. He had just unlocked the front entrance and walked into the building when the smell hit him. Now this man was old and normally did not trust his senses very well; but there was no mistaking this, not even in this most inland of inland towns: it was the smell of ocean—deep ocean, far out, the ocean of green water, kelp and brine.

And strangely, because the janitor was old and tired, and because this was the part of early morning that seems unreal to many old men, the first thing the smell made him feel was a small, almost undetectable thrilling in his old nerves, a memory deeper than blood of a time fifty years before when he had gone once, as a boy, to San Francisco and had watched the ships in the bay and had discovered the fine old dirty smell of sea water. But this feeling lasted only an instant. It was replaced immediately with amazement—and then anger, although it would have been impossible to say with what he was angry, here in this desert town, in the dressing rooms of the large public swimming pool at morning, being reminded of his youth and of the ocean.

'What the hell's going on here?' the janitor said.

There was no one to hear this, except perhaps the small boy who had been standing outside, staring through the wire fence into the pool and clutching a brown paper sack in one grubby hand, when the janitor had come up to the building. The man had paid no attention to the boy; small boys were always around the swimming pool in summer—a nuisance. The boy, if he had heard the man or not, did not reply.

The janitor walked on through the concrete-floored dressing rooms, not even stopping to read the morning's crop of obscenities scribbled on the walls of the little wooden booths. He walked into the tiled anteroom, stepped across the disinfectant foot bath, and out onto the wide concrete edge of the swimming pool itself.

Some things are unmistakable. There was a whale in the pool.

And no ordinary, everyday whale. This was a monumental creature, a whale's whale, a great, blue-gray leviathan, ninety feet long and thirty feet across the back, with a tail the size of a flatcar and a head like the smooth fist of a titan. A blue whale, an old shiny, leathery monster with barnacles on his gray underbelly and his eyes filmed with age and wisdom and myopia, with brown seaweed dribbling from one corner of his mouth, marks of the suckers of squid on his face, and a rusted piece of harpoon sunk in the unconscious blubber of his back. He rested on his belly in the pool, his back way out of the water and with his monstrous gray lips together in an expression of contentment and repose. He was not asleep; but he was asleep enough not to care where he was.

And he stank—with the fine old stink of the sea, the mother of us all; the brackish, barnacled, grainy salt stink of creation and old age, the stink of the world that was and of the world to come. He was beautiful.

The janitor did not freeze when he saw him; he froze a moment afterwards. First he said, aloud, his voice matter-of-fact, 'There's a whale in the swimming pool. A God damn whale.' He said this to no one—or to everyone—and perhaps the boy heard him, although there was no reply from the other side of the fence.

After speaking, the janitor stood where he was for seven minutes, thinking. He thought of many things, such as what he had eaten for breakfast, what his wife had said to him when she had awakened him that morning. Somewhere, in the corner of his vision, he saw the little boy with the paper sack, and his mind thought, as minds will do at such times, *Now that boy's about six years old. That's probably his lunch in that sack. Egg salad sandwich. Banana. Or apple.* But he did not think about the whale, because there was nothing to be thought about the whale. He stared at its unbelievable bulk, resting calmly, the great head in the deep water under the diving boards, the corner of one tail fluke being lapped gently by the shallow water of the wading pool.

The whale breathed slowly, deeply, through its blow hole. The janitor breathed slowly, shallowly, staring, not blinking even in the rising sunlight, staring with no comprehension at the eighty-five ton miracle in the swimming pool. The boy held his paper sack tightly at the top, and his eyes, too, remained fixed on the whale. The sun was rising in the sky over the desert to the east, and its light glinted in red and purple iridescence on the oily back of the whale.

And then the whale noticed the janitor. Weak-visioned, it peered at him filmily for several moments from its grotesquely small eye. And then it arched its back in a ponderous, awesome, and graceful movement, lifted its tail twenty feet in the air, and brought it down in a way that seemed strangely slow, slapping gently into the water with it. A hundred gallons of water rose out of the pool, and enough of it drenched the janitor to wake him from the state of partial paralysis into which he had fallen.

Abruptly the janitor jumped back, scrambling from the water, his eyes looking, frightened, in all directions, his lips white. There was nothing to see but the whale and the boy. 'All right,' he said, 'all right,' as if he had somehow seen through the plot, as if he knew, now, what a whale would be doing in the public swimming pool, as if no one was going to put anything over on *him*. 'All right,' the janitor said to the whale, and then he turned and ran.

He ran back into the center of town, back toward Main Street, back toward the bank, where he would find the chairman of the board of the City Parks Commission, the man who could, somehow —perhaps with a memorandum—save him. He ran back to the town where things were as they were supposed to be; ran as fast as he had ever run, even when young, to escape the only miracle he would ever see in his life and the greatest of all God's creatures . . .

After the janitor had left, the boy remained staring at the whale for a long while, his face a mask and his heart racing with all the peculiar excitement of wonder and love—wonder for all whales, and love for the only whale that he, an Arizona boy of six desert years, had ever seen. And then, when he realized that there would be men there soon and his time with his whale would be over, he lifted the paper sack carefully close to his face, and opened its top about an inch, gingerly. A commotion began in the sack, as if a small animal were in it that wanted desperately to get out.

'Stop that!' the boy said, frowning.

The kicking stopped. From the sack came a voice—a high-pitched, irascible voice, with a Gaelic accent. 'All right, whatever-your-name-is,' the voice said, 'I suppose you're ready for the second one.'

The boy held the sack carefully with his thumb and forefinger. He frowned at the opening in the top. 'Yes,' he said, 'I think so . . .'

When the janitor returned with the two other men, the whale was no longer there. Neither was the small boy. But the seaweed smell and the splashed, brackish water were there still, and in the pool were several brownish streamers of seaweed, floating aimlessly in the chlorinated water, far from home.

MY DEAR EMILY

Joanna Russ

S AN FRANCISCO, 188-

I am so looking forward to seeing my dear Emily at last, now she is grown, a woman, although I'm sure I will hardly recognize her. She must not be proud (as if she could be!) but will remember her friends, I know, and have patience with her dear Will who cannot help but remember the girl she was, and the sweet influence she had in her old home. I talk to your father about you every day, dear, and he longs to see you as I do. Think! a learned lady in our circle! But I know you have not changed . . .

Emily came home from school in April with her bosom friend Charlotte. They had loved each other in school, but they didn't speak much on the train. While Emily read Mr. Emerson's poems, Charlotte examined the scenery through opera-glasses. She expressed her wish to see 'savages.'

'That's foolish,' says Emily promptly.

'If we were carried off,' says Charlotte. 'I don't think you would notice it in time to disapprove.'

'That's very foolish,' says Emily, touching her round lace collar with one hand. She looks up from Mr. Emerson to stare Charlotte out of countenance, properly, morally, and matter-of-course young lady. It has always been her style.

'The New England look,' Charlotte snaps resentfully. She makes her opera-glasses slap shut.

'I should like to be carried off,' she proposes; 'but then I don't have an engagement to look forward to. A delicate affair.'

'You mustn't make fun,' says Emily. Mr. Emerson drops into her lap. She stares unseeing at Charlotte's opera-glasses.

'Why do they close?' she asks helplessly.

'I beg your pardon?' blankly, from Charlotte.

'Nothing. You're much nicer than I am,' says Emily.

'Look,' urges Charlotte kindly, pressing the toy into her friend's hand.

'For savages?'

Charlotte nods, Emily pushes the spring that will open the little machine, and a moment later drops them into her lap where they fall on Mr. Emerson. There is a cut across one of her fingers and a blue pinch darkening the other.

'They hurt me,' she says without expression, and as Charlotte takes the glasses up quickly, Emily looks with curious sad passivity at the blood from her little wound, which has bled an incongruous passionate drop on Mr. Emerson's clothbound poems. To her friend's surprise (and her own, too) she begins to cry, heavily, silently, and totally without reason.

He wakes up slowly, mistily, dizzily, with a vague memory of having fallen asleep on plush. He is intensely miserable, bound down to his bed with hoops of steel, and the memory adds nausea to his misery, solidifying ticklishly around his bare hands and the back of his neck as he drifts towards wakefulness. His stomach turns over with the dry brushy filthiness of it. With the caution of the chronically ill, he opens his eyelids, careful not to move, careful even to keep from focusing his gaze until—he thinks to himself —his bed stops holding him with the force of Hell and this intense miserable sickness goes down, settles . . . Darkness. No breath. A glimmer of light, a stone wall. He thinks: *I'm dead and buried, dead and buried, dead and*—With infinite care he attempts to breathe, sure that this time it will be easy; he'll be patient, discreet, sensible, he won't do it all at once—

He gags. Spasmodically he gulps, cries out, and gags again, springing convulsively to his knees and throwing himself over the low wall by his bed, laboring as if he were breathing sand. He starts to sweat. His heartbeat comes back, then pulse, then seeing, hearing, swallowing . . . High in the wall a window glimmers, a star is out, the sky is pale evening blue. Trembling with nausea he rises to his feet, sways a little in the gloom, then puts out one arm and steadies himself against the stone wall. He sees the window, sees the door ahead of him. In his tearing eyes the star suddenly blazes and lengthens like a knife; his head is whirling, his heart painful as a man's; he throws his hands over his face, longing for life and strength to come back, the overwhelming flow of force that will crest at sunrise, leaving him raging at the world and ready to kill anyone, utterly proud and contemptuous, driven to sleep as the last resort of a balked assassin. But it's difficult to stand, difficult to breathe: *I wish I were dead and buried, dead and buried, dead and buried—But there!* he whispers to himself like a charm, *There, it's going, it's going away.* He smiles slyly round at his companionable, merciful stone walls. With an involuntarily silent, gliding gait he moves towards the door, opens the iron gate, and goes outside. Life is coming back. The trees are black against the sky, which yet holds some light; far away in the West lie the radiant memories of a vanished sun. An always vanished sun.

'Alive!' he cries, in triumph. It is—as usual—his first word of the day.

Dear Emily, sweet Emily, met Martin Guevara three days after she arrived home. She had been shown the plants in the garden and the house plants in stands and had praised them; she had been shown the sun pictures and had praised *them;* she had fingered antimacassars, promised to knit, exclaimed at gaslights, and passed two evenings at home, doing nothing. Then in the hall that led to the pantry sweet Will had taken her hand and she had dropped her eyes because you were supposed to and that was her style. Charlotte (who slept in the same room as her friend) embraced her at bedtime, wept over the handtaking, and then Emily said to her dear, dear friend (without thinking):

'Sweet William.'

Charlotte laughed.

'It's not a joke!'

'It's so funny.'

'I love Will dearly.' She wondered if God would strike her dead for a hypocrite. Charlotte was looking at her oddly, and smiling.

'You mustn't be full of levity,' said Emily, peeved. It was then that sweet William came in and told them of tomorrow's garden-party, which was to be composed of her father's congregation. They were lucky, he said, to have acquaintances of such position and character. Charlotte slipped out on purpose and Will, seeing they were alone, attempted to take Emily's hand again.

'Leave me alone!' Emily said angrily. He stared.

'I said leave me alone!'

And she gave him such a look of angry pride that, in fact, he did.

Emily sees Guevara across the parlor by the abominable cherry-red sofa, talking animatedly and carelessly. In repose he is slight, undistinguished, and plain, but no one will ever see him in repose;

Emily realizes this. His strategy is never to rest, to bewilder, he would (she thinks) slap you if only to confuse you, and when he can't he's always out of the way and attacking, making one look ridiculous. She knows nobody and is bored; she starts for the door to the garden.

At the door his hand closes over her wrist; he has somehow gotten there ahead of her.

'The lady of the house,' he says.

'I'm back from school.'

'And you've learned—?'

'Let me go, please.'

'Never.' He drops her hand and stands in the doorway. She says:

'I want to go outside.'

'Never.'

'I'll call my father.'

'Do.' She tries and can't talk; I wouldn't *bother,* she thinks to herself, loftily. She goes out into the garden with him. Under the trees his plainness vanishes like smoke.

'You want lemonade,' he says.

'I'm not going to talk to you,' she responds. 'I'll talk to Will. Yes! I'll make him—'

'In trouble,' says Mr. Guevara, returning silently with lemonade in a glass cup.

'No thank you.'

'She wants to get away,' says Martin Guevara. 'I know.'

'If I had your trick of walking like a cat,' she says, 'I could get out of anything.'

'I *can* get out of anything,' says the gentleman, handing Emily her punch, 'Out of an engagement, a difficulty. I can even get *you* out of anything.'

'I loathe you,' whispers Emily suddenly. 'You walk like a cat. You're ugly.'

'Not out here,' he remarks.

'Who has to be afraid of lights?' cries Emily energetically. He stands away from the paper lanterns strung between the trees, handsome, comfortable and collected, watching Emily's cut-glass cup shake in her hand.

'I can't move,' she says miserably.

'Try.' She takes a step towards him. 'See; you can.'

'But I wanted to go *away!*' With sudden hysteria she flings the lemonade (cup and all) into his face, but he is no longer there.

'What are you doing at a church supper, you hypocrite!' she shouts tearfully at the vacancy.

Sweet William has to lead her in to bed.

'You thought better of it,' remarks Martin, head framed in an evening window, sounds of footsteps outside, ladies' heels clicking in the streets.

'I don't know you,' she says miserably, 'I just don't.' He takes her light shawl, a pattern in India cashmere.

'That will come,' he says, smiling. He sits again, takes her hand, and squeezes the skin on the wrist.

'Let me go, please?' she says like a child.

'I don't know.'

'You talk like the smart young gentlemen at Andover; they were all fools.'

'Perhaps you overawed them.' He leans forward and puts his hand around the back of her neck for a moment. 'Come on, dear.'

'What are you talking about!' Emily cries.

'San Francisco is a lovely city. I had ancestors here three hundred years ago.'

'Don't think that because I came here—'

'She doesn't,' he whispers, grasping her shoulder, 'she doesn't know a thing.'

'God damn you!'

He blinks and sits back. Emily is weeping. The confusion of the room—an over-stuffed, over-draped hotel room—has gotten on her nerves. She snatches for her shawl, which is still in his grasp, but he holds it out of her reach, darting his handsome, unnaturally young face from side to side as she tries to reach round him. She falls across his lap and lies there, breathless with terror.

'You're cold,' she whispers horrified, 'you're cold as a corpse.' The shawl descends lightly over her head and shoulders. His frozen hands help her to her feet. He is delighted; he bares his teeth in a smile.

'I think,' he says, tasting it, 'that I'm going to visit your family.'

'But you don't—'she stumbles—'you don't want to . . . sleep with me. I know it.'

'I can be a suitor like anyone else,' he says.

That night Emily tells it all to Charlotte, who, afraid of the roué, stays up and reads a French novel as the light drains from the windows and the true black dark takes its place. It is towards dawn and Charlotte has been dozing, when Emily shakes her friend awake, kneeling by the bed with innocent blue eyes reflecting the dying night.

'I had a terrible dream,' she complains.

'Hmmmm?'

'I dreamed,' says Emily tiredly. 'I had a nightmare. I dreamed I was walking by the beach and I decided to go swimming and then a . . . a thing, I don't know . . . it took me by the neck.'

'Is that all?' says Charlotte peevishly.

'I'm sick,' says Emily with childish satisfaction. She pushes Charlotte over in the bed and climbs in with her. 'I won't have to see that man again if I'm sick.'

'Pooh, why not?' mumbles Charlotte.

'Because I'll have to stay home.'

'He'll visit you.'

'William won't let him.'

'Sick?' says Charlotte then, suddenly waking up. She moves away from her friend, for she has read more bad fiction than Emily and less moral poetry.

'Yes, I feel awful,' says Emily simply, resting her head on her knees. She pulls away in tired irritation when her friend reaches for the collar of her nightdress. Charlotte looks and jumps out of bed.

'Oh,' says Charlotte. 'Oh—goodness—oh—' holding out her hands.

'What on earth's the matter with you?'

'He's—' whispers Charlotte in horror, 'He's—'

In the dim light her hands are black with blood.

'You've come,' he says. He is lying on his hotel sofa, reading a newspaper, his feet over one arm and a hand trailing on the rug.

'Yes,' she answers, trembling with resolution.

'I never thought this place would have such a good use. But I never know when I'll manage to pick up money—'

With a blow of her hand, she makes a fountain of the newspaper; he lies on the sofa, mildly amused.

'Nobody knows I came,' she says rapidly. 'But I'm going to finish you off. I know how.' She hunts feverishly in her bag.

'I wouldn't,' he remarks quietly.

'Ah!' Hauling out her baby cross (silver), she confronts him with it like Joan of Arc. He is still amused, still mildly surprised.

'In your hands?' he says delicately. Her fingers are loosening, her face pitiful.

'My dear, the significance is in the feeling, the faith, not the

symbol. You use that the way you would use a hypodermic needle.
Now in your father's hands—'

'I dropped it,' she says in a little voice. He picks it up and hands
it to her.

'You can touch—' she says, her face screwing up for tears.

'I can.'

'Oh my God!' she cries in despair.

'My dear.' He puts one arm around her, holding her against him,
a very strong man for she pushes frantically to free herself. 'How
many times have I said that! But you'll learn. Do I sound like the
silly boys at Andover?' Emily's eyes are fixed and her throat
contracts; he forces her head between her knees. 'The way you go
on, you'd think I was bad luck.'

'I—I—'

'And you without the plentiful lack of brains that characterizes
your friend. She'll be somebody's short work and I think I know
whose.'

Emily turns white again.

'I'll send her around to you afterwards. Good God! What do you
think will happen to her?'

'She'll die,' says Emily clearly. He grasps her by the shoulders.

'Ah!' he says with immense satisfaction. 'And after that? Who
lives forever after that? Did you know that?'

'Yes, people like you don't die,' whispers Emily. 'But you're not
people—'

'No,' he says intently, 'No. We're not.' He stands Emily on her
feet. 'We're a passion!' Smiling triumphantly, he puts his hands on
each side of her head, flattening the pretty curls, digging his fingers
into the hair, in a grip Emily can no more break than she could
break a vise.

'We're passion,' he whispers, amused. 'Life is passion. Desire
makes life.'

'Ah, let me go,' says Emily.

He smiles ecstatically at the sick girl.

'Desire,' he says dreamily, 'lives; *that* lives when nothing else
does, and we're desire made pure, desire walking the Earth. Can a
dead man walk? Ah! If you want, want, want . . .'

He throws his arms around her, pressing her head to his chest
and nearly suffocating her, ruining her elaborate coiffure and
crushing the lace at her throat. Emily breathes in the deadness
about him, the queer absence of odor, or heat, or presence; her
mouth is pressed against the cloth of his fashionable suit, expensive

stuff, a good dollar a yard, gotten by—what? But his hands are strong enough to get anything.

'You see,' he says gently, 'I enjoy someone with intelligence, even with morals; it adds a certain—And besides—' here he releases her and holds her face up to his—'we like souls that come to us; these visits to the bedrooms of unconscious citizens are rather like frequenting a public brothel.'

'I abhor you,' manages Emily. He laughs. He's delighted.

'Yes, yes, dear,' he says, 'But don't imagine we're callous parasites. Followers of the Marquis de Sade, perhaps—you see Frisco has evening hours for its bookstores!—but sensitive souls, really, and apt to long for a little conscious partnership.' Emily shuts her eyes. 'I said,' he goes on, with a touch of hardness, 'that I am a genuine seducer. I flatter myself that I'm not an animal.'

'You're a monster,' says Emily, with utter conviction. Keeping one hand on her shoulder, he steps back a pace.

'Go.' She stands, unable to believe her luck, then makes what seems to her a rush for the door; it carries her into his arms.

'You see?' He's pleased; he's proved a point.

'I can't,' she says, with wide eyes and wrinkled forehead . . .

'You will.' He reaches for her and she faints.

Down in the dark where love and some other things make their hidingplace, Emily drifts aimlessly, quite alone, quite cold, like a dead woman without a passion in her soul to make her come back to life.

She opens her eyes and finds herself looking at his face in the dark, as if the man carried his own light with him.

'I'll die,' she says softly.

'Not for a while,' he drawls, sleek and content.

'You've killed me.'

'I've loved.'

'Love!'

'Say "taken" then, if you insist.'

'I do! I do!' she cried bitterly.

'You decided to faint.'

'Oh the hell with you!' she shouts.

'Good girl!' And as she collapses, weeping hysterically, 'Now, now, come here, dear . . . ' nuzzling her abused little neck. He kisses it in the tenderest fashion with an exaggerated, mocking sigh; she twists away, but is pulled closer and as his lips open over the teeth of inhuman, dead desire, his victim finds—to her surprise

—that there is no pain. She braces herself and then, unexpectedly, shivers from head to foot.

'Stop it!' she whispers, horrified. 'Stop it! Stop it!'

But a vampire who has found a soul-mate (even a temporary one) will be immoderate. There's no stopping them.

Charlotte's books have not prepared her for *this*.

'You're to stay in the house, my dear, because you're ill.'

'I'm not,' Emily says, pulling the sheet up to her chin.

'Of course you are.' The Reverend beams at her, under the portrait of Emily's dead mother which hangs in Emily's bedroom. 'You've had a severe chill.'

'But I have to get out!' says Emily, sitting up. 'Because I have an appointment, you see.'

'Not now,' says the Reverend.

'But I *can't* have a severe chill in the *summer!*'

'You look so like your mother,' says the Reverend, musing. After he has gone away, Charlotte comes in.

'I have to stay in the damned bed,' says Emily forcefully, wiggling her toes under the sheet. Charlotte, who has been carrying a tray with tea and a posy on it, drops it on the washstand.

'Why, Emily!'

'I have to stay in the damned bed the whole damned day,' Emily adds.

'Dear, why do you use those words?'

'Because the whole world's damned!'

After the duties of his employment were completed at six o'clock on a Wednesday, William came to the house with a doctor and introduced him to the Reverend and Emily's bosom friend. The street lamps would not be lit for an hour but the sun was just down and the little party congregated in the garden under remains of Japanese paper lanterns. No one ever worried that these might set themselves on fire. Lucy brought tea—they were one of the few civilized circles in Frisco—and over the tea, in the darkening garden, to the accompaniment of sugar-tongs and plopping cream (very musical) they talked.

'Do you think,' says the Reverend, very worried, 'that it might be consumption?'

'Perhaps the lungs are affected,' says the doctor.

'She's always been such a robust girl.' This is William, putting down the teapot which has a knitted tube about the handle, for insulation. Charlotte is stirring her tea with a spoon.

'It's very strange,' says the doctor serenely, and he repeats 'it's very strange' as shadows advance in the garden. 'But young ladies, you know—especially at twenty—young ladies often take strange ideas into their heads; they do, they often do; they droop; they worry.' His eyes are mild, his back sags, he hears the pleasant gurgle of more tea. A quiet consultation, good people, good solid people, a little illness, nothing serious—

'No,' says Charlotte. Nobody hears her.

'I knew a young lady once—' ventures the doctor mildly.

'No,' says Charlotte, more loudly. Everyone turns to her, and Lucy, taking the opportunity, insinuates a plate of small-sized muffins in front of Charlotte.

'I can tell you all about it,' mutters Charlotte, glancing up from under her eyebrows. 'But you'll *laugh*.'

'Now, dear—' says the Reverend.

'Now, miss—' says the doctor.

'As a friend—' says William.

Charlotte begins to sob.

'Oh,' she says, 'I'll—I'll tell you about it.'

Emily meets Mr. Guevara at the Mansion House at seven, having recovered an appearance of health (through self-denial) and a good solid record of spending the evenings at home (through self-control). She stands at the hotel's wrought-iron gateway, her back rigid as a stick, drawing on white gloves. Martin materializes out of the blue evening shadows and takes her arm.

'I shall like living forever,' says Emily, thoughtfully.

'God deliver me from Puritans,' says Mr. Guevara.

'What?'

'You're a lady. You'll swallow me up.'

'I'll do anything I please,' remarks Emily severely, with a glint of teeth.

'Ah.'

'I will.' They walk through the gateway. 'You don't care two pins for me.'

'Unfortunately,' says he, bowing.

'It's not unfortunate as long as *I* care for me,' says Emily, smiling with great energy. 'Damn them all.'

'You proper girls would overturn the world.' Along they walk in the evening, in a quiet, respectable rustle of clothes. Halfway to the restaurant she stops and says breathlessly:

'Let's go—somewhere else!'

'My dear, you'll ruin your health!'

'You know better. Three weeks ago I was sick as a dog and much you cared; I haven't slept for days and I'm fine.'

'You look fine.'

'Ah! You mean I'm beginning to look dead, like you.' She tightens her hold on his arm, to bring him closer.

'Dead?' says he, slipping his arm around her.

'Fixed. Bright-eyed. Always at the same heat and not a moment's rest.'

'It agrees with you.'

'I adore you,' she says.

When Emily gets home, there's a reckoning. The Reverend stands in the doorway and sad William, too, but not Charlotte, for she is on the parlor sofa, having had hysterics.

'Dear Emily,' says the Reverend. 'We don't know how to tell you this—'

'Why, Daddy, *what?*' exclaims Emily, making wide-eyes at him.

'Your little friend told us—'

'Has something happened to Charlotte?' cries Emily. 'Oh tell me, tell me, what happened to Charlotte?' And before they can stop her she has flown into the parlor and is kneeling beside her friend, wondering if she dares pinch her under cover of her shawl. William, quick as a flash, kneels on one side of her and Daddy on the other.

'Dear Emily!' cries William with fervor.

'Oh sweetheart!' says Charlotte, reaching down and putting her arms around her friend.

'You're well!' shouts Emily, sobbing over Charlotte's hand and thinking perhaps to bite her. But the Reverend's arms lift her up.

'My dear,' says he, 'you came home unaccompanied. You were not at the Society.'

'But,' says Emily, smiling dazzlingly, 'two of the girls took all my hospital sewing to their house because we must finish it right away and I have not—'

'You have been lying to us,' the Reverend says, *Now*, thinks Emily, *sweet William will cover his face*. Charlotte sobs.

'She can't help it,' says Charlotte brokenly. 'It's the spell.'

'Why, I think everyone's gone out of their minds,' says Emily, frowning. Sweet William takes her from Daddy, leading her away from Charlotte.

'Weren't you with a gentleman tonight?' says Sweet Will firmly. Emily backs away.

'For shame!'

'She doesn't remember it,' explains Charlotte; 'it's part of his spell.'

'I think you ought to get a doctor for *her*,' observes Emily.

'You were with a gentleman named Guevara,' says Will, showing less tenderness than Emily expects. 'Weren't you? Well—weren't you?'

'Bad cess to you if I was!' snaps Emily, surprised at herself. The other three gasp. 'I won't be questioned,' she goes on, 'and I won't be spied upon. And I think you'd better take some of Charlotte's books away from her; she's getting downright silly.'

'You have too much color,' says Will, catching her hands. 'You're ill but you don't sleep. You stay awake all night. You don't eat. But look at you!'

'I don't understand you. Do you want me to be ugly?' says Emily, trying to be pitiful. Will softens; she sees him do it.

'My dear Emily,' he says. 'My dear girl—we're afraid for you.'

'Me?' says Emily, enjoying herself.

'We'd better put you to bed,' says the Reverend kindly.

'You're so kind,' whispers Emily, blinking as if she held back tears.

'That's a good girl,' says Will, approving. 'We know you don't understand. But we'll take care of you, Em.'

'*Will* you?'

'Yes, dear. You've been near very grave danger, but luckily we found out in time, and we found out what to do; we'll make you well, we'll keep you safe, we'll—'

'Not with *that* you won't,' says Emily suddenly, rooting herself to the spot, for what William takes out of his vest pocket (where he usually keeps his watch) is a broad-leaved, prickle-faced dock called wolfsbane; it must distress any vampire of sense to be so enslaved to pure superstition. But enslaved they are, nonetheless.

'Oh, no!' says Emily swiftly. 'That's silly, perfectly silly!'

'Common sense must give way in such a crisis,' remarks the Reverend gravely.

'You bastard!' shouts Emily, turning red, attempting to tear the charm out of her fiance's hand and jump up and down on it. But the Reverend holds one arm and Charlotte the other and between them they pry her fingers apart and William puts his property gently in his vest-pocket again.

'She's far gone,' says the Reverend fearfully, of his angry daughter. Emily is scowling, Charlotte stroking her hair.

'Ssssh' says Will with great seriousness. 'We must get her to bed,' and between them they half-carry Emily up the stairs and put her, dressed as she is, in the big double bed with the plush headboard that she has shared so far with Charlotte. Daddy and fiancé confer in the room across the long, low rambling hall, and Charlotte sits by her rebellious friend's bed and attempts to hold her hand.

'I won't permit it; you're a damned fool!' says Emily.

'Oh, Emmy!'

'Bosh.'

'It's true!'

'Is it?' With extraordinary swiftness, Emily turns round in the bed and rises to her knees. 'Do you know anything about it?'

'I know it's horrid, I—'

'Silly!' Playfully Emily puts her hands on Charlotte's shoulders. Her eyes are narrowed, her nostrils widened to breathe; she parts her lips a little and looks archly at her friend. 'You don't know anything about it,' she says insinuatingly.

'I'll call your father,' says Charlotte quickly.

Emily throws an arm around her friend's neck.

'Not yet! Dear Charlotte!'

'We'll save you,' says Charlotte doubtfully.

'Sweet Charrie; you're my friend, aren't you?'

Charlotte begins to sob again.

'Give me those awful things, those leaves.'

'Why, Emily, I *couldn't!*'

'But he'll come for me and I have to protect myself, don't I?'

'I'll call your father,' says Charlotte firmly.

'No, I'm *afraid.*' And Emily wrinkles her forehead sadly.

'Well—'

'Sometimes I—I—' falters Emily. 'I can't move or run away and everything looks so—so strange and *horrible*—'

'Oh, here!' Covering her face with one hand, Charlotte holds out her precious dock leaves in the other.

'Dear, dear! Oh, sweet! Oh thank you! Don't be afraid. He isn't after you.'

'I hope not,' says the bosom friend.

'Oh no, he told me. It's me he's after.'

'How awful,' says Charlotte, sincerely.

'Yes,' says Emily. 'Look.' And she pulls down the collar of her dress to show the ugly marks, white dots unnaturally healed up, like the pockmarks of a drug addict.

'Don't!' chokes Charlotte.

Emily smiles mournfully. 'We really ought to put the lights out,' she says.

'Out!'

'Yes, you can see him better that way. If the lights are on, he could sneak in without being seen; he doesn't mind lights, you know.'

'I don't know, dear—'

'I do.' (Emily is dropping the dock leaves into the washstand, under cover of her skirt.) 'I'm afraid. Please.'

'Well—'

'Oh, you must!' And leaping to her feet, she turns down the gas to a dim glow; Charlotte's face fades into the obscurity of the deepening shadows.

'So. The lights are out,' says Emily quietly.

'I'll ask Will—' Charlotte begins . . .

'No, dear.'

'But, Emily—'

'He's coming, dear.'

'You mean Will is coming.'

'No, not Will.'

'Emily, you're a—'

'I'm a sneak,' says Emily, chuckling. 'Ssssh!' And, while her friend sits paralyzed, one of the windows swings open in the night breeze, a lead-paned window that opens on a hinge, for the Reverend is fond of culture and old architecture. Charlotte lets out a little noise in her throat; and then—with the smash of a pistol shot—the gaslight shatters and the flame goes out. Gas hisses into the air, quietly, insinuatingly, as if explaining the same thing over and over. Charlotte screams with her whole heart. In the dark a hand clamps like a vise on Emily's wrist. A moment passes.

'Charlotte?' she whispers.

'Dead,' says Guevara.

Emily has spent most of the day asleep in the rubble, with his coat rolled under her head where he threw it the moment before sunrise, the moment before he staggered to his place and plunged into sleep. She has watched the dawn come up behind the rusty barred gate, and then drifted into sleep herself with his face before her closed eyes—his face burning with a rigid, constricted, unwasting vitality. Now she wakes aching and bruised, with the sun of late afternoon in her face. Sitting against the stone wall, she sneezes twice and tries, ineffectually, to shake the dust from her silk skirt.

Oh, how—she thinks vaguely—*how messy.* She gets to her feet. *There's something I have to do.* The iron gate swings open at a touch.

Trees and gravestones tilted every which way. What did he say? Nothing would disturb it but a Historical Society.

Having tidied herself as best she can, with his coat over her arm and the address of his tailor in her pocket, she trudges among the erupted stones, which tilt crazily to all sides as if in an earthquake. Blood (Charlotte's, whom she does not think about) has spread thinly on to her hair and the hem of her dress, but her hair is done up with fine feeling, despite the absence of a mirror, and her dress is dark gray; the spot looks like a spot of dust. She folds the coat into a neat package and uses it to wipe the dust off her shoes, then lightens her step past the cemetery entrance, trying to look healthy and respectable. She aches all over from sleeping on the ground.

Once in town and having ascertained from a shop window that she will pass muster in a crowd, Emily trudges up hills and down hills to the tailor, the evidence over her arm. She stops at other windows, to look or to admire herself; thinks smugly of her improved coloring; shifts the parcel on her arm to show off her waist. In one window there is a display of religious objects—beads and crosses, books with fringed gilt bookmarks, a colored chromo of the Madonna and Child. In this window Emily admires herself.

'It's Emily, dear!'

A Mrs. L———appears in the window beside her, with Constantia, Mrs. L———'s twelve-year-old offspring.

'Why, dear, whatever happened to you?' says Mrs. L———, noticing no hat, no gloves, and no veil.

'Nothing; whatever happened to you?' says Emily cockily. Constantia's eyes grow wide with astonishment at the fine, free audacity of it.

'Why, you look as if you'd been—'

'Picknicking,' says Emily, promptly. 'One of the gentlemen spilled beer on his coat.' And she's in the shop now and hanging over the counter, flushed, counting the coral and amber beads strung around a crucifix.

Mrs. L———knocks doubtfully on the window-glass.

Emily waves and smiles.

Your father—form Mrs. L———'s lips in the glass.

Emily nods and waves cheerfully.

They do go away, finally.

'A fine gentleman,' says the tailor earnestly, 'a very fine man.' He lisps a little.

'Oh very fine,' agrees Emily, sitting on a stool and kicking the rungs with her feet. 'Monstrous fine.'

'But very careless,' says the tailor fretfully, pulling Martin's coat nearer the window so he can see it, for the shop is a hole-in-the-wall and dark. 'He shouldn't send a lady to this part of the town.'

'I was a lady once,' says Emily.

'Mmmmm.'

'It's fruit stains—something awful, don't you think?'

'I cannot have this ready by tonight,' looking up.

'Well, you must, that's all,' says Emily calmly. 'You always have and he has a lot of confidence in you, you know. He'd be awfully angry if he found out.'

'Found out?' sharply.

'That you can't have it ready by tonight.'

The tailor ponders.

'I'll positively stay in the shop while you work,' says Emily flatteringly.

'Why, Reverend, I saw her on King Street as dirty as a gypsy, with her hair loose and the wildest eyes and I *tried* to talk to her, but she dashed into a shop—'

The sun goes down in a broad belt of gold, goes down over the ocean, over the hills and the beaches, makes shadows lengthen in the street near the quays where a lisping tailor smooths and alters, working against the sun (and very uncomfortable he is, too), watched by a pair of unwinking eyes that glitter a little in the dusk inside the stuffy shop. (*I think I've changed*, meditates Emily.)

He finishes, finally, with relief, and sits with an *ouf!* handing her the coat, the new and beautiful coat that will be worn as soon as the eccentric gentleman comes out to take the evening air. The eccentric gentleman, says Emily incautiously, will do so in an hour by the Mansion House when the last traces of light have faded from the sky.

'Then, my dear Miss,' says the tailor unctuously, 'I think a little matter of pay—'

'You don't think,' says Emily softly, 'or you wouldn't have gotten yourself into such a mess as to be this eccentric gentleman's tailor.' And out she goes.

Now nobody can see the stains on Emily's skirt or in her hair;

street lamps are being lit, there are no more carriages, and the number of people in the streets grows—San Francisco making the most of the short summer nights. It is perhaps fifteen minutes back to the fashionable part of the town where Emily's hatless, shawlless state will be looked on with disdain; here nobody notices. Emily dawdles through the streets, fingering her throat, yawning, looking at the sky, thinking: I love, I love, I love—

She has fasted for the day but she feels fine; she feels busy, busy inside as if the life inside her is flowering and bestirring itself, populated as the streets. She remembers—

I love you. I hate you. You enchantment, you degrading necessity, you foul and filthy life, you promise of endless love and endless time . . .

What words to say with Charlotte sleeping in the same room, no, the same bed, with her hands folded under her face! Innocent sweetheart, whose state must now be rather different.

Up the hills she goes, where the view becomes wider and wider, and the lights spread out like sparkles on a cake, out of the section which is too dangerous, too low, and too furtive to bother with a lady (or is it something in her eyes?), into the broader by-streets where shore-leave sailors try to make her acquaintance by falling into step and seizing her elbow; she snakes away with unbounded strength, darts into shadows, laughs in their faces: 'I've got what I want!'

'Not like me!'

'Better!'

This is the Barbary Coast, only beginning to become a tourist attraction; there are barkers outside the restaurants advertising pretty waiter girls, dance halls, spangled posters twice the height of a man, crowds upon crowds of people, one or two guides with tickets in their hats, and Emily—who keeps to the shadows. She nearly chokes with laughter: *What a field of ripe wheat!* One of the barkers hoists her by the waist onto his platform.

'Do you see this little lady? Do you see this—'

'Let me go, God damn you!' she cries indignantly.

'This angry little lady—' pushing her chin with one sunburned hand to make her face the crowd. 'This—' But here Emily hurts him, slashing his palm with her teeth, quite pleased with herself, but surprised, too, for the man was holding his hand cupped and the whole thing seemed to happen of itself. She escapes instantly into the crowd and continues up through the Coast, through the old Tenderloin, drunk with self-confidence, slipping like a shadow through the now genteel streets and arriving at the Mansion House gate having seen no family spies and convinced that none has seen her.

But nobody is there.

Ten by the clock, and no one is there, either; eleven by the clock and still no one. *Why didn't I leave this life when I had the chance!* Only one thing consoles Emily, that by some alchemy or nearness to the state she longs for, no one bothers or questions her and even the policemen pass her by as if in her little corner of the gate there is nothing but a shadow. Midnight and no one, half-past and she dozes; perhaps three hours later, perhaps four, she is startled awake by the sound of footsteps. She wakes: nothing. She sleeps again and in her dream hears them for the second time, then she wakes to find herself looking into the face of a lady who wears a veil.

'What!' Emily's startled whisper.

The lady gestures vaguely, as if trying to speak.

'What is it?'

'Don't—' and the lady speaks with feeling but, it seems, with difficulty also—'don't go home.'

'Home?' echoes Emily, stupefied, and the stranger nods, saying:

'In danger.'

'Who?' Emily is horrified.

'He's in danger.' Behind her veil her face seems almost to emit a faint light of its own.

'You're one of them,' says Emily. 'Aren't you?' and when the woman nods, adds desperately, 'Then you must save him!'

The lady smiles pitifully; that much of her face can be seen as the light breeze plays with her net veil.

'But you must!' exclaims Emily, 'You know how; I don't; you've got to!'

'I don't dare,' very softly. Then the veiled woman turns to go, but Emily—quite hysterical now—seizes her hand, saying:

'Who are you? Who are you?'

The lady gestures vaguely and shakes her head.

'Who are you!' repeats Emily with more energy. 'You tell me, do you hear?'

Sombrely the lady raises her veil and stares at her friend with a tragic, dignified, pitiful gaze. In the darkness her face burns with unnatural and beautiful color.

It is Charlotte.

Dawn comes with a pellucid quickening, glassy and ghostly. Slowly, shapes emerge from darkness and the blue pours back into the world—twilight turned backwards and the natural order reversed. Destruction, which is simple, logical, and easy, finds a kind of mocking parody in the morning's creation. Light has no business coming back, but light does.

Emily reaches the cemetery just as the caldron in the east overflows, just as the birds (idiots! she thinks) begin a tentative cheeping and chirping. She sits at the gate for a minute to regain her strength, for the night's walking and worry have tried her severely. In front of her the stones lie on graves, almost completely hard and real, waiting for the rising of the sun to finish them off and make complete masterpieces of them. Emily rises and trudges up the hill, slower and slower as the ground rises to its topmost swell, where three hundred years of peaceful Guevaras fertilize the grass and do their best to discredit the one wild shoot that lives on, the only disrespectful member of the family. Weeping a little to herself, Emily lags up the hill, raising her skirts to keep them off the weeds, and murderously hating in her heart the increasing light and the happier celebrating of the birds. She rounds the last hillock of ground and raises her eyes to the Guevaras' eternal mansion, expecting to see nobody again. There is the corner of the building, the low iron gate—

In front of it stands Martin Guevara between her father and sweet sweet Will, captived by both arms, his face pale and beautiful between two gold crosses that are just beginning to sparkle in the light of day.

'We are caught,' says Guevara, seeing her, directing at her his fixed, white smile.

'You let him go,' says Emily—very reasonably.

'You're safe, my Emily!' cries sweet Will.

'Let him go!' She runs to them, stops, look at them, perplexed to the bottom of her soul.

'Let him go,' she says. 'Let him go, let him go!'

Between the two bits of jewelry, Emily's life and hope and only pleasure smiles painfully at her, the color drained out of his face, desperate eyes fixed on the east.

'You don't understand,' says Emily, inventing. 'He isn't dangerous now. If you let him go, he'll run inside and then you can come back any time during the day and finish him off. I'm sick. You—'

The words die in her throat. All around them, from every tree and hedge, from boughs that have sheltered the graveyard for a hundred years, the birds begin their morning noise. A great hallelujah rises; after all, the birds have nothing to worry about. Numb, with legs like sticks, Emily sees sunlight touch the top of the stone mausoleum, sunlight slide down its face, sunlight reach the level of a standing man—

'I adore you,' says Martin to her. With the slow bending over of a drowning man, he doubles up, like a man stuck with a knife in a dream; he doubles up, falls—

And Emily screams; What a scream! as if her soul were being haled out through her throat; and she is running down the other side of the little hill to regions as yet untouched by the sun, crying inwardly: I need help! help! help! She knows where to get it. Three hundred feet down the hill in a valley, a wooded protecting valley sunk below the touch of the rising sun, there she runs through the trees, past the fence that separates the old graveyard from the new, expensive, cast-iron-and-polished granite—

There, just inside the door (for they were rich people and Charlotte's mother's sister lived in Frisco) lies Emily's good friend, her old friend, with her hat and cloak off and her blonde hair falling over the bier to her knees—Charlotte in a white wrap like a slip. Emily stops inside the door, confused; Charlotte regards her fixedly.

'There's not much time,' says Charlotte.

'Help him!' whispers Emily.

'I can't; he's already gone.'

'Please—please—' but Charlotte only rises glidingly on her couch, lifting her beautiful bare shoulders out of the white silk, fixedly regarding her friend with that look which neither time nor age will do anything to dim.

'I won't,' says Emily, frightened, 'I don't think—' taking a few unwilling steps towards the coffin, 'I don't think that now—'

'You have only a moment,' says Charlotte. Emily is now standing by her friend and slowly, as if through tired weakness, she sinks to her knees.

'Quickly,' says Charlotte, scarcely to be heard at all. Looping one arm around her friend's neck, she pulls the face up to hers.

'But not without him'—Emily is half suffocated—'Not without him! Not this way!' She tries to break the grip and cannot.

'Not without him,' (her voice dying away faintly) 'not without him . . . not without . . . without . . . .'

Sunlight touches the door, a moment too late.

THE MAN WHO PAINTED THE DRAGON GRIAULE

Lucius Shepard

O ther than the Sichi Collection, Cattanay's only surviving works are to be found in the Municipal Gallery at Regensburg, a group of eight oils-on-canvas, most notable among them being *Woman With Oranges*. These paintings constitute his portion of a student exhibition hung some weeks after he had left the city of his birth and traveled south to Teocinte, there to present his proposal to the city fathers; it is unlikely he ever learned of the disposition of his work, and even more unlikely that he was aware of the general critical indifference with which it was received. Perhaps the most interesting of the group to modern scholars, the most indicative as to Cattanay's later preoccupations, is the *Self Portrait*, painted at the age of twenty-eight, a year before his departure.

'The majority of the canvas is a richly varnished black in which the vague shapes of floorboards are presented, barely visible. Two irregular slashes of gold cross the blackness, and within these we can see a section of the artist's thin features and the shoulder panel of his shirt. The perspective given is that we are looking down at the artist, perhaps through a tear in the roof, and that he is looking up at us, squinting into the light, his mouth distorted by a grimace born of intense concentration. On first viewing the painting, I was struck by the atmosphere of tension that radiated from it. It seemed I was spying upon a man imprisoned within a shadow having two golden bars, tormented by the possibilities of light beyond the walls. And though this may be the reaction of the art historian, not the less knowledgeable and therefore more trustworthy response of the gallery-goer, it also seemed that this imprisonment was self-imposed, that he could have easily escaped his confine; but that he had realized a feeling of stricture was an essential fuel to his

ambition, and so had chained himself to this arduous and thoroughly unreasonable chore of perception . . .'

—from *Meric Cattany:*
The Politics of Conception
by Reade Holland, Ph.D

1.

In 1853, in a country far to the south, in a world separated from
this one by the thinnest margin of possibility, a dragon named
Griaule dominated the region of the Carbonales Valley, a fertile area
centering upon the town of Teocinte and renowned for its production of silver, mahogany, and indigo. There were other dragons in
those days, most dwelling on the rocky islands west of Patagonia
—tiny, irascible creatures, the largest of them no bigger than a
swallow. But Griaule was one of the great Beasts who had ruled an
age. Over the centuries he had grown to stand 750 feet high at the
midback, and from the tip of his tail to his nose he was 6,000 feet
long. (It should be noted here that the growth of dragons was due
not to caloric intake, but to the absorption of energy derived from
the passage of time.) Had it not been for a miscast spell, Griaule
would have died millennia before. The wizard entrusted with the
task of slaying him—knowing his own life would be forfeited as a
result of the magical backwash—had experienced a last-second
twinge of fear, and, diminished by this ounce of courage, the spell
had flown a mortal inch awry. Though the wizard's whereabouts
were unknown, Griaule had remained alive. His heart had stopped,
his breath stilled, but his mind continued to seethe, to send forth
the gloomy vibrations that enslaved all who stayed for long within
range of his influence.

This dominance of Griaule's was an elusive thing. The people of
the valley attributed their dour character to years of living under his
mental shadow, yet there were other regional populations who
maintained a harsh face to the world and had no dragon on which to
blame the condition; they also attributed their frequent raids
against the neighboring states to Griaule's effect, claiming to be a
peaceful folk at heart—but again, was this not human nature?
Perhaps the most certifiable proof of Griaule's primacy was the fact
that despite a standing offer of a fortune in silver to anyone who

could kill him, no one had succeeded. Hundreds of plans had been put forward, and all had failed, either through inanition or impracticality. The archives of Teocinte were filled with schematics for enormous steam-powered swords and other such improbable devices, and the architects of these plans had every one stayed too long in the valley and become part of the disgruntled populace. And so they went on with their lives, coming and going, always returning, bound to the valley, until one spring day in 1853, Meric Cattanay arrived and proposed that the dragon be painted.

He was a lanky young man with a shock of black hair and a pinched look to his cheeks; he affected the loose trousers and shirt of a peasant, and waved his arms to make a point. His eyes grew wide when listening, as if his brain were bursting with illumination, and at times he talked incoherently about 'the conceptual statement of death by art.' And though the city fathers could not be sure, though they allowed for the possibility that he simply had an unfortunate manner, it seemed he was mocking them. All in all, he was not the sort they were inclined to trust. But, because he had come armed with such a wealth of diagrams and charts, they were forced to give him serious consideration.

'I don't believe Griaule will be able to perceive the menace in a process as subtle as art,' Meric told them. 'We'll proceed as if we were going to illustrate him, grace his side with a work of true vision, and all the while we'll be poisoning him with the paint.'

The city fathers voiced their incredulity, and Meric waited impatiently until they quieted. He did not enjoy dealing with these worthies. Seated at their long table, sour-faced, a huge smudge of soot on the wall above their heads like an ugly thought they were sharing, they reminded him of the Wine Merchants Association in Regensburg, the time they had rejected his group portrait.

'Paint can be deadly stuff,' he said after their muttering had died down. 'Take vert Veronese, for example. It's derived from oxide of chrome and barium. Just a whiff would make you keel over. But we have to go about it seriously, create a real piece of art. If we just slap paint on his side, he might see through us.'

The first step in the process, he told them, would be to build a tower of scaffolding, complete with hoists and ladders, that would brace against the supraocular plates above the dragon's eye; this would provide a direct route to a seven-hundred-foot-square loading platform and base station behind the eye. He estimated it would take eighty-one thousand board feet of lumber, and a crew of ninety men should be able to finish construction within five months. Ground crews accompanied by chemists and geologists would search out limestone deposits (useful in priming the scales) and sources of pigments, whether organic or minerals such as azurite and hematite. Other teams would be set to scraping the dragon's side clean of algae, peeled skin, any decayed material, and afterward would laminate the surface with resins.

'It would be easier to bleach him with quicklime,' he said. 'But that way we lose the discolorations and ridges generated by growth and age, and I think what we'll paint will be defined by those shapes. Anything else would look like a damn tattoo!'

There would be storage vats and mills: edge-runner mills to separate pigments from crude ores, ball mills to powder the pigments, pug mills to mix them with oil. There would be boiling vats and calciners—fifteen-foot-high furnaces used to produce caustic lime for sealant solutions.

'We'll build most of them atop the dragon's head for purposes of access,' he said. 'On the frontoparital plate.' He checked some figures. 'By my reckoning, the plate's about 350 feet wide. Does that sound accurate?'

Most of the city fathers were stunned by the prospect, but one managed a nod, and another asked, 'How long will it take for him to die?'

'Hard to say,' came the answer. 'Who knows how much poison he's capable of absorbing. It might just take a few years. But in the worst instance, within forty or fifty years, enough chemicals will have seeped through the scales to have weakened the skeleton, and he'll fall in like an old barn.'

'Forty years!' exclaimed someone. 'Preposterous!'

'Or fifty.' Meric smiled. 'That way we'll have time to finish the painting.' He turned and walked to the window and stood gazing out at the white stone houses of Teocinte. This was going to be the sticky part, but if he read them right, they would not believe in the plan if it seemed too easy. They needed to feel they were making a sacrifice, that they were nobly bound to a great labor. 'If it does take forty or fifty years,' he went on, 'the project will drain your resources. Timber, animal life, minerals. Everything will be used up by the work. Your lives will be totally changed. But I guarantee you'll be rid of him.'

The city fathers broke into an outraged babble.

'Do you really want to kill him?' cried Meric, stalking over to them and planting his fists on the table. 'You've been waiting centuries for someone to come along and chop off his head or send him up in a puff of smoke. That's not going to happen! There is no easy solution. But there is a practical one, an elegant one. To use the stuff of the land he dominates to destroy him. It will *not* be easy, but you *will* be rid of him. And that's what you want, isn't it?'

They were silent, exchanging glances, and he saw that they now believed he could do what he proposed and were wondering if the cost was too high.

'I'll need five hundred ounces of silver to hire engineers and artisans,' said Meric. 'Think it over. I'll take a few days and go see this dragon of yours . . . inspect the scales and so forth. When I return, you can give me your answer.'

The city fathers grumbled and scratched their heads, but at last they agreed to put the question before the body politic. They asked for a week in which to decide and appointed Jarcke, who was the mayoress of Hangtown, to guide Meric to Griaule.

The valley extended seventy miles from north to south, and was enclosed by jungled hills whose folded sides and spiny backs gave rise to the idea that beasts were sleeping beneath them. The valley floor was cultivated into fields of bananas and cane and melons, and where it was not cultivated, there were stands of thistle palms and berry thickets and the occasional giant fig brooding sentinel over the rest. Jarcke and Meric tethered their horses a half hour's ride from town and began to ascend a gentle incline that rose into the notch between two hills. Sweaty and short of breath, Meric stopped a third of the way up; but Jarcke kept plodding along, unaware he was no longer following. She was by nature as blunt as her name—a stump beer keg of a woman with a brown, weathered face. Though she appeared to be ten years older than Meric, she was nearly the same age. She wore a gray robe belted at the waist with a leather band that held four throwing knives, and a coil of rope was slung over her shoulder.

'How much farther?' called Meric.

She turned and frowned. 'You're standin' on his tail. Rest of him's around back of the hill.'

A pinprick of chill bloomed in Meric's abdomen, and he stared down at the grass, expecting it to dissolve and reveal a mass of glittering scales.

'Why don't we take the horses?' he asked.

'Horses don't like it up here.' She grunted with amusement. 'Neither do most people, for that matter.' She trudged off.

Another twenty minutes brought them to the other side of the hill high above the valley floor. The land continued to slope upward, but more gently than before. Gnarled, stunted oaks pushed up from thickets of chokecherry, and insects sizzled in the weeds. They might have been walking on a natural shelf several hundred feet across; but ahead of them, where the ground rose abruptly, a number of thick, greenish black columns broke from the earth. Leathery folds hung between them, and these were encrusted with clumps of earth and brocaded with mold. They had the look of a collapsed palisade and the ghosted feel of ancient ruins.

'Them's the wings,' said Jarcke. 'Mostly they's covered, but you can catch sight of 'em off the edge, and up near Hangtown there's places where you can walk in under 'em . . . but I wouldn't advise it.'

'I'd like to take a look off the edge,' said Meric, unable to tear his eyes away from the wings; though the surfaces of the leaves gleamed in the strong sun, the wings seemed to absorb the light, as if their age and strangeness were proof against reflection.

Jarcke led him to a glade in which tree ferns and oaks crowded together and cast a green gloom, and where the earth sloped sharply downward. She lashed her rope to an oak and tied the other end around Meric's waist. 'Give a yank when you want to stop, and another when you want to be hauled up,' she said, and began paying out the rope, letting him walk backward against her pull.

Ferns tickled Meric's neck as he pushed through the brush, and the oak leaves pricked his cheeks. Suddenly he emerged into bright sunlight. On looking down, he found his feet were braced against a fold of the dragon's wing, and on looking up, he saw that the wing vanished beneath a mantle of earth and vegetation. He let Jarcke lower him a dozen feet more, yanked, and gazed off northward along the enormous swell of Griaule's side.

The swells were hexagonals thirty feet across and half that distance high; their basic color was a pale greenish gold, but some were whitish, draped with peels of dead skin, and others were overgrown by viridian moss, and the rest were scrolled with patterns of lichen and algae that resembled the characters of a serpentine alphabet. Birds had nested in the cracks, and ferns plumed from the interstices, thousands of them lifting in the breeze. It was a great hanging garden whose scope took Meric's breath away—like looking around the curve of a fossil moon. The sense of all the centuries accreted in the scales made him dizzy, and he found he could not turn his head, but could only stare at the panorama, his soul shriveling with a comprehension of the timelessness and bulk of this creature to which he clung like a fly. He lost perspective on the scene—Griaule's side was bigger than the sky, possessing its own potent gravity, and it seemed completely reasonable that he should be able to walk out along it and suffer no fall. He started to do so, and Jarcke, mistaking the strain on the rope for signal, hauled him up, dragging him across the wing, through the dirt and ferns, and back into the glade. He lay speechless and gasping at her feet.

'Big 'un, ain't he,' she said, and grinned.

After Meric had gotten his legs under him, they set off toward Hangtown; but they had not gone a hundred yards, following a trail that wound through the thickets, before Jarcke whipped out a knife and hurled it at a raccoon-sized creature that leaped out in front of them.

'Skizzer,' she said, kneeling beside it and pulling the knife from its neck. 'Calls 'em that 'cause they hisses when they runs. They eats snakes, but they'll go after children what ain't careful.'

Meric dropped down next to her. The skizzer's body was covered with short black fur, but its head was hairless, corpse-pale, the skin wrinkled as if it had been immersed too long in water. Its face was squinty-eyed, flat-nosed, with a disproportionately large jaw that hinged open to expose a nasty set of teeth.

'They's the dragon's critters,' said Jarcke. 'Used to live in his bunghole.' She pressed one of its paws, and claws curved like hooks slid forth. 'They'd hang around the lip and drop on other critters what wandered in. And if nothin' wandered in . . .' She pried out the tongue with her knife—its surface was studded with jagged points like the blade of a rasp. 'Then they'd lick Griaule clean for their supper.'

Back in Teocinte, the dragon had seemed to Meric a simple thing, a big lizard with a tick of life left inside, the residue of a dim sensibility; but he was beginning to suspect that this tick of life was more complex than any he had encountered.

'My gram used to say,' Jarcke went on, 'that the old dragons could fling themselves up to the sun in a blink and travel back to their own world, and when they come back, they'd bring the skizzers and all the rest with 'em. They was immortal, she said. Only the young ones came here 'cause later on they grew too big to fly on Earth.' She made a sour face. 'Don't know as I believe it.'

'Then you're a fool,' said Meric.

Jarcke glanced up at him, her hand twitching toward her belt.

'How can you live here and *not* believe it!' he said, surprised to hear himself so fervently defending a myth. 'God! This . . .' He broke off, noticing the flicker of a smile on her face.

She clucked her tongue, apparently satisfied by something. 'Come on,' she said. 'I want to be at the eye before sunset.'

The peaks of Griaule's folded wings, completely overgrown by grass and shrubs and dwarfish trees, formed two spiny hills that cast a shadow over Hangtown and the narrow lake around which it sprawled. Jarcke said the lake was a stream flowing off the hill behind the dragon, and that it drained away through the membranes of his wing and down onto his shoulder. It was beautiful beneath the wing, she told him. Ferns and waterfalls. But it was reckoned an evil place. From a distance the town looked picturesque—rustic cabins, smoking chimneys. As they approached, however, the cabins resolved into dilapidated shanties with missing boards and broken windows; suds and garbage and offal floated in the shallows of the lake. Aside from a few men idling on the stoops, who squinted at Meric and nodded glumly at Jarcke, no one was about. The grass blades stirred in the breeze, spiders scuttled under the shanties, and there was an air of torpor and dissolution.

Jarcke seemed embarrassed by the town. She made no attempt at introductions, stopping only long enough to fetch another coil of rope from one of the shanties, and as they walked between the wings, down through the neck spines—a forest of greenish gold spikes burnished by the lowering sun—she explained how the townsfolk grubbed a livelihood from Griaule. Herbs gathered on his back were valued as medicine and charms, as were the peels of dead skin; the artifacts left by previous Hangtown generations were of some worth to various collectors.

'Then there's scale hunters,' she said with disgust. 'Henry Sichi from Port Chantay'll pay good money for pieces of scale, and though it's bad luck to do it, some'll have a go at chippin' off the loose 'uns.' She walked a few paces in silence. 'But there's others who've got better reasons for livin' here.'

The frontal spike above Griaule's eyes was whorled at the base like a narwhal's horn and curved back toward the wings. Jarcke attached the ropes to eyebolts drilled into the spike, tied one about her waist, the other about Meric's; she cautioned him to wait, and rappelled off the side. In a moment she called for him to come down. Once again he grew dizzy as he descended; he glimpsed a clawed foot far below, mossy fangs jutting from an impossibly long jaw; and then he began to spin and bash against the scales. Jarcke gathered him in and helped him sit on the lip of the socket.

'Damn!' she said, stamping her foot.

A three-foot-long section of the adjoining scale shifted slowly away. Peering close, Meric saw that while in texture and hue it was indistinguishable from the scale, there was a hairline division between it and the surface. Jarcke, her face twisted in disgust, continued to harry the thing until it moved out of reach.

'Call 'em flakes,' she said when he asked what it was. 'Some kind of insect. Got a long tube that they pokes down between the scales and sucks the blood. See there?' She pointed off to where a flock of birds were wheeling close to Griaule's side; a chip of pale gold broke loose and went tumbling down to the valley. 'Birds pry 'em off, let 'em bust open, and eats the innards.' She hunkered down beside him and after a moment asked, 'You really think you can do it?'

'What? You mean kill the dragon?'

She nodded.

'Certainly,' he said, and then added, lying, 'I've spent years devising the method.'

'If all the paint's goin' to be atop his head, how're you goin' to get it to where the paintin's done?'

'That's no problem. We'll pipe it to wherever it's needed.'

She nodded again. 'You're a clever fellow,' she said; and when Meric, pleased, made as if to thank her for the compliment, she cut in and said, 'Don't mean nothin' by it. Bein' clever ain't an accomplishment. It's just somethin' you come by, like bein' tall.' She turned away, ending the conversation.

Meric was weary of being awestruck, but even so he could not help marveling at the eye. By his estimate it was seventy feet long and fifty feet high, and it was shuttered by an opaque membrane that was unusually clear of algae and lichen, glistening, with vague glints of color visible behind it. As the westering sun reddened and sank between two distant hills, the membrane began to quiver and then split open down the center. With the ponderous slowness of a theater curtain opening, the halves slid apart to reveal the glowing humor. Terrified by the idea that Griaule could see him, Meric sprang to his feet, but Jarcke restrained him.

'Stay still and watch,' she said.

He had no choice—the eye was mesmerizing. The pupil was slit and featureless black, but the humor . . . he had never seen such fiery blues and crimsons and golds. What had looked to be vague glints, odd refractions of the sunset, he now realized were photic reactions of some sort. Fairy rings of light developed deep within the eye, expanded into spoked shapes, flooded the humor, and faded—only to be replaced by another and another. He felt the pressure of Griaule's vision, his ancient mind, pouring through him, and as if in response to this pressure, memories bubbled up in his thoughts. Particularly sharp ones. The way a bowlful of brush water had looked after freezing over during a winter's night—a delicate, fractured flower of murky yellow. An archipelago of orange peels that his girl had left strewn across the floor of the studio. Sketching atop Jokenam Hill one sunrise, the snow-capped roofs of Regensburg below pitched at all angles like broken paving stones, and silver shafts of the sun striking down through a leaden overcast. It was as if these things were being drawn forth for his inspection. Then they were washed away by what also seemed a memory, though at the same time it was wholly unfamiliar. Essentially, it was a landscape of light, and he was plunging through it, up and up. Prisms and lattices of iridescent fire bloomed around him, and everything was a roaring fall into brightness, and finally he was clear into its white furnace heart, his own heart swelling with the joy of his strength and dominion.

It was dusk before Meric realized the eye had closed. His mouth hung open, his eyes ached from straining to see, and his tongue was glued to his palate. Jarcke sat motionless, buried in shadow.

'Th . . .' He had to swallow to clear his throat of mucus. 'This is the reason you live here, isn't it?'

'Part of the reason,' she said. 'I can see things comin' way up here. Things to watch out for, things to study on.'

She stood and walked to the lip of the socket and spat off the edge; the valley stretched out gray and unreal behind her, the folds of the hills barely visible in the gathering dusk.

'I seen you comin',' she said.

A week later, after much exploration, much talk, they went down into Teocinte. The town was a shambles—shattered windows, slogans painted on the walls, glass and torn banners and spoiled food littering the streets—as if there had been both a celebration and a battle. Which there had. The city fathers met with Meric in the town hall and informed him that his plan had been approved. They presented him a chest containing five hundred ounces of silver and said that the entire resources of the community were at his disposal. They offered a wagon and a team to transport him and the chest to Regensburg and asked if any of the preliminary work could be begun during his absence.

Meric hefted one of the silver bars. In its cold gleam he saw the object of his desire—two, perhaps three years of freedom, of doing the work he wanted and not having to accept commissions. But all that had been confused. He glanced at Jarcke; she was staring out the window, leaving it to him. He set the bar back in the chest and shut the lid.

'You'll have to send someone else,' he said. And then, as the city fathers looked at each other askance, he laughed and laughed at how easily he had discarded all his dreams and expectations.

'. . . It had been eleven years since I had been to the valley, twelve since work had begun on the painting, and I was appalled by the changes that had taken place. Many of the hills were scraped brown and treeless, and there was a general dearth of wildlife. Griaule, of course, was most changed. Scaffolding hung from his back; artisans, suspended by webworks of ropes, crawled over his side; and all the scales to be worked had either been painted or primed. The tower rising to his eye was swarmed by laborers, and at night the calciners and vats atop his head belched flame into the sky, making it seem there was a mill town in the heavens. At his feet was a brawling shantytown populated by prostitutes, workers, gamblers, ne'er-do-wells of every sort, and soldiers: the burdensome cost of the project had encouraged the city fathers of Teocinte to form a regular militia, which regularly plundered the adjoining states and had posted occupation forces to some areas. Herds of frightened animals milled in the slaughtering pens, waiting to be rendered into oils and pigments. Wagons filled with ores and vegetable products rattled in the streets. I myself had brought a cargo of madder roots from which a rose tint would be derived.

'It was not easy to arrange a meeting with Cattanay. While he did none of the actual painting, he was always busy in his office consulting with engineers and artisans, or involved in some other part of the logistical process. When at last I did meet with him, I found he had changed as drastically as Griaule. His hair had gone gray, deep lines scored his features, and his right shoulder had a peculiar bulge at its midpoint—the product of a fall. He was amused by the fact that I wanted to buy the painting, to collect the scales after Griaule's death, and I do not believe he took me at all seriously. But the woman Jarcke, his constant companion, informed him that I was a responsible businessman, that I had already bought the bones, the teeth, even the dirt beneath Griaule's belly (this I eventually sold as having magical properties).

'"Well," said Cattanay, "I suppose someone has to own them."

'He led me outside, and we stood looking at the painting.

'"You'll keep them together?" he asked.

'I said, "Yes."

'"If you'll put that in writing," he said, "then they're yours."

'Having expected to haggle long and hard over the price, I was flabbergasted; but I was even more flabbergasted by what he said next.

'"Do you think it's any good?" he asked.

'Cattanay did not consider the painting to be the work of *his* imagination; he felt he was simply illuminating the shapes that appeared on Griaule's side and was convinced that once the paint was applied, new shapes were produced beneath it, causing him to make constant changes. He saw himself as an artisan more than a creative artist. But to put his question into perspective, people were beginning to flock from all over the world and marvel at the painting. Some claimed they saw intimations of the future in its gleaming surface; others underwent transfiguring experiences; still others—artists themselves—attempted to capture something of the work on canvas, hopeful of establishing reputations merely by being competent copyists of Cattanay's art. The painting was nonrepresentational in character, essentially a wash of pale gold spread across the dragon's side; but buried beneath the laminated surface were a myriad tints of iridescent color that, as the sun passed through the heavens and the light bloomed and faded, solidified into innumerable forms and figures that seemed to flow back and forth. I will not try to categorize these forms, because there was no end to them; they were as varied as the conditions under which they were viewed. But I will say that on the morning I met with Cattanay, I—who was the soul of the practical man, without a visionary bone in my body—felt as though I were being whirled away into the painting, up through geometries of light, latticeworks of rainbow color that built the way the edges of a cloud build, past orbs, spirals, wheels of flame . . .'

—from *This Business of Griaule*
by Henry Sichi

2.

There had been several women in Meric's life since he arrived in the valley; most had been attracted by his growing fame and his association with the mystery of the dragon, and most had left him for the same reasons, feeling daunted and unappreciated. But Lise was different in two respects. First, because she loved Meric truly and well; and second, because she was married—albeit unhappily

—to a man named Pardiel, the foreman of the calciner crew. She did not love him as she did Meric, yet she respected him and felt obliged to consider carefully before ending the relationship. Meric had never known such an introspective soul. She was twelve years younger than he, tall and lovely, with sun-streaked hair and brown eyes that went dark and seemed to turn inward whenever she was pensive. She was in the habit of analyzing everything that affected her, drawing back from her emotions and inspecting them as if they were a clutch of strange insects she had discovered crawling on her skirt. Though her penchant for self-examination kept her from him, Meric viewed it as a kind of baffling virtue. He had the classic malady and could find no fault with her. For almost a year they were as happy as could be expected; they talked long hours and walked together, and on those occasions when Pardiel worked double shifts and was forced to bed down by his furnaces, they spent the nights making love in the cavernous spaces beneath the dragon's wing.

It was still reckoned an evil place. Something far worse than skizzers or flakes was rumored to live there, and the ravages of this creature were blamed for every disappearance, even that of the most malcontented laborer. But Meric did not give credence to the rumors. He half-believed Griaule had chosen him to be his executioner and that the dragon would never let him be harmed; and besides, it was the only place where they could be assured of privacy.

A crude stair led under the wing, handholds and steps hacked from the scales—doubtless the work of scale hunters. It was a treacherous passage, six hundred feet above the valley floor; but Lise and Meric were secured by ropes, and over the months, driven by the urgency of passion, they adapted to it. Their favorite spot lay fifty feet in (Lise would go no farther; she was afraid even if he was not), near a waterfall that trickled over the leathery folds, causing them to glisten with a mineral brilliance. It was eerily beautiful, a haunted gallery. Peels of dead skin hung down from the shadows like torn veils of ectoplasm; ferns sprouted from the vanes, which were thicker than cathedral columns; swallows curved through the black air. Sometimes, lying with her hidden by a tuck of the wing, Meric would think the beating of their hearts was what really animated the place, that the instant they left, the water ceased flowing and the swallows vanished. He had an unshakable faith in the transforming power of their affections, and one morning as they dressed, preparing to return to Hangtown, he asked her to leave with him.

'To another part of the valley?' She laughed sadly. 'What good would that do? Pardiel would follow us.'

'No,' he said. 'To another country. Anywhere far from here.'

'We can't,' she said, kicking at the wing. 'Not until Griaule dies. Have you forgotten?'

'We haven't tried.'

'Others have.'

'But we'd be strong enough. I know it!'

'You're a romantic,' she said gloomily, and stared out over the slope of Griaule's back at the valley. Sunrise had washed the hills to crimson, and even the tips of the wings were glowing a dull red.

'Of course I'm a romantic!' He stood, angry. 'What the hell's wrong with that?'

She sighed with exasperation. 'You wouldn't leave your work,' she said. 'And if we did leave, what work would you do? Would. . . .'

'Why must everything be a problem in advance!' he shouted. 'I'll tattoo elephants! I'll paint murals on the chests of giants, I'll illuminate whales! Who else is better qualified?'

She smiled, and his anger evaporated.

'I didn't mean it that way,' she said. 'I just wondered if you could be satisfied with anything else.'

She reached out her hand to be pulled up, and he drew her into an embrace. As he held her, inhaling the scent of vanilla water from her hair, he saw a diminutive figure silhouetted against the backdrop of the valley. It did not seem real—a black homunculus —and even when it began to come forward, growing larger and larger, it looked less a man than a magical keyhole opening in a crimson set hillside. But Meric knew from the man's rolling walk and the hulking set of his shoulders that it was Pardiel; he was carrying a long-handled hook, one of those used by artisans to maneuver along the scales.

Meric tensed, and Lise looked back to see what had alarmed him. 'Oh, my God!' she said, moving out of the embrace.

Pardiel stopped a dozen feet away. He said nothing. His face was in shadow, and the hook swung lazily from his hand. Lise took a step toward him, then stepped back and stood in front of Meric as if to shield him. Seeing this, Pardiel let out an inarticulate yell and charged, slashing with the hook. Meric pushed Lise aside and ducked. He caught a brimstone whiff of the calciners as Pardiel rushed past and went sprawling, tripped by some irregularity in the scale. Deathly afraid, knowing he was no match for the foreman, Meric seized Lise's hand and ran deeper under the wing. He hoped

Pardiel would be too frightened to follow, leery of the creature that was rumored to live there; but he was not. He came after them at a measured pace, tapping the hook against his leg.

Higher on Griaule's back, the wing was dimpled downward by hundreds of bulges, and this created a maze of small chambers and tunnels so low that they had to crouch to pass along them. The sound of their breathing and the scrape of their feet were amplified by the enclosed spaces, and Meric could no longer hear Pardiel. He had never been this deep before. He had thought it would be pitch-dark; but the lichen and algae adhering to the wing were luminescent and patterned every surface, even the scales beneath them, with whorls of blue and green fire that shed a sickly radiance. It was as if they were giants crawling through a universe whose starry matter had not yet congealed into galaxies and nebulas. In the wan light, Lise's face—turned back to him now and again —was teary and frantic; and then, as she straightened, passing into still another chamber, she drew in breath with a shriek.

At first Meric thought Pardiel had somehow managed to get ahead of them; but on entering he saw that the cause of her fright was a man propped in a sitting position against the far wall. He looked mummified. Wisps of brittle hair poked up from his scalp, the shapes of his bones were visible through his skin, and his eyes were empty holes. Between his legs was a scatter of dust where his genitals had been. Meric pushed Lise toward the next tunnel, but she resisted and pointed at the man.

'His eyes,' she said, horror-struck.

Though the eyes were mostly a negative black, Meric now realized they were shot through by opalescent flickers. He felt compelled to kneel beside the man—it was a sudden, motiveless urge that gripped him, bent him to its will, and released him a second later. As he rested his hand on the scale, he brushed a massive ring that was lying beneath the shrunken fingers. Its stone was black, shot through by flickers identical to those within the eyes, and incised with the letter S. He found his gaze was deflected away from both the stone and the eyes, as if they contained charges repellent to the senses. He touched the man's withered arm; the flesh was rock-hard, petrified. But alive. From that brief touch he gained an impression of the man's life, of gazing for centuries at the same patch of unearthly fire, of a mind gone beyond mere madness into a perverse rapture, a meditation upon some foul principle. He snatched back his hand in revulsion.

There was a noise behind them, and Meric jumped up, pushing Lise into the next tunnel. 'Go right,' he whispered. 'We'll circle back toward the stair.' But Pardiel was too close to confuse with such tactics, and their flight became a wild chase, scrambling, falling, catching glimpses of Pardiel's smoke-stained face, until finally—as Meric came to a large chamber—he felt the hook bite into his thigh. He went down, clutching at the wound, pulling the hook loose. The next moment Pardiel was atop him; Lise appeared over his shoulder, but he knocked her away and locked his fingers in Meric's hair and smashed his head against the scale. Lise screamed, and white lights fired through Meric's skull. Again his head was smashed down. And again. Dimly, he saw Lise struggling with Pardiel, saw her shoved away, saw the hook raised high and the foreman's mouth distorted by a grimace. Then the grimace vanished. His jaw dropped open and he reached behind him as if to scratch his shoulder blade. A line of dark blood eeled from his mouth and he collapsed, smothering Meric beneath his chest. Meric heard voices. He tried to dislodge the body, and the effects drained the last of his strength. He whirled down through a blackness that seemed as negative and inexhaustible as the petrified man's eyes.

Someone had propped his head on their lap and was bathing his brow with a damp cloth. He assumed it was Lise, but when he asked what had happened, it was Jarcke who answered, saying, 'Had to kill him.' His head throbbed, his leg throbbed even worse, and his eyes would not focus. The peels of dead skin hanging overhead appeared to be writhing. He realized they were out near the edge of the wing.

'Where's Lise?'

'Don't worry,' said Jarcke. 'You'll see her again.' She made it sound like an indictment.

'Where is she?'

'Sent her back to Hangtown. Won't do you two bein' seen hand in hand the same day Pardiel's missin'.'

'She wouldn't have left. . . .' He blinked, trying to see her face; the lines around her mouth were etched deep and reminded him of the patterns of lichen on the dragon's scale. 'What did you do?'

'Convinced her it was best,' said Jarcke. 'Don't you know she's just foolin' with you?'

'I've got to talk with her.' He was full of remorse, and it was unthinkable that Lise should be bearing her grief alone; but when he struggled to rise, pain lanced through his leg.

'You wouldn't get ten feet,' she said. 'Soon as your head's clear, I'll help you with the stairs.'

He closed his eyes, resolving to find Lise the instant he got back to Hangtown—together they would decide what to do. The scale beneath him was cool, and that coolness was transmitted to his skin, his flesh, as if he were merging with it, becoming one of its ridges.

'What was the wizard's name?' he asked after a while, recalling the petrified man, the ring and its incised letter. 'The one who tried to kill Griaule. . . .'

'Don't know as I ever heard it,' said Jarcke. 'But I reckon it's him back there.'

'You saw him?'

'I was chasin' a scale hunter once what stole some rope, and I found him instead. Pretty miserable sort, whoever he is.'

Her fingers trailed over his shoulder—a gentle, treasuring touch. He did not understand what it signaled, being too concerned with Lise, with the terrifying potentials of all that had happened; but years later, after things had passed beyond remedy, he cursed himself for not having understood.

At length Jarcke helped him to his feet, and they climbed up to Hangtown, to bitter realizations and regrets, leaving Pardiel to the birds or the weather or worse.

'. . . It seems it is considered irreligious for a woman in love to hesitate or examine the situation, to do anything other than blindly follow the impulse of her emotions. I felt the brunt of such an attitude—people judged it my fault for not having acted quickly and decisively one way or another. Perhaps I was overcautious. I do not claim to be free of blame, only innocent of sacrilege. I believe I might have eventually left Pardiel—there was not enough in the relationship to sustain happiness for either of us. But I had good reason for cautious examination. My husband was not an evil man, and there were matters of loyalty between us.

'I could not face Meric after Pardiel's death, and I moved to another part of the valley. He tried to see me on many occasions, but I always refused. Though I was greatly tempted, my guilt was greater. Four years later, after Jarcke died—crushed by a runaway wagon—one of her associates wrote and told me Jarcke had been in love with Meric, that it had been she who had informed Pardiel of the affair, and that she may well have staged the murder. The letter acted somewhat to expiate my guilt, and I weighed the possibility of seeing Meric again. But too much time had passed, and we had both assumed other lives. I decided against it. Six years later, when Griaule's influence had weakened sufficiently to allow emigration, I moved to Port Chantay. I did not hear from Meric for almost twenty years after that, and then one day I received a letter, which I will reproduce in part.

' ". . . My old friend from Regensburg, Louis Dardano, has been living here for the past few years, engaged in writing my biography. The narrative has a breezy feel, like a tale being told in a tavern, which—if you recall my telling you how this all began—is quite appropriate. But on reading it, I am amazed my life has had such a simple shape. One task, one passion. God, Lise! Seventy years old, and I still dream of you. And I still think of what happened that morning under the wing. Strange, that it has taken me all this time to realize it was not Jarcke, not you or I who were culpable, but Griaule. How obvious it seems now. I was leaving, and he needed me to complete the expression on his side, his dream of flying, of escape, to grant him the death of his desire. I am certain you will think I have leaped to this assumption, but I remind you that it has been a leap of forty years' duration. I know Griaule, know his monstrous subtlety. I can see it at work in every action that has taken place in the valley since my arrival. I was a fool not to understand that his powers were at the heart of our sad conclusion."

' "The army now runs everything here, as no doubt you are aware. It is rumored they are planning a winter campaign against Regensburg. Can you believe it! Their fathers were ignorant, but this generation is brutally stupid. Otherwise, the work goes well and things are as usual with me. My shoulder aches, children stare at me on the street, and it is whispered I am mad . . ." '

—from *Under Griaule's Wing*
by Lise Claverie

3.

Acne-scarred, lean, arrogant, Major Hauk was a very young major with a limp. When Meric had entered, the major had been practicing his signature—it was a thing of elegant loops and flourishes, obviously intended to have a place in posterity. As he strode back and forth during their conversation, he paused frequently to admire himself in the window glass, settling the hang of his red jacket or running his fingers along the crease of his white trousers. It was the new style of uniform, the first Meric had seen at close range, and he noted with amusement the dragons embossed on the epaulets. He wondered if Griaule was capable of such an irony, if his influence was sufficiently discreet to have planted the idea for this comic opera apparel in the brain of some general's wife.

'. . . not a question of manpower,' the major was saying, 'but of. . . .' He broke off, and after a moment cleared his throat.

Meric, who had been studying the blotches on the backs of his hands, glanced up; the cane that had been resting against his knee slipped and clattered to the floor.

'A question of *matériel*,' said the major firmly. 'The price of antimony, for example. . . .'

'Hardly use it anymore,' said Meric. 'I'm almost done with the mineral reds.'

A look of impatience crossed the major's face. 'Very well,' he said; he stooped to his desk and shuffled through some papers. 'Ah! Here's a bill for a shipment of cuttlefish from which you derive. . . .' He shuffled more papers.

'Syrian brown,' said Meric gruffly. 'I'm done with that, too. Golds and violets are all I need anymore. A little blue and rose.' He wished the man would stop badgering him; he wanted to be at the eye before sunset.

As the major continued his accounting, Meric's gaze wandered out the window. The shantytown surrounding Griaule had swelled into a city and now sprawled across the hills. Most of the buildings were permanent, wood and stone, and the cant of the roofs, the smoke from the factories around the perimeter, put him in mind of Regensburg. All the natural beauty of the land had been drained into the painting. Blackish gray rain clouds were muscling up from the east, but the afternoon sun shone clear and shed a heavy gold radiance on Griaule's side. It looked as if the sunlight were an extension of the gleaming resins, as if the thickness of the paint were becoming infinite. He let the major's voice recede to a buzz and followed the scatter and dazzle of the images; and then, with a start, he realized the major was sounding him out about stopping the work.

The idea panicked him at first. He tried to interrupt, to raise objections; but the major talked through him, and as Meric thought it over, he grew less and less opposed. The painting would never be finished, and he was tired. Perhaps it was time to have done with it, to accept a university post somewhere and enjoy life for a while.

'We've been thinking about a temporary stoppage,' said Major Hauk. 'Then if the winter campaign goes well. . . .' He smiled. 'If we're not visited by plague and pestilence, we'll assume things are in hand. Of course we'd like your opinion.'

Meric felt a surge of anger toward this smug little monster. 'In my opinion, you people are idiots,' he said. 'You wear Griaule's image on your shoulders, weave him on your flags, and yet you don't have the least comprehension of what that means. You think it's just a useful symbol. . . .'

'Excuse me,' said the major stiffly.

'The hell I will!' Meric groped for his cane and heaved up to his feet. 'You see yourselves as conquerors. Shapers of destiny. But all your rapes and slaughters are Griaule's expressions. *His* will. You're every bit as much his parasites as the skizzers.'

The major sat, picked up a pen, and began to write.

'It astounds me,' Meric went on, 'that you can live next to a miracle, a source of mystery, and treat him as if he were an oddly shaped rock.'

The major kept writing.

'What are you doing?' asked Meric.

'My recommendation,' said the major without looking up.

'Which is?'

'That we initiate stoppage at once.'

They exchanged hostile stares, and Meric turned to leave; but as he took hold of the doorknob, the major spoke again.

'We owe you so much,' he said; he wore an expression of mingled pity and respect that further irritated Meric.

'How many men have you killed, Major?' he asked, opening the door.

'I'm not sure. I was in the artillery. We were never able to be sure.'

'Well, I'm sure of my tally,' said Meric. 'It's taken me forty years to amass it. Fifteen hundred and ninety-three men and women. Poisoned, scalded, broken by falls, savaged by animals. Murdered. Why don't we—you and I—just call it even.'

Though it was a sultry afternoon, he felt cold as he walked toward the tower—an internal cold that left him light-headed and weak. He tried to think what he would do. The idea of a university post seemed less appealing away from the major's office; he would soon grow weary of worshipful students and in-depth dissections of his work by jealous academics. A man hailed him as he turned into the market. Meric waved but did not stop, and heard another man say, '*That's* Cattanay?' (That ragged old ruin?)

The colors of the market were too bright, the smells of charcoal cookery too cloying, the crowds too thick, and he made for the side streets, hobbling past one-room stucco houses and tiny stores where they sold cooking oil by the ounce and cut cigars in half if you could not afford a whole one. Garbage, tornados of dust and flies, drunks with bloody mouths. Somebody had tied wires around a pariah dog—a bitch with slack teats; the wires had sliced into her flesh, and she lay panting in an alley mouth, gaunt ribs flecked with pink lather, gazing into nowhere. She, thought Meric, and not Griaule, should be the symbol of their flag.

As he rode the hoist up the side of the tower, he fell into his old habit of jotting down notes for the next day. *What's that cord of wood doing on level five? Slow leak of chrome yellow from pipes on level twelve.* Only when he saw a man dismantling some scaffolding did he recall Major Hauk's recommendation and understand that the order must already have been given. The loss of his work struck home to him then, and he leaned against the railing, his chest constricted and his eyes brimming. He straightened, ashamed of himself. The sun hung in a haze of iron-colored light low above the western hills, looking red and bloated and vile as a vulture's ruff. That polluted sky was his creation as much as was the painting, and it would be good to leave it behind. Once away from the valley, from all the influences of the place, he would be able to consider the future.

A young girl was sitting on the twentieth level just beneath the eye. Years before, the ritual of viewing the eye had grown to cultish proportions; there had been group chanting and praying and discussions of the experience. But these were more practical times, and no doubt the young men and women who had congregated here were now manning administrative desks somewhere in the burgeoning empire. They were the ones about whom Dardano should write; they, and all the eccentric characters who had played roles in this slow pageant. The gypsy woman who had danced every night by the eye, hoping to charm Griaule into killing her faithless lover—she had gone away satisfied. The man who had tried to extract one of the fangs—nobody knew what had become of him. The scale hunters, the artisans. A history of Hangtown would be a volume in itself.

The walk had left Meric weak and breathless; he sat down clumsily beside the girl, who smiled. He could not remember her name, but she came often to the eye. Small and dark, with an inner reserve that reminded him of Lise. He laughed inwardly—most women reminded him of Lise in some way.

'Are you all right?' she asked, her brow wrinkled with concern.

'Oh, yes,' he said; he felt a need for conversation to take his mind off things, but he could think of nothing more to say. She was so young! All freshness and gleam and nerves.

'This will be my last time,' she said. 'At least for a while. I'll miss it.' And then, before he could ask why, she added, 'I'm getting married tomorrow, and we're moving away.'

He offered congratulations and asked her who was the lucky fellow.

'Just a boy.' She tossed her hair, as if to dismiss the boy's importance; she gazed up at the shuttered membrane. 'What's it like for you when the eye opens?' she asked.

'Like everyone else,' he said. 'I remember . . . memories of my life. Other lives, too.' He did not tell her about Griaule's memory of flight; he had never told anyone except Lise about that.

'All those bits of souls trapped in there,' she said, gesturing at the eye. 'What do they mean to him? Why does he show them to us?'

'I imagine he has his purposes, but I can't explain them.'

'Once I remembered being with you,' said the girl, peeking at him shyly through a dark curl. 'We were under the wing.'

He glanced at her sharply. 'Tell me.'

'We were . . . together,' she said, blushing. 'Intimate, you know. I was very afraid of the place, of the sounds and shadows. But I loved you so much, it didn't matter. We made love all night, and I was surprised because I thought that kind of passion was just in stories, something people had invented to make up for how ordinary it really was. And in the morning even that dreadful place had become beautiful, with the wing tips glowing red and the waterfall echoing . . .' She lowered her eyes. 'Ever since I had that memory, I've been a little in love with you.'

'Lise,' he said, feeling helpless before her.

'Was that her name?'

He nodded and put a hand to his brow, trying to pinch back the emotions that flooded him.

'I'm sorry.' Her lips grazed his cheek, and just that slight touch seemed to weaken him further. 'I wanted to tell you how she felt in case she hadn't told you herself. She was very troubled by something, and I wasn't sure she had.'

She shifted away from him, made uncomfortable by the intensity of his reaction, and they sat without speaking. Meric became lost in watching how the sun glazed the scales to reddish gold, how the light was channeled along the ridges in molten streams that paled as the day wound down. He was startled when the girl jumped to her feet and backed toward the hoist.

'He's dead,' she said wonderingly.

Meric looked at her, uncomprehending.

'See?' She pointed at the sun, which showed a crimson sliver above the hill. 'He's dead,' she repeated, and the expression on her face flowed between fear and exultation.

The idea of Griaule's death was too large for Meric's mind to encompass, and he turned to the eye to find a counterproof—no glints of color flickered beneath the membrane. He heard the hoist creak as the girl headed down, but he continued to wait. Perhaps only the dragon's vision had failed. No. It was likely not a coincidence that work had been officially terminated today. Stunned, he sat staring at the lifeless membrane until the sun sank below the hills; then he stood and went over to the hoist. Before he could throw the switch, the cables thrummed—somebody heading up. Of course. The girl would have spread the news, and all the Major Hauks and their underlings would be hurrying to test Griaule's reflexes. He did not want to be here when they arrived, to watch them pose with their trophy like successful fishermen.

It was hard work climbing up to the frontoparietal plate. The ladder swayed, the wind buffeted him, and by the time he clambered onto the plate, he was giddy, his chest full of twinges. He hobbled forward and leaned against the rust-caked side of a boiling vat. Shadowy in the twilight, the great furnaces and vats towered around him, and it seemed this system of fiery devices reeking of cooked flesh and minerals was the actual machinery of Griaule's thought materialized above his skull. Energyless, abandoned. They had been replaced by more efficient equipment down below, and it had been—what was it?—almost five years since they were last used. Cobwebs veiled a pyramid of firewood; the stairs leading to the rims of the vats were crumbling. The plate itself was scarred and coated with sludge.

'Cattanay!'

Someone shouted from below, and the top of the ladder trembled. God, they were coming after him! Bubbling over with congratulations and plans for testimonial dinners, memorial plaques, specially struck medals. They would have him draped in bunting and bronzed and covered with pigeon shit before they were done. All these years he had been among them, both their slave and their master, yet he had never felt at home. Leaning heavily on his cane, he made his way past the frontal spike—blackened by years of oily smoke—and down between the wings to Hangtown. It was a ghost town, now. Weeds overgrowing the collapsed shanties; the lake a stinking pit, drained after some children had drowned in the summer of '91. Where Jarcke's home had stood was a huge pile of animal bones, taking a pale shine from the half-light. Wind keened through the tattered shrubs.

'Meric!' 'Cattanay.'

The voices were closer.

Well, there was one place where they would not follow.

The leaves of the thickets were speckled with mold and brittle, flaking away as he brushed them. He hesitated at the top of the scale hunters' stair. He had no rope. Though he had done the climb unaided many times, it had been quite a few years. The gusts of wind, the shouts, the sweep of the valley and the lights scattered across it like diamonds on gray velvet—it all seemed a single inconstant medium. He heard the brush crunch behind him, more voices. To hell with it! Gritting his teeth against a twinge of pain in his shoulder, hooking his cane over his belt, he inched onto the stair and locked his fingers in the handholds. The wind whipped his clothes and threatened to pry him loose and send him pinwheeling off. Once he slipped; once he froze, unable to move backward or forward. But at last he reached the bottom and edged upslope until he found a spot flat enough to stand.

The mystery of the place suddenly bore in upon him, and he was afraid. He half-turned to the stair, thinking he would go back to Hangtown and accept the hurly-burly. But a moment later he realized how foolish a thought that was. Waves of weakness poured through him, his heart hammered, and white dazzles flared in his vision. His chest felt heavy as iron. Rattled, he went a few steps forward, the cane pocking the silence. It was too dark to see more than outlines, but up ahead was the fold of wing where he and Lise had sheltered. He walked toward it, intent on revisiting it; then he remembered the girl beneath the eye and understood that he had already said that good-bye. And it *was* good-bye—that he understood vividly. He kept walking. Blackness looked to be welling from the wing joint, from the entrances to the maze of luminous tunnels where they had stumbled onto the petrified man. Had it really been the old wizard, doomed by magical justice to molder and live on and on? It made sense. At least it accorded with what happened to wizards who slew their dragons.

'Griaule?' he whispered to the darkness, and cocked his head, half-expecting an answer. The sound of his voice pointed up the immensity of the great gallery under the wing, the emptiness, and he recalled how vital a habitat it had once been. Flakes shifting over the surface, skizzers, peculiar insects fuming in the thickets, the glum populace of Hangtown, waterfalls. He had never been able to picture Griaule fully alive—that kind of vitality was beyond the powers of the imagination. Yet he wondered if by some miracle the dragon were alive now, flying up through his golden night to the sun's core. Or had that merely been a dream, a bit of tissue glittering deep in the cold tons of his brain? He laughed. Ask the stars for their first names, and you'd be more likely to receive a reply.

He decided not to walk any farther—it was really no decision. Pain was spreading through his shoulder, so intense he imagined it must be glowing inside. Carefully, carefully, he lowered himself and lay propped on an elbow, hanging onto the cane. Good, magical wood. Cut from a hawthorn atop Griaule's haunch. A man had once offered him a small fortune for it. Who would claim it now? Probably old Henry Sichi would snatch it for his museum, stick it in a glass case next to his boots. What a joke! He decided to lie flat on his stomach, resting his chin on an arm—the stony coolness beneath acted to muffle the pain. Amusing, how the range of one's decision dwindled. You decided to paint a dragon, to send hundreds of men searching for malachite and cochineal beetles, to love a woman, to heighten an undertone here and there, and finally to position your body a certain way. He seemed to have reached the end of the process. What next? He tried to regulate his breathing, to ease the pressure on his chest. Then, as something rustled out near the wing joint, he turned on his side. He thought he detected movement, a gleaming blackness flowing toward him . . . or else it was only the haphazard firing of his nerves playing tricks with his vision. More surprised than afraid, wanting to see, he peered into the darkness and felt his heart beating erratically against the dragon's scale.

'. . . It's foolish to draw simple conclusions from complex events, but I suppose there must be both moral and truth to this life, these events. I'll leave that to the gadflies. The historians, the social scientists, the expert apologists for reality. All I know is that he had a fight with his girlfriend over money and walked out. He sent her a letter saying he had gone south and would be back in a few months with more money than she could ever spend. I had no idea what he'd done. The whole thing about Griaule had just been a bunch of us sitting around the Red Bear, drinking up my pay—I'd sold an article—and somebody said, "Wouldn't it be great if Dardano didn't have to write articles, if we didn't have to paint pictures that color-coordinated with people's furniture or slave at getting the gooey smiles of little nieces and nephews just right?" All sorts of improbable moneymaking schemes were put forward. Robberies, kidnappings. Then the idea of swindling the city fathers of Teocinte came up, and the entire plan was fleshed out in minutes. Scribbled on napkins, scrawled on sketchpads. A group effort. I keep trying to remember if anyone got a glassy look in their eye, if I felt a cold tendril of Griaule's thought stirring my brains. But I can't. It was a half hour's sensation, nothing more. A drunken whimsy, an art-school metaphor. Shortly thereafter, we ran out of money and staggered into the streets. It was snowing—big wet flakes that melted down our collars. God, we were drunk! Laughing, balancing on the icy railing of the University Bridge. Making faces at the bundled-up burghers and their fat ladies who huffed and puffed past, spouting steam and never giving us a glance, and none of us—not even the burghers—knowing that we were living our happy ending in advance. . . .'

—from *The Man Who Painted*
The Dragon Griaule
by Louis Dardano

For Jamie and Laura

THE VANISHING AMERICAN

Charles Beaumont

He got the notion shortly after five o'clock; at least, a part of him did, a small part hidden down beneath all the conscious cells—*he* didn't get the notion until sometime later. At exactly 5 P.M. the bell rang. At two minutes after, the chairs began to empty. There was the vast slamming of drawers, the straightening of rulers, the sound of bones snapping and mouths yawning and feet shuffling tiredly.

Mr. Minchell relaxed. He rubbed his hands together and relaxed and thought how nice it would be to get up and go home, like the others. But of course there was the tape, only three-quarters finished. He would have to stay.

He stretched and said good night to the people who filed past him. As usual, no one answered. When they had gone, he set his fingers pecking again over the keyboard. The click-clicking grew loud in the suddenly still office, but Mr. Minchell did not notice. He was lost in the work. Soon, he knew, it would be time for the totaling, and his pulse quickened at the thought of this.

He lit a cigarette. Heart tapping, he drew in smoke and released it.

He extended his right hand and rested his index and middle fingers on the metal bar marked TOTAL. A mile-long ribbon of paper lay gathered on the desk, strangely festive. He glanced at it, then at the manifest sheet. The figure 18037448 was circled in red. He pulled breath into his lungs, locked it there; then he closed his eyes and pressed the TOTAL bar.

There was a smooth low metallic grinding, followed by absolute silence.

Mr. Minchell opened one eye, dragged it from the ceiling on down to the adding machine.

He groaned, slightly.

The total read: 18037447.

'God.' He stared at the figure and thought of the fifty-three pages of manifest, the three thousand separate rows of figures that would have to be checked again. 'God.'

The day was lost, now. Irretrievably. It was too late to do anything. Madge would have supper waiting, and F.J. didn't approve of overtime; also——

He looked at the total again. At the last two digits.

He sighed. Forty-seven. And thought, startled: Today, for the Lord's sake, is my birthday! Today I am forty—what? forty-seven. And that explains the mistake, I suppose. Subconscious kind of thing . . .

Slowly he got up and looked around the deserted office.

Then he went to the dressing room and got his hat and his coat and put them on, carefully.

'Pushing fifty now . . .'

The outside hall was dark. Mr. Minchell walked softly to the elevator and punched the *down* button. 'Forty-seven,' he said, aloud; then, almost immediately, the light turned red and the thick door slid back noisily. The elevator operator, a bird-thin, tan-fleshed girl, swiveled her head, looking up and down the hall. 'Going down,' she said.

'Yes,' Mr. Minchell said, stepping forward.

'Going down.' The girl clicked her tongue and muttered, 'Damn kids.' She gave the lattice gate a tired push and moved the smooth wooden-handled lever in its slot.

Odd, Mr. Minchell decided, was the word for this particular girl. He wished now that he had taken the stairs. Being alone with only one other person in an elevator had always made him nervous: now it made him very nervous. He felt the tension growing. When it became unbearable, he cleared his throat and said, 'Long day.'

The girl said nothing. She had a surly look, and she seemed to be humming something deep in her throat.

Mr. Minchell closed his eyes. In less than a minute—during which time he dreamed of the cable snarling, of the car being caught between floors, of himself trying to make small talk with the odd girl for six straight hours—he opened his eyes again and walked into the lobby, briskly.

The gate slammed.

He turned and started for the doorway. Then he paused, feeling a sharp increase in his heartbeat. A large, red-faced, magnificently groomed man of middle years stood directly beyond the glass, talking with another man.

Mr. Minchell pushed through the door, with effort. He's seen me now, he thought. If he asks any questions, though, or anything, I'll just say I didn't put it on the time card; that ought to make it all right. . . .

He nodded and smiled at the large man. 'Good night, Mr. Diemel.'

The man looked up briefly, blinked, and returned to his conversation.

Mr. Minchell felt a burning come into his face. He hurried on down the street. Now the notion—though it was not even that yet, strictly: it was more a vague feeling—swam up from the bottom of his brain. He remembered that he had not spoken directly to F.J. Diemel for over ten years, beyond a good morning. . . .

Ice-cold shadows fell off the tall buildings, staining the streets, now. Crowds of shoppers moved along the pavement like juggernauts, exhaustedly, but with great determination. Mr. Minchell looked at them. They all had furtive appearances, it seemed to him, suddenly, even the children, as if each was fleeing from some hideous crime. They hurried along, staring.

But not, Mr. Minchell noticed, at him. Through him, yes. Past him. As the elevator operator had done, and now F.J. And had anyone said good night?

He pulled up his coat collar and walked toward the drugstore, thinking. He was forty-seven years old. At the current life-expectancy rate, he might have another seventeen or eighteen years left. And then death.

If you're not dead already.

He paused and for some reason remembered a story he'd once read in a magazine. Something about a man who dies and whose ghost takes up his duties, or something; anyway, the man didn't know he was dead—that was it. And at the end of the story, he runs into his own corpse.

Which is pretty absurd: he glanced down at his body. Ghosts don't wear $36 suits, nor do they have trouble pushing doors open, nor do their corns ache like blazes, and what the devil is wrong with me today?

He shook his head.

It was the tape, of course, and the fact that it was his birthday. That was why his mind was behaving so foolishly.

He went into the drugstore. It was an immense place, packed

with people. He walked to the cigar counter, trying not to feel intimidated, and reached into his pocket. A small man elbowed in front of him and called loudly: 'Gimme coupla nickels, will you, Jack?' The clerk scowled and scooped the change out of his cash register. The small man scurried off. Others took his place. Mr. Minchell thrust his arm forward. 'A pack of Luckies, please,' he said. The clerk whipped his fingers around a pile of cellophaned packages and, looking elsewhere, droned: 'Twenty-six.' Mr. Minchell put his twenty-six cents exactly on the glass shelf. The clerk shoved the cigarettes toward the edge and picked up the money, deftly. Not once did he lift his eyes.

Mr. Minchell pocketed the Luckies and went back out of the store. He was perspiring now, slightly, despite the chill wind. The word 'ridiculous' lodged in his mind and stayed there. Ridiculous, yes, for heaven's sake. Still, he thought—now just answer the question—isn't it true? Can you honestly say that that clerk saw you?

Or that anyone saw you today?

Swallowing dryly, he walked another two blocks, always in the direction of the subway, and went into a bar called the Chez When. One drink would not hurt, one small, stiff, steadying shot.

The bar was a gloomy place, and not very warm, but there was a good crowd. Mr. Minchell sat down on a stool and folded his hands. The bartender was talking animatedly with an old woman, laughing with boisterous good humor from time to time. Mr. Minchell waited. Minutes passed. The bartender looked up several times, but never made a move to indicate that he had seen a customer.

Mr. Minchell looked at his old gray overcoat, the humbly floraled tie, the cheap sharkskin suit-cloth, and became aware of the extent to which he detested this ensemble. He sat there and detested his clothes for a long time. Then he glanced around. The bartender was wiping a glass, slowly.

All right, the hell with you. I'll go somewhere else.

He slid off the stool. Just as he was about to turn he saw the mirrored wall, pink-tinted and curved. He stopped, peering. Then he almost ran out of the bar.

Cold wind went into his head.

Ridiculous. The mirror was curved, you jackass. How do you expect to see yourself in curved mirrors?

He walked past high buildings, and now past the library and the stone lion he had once, long ago, named King Richard; and he did not look at the lion, because he'd always wanted to ride the lion, ever since he was a child, and he'd promised himself he would do that, but he never did.

He hurried on to the subway, took the stairs by twos, and clattered across the platform in time to board the express.

It roared and thundered. Mr. Minchell held onto the strap and kept himself from staring. No one watched him. No one even glanced at him when he pushed his way to the door and went out onto the empty platform.

He waited. Then the train was gone, and he was alone.

He walked up the stairs. It was fully night now, a soft, unshadowed darkness. He thought about the day and the strange things that were gouging into his mind and thought about all this as he turned down a familiar street which led to his familiar apartment.

The door opened.

His wife was in the kitchen, he could see. Her apron flashed across the arch, and back, and across. He called: 'Madge, I'm home.'

Madge did not answer. Her movements were regular. Jimmy was sitting at the table, drooling over a glass of pop, whispering to himself.

'I said——' Mr. Minchell began.

'Jimmy, get up and go to the bathroom, you hear? I've got your water drawn.'

Jimmy promptly broke into tears. He jumped off the chair and ran past Mr. Minchell into the bedroom. The door slammed viciously.

'Madge.'

Madge Minchell came into the room, tired and lined and heavy. Her eyes did not waver. She went into the bedroom, and there was a silence; then a sharp slapping noise, and a yelling.

Mr. Minchell walked to the bathroom, fighting down the small terror. He closed the door and locked it and wiped his forehead with a handkerchief. Ridiculous, he thought, and ridiculous and ridiculous. I am making something utterly foolish out of nothing. All I have to do is look in the mirror, and——

He held the handkerchief to his lips. It was difficult to breathe.

Then he knew that he was afraid, more so than ever before in a lifetime of being afraid.

Look at it this way, Minchell: why shouldn't *you vanish?*

'Young man, just you wait until your father gets here!'

He pushed the handkerchief against his mouth and leaned on the door and gasped.

'*What do you mean, vanish?*'
Go on, take a look. You'll see what I mean.
He tried to swallow, couldn't. Tried to wet his lips, they stayed dry.
'*Lord——*'
He slitted his eyes and walked to the shaving mirror and looked in.
His mouth fell open.
The mirror reflected nothing. It held nothing. It was dull and gray and empty.
Mr. Minchell stared at the glass, put out his hand, drew it back hastily.
He squinted. Inches away. There was a form now: vague, indistinct, featureless: but a form.
'Lord,' he said. He understood why the elevator girl hadn't seen him, and why F.J. hadn't answered him, and why the clerk at the drugstore and the bartender and Madge . . .
'*I'm not dead.*'
Of course you're not dead—not that way.
'—tan your hide, Jimmy Minchell, when he gets home.'
Mr. Minchell suddenly wheeled and clicked the lock. He rushed out of the steam-filled bathroom, across the room, down the stairs, into the street, into the cool night.
A block from home he slowed to a walk.
Invisible! He said the word over and over, in a half-voice. He said it and tried to control the panic that pulled at his legs, and at his brain, and filled him.
Why?
A fat woman and a little girl passed by. Neither of them looked up. He started to call out and checked himself. No. That wouldn't do any good. There was no question about it now. He was invisible.
He walked on. As he did, forgotten things returned; they came and they left, too fast. He couldn't hold onto them. He could only watch, and remember. Himself as a youngster, reading: the Oz books, and Tarzan, and Mr. Wells. Himself, going to the University, wanting to teach, and meeting Madge; then not planning any more, and Madge changing, and all the dreams put away. For later. For the right time. And then Jimmy—little strange Jimmy, who ate filth and picked his nose and watched television, who never read books, never; Jimmy, his son, whom he would never understand . . .
He walked by the edge of the park now. Then on past the park, through a maze of familiar and unfamiliar neighborhoods. Walking,

remembering, looking at the people and feeling pain because he knew that they could not see him, not now or ever again, because he had vanished. He walked and remembered and felt pain.

All the stagnant dreams came back. Fully. The trip to Italy he'd planned. The open sports car, bad weather be damned. The first-hand knowledge that would tell him whether he did or did not approve of bullfighting. The book . . .

Then something occurred to him. It occurred to Mr. Minchell that he had not just suddenly vanished, like that, after all. No; he had been vanishing gradually for a long while. Every time he said good morning to that bastard Diemel he got a little harder to see. Every time he put on this horrible suit he faded. The process of disappearing was set into action every time he brought his pay check home and turned it over to Madge, every time he kissed her, or listened to her vicious unending complaints, or decided against buying that novel, or punched the adding machine he hated so, or . . .

Certainly.

He had vanished for Diemel and the others in the office years ago. And for strangers right afterwards. Now even Madge and Jimmy couldn't see him. And he could barely see himself, even in a mirror.

It made terrible sense to him. *Why* shouldn't *you disappear?* Well, why, indeed? There wasn't any very good reason, actually. None. And this, in a nightmarish sort of a way, made it as brutally logical as a perfect tape.

Then he thought about going back to work tomorrow and the next day and the day after that. He'd have to, of course. He couldn't let Madge and Jimmy starve; and besides, what else would he do? It wasn't as if anything important had changed. He'd go on punching the clock and saying good morning to people who didn't see him, and he'd run the tapes and come home beat, nothing altered, and someday he'd die and that would be that.

All at once he felt tired.

He sat down on a cement step and sighed. Distantly he realized that he had come to the library. He sat there, watching the people, feeling the tiredness seep through him, thickly.

Then he looked up.

Above him, black and regal against the sky, stood the huge stone lion. Its mouth was open, and the great head was raised proudly.

Mr. Minchell smiled. King Richard. Memories scattered in his mind: old King Richard, well, my God, here we are.

He got to his feet. Fifty thousand times, at least, he had passed this spot, and every time he had experienced that instant of wild craving. Less so of late, but still, had it ever completely gone? He was amazed to find that now the childish desire was welling up again, stronger than ever before. Urgently.

He rubbed his cheek and stood there for several minutes. It's the most ridiculous thing in the world, he thought, and I must be going out of my mind, and that must explain everything. But, he inquired of himself, even so, why not?

After all, I'm invisible. No one can see me. Of course, it didn't have to be this way, not really. I don't know, he went on, I mean, I believed that I was doing the right thing. Would it have been right to go back to the University and the hell with Madge? I couldn't change that, could I? Could I have done anything about that, even if I'd known?

He nodded sadly.

All right, but don't make it any worse. Don't for God's sake *dwell* on it!

To his surprise, Mr. Minchell found that he was climbing up the concrete base of the statue. It ripped the breath from his lungs —and he saw that he could much more easily have gone up a few extra steps and simply stepped on—but there didn't seem anything else to do but just this, what he was doing. Once upright, he passed his hand over the statue's flank. The surface was incredibly sleek and cold, hard as a lion's muscles ought to be, and tawny.

He took a step backwards. Lord! Had there ever been such power? Such marvelous downright power and . . . majesty, as was here? From stone—no, indeed. It fooled a good many people, but it did not fool Mr. Minchell. He knew. This lion was no mere library decoration. It was an animal, of deadly cunning and fantastic strength and unbelievable ferocity. And it didn't move for the simple reason that it did not care to move. It was waiting. Someday it would see what it was waiting for, its enemy, coming down the street. Then look out, people!

He remembered the whole yarn now. Of everyone on Earth, only he, Henry Minchell, knew the secret of the lion. And only he was allowed to sit astride this mighty back.

He stepped onto the tail, experimentally. He hesitated, gulped, and swung forward, swiftly, on up to the curved rump.

Trembling, he slid forward, until finally he was over the shoulders of the lion, just behind the raised head.

His breath came very fast.

He closed his eyes.

It was not long before he was breathing regularly again. Only now it was the hot, fetid air of the jungle that went into his nostrils. He felt the great muscles ripple beneath him and he listened to the fast crackle of crushed foliage, and he whispered?

'Easy, fellow.'

The flying spears did not frighten him. He sat straight, smiling, with his fingers buried in the rich, tawny mane of King Richard, while the wind tore at his hair. . . .

Then, abruptly, he opened his eyes.

The city stretched before him, and the people, and the lights. He tried quite hard not to cry, because he knew that forty-seven-year-old men never cried, not even when they had vanished, but he couldn't help it. So he sat on the stone lion and lowered his head and cried.

He didn't hear the laughter at first.

When he did hear it, he thought that he was dreaming. But it was true: somebody was laughing.

He grasped one of the statue's ears for balance and leaned forward. He blinked. Below, some fifteen feet, there were people. Young people. Some of them with books. They were looking up and smiling and laughing.

Mr. Minchell wiped his eyes.

A slight horror came over him, and fell away. He leaned farther out.

One of the boys waved and shouted: 'Ride him, Pop!'

Mr. Minchell almost toppled. Then, without understanding, without even trying to understand—merely knowing—he grinned, widely, showing his teeth, which were his own and very white.

'You . . . see me?' he called.

The young people roared.

'You do!' Mr. Minchell's face seemed to melt upwards. He let out a yell and gave King Richard's shaggy stone mane an enormous hug.

Below, other people stopped in their walking and a small crowd began to form. Dozens of eyes peered sharply, quizzically.

A woman in gray furs giggled.

A thin man in a blue suit grunted something about these damned exhibitionists.

'You pipe down,' another man said. 'Guy wants to ride the god-damn lion it's his own business.'

There were murmurings. The man who had said pipe down was small and he wore black-rimmed glasses. 'I used to do it all the time.' He turned to Mr. Minchell and cried: 'How is it?'

Mr. Minchell grinned. Somehow, he realized, in some mysterious way, he had been given a second chance. And this time he knew what he would do with it. 'Fine!' he shouted, and stood up on King Richard's back and sent his derby spinning out over the heads of the people. 'Come on up!'

'Can't do it,' the man said. 'Got a date.' There was a look of profound admiration in his eyes as he strode off. Away from the crowd he stopped and cupped his hands and cried: 'I'll be seeing you!'

'That's right,' Mr. Minchell said, feeling the cold new wind on his face. 'You'll be seeing me.'

Later, when he was good and ready, he got down off the lion.

THE CLOUD-SCULPTORS OF CORAL D

J. G. Ballard

All summer the cloud-sculptors would come from Vermilion Sands and sail their painted gliders above the coral towers that rose like white pagodas beside the highway to Lagoon West. The tallest of the towers was Coral D, and here the rising air above the sand-reefs was topped by swan-like clumps of fair-weather cumulus. Lifted on the shoulders of the air above the crown of Coral D, we would carve sea-horses and unicorns, the portraits of presidents and film-stars, lizards and exotic birds. As the crowd watched from their cars, a cool rain would fall on to the dusty roofs, weeping from the sculptured clouds as they sailed across the desert floor towards the sun.

Of all the cloud-sculptures we were to carve, the strangest were the portraits of Leonora Chanel. As I looked back to that afternoon last summer when she first came in her white limousine to watch the cloud-sculptures of Coral D, I know we barely realized how seriously this beautiful but insane woman regarded the sculptures floating above her in that calm sky. Later her portraits, carved in the whirlwind, were to weep their storm-rain upon the corpses of their sculptors.

I had arrived in Vermilion Sands three months earlier. A retired pilot, I was painfully coming to terms with a broken leg and the prospect of never flying again. Driving into the desert one day, I stopped near the coral towers on the highway to Lagoon West. As I gazed at these immense pagodas stranded on the floor of this fossil sea, I heard music coming from a sand-reef two hundred yards away. Swinging on my crutches across the sliding sand, I found a shallow basin among the dunes where sonic statues had run to seed beside a ruined studio. The owner had gone, abandoning the hangar-like building to the sandrays and the desert, and on some half-formed impulse. I began to drive out each afternoon. From the lathes and joists left behind I built my first giant kites and, later, gliders with cockpits. Tethered by their cables, they would hang above me in the afternoon air like amiable ciphers.

One evening, as I wound the gliders down on to the winch, a sudden gale rose over the crest of Coral D. While I grappled with the whirling handle, trying to anchor my crutches in the sand, two figures approached across the desert floor. One was a small hunchback with a child's overlit eyes and a deformed jaw twisted like an anchor barb to one side. He scuttled over to the winch and wound the tattered gliders towards the ground, his powerful shoulders pushing me aside. He helped me on to my crutches and peered into the hangar. Here my most ambitious glider to date, no longer a kite but a sail-plane with elevators and control lines, was taking shape on the bench.

He spread a large hand over his chest. 'Petit Manuel—acrobat and weight-lifter. Nolan!' he bellowed. 'Look at this!' His companion was squatting by the sonic statues, twisting their helixes so that their voices became more resonant. 'Nolan's an artist,' the hunchback confided to me. 'He'll build you gliders like condors.'

The tall man was wandering among the gliders, touching their wings with a sculptor's hand. His morose eyes were set in a face like a bored Gauguin's. He glanced at the plaster on my leg and my faded flying jacket, and gestured at the gliders. 'You've given cockpit to them, major.' The remark contained a complete understanding of my motives. He pointed to the coral towers rising above us into the evening sky. 'With silver iodide we could carve the clouds.'

The hunchback nodded encouragingly to me, his eyes lit by an astronomy of dreams.

So were formed the cloud-sculptors of Coral D. Although I considered myself one of them, I never flew the gliders, but I taught Nolan and little Manuel to fly, and later, when he joined us, Charles Van Eyck. Nolan had found this blond-haired pirate of the cafe terraces in Vermilion Sands, a laconic teuton with droll eyes and a weak mouth, and brought him out to Coral D when the season ended and the well-to-do tourists and their nubile daughters returned to Red Beach. 'Major Parker—Charles Van Eyck.

He's a head-hunter,' Nolan commented with cold humour, '—maidenheads.' Despite their uneasy rivalry I realized that Van Eyck would give our group a useful dimension of glamour.

From the first I suspected that the studio in the desert was Nolan's, and that we were all serving some private whim of this dark-haired solitary. At the time, however, I was more concerned with teaching them to fly—first on cable, mastering the updraughts that swept the stunted turret of Coral A, smallest of the towers, then the steeper slopes of B and C, and finally the powerful currents of Coral D. Late one afternoon, when I began to wind them in, Nolan cut away his line. The glider plummeted onto its back, diving down to impale itself on the rock spires. I flung myself to the ground as the cable whipped across my car, shattering the windshield. When I looked up, Nolan was soaring high in the tinted air above Coral D. The wind, guardian of the coral towers, carried him through the islands of cumulus that veiled the evening light.

As I ran to the winch, the second cable went, and little Manuel swerved away to join Nolan. Ugly crab on the ground, in the air the hunchback became a bird with immense wings, outflying both Nolan and Van Eyck. I watched them as they circled the coral towers, and then swept down together over the desert floor, stirring the sand-rays into soot-like clouds. Petit Manuel was jubilant. He strutted around me like a pocket Napoleon, contemptuous of my broken leg, scooping up handfuls of broken glass and tossing them over his head like bouquets to the air.

Two months later, as we drove out to Coral D on the day we were to meet Leonora Chanel, something of this first feeling of exhilaration had faded. Now that the season had ended few tourists travelled to Lagoon West, and often we would perform our cloud-sculpture to the empty highway. Sometimes Nolan would remain behind in his hotel, drinking by himself on the bed, or Van Eyck would disappear for several days with some widow or divorcee, and Petit Manuel and I would go out alone.

Nonetheless, as the four of us drove out in my car that afternoon and saw the clouds waiting for us above the spire of Coral D, all my depression and fatigue vanished. Ten minutes later the three cloud-gliders rose into the air and the first cars began to stop on the highway. Nolan was in the lead in his black-winged glider, climbing straight to the crown of Coral D two hundred feet above, while Van Eyck soared to and fro below, showing his blond mane to a middle-aged woman in a topaz convertible. Behind them came little Manuel, his candy-striped wings slipping and churning in the disturbed air. Shouting happy obscenities, he flew with his twisted knees, huge arms gesticulating out of the cockpit.

The three gliders, brilliant painted toys, revolved like lazing birds above Coral D, waiting for the first clouds to pass overhead. Van Eyck moved away to take a cloud. He sailed around its white pillow, spraying the sides with iodide crystals and cutting away the flock-like tissue. The steaming shards fell towards us like crumbling ice-drifts. As the drops of condensing spray fell on my face, I could see Van Eyck shaping an immense horse's head. He sailed up and down the long forehead and chiselled out the eyes and ears.

As always, the people watching from their cars seemed to enjoy this piece of aerial marzipan. It sailed overhead, carried away on the wind from Coral D. Van Eyck followed it down, wings lazing around the equine head. Meanwhile, Petit Manuel worked away at the next cloud. As he sprayed its sides, a familiar human head appeared through the tumbling mist. Manuel caricatured the high wavy mane, strong jaw but slipped mouth from the cloud with a series of deft passes, wing-tips almost touching each other as he dived in and out of the portrait.

The glossy white head, an unmistakable parody of Van Eyck in his own worst style, crossed the highway towards Vermilion Sands. Manuel slid out of the air, stalling his glider to a landing beside my car as Van Eyck stepped from his cockpit with a forced smile.

We waited for the third display. A cloud formed over Coral D, within a few minutes had blossomed into a pristine fair-weather cumulus. As it hung there Nolan's black-winged glider plunged out of the sun. He soared around the cloud, cutting away its tissues. The soft fleece fell towards us in a cool rain.

There was a shout from one of the cars. Nolan turned from the cloud, his wings slipping as if unveiling his handiwork. Illuminated by the afternoon sun was the serene face of a three-year-old child. Its wide cheeks framed a placid mouth and plump chin. As one or two people clapped, Nolan sailed over the cloud and rippled the roof into ribbons and curls.

However, I knew that the real climax was yet to come. Cursed by some malignant virus, Nolan seemed unable to accept his own handiwork, always destroying it with the same cold humour. Petit Manuel had thrown away his cigarette, and even Van Eyck had turned his attention from the women in the cars.

Nolan soared above the child's face, following like a matador waiting for the moment of the kill. There was silence for a minute as he worked away at the cloud, and then someone slammed a car door in disgust.

Hanging above us was the white image of a skull.

The child's face, converted by a few strokes, had vanished, but in the notched teeth and gaping orbits, large enough to hold a car, we could still see an echo of its infant features. The spectre moved past us, the spectators frowning at this weeping skull whose rain fell upon their faces.

Half-heartedly I picked my old flying helmet off the back seat and began to carry it around the cars. Two of the spectators drove off before I could reach them. As I hovered about uncertainly, wondering why on earth a retired and well-to-do Air Force officer should be trying to collect these few dollar bills, Van Eyck stepped behind me and took the helmet from my hand.

'Not now, major. Look at what arrives—my apocalypse . . .'

A white Rolls-Royce, driven by a chauffeur in braided cream livery, had turned off the highway. Through the tinted communication window a young woman in a secretary's day suit spoke to the chauffeur. Beside her, a gloved hand still holding the window strap, a white-haired woman with jewelled eyes gazed up at the circling wings of the cloud-glider. Her strong and elegant face seemed sealed within the dark glass of the limousine like the enigmatic madonna of some marine grotto.

Van Eyck's glider rose into the air, soaring upwards to the cloud that hung above Coral D. I walked back to my car, searching the sky for Nolan. Above, Van Eyck was producing a pastiche Mona Lisa, a picture postcard gioconda as authentic as a plaster virgin. Its glossy finish shone in the over-bright sunlight as if enamelled together out of some cosmetic foam.

Then Nolan dived from the sun behind Van Eyck. Rolling his black-winged glider past Van Eyck's, he drove through the neck of the gioconda, and with the flick of a wing toppled the broad-cheeked head. It fell towards the cars below. The features disintegrated into a flaccid mess, sections of the nose and jaw tumbling through the steam. Then wings brushed. Van Eyck fired his spray gun at Nolan, and there was a flurry of torn fabric. Van Eyck fell from the air, steering his glider down to a broken landing.

I ran over to him. 'Charles, do you have to play Von Richthofen? For God's sake, leave each other alone!'

Van Eyck waved me away. 'Talk to Nolan, major. I'm not responsible for his air piracy.' He stood in the cockpit, gazing over the cars as the shreds of fabric fell around him.

I walked back to my car, deciding that the time had come to

disband the cloud-sculptors of Coral D. Fifty yards away the young secretary in the Rolls-Royce had stepped from the car and beckoned to me. Through the open door her mistress watched me with her jewelled eyes. Her white hair lay in a coil over one shoulder like a nacreous serpent.

I carried my flying helmet down to the young woman. Above a high forehead her auburn hair was swept back in a defensive bun, as if she were deliberately concealing part of herself. She stared with puzzled eyes at the helmet held out in front of her.

'I don't want to fly—what is it?'

'A grace,' I explained. 'For the repose of Michelangelo, Ed Keinholz and the cloud-sculptors of Coral D.'

'Oh, my God. I think the chauffeur's the only one with any *money*. Look, do you perform anywhere else?'

'Perform?' I glanced from this pretty and agreeable young woman to the pale chimera with jewelled eyes in the dim compartment of the Rolls. She was watching the headless figure of the Mona Lisa as it moved across the desert floor towards Vermilion Sands. 'We're not a professional troupe, as you've probably guessed. And obviously we'd need some fair-weather cloud. Where, exactly?'

'At Lagoon West.' She took a snake-skinned diary from her handbag. 'Miss Chanel is holding a series of garden parties. She wondered if you'd care to perform. Of course there would be a large fee.'

'Chanel . . . Leonora Chanel, the . . .?'

The young woman's face again took on its defensive posture, dissociating her from whatever might follow. 'Miss Chanel is at Lagoon West for the summer. By the way, there's one condition I must point out—Miss Chanel will provide the sole subject matter. You do understand?'

Fifty yards away Van Eyck was dragging his damaged glider towards my car. Nolan had landed, a caricature of Cyrano abandoned in mid-air. Petit Manuel limped to and fro, gathering together the equipment. In the fading afternoon light they resembled a threadbare circus troupe.

'All right,' I agreed. 'I take your point. But what about the clouds, Miss—?'

'Lafferty. Beatrice Lafferty. Miss Chanel will provide the clouds.'

I walked around the cars with the helmet, then divided the money between Nolan, Van Eyck and Manuel. They stood in the gathering dusk, the few bills in their hands, watching the highway below.

Leonora Chanel stepped from the limousine and strolled into the desert. Her white-haired figure in its cobra-skinned coat wandered among the dunes. Sand-rays lifted around her, disturbed by the random movements of this sauntering phantasm of the burnt afternoon. Ignoring their open stings around her legs, she was gazing up at the aerial bestiary dissolving in the sky, and at the white skull a mile away over Lagoon West that had smeared itself across the sky.

At the time I first saw her, watching the cloud-sculptors of Coral D, I had only a half-formed impression of Leonora Chanel. The daughter of one of the world's leading financiers, she was an heiress both in her own right and on the death of her husband, a shy Monacan aristocrat, Comte Louis Chanel. The mysterious circumstances of his death at Cap Ferrat on the Riviera, officially described as suicide, had placed Leonora in a spotlight of publicity and gossip. She had escaped by wandering endlessly across the globe, from her walled villa in Tangier to an Alpine mansion in the snows above Pontresina, and from there to Palm Springs, Seville and Mykonos.

During these years of exile something of her character emerged from the magazine and newspaper photographs: moodily visiting a Spanish charity with the Duchess of Alba, or seated with Saroya and other members of cafe society on the terrace of Dali's villa at Port Lligat, her self-regarding face gazing out with its jewelled eyes at the diamond sea of the Costa Brava.

Inevitably her Garbo-like role seemed over-calculated, forever undermined by the suspicions of her own hand in her husband's death. The Count had been an introspective playboy who piloted his own aircraft to archaeological sites in the Peloponnese and whose mistress, a beautiful young Lebanese, was one of the world's pre-eminent keyboard interpreters of Bach. Why this reserved and pleasant man should have committed suicide was never made plain. What promised to be a significant exhibit at the coroner's inquest, a mutilated easel portrait of Leonora on which he was working, was accidentally destroyed before the hearing. Perhaps the painting revealed more of Leonora's character than she chose to see.

A week later, as I drove out to Lagoon West on the morning of the first garden party, I could well understand why Leonora Chanel had come to Vermilion Sands, to this bizarre, sand-bound resort with its lethargy, beach fatigue and shifting perspectives. Sonic statues grew wild along the beach, their voices keening as I swept past along the shore road. The fused silica on the surface of the lake formed an immense rainbow mirror that reflected the deranged colours of the sand-reefs, more vivid even than the cinnabar and cyclamen wing-panels of the cloud-gliders overhead. They soared in the sky above the lake like fitful dragonflies as Nolan, Van Eyck and Petit Manuel flew them from Coral D.

We had entered an inflamed landscape. Half a mile away the angular cornices of the summer house jutted into the vivid air as if distorted by some faulty junction of time and space. Behind it, like an exhausted volcano, a broad-topped mesa rose into the glazed air, its shoulders lifting the thermal currents high off the heated lake.

Envying Nolan and little Manuel these tremendous updraughts, more powerful than any we had known at Coral D, I drove towards the villa. Then the haze cleared along the beach and I saw the clouds.

A hundred feet above the roof of the mesa, they hung like the twisted pillows of a sleepless giant. Columns of turbulent air moved within the clouds, boiling upwards to the anvil heads like liquid in a cauldron. These were not the placid, fair-weather cumulus of Coral D, but storm-nimbus, unstable masses of overheated air that could catch an aircraft and lift it a thousand feet in a few seconds. Here and there the clouds were rimmed with dark bands, their towers crossed by valleys and ravines. They moved across the villa, concealed from the lakeside heat by the haze overhead, then dissolved in a series of violent shifts in the disordered air.

As I entered the drive behind a truck filled with *son et lumiere* equipment, a dozen members of the staff were straightening lines of gilt chairs on the terrace and unrolling panels of a marquee.

Beatrice Lafferty stepped across the cables. 'Major Parker —there are the clouds we promised you.'

I looked up again at the dark billows hanging like shrouds above the white villa. 'Clouds, Beatrice? Those are tigers, tigers with wings. We're manicurists of the air, not dragon-tamers.'

'Don't worry, a manicure is exactly what you're expected to carry out.' With an arch glance, she added: 'Your men do understand that there's to be only one subject?'

'Miss Chanel herself? Of course.' I took her arm as we walked towards the balcony overlooking the lake. 'You know, I think you enjoy these snide asides. Let the rich choose their materials —marble, bronze, plasma or cloud. Why not? Portraiture has always been a neglected art.'

'My God, not here.' She waited until a steward passed with a tray of table-cloths. 'Carving one's portrait in the sky out of the sun and air—some people might say that smacked of vanity, or even worse sins.'

'You're very mysterious. Such as?'

She played games with her eyes. 'I'll tell you in a month's time when my contract expires. Now, when are your men coming?'

'They're here.' I pointed to the sky over the lake. The three gliders hung in the overheated air, clumps of cloud-cotton drifting past them to dissolve in the haze. They were following a sand-yacht that approached the quay, its tyres throwing up the cerise dust. Behind the helmsman sat Leonora Chanel in a trouser suit of yellow alligator skin, her white hair hidden inside a black raffia toque.

As the helmsman moored the craft, Van Eyck and Petit Manuel put on an impromptu performance, shaping the fragments of cloud-cotton a hundred feet above the lake. First Van Eyck carved an orchid, then a heart and a pair of lips, while Manuel fashioned the head of a parakeet, two identical mice and the letters 'L.C.' As they dived and plunged around her, their wings sometimes touching the lake, Leonora stood on the quay, politely waving at each of these brief confections.

When they landed beside the quay, Leonora waited for Nolan to take one of the clouds, but he was sailing up and down the lake in front of her like a weary bird. Watching this strange chatelaine of Lagoon West, I noticed that she had slipped off into some private reverie, her gaze fixed on Nolan and oblivious of the people around her. Memories, caravels without sails, crossed the shadowy deserts of her burnt-out eyes.

Later that evening Beatrice Lafferty led me into the villa through the library window. There, as Leonora greeted her guests on the terrace, wearing a topless dress of sapphires and organdy, her breasts covered only by their contour jewellery, I saw the portraits that filled the villa. I counted more than twenty, from the formal society portraits in the drawing rooms, one by the President of the Royal Academy, another by Annigoni, to the bizarre psychological studies in the bar and dining room by Dali and Francis Bacon. Everywhere we moved, in the alcoves between the marble semi-columns, in gilt miniatures on the mantle shelves, even in the ascending mural that followed the staircase, we saw the same beautiful, self-regarding face. This colossal narcissism seemed to have become her last refuge, the only retreat for her fugitive self in its flight from the world.

Then, in the studio on the roof, we came across a large easel portrait that had just been varnished. The artist had produced a deliberate travesty of the sentimental and powder-blue tints of a fashionable society painter, but beneath this gloss he had visualized Leonora as a dead Medea. The stretched skin below her right cheek, the sharp forehead and slipped mouth gave her the numbed and luminous appearance of a corpse.

My eyes moved to the signature. 'Nolan! My God, were you here when he painted this?'

'It was finished before I came—two months ago. She refused to have it framed.'

'No wonder.' I went over to the window and looked down at the bedrooms hidden behind their awnings. 'Nolan was *here*. The old studio near Coral D was his.'

'But why should Leonora ask him back? They must have—'

'To paint her portrait again. I know Leonora Chanel better than you do, Beatrice. This time, though, the size of the sky.'

We left the library and walked past the cocktails and canapes to where Leonora was welcoming her guests. Nolan stood beside her, wearing a suit of white suede. Now and then he looked down at her as if playing with the possibilities this self-obsessed woman gave to his macabre humour. Leonora clutched at his elbow. With the diamonds fixed around her eyes she reminded me of some archaic priestess. Beneath the contour jewelery her breasts lay like eager snakes.

Van Eyck introduced himself with an exaggerated bow. Behind him came Petit Manuel, his twisted head ducking nervously among the tuxedos.

Leonora's mouth shut in a rictus of distaste. She glanced at the white plaster on my foot. 'Nolan, you fill your world with cripples. Your little dwarf—will he fly too?'

Petit Manuel looked at her with eyes like crushed flowers.

The performance began an hour later. The dark-rimmed clouds were lit by the sun setting behind the mesa, the air crossed by wraiths of cirrus like the gilded frames of the immense paintings to come. Van Eyck's glider rose in a spiral towards the face of the first cloud, stalling and climbing again as the turbulent updraughts threw him across the air.

As the cheekbones began to appear, as smooth and lifeless as carved foam, applause rang out from the guests seated on the terrace. Five minutes later, when Van Eyck's glider swooped down onto the lake, I could see that he had excelled himself. Lit by the searchlights, and with the overture to Tristan sounding from the loudspeaker on the slopes of the mesa, as if inflating this huge bauble, the portrait of Leonora moved overhead, a faint rain falling from it. By luck the cloud remained stable until it passed the shoreline, and then broke up in the evening air as if ripped from the sky by an irritated hand.

Petit Manuel began his ascent, sailing in on a dark-edged cloud like an urchin accosting a bad-tempered matron. He soared to and fro, as if unsure how to shape this unpredictable column of vapour, then began to carve it into the approximate contours of a woman's head. He seemed more nervous than I had ever seen him. As he finished a second round of applause broke out, soon followed by laughter and ironic cheers.

The cloud, sculptured into a flattering likeness of Leonora, had begun to tilt, rotating in the disturbed air. The jaw lengthened, the glazed smile became that of an idiot's. Within a minute the gigantic head of Leonora Chanel hung upside down above us.

Discreetly I ordered the searchlights switched off, and the audience's attention turned to Nolan's black-winged glider as it climbed towards the next cloud. Shards of dissolving tissue fell from the darkening air, the spray concealing whatever ambiguous creation Nolan was carving. To my surprise, the portrait that emerged was wholly lifelike. There was a burst of applause, a few bars of Tannhauser, and the searchlights lit up the elegant head. Standing among her guests, Leonora raised her glass to Nolan's glider.

Puzzled by Nolan's generosity, I looked more closely at the gleaming face, and then realized what he had done. The portrait, with cruel irony, was all too lifelike. The downward turn of Leonora's mouth, the chin held up to smooth her neck, the fall of flesh below her right cheek—all these were carried on the face of the cloud as they had been in his painting in the studio.

Around Leonora the guests were congratulating her on the performance. She was looking up at her portrait as it began to break up over the lake, seeing it for the first time. The veins held the blood in her face.

Then a fireworks display on the beach blotted out these ambiguities in its pink and blue explosions.

Shortly before dawn Beatrice Lafferty and I walked along the beach among the shells of burnt-out rockets and catherine wheels. On the deserted terrace a few lights shone through the darkness onto the scattered chairs. As we reached the steps, a woman's voice cried out somewhere above us. There was the sound of smashed glass. A french window was kicked back, and a dark-haired man in a white suit ran between the tables.

As Nolan disappeared along the drive, Leonora Chanel walked out into the centre of the terrace. She looked at the dark clouds surging over the mesa, and with one hand tore the jewels from her eyes. They lay winking in the tiles at her feet. Then the hunched figure of Petit Manuel leapt from his hiding place in the bandstand. He scuttled past, racing on his bent legs.

An engine started by the gates. Leonora began to walk back to the villa, staring at her broken reflections in the glass below the window. She stopped as a tall, blond-haired man with cold and eager eyes stepped from the sonic statues outside the library. Disturbed by the noise, the statues had begun to whine. As Van Eyck moved towards Leonora they took up the slow beat of his steps.

The next day's performance was the last by the cloud-sculptors of Coral D. All afternoon, before the guests arrived, a dim light lay over the lake. Immense tiers of storm-nimbus were massing behind the mesa, and any performance at all seemed unlikely.

Van Eyck was with Leonora. As I arrived, Beatrice Lafferty was watching their sand-yacht carry them unevenly across the lake, its sails shipped by the squalls.

'There's no sign of Nolan or little Manuel,' she told me. 'The party starts in three hours.'

I took her arm. 'The party's already over. When you're finished here, Bea, come and live with me at Coral D. I'll teach you to sculpt the clouds.'

Van Eyck and Leonora came ashore half an hour later. Van Eyck stared through my face as he brushed past. Leonora clung to his arm, the day-jewels around her eyes scattering their hard light across the terrace.

By eight, when the first guests began to appear, Nolan and Petit Manuel had still not arrived. On the terrace the evening was warm and lamplit, but overhead the storm-clouds sidled past each other like uneasy giants. I walked up the slope to where the gliders were tethered. Their wings shivered in the updraughts.

Barely half a minute after he rose into the darkening air, dwarfed by an immense tower of storm-nimbus, Charles Van Eyck was spinning towards the ground, his glider toppled by the crazed air. He recovered fifty feet from the villa and climbed on the updraughts from the lake, well away from the spreading chest of the cloud. He soared in again. As Leonora and her guests watched from their seats, the glider was hurled back over their heads in an explosion of vapour, then fell towards the lake with a broken wing.

I walked towards Leonora. Standing by the balcony were Nolan and Petit Manuel, watching Van Eyck climb from the cockpit of his glider three hundred yards away.

To Nolan I said: 'Why bother to come? Don't tell me you're going to fly?'

Nolan leaned against the rail, hands in the pockets of his suit. 'I'm not—that's why I'm here.'

Leonora was wearing an evening dress of peacock feathers that lay around her legs in an immense train. The hundreds of eyes gleamed in the electric air before the storm, sheathing her body in their blue flames.

'Miss Chanel, the clouds are like madmen,' I apologised. 'There's a storm on its way.'

She looked up at me with unsettled eyes. 'Don't you people expect to take risks?' She gestured at the storm-nimbus that swirled over our heads. 'For clouds like these I need a Michelangelo of the sky . . . What about Nolan? Is he too frightened as well?'

As she shouted his name, Nolan stared at her, then turned his back to us. The light over Lagoon West had changed. Half the lake was covered by a dim pall.

There was a tug on my sleeve. Petit Manuel looked up at me with his crafty child's eyes. 'Raymond, I can go. Let me take the glider.'

'Manuel, for God's sake. You'll kill—'

He darted between the gilt chairs. Leonora frowned as he plucked her wrist.

'Miss Chanel . . .' His loose mouth formed an encouraging smile. 'I'll sculpt for you. Right now, a big storm-cloud, eh?'

She stared down at him, half-repelled by this eager hunchback ogling her beside the hundred eyes of her peacock train. Van Eyck was limping back to the beach from his wrecked glider. I guessed that in some strange way Manuel was pitting himself against Van Eyck.

Leonora grimaced, as if swallowing some poisonous phlegm. 'Major Parker, tell him to—' She glanced at the dark cloud boiling over the mesa like the effluvium of some black-hearted volcano.

'Wait! Let's see what the little cripple can do!' She turned on Manuel with an over-bright smile. 'Go on, then. Let's see you sculpt a whirlwind!'

In her face the diagram of bones formed a geometry of murder.

Nolan ran past across the terrace, his feet crushing the peacock feathers as Leonora laughed. We tried to stop Manuel, but he raced up the slope. Stung by Leonora's taunt, he skipped among the rocks, disappearing from sight in the darkening air. On the terrace a small crowd gathered to watch.

The yellow and tangerine glider rose into the sky and climbed across the face of the storm-cloud. Fifty yards from the dark billows it was buffeted by the shifting air, but Manuel soared in and began to cut away at the dark face. Drops of black rain fell across the terrace at our feet.

The first outline of a woman's head appeared, satanic eyes lit by the open vents in the cloud, a sliding mouth like a dark smear as the huge billows boiled forwards. Nolan shouted in warning from the lake as he climbed into his glider. A moment later little Manuel's craft was lifted by a powerful updraught and tossed over the roof of the cloud. Fighting the insane air, Manuel plunged the glider downwards and drove into the cloud again. Then its immense face opened, and in a sudden spasm the cloud surged forward and swallowed the glider.

There was silence on the terrace as the crushed body of the craft revolved in the centre of the cloud. It moved over our heads, dismembered pieces of the wings and fuselage churned about in the dissolving face. As it reached the lake, the cloud began its violent end. Pieces of the face slewed sideways, the mouth was torn off, an eye exploded. It vanished in a last brief squall.

The pieces of Petit Manuel's glider fell from the bright air.

Beatrice Lafferty and I drove across the lake to collect Manuel's body. After the spectacle of this death within the exploding replica of their hostess's face, the guests began to leave. Within minutes the drive was full of cars. Leonora watched them go, standing with Van Eyck among the deserted tables.

Beatrice said nothing as we drove out. The pieces of the shattered glider lay over the fused sand, tags of canvas and broken struts, control lines tied into knots. Then yards from the cockpit I found Petit Manuel's body, lying in a wet ball like a drowned monkey.

I carried him back to the sand-yacht.

'Raymond!' Beatrice pointed to the shore. Storm-clouds were

massed along the entire length of the lake, and the first flashes of lightning were striking in the hills behind the mesa. In the electric air the villa had lost its glitter. Half a mile away a tornado was moving along the valley floor, its trunk swaying towards the lake.

The first gusts of air struck the yacht. Beatrice shouted again: 'Raymond! Nolan's there—he's flying inside it!'

Then I saw the black-winged glider circling under the umbrella of the tornado, Nolan himself riding in the whirlwind. His wings held steady in the revolving air around the funnel. Like a pilot fish he soared in, as if steering the tornado towards Leonora's villa.

Twenty seconds later, when it struck the house, I lost sight of him. An explosion of dark air overwhelmed the villa, a churning centrifuge of shattered chairs and tiles that burst over the roof. Beatrice and I ran from the yacht, and lay together in a fault in the glass surface. As the tornado moved away, fading into the storm-filled sky, a dark squall hung over the wrecked villa, now and then flicking the debris into the air. Shreds of canvas and peacock feathers fell around us.

We waited half an hour before approaching the house. Hundreds of smashed glasses and broken chairs littered the terrace. At first I could see no signs of Leonora, although her face was everywhere, the portraits with their slashed profiles strewn on the damp tiles. An eddying smile floated towards me from the disturbed air, and wrapped itself around my leg.

Leonora's body lay among the broken tables near the bandstand, half-wrapped in a bleeding canvas. Her face was as bruised now as the storm-cloud Manuel had tried to carve.

We found Van Eyck in the wreck of the marquee. He was suspended by the neck from a tangle of electric wiring, his pale face wreathed in a noose of light bulbs. The current flowed intermittently through the wiring, lighting up his strangled eyes.

I leaned against the overturned Rolls, holding Beatrice's shoulders. 'There's no sign of Nolan—no pieces of his glider.'

'Poor man. Raymond, he was driving that whirlwind here. Somehow he was controlling it.'

I walked across the damp terrace to where Leonora lay. I began silently to cover her with the shreds of canvas, the torn faces of herself.

I took Beatrice Lafferty to live with me in Nolan's studio in the desert near Coral D. We heard no more of Nolan, and never flew the gliders again. The clouds carry too many memories. Three months ago a man who saw the derelict gliders outside the studio stopped near Coral D and walked across to us. He told us he had seen a man flying a glider in the sky high above Red Beach, carving the strato-cirrus into images of jewels and children's faces. Once there was a dwarf's head.

On reflection, that sounds rather like Nolan, so perhaps he managed to get away from the tornado. In the evenings Beatrice and I sit among the sonic statues, listening to their voices as the fair-weather clouds rise above Coral D, waiting for a man in a dark-winged glider, perhaps painted like candy now, who will come in on the wind and carve for us images of sea-horses and unicorns, dwarfs and jewels and children's faces.

THE INVASION OF THE CHURCH OF THE HOLY GHOST

Russell Kirk

Some say no evil thing that walks by night
In fog, or fire, by lake, or moorish fen,
Blew meager Hag, or stubborn unlaid
  ghost,
No Goblin, or swart Faery of the mine,
Hath hurtful power o'er true virginity.
            —*Comus*

What occurred in my church last night must be committed to writing without delay. Having discovered my own feebleness, I do not know how long I might resist, should some other presence enter the church. Fork cast out the nightwalkers, and the girl, too, has gone, but there is no discharge in this war.

Perhaps the one devil who stared me in the face may gather seven other spirits more wicked than himself, so that my last state should be worse than my first. If such ruin comes to pass, at least I will have set down these happenings. Knowledge of them might preserve my successor at this Church of the Holy Ghost.

Successor? No likely prospect. Were I to depart, the bishop would lock the bronze doors—and soon demolish the hulking church, supposing him able to pay the wreckers' bills. Our bishop, saints forgive him, spends his days comminating the president of the United States and ordaining lesbians. The Right Reverend Soronson Hickey regards me as a disagreeable, if exotic, eccentric who fancies that he has a cure of souls—when every right-thinking cleric in this diocese has been instructed that the notion of souls is a fable. Had I been born white, the bishop would have thrust me out of the Church of the Holy Ghost months ago.

Whoever you are, reading these scribbled pages—why, I may be dead or vanished, and the dear bishop may be my reader—I must first set down my name and station. I am Raymond Thomas Montrose, doctor of divinity, rector of the Church of the Holy Ghost in the parish of Hawkhill. This parish and the neighboring districts make up the roughest quarter of what is called the 'inner city.' I am an Episcopalian priest, the only reasonably orthodox clergyman remaining in Hawkhill, which Satan claims for his own.

Thomas is my confirmation name, and my patron is Saint Thomas of Canterbury. Like my patron, I stand six feet four in my armor. Yes, armor; but my mail is black leather, and I sleep with a pistol hanging from my bedhead.

A sergeant's son, I was born in Spanishtown, Jamaica, and I am shiny black: nobody excels me in negritude. The barmaids of Pentecost Road say I have a 'cute British accent.' I believe in the Father, the Son, and the Holy Ghost; the resurrection of the dead; and the life everlasting. I am celibate, not quite forty years of age, and since my ordination chaste of body. I have survived in Hawkhill a whole year.

My rectory is a safe-house, after a fashion. Occasionally I lodge behind its thick walls and barred windows—the builders of a century gone built more wisely than they knew—girls off Pentecost Road, fugitive from their pimps. The bishop admonishes me that this unseemly hospitality may give rise to scandal. I have replied that I do not desire carnal knowledge of these young women. It is their souls I am after. At such superstitious discourse the bishop scowls. Were I a pathic, he would not reprove me.

My Church of the Holy Ghost is Richardsonian Romanesque in style, erected more than a century ago, when red sandstone and Hawkhill were fashionable. The bishop has exiled me to the farthest frontier of his diocese, no other clergyman applying for my present rectorship. I accepted cheerfully enough a cure of souls in what the humorists of our daily press call the Demilitarized Zone of our city. Would that it really had been demilitarized. I did not obtain a permit for a pistol out of mere bravado.

The Church of the Holy Ghost, Protestant Episcopal, looms handsomely though grimly over Merrymont Avenue, three blocks east of the junction with Pentecost Road. (In the believing early years of our city, those names were not thought absurd.) Some fine old houses still stand on Merrymont: many more have been burned by arsonists (often hired arsonists) or have fallen into hopeless ruin.

Where once our upper classes gloried and drank deep, the owl and bat their revel keep—or, more literally, the poorest of our poor get drunk and disorderly whenever they can.

I make no claim to have cured many souls near the junction of Pentecost and Merrymont. Occasionally my Sunday services are attended by as many as seventy persons (in a building that might seat seven hundred), a good many of them immigrants (chiefly illegal) from the Caribbean like myself. There is a peppering of quiet little people from southeastern Asia, and a salting of old white folk stranded in Hawkhill by the pace of change in our city. One of the last group, Mrs. Simmons, still has money, which enables me to keep the church doors open. The bishop doles me out next to nothing for any purpose.

The sheltered broad steps ascending to the magnificent doors of my church are carpeted wall to wall, on clement days, by the Old Soldiers, winos and other derelicts; some bums sleep on those steps all night in summer, though not at this season. (Were I to let them lodge inside, they'd have the church befouled, looted, and desecrated within an hour.) A brace of policemen clear the Old Soldiers off the steps for my Sunday morning service. Some few of these Ancient Pistols even join my congregation, to escape snow or wind. I have made Anglo-Catholics of two or three.

Though less poverty-racked than Merrymont Avenue, Pentecost Road is more dreadful. For Pentecost Road has become the heart of the domain of the pushers and the pimps. Young women and female children of several colors parade on Pentecost in hope of custom; so do a number of boys, also for general hire. 'If you want it, we've got it,' is the legend painted above the entrance to the best-patronized bar on Pentecost Road. At the devil's booth all things are sold.

Besides believing earnestly in the doctrine of the soul, I believe with all my heart in Satan, whose territories are daily enlarged. I know myself for a castellan of Castle Perilous—my Church of the Holy Ghost looks like a mighty fortress—beset every hour by Satan's minions.

Reader, whoever you are, you might call me an educated Salvation Nigger. I am called worse than that, frequently, on Pentecost Road. Few of Satan's minions on that street know me for a man of the cloth; they are not numbered among my communicants. In vestments, and with my hair brushed, I look unlike myself in my Pentecost Road armor. When I tour the Pentecost bars I wear a greasy broad-brim hat and a very loud suit under my leather jacket. Somehow the word has been passed round that I am an unsuccessful chiropractor who likes his rum drinks.

I frequent Pentecost Road to snatch from the burning what brands I may. In this thankless labor I found an impossible coadjutor in the person of Fork Causland.

A source of the rumor that I am a chiropractor is Fork Causland's custom of addressing me as Doc. But I am in his debt for much more than that.

The first time I saw Fork, who will loom large in the pages of this document, he was descending nimbly from a bus—nimbly for a blind man, that is. Under his left arm he gripped a sheaf of placards announcing a wrestling match; these he was posting in the windows of barbershops and other small businesses. This bill-posting was one of the several means by which Causland supported himself, accepting no welfare payments.

I watched while he clanked his brass-shod stick upon the sidewalk and cried out to the world, in jovial defiance, 'Northwest corner of Beryl and Clemens! Don't tell me I don't know where I am!'

Fork wore black goggles that fitted tight to his broad half-Indian face. Quite as invariably he wore, outdoors and in, a black derby hat—what would have been called a bowler, down where I was born. Although not tall, Fork was formidably constructed and in prime condition. His face-mask was the hardest visage that ever I have looked upon: 'tough as nails,' as they say. Also, it was a face humorously stoical.

On that street corner I merely stared at Fork, who brushed past me to enter a cafeteria. It was a week later that I first conversed with him, in the Mustang Bar, Pentecost Road.

I was sipping a daiquiri—'pansy drink,' a mugger type at the bar had growled, but I had stared him down—when somebody outside shouted, 'The old Mustang! Wahoo!' Something rang upon concrete, and there bounced into view Fork Causland. I write 'bounced': that is what he did. The burly blind man flung himself into the air, his left hand clutching the head of his stick; and he seemed to hold himself suspended in the air for half a minute, miraculously, his soles a foot or more above the pavement. Either Causland had a marvelously strong left wrist, or there was something preternatural about this blind man who could set at defiance the law of gravity.

Nobody else happened to be watching Fork's performance at that moment, but later I inquired among barflies about him. Some thought that Causland had been a circus performer in his youth, and had fallen from a high wire, destroying his eyes. Others said that he had been a sergeant of military police, blinded in line of duty. (If so, where was his pension?) Yet others suggested that acid had been thrown in his eyes when he was a strikebreaker, or perhaps a striker. Fork kept his own counsel. Surely that levitation-performance was odd, extremely odd; so were other feats of his, I was to learn.

'This old Mustang!' Fork announced again, very loudly, to an uncaring Pentecost Road. He passed through the open doorway of the Mustang to seat himself at the blond piano in the middle of the smoky room. (The Mustang reeks with marijuana.) 'The regular, Ozzie,' Fork called to the barman. A waitress fetched him a tumbler of cheap whiskey. Having tossed off half his drink, Fork began to play that battered piano.

I remember that he played 'Redwing'—the taste of the elder spirits among the Mustang's patrons being oldfangled and senti-mental; and he sang the lyrics in a melodious deep voice. 'The breeze is sighing, the night birds crying . . .' He elevated the lyrics from bathos to pathos. He was not a piano player merely, but a pianist, this blind chap.

I asked the waitress the man's name. 'Homer Causland, but for the last two years they've all called him Fork.' She added, sotto voce, 'Don't give him no cause to take offense.'

I shifted to a table beside the piano. 'Mr. Causland,' I said to him, 'have you ever played the organ?'

'You're from Jamaica?' he responded, without hesitation. His head turned in my direction, the hard, taut face inscrutable.

'Not Long Island,' I answered. 'You've a good ear for speech, friend.'

'That's part of my survival strategy. You a doctor, maybe?'

'Of divinity, Mr. Causland. I'm rector of Holy Ghost Church.'

'If you need somebody to play the organ there, Doc, you could look further than me and do worse. What do you pay?'

We settled on five dollars a Sunday, all I could manage, but a substantial augmenting of Fork's income. I found that he could play Bach and Handel tolerably well from memory. Where Fork learned piano and organ, he never confided to me.

Pentecost Road took it for granted that Fork had 'blown his lid' on some narcotic, so accepting his eccentricity. I found him neither mad nor half-mad, odd though he was. He was quick-witted, shrewd, and capable of serious reflection. From listening to records and tapes for the blind, he had picked up a miscellany of literary and philosophical knowledge. The recurrent extreme oddity of his public conduct—his acrobatic tricks (if such they were) and his shouting—I judged to be part of a general pose or blind (not to pun). Yet for what purpose this concealment of his real nature?

In the course of a month, I extracted from Fork and from others the explanation of his sobriquet 'Fork.' That account, set down below, may seem a digression; but it is bound up with the unnerving things that occurred during the past week at my church.

Pentecost Road respects one thing chiefly: successful violence, better even than riches. From such an act Fork Causland had obtained his familiar name and his high repute on Pentecost Road.

Occasionally fragments of conversation of a sinister bent may be overheard by a sharp-eared man who for drinks and tips plays the piano in rough saloons. In the Mustang, Homer Causland happened to gather enough of one tipsy dialogue to recognize it as a conspiracy to murder. He informed the police.

It was a gruesome, interesting case, that conspiracy to murder; but I am trying to be succinct. Despite Causland's warning, the murder in question actually was perpetrated—while the police were trying to fit Causland's testimony into the jigsaw puzzle of the suspected conspiracy. It was the killing, the prolonged and hideous slaughter, of a disobedient young prostitute.

Although Causland's evidence did not prevent the crime, it did enable the police to identify the three principal criminals, leaders of a 'vice ring.' They had been often arrested, yet scarcely ever convicted. Now the charge was homicide in the first degree.

With his accustomed stoic courage, Causland testified fully in open court; the police rarely had been able to produce so convincing a witness. Nevertheless, an intimidated jury and a judge who disgraced the bench found the three accused not guilty.

One of the accused was a Big Man on Pentecost Road: big in narcotics, big in prostitution. Generally he was called Sherm; sometimes Sherm the Screamer, from his accustomed mode of addressing young women under his control; also, perhaps, because of his talent for compelling other people to scream. He had been tried under the name (doubtless an alias, his original name being unknown in our city) of Sherman Stanton. He was a youngish man, lean, curly-haired, even handsome except for the persistent sneer on his face. Nobody knew where Sherm had come from before he began to dominate Pentecost Road's traffic in drugs and flesh.

Such talented and agressive criminals build up a following of young men and women, moved by the emulatory passion, in such districts as Hawkhill. Sherm, despite his nasty manners and ways, obtained a large and devoted following. What was less usual, he riveted his grip upon his dupes by posing as an occult prophet of sorts. Oh, he was clever!

We have a sufficient number of queer creeds in Jamaica, but Sherm's pseudo-religion was worse than any of those. In some ways his rubbish—cribbed from paperback novels, possibly—resembled the cult of Thuggee. How much of his own mystagogy about Kali and Ishtar did Sherm the Screamer actually believe? He was after domination of minds and bodies—especially bodies, but he seems to have subscribed to some of his own devilish dogmas. He claimed to be able to project his essence out of the body, and to travel as pure kinetic energy through space and time. Also, he declared that he could not perish.

The pretense of exotic religiosity was of some utility to him. I am told that he tried to obtain exemption from property taxes for the storefront 'church' that was his ring's headquarters; and he hired a lawyer to plead the first clause of the First Amendment when police asked for a warrant to search that 'church.' One detective remarked unguardedly to a reporter, 'Hell, that "Church of Ishtar and Kali" is just a kinky bawdy house.'

When I write that some of us are engaged in a holy war, I mean that literally. We are a scant rear guard, and we are losing, here below, in this fallen age. Like the Celts of the Twilight, we go forth often to battle, but rarely to victory.

Satan is come among us as a raging lion, having great wrath. Sherm was a limb of Satan: that, too, I mean literally. He corrupted and peddled young girls for the pleasure of seeing them destroyed. He laughed whenever he had persuaded some fool to burn out his own brains on hard drugs. In our day the Sherms multiply and prosper. You have only to spend a year in the neighborhood of Pentecost Road to understand that Satan is a person and a conscious force, no figure of myth merely. He takes possession of empty vessels. On Pentecost Road I learned that the time is out of joint—and that though I could not set it right, still might I set my face against temptation, as did my patron Thomas à Becket. I digress: I must keep to the point, for the night cometh when no man shall work.

> But at my back in a cold blast I hear
> The rattle of the bones, and chuckle
> spread from ear to ear.

Yes, Sherm and his friends were set at liberty. This enabled them to deal with Causland, whose testimony had come near to getting them life sentences. Sherm the Screamer did not tolerate informers on Pentecost Road. Blind Homer Causland knew what to expect.

Prosecutor and police conveniently forgot Causland, when the trial had ended in acquittal; they had plenty of fish to fry. Had he gone to the prosecutor's office, perhaps some nominal protection might have been extended to him; but Causland, a lone wolf, didn't bother. He hadn't the money, or perhaps the will, to leave the city altogether. Once upon a time Causland may have been good with a gun, possibly in the line of duty but a blind man has no use for such toys. All Causland could do was to wait upon the event, which might lie in the hand of God or in the hand of Satan.

On his way home from bill-posting one afternoon, Causland halted at a tumbledown secondhand shop. He had a speaking acquaintance with the proprietress, an alcoholic crone.

'What you rummagin' for today, Homer?'

'Garden tools, Mrs. Mattheson.'

'Pardon me sayin' so, but I didn't never hear of no blind man growin' no garden.' Mrs. Mattheson tittered at her own wit.

'Why, Mrs. Mattheson, a blind beggar can make a compost heap. Do you have in stock such a thing as a pitchfork?'

She did: an old rusty one, the upper part of its hickory shaft somewhat split. Causland fingered the crack, asked for a small saw, and skillfully sawed off the upper portion of the shaft, shortening the tool by a foot. He paid Mrs. Mattheson sixty-five cents for this purchase, and a quarter more for a little old greasy whetstone.

Causland lived in a tall brick house that had seen better days—much better. So had his ancient Christian Science landlady. A battered cast-iron fence still surrounded the yard. The several tenants, whatever their moral attributes, were tolerably clean and quiet. Three effeminate young men occupied most of the ground floor. Causland had one room on the top floor; a narrow staircase was the only normal means of access. But Causland's room was one of three in which the Christian Science landlady, Mrs. Bauer, took a peculiar pride. Those three had, or could have had, dumbwaiter service. The dumbwaiter was a forgotten token of genteel living on Merrymont Avenue. Though nothing much had gone up or down the dumbwaiter for years, its electric controls remained operable.

Causland's room (which I saw for the first time only last week, when we had important matters to discuss) had been furnished by the landlady. It was an old-fashioned widow's room, actually, with austere straight-backed chairs, cane-seated, bought cheaply about

1900; a vast, heavy, venerable wardrobe; an old chest; a pine table; a narrow iron bedstead. Everything was desiccated, and the lace curtains seemed ready to disintegrate. Yet the room was clean. Blind men, I suppose, are indifferent to furniture styles and the hues of wallpaper.

The one feature of that room to relieve the eye was the glossy-varnished oaken door to the dumbwaiter. It was a large dumbwaiter—possibly it had been used for carrying firewood and coals, before the house's fireplaces had been bricked up and papered over—so that a slim man might open the door and climb into the contraption, if he chose.

Causland's lodging house stood on Merrymont, only three blocks east of my church. Here, in point of continuity, I digress again. By chance, one midnight I found myself strolling a few yards to Fork Causland's rear as he proceeded home. He was accompanied by boon companions, Old Soldiers, one on either side of him. It was a slippery winter night. The Old Soldiers reeled and staggered alarmingly, but Causland swaggered confidently between them, striking the sidewalk with his stick as he went, his derby roofed with snow.

'Where you livin' now, Fork?' one Old Soldier ventured. 'Same place where—where you give it to 'em?'

'Same place, my friend; old Mother Bauer's, top floor, hot as a frypan in summer and cold as James Bay these winter months.'

'You don't have no bad feelin' about stayin' on there, Mr. Causland?' the other Old Soldier inquired. (This latter comrade was a white-bearded character known on Pentecost Road as The Ambassador from Poland.) 'I don't mean a troubled conscience, like they say. I mean—well, like sumpthin might jump out an' grab you?'

'Ambassador,' Fork Causland said to his second henchman, 'keep on that way, and you'll earn yourself a split lip. Wahoo! Take me to old Mother Bauer's, boys, or I'll jump out and grab *you!* Wahoo!'

Then Fork performed another of those astonishing tricks of his. He took his stick between his teeth; flung himself straight upward with a muscular jump; as he descended, he thrust his rigid forefingers upon the arms of his tipsy companions. Then he rode along as if those two were his native bearers, his feet well clear of the ground, he seemingly supported only by those strong forefingers of his resting on the Old Soldiers' forearms.

His companions did not seem oppressed by his weight, though they kept their forearms extended and parallel with the ground, as if they had done Fork like service before. On they reeled for another block, Fork riding between them, chanting some old tune I did not recognize. When they were about to cross Thistle Street, Fork dropped back to the sidewalk to swagger along as before.

I never have seen such a thing done by anybody else. I do not know if this may have been some sort of acrobatic play. Surely the two Old Soldiers were no acrobats. I don't know how to convey the wonder that I felt at that moment. Was I wandering in a world of maya, of illusion? Could any man make himself weightless when he chose?

At some distance I followed the three companions to the walk that led up to Mrs. Bauer's house with the cast-iron railings. Causland slapped his comrades on the back, roared good night, and positively trotted all by himself up the steep steps of the porch, to vanish behind a handsome antique door. The Old Soldiers reeled onward, probably toward some cheap lodging house or Salvation Army hostel; I retreated to my citadel of a rectory.

But I am running ahead of my proper narrative. Of course the above nocturnal mystery occurred long after the battle at Mrs. Bauer's lodging house, which converted Homer Causland into Fork Causland. I turn back to the dumbwaiter and the compost fork. Causland had whetted well the prongs' points. I surmise that there must have been a faint smile on his hard-as-nails sightless face as he fingered the tines.

No police patrol cars rove Hawkhill at three of the morning. As Sergeant Shaugnessy said to me the other day, when I was imploring him for some effective help rescuing girls, 'What's all the world to a man when his wife's a widdy?' At that hour especially, Hawkhill belongs to Satan's limbs like Sherm the Screamer.

Sherm brought with him to Mrs. Bauer's house, at three of the morning, nine of his boys. As matters turned out, it would have been more prudent to have fetched fewer helpers; but hubris now afflicted Sherm the Screamer. Having special plans for the informing blind piano player, he prepared to fend off any interference. Probably the original design was to snatch Causland, lock him into the trunk of one of the cars, and transport him elsewhere, to be tormented at leisure—perhaps in Sherm's 'church.' Sherm left the drivers in both of the cars, with the motors running quietly.

A merciful providence had sent Mrs. Bauer crosstown that weekend to visit a niece. Sherm's boys had successfully jimmied the front door when one of the three limp-wristed young men living on the ground floor happened to open the door of their apartment, intending to put out a milk bottle.

'What do you guys want?' he demanded. Eight men were filing into the corridor, all of them high on something costly. The tenant made out their faces. 'Oh God! Billie, call the cops!' he screeched back to one of his friends.

They sapped him the next moment, and burst over his body into the ground-floor apartment. This taste of blood broke the invaders' fragile control over themselves. Roaring, they worked over the other two young men with blackjacks and bars. (One of those unfortunates was crippled life-long, after that night.) The victims' screams roused the tenant at the top of the house. Causland always had been a light sleeper.

Instantly he understood what must be occurring below. In no way could he assist the ground-floor trio. The diversion downstairs gave him three or four minutes' grace, and for such an event he had made some preparation. Being a very strong man, he was able to thrust the huge wardrobe hard against his door. Back of the wardrobe he forced the iron bedstead. Thus, he filled completely the space between the doorway and the outer wall of his room. His door opening inward, this defensive strategy made it impossible for the door to be opened by his enemies, no matter how numerous and frantic they were: they might have to chop their way through with axes, or else use explosives. Either method would require time and noise. He was well aware of the possibility that so baffled, they might instead burn down the whole house, with him inside.

There was no salvation for him through a window—not three flights up, with no fire escape, and he blind. With admirable presence of mind, Causland took his whole cash reserve, seventy dollars, from his money belt. The bills and some private papers he concealed under the carpet. Then he took up his pitchfork.

Now the gang came roaring up the stairs and burst against his barricaded door. He recognized some of the voices: they were careless in their howling, which signified that they did not mean him to come alive out of this, to bear witness against them. In particular he knew the torturer's voice of Sherm the Screamer.

'Come on, open up, Causland!' they were shouting, surprised at not being able to budge his door. 'We're just going to ask you some questions.' Causland said nothing in reply. He had no telephone in his room; and though he might shriek from a window, no one would rush to his assistance in this neighborhood, at this hour. No neighbor would venture so much involvement as to call the police, for that matter—not unless the tumult at Mrs. Bauer's house should threaten to spread to the adjacent houses.

Those smashing at his door were up to their eyes in heroin, he guessed. Somebody out there was clearheaded enough to grunt, 'Get the door off the hinges!' But their superfluity of numbers hampered the assailants in that narrow corridor. Then someone screamed—oh, he knew that voice—'There's another way!' Causland heard three or four men pounding back down the stairs. Meanwhile, the savage smashing at the door continued.

Yes, there was another way: Sherm's men must have learned about Mrs. Bauer's dumbwaiter. That device was no escape route for Homer Causland, for its mechanism could not be operated from within the dumbwaiter itself; and besides, what figure would a blind man make, emerging below, helpless before his enemies? Therefore, Causland took his stand in a shadowy convenient corner, as he planned, awaiting the event.

The clanking of the dumbwaiter's chain and the growling of its motor, like Halloween sound effects, gave Causland plenty of notice of his enemy's approach. The car in the shaft halted opposite the aperture of Causland's room now; the man within knew what he was doing. It still might have been possible for Causland to press the 'down' button by the dumbwaiter door, in hope of returning the car to the ground floor. But Causland preferred tactics more decisive.

'Hold it, Ralph!' the man in the car shouted to his helper below. 'I'm getting out.' It was the Screamer's dreadful voice.

Sherm had risen by audacity. And after all, how much resistance could be offered by a blind piano player, twice Sherm's years?

Sherm banged open the dumbwaiter door and began to scramble through the narrow opening, into the total darkness of Causland's room. He cracked his head against the oaken doorframe, trying to emerge quickly, and cursed. Happily for Fork, as matters turned out, Sherm was carrying a sawed-off shotgun. 'Homer Causland, you old stoolie,' the Screamer screamed, 'get down on your knees and start begging!'

'Hi!' said Causland, softly, from the shadows. 'I've got something here for you, Screamer.' As Sherm swung toward him, raising the shotgun, Causland lunged. He contrived to drive the prongs of the fork straight through Sherm's lean belly. The force of Causland's rush bowled Sherm over, and Causland fell upon him. 'Good-bye, Sherm,' Causland panted.

Then Sherm the Screamer screamed his loudest ever. Causland

heard the shotgun crash to the floor of his room. Groping about, he encountered the shaft of the fork; he tried to extract it from the belly of his enemy, whose heels were drumming on the floor. But this was an awkward undertaking, and Causland feared that meanwhile the door of his room might be taken off behind him.

So, panting, he managed in the darkness to thrust the dying Sherm, headfirst, back into the dumbwaiter. Blind Homer pressed the 'down' button, sending the fatal car on its return journey, to bear back to his disciples the Screamer, perforated, with the fork still in him. Like the beasts, the Prophet Sherm could perish, after all.

Disposing of Sherm had required about one minute. Yes, the door had been lifted off its hinges now; Causland's ears informed him that his adversaries were trying to kick their way through the second barrier, the sturdy back of the enormous wardrobe.

From the bottom of the stairs, a member of the gang shouted up, desperate, *'Christ, guys, he's gutted Sherm!* Get through that door and smash him!'

Causland had the shotgun in his hands: a double-barreled repeater. His fingers checked its triggers and magazine. This gun would do very well.

Shifting his station to the foot of the iron bedstead, seven feet from the tottering wardrobe, he pointed the barrels carefully. There was mighty confusion beyond that blocked doorway, some men running upstairs and others downstairs. Sherm's screams from below seemed less vigorous: Causland had angled his fork somewhat upward when he had made that dread thrust.

Now the carved doors of the wardrobe splintered into fragments, and a big body became entangled with the bedhead, struggling to enter the room. Causland gave this intruder one barrel.

In the little bedroom that reverberation was exquisitely painful to Causland's sensitive auditory nerves; but the result of his discharge was exquisitely gratifying. A body crashed backward. Later Causland learned that he had aimed a trifle high, so taking off the man's face.

Now Causland must carry the war into Africa. Risky strategy, that; yet not so risky as to wait for the gang to set the house afire. Gun at the ready, Causland clambered over some bloody bulky thing, through the demolished wardrobe. To clear the way, he fired the second barrel at a venture into the corridor beyond.

Someone else shrieked, fell, lay groaning hideously. Causland heard the whole crowd of them tumbling back down the stairs. Kneeling to thrust his weapon between the wooden balusters, the blind champion fired downward, both barrels. To judge by the anguished complaints, he had severely damaged one or two of the enemy.

Somebody fired back—a pistol, Causland judged—but missed him. Vexed, Causland gave them both barrels a second time: more screaming. It was like old times overseas.

At that moment, the horn of one car waiting at the curb began to honk furiously; then the horn of the second car. Later he was told that the drivers, on edge, had heard the siren of an ambulance on Pentecost Road, and had taken that for a patrol car.

Causland struggled back into his room. A small window looked toward Merrymont Avenue. Flinging up the sash, Causland fired into the blackness toward the honking. He heard the cars begin to pull away; again Causland fired in their direction. To his pleased surprise, there came a loud resounding bang, but not a gunshot: he must have hit a tire. A moment later a crash followed, for the car with a blown front tire, in fact, had careened across the street and struck a tree.

The other car roared away. Causland heard the running feet of the members of the gang abandoned by the driver. Then the house fell silent except for the horrid moaning of the man whom Causland had shot in the third-floor corridor.

Having made his way down to Mrs. Bauer's telephone, Causland called the police. After five or six minutes, some of the bolder spirits in the neighborhood actually ventured out of their lairs and began to converse in hushed tones, before Mrs. Bauer's house. But nobody dared ascend the steps until the police arrived.

Sergeant Shaugnessy and his men found one man dead, three dying, one shot in the legs and unable to walk, one stunned in a car that had rammed a tree, and gouts of blood on the sidewalk from one or two others who had escaped. Sherm the Screamer gave up the ghost in the ambulance bearing him to the hospital.

In Causland's phrase, 'Sergeant Shaugnessy was flabbergasted but appreciative. They didn't indict me for anything.'

After that he was 'Fork' to boon companions and 'Mr. Causland' to the less privileged. Nobody gave him trouble thereafter. He had attained the equivocal distinction of general recognition as Hawkhill's most accomplished resident. It is said in the Mustang that Fork sent a basket of poison ivy to Sherm's funeral; but that report I doubt. Wondrous to relate, all but two of the survivors of the attempt on Fork Causland were convicted on charges of attempted murder, criminal assault, unlicensed possession of a deadly weapon, or breaking and entering.

Fork Causland's fearsome reputation enabled him to walk the streets of Hawkhill at any hour, unmugged. There arose a popular belief that in reality he was not blind at all, but had especially keen sight behind those dark goggles. Some took him for an undercover detective. Who could have killed Sherm and his boys without even seeing them? Or conceivably—this suggestion occurring particularly among Hawkhill's West Indian element—Causland was a conjure-man, invulnerable and deadly.

Yes, he swaggered along the nocturnal streets. Yet the Screamer's band was not extinct; and those two who had survived the encounter at Mrs. Bauer's, and had not been imprisoned, would not forget. Fearsomeness wears thin with time, and the disciples of Sherm might take heart again. But Fork said no word of that.

No one could enter my church without my knowledge. I must make that point wholly clear. Were it not so, there might be some quasi-rational explanation of last night's events.

What is rare in American churches of the Romanesque revival, the Church of the Holy Ghost has a narthex, or galilee. (I prefer the latter term.) Above the broad steps frequented by the Old Soldiers of Merrymount Avenue, the great doors open upon this galilee, which traditionally is less sacred than the body of the church.

Within this interior porch, or galilee, I conduct most of my business with comers to the church—particularly with the street girls. In a vaulted chamber off the galilee I maintain a desk, some chairs, and a typewriter; this chamber has a functioning fireplace. I frequent this sentry post (so to speak) of the Holy Ghost because it is situated near the grand entrance to the church's west front. Only at this point may the whole church complex be entered nowadays.

For I have sealed the several other entrances, even that to the 'service' regions of the complex, although closing the other doors has made it necessary for Lin, the Cambodian man whom I have appointed verger (janitor, in reality), to transport rubbish in a barrow to the west front. When I write 'sealed,' I mean bricked up. No doubt I have violated fire inspectors' rules; but the public authorities winking at worse offenses in Hawkhill, they have not troubled me concerning my precautions.

The small roundheaded windows of the church, on the northern side, are set too high for burglars to operate without ladders; also, they are narrow, with a stone pillar fixed in the middle of each window arch. The rector who preceded me in this benefice had a heavy wire screen attached to the outer side of every window, to protect the painted glass from boys' stones. The southern windows face upon the cloister, not upon a street, and in effect are protected by the tall rectory.

A benefaction from old Mrs. Simmons enabled me to secure the windows of the adjoining rectory with interior steel shutters. I have sealed the rectory's street doors, now reaching my rooms there by passing through the galilee and the cloister on the church's south side. Need I remark that no building is entirely secure against intruders who possess special tools for burglary? However that may be, on the nights to which I refer below, these defenses of the Holy Ghost were undisturbed, and no alarm sounded on the electronic warning system purchased out of the Simmons benefaction. I am satisfied that no one could have entered the church except through the galilee.

In one of the great bronze doors (opened only on great feast days) of the west front is set a kind of postern door, also of bronze, so narrow as to admit only one person at a time. It is this small door through which everybody and everything pass ordinarily. Only the verger and I possess keys to this door, which moreover is secured within, when I am there, by a police lock and other devices. My small vaulted reception chamber or office is situated close to this postern, so that when I am at my desk I may see who enters and leaves the church. I am as much porter as rector. Thus all of my parishioners, and other callers, must pound the enormous bronze knocker or ring the electric bell if they would see me.

The sacred vessels, the tapestries, and other furnishings of the Church of the Holy Ghost being highly valuable, efficient robbers might be attracted—were it not for the smoke grimed exterior of the building, which suggests impoverishment and dereliction. I have provided as best I might against casual thieves, and for the safety of the complex's temporary or permanent inmates. Yet all these precautions seemed futile last night.

It should be understood that during daylight hours I make the nave accessible for private devotions (not that many take advantage of the opportunity) or for the rare visitor interested in the architecture of Holy Ghost Church. I do try to make sure that either the verger or his Cambodian wife (who does our mopping and the like) is present in nave or galilee during hours when the postern door is unlocked. So it is barely conceivable that some person might have crept into the church and concealed himself until yesterday night, perhaps in the blind-story. Yet such an explanation is even more improbable than the supposition I will imply toward the close of this document.

When Fork Causland became our church organist, I offered him a key to the church, but he refused it, saying that he could ring for the verger or myself. From the first I was confident of his honesty. In corrupted Hawkhill, he appeared to have no corrupt habits. Though fond of whiskey, Fork never was drunken. He paid little or no attention to the girls hanging about the bars when he played the piano. The pushers feared him. His conversation was always decent and sometimes amusing. Considerably to my surprise, I found that he was familiar with our liturgy, and that he prayed in church.

From asides in his talk, I gathered that he had been a wanderer, a beggar, a peddler, an acrobat, a carnival hand, a soldier—not in that order, presumably, but at one time or another. Was his proficiency at killing derived from military experience only? Two or three times I entered the church to hear the *Dies Irae* pouring from the organ: Fork at practice in his grim humorous fashion. 'Doc,' he would say, descending from his bench, 'it will be with this city as with the cities of the plain.' He was apt at biblical quotations and curious applications of them.

Yet I cannot say that we grew intimate. My situation is lonely; I have no Hawkhill friends; I would have been glad if Fork had accepted my offer of a room in the rectory, that echoing habitation not being less homelike than his room at Mrs. Bauer's. He thanked me, but said, 'I'm not a comfortable neighbor, Doc.'

I do not think that he held my color against me—not that he could discern it literally. And aside from chance drinking companions, clearly he had no friends of his own. He seemed armored by a self-sufficient stoicism. I envied him that.

I inquired discreetly about Fork among my parishioners and among the denizens of Pentecost Road. Nobody seemed to know how long Causland had lived in Hawkhill. Some said, 'Always, I guess'; others, 'Three years, maybe'; yet others, 'Never noticed him till this past winter.' So far as I could ascertain, nobody ever had conversed seriously with Fork longer than I had. His oddity had tended to deter familiarities even before his bloody amazing victory at Mrs. Bauer's house. After Fork had killed Sherm and his chums, a certain deadliness seemed to hang about the piano player. (I did not sense it myself; I refer to a discernible reverent uneasiness among the habitués of the Pentecost bars). Despite Fork's isolation, somehow I fancied that of all the grotesques of Pentecost Road, he alone was permanent, the rest evanescent.

Occasionally, after he had practiced at the creaky old vast organ, Causland and I talked in a parlor of the rectory, over tea brewed by the Cambodian woman. (Both of us took rum in our tea, in that damp stone building.) Fork could converse sensibly; also somewhat mystically. He knew all of Hawkhill's secrets, and sometimes hinted at mysteries of the world beyond the world, as if he were Tiresias, or Homer, or some other blind seer. Now and again he deferred, during these talks, to my theological learning—or what he took for my erudition.

'Doc,' he inquired at the session I best recollect, 'what's possession? Being possessed by a spirit, I mean.'

I endeavored to explain the church's doctrine concerning this, but that was not what he wished to know.

'I mean, Doc, how does it *feel?* Can something get inside you, and yet leave room enough for yourself? Can you be comfortable with it? Can you live with it as if it were your own brother? Can it help you?'

Naturally I was startled by this. 'Are you talking about yourself, Fork?'

He nodded. 'I think there's been somebody else with me for years now. Once, Doc, you said something about "levitation" and that jumping I do—but then you beat around the bush. Well, it's not Saint Vitus's dance, Doc. Something that's got into me does the jumping—not that I object much. And when I was in real need, it lent me its sight.'

I drew a long breath. 'You're talking about the time Sherm came for you?'

'That's it. I know the Old Soldiers say I can really see whenever I want to. But that's a lie.' He tapped his goggles. 'I could take these off to show you what's underneath my eyelids, Doc; but that would give you a turn. All the same, somebody or something lent me sight that rough time.'

Fork's one indulgence, not counting the free whiskies, was Brazilian cigars. He unwrapped one now, and I lit it for him.

He puffed on the black wrinkled thing. 'I've told this to nobody but you, Doc. Let me tell you, it came as a blessed shock to me. I'd made my preparations blinder than any bat, and I didn't expect miracles. But when it happened, everything was coming at me so quick that I just accepted the sight, no questions asked at the moment. It didn't come upon me until the last chance. You better believe me, Doc.' He blew smoke from his nostrils.

'I kept this quiet because anybody that dared would have called me a damned liar. The moment Sherm pushed open that dumbwaiter door, sight came to me.

'Or maybe I shouldn't say "sight": well, "perception"—that's more the word. I seemed to see outlines. There was a twenty-watt bulb dangling in the dumbwaiter, and Sherm was outlined against it. That was no time for musing on miracles. I knew he couldn't make out hide nor hair of me. His outline, sort of like a paper doll, turned toward me, blindlike, when I spoke to him, and the outline of a shotgun went up to his shoulder. That cleared the way for me to dive under the gun and run him through the belly.'

Deftly he relit his cigar.

'Mind you, Doc, I could make out only movement. So once I sent the elevator back down to the ground floor, I was blind as before. But when one of the gang broke through the wardrobe, I made out the shape of him plain, and blew the face off him. Then when I pushed into the corridor myself, I could—well, perceive, I guess—perceive the lot of Sherm's boys running downstairs, and I fired into the midst of them. And when I gave both barrels to that car outside the house, I could see the thing moving away from the curb. After that, right after that last shot, whatever lent the perception to me took it back again. Is there a name for what happened to me, Doc?'

'Not a medical term, Fork,' I said to him. 'There's a psychological term: extrasensory perception. Lord knows what that means.'

'You half-believe me, don't you, Doc? Nobody else would. Well, what about the possession? Do you half-believe that, too?'

Now the sun had sunk beneath the level of the barred windows of my rectory; we had no light but the glow from the coals in my fireplace. I shivered. 'What could it be that's got into you? Maybe it be a devil, do you think?'

'I'm asking you, Doc. How the hell should I know?' Fork sprang up and performed a little song-and-dance routine in my parlor, chanting—

He's a devil, he's a devil,
He's a devil in his own home town.
On the level, he's a devil . . .

Then Fork sat down as abruptly as he had risen.

'Look out, Doc: that was it, the thing in me, just now. He hears you. But no, I don't think it's a demon. It's a killer, though, and not pretty.'

The parlor door swung open; we both jumped at the sound and the draft of cold air. But it was only the verger's wife, my housekeeper, come to carry off the tea things. Evidently Fork thought that he had uttered too much already, for he clapped his derby on his large head and went out, back toward Pentecost Road.

We never had opportunity to resume that chilling conversation about the possessed and the possessors. I suspect that Fork may have been capable of elaborate hoaxes, for the fun of them—but not on that dark subject.

How often, my gun under my jacket, have I strolled almost the length of Pentecost Road, praying as I ambled! Desperate though the neighborhood is, some franchise eating houses make a good profit there, at high nocturnal risk of their cashiers. Much of the Road is brightly lit by neon. 'Twenty Gorgeous Bottomless Dancers, Stark Naked or Your Money Back,' one sign blinks on and off. I pass four or five massage parlors.

Shoddy little theaters for X-rated films (their marquees promising more than they can deliver, in competition with the living flesh next door or down the road); 'adult' bookshops for retarded adolescents and middle-aged illiterates; scantly stocked tiny 'notion' shops that are fronts for narcotics-peddling—these are the thriving enterprises of Pentecost Road, in this year of our Lord. The hideousness of it hurts as much as the depravity.

Now I have to write about Julie Tilton.

There is no coincidence: everything that occurs is part of a most intricate design.

The Mustang, where the daiquiris are good (though nothing else there has any admixture of good in it), is situated at the intersection of Pentecost and Merrymont. A great deal of money changes hands, more or less surreptitiously, at those corners. For that reason the sidewalk outside the Mustang is frequented by mendicants. I usually give something to the old man with no legs, selling pencils, who rides a board to which four roller skates are fixed; he is there on the bitterest days. Another begging habitué is the idiot woman shaped like an interrogation point. Also, 'religious' freaks are to be seen, especially an Indian fakir in nothing but a loincloth.

The beggars and the madmen are outnumbered by the street girls, some promenading, some lounging against the wall, awaiting custom. Few are birds of paradise. I labor under no delusion about harlots. With very rare exceptions, the kindly prostitute is a creation of novelists and playwrights. As a class, such women are psychopathic, devouring, and treacherous. They have their uses, particularly to the police: in the hope of reward, or out of unblemished malice, they betray their bullies and lovers. I have discovered among them, on Pentecost Road, no heroic repentant Magdalene. All that I can accomplish among them, pastorally, is to persuade a few of the young ones, strutting down Pentecost under compulsion, to go back to their parents or to whomever in the home town might receive them. I have facilitated a number of such escapes, after conversations at my office in the galilee. The first stage on my underground railway is a lodging for a night in that safe-house, my rectory. They do not tempt me. Ever since my ordination, I have kept myself under a most strict discipline; and even had I not vowed myself to celibacy and chastity, still I would be no fool—though sensual, more sensual than most by nature.

On Monday evening, as I approached the Mustang, the girls were particularly numerous and importunate. I shouldered my way among them—black hat, black face, black leather jacket—in my role of hard-drinking impecunious chiropractor. Just outside the door of the Mustang someone gripped me by the arm—but not with the customary unimaginative 'Want to have some fun, honey?' This person was saying, 'Brother, have you been washed in the blood of the Lamb?'

I swung round. It was a young black man, fantastically dressed, a street preacher, wild-eyed. He had a companion.

This colleague, seated in a sort of primitive wheelchair, was paler than death. He did not move a muscle, not even of lips or eyes. At first I took him for a paralytic, trundled about for a holy show by his preacher-captor. Then the thought flashed through my mind that this white boy, bareheaded, neatly dressed, might be a corpse: things not much less shocking are seen from time to time at Pentecost and Merrymont.

'Brother, have you been saved?' the mad preacher was demanding of me. 'Have you been washed in the blood of the Lamb?'

I unfixed his hand from my arm. 'Nobody can answer that question with full knowledge, brother,' I told him.

But already he had turned from me and was addressing the passing stream of tarts, procurers, pushers, drunkards, and males of various ages 'out for a little fun.' 'Brothers and sisters,' he was crying, 'where'll you spend eternity? Wine is a mocker, strong drink is raging, and whoever is deceived thereby is not wise.'

He then plucked the white boy out of his chair and exhibited him at arm's length to the street people. Praise be, the pallid thing was an inanimate mannequin, marvelously realistic, after all. I wouldn't have to telephone Shaugnessy.

''Cept you take the Lord Jesus for your personal savior, you're no better 'n this here dummy!' the wild-eyed preacher was shouting. 'Where you goin' to spend eternity? You want to spend it with the Whore o' Babylon and the Beast, whose number is six-six-six? The wages of sin is death. You want to be like this here dummy, no brains in your head? You want to be cast into the fire eternal? Brothers and sisters, death is all around us. Old Mister Death, he grabs you when you're on a high, when you're drinkin' and fornicatin', and he takes the breath out o' your body, leavin' you no better than this here dummy! He takes you where the worm never dieth and the fire is not quenched. 'Cept you follow the Lord Jesus, Ol' Man Death put his bony hand on you, and you curl up like a worm. . . .'

Two mighty hands took me by the shoulders, from behind. Their clutch was terribly painful; a shock like electricity ran through me. 'Gottcha, Doc!' said Fork. 'You come along with me into this hell on earth they call the Mustang. Wahoo!'

His ears had singled me out in the crowd by my few words in retort to the street preacher.

'In a minute, Fork, you Beast from the Abyss,' I muttered.

With his stick tucked under his arm, the blind man stood beside me, listening to the crazy preacher. 'It always was a scandal, that faith, eh, Doc?' He poked me in the ribs with the head of his stick. 'That there raving and ranting fellow—sort of like a caricature of you, eh, Doc?'

'Go to hell, Fork,' I told him.

'All in good time, Doc; all in God's own good time.' He chuckled harshly.

''Cept you repent, brothers and sisters, you gonna die the body of this death,' the crazy preacher was exhorting some tarts and three beggars. He brandished the mannequin. 'No brains, jes' like this here dummy; no heart, no guts, no nothin'. If you don't have no immortal soul washed in the blood of the Lamb, you got nothin'. Old Mister Death, he got your 'pointed day writ down on his calendar, you poor dummies. . . .'

'You've got some competition in the soul business, Doc,' said Fork, half-needling me, half-serious. We were entering the Mustang. 'You ever repent of taking up this line of work? Feel sorry about not marrying and taking up the cross in Hawkhill?'

'It's a calling, Mr. Homer Causland; I wouldn't have it any other way. What's your calling? Speaking of Old Man Death, killing seems to be your talent.'

'In the line of duty, Doc: add that qualification. You're welcome to call me a rat, Reverend Doc. On one of those records for no-eyes, once, I heard a poem by some Scotchman about a rat's prayer:

> 'God grant me that
> I carrion find,
> And may it stink:
> O Father, kind,
> Permit me drink
> Of blood ensoured . . .
> There is no waste
> Where rats are fed,
> And, for all haste,
> Grace shall be said.'

Fork had astounded me once again. 'In what corner of hell did you hear that, you blind devil?'

'Devil?' Not quite that, Doc; devil's cousin, maybe. Wahoo!'

He sat down at his piano, called for his whiskey, and began to play. I took a table near him. The Mustang was two-thirds full, that night, of the lost. The blind devil played for them like an angel. Even to acid rock he imparted a somber pathos; or so it sounded to my priestly ears.

I was roused out of a reverie brought on by Fork's 'not marrying' when a girl's voice, a sweet one, said, 'Excuse me, sir.' She withdrew a chair from my table, turned it in Fork's direction, and sat waiting for him to pause in his playing. I saw her in profile.

She was beautiful, but more than beautiful: lovely. She wore her blond hair long, very long. Nose, lips, and chin all were delicate and perfect; so was her figure. She was six feet tall at least. Her blue eyes were impossibly innocent. I judged her to be sixteen or seventeen years old. This was nobody off Pentecost Road. Face aside, she was dressed too decently for that.

When Fork had stopped playing, she said to him, 'Excuse me, sir. Maybe you can help me. Have you seen Alexander Tilton?'

Fork turned toward her his poker face with its black goggles, taking the cigar from his mouth. He removed his derby. 'Why do you ask a blind man a question like that, lady?'

I watched her blush. Her fair skin was suffused with a soft delicious pink. 'Oh, I'm sorry; I didn't know. I thought you looked like a man who might have met a good many people in this part of town.'

'I do, lady, but I never met anybody by that name. Doc, could you check at the bar?'

I rose. Who wouldn't do anything for this young lady? Indeed, I bowed the first bow ever executed in the Mustang.

'Meet the Reverend Raymond Montrose, rector of Holy Ghost Church, lady, even if he doesn't look it.'

'I don't want to disturb you, Reverend Montrose,' the beauty said. She blushed again.

'It's a pleasure, young lady,' I assured her, stuttering a little. 'But not "Reverend Montrose," if you please. Father Montrose, or Dr. Montrose, or even Mr. Montrose; but never Reverend Montrose. I'm a stickler for forms, being an Anglo-Catholic.'

'Oh, I'm a Methodist, I'm afraid, Father.'

'Don't be afraid, not even in this bar. Excuse me, Miss . . .'

'I'm Julie Tilton, and Alexander Tilton is my brother, twelve years older. The last letter he sent us was on the stationery of the Tangiers Motel, Pentecost Road, and so I got a room there, half an hour ago, but they hadn't heard of him, and said somebody at the Mustang Bar might know him. I took a taxi straight here.' She was genuine!

'You better check out of the Tangiers Motel, lady: they got something worse than the veterans' disease there. Doc, stop your bowing and scraping, and ask after one Alexander Tilton at the bar. I'll keep an eye on this Miss Tilton, in a manner of speaking.' Fork resumed his derby.

The bartender and the waitresses hadn't ever heard of an Alexander Tilton, they informed me. When I returned to the piano, I found three unpleasant young toughs standing by Fork and the girl, flies drawn to honey.

'How about a dance, baby?' said the biggest of them.

'Move on, brothers,' I told them. They stared at me.

'You heard Doc,' Fork growled. 'Scoot, boys.'

They went, swearing, but softly.

'Pay them no mind, lady,' said Fork. 'They'll get their comeuppance before long, I promise you. Now this brother of yours—what did he look like?'

'My grandmother and I haven't seen him for nearly ten years, but he must be very good-looking. He's about as tall as I am, and slim. The girls back home were wild about him. He got one—but that doesn't matter now.' Another blush.

'He used to write about once a year,' she went on; 'then, better than two years ago, he stopped writing. I thought everybody around here must know him, because he did so well in this city. He sent lots and lots of money home for us to keep for him. "Bury it in the cellar in tight cans," he wrote to us. Some people don't trust banks, I guess, and he's one of them. He even sends the cash in little sealed boxes, by special messengers! Except for letting us know his money was on its way, Sherm never told us much in his letters.'

'*Sherm?*' said Fork, drawling out the name.

'Here in Hawkhill, Miss Tilton,' I put in, 'A good many people get lost—and not found. I thought you said your brother's name was Alexander.'

'Oh, it is, Father Montrose: Alexander Sherman Tilton. But we've called him Sherm in the family ever since I can remember.'

Fork, silent, relit his cigar.

'Possibly there are other ways you might identify your brother, Miss Tilton,' I continued. 'His voice, for instance: was it soft as yours?'

She smiled angelically. 'Oh, no. Sherm always spoke very loudly—loud enough to hurt some people's ears. When he was angry, could he ever yell!'

'Ummm,' from Fork. 'Now this brother Sherm, lady: did he ever use any other names?'

'Not that I know of. Why should he? But perhaps he used the "Alexander" in this town, because he always signed his letters to us that way, as if he had gotten more formal. It was just "Alexander," not signing his last name. We mailed back letters to Alexander Tilton, at the post office box number he gave us; but he never answered until he decided to send more money home.'

I presented to her my engraved card, in the hope of achieving in Miss Tilton's admirable eyes a respectability that my beard and my fancy boots would not convey to her. Or might she, untraveled, fancy that all doctors of divinity went about so attired? 'Did you have some particular reason,' I inquired, 'for coming all this distance to look for your brother?'

'No, Father: it's just that he's my only brother, and I haven't any sisters, and Dad and Mom died five years ago. In his last letter, Sherm told me that I ought to come to the big city and live with him; that I'd really go places here. He practically ordered me to come. I wrote back that I would, whenever he wanted me to. He didn't answer me, though, so I waited until after graduation, and at last I decided that the thing for me to do was simply to come here and look him up. Here I am!'

Yes, here she was, Iphigenia in Aulis, come unwittingly to the sacrifice. Here she was, a brand for me to snatch pastorally before she had been singed!

'This gentleman at the piano is our church organist, Mr. Fork

Causland,' I informed her. I gave Fork a gentle, stealthy dig in his ribs. 'He and I will do what we can to help you.'

'Sure, lady,' Fork said. 'I wouldn't go asking around this here bar, if I were you.'

The three unpleasant young men had not scooted very far: I noticed them standing at the bar, scowling at us. I recollected, or thought I recollected, that two of them had been surreptitiously pointed out to me, months ago, as survivors of the Screamer's gang. It wouldn't do to linger. I put my hand on Fork's shoulder.

'The two of us had best take Miss Tilton back in a taxi to the Tangiers Motel, Fork, and get her bags now. I can put her up at the rectory, if she doesn't mind.'

'Right, Doc—I guess. There's too many vermin at the Tangiers, lady. Just one more question, before we go.' Fork swallowed the remnant of his whiskey. 'Brother Sherm—in his last letter, better than two years ago, did he give you any idea of what he was going to have you do in this town?'

'I'm quite a good typist, Mr. Fork, but Sherm didn't mention that. All he suggested was that he knew a lot of interesting boys to take me out.' Here she colored more furiously than before.

We made our way to the door, I running interference. All the men in the Mustang were staring, and three or four whistled loudly. 'Where you takin' that kid, Fork?' somebody called out. Someone else muttered, 'For Christ's sake, don't rile him.'

A taxi was at the curb, letting out a drunken fare. Julie Tilton got in with us two strangers, ingenuously. Possibly my 'cute British accent' was reassurance of sorts. With no other two men from the Mustang would she have been able to check out of the Tangiers uninsulted—or worse than that. Coincidence again? I think not.

'I fancy you come from a rather small town, Miss Tilton,' I said on our way to the motel.

'How did you know, Father? Titus isn't much more than a church, a general store, and a dozen houses. Sherm used to call it Hicksville or Endsville.'

'How you gonna keep 'em down on the farm, after they've seen Hawkhill?' Fork had been humming. He ceased, saying, 'Julie, pardon my asking, but was this brother Sherm in more sorts of trouble than one, when he left Titus nearly ten years ago?'

'He got himself into a peck of troubles, Mr. Fork. But he must have straightened himself up, or he couldn't have earned all that money to send home.'

At the flashy Tangiers, I thought it prudent to go with Julie to her room for her suitcase. I was pleased and somewhat surprised to find the bag still there; they had not given her a key for her room. While Julie and I were down the hall, the desk clerk tried to make trouble about this guest being taken away by two men, but Fork gave him the rough side of his tongue. Undoubtedly the desk clerk had plans for the lady guest. He asked her to come back any time; he meant it.

'How you goin' to keep 'em away from Pentecost, jazzin' around, paintin' the town?' Fork was humming as we drew up before the Church of the Holy Ghost.

The lovely big girl was overwhelmed by the scale of my church. 'This must be a very religious town, Father Montrose! I hope I'm not causing your wife too much trouble.'

'Once upon a time, it was. I'm celibate, Miss Tilton. Our housekeeper, the verger's wife, will get your room in order and bring you tea—and a sandwich, if you'd care for one.' Providentially, no fugitive street girl was lodged in the rectory that night. I unlocked the postern door, and we three entered.

The galilee of my church had taken the galilee of Durham Cathedral for its model, in part. The rows of pillars, and the roundheaded arches with their chevron moldings, took Julie's breath away. From my office I rang a bell connected with the verger's rooms at the top of the rectory, summoning the little Cambodian woman, whose English was tolerable.

We had our ingenue safe out of the Mustang, safe out of the Tangiers Motel. What next?

'Will it be all right for me to stay here until I find my brother?' Julie asked, as the verger's wife waited to lead her across the cloister. 'I don't know how to repay you, Father. I'm sure Sherm's somewhere very close; I just simply feel it.'

'We could have ridden on to Mrs. Simmons's, Doc. She'd have taken the girl in if you'd asked her. It wouldn't have been like imposing a streetwalker on the old lady.'

'She's safer in the rectory, Fork.'

We two sat in my office off the galilee. It was midnight, and Miss Tilton doubtless was sleeping the sleep of the guiltless—a few rods distant from me.

'Maybe,' said Fork. 'Probably they're looking for her right now.'

'Who in particular?'

'Those three that wanted to dance with her at the Mustang. The guy that spoke to her and gave us some lip—I knew his voice. He was one of the two acquitted after my fracas at Mrs. Bauer's. His name's Franchetti. He's getting his nerve back, two years after the treatment I gave his pals. Sherm's sister would be worth plenty to him.'

'Is she actually Sherm's sister?'

'Why not? It all fits together. I bet Franchetti saw they were two peas in a pod. Sherm must have told him she'd be along. What does the girl look like?'

'A rose in bloom.' I had not been able to keep my eyes off young Miss Tilton; I supplied particulars, perhaps too enthusiastically.

'That's enough detail, Doc. Sherm was a good-looking goon, except for the smirk, they tell me. He was her height, her coloring, and "Sherman Stanton" is close enough to "Sherman Tilton."''

'But her coming straight to the man who executed her brother? That's too much of a coincidence, Fork.'

'There's wheels within wheels, Doc. She was sent, God knows why. It did give me a jolt when she said "Sherm," let me tell you.'

We fell silent for a minute or two.

'We can't let Julie know what her brother was, nor how he ended,' I said then.

Fork nodded. 'She's got to go back to Titus, pronto.'

'It won't be simple to persuade her of that, at least for a few days. She says her intuition tells her that Sherm's near at hand. Girls and their notions!'

'She may not be so far wrong, Doc. That's been my intuition, too.'

'Don't be a fool, Fork.'

'I never would have lasted this long if I'd been a fool, not with the life I've led. Now look: in this here Middle Ages church of yours, you've talked to me more than once about death and judgment. You're a Middle Ages parson, Doc, and I'm with you. What's the teaching about what you've called "the interval"?'

He had cornered me with my own doctrine. 'I know what you're thinking, Fork. Once upon a time, everybody believed it. When a man dies, that's not the end of his personality—not until the Last Judgment. There may be a kind of half-life, though the body has perished. After all, in the twentieth century we know what we call 'matter' is a collection of a power we don't understand. That arrangement falls apart when a body disintegrates; but the particles, the energy . . . ah, there's the rub, Fork. Even a consciousness may survive, Fork, in a twilight realm of which we receive glimpses, sometimes, that startle us, the living. Until the Last Judgment, what we call ghost . . .'

'All right, Doc: that's your teaching. You believe it?'

'Yes.'

'And you believe in possession?'

'Yes.'

'Sherm was possessed, Doc, if ever a man was. Maybe I am, though not in the same way. Something might possess you. Watch your step.'

'What do you mean?'

'You ought to know, Doc.'

I shrugged that off. Another interval of silence followed. Then I said, 'Why did Sherm tell Julie to come to Hawkhill?'

'Unnatural affection, Doc. After he'd taken his pleasure with her, he'd have peddled her on Pentecost Road.'

I crossed myself. 'Lord! And this girl!'

'Sherm drove out any goodness that had been in him, leaving himself empty. A demon entered in. You better believe me, Doc.'

I let my friend out of the church then, and he went his way into the darkness intrepidly; standing at the postern, I heard his stick striking the sidewalk occasionally as he made his way toward that desiccated room at Mrs. Bauer's.

Having secured the door, I passed through nave and choir to the apse. Tall archaic carvings of saints loomed above me. For half an hour I knelt in prayer. 'Pray for us sinners now and at the hour of our death.' I prayed even for Sherm, unlikely creature. As I passed back through the nave, my eye somehow was drawn upward to the blindstory along the north wall. But if there had been any slight movement, it must have been a rat's: the vermin plagued us; I had extirpated them from the rectory, but they continued, a few of them, to haunt the church itself.

In my rectory, I paused at Julie's door. The keys to the rectory's interior doors had been lost years ago. Should I knock? Should I simply look in upon her, silently, to make sure she was all right—and for a moment's glimpse of that perfect face in sleep? But restraining myself, I went on to my own whitewashed room (ascetic as any monk's cell), three doors farther on.

The rectory was so well built, and fitted with such heavy doors and draperies, that the Cambodians on the top floor could hear nothing of noise on this ground floor, I reflected.

On Tuesday morning the housekeeper served a decent breakfast to Julie and me in the dining room, so seldom used, musty and sepulchral. I found the young lady surprisingly perceptive; and she could converse animatedly. She was interested in my Church of the Holy Ghost; I, in her charms. Her face helped me somewhat to drive out gross images from my thoughts: its purity was foreign to

Hawkhill. The delicate flair of the tall beauty's nostrils! I thought of her dead brother, so like, so different.

She insisted upon combing the city for her brother. It would have been perilous to have taken her walking on the streets of Hawkhill, especially if the remnants of her brother's gang were looking for her. Having persuaded her to visit officialdom instead, I called a taxi and took the darling on a tour of police headquarters, city hall, the central post office, the county coroner's office. Nobody had heard of a youngish man called Alexander Tilton. Of course I did not inquire after a person called Sherman Stanton. Only four Tiltons were listed in the telephone directory, and from downtown we rang up all of those, unavailing.

Sergeant Shaugnessy, Vice and Homicide Squad gave us half an hour of his time. That visit was risky; but though Shaugnessy stared at Julie fixedly, apparently he could not place the resemblance between this lovely innocent and the worst man in Hawkhill. He told us that if we would come back another day, he would try to go through his 'morgue' of photographs with us. I did not mention that I intended to ship the girl back to Titus before that might occur. Happily Julie did not mention to the Sergeant that her brother's middle name was Sherman—though it is unlikely that he would have been quick-witted enough to make that improbable connection. Also, she said nothing about the money he sent home.

I took her to dinner at a cafeteria downtown, and then we returned to the rectory. Fork stopped by a few minutes after we had got back; we reported to him our failure.

'For all you know, Julie,' said Fork, 'your brother may have moved on east, or west. There's an Amtrak train tomorrow noon that could take you within ten miles of Titus; I stopped by the station. Oh, you know about that? Take it, girl, take it.'

It entered my mind that I did not wish to let her go so soon. She was protesting to Fork that she was ready to stay here a week, if there were any chance of finding Brother Sherm.

'There'll be other trains, Fork,' I said. 'Or she could fly back, about the end of this week.'

'And you'll comfort Julie spiritually until then?' Fork inquired, in his most sardonic way. But the girl appeared to catch no imputation. I could have struck Fork.

'Father Montrose already has given me such good advice!' she told the old blind devil. 'He's taken me to see everybody who might know something about Sherm. I don't know what I can ever do to make it up to him for all his trouble.'

I almost said at that point, 'I do know.'

'If you're going to hang on here, Julie,' Fork was telling her, 'don't go outdoors by yourself. Any girl's in danger on these streets, even in daylight—and you in particular, sweet girl graduate of Titus Rural High.'

'Why especially?' Her eyes widened.

Fork ignored that question. 'And if anything should happen to the reverend ecclesiastic here, call a taxi and go to Mrs. Simmons's house. Doc will write down the address for you.'

She was startled and concerned. 'Why, whatever could happen to Father Montrose?'

'Some of the boys at the Mustang Bar have it in for him now, and I'm told they've learned where he lives. That's one thing possible; there are other possibilities. Doc, take out your notepad and give her Mrs. Simmons's address right now.'

I did that.

Julie was puzzled and shaken. 'Ah, well,' I told her, 'that's merely for emergencies, which don't happen. But I'll telephone Mrs. Simmons to tell her about you.'

'I'll be off,' Fork said, 'and back tomorrow evening.' Wednesday was his night for prolonged practice on the organ. 'Keep her indoors, Doc. Tell her about Ol' Mister Death putting his bony hands on you here in Hawkhill. And Doc, exert your will, as you're given to saying in your sermons: don't let anything occupy you.'

He sauntered away down Merrymont—tapping past its boarded-up storefronts, its derelict gasoline stations, its fire-gutted mansions, its wastelands of unprofitable parking lots—a deadly, kind man. At that moment I hated him: he surmised too much. Now I most bitterly repent that malign emotion.

It being nearly time for evensong, I must put on my vestments. I conscientiously perform my daily offices, although no one attends my services except on Sundays. Somehow I did not wish to have Julie at my vespers: I suppose now that I sensed, given my growing desire for her, how Julie for a congregation might have made evensong a mockery.

'What shall we do with you while I'm in the church, Julie?' (The phrase itself sounded erotic to me.) 'Possibly you need to write a letter home? Do you play dominoes? Perhaps we'll have a match when I come back.'

Or perhaps we'll have a match of something else, I added for my own delection, silently. I had begun to lose control of my fancies about this Miss Julie Tilton, kid sister of the pillar of unrighteousness. Othello, Desdemona, and the beast with two backs were only the beginning.

That she was so innocent, and I under a vow, made these prospects yet more attractive. Abelard and Heloise! Or, from *Notre Dame*, the lascivious archdeacon and virginal Esmeralda. I would laugh, toying with her in the beginning, tugging at her long hair . . .

Fork, the homicidal old devil, damn him, must have sensed my change of mood—my change of character, almost. What had he meant by his 'don't let anything occupy you'? But Fork would not return until tomorrow evening. Meanwhile, Julie and I could have a very lively time. Perhaps. There were risks. . . .

While sinking into these amorous reveries, I had put on my vestments. I was about to enter the church, to celebrate evensong at the apsidal chapel of Saint Thomas of Canterbury, when the electric bell rang at the great doors. The Cambodian couple were out for the evening, at the cinema—a thoughtful suggestion of mine, that. Damn the bell: let it ring! But then, Julie might hear it and foolishly open the postern; Lord knows who might enter. No, I had best respond myself.

I endeavored, while passing through the galilee to put Julie out of my mind. Her body had become an obsession, all six feet of her young inexperience. My amorous images were turning toward violent acts, in my mind's eye. It was as if the appetites of someone else . . .

Releasing the several locks, I swung open the postern door. A big man stood there. By the light of the small bulb that burns above the door, I made out his face. It was Franchetti, once Sherm's chief enforcer, the man who had accosted Julie in the Mustang the previous night.

Though not so massive as I am, Franchetti was tall and tough: that pleased me. Rather than slamming the door in his face, I said to him, 'Good evening, Mr. Franchetti. You've come to evensong?'

He seemed taken aback at my knowing his name, and he did not understand my invitation. Also, he may have been confused as to my identity: as I mentioned earlier, I look different in cassock and surplice.

'Hi, Doc—I mean, Rev,' he began. 'You're the chief honcho here, right? I got a deal to make with you.'

'Do come in, Franchetti.' I stood back to admit him.

The spectacle of the dimly lit galilee obviously bewildered my visitor. To him this splendid Romanesque porch, with its shadows and mysterious columns and many arches, must have seemed like the setting for a horror movie—not that any mere film could be more horrid than Franchetti's own mode of existence. Locking automatically, the door closed behind him.

'You've come to divine worship, Franchetti?'

He snorted. 'Some joker! Rev, we could do you a lot of damage.'

'I'm aware of that, Brother Franchetti. You might even murder me—or try to. It could turn out like your attempt on Causland.'

He stared at me; decided on a new tack. 'OK, Rev, let's drop that line. I came here to give you money, real money.'

'How much?'

'A thousand bucks, right now, Rev.'

'For the succor of the poor?'

He snorted again. 'If that's the way you like to kid, Rev.'

'Possibly you expect something in exchange?'

'We sure do. You're goin' to give us that young blonde you been amusin' yourself with. You got no claim on her.'

'You have?'

'Sure. Sherm promised her to the boys two years ago, and he took it in the guts, but now we're goin' to collect her.'

'You take her to be Sherm's sister?'

'Sure, Rev. Sherm was goin' to have his kinky fun with her, and then turn her over to us to be eddicated for the street, understand? You didn't never meet Sherm? Well, her and Sherm coulda been identical twins, see, 'cept for differences in the right places. She's our stuff. You already had your pleasure, Rev, with what she's got.'

I sucked in my breath: he had shot near the mark. My adrenalin could not be restrained much longer. Yet I contrived to prolong our conversation for a few moments.

'What makes you say that, dear Brother Franchetti?'

'Hell, Rev, we found out you took in four or five kids, two of 'em our property, for your private use in this here crazyhouse of yours. None of 'em ever showed up on Pentecost again. What'd you do with 'em, Rev? Got 'em chained in the cellar? Buried in the cellar? I hate to think of what you done with them girls, Rev—and one of 'em a gold mine. Why, you're a public menace. Somebody ought to turn you in to the pigs.'

At this point in our dialogue I burst into laughter, hearty if hysterical. The sound echoed through the crepuscular galilee. Franchetti joined somewhat uneasily in the dismal mirth.

If we poor feeble sinners—of whom I am the chief—are engaged in a holy war against the forces of Satan, we ought to ensure that not all the casualties fall on our side.

'Franchetti,' I said, 'I have been unfair to you. Before you entered this place, I ought to have informed you that from the age of four upward, I was trained in the manly and martial arts by my sergeant-father, at Spanishtown. The door is locked. Do you think you can contrive to get out of this place alive?'

Being an old hand at such encounters, Franchetti reached very swiftly for what he carried within his jacket. Yet I, strung up for this contest, was swifter. I gave him a left in the belly, a right to the jaw, took him by the throat and pounded his head against the sandstone wall. He collapsed without being able to draw, and I disarmed him. He slumped down to the flags.

'You mistook me for a Creeping Jesus, perhaps,' I remarked. I dragged him up and knocked him down again. Then I proceeded to kick and trample my victim, with truly hellish fury.

I have been in many fights, principally before I was ordained, but never before had I treated a fallen adversary in that fashion. What was it Fork had said? 'Watch out—something might get inside you, Doc?' I didn't care now.

Having unlocked the door, I took the broken man by his ankles and dragged him outside, face down. I pulled him some distance, round the corner to the lane that runs alongside the north wall of the church. A large trash bin is chained there. In the chill rain, no witnesses passed. Having administered several more kicks to Franchetti, I heaved him into the bin, head down. The garbage truck would find him in the morning, if no one noticed the wreck before then. One more of the mugged would rouse no great sensation in Hawkhill. What Franchetti had done to others, now had been done to him.

On my way back to the postern, I noticed that Franchetti's billfold had fallen on the sidewalk. In it I found nearly two thousand dollars in hundred-dollar bills. The wallet and Franchetti's gun I flung down the opening of a convenient storm sewer. The bills I stuffed into our poor box within the galilee, so laying up treasure in heaven for Franchetti.

I felt like Hercules or Thomas à Becket. Should I swagger down to Pentecost Road, seeking out Franchetti's two particular chums, to give them a dose of the same medicine? But I was weary: it was as if abruptly the destructive energy were being drained out of me. Instead, I went back into the church, forgetting even-song for the first time, and strode through the cloister to my rectory.

Libido dominandi, for the time being, had driven out a differ-ent lust. Besides, exhaustion and disgust had begun to set in. I passed Julie's door, reeled into my own room, and slept in my vestments.

Before breakfast, Sergeant Shaugnessy telephoned me to report that a man named Franchetti, who had a long criminal record, had been found badly damaged near my church, and now lay in critical condition in Receiving Hospital. He wondered if I had heard anything outside in the street, during the night. I informed him that no sounds penetrated through our great bronze doors. This seemed to satisfy the Sergeant, not solicitous for Franchetti's well-being. 'Franchetti's got the d.t.'s,' he informed me. 'He keeps groaning that a nigger preacher who breaks bones took his money and beat his brains out.'

I contrived to be urbane with Julie at breakfast. My ambition to conquer somehow was diminished in the morning; I felt affection more than appetite. We spent the day visiting, by taxi, the city office of the FBI, the state police headquarters, and the hospitals: no discoveries about any Tilton.

But as evening approached, images of concupiscence rose strong again in my head. I arranged for the verger and his wife, to their surprise, a second expedition to the flicks, in a suburb. They protested that the taxis would cost too much; I brushed that aside, handing them forty dollars. I would have Julie at my undisturbed disposal for at least three hours. Miss Tilton would be worth two twenties.

Yet there was Fork to be reckoned with: I had almost forgotten that he would arrive about nine or nine-thirty to practice on the organ. Well, he had no key to the church: let him ring in vain for admittance. I would not be diverted from what Julie had to offer.

I took the trouble to book a taxi, for precisely eight-thirty, to come to the church door and take the Cambodian couple to the suburban movie house. I would take Julie into the church itself, the moment they left: a piquant setting for what I intended. Tuesday night I had enjoyed battering Franchetti in the galilee; this night I would have the relish of sacrilege with Julie in the sanctuary.

I knew what I was doing and just how I would go about everything, rejoicing in outrage. Yet something else in me still protested against this wildness.

About seven o'clock, I went into the church, took some kneeler-cushions from pews, and laid them conveniently before the little altar in the apse-chapel of Thomas of Canterbury. Here I meant to celebrate my peculiar evensong with Julie Tilton.

An interesting architectural feature of my Church of the Holy Ghost is a large entrance, at the crossing, to the crypt. The stair downward, and the balustrades that guard it, are of splendid marble. I am told that this construction closely resembles the approach to the tombs at a church in Padua, which I have not visited.

As I returned from the apse toward the nave, I thought for a moment that I heard a voice down the sepulchral stair. Could it be the verger? My impression of a voice was so strong that I descended into the large low-vaulted crypt. I found everything in order, and no man or woman. My conflict of emotions must be affecting my perceptions. Julie would have to pay for that, in precisely an hour and a half.

The two of us ate a simple dinner in the rectory; I told the Cambodian housekeeper not to bother with the dishes until she came back from the cinema. Julie must have thought my manner odd: I talked confusedly of everything under the sun and the moon—theology, Jamaica, low life in Hawkhill, the bishop, Fork (but there I checked my tongue), Mrs. Simmons, the lonely existence of a celibate. I stared hard at her all the while. Though presumably a little disturbed by my eccentricity, Julie remained pleasant, now and again asking a sensible question, and occasionally a naive one. I must have her.

'I don't suppose you've ever been present at a liturgy of the sort we celebrate in this church, Julie.'

'Oh, no, Father Montrose, I haven't; but I'd just love to.'

'It happens that I have arranged a special evensong liturgy for you alone, Julie. You'll be my whole congregation, a few minutes from now, at our Chapel of Saint Thomas of Canterbury.'

Her assent was delicious. What was to follow might be rather rough on Miss Tilton, but delicious for me. Let the consequences be damned.

I took my prize by the hand and led her to the galilee. My grasp did not startle her; quite possibly she thought it part of the liturgy.

It was nearly half-past eight. The old Cambodian verger was unlocking the postern door.

'Taxi honk, Father,' he told me. 'My wife, she come down in minute.'

I had held open the carved wooden doors to the nave, but Julie hung back. 'Just a minute, Father: I'll say "Have a good time" to the housekeeper when she comes down.'

Gripping her slender hand so that she winced a trifle, I tugged

Julie through the entrance to the nave. 'Come on, kid,' I heard myself saying harshly, 'we've got no time to waste.'

'Oh!' she cried.

'What's wrong, Julie, you little fool?'

'It's funny: you sounded just like Sherm then. It could have been his own voice, Father Montrose.'

We two stood at the foot of the central aisle. The Norman pillars of the nave interrupted the beams of dim religious light from such concealed fixtures as I had chosen to switch on. Far ahead of us, a huge ornate sanctuary lamp shone upon the high altar; and smaller sanctuary lamps glimmered from the side chapels.

I squeezed her hand. 'This is going to be a totally new experience for you, Julie. Perhaps you'll not enjoy all of it so much as I intend to.'

'Father, I just know it's going to be marvelous!'

I had begun to lead her down that broad aisle.

Then for a second time I heard a harsh, incoherent voice from the crypt stair near the crossing.

I stopped dead. Julie almost tripped.

'What's wrong, Father?'

'I don't know . . . What can have spoken?'

'Spoken, Father? I didn't hear anyone at all.'

Then came the first scream, so terrible that I reeled against a bench end. Ah, the ghastly echoes of it in the nave, in the aisles, in the choir, back from the blindstory!

'Oh, Father, are you all right? What's happening?'

'My God, Julie, didn't you hear that howl?' I could do no more than whisper the inquiry to her.

'I don't know what you mean. For just the littlest fraction of a second, though, I thought I heard my brother whispering in my ear.'

At that moment, in this dim sanctuary light, a head emerged above the balustrade of the crypt stair. Other heads followed it. They seemed like jelly, glistening.

In the horror of that moment, I broke free from the spirit that had entered into me. I knew all of a sudden that I had been occupied and made an agent. Whether from shock or from grace, I was enabled to regain my will. Through me, these things from below had schemed to take Julie.

Swinging round, I snatched up Julie and ran with her, bursting through the doors into the galilee. The verger and his wife were going out the door to take the taxi. Upon them I thrust my Julie.

'Drive her to Mrs. Simmons's quick!' I ordered them. It seemed to me as if I were grunting like a hog. 'Quick!' And to Julie, 'Good-bye, my darling. Don't ever come back here!'

Before I slammed the door behind them, I had one last glimpse of her astounded, pallid, lovely face, forbidden to me ever after.

Then I ran back into the nave, to impede the damned invaders.

Having emerged from the stair, the things were wavering slowly up the aisle toward me. In their insubstantiality they seemed to shimmer. There came four of them, inexpressibly loathsome. I knew they must be the men who had died on Causland's fork or by his gun.

As they drew nearer, I could make out the face of the first only. Lips and nostrils were hideously contorted; yet the resemblance to Julie could not be denied. From the four wounds, gouts of blood had run down the thing's middle.

In my extremity, I tried to stammer out the Third Collect;

Lighten our darkness, we beseech thee, O Lord, and by thy great mercy defend us from all perils and dangers of this night, for the love of thy only Son, our Savior Jesus Christ.

Yet the words, inaudible, stuck in my craw. Then came the Screamer's second tremendous howl, surely from the Pit. This thing had told his disciples that his essence could transcend space and time.

I clutched a pillar. These 'beasts with the souls of damned men' would overcome me, for too much of them had entered into me already. We were sib.

That second screech was followed by an unbearable silence. The Sherm-thing's tormented face drew nearer mine. He would enter. We would be one.

In that silence rang out the sound of brass upon stone. Fork thrust himself between me and the Screamer. 'Wahoo!'

It seemed to my eyes that Fork leaped twenty feet into the air; lingered suspended there; then returned, laughing as a hyena laughs.

The four dead things shrank from him. They seemed gelatinous, deliquescent: no word might express the ghastliness of them.

But Fork was all compact, glowing with energy, transfigured and yet in semblance himself, that hard, taut face invincible.

'So must you ever be,' said Fork, pointing at the four with his blindman's stick. 'This place and this man are too much for you. Into the fire, Sherm and all!'

They receded. Screaming, they were swept into nothingness. I fell.

If it was consciousness I regained, that was an awareness of the world beyond the world. Incapable of speech or movement, I seemed to be lying in some shadowy, cold, enclosed, unknown place. Was it a sepulcher? The form of Fork Causland—derby, stick, cigar, and all—seemed to stand before me.

'In the hour of need, you were a man, Doc,' he said to me, 'a man in the mold of your friend Thomas à Becket. It was the old Adam in you that admitted those four spirits from below, but the better part in you withstood them. I take off my hat to you'—and so he did, sweepingly, in Fork's sardonic way.

'You'll not see the girl again, Doc, here below, nor Fork Causland. His time came; it would have come more terribly two years ago, had I not occupied him then and thereafter. The end arrived in a moment of grace, while he was on his way to reinforce you; and it will be well with poor Fork.'

Though I strove to speak, I failed; the semblance of Fork shook its head. 'Listen. That you should see me without your blood freezing, I have come to you in the mask of your friend Fork. I shall come to you once more, Thomas Montrose—no, priest, I'll not specify the year, the day, the hour, humankind not being able to stand much reality—and then as a friend, civilly inviting you to enter upon eternity. Why, I'll stand then hat in hand before you, Doc, as I stand now. Shall I come in the semblance of Fork Causland on that occasion, too? I would please you.'

Lying rigid with fright, I could not reply to this being. He smiled Fork's stoical, humorous smile.

'Do you take me for a demon, Doc? No, I'm not what possessed Sherm, or what came close to possessing you. Through Fork's lips I told you that I was only cousin to devils. I'm a messenger, penetrating Time, taking such shapes as I am commanded: sometimes merciful, sometimes retributory.

'The old Greeks called me Thanatos. The Muslims call me Azrael. You may as well call me—why, Fork will do as well as any other name. Fast and pray, Doc. You have been tried, but not found wanting. In the fullness of time, as our blind friend Fork would have put it, "I'll be seeing you." '

Then he was gone, taking everything with him.

*   *   *

The ringing telephone on my bedside table woke me. Somehow the returned Cambodian church mice, taking me to be drunken merely, had contrived to drag me to my bed.

'Reverend Montrose?' the efficient voice of a woman inquired from the receiver. 'Do you know somebody named Homer Causland? We found your name and number in one of his pockets.'

'Yes. Something happened?'

'Mr. Causland was struck by a hit-and-run driver shortly after eight-thirty last night. His body was taken to Receiving Hospital, but there wasn't anything we could do for him here. He didn't suffer. The police have got the driver and booked him for murder. Can you make the arrangements—that is, was Mr. Causland a friend of yours?'

'My only one,' I told her. '*Requiescat in pace.*'

I have sent Julie Tilton's bag by taxi to Mrs. Simmons's big house, and Mrs. Simmons will see that Julie flies home, however bewildered, this evening.

If an energumen from below may penetrate even to the fastness of the church, how shall we prevail? Yet I fast and pray as one should who has been in the company of the dead damned, and has heard the speech of the Death Angel.

In all of us sinners the flesh is weak; and the future, unknowable, has its many contrived corridors and issues. Lord, I am a miserable thing, and I am afraid.

Puffed up with pride of spirit, by which fault fell the angels, I came near to serving the Prince of the Air. From the ravenous powers of darkness, O Lord, let me be preserved; and I entreat thee, do cast the lurking unclean spirits, instead, into the swine of Gadara.

For hours I have sat here, meditating, now and again scribbling these pages at my table in the galilee. The coals having expired in the grate, I am cold now.

The race is not to the swift, nor the battle to the strong.

Winter coming on, this is a night of sleet. What is tapping now, so faintly, at the great knocker on the bronze door? It never can be she. Has the order of release been sent? 'Watch ye, stand fast in the faith, quit you like men, be strong.' I'll unbar the little door. Pray for us sinners now and at the hour of death.

THE ACCOUNTANT

Robert Sheckley

Mr. Dee was seated in the big armchair, his belt loosened, the evening papers strewn around his knees. Peacefully he smoked his pipe, and considered how wonderful the world was. Today he had sold two amulets and a philter; his wife was bustling around the kitchen, preparing a delicious meal; and his pipe was drawing well. With a sigh of contentment, Mr. Dee yawned and stretched.

Morton, his nine-year-old son, hurried across the living room, laden down with books.

'How'd school go today?' Mr. Dee called.

'O.K.' the boy said, slowing down, but still moving toward his room.

'What have you got there?' Mr. Dee asked, gesturing at his son's tall pile of books.

'Just some more accounting stuff,' Morton said, not looking at his father. He hurried into his room.

Mr. Dee shook his head. Somewhere, the lad had picked up the notion that he wanted to be an accountant. An accountant! True, Morton was quick with figures; but he would have to forget this nonsense. Bigger things were in store for him.

The doorbell rang.

Mr. Dee tightened his belt, hastily stuffed in his shirt and opened the front door. There stood Miss Greeb, his son's fourth-grade teacher.

'Come in, Miss Greeb,' said Dee. 'Can I offer you something?'

'I have no time,' said Miss Greeb. She stood in the doorway, her arms akimbo. With her gray, tangled hair, her thin, long-nosed face and red runny eyes, she looked exactly like a witch. And this was as it should be, for Miss Greeb *was* a witch.

'I've come to speak to you about your son,' she said.

At this moment Mrs. Dee hurried out of the kitchen, wiping her hands on her apron.

'I hope he hasn't been naughty,' Mrs. Dee said anxiously.

Miss Greeb sniffed ominously. 'Today I gave the yearly tests. Your son failed miserably.'

'Oh dear,' Mrs. Dee said. 'It's spring. Perhaps——'

'Spring has nothing to do with it,' said Miss Greeb. 'Last week I assigned the Greater Spells of Cordus, section one. You know how easy *they* are. He didn't learn a single one.'

'Hm,' said Mr. Dee succinctly.

'In Biology, he doesn't have the slightest notion which are the basic conjuring herbs. Not the slightest.'

'This is unthinkable,' said Mr. Dee.

Miss Greeb laughed sourly. 'Moreover, he has forgotten all the Secret Alphabet which he learned in third grade. He has forgotten the Protective Formula, forgotten the names of the 99 lesser imps of the Third Circle, forgotten what little he knew of the Geography of Greater Hell. And what's more, he doesn't want to learn.'

Mr. and Mrs. Dee looked at each other silently. This was very serious indeed. A certain amount of boyish inattentiveness was allowable; encouraged, even, for it showed spirit. But a child *had* to learn the basics, if he ever hoped to become a full-fledged wizard.

'I can tell you right here and now,' said Miss Greeb, 'if this were the old days, I'd flunk him without another thought. But there are so few of us left.

Mr. Dee nodded sadly. Witchcraft had been steadily declining over the centuries. The old families died out, or were snatched by demonic forces, or became scientists. And the fickle public showed no interest whatsoever in the charms and enchantments of ancient days.

Now, only a scattered handful possesed the Old Lore, guarding it, teaching it in places like Miss Greeb's private school for the children of wizards. It was a heritage, a sacred trust.

'It's this accounting nonsense,' said Miss Greeb. 'I don't know where he got the notion.' She stared accusingly at Dee. 'And I don't know why it wasn't nipped in the bud.'

Mr. Dee felt his cheeks grow hot.

'But I do know this. As long as Morton has *that* on his mind, he can't give his attention to Thaumaturgy.'

Mr. Dee looked away from the witch's red eyes. It was his fault. He should never have brought home that toy adding machine. And when he first saw Morton playing at double entry bookkeeping, he should have burned the ledger.

But how could he know it would grow into an obsession?

Mrs. Dee smoothed out her apron, and said, 'Miss Greeb, you know you have our complete confidence. What would you suggest?'

'All I can do I have done,' said Miss Greeb. 'The only remaining thing is to call up Boarbas, the Demon of Children. And that, naturally, is up to you.'

'Oh, I don't think it's that serious yet,' Mr. Dee said quickly. 'Calling up Boarbas is a serious measure.'

'As I said, that's up to you,' Miss Greeb said. 'Call Boarbas or not, as you see fit. As things stand now, your son will never be a wizard.' She turned and started to leave.

'Won't you stay for a cup of tea?' Mrs. Dee asked hastily.

'No, I must attend a Witches' Coven in Cincinnati,' said Miss Greeb, and vanished in a puff of orange smoke.

Mr. Dee fanned the smoke with his hands and closed the door. 'Phew,' he said. 'You'd think she'd use a perfumed brand.'

'She's old-fashioned,' Mrs. Dee murmured.

They stood beside the door in silence. Mr. Dee was just beginning to feel the shock. It was hard to believe that his son, his own flesh and blood, didn't want to carry on the family tradition. It couldn't be true!

'After dinner,' Dee said, finally, 'I'll have a man-to-man talk with him. I'm sure we won't need any demoniac intervention.'

'Good,' Mrs. Dee said. 'I'm sure you can make the boy understand.' She smiled, and Dee caught a glimpse of the old witch-light flickering behind her eyes.

'My roast!' Mrs. Dee gasped suddenly, the witch-light dying. She hurried back to her kitchen.

Dinner was a quiet meal. Morton knew that Miss Greeb had been there, and he ate in guilty silence, glancing occasionally at his father. Mr. Dee sliced and served the roast, frowning deeply. Mrs. Dee didn't even attempt any small talk.

After bolting his dessert, the boy hurried to his room.

'Now we'll see,' Mr. Dee said to his wife. He finished the last of his coffee, wiped his mouth and stood up. 'I am going to reason with him now. Where is my Amulet of Persuasion?'

Mrs. Dee thought deeply for a moment. Then she walked across the room to the bookcase. 'Here it is,' she said, lifting it from the pages of a brightly jacketed novel. 'I was using it as a marker.'

Mr. Dee slipped the amulet into his pocket, took a deep breath, and entered his son's room.

Morton was seated at his desk. In front of him was a notebook, scribbled with figures and tiny, precise notations. On his desk were six carefully sharpened pencils, a soap eraser, an abacus and a toy adding machine. His books hung precariously over the edge of the desk; there was *Money*, by Rimraamer, *Bank Accounting Practice*, by Johnson and Calhoun, *Ellman's Studies for the CPA*, and a dozen others.

Mr. Dee pushed aside a mound of clothes and made room for himself on the bed. 'How's it going, son?' he asked, in his kindest voice.

'Fine, Dad,' Morton answered eagerly. 'I'm up to chapter four in *Basic Accounting*, and I answered all the questions——'

'Son,' Dee broke in, speaking very softly, 'how about your regular homework?'

Morton looked uncomfortable and scuffed his feet on the floor.

'You know, not many boys have a chance to become wizards in this day and age.'

'Yes sir, I know.' Morton looked away abruptly. In a high, nervous voice he said, 'But, Dad, I want to be an accountant. I really do. Dad?'

Mr. Dee shook his head. 'Morton, there's always been a wizard in our family. For eighteen hundred years, the Dees have been famous in supernatural circles.'

Morton continued to look out the window and scuff his feet.

'You wouldn't want to disappoint me, would you, son?' Dee smiled sadly. 'You know, anyone can be an *accountant*. But only a chosen few can master the Black Arts.'

Morton turned away from the window. He picked up a pencil, inspected the point, and began to turn it slowly in his fingers.

'How about it, boy? Won't you work harder for Miss Greeb?'

Morton shook his head. 'I want to be an accountant.'

Mr. Dee contained his sudden rush of anger with difficulty. What was wrong with the Amulet of Persuasion? Could the spell have run down? He should have recharged it. Nevertheless, he went on.

'Morton,' he said in a husky voice, 'I'm only a Third Degree Adept, you know. My parents were very poor. They couldn't send me to The University.'

'I know,' the boy said in a whisper.

'I want you to have all the things I never had. Morton, you can be a First Degree Adept.' He shook his head wistfully. 'It'll be difficult. But your mother and I have a little put away, and we'll scrape the rest together somehow.'

Morton was biting his lip and turning the pencil rapidly in his fingers.

'How about it, son? You know, as a First Degree Adept, you won't have to work in a store. You can be a Direct Agent of The Black One. A Direct Agent! What do you say, boy?'

For a moment, Dee thought his son was moved. Morton's lips were parted, and there was a suspicious brightness in his eyes. But then the boy glanced at his accounting books, his little abacus, his toy adding machine.

'I'm going to be an accountant,' he said.

'We'll see!' Mr. Dee shouted, all patience gone. 'You will *not* be an accountant, young man. You will be a wizard. It was good enough for the rest of your family, and by all that's damnable, it'll be good enough for you. You haven't heard the last of this, young man.' And he stormed out of the room.

Immediately, Morton returned to his accounting books.

Mr. and Mrs. Dee sat together on the couch, not talking. Mrs. Dee was busily knotting a wind-cord, but her mind wasn't on it. Mr. Dee stared moodily at a worn spot on the living room rug.

Finally, Dee said, 'I've spoiled him. Boarbas is the only solution.'

'Oh, no,' Mrs. Dee said hastily. 'He's so young.'

'Do you want your son to be an accountant?' Mr. Dee asked bitterly. 'Do you want him to grow up scribbling with figures instead of doing The Black One's important work?'

'Of course not,' said Mrs. Dee. 'But Boarbas——'

'I know. I feel like a murderer already.'

They thought for a few moments. Then Mrs. Dee said, 'Perhaps his grandfather can do something. He was always fond of the boy.'

'Perhaps he can,' Mr. Dee said thoughtfully. 'But I don't know if we should disturb him. After all, the old gentleman has been dead for three years.'

'I know,' Mrs. Dee said, undoing an incorrect knot in the wind-cord. 'But it's either that or Boarbas.'

Mr. Dee agreed. Unsettling as it would be to Morton's grandfather, Boarbas was infinitely worse. Immediately, Dee made preparations for calling up his dead father.

He gathered together the henbane, the ground unicorn's horn, the hemlock, together with a morsel of dragon's tooth. These he placed on the rug.

'Where's my wand?' he asked his wife.

'I put it in the bag with your golfsticks,' she told him.

Mr. Dee got his wand and waved it over the ingredients. He muttered the three words of The Unbinding, and called out his father's name.

Immediately a wisp of smoke arose from the rug.

'Hello, Grandpa Dee,' Mrs. Dee said.

'Dad, I'm sorry to disturb you,' Mr. Dee said. 'But my son—your grandson—refuses to become a wizard. He wants to be an—accountant.'

The wisp of smoke trembled, then straightened out and described a character of the Old Language.

'Yes,' Mr. Dee said. 'We tried persuasion. The boy is adamant.'

Again the smoke trembled, and formed another character.

'I suppose that's best,' Mr. Dee said. 'If you frighten him out of his wits once and for all, he'll forget this accounting nonsense. It's cruel—but it's better than Boarbas.'

The wisp of smoke nodded, and streamed toward the boy's room. Mr. and Mrs. Dee sat down on the couch.

The door of Morton's room was slammed open, as though by a gigantic wind. Morton looked up, frowned, and returned to his books.

The wisp of smoke turned into a winged lion with the tail of a shark. It roared hideously, crouched, snarled, and gathered itself for a spring.

Morton glanced at it, raised both eyebrows, and proceeded to jot down a column of figures.

The lion changed into a three-headed lizard, its flanks reeking horribly of blood. Breathing gusts of fire, the lizard advanced on the boy.

Morton finished adding the column of figures, checked the result on his abacus, and looked at the lizard.

With a screech, the lizard changed into a giant gibbering bat. It fluttered around the boy's head, moaning and gibbering.

Morton grinned, and turned back to his books.

Mr. Dee was unable to stand it any longer. 'Damn it,' he shouted, 'aren't you scared?'

'Why should I be?' Morton asked. 'It's only Grandpa.'

Upon the word, the bat dissolved into a plume of smoke. It nodded sadly to Mr. Dee, bowed to Mrs. Dee, and vanished.

'Goodbye, Grandpa,' Morton called. He got up and closed his door.

'That does it,' Mr. Dee said. 'The boy is too cocksure of himself. We must call up Boarbas.'

'No!' his wife said.

'What, then?'

'I just don't know any more,' Mrs. Dee said, on the verge of tears. 'You *know* what Boarbas does to children. They're never the same afterwards.'

Mr. Dee's face was hard as granite. 'I know. It can't be helped.'

'He's so young!' Mrs. Dee wailed. 'It—it will be traumatic!'

'If so, we will use all the resources of modern psychology to heal him,' Mr. Dee said soothingly. 'He will have the best psychoanalysts money can buy. But the boy must be a wizard!'

'Go ahead then,' Mrs. Dee said, crying openly. 'But please don't ask me to assist you.'

How like a woman, Dee thought. Always turning into jelly at the moment when firmness was indicated. With a heavy heart, he made the preparations for calling up Boarbas, Demon of Children.

First came the intricate sketching of the pentagon, and the twelve-pointed star within it, and the endless spiral within that. Then came the herbs and essences; expensive items, but absolutely necessary for the conjuring. Then came the inscribing of the Protective Spell, so that Boarbas might not break loose and destroy them all. Then came the three drops of hippogriff blood——

'Where is my hippogriff blood?' Mr. Dee asked, rummaging through the living-room cabinet.

'In the kitchen, in the aspirin bottle,' Mrs. Dee said, wiping her eyes.

Dee found it, and then all was in readiness. He lighted the black candles and chanted the Unlocking Spell.

The room was suddenly very warm, and there remained only the Naming of the Name.

'Morton,' Mr. Dee called. 'Come here.'

Morton opened the door and stepped out, holding one of his accounting books tightly, looking very young and defenseless.

'Morton, I am about to call up the Demon of Children. Don't make me do it, Morton.'

The boy turned pale and shrank back against the door. But stubbornly he shook his head.

'Very well,' Mr. Dee said. 'BOARBAS!'

There was an ear-splitting clap of thunder and a wave of heat, and Boarbas appeared, as tall as the ceiling, chuckling evilly.

'Ah!' cried Boarbas, in a voice that shook the room. 'A little boy.'

Morton gaped, his jaw open and eyes bulging.

'A naughty little boy,' Boarbas said, and laughed. The demon marched forward, shaking the house with every stride.

'Send him away!' Mrs. Dee cried.

'I can't,' Dee said, his voice breaking. 'I can't do anything until he's finished.'

The demon's great horned hands reached for Morton; but quickly the boy opened the accounting book. 'Save me!' he screamed.

In that instant, a tall, terribly thin old man appeared, covered with worn pen points and ledger sheets, his eyes two empty zeroes.

'*Zico Pico Reel!*' chanted Boarbas, turning to grapple with the newcomer. But the thin old man laughed, and said, 'A contract of a corporation which is *ultra vires* is not voidable only, but utterly void.'

At these words, Boarbas was flung back, breaking a chair as he fell. He scrambled to his feet, his skin glowing red-hot with rage, and intoned the Demoniac Master-Spell: 'VRAT, HAT, HO!'

But the thin old man shielded Morton with his body, and cried the words of Dissolution. 'Expiration, Repeal, Occurrence, Surrender, Abandonment and Death!'

Boarbas squeaked in agony. Hastily he backed away, fumbling in the air until he found The Opening. He jumped through this, and was gone.

The tall, thin old man turned to Mr. and Mrs. Dee, cowering in a corner of the living room, and said, 'Know that I am The Accountant. And Know, Moreover, that this Child has signed a Compact with Me, to enter My Apprenticeship and be My Servant. And in return for Services Rendered, I, The Accountant, am teaching him the Damnation of Souls, by means of ensnaring them in a cursed web of Figures, Forms, Torts and Reprisals. And behold, this is My Mark upon him!'

The Accountant held up Morton's right hand, and showed the ink smudge on the third finger.

He turned to Morton, and in a softer voice said, 'Tomorrow, lad, we will consider some aspects of Income Tax Evasion as a Path to Damnation.'

'Yes *sir*,' Morton said eagerly.

And with another sharp look at the Dees, The Accountant vanished.

For long seconds there was silence. Then Dee turned to his wife.

'Well,' Dee said, 'if the boy wants to be an accountant *that* badly, I'm sure I'm not going to stand in his way.'

THE FIRE WHEN IT COMES

Parke Godwin

Got to wake up soon.

I've been sick a long time, I mean really sick. Hard to remember why or how long, but it feels like that time I had hundred-and-three fever for a week. Sleep wasn't rest but endless, meaningless movement, and I'd wake up to change my sweaty nightdress for a clean one which would be soaked by sunup.

But this boring, weary dream has gone on for ages. I'm walking up and down the apartment trying to find the door. The furniture isn't mine. People come and go, replaced by others with even tackier sofas in colors loud enough to keep them awake, and I flutter around and past them on my own silly route as if I'd lost an earring and had to find it before I could get on with life. None of it's very real, murky as *cinema-verité* shot in a broom closet. I have to strain to recognize the apartment, and the sound track just mumbles. No feeling at all.

Just that it's gone on so long.

All right, enough of this. Lying around sick and fragile is romantic as hell, but I have to get it together, drop the needle on the world again and let it play. I'm—

Hell, I am out of it, can't even remember my name, but there's a twinge of pain in trying. Never mind, start with simple things. Move your hand, spider your fingers out from under the covers. Rub your face, open your eyes.

That hasn't worked the last thousand times. I can't wake up, and in a minute the stupid dream will start again with a new cast and no script, and I'll be loping up and down after that earring or the lost door. Hell, yes. Here it comes. Again.

No. It's different this time. I'd almost swear I was awake,

standing near the balcony door with the whole long view of
my apartment stretching out before me: living room, pullman
kitchen, the bedroom, bathroom like an afterthought in the
rear. It's clear daylight, and the apartment is bare. Sounds are
painfully sharp. The door screams open and shuts like thunder.

A boy and a girl.

She's twenty-two at the outside, he's not much older. He looks
sweet, happy and maybe a little scared. Nice face, the kind of
sensitive expression you look at twice. The girl's mouth is firmer.
Small and blonde and compact. I know that expression, tentative
only for a moment before she begins to measure my apartment for
possibilities, making it hers.

'Really a lot of room,' she says. 'I could do things with this place
if we had the money.'

My God, they're so *loud*. The boy drifts toward me while she
bangs cupboard doors, checks out the bathroom, flushes the toilet.

'The john works. No plumbing problems.'

'Al, come here. Look, a balcony.'

'Wow, Lowen, is that for real?'

Of course it's real, love. Open the door, take a look and then get
the hell out of my dreams.

'Let's look, Al.' He invites the girl with one hand and opens the
balcony door. He's in love with her and doesn't quite know how to
handle it all yet. They wander out onto my tiny balcony and look
down at 77th Street and out over the river where a garbage scow is
gliding upstream. It's a lovely day. Jesus, how long since I've seen
the sun? Kids are romping in the playground across Riverside
Drive. Lowen and Al stand close together. When he pulls her
to him, her hand slips up over his shoulder. The gold ring looks
new.

'Can we afford it, Lowen?'

'We can if you want it.'

'If? I never wanted anything so much in my life.'

They hold each other and talk money as if it were a novel-
ty, mentioning a rent way over what I pay. The frigging land-
lord would love to hang that price tag on this place. Lowen
points to the drainpipe collar bedded in a patch of cement,
monument stone to my epic battle with that bastard to clear the
drain and anchor it so every rain didn't turn my balcony
into a small lake. Lowen's pointing to letters scratched in the cement.

'GAYLA.'

That's right, that's me. I remember now.

They look through the apartment again, excited now that they think they want it. Yes, if they're careful with their budget, if they get that cash wedding present from Aunt Somebody, they can work it. I feel very odd; something is funny here. They're too real. The dream is about them now.

Hey, wait a minute, you two.

The door bangs shut after them.

Hey, wait!

I run out onto the balcony and call to them in the street, and for the first time in this fever dream, I'm conscious of arms and legs that I still can't feel, and a fear growing out of a clearing memory.

Hey, hello. It's me, Gayla Damon.

Lowen turns and tilts his head as if he heard me, or perhaps for one more look at where he's going to live with Al-short-for-Alice. I can't tell from his smile, but I lean to it like a fire in winter, out over the low stone parapet—and then, oh Christ, I remember. For one terrible, sufficient flash, the memory flicks a light switch.

If I could cry or be sick, I'd do that. If I screamed loud enough to crack the asphalt on West End Avenue, nobody would hear. But I let it out anyway, and my scream fills the world as Lowen and Al stroll away toward Riverside Drive.

As if they could actually see me hunched over the balcony edge, head shaking back and forth in despair. They could will their real bodies to stop, real eyes lift again to a real, vacant balcony.

Because they're real. I'm not. Not sick or dreaming, just not.

You died, Gayla baby. You're dead.

The last couple of days have been bad. Panic, running back and forth, scared to death or life, I don't know which, trying to find a way out without knowing where to go or why. I know I died, God, am I sure of that, but not how or how to get out.

There's no frigging door! Lowen and Al sail in and out unloading their junk, but when I try to find the door, it's Not, like me. I'm stuck here. I guess that's what frightens all of us because you can't imagine Not. I never bought the MGM version of heaven. For me, being dead was simply not being, zero, zilch, something you can't imagine. The closest you can come is when a dentist knocks you out with pentothol or how you felt two years before you were born.

No. I don't end, you say. Not me, not the center of the universe. And yet it's happened and I'm stuck with it, no way out, trying to hack the whole thing at once, skittering back and forth from the bedroom to the living room, through the kitchen with its new cream paint, crawling like cigarette smoke in the drapes, beating my nothing-fists against the wall sometimes, collapsing out of habit and exhaustion into a chair or bed I can't feel under me, wearing myself out with the only sensation left, exhaustion and terror.

I'm not dead. I can't be dead, because if I am, why am I still here. Let me out!

To go where, honey?

There's a kind of time again. Al's pinned up a Japanese art calendar in the kitchen, very posh. This month it's a samurai warrior drawing his sword; either that or playing with himself. I can't see it that well, but the date is much too clear. 1981. No wonder the rent's gone up. Seven years since I—

No, that word is a downer. Exited is better. Just how is still a big fat blank wrapped in confusion. All I remember is my name and a few silly details about the apartment. No past, no memory to splice the little snippets of film that flash by too swiftly to catch. Not that it matters, but where's my body? Was I buried or burned, scattered or canned in memoriam in some mausoleum? Was there a husband, a lover? What kind of life did I have?

When I think hard, there's the phantom pain of someone gone, someone who hurt me. That memory is vaguely connected with another of crying into the phone, very drunk. I can't quite remember, just how it made me feel. Got to organize and think, I've worn myself out running scared, and still no answers. The only clear thought is an odd little thing; there must have been a lot of life in me to be kept so close to it.

Don't ask me about death. The rules are all new. I might be the first of the breed. It's still me, but unable to breathe or sleep or get hungry. Just energy that can still run down from overuse, and when that happens, Lowen and Al grow faint. That's all there is to me now, energy, and not much of that. I have to conserve, just float here by Al's painfully correct window drapes and think.

Does anyone know I'm here. I mean, Anyone?

A few more days. Al and Lowen are all moved in. Al's decor works very hard at being House Beautiful, an almost militant graciousness. Style with clenched teeth. And all her china matches—hell, yes, it would. But let's face it: whatever's happening to me is because of them. When they're close, I get a hint of solid objects around me, as if I could reach out and touch tables and chairs or

Lowen, but touching life costs me energy. The degree of nearness determines how much of my pitiful little charge is spent. Like being alive in a way. Living costs. I learned that somewhere.

Just got the hell scared out of me. Al has a mirror in the bedroom, a big antique affair. Sometimes when she brushes her hair, I stand behind her, aching out of habit to get that brush into my own mop. Tonight as I watched, I saw myself behind her.

I actually jumped with fright, but Al just went on pumping away with the brush while I peered over her head at Gayla Damon. Thirty-three—I remember that now—and beginning to look it. Thank God that won't bother me any more. Yes, I was tall. Brownish-black hair not too well cut. Thin face, strong jaw, eyes large and expressive. They were my best feature, they broadcast every feeling I ever had. Lines starting around my mouth. Not a hard mouth but beginning to turn down around the edges, a little tired. Hardness would have helped, I guess. Some of Natalie Bond's brass balls.

Nattie Bond: a name, another memory.

No, it's gone, but there was a kind of pain with it. I stared at the mirror. Cruddy old black sweater and jeans: was I wearing them? You'd think I could check out in something better. Hey, brown eyes, how did they do you for the curtain call? Touch of pancake, I hope. You always looked dead without it. Oh, shit . . .

A little crying helps. Even dry it's something.

I watch Lowen more and more, turning to him as a flower follows the sun, beginning to learn why I respond to him. Lowen's a listener and a watcher. He can be animated when he's feeling good or way down if he's not. Tired, depressed or angry, his brown eyes go almost black. Not terribly aggressive, but he does sense and respond to the life going on around him.

He likes the apartment and being quiet in it. He smokes, too, not much but enough to bother Al. They've worked out a compromise: anywhere but the bedroom. So, sometimes, I get a surprise visit in the living room when Lowen wakes up and wants a smoke. He sits for a few minutes in the dark, cigarette a bright arc from his mouth to the ashtray. I can't tell, but sometimes it seems he's listening to pure silence. He turns his head this way and that—toward me sometimes—and I feel weird; like he was sifting the molecules of silence, sensing a weight in them. Sometimes in the evening when he and Al are fixing dinner, Lowen will raise his head in that listening way.

It's a long-shot hope, but I wonder if he can feel *me*.

Why has he brought me back to time and space and caring? All these years there's been only blurred shadows and voices faint as a radio in the next room. Real light and sound and thought came only when he walked in. When Lowen's near, I perk up and glow; when he leaves, I fade to drift, disinterested, by the balcony door.

Lowen Sheppard: twenty-four at most, gentle, unconsciously graceful, awkward only when he tries to be more mature than he is. Don't work at it, lover, it'll come. Soft, straight brown hair that he forgets to cut until Al reminds him, which is often. She's great on detail, lives by it. Faces this apartment like a cage of lions to be tamed. Perhaps it's the best she ever had.

Lowen seems used to this much or maybe better. Mister nice guy, not my type at all, and yet I'm bound to him by a kind of fascination, bound without being able to touch his hair or speak to him. And it's no use wondering why, I'm learning that, too. Like that old Bergman flick where Death comes to collect Max von Sydow. Max says, 'Tell me what eternity is like.' And Death says, 'Who knows? I just work here.'

Don't call us. We'll call you.

Well, damnit, *someone* is going to know I'm here. If I can think, I can do, and I'm not going to sit here forever just around the corner from life. Lowen and Al are my world now, the only script left to work with. I'm a part of their lives like a wart on the thigh, somewhere between God and a voyeur.

Wait, a memory just . . . no. Gone too quick again.

If I could touch Lowen somehow. Let him know.

Lowen and Al are settled in, place for everything and everything in its place, and Al daring it to get out of line. Lowen works full time, and Al must do some part-time gig. She goes out in the early afternoon. The lights dim then. Just as well; I don't like what she's done with my apartment. Everything shrieks its price at you, but somehow Al's not comfortable with it. Maybe she never will be. That mouth is awful tight. She wanted to keep plastic covers over the sofa and chairs, the kind that go *crunkle* when you sit on them and make you feel like you're living in a commercial. But Lowen put his foot down on that.

'But, Al, they're to use, not just to look at.'

'I know, but they're so nice and new.'

'Look, I wear a rubber when we make love. I don't need them on the furniture.'

She actually blushed. 'Really, Lowen.'

Son of a—she makes him—? Do guys still wear those things? Whatever happened to the sexual revolution?

It's indicative of their upbringing the way each eats, too. Al sits erect at the table and does the full choreography with her knife and fork, as if disapproving mama was watching her all the time. Cut the meat, lay the knife down, cross the fork to her right hand, spear, chew, swallow, and the whole thing over again. Left hand demurely in her lap.

Lowen leans slightly into his plate, what-the-hell elbows on the table. More often than not, he uses the fork in his left hand, placing things on it with his knife. The way he handles them both, he's definitely lived in England or Europe. Not born there, though. The fall of his speech has a hint of softness and mid-South nasal. Virginia or Maryland. Baltimore, maybe.

Perhaps it's just plain jealousy that puts me off Alice. She's alive. She can reach out and touch, hold, kiss what I can only look at. She's the strength in this marriage, the one who'll make it work. Lowen's softer, easier, with that careless assurance that comes from never having to worry about the rent or good clothes. He's been given to; Al's had to grab and fight. Now he's got a job and trying to cut it on his own for the first time. That's scary, but Al helps. She does a pretty fair job of supporting Lowen without letting him notice it too much.

She has her problems, but Lowen comes first. She gets home just before him, zips out to get fresh flowers for the table. A quick shower and a spritz of perfume, another swift agony at the mirror. And then Lowen is home and sitting down to dinner, telling her about the day. And Al listens, not so much to the words but the easy, charming sound, the quality she loves in him, as if she could learn it for herself. She's from New York, probably the Bronx. I remember the accent somehow. Petite and pretty, but she doesn't believe it no matter how much attention Lowen gives her. Spends a lot of time at the mirror when he's gone, not admiring but wondering. What does she really look like. What type is she, what kind of an image does she, should she, project; and can she do it? Lipstick: this shade or that? So she fiddles and narrows her eyes, scrutinizing the goods, hopes for the advertised magic of Maybelline and ends up pretty much the same: more attractive than she thinks, not liking what she sees.

Except she doesn't see. She's carried it around all her life, too busy, too nervous and insecure to know what she's got. Stripped down for a bath, Al looks like she never had a pimple or a pound of fat in her life, but I swear she'll find something wrong, something not to like.

Don't slop that goo on your face, girl. You're great already. God,

I only wish I had your skin. The crap I had to put on and take off every night, playing parts like—

Parts like. . . .

My God, I remember!

I was an actress. That's what I remember in quick flashes of hard light. The pictures whiz by like fast cars, but they're slowing down: stage sets, snatches of dialogue, dim faces in the front rows. Bill Wrenn giving me a piece of business to work out. Fragments of me like a painting on shattered glass. I grope for the pieces, fitting them together one by one.

Bill Wrenn: there's a warm feeling when I think of him, a trusting. Where did I meet him? Yes, it's coming back.

Bill directed that first season at Lexington Rep. Gentle and patient with a weariness that no longer expected any goodies from life, he always reminded me of a harried sheepdog with too many sheep to hustle. Forty years old, two marriages and struck out both times, not about to fall hard again.

But he did for me. I made it easy for him. We were out of the same mold, Bill and I. He sensed my insecurity as a woman and found ways to make it work for me onstage, found parts in me I'd never dream of playing. With most men, my whole thing began in bed and usually ended there. Bill and I didn't hurry; there was a love first. We enjoyed and respected each other's work, and theater was a church for us. We'd rehash each performance, sometimes staying up all night to put an extra smidge of polish on business or timing, to get a better laugh, to make something good just a hair better. We started with a love of something beyond us that grew toward each other, so that bed, when it came, was natural and easy as it was gorgeous.

I made him love me, my one genuine conquest. We even talked about getting married—carefully skirting around a lot of if's. I seem to remember him asking me one night in Lexington. I *think* he asked then; there's a thick haze of vodka and grass over that night. Did I say yes? Not likely; by that time the old habits were setting in.

It was too good with Bill. That's not funny. Perfection, happiness, these are frightening things. Very few of us can live with them. After a while, I began to resent Bill. I mean, who the hell was he to take up so much of my life? I began to pick at him, finding things not to like, irritating habits like the nervous way he cleared his throat or dug in his ear when he was thinking out some stage problem; the way he picked his feet in bed and usually left the bathroom a mess. Just bitchiness. I even over reacted when he gave me notes after a performance. All bullshit and panic; just looking for a way out. How dare you love me, Bill Wrenn? Who asked you? Where did I get that way, where did it begin?

When Nick Charreau came into the company, he was tailor-made for me.

He was alone onstage the first time I saw him, a new cast replacement going through his blocking with the stage manager. Everything his predecessor did, Nick adjusted to show himself in a better light. He wasn't a better actor, but so completely, insolently sure of himself that he could pull off anything and make it look good, even a bad choice. Totally self-centered: if there were critics in the house, Nick lit up like a sign, otherwise it was just another working night in the sticks.

Nick was a lot better looking than Bill and eighteen years younger. Even-featured with a sharp, cool, detached expression. Eyes that looked right through you. He could tell me things wrong with myself that would earn Bill Wrenn a reaming out, but I took it from Nick. He didn't get close or involved all the way down. Perhaps that's why I chose him, out of cowardice. He wouldn't ever ask me to be a person.

When he finished the blocking session, I came down to lean on the stage apron. 'You play that far back, you'll upstage everyone else in the scene.'

'It's my scene. I'm beautifully lit up there.' Nick's smile was friendly with just the right soupçon of cockiness. A little above us all, just enough to tickle my own self-doubt and make me want to take him on. I can handle you, mister. You're not so tough.

But he was. There was always part of Nick I couldn't reach or satisfy. I started out challenged, piqued, to cut him down to size in bed and ended up happy if he'd just smile at me.

Looking over Al's shoulder in the mirror, I know it's not what we're born but what we're made into. The game is called Hurt me, I haven't suffered enough. I needed a son of a bitch like Nick. You don't think I'd go around deserving someone like Bill, do you?

Call that weird, Alice? You're the same song, different verse. You have that wary, born-owing-money look yourself. You handle it better than I did—you knew a good man when you saw one—but you still feel like a loser.

The fights with Bill grew large, bitter and frequent. He knew what was happening and it hurt him. And one night we split.

'When will you grow up, Gayla?'

'Bill, don't make it harder than it has to be. Just wish me luck.'

Dogged, tired, plopping fresh ice-cubes into his drink. 'I care about you. About you, Gayla. That makes it hard. Nick's twenty-two and about an inch deep. He'll split in six months and you'll be out in the cold. When will you learn, Gay? It's not a game, it's not a great big candy store. It's people.'

'I'm sorry, Bill.'

'Honey,' he sighed, 'you sure are.'

I still hovered, somehow needing his blessing. 'Please? Wish me luck?'

Bill raised his glass, not looking up. 'Sure, Gay. With Nick you'll need it.'

'What's that mean?'

'Nothing, forget it.'

'No, you don't just say things like that.'

'Sorry, I'm all out of graciousness.'

'What did you mean? I'll need it.'

Bill paused to take a swallow of his drink. 'Come on, Gay. You're not blind.'

'Other women? So what.'

'Other anybody.'

'Oh boy, you're—'

'Nick swings both ways.'

'That's a lie!'

'He'd screw a light socket if it helped him to a part.'

That was the nastiest thing Bill ever said about anyone. I felt angry and at the same time gratified that he made it easier to walk out mad. 'Good-bye, Bill.'

And then he looked up at me, showing what was hidden before. Bill Wrenn was crying. Crying for me, the only person in this fucking world who ever did. All the pain, anger, loss, welling up in those sad sheepdog eyes. I could have put my arms around him and stayed . . . no, wait, the picture's changing. I'm here in the apartment. *Get him out of here, Nick—*

No, it goes too fast or I will it to go. I can't, won't remember that yet because it hurts too much, and like a child I reach, cry out for the one thing I could always trust.

Bill-l-l—

Not a scream, just the memory of sound.

Lowen looks up from his book, puzzled. 'Al? You call me?'

No answer. It's late, she's asleep.

Once more Lowen seems to listen, feeling the air and the silence, separating its texture with his senses. Searching. Then he goes back to his book, but doesn't really try to read.

He heard me. He heard *me*. I can reach him.

Sooner or later, he'll know I'm here. Bust my hump or break my heart, I'll do it. Somehow. I've got to live, baby. Even dead, it's all I know how to do.

I've hit a new low, watched Lowen and Al make love. At first I avoided it, but gradually the prospect drew me as hunger draws you to a kitchen; hunger no longer a poignant memory but sharp need that grows with my strength.

I've never watched love-making before. Porn, yes, but that's for laughs, a nowhere fantasy. One of the character men in Lexington had a library of films we used to dig sometimes after a show, hooting at their ineptness. They could make you laugh or even horny now and then, but none of them ever dealt with reality. Porn removes you from the act, puts it at a safe distance.

Real sex is awkward, banal and somehow very touching to watch. It's all the things we are and want: involvement, commitment, warmth, passion, clumsiness, generosity or selfishness. Giving and receiving or holding back, all stained with the colors of openness or fear, lovely—and very vulnerable. All that, and yet the words are inadequate; you can't get any of that from watching. Like the man said, you had to be there.

Rogers and Astaire these two are not. It's all pretty straight missionary and more of an express than a local. Lowen does certain things and Al tries a few herself, sort of at arm's length and without much freedom. I don't think Lowen's had much experience, and Al, though she needs sex, probably learned somewhere that she oughtn't like it all that much. She's the new generation; she's heard it's her right and prerogative, but the no-no was bred in early. So she compromises by not enjoying it, by making it uphill for both of them. She inhibits Lowen without meaning to. He has to wait so long for her to relax and then work so hard to get her going. And of course at the best moment, like an insurance commercial in the middle of a cavalry charge, he has to stop and put on that stupid rubber. I wonder if Al's Catholic, she never heard of a diaphragm? Or maybe it's money. That's not so far out. Maybe she's up-tight about getting pregnant because she remembers how it was to grow up poor. Maybe it's a lot of things adding up to tense ambivalence, wondering why the bells don't ring and the earth shake like she read in *Cosmopolitan*. I seem to remember that trip.

She doesn't give herself much time to relish it afterward, either. Kiss-kiss-bang-bang, then zip with the kleenex and pit-pat into the shower as if someone might catch them. Maybe that's the way it was before they married, a habit that set before either of them realized it.

But I've touched Lowen. God, yes, for one galvanized split-second I felt his body against me. I paid for it, but it had to be.

It was after they made love and Al did her sprint from bed through the shower and into her nightie-cocoon. Lowen went into the bathroom then. I heard the shower running and drifted in after him.

His body looked marvelous; smooth light olive against Al's blue flower-patterned bath curtains, the soap lather standing out sharp white against the last of his summer tan. Not too muscular; supple like Nick. It'll be a while before he has to worry about weight.

Lowen soaped and rinsed, and I enjoyed the shape of his chest and shoulders when he raised his arms over his head.

You're beautiful, Mr. Sheppard.

I had to do it then. I moved in and kissed him, *felt* his chest, stomach, his hardness against the memory of my pelvis. Only a second, a moment when I had to hold him.

The sensation that shivered through me was like a sudden electric shock. I pulled back, frightened and hurt, hovering in the shower curtain. Lowen jerked, grabbing for the towel rack, taut, scared as myself. Then, slowly, the fear faded and I saw that listening, probing attitude in the lift of his head before the instinctive fear returned. Lowen snapped the water off, stumbled out of the tub and just sat down on the john, dripping and shaking. He sat there for minutes, watching the water drying on his skin, runneling down the sides of the tub. Once he put a hand to his lips. They moved, forming a word I couldn't hear.

You felt me, damn you. You know I'm here. If I could just talk to you.

But the exhaustion and pain ebbed me. We slumped at opposite ends of the small bathroom, Lowen staring through me, not hearing the sob, the agony of the pictures that flashed into life. Touching him, I remember. After the shock of life comes the memory, filling me out by one more jagged fragment, measuring me in pain.

Al, Al, frowning at your mirror, wondering what magic you lack—I should have your problem. The guys probably lined up around the block when you were in school. Not for Gayla Damon; hell, that wasn't even my real name, not for a long, hard time. First there was big, fat Gail Danowski from the Bronx like you, and at seventeen what your men prayed for and likely never got, I couldn't give away.

Why do I have to remember that? Please, I tried so hard to get away from it. My father who worked for the city as a sandhog, my dumpy mother with her permanent look of washed-out disgust, both of them fresh off the boat in 1938. My sister Sasha who got married at seventeen to get away from them. Big change: all Zosh did after that was have kids for that beer-drinking slob husband of hers. Jesus, Charlie disgusted me. Sunday afternoons he'd come over and watch football with my father, swill beer and stuff potato chips. Every once in a while he'd let out a huge belch, then sigh and pat his pot gut like he was so goddamn pleased with himself. For years, while Zosh's teeth went and her skin faded to chalk delivering five kids.

And me growing up in the middle of it, waiting for the big event of the day in the south Bronx, the Good Humor truck out on the street.

'Mommy, Mommy, the goojoomer's here! C'n I have a dime for the goojoomer?'

'Y'fadda din leave me no money.'

Urgent jingling from the Good Humor, ready to leave and take excitement with it. 'Mommy!'

'Geddouda here. I ain't got no dime, now shaddup.'

I used to think about that a lot: a lousy dime. So little and so much to a kid. Go to hell, Momma. Not for the dime, but for a whole beauty you never had and never missed. You weren't going to keep me from it.

It wasn't much better in high school. I was embarrassed to undress for gym because of the holes in my underwear. And the stains sometimes because I had to use Momma's Kotex and she didn't care if she ran out. I could have used Tampax; virgin or not, I was a big, healthy ox like her and Zosh. I could have conceived an army. When Momma found the Tampax I bought, she slapped me halfway across the room.

'What's this, hah? *Hah?* I ain't got enough trouble, you started already? You sneakin around, you little bitch?'

No such luck, Momma. They didn't want me. The closest I got to boys was talking about them. Sitting in a coffee shop over the debris of my cheap, starchy lunch, the table a garbage dump of bread crusts, spilled sugar and straw wrappers, shredding food bits and paper ends like our envious gossip dissected the girls we knew and the boys we wanted to know.

I never had any sense about men or myself. That happens when you're five foot seven in high school and still growing. A sequoia in a daisy bed, lumpy and lumbering, addicted to food, my refuge when I lost the courage for school dances. I fled home to the ice box and stayed there, eating myself out of my clothes, smearing my acne with Vis-o-Hex, or huddled for hours in a movie, seeing it twice over to pretend I was Hepburn or Bacall, slim, brittle and clever. Or Judith Anderson, tearing hell out of *Medea*. I read the play and practiced the lines at my mirror with stiff approximations of her gestures.

But it was *A Streetcar Named Desire* that changed my life. I hardly spoke for days after seeing it. The play stabbed me deep and sparked something that was going to be. I bought more plays and devoured them. Fewer trips to the movies now and more downtown to Broadway and the Village. Live theater, not unreeling on a spool, but happening the moment I saw it.

I was still a lump, still a hundred and fifty pounds of un-lusted-after virgin bohunk, and nobody was going to star Gail Danowski in anything but lunch. I walked alone with my dreams while the hungers grew.

You can go a little mad with loneliness, past caring. Virginity? I couldn't give it away, Momma; so I threw it away. No big Zanuck production, just a boy and a party I can't picture too clearly. We were drinking and wrestling, and I thought: all right, why not? Just once I'm gonna grab a little happiness even if it's just getting laid, what am I saving it for? But I had to get drunk before he fumbled at me. If there was pain or pleasure, I barely felt them, only knew that at last I tasted life where it sprang from the fountain. A meager cup, the cut version, the boy pulling at his clothes afterward, distant, disgusted.

'Shit, whyn't you tell me, Gail?'

Tell you what, lover? That I was a virgin, that by accident you were first? Is that a guilt trip? Whatever I lost, don't mourn it. Cry for the other things we lose in parked cars and motel beds because we're too drunk or there's too much guilt or fear for beauty. It was the beauty I missed. Be first any time, score up a hundred stiff, clumsy girls, say the silly words, break a hundred promises, brag about it afterwards. But leave something of yourself, something of beauty. Only that, and you part with a blessing.

He didn't.

The next morning, hung over and miserable, I looked at that frazzled thing in the mirror, had clean through and down to rock bottom, and knew from here on out I'd have to be me or just another Zosh. That day I started to build Gayla Damon.

I graduated an inch taller and thirty pounds lighter, did hard one-week stock as an apprentice. Seventeen hours a day of walk-ons, painting scenery, fencing and dance classes. Diction: practicing for hours with a cork between my teeth—

'Baby, the word is dance. DAAnce, hear the A? Not de-e-ance. Open your mouth and *use* it when you speak.'

—Letting my hair grow and moving down to Manhattan, always running away from that lump in the mirror. I never outran her. She was always there, worrying out of my eyes at a thousand auditions, patting my stomach and thighs, searching a hundred dressing room mirrors, plastering pancake on imagined blemishes, grabbing any man's hand because it was there. The years just went, hurrying by like strangers on a street, trailing bits of memory like broken china from a dusty box: buses, planes, snatches of rehearsal, stock, repertory, old reviews.

Miss Damon's talent is raw but unmistakable. When she's right, she *is* theater, vivid, filled with primordial energy that can burn or chill. If she can learn to control . . . she was superbly cast as . . .

—A self-driven horse record-time springing from nowhere to noplace. Life? I lived it from eight to eleven o'clock every night and two matinees a week. For three hours each night, I loved, hated, sang, sorrowed enough for three lifetimes. Good houses, bad houses, they all got the best of me because my work had a love behind it. The rest was only fill, and who cared? Season after season of repertory, a dozen cities, a dozen summer towns barely glimpsed from opening night to closing, a blur of men and a lot of beds, flush or broke, it didn't matter.

Zosh caught a show once when I was playing in Westchester. Poor Zosh: pasty and fat as Momma by then, busting out of her dresses and her teeth shot. She came hesitantly into my dressing room, wondering if someone might throw her out. The first stage play she ever saw. She didn't know really what to make of it.

'Oh, it was great and all. You look good, Gail. God, you really got some figure now, what size you wear? I never knew about plays. You know me'n school, I always got my girlfriend to write my reports.'

She barely sipped the scotch I poured for her. 'Charlie never buys nothin' but beer.' I wanted to take her out for a good dinner, but, no, she had a sitter at home and it was expensive, and Charlie would yell if she came home too late when he was out bowling.

'Let the dumb ox yell. You're entitled once in a while.'

'Hey, you really gettin' a mouth on you, Gail.'

'Speaking of that, doesn't Charlie ever look at yours? Doesn't he know you need a dentist?'

'Well, you know how it is. The kids take it out of you.'

I gave Zosh a hundred dollars to get her teeth fixed. She wrote that she spent it on the house and kids. *There was the gas bill and Christmas. You cant complain theres nobody on the other end of the phone. Ha-ha. My friends all want to know when your on TV.*

Are you still around, Zosh? Not that it matters. They buried you years ago. No one was going to do that to me.

And then suddenly I was thirty, that big, scary number. Working harder, running harder without knowing where, doing the where-did-it-all-go bit now and then (while the lights caught her best, most expressive angle). Where are you now, Bill? You must be pushing fifty. Did you find someone like me or just the opposite. I wouldn't blame you.

And how about you, Nick?

He'll split in six months. You'll be out in the cold.

When Bill said that, I remember thinking: hell, he's right. I'm thirty-two and after that comes thirty-three. Fourteen years, seven dollars in the bank, and where the hell am I?

But I was hung up on Nick's body and trying to please him. Perhaps there were other, unspoken things that have nothing to do with loving or sex. You get used very early to not liking yourself. You know you're a fraud, someday they'll all know. The Lump hiding inside your dieted figure and with-it clothes knows you haven't changed, no matter what. The Lump doesn't want to like you. How can she tolerate anyone who does? No, she'll sniff out someone who'll keep her in her lovely place.

Crimes and insanities. Hurting Bill was a very countable sin, but I knew what I needed. So it was Nick, not Bill, who moved in here with me.

And where are you this dark night, Nick? Did you make the big time? I hope so. You're almost thirty now. That's getting on for what you had to sell. Your kind of act has a short run.

My mind wanders like that when Lowen's not around.

Energy builds again, the lights dim up. I drift out onto the balcony, feeling that weight of depression it always brings. My sense of color is dimmed because the kids are asleep. 77th Street is a still shot in black and white. Not a soul, not even a late cab whispering up Riverside Drive.

Hey, look: there's a meteor, a falling star. Make a wish: be happy, Bill Wrenn.

And listen! A clock tower. Even with Lowen asleep, I can hear it. Two-three-four o'clock. Definitely, I'm getting stronger. More and more I can feel and sometimes see my legs when I walk, less like floating in a current. I move back through the apartment to hover over Lowen as he sleeps. Wanting. Wondering.

After all this time, why should it be Lowen who wakes me? Nothing's clear but that I can touch life again with him. If that's wrong, I didn't write the script. Name any form of life you want. A cold germ is just a bug trying to make a living in the only way it knows, in a place it doesn't understand, and it only takes a little out of the place trying. That's me, that's all of us. I'll take what I need to live. If there's air to breathe, don't tell me I can't. That's academic.

Al sleeps tiny and still beside Lowen, hardly a bump under the covers. It must be wonderful to sleep like that. I could never stay out more than two hours at a time. No, wait: here she comes up out of it with a sigh and turnover that barely whispers the covers. She slides out of bed and pit-pats to the bathroom. Bladder the size of an acorn, up three times a night like I was.

When the john flushes, Lowen stirs and mumbles, flops over and sinks again. The bathroom door creaks, Al slips back in beside him. She doesn't settle down yet, but rests on one elbow, a momentary vigil over Lowen, a secret protecting. I'll bet he doesn't know she watches him like that. Then she slides under the covers very close, one arm over him, fingers spread lightly on his skin.

To lie beside Lowen like that, to touch him simply by willing it. If that were my hand resting on his skin. What wouldn't I give for that?

The idea is sudden and frightening. Why not?

If I could get inside Al, stretch out my arm inside hers, wear it like a glove; just for a moment move one real finger over Lowen's skin. It couldn't hurt her, and I need it so.

I wait for Al to fall asleep, scared of the whole notion. It could hurt. It hurt to touch Lowen before. Maybe it's against some natural law. They're flesh, I'm a memory. Lots of maybe's, but I have to try. Slow and scared, I drift down over Al and will what shape there is to me into the attitude of her body. There's no shock when I touch her, but a definite sensation like dipping into swift-running water. So weird, I pull away and have to build up my nerve to try again, settling like a sinking ship as the current of Al's healthy young life surges and tingles around me, and her chest rises and falls like a warm blanket over cozy sleep. My breasts nestle into hers, my arm stretching slowly to fill out the slim contour of her shoulder, elbow, wrist. It's hard and slow, like half-frozen syrup oozing through a hose. My fingers struggle one by one into hers.

So tired. Got to rest.

But I feel life, I *feel* it, humming and bubbling all around me. Jesus, I must have sounded like a steel mill inside, the way I drove myself. The power, such a wonder. Why did I waste so much time feeling miserable?

The electric clock glows at 5:03. More minutes pass while each finger tests itself in Al's, and then I try to move one on Lowen's skin.

The shock curdles me. I cringe away from it, shiveling back up Al's arm, all of me a shaky little ball in her middle. Just as in the shower, I felt skin against skin, even the tiny moisture of pores, but it drains me as if I've run five miles.

Rest and try again. Slow, so slow, so hard, but my fingers creep forward into Al's again. Same thing: the instant I let myself feel with Al's flesh, there's a bright shock and energy drains. If that's not enough, those delicate fingers weigh ten pounds each. I push, poop out, rest, try again, the hardest battle of my life, let alone death, and all in dogged silence broken only by their breathing and the muted *whir* of the clock.

6:32. The dark bedroom grays up to morning. I can see Lowen's face clearly now: very young, crumpled with sleep. He can't hear my soundless, exhausted panting like the heartbeat of a humming-bird.

6:48. Twelve minutes before the clock beeps the beginning of their day, one finger, one slender thread binding me to Lowen . . . moves. Again. I go dizzy with the sensation but hang on, pouring the last strength into one huge effort. The small hand flexes all five fingers like a crab, sliding over the sparse hair on Lowen's chest. A flash-frame of Bill, of Nick, and a thrill of victory.

Hi, baby. I made it.

Then Al stirs, moves, *don't, please, wait!* and flips over on her other side, unconcerned as a pancake. I let go, used up, drifting out to nowhere again, barely conscious of space or objects, too burned out even to feel frustrated after all that work.

But I did it. I know the way now. I'll be back.

Night after night I kept at it, fitting to Al's body, learning how to move her fingers without burning myself out. Stronger and surer, until I could move the whole hand and then the arm, and even if

Lowen pressed the hand to his mouth or nestled his cheek against it, I could hold on.

And then I blew it, the story of my life. Klutz-woman strikes again. I tried to get in when they were making love.

I said before they're not too dexterous in the bedroom. Al gets uptight from the start, and I can see her lying there, eyes tight shut over Lowen's shoulder, hoping he'll come soon and get it over with. Not always; sometimes she wants it as much as him, but the old hangups are always there. She holds back, so he holds back. It's usually one-sided and finished soon.

But that evening everything seemed perfect. They had a light supper, several drinks rather than the usual one, and Lowen didn't spare the vodka. They just naturally segued to the bedroom, not rushed or nervous, undressing each other slowly, enjoyably, melting into each other's arms. Al brought in a candle from the supper table. Nice touch: Nick and I used to do that. They lie there caressing each other, murmuring drowsily. Lowen looks gorgeous in the soft glow, Al like a little Dresden doll. And me—poor, pathetic afterthought—watching it all and yearning.

Jesus, Al, act like you're alive. That's a man. Take hold of him.

Damn, it was too much. The hell with consequences. I draped myself over Al with the ease of practice, stretched my arms and legs along hers. Foolhardy, yes, but at last *my* arms went around Lowen, smoothing, then clawing down his back.

Love me, baby. Love all of me.

My mouth opened hungrily under his, licking his lips and then nipping at them. I writhed Al's slim body under his, pushed her hands to explore him from shoulders to thighs. I never had much trouble in bed. If the guy had anything going and didn't run through it like a fire drill, I could come half a dozen times, little ones and big ones, before he got there.

With Lowen it was like all the best orgasms I ever had. The moment before you start to go, you want to hold back, prolong it, but you can't. I was dependent on Al's chemistry now. Her body was strangely stiff as I hauled her over on top of Lowen. Something new for her. She went taut, resisting it.

'Lowen, wait.'

He can't wait, though I'm the only one who sees the irony and the lie. Lowen is coming, I certainly want to, but Al is out of it. I want to *scream* at her, though I should have guessed it long before this. She always times her cries with his, as if they came together.

But it's a lie. She's faking it. She's learned that much.

My God, you're alive, the greatest gift anyone ever got. Does a past tense like me have to show you how?

With a strength like life itself, I churned her up and down on Lowen, hard, burning myself out to tear Al's careful controls from her emotions. She moaned, fighting me, afraid.

'Lowen, stop. Please, stop.'

You don't fake tonight, kid.

'Stop!'

No way. Go . . . *go!*

Lowen gripped her spasmodically, and I felt his hips tremble under mine/hers. He couldn't hold back any longer. With the last ounce of my will, I bent Al's body down over his, mouth to mouth.

'Now, Lowen. Now!'

Not Al's voice but mine, the first time I've heard it in seven years. Deeper, throatier than Al's. In the middle of coming, an alien bewilderment flooded Lowen's expression. Al stiffened like she was shot. With a cry of bleak terror, she tore herself loose and leaped clear off the bed, clawing for the lamp switch, big-eyed and terrified in the hard light.

'Oh, God. Oh, Jesus, what's happening?'

Confused, a little out of it himself now, Lowen sat up to stare back at her. 'Al, what's the matter?'

She shuddered. 'It's not me.'

'What?'

'It's not *me.*' She snatched up her bathrobe like the last haven in the world. Lowen reached for his instinctively, comforting.

'It's all right, honey, it's—'

'No. It's like something hot inside me.'

He went on soothing her, but he knew. I could see that in his eyes as he pulled Al down beside him. He knew: the last thing I saw, because the lights were going down for me, their last spill playing over memory-fragments before fading. A confused montage: Nick putting on his jacket, me fumbling for the phone, then pulling at the balcony door, and the darkness and the silence then were like dying again.

I've had some hangovers in my time, mornings of agony after a messy, screaming drunk. Coming back to queasy consciousness while the night's party repeats in your mind like a stupid film loop, and you wonder, in a foggy way, if you really spilled that drink on somebody, and—oh, no—you couldn't have said *that* to him, and if you're going to be sick right then or later.

Then the smog clears and you remember. Yeah. You spilled it and did it and you sure as hell said it, and the five best bloody mary's in the world won't help.

I blew it good this time, a real production number. Now they both know I'm here.

December 23. I know the date because Al's carefully crossed the days off her calendar where she never bothered before. I've been turned off for days. Almost Christmas, but you'd never know it around here. No holly, no tree, just a few cards opened and dropped on the little teakwood desk where they keep their bills. When Lowen brushes one aside, I can see a thin line of dust. Al hasn't been cleaning.

The kitchen is cluttered. The morning's dishes are still in the sink. Three cardboard boxes stand on the floor, each half full of wrapped dishes and utensils.

So that's it. They're moving. A moment of panic: where do I go from here, then? All right, it was my fault, but . . . don't go, Lowen. I'm not wild about this script myself, but don't ask me to turn out the lights and die again. Because I won't.

There's a miasma of oppression and apprehension all through the apartment. Al's mouth is tighter, her eyes frightened. Lowen comes out into the living room, reluctant and dutiful. Furtively, he tests the air as if to feel me in it. He sits down in his usual chair; 3:13 by the miniature grandfather clock on the book case. The lights and sound come up slowly with Lowen's nearness. He's home early this afternoon.

Al brings out the Waterford sherry set and puts it on the coffee table. She sits down, waiting with Lowen. The whole scene reminds me of actors taking places before the curtain rises; Al poised tensely on the sofa, revolving her sherry glass in white fingers: Lowen distant, into his own thoughts. The sound is still lousy.

'. . . feel silly,' Lowen ventures. '. . . all this way . . . time off from . . . just to . . .'

'No! . . . live here like this, not with . . .' Al is really shook; takes a cigarette from Lowen's pack on the coffee table and smokes it in quick, inexpert puffs. 'You say you can feel her?'

Lowen nods, unhappy. He doesn't like any of this. 'I loved this place from the first day.'

'Lowen, answer me. Please.'

'Yes.'

'Where?'

'Somewhere close. Always to me.'

Al stubs out the cigarette. 'And we sure know it's *she*, don't we?'

'Al—'

'Oh, hell! I loved this place too, but this is crazy. I'm *scared*, Lowen. How long have you known?'

'Almost from the start.'

'And you never told me.'

'Why?' Lowen looks up at her. 'I'm not a medium; nothing like this ever happened before. It was weird at first, but then I began to feel that she was just *here*—'

'What!'

'. . . and part of things . . . like the walls. I didn't even know it was a woman at first.'

'Until that time in the shower,' Al finishes for him. 'Bitch.'

Thanks a lot, kid. At least I know what to do with him.

'Look, Al, I can't tell you how I know, but I don't think she means any harm.'

Al gulps down her sherry and fills the glass. 'The—hell—she —doesn't. I'm not into church anymore. Even if I were, I wouldn't go running for the holy water every time a floor creaked, but don't tell me she doesn't mean anything, Lowen. You know what I'm talking about.' Her hands dry-wash each other jerkily. 'I mean that night, the way we made love. I—always wanted to make love to you like that. That . . . free.'

The best you ever had, love.

Al gets up and paces, nervous. 'All right, I've got these god-damned problems. You get taught certain things are wrong. If it's not for babies, it's wrong. It's wrong to use contraceptives, but we can't afford a baby, and—I don't know, Lowen. The world is crazy. But that night, it wasn't me. Not even my voice.'

'No, it wasn't.'

Lowen must be way down, depressed, because my energy is wavering with his, and sound fades in and out. There's a muffled knock at the door. Lowen opens it to a bald little man like a wizened guru in a heavy, fur-collared overcoat.

Wait, I know this guy. It's that little weasel, Hirajian, from Riverside Realty. He rented me this place. Hirajian settles himself in a chair, briefcase on his knee, declining the sherry Al offers. He doesn't look too happy about being here, but the self-satisfied little bastard doesn't miss Al's legs, which make mine look bush league in retrospect.

8888888888888

I can't catch everything, but Hirajian's puzzled by something. Al's saying. No problem about the lease, he allows, apartments rent in two days now, but she's apparently thrown him a curve.

Al now: '. . . not exactly our wish, but . . .'

'Unusual request . . . never anything. . . .'

Now Al is flat and clear: 'Did you find out?'

Hirajian opens his briefcase and brings out a sheet of paper while I strain at his through-the-wall mumble.

'Don't know why . . . however . . . before you. . . .' He runs through a string of names until I make the connection. The tenants who came after me, all those damned extras who wandered through my dreams before Lowen.

Lowen stops him suddenly. He's not as depressed as Al; there's an eagerness in the question. 'Did anyone die here?'

'Die?'

'It's very important,' Al says.

Hirajian looks like an undertaker's assistant now, all professional solemnity and reluctance. 'As a matter of fact, yes. I was getting to that. In 1974, a Miss Danowski.'

Lowen's head snaps up. 'First name?'

'Gail.'

'Anyone named Gayla? Someone cut the name Gayla in the cement on the balcony.'

'That was the Danowski woman. Gayla Damon was her stage name. She was an actress. I remember because she put that name on the lease and had to do it again with her legal signature.'

'Gayla.'

'You knew her, Mr. Sheppard?'

'Gayla Damon. I should, it's awfully familiar, but—'

'Single?' Al asks. 'What sort of person was she?'

Hirajian cracks his prim little smile like a housewife leaning over a back fence to gossip. 'Yes and no, you know show people. Her boyfriend moved in with her. I know it's the fashion nowadays, but *we*,' evidently Riverside and God, 'don't approve of it.'

There's enough energy to laugh, and I wish you could hear me, you little second-string satyr. You made a pass when you showed me this place. I remember: I was wearing that new tan suit from Bergdorf's, and I couldn't split fast enough. But it was the best place yet for the money, so I took it.

Damn it, how did I die? What happened. Don't fade out, weasel. Project, let me hear you.

Al sets down her sherry glass. 'We just can't stay here. It's impossible.'

Don't go, Lowen. You're all I have, all there is. I won't touch Al, I promise never again. But don't go.

Of course there were promises, Nick. There's always a promise. No one has to spell it out.

I said that once. I'm starting to remember.

While Hirajian patters on, Lowen's lost in some thought. There's something in his eyes I've never seen before. A concern, a caring.

'You mean he didn't come back even when he heard Gayla was dead?'

I love the way he says my name. Like a song, new strength.

'No end of legal trouble,' Hirajian clucks. 'We couldn't locate him or any family at first. A Mister . . . yes, a Mister Wrenn came and made all the arrangements. An old boyfriend, I suppose.'

You did that for me, Bill? You came back and helped me out. Boy, what I had and threw away. Sand through my fingers.

'Gayla. Gayla Damon.' I grow stronger as Lowen repeats my name, stronger yet as he rises and takes a step toward the balcony door. I could touch him, but I don't dare now. 'Yes. Just the name I forgot. It's hard to believe, Al, but it's the only thing I can believe.'

Such a queer, tender look. Al reads it too. 'What, Lowen?'

He strides quickly away to the bedroom, and the lights dim a little. Then he's back with a folded paper, so lost in some thought that Al just stares at him and Hirajian is completely lost.

'The things we learn about life,' Lowen says. 'An English professor of mine said once that life is too coincidental for art; that's why art is structured. Mr. Hirajian, you said no one else ever complained of disturbances in this apartment. I'm not a medium, can't even predict the weather. But I'm beginning to understand a little of this.'

Will you tell me, for Christ's sake?

He hands the paper to Al. It looks like an old theater program. 'You see, Mister Hirajian, she's still here.'

He has to say it again, delicately as possible. Hirajian poohpoohs the whole notion. 'Oh, really, now, you can't be sure of something like that.'

'We know,' Al says in a hard voice. 'We haven't told you everything. She, it, something's here, and it's destructive.'

'No, I don't think so.' Lowen nods to the program. I can't see it too well. 'Eagle Lake Playhouse, 1974. I saw her work.'

You couldn't have. You were only—

'She played Gwendolyn in *Becket*. That's her autograph by her name.'

Where the hell is Eagle Lake? Wait a minute. Wait—a—minute. I'm remembering.

'My father was taking me back to school. I spent my whole life in boarding schools all the way through college. Dad thought for our last night together, he'd take me to an uplifting play and save himself making conversation. My parents were very efficient that way.

'Gayla only had one scene, but she was so open, so completely translucent that I couldn't take my eyes off her.'

I did play Eagle Lake, and there's a faint memory of some double-breasted country-club type coming back for an autograph for his kid.

'I still remember, she had a line that went: 'My lord cares for nothing in this world, does he?' She turned to Becket then, and you could see a *line* in that turn, a power that reached the other actor and came out to the audience. The other actors were good, but Gayla lit up the stage with something—unbearably human.'

Damn right, love. I was gangbusters in that role. And you saw me? I could almost believe in God now, though He hasn't called lately.

'I was sixteen, and I thought I was the only one in the world who could be so lonely. She showed me we're all alike in that. All our feelings touch. Next day I hitchhiked all the way back to the theater from school. . . .' Lowen trails off, looking at Al and the apartment. 'And this was her place. She wasn't very old. How did she die?'

'Depressing,' Hirajian admits. 'Very ugly and depressing, but then suicide always is.'

What!

'But as regards your moving out just because—'

The hell I did, no *way*, mister. No. No. NO! I won't listen to any more. Don't believe him, Lowen.

Lowen's on his feet, head tilted in that listening attitude. Al puts down her glass, pale and tense. 'What is it?'

'She's here now. She's angry.'

'How do you know?'

'Don't ask me how, dammit. I know. She's here.'

No, Lowen. On the worst, weakest day of my life, I couldn't do that. Listen. Hear me. Please.

Then Al's up, frightened and desperate. 'Go away, whoever you are. For the love of God, go away.'

I barely hear her, flinging myself away from them out onto the balcony; silent mouth screaming at the frustration and stupid injustice of it. A lie, a lie, and Lowen is leaving, sending me back to nothing and darkness. But the strength is growing, born of rage and terror. Lowen. Lowen, Lowen. Hear me. I didn't. *Hear me*.

'Lowen, don't!'

I hear Al's voice, then the sudden, sharp sound of the balcony door wrenching open. And as I turn to Lowen, the whole, uncut film starts to roll. And, oh Jesus, I remember.

Eagle Lake. That's where it ended, Lowen. Not here, no matter what they tell you. That's where all the years, parts, buses, beds, the whole game came to an end. When I found that, no matter what, none of it worked any more. Maybe I was growing up a little at last, looking for the *me* in all of it.

Funny: I wasn't even going to audition for stock that summer. Bill called me to do a couple of roles at Eagle Lake, and Nick urged me to go. It was a good season, closing with *A Streetcar Named Desire*. The owner, Ermise Stour, jobbed in Natalie Bond for Blanche DuBois, and I was to be her understudy. Nattie's name wasn't smash movie box office any more, but still big enough for stock and star-package houses. She's be Erm's insurance to make up whatever they lost on the rest of the season.

Erm, you tough old bag. You were going to sell that broken-down theater after every season. I'll bet you're still there, chain-smoking over a bottle of Chivas and babying that ratty poodle.

Ermise lived in a rambling ex-hotel with a huge fireplace in the lounge. We had all our opening-night parties there with a big blaze going because Eagle Lake never warmed up or dried out even in August.

At the opening party for *Becket,* all of us were too keyed up to get drunk, running on adrenaline from the show, slopping drinks and stuffing sandwiches, fending off the local reviewers, horny boy scouts with a course in journalism.

Dinner? No thanks. I've got a horrible week coming up, and it's all I can do to shower and fall into bed. Bill, let's get *out* of here. Thanks, you're a jewel, I needed a refill. Gimme your sweater. Jesus, doesn't it ever get warm in this place? You could age beef in our dressing room.

Nick was down for a few days the week before. Bill rather pointedly made himself scarce. He was still in love with me. That must have hurt, working with me day after day, keeping it inside, and I didn't help matters by dragging Nick everywhere like a prize bull: hey, look what I got! Smart girl, Gayla. With a year's study, you could be an idiot.

But Nick was gone, and we'd managed to get *Becket* open despite failing energy, colds, frayed nerves and lousy weather. It was good just to stand with Bill against the porch railing, watching moths bat themselves silly against the overhead light. Bill was always guarded when we were alone now. I kept it light and friendly, asked about his preparations for *Streetcar*. He sighed with an Old Testament flavor of doom.

'Don't ask. Erm had to cut the set budget, first read-through is tomorrow morning, and Nattie's plane won't get in until one. I'm going to be up all night and I'll still only be about five pages ahead of you people on blocking.'

'Why's she late?'

'Who the hell knows? Business with her agent or something. You'll have to read in for her.'

Good. One more precious rehearsal on my Blanche, one more time to read those beautiful words and perhaps find one more color in them before Natalie Bond froze it all in star glitter. That was all I had to look forward to now. The fatigue, the wet summer, lousy houses, all of it accumulated to a desolation I couldn't shrug off. I had a small part in *Streetcar*, but understudying Natalie Bond meant watching her do my role, never to touch the magic myself. Maybe her plane could crash—just a little—but even then, what? Somehow even the thought of Nick depressed me. Back in New York he'd get in to see the right agents where I couldn't, landing commercials, lining up this, grabbing that, always smarter at business than me.

That night before the party, I sat on my bed, staring glumly at the yellow-green wallpaper and my battered Samsonite luggage, and thought: *I'm tired of you. Something's gone. There's gotta be more than this.* And I curled up in my old gray bathrobe, wallowing in self-pity. Nick, you want to get married? Bring me the towel and wash my back? Baby me a little when I feel rotten, like now? There's a big empty place in me wants to be pregnant with more than a part. Tired, negative, I knew Nick would *never* marry me; I was kidding myself.

So it was good to have Bill there on the porch for a minute. I leaned against him and he put an arm around me. We should have gone to bed and let it be beautiful one more time. It would have been the last.

'Tired, Gay?'

'I want to go home.'

Except I never in my whole life found where it was.

Natalie Bond came and conquered. She knew her lines pretty well going in and crammed the rest with me in her room or the restaurant down our street. No one recognized her at first with her hair done just the right shade of fading dishwater blonde for Blanche, most of her thin face hidden behind a huge pair of prescription sunglasses.

She was near-sighted to blindness; some of her intensity on film must have come from trying to feel out the blocking by Braille. But a pro she was. She soaked up Bill's direction, drove herself and us, and I saw the ruthless energy that made Nattie a star.

I saw other things, too. Nattie hadn't been on a live stage for a lot of years. She missed values left and right in Blanche and didn't have time to pick them up on a two-week stock schedule. Film is a director's medium. He can put your attention where he wants with the camera. Stage work takes a whole different set of muscles, and hers were flabby, unused to sustaining an action or mood for two and a half hours.

But for the first time that season, we were nearly sold out at the box office. Erm was impressed. Bill wasn't.

'They're coming to see a star. She could fart her way through Blanche and they'll still say she's wonderful.'

Maybe, but life wasn't all skittles for Nattie. She had two children in expensive schools and got endless phone calls from her manager in California about taxes.

'I gotta work, honey,' she told me over black coffee and dry toast. 'The wolf's got my ass in his chops already.'

She meant it. Another phone call, and that same afternoon between lunch and rehearsal call, Nattie Bond was gone, and I was sitting in Ermise's living room again while Erm swore back and forth across the worn carpet, waving her drink like a weapon, and Bill tried to look bereaved. He always wanted me for Blanche. He had me now.

'Screwed me from the word go.' Ermise sprayed ashes over the rug and her poodle. 'She knew this when she signed and never said a goddamn word.'

The facts filtered through my rosy haze. Natalie's agent had a picture deal on the coast so close to signing that it was worth it to let Ermise sue. They'd just buy up her contract—if she could be in Los Angeles tomorrow.

Ermise hurled her cigarette into the trash-filled fireplace, gulped the last of her drink and turned a mental page. Nattie was one problem, the show another. 'You ready to go, Gayla?'

'In my sleep, love.'

I was already readjusting the role to the Blanche in my ear and not as sorry for the box office as Erm. Screw 'em all, they were going to see ten times the Blanche Nattie Bond could give them on the best day she ever worked.

'Bill wants me to give you a raise,' Ermise said. 'Wish I could, Gay, but things are tight.'

I pulled the worn script out of my jeans, grinning like a fool back at Bill, who couldn't hide his glee any more. 'Just pay on time, Erm. Keep out of my hair and don't clutter up my stage. Bill, let's go to work.'

From my first rehearsal, the play convulsed and became a different animal. The whole cast had to shift gears for me, but no longer suffused by Nattie's hard light they began to find themselves and glimmer with life. I ate and slept with the script while Blanche came sure and clear. Hell, I'd been rehearsing her for fourteen years. It wasn't hard to identify: the hunger for love half appeased in bed-hopping and sexual junk food, and what that does to a woman. The blurred, darkening picture of a girl waiting in her best dress to go to the dance of life with someone who never came.

Then, just as it seemed to be coming together, it went flat, deader than I am now. But out of that death came a beautiful, risky answer.

Blanche DuBois is a bitch of a role and demands a powerhouse actress. That's the problem. Like the aura that surrounds Hamlet, the role accumulates a lot of star-shtick, and something very subtle can get lost. I determined to strip away the layers of gloss and find what was there to begin with.

'The part's a trap, Bill. All those fluttery, curlicued lines reach out and beg you to *act* them. And you wind up with dazzle again, a concert performance.'

'Cadenzas,' he agreed with me. 'The old Williams poetry.'

'Right! Cadenzas, scales. No, by God. I've played the Deep South. There's a smothered quality to those women that gets lost that way. The script describes her as a moth. Moths don't dazzle. They don't glitter.'

'Remember that night on the porch,' Bill said thoughtfully. 'They don't glitter, but they do need the light.'

And that was it. Blanche aspired to the things she painted with foolish words. A dream of glitter seen by a near-sighted person by a failing candle. The lines are ornate, but just possibly, Blanche is not quite as intelligent as she's been played.

A long artistic chance, but they're the only ones worth taking. If you don't have the guts to be wrong, take up accounting.

So my Blanche emerged a very pathetic woman, a little grotesque as such women are, not only desperate for love but logical in her hopes for Mitch. For all Belle Reeve and the inbred magnolias, she's not that far above him. Bill gave me my head knowing that by finding my own Blanche, even being wrong for a while, I'd find the play's as well. On my terms and with my own reality.

I had three lovely labor-pained days of seeing her come alive. On the third day, I was sitting in a corner of the stage with coffee and a sandwich, digging at the script while the others lunched. When Sally Kent walked in, I snapped at her.

'Where's the rest? It's two o'clock. Let's go.'

'They want you over at the office, Gay.'

'What the hell for? I don't have time. Where's Bill?'

'At the office,' Sally admitted reluctantly. 'Natalie Bond is here. She's back in the show.'

The kiss of death. Even as I shook my head, no, Erm wouldn't do this to me, I knew she would.

Ermise hunched in a chair by the fireplace, bitter with what she had to do, trying not to antagonize Bill any further. He poised on the sofa, seething like a malevolent cat.

'Nattie will do the show after all,' Ermise said. 'I have to put her back in, Gay.'

I couldn't speak at first; sick, quivering on my feet with that horrible end-of-the-rope hollowness in my stomach. No place to go from here. No place. . . .

'When we pulled her name off the advertising, we lost more than a third of our reservations.' Erm snorted. 'I don't like it. I don't like her right now, but she's the only thing'll keep my theater open.'

Bill's comment cut with the hard edge of disgust. 'You know what this does to the cast, don't you? They've readjusted once. Now they have to do it again and open in two days. They were an ensemble with Gayla. Now they're the tail of a star vehicle.'

Bill knew it was already lost, but he was doing this for me.

Ermise shook her head. 'Gay, honey, I can't afford it, but I'm gonna raise you retroactive to the first week of your contract.' Her hands fluttered in an uncharacteristically helpless gesture. 'I owe you that. And you'll go back in as Eunice. But next season—'

I found my voice. It was strange, old. 'Don't do this to me. This role, it's mine, I earned it. She'll ruin it.'

'Don't look at me,' Bill snapped to Ermise. 'She's right.'

Ermise went defensive. 'I don't care who's right. You're all for Gay. Fine, but I can't run a theater that way. Lucky to break even as it is. Nattie's back, she plays, and that's the end of it. Gay's contract reads 'as cast.' She's Eunice. What else can I say?'

I showed her what else. I ripped the *Streetcar* script in four parts and threw them in the fireplace. 'You can say good-by, Ermise. Then you can take your raise and shove it.' I was already lurching toward the door, voice breaking. 'Then you can put someone in my roles, because I'm leaving.'

I meant it. Without Blanche, there was no reason to stay another minute. Finished. Done.

Except for Natalie Bond. I found her in her hotel room, already dressed for rehearsal and running over the script.

'Come on in, Gayla. Drink?'

'No.'

She read my tension as I crouched with my back against the door. 'All right, hon. Get it off your chest.'

'I will.'

I told the bitch what I felt and what I thought and didn't leave anything out. It was quite a speech for no rehearsal, beginning with my teens when I first knew I had to play Blanche, and the years and hard work that made me worthy of it. There wasn't a rep company in the east I hadn't worked, or a major role from Rosalind to Saint Joan I hadn't played. To walk out on the show like she did was pure shit. To crawl back was worse.

'Right,' said Nattie. She faced me all through it, let me get it all out. I was crying when I finished. I sank down on a chair, grabbing for one of her Kleenex.

'Now do you want a drink?'

'Yes, what the hell.'

She wasn't all rat, Nattie. She could have put me down with the star routine, but she fixed me a stiff gin and soda without a word. I remember her fixing that drink: thick glasses and no make up, gristly thin. She had endless trouble with her uterus, infection after painful infection and a work schedule that never allowed her to heal properly. A hysterectomy ended the whole thing. Nattie's face was thinner than mine, all the softness gone, mouth and cheeks drawn tight. No matter how sincere, the smile couldn't unclench.

And this, I thought, is what I want to be? Help me, Nick. Take me home. There's gotta be a home somewhere, a little rest.

'Know what we're like?' Nattie mused. 'A little fish swimming away from a big, hungry fish who's just about to be eaten by a bigger fish. That's us, honey. And that's me in the middle.'

She screwed Ermise, but someone shafted her too. The picture deal was a big fat fake. The producer wanted someone a little bigger and hustled Nattie very plausibly to scare the lady into reaching for a pen.

'I'm broke, Gayla. I owe forty thousand in back taxes, my house is on a second mortgage, and my kids' tuition is overdue. Those kids are all I have. I don't know where the hell to go from here, but Ermise needs me and I sure as hell need the job.'

While I huddled over my drink, unable to speak, Nattie scribbled something on a memo pad.

'You're too good to waste, you're not commercial, and you'll probably die broke. But I saw your rehearsal this morning.'

I looked up at her in weepy surprise. The smile wasn't quite so hard just then.

'If I can do it half that well, Gay. Half.'

She shoved the paper into my hand. 'That's my agent in New York. He's with William Morris. If he can't get you work, no one can. I'll call him myself.' She glanced at her dressing table clock. 'Time, gotta run.'

Nattie divined the finality in my shoulders as I sagged toward the door. 'You going to play Eunice?'

'No. I'm leaving.'

Pinning her hair, she shot me a swift, unsmiling appraisal through the mirror. 'Good for you. You got a man in New York?'

'Yeah.'

'Get married,' she mumbled through a mouthful of pins. 'It's not worth it.' As the door closed, she raised her voice. 'But call my agent.'

My bags were packed, but I hadn't bothered to change clothes. That's why my permanent costume, I suppose. Who knew then I'd get very tired of black. Bill insisted on driving me to the airport. When he came for me, I must have looked pathetic, curled up on the bed in one more temporary, damp summer room just waiting to eject me. No love lost; I got damned sick of yellow-green wallpaper.

Bill sat on the edge of the bed. 'Ready, love?'

I didn't move or answer. Done, finished. Bill put aside the old hurt and lay down beside me, bringing me into his arms. I guess something in him had to open in spite of his defenses. He opened my heart gently as a baby's hand clutched around something that might harm it, letting me cry the last of it out against his shoulder. The light faded in the room while we lay together.

We kissed good-by like lovers at the departure gate. Bill was too much a part of me for anything less. Maybe he knew better than I how little was waiting for me.

'Be good, Gay.'

'You too.' I fiddled with his collar. 'Don't forget to take your vitamins, you need them. Call me when you get back.'

He hugged me one last time. 'Why don't you marry me sometime?'

For a lot of reasons, Bill. Because I was a fool and something of a coward. The stunting begins in the seed when we learn not to like ourselves. The sad thing about life is that we usually get what we really want. Let it be.

Funny, though: that was my first and last proposal, and I kissed him good-by, walked out of his life, and four hours later I was dead.

There was time on the plane to get some of it together. Natalie was a star, at the top where I wanted to be, and look at her: most of the woman cut out of her, flogged to work not by ambition but need. Driven and used. She reminded me of a legless circus freak propelling herself on huge, overdeveloped arms, the rest of her a pitiful afterthought cared for by an expensive gynecologist. I thought: at least when I get home there'll be Nick. Don't call him from the airport; let it be a surprise. We'll get some coffee and cold-cuts, make love and talk half the night. I needed to talk, to see us plain.

Get married, Nattie said. It isn't worth it.

Maybe not the way I chased it for fourteen years. I'd call her agent, keep working, but more New York jobs with time left over to be with Nick, to sit on my balcony and just breathe or read. To make a few friends outside of theater. To see a doctor and find out how tough I really am, and if everything in the baby box is working right, so that maybe—

Like she said, so maybe get married and have kids while I can. A little commitment, Nick, a little tomorrow. If the word sounds strange, I just learned it. Give me this, Nick. I need it.

The light was on in our living room as I hauled my suitcase out of the cab and started up. Hell, I won't even buzz, just turn the key in the lock and reach for him.

I did that.

There was—yes, I remember—one blessed moment of breathing the good, safe air of my own living room as I set down the luggage. I heard a faint stirring from the bedroom. Good, I've surprised him.

If Nick was just waking from a nap, we'd have that much more time to touch each other.

'It's me, baby.'

I crossed to the bedroom door, groping inside for the light switch. 'I'm home.'

I didn't need the switch. There was enough light to see them frozen on the torn-up bed. The other one was older, a little flabby. He muttered something to Nick. I stood there, absurd myself, and choked: 'Excuse me.'

Then, as if someone punched me in the stomach, I stumbled to the bathroom, pushed the door shut and fell back against it.

'Get him out of here, Nick!'

The last word strangled off as I doubled over the john and vomited all the horrible day out of me, with two hours left to live, retching and sobbing, not wanting to hear whatever was said beyond the door. After a short time, the front door closed. I washed my face, dried it with the stiff, clumsy movements of exhaustion, and got out to the living room somehow, past the bed where Nick was smoking a cigarette, the sheet pulled up over his lean thighs.

I remember pouring a drink. That was foolish on an empty stomach, the worst thing anyone could have done. I sat on the sofa, waiting.

'Nick.' The silence from the bedroom was the only thing I could feel in my shock. 'Nick, please come out. I want to talk to you.'

I heard him rustle into his clothes. In a moment Nick came out, bleak and sullen.

'Why are you back so early?'

'No, they—' My reactions were still disjointed, coming out of shock, but the anger was building. 'They put Nattie Bond back in the show. I walked out.'

That seemed to concern him more than anything else. 'You just walked out? They'll get Equity on you.'

'Never mind about Equity, what are *we* gonna do?'

'What do you mean?' he asked calmly.

'Oh, man, are you for real?' I pointed at the door. 'What was that?'

'That may be a Broadway job.' He turned away into the kitchen. 'Now get off my back.'

'The hell I—'

'Hey look, Gayla. I haven't made any promises to you. You wanted me to move in. Okay, I moved in. We've had it good.'

I began to shake. 'Promises? Of course there were promises.

There's always a promise, nobody has to spell it out. I could have gone to bed with Bill Wrenn plenty of times this summer, but I didn't.'

He only shrugged. 'So whose fault is that? Not mine.'

'You bastard!' I threw my glass at him. He ducked, the thing went a mile wide, then Nick was sopping up whisky and bits of glass while I shook myself apart on the couch, teeth chattering so hard I had to clamp my mouth tight shut. It was all hitting me at once, and I couldn't handle half of it. Nick finished cleaning up without a word, but I could see even then the tight line of his mouth and the angry droop of his eyelids. He had guts of a kind, Nick. He could face anything because it didn't matter. All the important things were outside, to be reached for. Inside I think he was dead.

'The meanest thing Bill ever said to me,' I stuttered. 'When I left him for you, h-he said you played both sides of the fence. And I c-called him a goddamn liar. I couldn't believe he'd be small enough to—Nick, I'm falling apart. They took my show, and I came home to you because I don't know what to do.'

Nick came over, sat down and held me in his arms. 'I'm not, Gayla.'

'Not what?'

'What Bill said.'

'Then w-what was this?'

He didn't answer, just kissed me. I clung to Nick like a lost child.

Why do we always try to rewrite what's happened? Even now I see myself pointing to the door and kissing him off with a real Bette Davis sizzler for a curtain. Bullshit. I needed Nick. The accounting department was already toting up the cost of what I wanted and saying: *I'll change him. It's worth it.*

I only cried wearily in his arms while Nick soothed and stroked me. 'I'm not that,' he said again. 'Just that so many guys are hung up on role-playing and all that shit. Oh, it's been said about me.'

I twisted in his lap to look at him 'Nick, why did you come to me?'

The question gave him more trouble than it should. 'I like you. You're the greatest girl I ever met.'

Something didn't add up. Nothing ever bugged Nick before; he could always handle it, but he was finding this hard.

'That's not enough,' I persisted. 'Not tonight.'

Nick disengaged himself with a bored sigh. 'Look, I have to go out.'

'Go out? Now?' I couldn't believe he'd leave me like this. 'Why?'

He walked away toward the bedroom. I felt the anger grow cold with something I'd never faced before, answers to questions that gnawed at the back of my mind from our first night. 'Why, Nick? Is it him? Did that fat queer tell you to come over after you ditched the hag?'

Nick turned on me, lowering. 'I don't like that word.'

'Queer.'

'I said—'

'Queer.'

'All right.' He kicked viciously at the bedroom door with all the force he wanted to spend stopping my mouth. 'It's a fact in this business. That's why I get in places you don't. It's a business, cut and dried, not an *aht fawm* like you're always preaching.'

'Come off it, Nick.' I stood up, ready for him and wanting the fight. 'That casting couch bit went out with Harlow. Is that how you get jobs? That, and the cheap, scene-stealing tricks you use when you know and I know I played you against the wall in Lexington, you hypocritical son of a bitch.'

Nick threw up a warning hand. 'Hey, wait just one damn minute, Bernhardt. I never said I was or ever could be as good as you. But I'll tell you one thing.' Nick opened the closet and snaked his jacket off a hanger. 'I'll be around and working when nobody remembers you, because I know the business. You've been around fourteen years and still don't know the score. You won't make rounds, you don't want to be bothered waiting for an agent to see you. You're a goddamn *ahtist*. You won't wait in New York for something to develop, hell no. You'll take any show going out to Noplaceville, and who the hell ever sees you but some jerkoff writing for a newspaper no one reads. Integrity? Bullshit, lady. You are *afraid* of New York, afraid to take a chance on it.'

Nick subsided a little. 'That guy who was here, he produces. He's got a big voice where it counts.' Again he looked away with that odd, inconsistent embarrassment. 'He didn't want to sleep with me, really. He's basically straight.'

That was too absurd for anger. 'Basically?'

'He only wanted a little affection.'

'And you, Nick. Which way do you go basically. I mean was it his idea or yours?'

That was the first totally vulnerable moment I ever saw in Nick. He turned away, leaning against the sink. I could barely hear him.

'I don't know. It's never made much difference. So what's the harm? I don't lose anything, and I may gain.'

He started for the door, but I stopped him. 'Nick, I need you. What's happened to me today, I'm almost sick. Please don't do this to me.'

'Do what? Look.' He held me a moment without warmth or conviction. 'I'll only be gone a little while. We'll talk tomorrow, okay?'

'Don't go, Nick.'

He straightened his collar carefully with a sidelong glance at the mirror. 'We can't talk when you're like this. There's no point.'

I dogged him desperately, needing something to hang onto. 'Please don't go. I'm sorry for what I said. Nick, we can work it out, but don't leave me alone.'

'I have to.' His hand was already on the door, cutting me off like a thread hanging from his sleeve.

'Why!' It ripped up out of the bottom, out of the hate without which we never love or possess anything. 'Because that fat faggot with his job means more than I do, right? How low do you crawl to make a buck in this business? Or is it all business? Jesus, you make me sick.'

Nick couldn't be insulted. Even at the end, he didn't have that to spare me. Just a look from those cool blue eyes I tried so hard to please, telling me he was a winner in a game he knew, and I just didn't make it.

'It's your apartment. I'll move.'

'Nick, don't go.'

The door closed.

What did I do then? I should remember, they were the last minutes of my life. The door closed. I heard Nick thumping down the carpeted stairs, and thank God for cold comfort I didn't run after him. I poured a straight shot and finished it in one pull.

A hollow, eye-of-the-storm calm settled on me and then a depression so heavy it was a physical pain. I wandered through the apartment drinking too much and too fast, talking to Nick, to Bill, to Nattie, until I collapsed, clumsy, hiccuping drunk on the floor with half an hour to live.

Another drink. Get blind, drunk enough to reach . . . something, to blot out the Lump. Yeah, she's still with you, the goddamn little loser. Don't you ever learn, loser? No, she won't ever learn. Yesterday did this day's madness prepare. What play was that and who cares?

I tried to think but nothing came together. My life was a scattered Tinkertoy, all joints and pieces without meaning or order. A sum of apples and oranges: parts played, meals eaten, clothes worn, he said and I said, old tickets, old programs, newspaper reviews yellowed and fragile as Blanche's love letters. Apples and oranges. Where did I leave anything of myself, who did I love, what did I have? No one. Nothing.

Only Bill Wrenn.

'Christ, Bill, help me!'

I clawed for the phone with the room spinning and managed to call the theater. One of the girl apprentices answered. I struggled to make myself understood with a thickening tongue. 'Yeah, Bill Wrenn, 'simportant. Gayla Damon. yeah, hi, honey. He's not? Goddammit, he's gotta be. I *need* him. When'll he be back? Yeah . . . yeah. Tell'm call Gayla, please. Please. Yeah, trouble, Real trouble. I need him.'

That's how it happened. I dropped the phone in the general vicinity of the hook and staggered to the pitching sink to make one more huge, suicidal drink, crying and laughing, part drunk, part hysteria. But Bill was going to bail me out like he always had, and, boy, ol' Gay had learned her lesson. I was a fool to leave him. He loved me. Bill loved me and I was afraid of that. Afraid to be loved. How dumb can you get?

'How dumb?' I raged mushily at the Lump in the mirror. 'You with the great, soulful eyes. You never knew shit, baby.'

I was sweating. The wool sweater oppressed my clammy skin. Some sober molecule said take it off, but no. It's cooler out on my balcony. I will go out on my beautiful, nighted balcony and present my case to the yet unknowing world.

I half fell through the door. The balcony had a low railing, lower than I judged as I stumbled and heaved my drunken weight behind the hand flung out to steady myself and—

Fell. No more time.

That's it, finished. Now I've remembered. It was that sudden, painless, meaningless. No fade out, no end title music resolving the conflict themes, only torn film fluttering past the projector light, leaving a white screen.

There's a few answers anyway. I could get a lump in my throat, if I had one, thinking how Bill came and checked me out. God, let's hope they kept me covered. I must have looked awful. Poor Bill; maybe I gave you such a rotten time because I knew you could take it and still hang in. That's one of the faces of love, Mister Wrenn.

But I'd never have guessed about Lowen. Just imagine: he saw me that long ago and remembered all those years because I showed him he wasn't alone. I still can't add it up. Apples and oranges.

Unless, just maybe. . . .

'Lowen!'

The sound track again, the needle dropped on time. The balcony door thunders open and slams shut. Al calls again, but Lowen ignores her, leaning against the door, holding it closed.

'Gayla?'

His eyes move searchingly over the balcony in the darkening winter afternoon. From my name etched in the cement, around the railing, Lowen's whole concentrated being probes the gray light and air, full of purpose and need.

'Gayla, I know you're here.'

As he says my name, sound and vision and my own strength treble. I turn to him, wondering if through the sheer power of his need he can see me yet.

Lowen, can you hear me?

'I think I know what this means.'

I stretch out my hand, open up, let it touch his face, and as I tingle and hurt with it, Lowen turns his cheek into the caress.

'Yes, I feel you close.'

Talk to me, love.

'Isn't it strange, Gayla?'

Not strange at all, not us.

'When I saw you that night, I wanted to reach out and touch you, but I was just too shy. Couldn't even ask for my own autograph.'

Why not? I could have used a little touching.

'But I hitched all the way from school next day just to catch a glimpse of you. Hid in the back of the theater and watched you rehearse.'

That was Blanche. You saw that?

'It was the same thing all over again. You had something that reached out and showed me how we're all alike. I never saw a lonelier person than you on that stage. Or more beautiful. I cried.'

You saw Blanche. She did have a beauty.

'Oh, Gayla, the letters I wrote you and never sent. Forgive me. I forgot the name but not the lesson. If you hear me: you were the first woman I ever loved, and you taught me right. It's a giving.'

I can hear Al's urgent knock on the other side of the door. 'Lowen, what is it? Are you all right?'

He turns his head and smiles. God, he's beautiful. 'Fine, Al. She loves this place, Gayla. Don't drive her away.'

I won't, but don't go. Now when I'm beginning to understand so much.

He shakes his head. 'This is our first house. We're new, all kinds of problems. Parents, religion, everything.'

Can you *hear* me?

'We were never loved by anyone before, either of us. That's new, too. You pray for it—'

Like a fire:

'. . . like a fire to warm yourself.'

You do hear me.

'But it's scary. What do you do with the fire when it comes?' Lowen's hands reach out, pleading. 'Don't take this away from her. Don't hurt my Al. You're stronger than us. You can manage.'

I stretch my hand to touch his. With all my will, I press the answer through the contact.

Promise, Lowen.

'Don't make me shut you out, I don't know if I could. Go away and keep our secret? Take a big piece of love with you?'

Yes. Just that I was reaching for something, like you, and I had it all the time. So do you, Lowen. You're a—

I feel again as I did when the star fell across the sky, joyful and new and big as all creation without needing a reason, as Lowen's real fingers close around the memory of mine.

You're a *mensche*, love. Like me.

Lowen murmurs: 'I feel your hand. I don't care what anyone says. Your kind of woman doesn't kill herself. I'll never believe it.'

Bet on it. And thank you.

So it was a hell of a lot more than apples and oranges. It was a giving, a love. Hear that, Bill? Nattie? What I called life was just the love, the giving, like kisses on the wind, thrown to the audience, to my work, to the casual men, to whom it may concern. I was a giver, and if the little takers like Nick couldn't dig that, tough. That's the way it went down. All the miserable, self-cheating years, something heard music and went on singing. If Nattie could do it half as well. If she was half as alive as me, she meant. I loved all my life, because they're the same thing. Man, I was beautiful.

That's the part of you that woke me, Lowen. You're green, but you won't go through life like a tourist. You're going to get hurt and do some hurting yourself, but maybe someday. . . .

That's it, Lowen. That's the plot. You said it: we all touch, and the touching continues us. All those nights, throwing all of myself at life, and who's to say I did it alone?

So when you're full up with life, maybe you'll wake like me to spill it over into some poor, scared guy or girl. You're full of life like me, Lowen. It's a beautiful, rare gift.

It's dark enough now to see stars and the fingernail sliver of moon. A lovely moment for Lowen and me, like a night with Bill a moment before we made love for the first time. Lowen and I holding hands in the evening. Understanding. His eyes move slowly from my hand up, up toward my face.

'Gayla, I can see you.'

Can you, honest?

'Very clear. You're wearing a sweater and jeans. And you're smiling.'

Am I ever!

'And very beautiful.'

Bet your ass, love. I feel great, like I finally got it together.

One last painful, lovely current of life as Lowen squeezes my hand. 'Good-by, Gayla.'

So long, love.

Lowen yanks open the door. 'Al, Mister Hirajian? Come on out. It's a lovely evening.'

Alice peeks out to see Lowen leaning over the railing, enjoying the river and the early stars. His chest swells; he's laughing and he looks marvelous, inviting Al into his arms the way he did on their first day here. She comes unsurely to nestle in beside him, one arm around his waist. 'Who were you talking to?'

'She's gone, Al. You've got nothing to be afraid of. Except being afraid.'

'Lowen, I'm not going to—'

'This is our house, and nobody's going to take it away from us.' He turns Al to him and kisses her. 'Nobody wants to, that's a promise. So don't run away from it or yourself.'

She shivers a little, still uncertain. 'Do you really think we can stay? I can't—'

'Hey, love.' Lowen leans into her, cocky and charming, but meaning it. 'Don't tell a *mensche* what you can't. Hey, Hirajian.'

When the little prune pokes his head out the door, Lowen sweeps his arm out over the river and the whole lit-up West Side. 'Sorry for all the trouble, but we've changed our minds. I mean, look at it! Who could give up a balcony with a view like this?'

He's the last thing I see before the lights change: Lowen holding

Al and grinning out at the world. I thought the lights were dimming, but it's something else, another cue coming up. The lights cross-fade up, up, more pink and amber, until—my God, it's gorgeous!

I'm not dead, not gone. I feel more alive than ever. I'm Gail and Gayla and Lowen and Bill and Al and all of them magnified, heightened, fully realized, flowing together like bright, silver streams into—

Will you look at that *set*. Fantastic. Who's on the lights?

So that's what You look like. Ri-i-ght. I'm with it now, and I love You too. Give me a follow-spot, Baby.

I'm on.

MY BOY FRIEND'S NAME IS JELLO

Avram Davidson

Fashion, nothing but fashion. Virus X having in the medical zodiac its course half i-run, the physician (I refuse to say 'doctor' and, indeed, am tempted to use the more correct 'apothecary')—the physician, I say, tells me I have Virus Y. No doubt in the Navy it would still be called Catarrhal Fever. They say that hardly anyone had appendicitis until Edward VII came down with it a few weeks before his coronation, and thus made it fashionable. He (the medical man) is dosing me with injections of some stuff that comes in vials. A few centuries ago he would have used herbal clysters. . . . Where did I read that old remedy for the quinsy ('putrescent sore throat,' says my dictionary)? *Take seven weeds from seven meads and seven nails from seven steeds.* Oh dear, how my mind runs on. I must be feverish. An ague, no doubt.

Well, rather an ague than a pox. A pox is something one wishes on editors . . . strange breed, editors. The females all have names like Lulu Ammabelle Smith or Minnie Lundquist Bloom, and the males have little horns growing out of their brows. They must all be Quakers, I suppose, for their letters invariably begin, 'Dear Richard Roe' or 'Dear John Doe,' as if the word *mister* were a Vanity . . . when they write at all, that is; and meanwhile Goodwife Moos calls weekly for the rent. If I ever have a son (than which nothing is more unlikely) who shows the slightest inclination of becoming a writer, I shall instantly prentice him to a fishmonger or a Master Chimney Sweep. Don't write about Sex, the editors say, and don't write about Religion, or about History. If, however, you *do* write about History, be sure to add Religion and Sex. If one sends in a story about a celibate atheist, however, do you think they'll buy it?

In front of the house two little girls are playing one of those clap-handie games. Right hand, left hand, cross hands on bosom, left hand, right hand . . . it makes one dizzy to watch. And singing the while:

> My *boy* friend's *name* is *Jell*o,
> He *comes* from *Cincinello,*
> With a *pim*ple on his *nose*
> And *three* fat toes;
> And *that's* the *way* my *story* goes!

There is a pleasing surrealist quality to this which intrigues me. In general I find little girls enchanting. What a shame they grow up to be *big* girls and make our lives as miserable as we allow them, and ofttimes more. Silly, nasty-minded critics, trying to make poor Dodgson a monster of abnormality, simply because he loved Alice and was capable of following her into Wonderland. I suppose they would have preferred him to have taken a country curacy and become another Pastor Quiverful. A perfectly normal and perfectly horrible existence, and one which would have left us all still on *this* side of the looking-glass.

Whatever was in those vials doesn't seem to be helping me. I suppose old Dover's famous Powders hadn't the slightest fatal effect on the germs, bacteria, or virus (viri?), but at least they gave one a good old sweat (ipecac) and a mild, non-habit-forming jag (opium). But they're old-fashioned now, and so there we go again, round and round, one's train of thought like a Japanese waltzing mouse. I used to know a Japanese who—now, stop that. Distract yourself. Talk to the little girls . . .

Well, that was a pleasant interlude. We discussed (quite gravely, for I never condescend to children) the inconveniences of being sick, the unpleasantness of the heat; we agreed that a good rain would cool things off. Then their attention began to falter, and I lay back again. Miss Thurl may be in soon. Mrs. Moos (perfect name, she lacks only the antlers) said, whilst bringing in the bowl of slops which the medicine man allows me for victuals, said, My Sister Is Coming Along Later And She's Going To Fix You Up Some Nice Flowers. Miss Thurl, I do believe, spends most of her time fixing flowers. Weekends she joins a confraternity of overgrown campfire girls and boys who go on hiking trips, comes back sunburned and sweating and carrying specimen samples of plant and lesser animal

life. However, I must say for Miss Thurl that she is quiet. Her
brother-in-law, the bull-Moos, would be in here all the time if I
suffered it. He puts stupid quotations in other people's mouths.
He will talk about the weather and I will not utter a word, then
he will say, Well, It's Like You Say, It's Not The Heat But The
Humidity.

Thinking of which, I notice a drop in the heat, and I see it
is raining. That should cool things off. How pleasant. A pity that
it is washing away the marks of the little girls' last game. They
played this one on the sidewalk, with chalked-out patterns and
bits of stone and broken glass. They chanted and hopped back
and forth across the chalkmarks and shoved the bits of stone
and glass—or were they potsherds—'potsie' from potsherd,
perhaps? I shall write a monograph, should I ever desire a Ph.D.
I will compare the chalkmarks with Toltec emblems and masons'
marks and the signs which Hindoo holy men smear on themselves
with wood ashes and perfumed cow dung. All this passes for erudition.

I feel terrible, despite the cool rain. Perhaps without it, I should
feel worse.

Miss Thurl was just here. A huge bowl of blossoms, arranged
on the table across the room. Intricately arranged, I should
say; but she put some extra touches to it, humming to herself. Something ever so faintly reminiscent about that tune, and
vaguely disturbing. Then she made one of her rare remarks.
She said that I needed a wife to take care of me. My blood ran
cold. An icy sweat (to quote Catullus, that wretched Priapist),
bedewed my limbs. I moaned. Miss Thurl at once departed,
murmuring something about a cup of tea. If I weren't so weak
I'd knot my bedsheets together and escape. But I am terribly
feeble.

It's unmanly to weep. . . .

Back she came, literally poured the tea down my throat. A
curious taste it had. Sassafras? Bergamot? Mandrake root? It is
impossible to say how old Miss Thurl is. She wears her hair parted
in the center and looped back. Ageless . . . ageless . . .

I thank whatever gods may be that Mr Ahyellow came in just
then. The other boarder (upstairs), a greengrocer, decent fellow, a
bit short-tempered. He wished me soon well. He complained he
had his own troubles, foot troubles . . . I scarcely listened, just
chattered, hoping the Thurl would get her hence. . . . Toes . . .
something about his toes. Swollen, three of them, quite painful. A
bell tinkled in my brain. I asked him how he spelt his name.

A-j-e-l-l-o. Curious, I never thought of that. Now, I wonder what he could have done to offend the little girls? Chased them from in front of his store, perhaps. There is a distinct reddish spot on his nose. By tomorrow he will have an American Beauty of a pimple.

Fortunately he and Miss Thurl went out together. I must think this through. I must remain cool. Aroint thee, thou mist of fever. This much is obvious: There are sorcerers about. Sorcer*esses,* I mean. The little ones made rain. And they laid a minor curse on poor Ajello. The elder one has struck me in the very vitals, however. If I had a cow it would doubtless be dry by this time. Should I struggle? Should I submit? Who knows what lies behind those moss-colored eyes, what thoughts inside the skull covered by those heavy tresses? Life with Mrs. and Mr. Moos is—even by itself—too frightful to contemplate. Why doesn't she lay her traps for Ajello? Why should I be selected as the milk-white victim for the Hymeneal sacrifice? Useless to question. Few men have escaped once the female cast the runes upon them. And the allopath has nothing in his little black bag, either, which can cure.

Blessed association of words! Allopath—Homeopath—*homoios,* the like, the same, *pathos,* feeling, suffering—*similia similibus curantur*—

The little girls are playing beneath my window once more, clapping hands and singing. Something about a boy friend named Tony, who eats macaroni, has a great big knife and a pretty little wife, and will always lead a happy life . . . that must be the butcher opposite; he's always kind to the children. . . . Strength, strength! The work of a moment to get two coins from my wallet and throw them down. What little girl could resist picking up a dime which fell in front of her? *'Cross my palm with silver, pretty gentleman!'* —eh? And now to tell them my tale . . .

I feel better already. I don't think I'll see Miss Thurl again for a while. She opened the door, the front door, and when the children had sung the new verse she slammed the door shut quite viciously.

It's too bad about Ajello, but every man for himself.

Listen to them singing away, bless their little hearts! I love little girls. Such sweet, innocent voices.

> My *boy* friend will *soon* be *heal*thy.
> He *shall* be *very weal*thy.
> No *wo*man shall *har*ry;

Or *seek* to *marry*;
Two and *two* is *four*, and *one* to *carry!*

It will be pleasant to be wealthy, I hope. I must ask Ajello where
Cincinello is.

SAN DIEGO LIGHTFOOT SUE

Tom Reamy

This all began about ten years ago in a house at the top of a flight of rickety wooden stairs in Laurel Canyon. It might be said there were two beginnings, though the casual sorcery in Laurel Canyon may have been the cause and the other merely the effect—if you believe in that sort of thing.

The woman sat cross-legged on the floor reading the book. The windows were open to the warm California night, and the only sounds that came through them was the distant, muffled, eternal roar of Los Angeles traffic. The brittle pages of the book crackled as she turned them carefully. She read slowly because her Latin wasn't what it used to be. She lit a cigarette and left it to burn unnoticed in the ashtray on the floor beside her.

'Here's a good one,' she said to the big orange tom curled in the chair she leaned against. 'You don't know where I can find a hazelnut bush with a nest of thirteen white adders under it, do you, Punkin?' The cat didn't answer; he only opened one eye slightly and twitched the tip of his tail.

She turned a page, and several two-inch rectangles of white paper fell into her lap. She picked them up and examined them, but they were blank. She stuck them back in the book and kept reading.

She found it a while later. It was a simple spell. All she had to do was write the word-square on a piece of white parchment with black ink and then burn it while thinking of the person she wished to summon.

'I wonder if Paul Newman is doing anything tonight,' she chuckled.

She stood up and went to the drafting table, opened a drawer and removed a pen and a bottle of india ink. She put a masking tape dispenser on the edge of the book to hold it open and carefully lettered the word-square on one of the pieces of paper stuck between the pages. She supposed that's why her mother, or whoever, had put them there—they looked like parchment, anyway.

The word-square was eight letters wide and eight letters high; eight, eight-letter words stacked on top of one another. She imagined they were words, though they were in no language she knew. The peculiar thing about the square was that it read the same sideways or upside down—even in a mirror image, it was the same.

She put the cap back on the ink and went to the ashtray, kneeling beside it. She lay the parchment on the dead cigarette butts. 'Well, here goes,' she said to the cat. 'I wonder if it's all right to burn it with a cigarette lighter? Maybe I need a black taper made of the wax of dead bees or something.'

She composed herself, trying to take it seriously, and thought of a man, not a specific man, just *the* man. 'I feel like Snow White singing "Someday My Prince Will Come,"' she muttered. She flicked the cigarette lighter and touched the flame to the corner of the piece of paper.

It flamed up so quickly and so brightly that she gasped and drew back. 'God!' she grunted and hurried to a window to escape the billows of black smoke that smelled of rotten eggs. The cat was already out, sitting on the farthest point of the deck railing, looking at her with round startled eyes.

The woman glanced back at the black smoke spreading like a carpet on the ceiling and then at the wide-eyed cat. She suddenly collapsed against the window sill in a fit of uncontrollable laughter. 'Come on back in, Punkin,' she gasped. 'It's all over.' The cat gave her an incredulous look and hopped off the railing into the shrubbery.

This also began about ten years ago in Kansas, the summer he was fifteen, when the air smelled like hot metal and rang with the cries of cicadas. It ended a month later when he was still fifteen, when the house in Laurel Canyon burned with a strange green fire that made no heat.

His name was John Lee Peacock, a good, old, undistinguished name in Southern Kansas. His mother and his aunts and his aunts' husbands called him John Lee. The kids in school called him Johnny, which he preferred. His father never called him anything.

His father had been by-passed by the world, but he wouldn't have cared, even if he had been aware of it. Wash Peacock was a dirt farmer who refused to abandon the land. The land repayed his taciturn loyalty with annual betrayal. Wash had only four desires to life: to work the land, three hot meals each day, sleep, and copulation when the pressures built high enough. The children were strangers who appeared suddenly, disturbed his sleep for a while, then faded into the gray house or the County Line Cemetery.

John Lee's mother had been a Willet. The aunts were her sisters: Rose and Lilah. Wash had a younger brother somewhere in Pennsylvania—or, had had one the last time he heard. That was in 1927, the year Wash's mother died. Grace Elizabeth Willet married Delbert Washburn Peacock in the fall of 1930. She did it because her father, old Judge Willet, thought it was a good idea. Grace Elizabeth was a plain, timid girl who, he felt, was destined to be the family's maiden aunt. He was right, but she would have been much happier if he hadn't interfered.

The Peacocks had owned the land for nearly a hundred years and were moderately prosperous. They had survived the Civil War, Reconstruction, and statehood, but wouldn't survive the Depression. Judge Willet felt that Wash was the best he could do for Grace Elizabeth. He was a nice-looking man, and what he lacked in imagination, he made up in hard work.

But the Peacocks had a thin, unfortunate blood line. Only a few of the many children lived. It was the same with Wash and Grace Elizabeth. She had given birth eight times, but there were only three of them left. Wash, Jr, her first born, had married one of the trashy O'Dell girls and had gone to Oklahoma to work in the oilfields. She hadn't heard from him in thirteen years. Dwayne Edward, the third born, had stayed in Los Angeles after his separation from the army. He sent a card every Christmas and she had kept them all. She wished some of the girls had lived. She would have liked to have a girl, to make pretty things for her, to have someone to talk to. But she had lost the three girls and two of the boys. She had trouble remembering their names sometimes, but it was all written in the big Bible where she could remind herself when the names began to slip away.

John Lee was the youngest. He had arrived late in her life, a comfort for her weary years. She wanted him to be different from the others. Wash, Jr., and Dwayne had both been disappointments; too much like their father: unimaginative plodding boys who had done badly in school and got into trouble with the law. She still loved them because they were her children, but she sometimes forgot why she was supposed to. She wanted John Lee to read books (God! How long since she'd read a book; she used to read all the time when she was a girl), to know about art and faraway places. She knew she hoped for too much, and so she was content when she got a part of it.

Wash didn't pay any more attention to John Lee than he had the others. He neither asked nor seemed to want the boy's help in the field. So Grace Elizabeth kept him around the house, helping with her chores, talking to him, having him share with her what he had learned in school. She gave him as much as she could. There wasn't money for much, but she managed to hold back a few dollars now and then.

She loved John Lee very much; he was probably the only thing she did love. So, on that shimmering summer day about ten years ago, when he was fifteen, she died for him.

She was cleaning up the kitchen after supper. Wash had gone back to the fields where he would stay until dark. John Lee was at the kitchen table, reading, passing on bits of information he knew she would like to hear. She leaned against the sink with the cup towel clutched in her hand and felt her supper turn over in her stomach. She had known it was coming for months. Now it was here.

He's too young, she thought. If he could only have a couple more years. She watched him bent over the book, the evening sun glinting on his brown hair. He's even better looking than his father, she thought. So like his father. But only on the outside. Only on the outside.

She spread the cup towel on the rack to dry and walked through the big old house. She hadn't really noticed the house in a long time. It had grown old and gray slowly, as she had, and so she had hardly noticed it happening. Then she looked at it again and it wasn't the house she remembered moving into all those years ago. Wash's father had built it in 1913 when the old one had been unroofed by a twister. He had built it like they did in those days: big, so generations could live in it. It had been freshly painted when she moved in, a big white box eight miles from Hawley, a mile from Miller's Corners.

Then the hard times began. But Wash had clung to the land during the Depression and the dust. He hadn't panicked like most of the others. He hadn't sold the land at give-away prices or lost it because he couldn't pay the taxes. Things had gotten a little better when the war began, but never as good as before the Depression.

Now they were bad again. At the end of each weary year there was only enough money to do it all over again.

She supposed that being the oldest, Wash, Jr, would get it. She was glad John Lee wouldn't. She went upstairs to his room and packed his things in a pasteboard box. She left it where he would find it and went to her own room. She opened a drawer in the old highboy that had belonged to her grandmother and removed an envelope from beneath her cotton slips. She took it to the kitchen and handed it to John Lee.

He took it and looked at her. 'What is it, Mama?'

'Open it in the morning, John Lee. You'd better go to bed now.'

'But it's not even dark yet.' There's something wrong, there's something wrong.

'Soon, then. I want to sit on the porch awhile and rest.' She kissed him and patted his shoulder and left the room. He watched the empty doorway and felt the blood singing in his ears. After a while, he got a drink of water from the cooler and went to his room. He lay on the bed, looking at the water spots on the ceiling paper, and clutched the envelope in his hands. Tears formed in his eyes and he tried to blink them away.

Grace Elizabeth sat on the porch in her rocker, moving gently, mending Wash's clothes until it got too dark to see. Then she folded them neatly in her lap, leaned back in the chair, and closed her eyes.

Wash found her the next morning only because he wondered why his breakfast wasn't waiting for him. She was buried in the County Line Cemetery with five of her children after a brief service at the First Baptist Church in Hawley. Aunt Rose and Aunt Lilah had a fine time weeping into black lace handkerchiefs and clucking over Poor John Lee.

On the way back from the funeral John Lee rode in the front seat of the '53 Chevrolet beside his father. Neither of them spoke until they had turned off the highway at Miller's Corners.

'Write a letter to Wash, Jr. Tell him to come home.' John Lee didn't answer. He could smell the dust rising up behind the car. Wash parked it in the old carriage house and hurried to change clothes, hurried to make up the half day he had lost. John Lee went to the closet in the front hall and took down a shoe box, in which his mother kept such things, and looked for an address. He found it after a bit, worked to the bottom, unused for thirteen years. He wrote the letter anyway.

He had left the envelope unopened under his pillow. Now he

opened it, although he had guessed what it was. He counted the carefully hoarded bills: a hundred and twenty-seven dollars. He sat on the edge of the bed, on the crazy quilt his mother had made for him, in the quiet room, in the silent weary house. He wiped his eyes with his knuckles, picked up the pasteboard box, and walked the mile to Miller's Corners.

His Sunday suit, worn to the funeral that morning, once belonging to Dwayne, and before that, Wash, Jr., was white at the cuffs from the dusty road. His shoes, his alone, were even worse. It was a scorcher. 'It's gonna be another scorcher,' she always used to say, looking out the kitchen window after putting away the breakfast dishes. He sat on the bench at the Gulf station, cleaning the dust off the best he could.

The cicadas screeched from the mesquite bushes, filling the hot still air with their insistent calls for a mate. John Lee rather liked the sound, but it had bothered his mother. 'Enough to drive a body ravin' mad,' she used to say. She always called them locusts, but he had learned in school their real name was cicada. And when they talked about a plague of locusts in the Bible, they really meant grasshoppers. 'Well, I'll declare,' she had said. 'Always wondered why locusts would be considered a plague. Far's I know, they don't do anything but sit in the bushes and make noise. Now, grasshoppers I can understand.' And she would smile at him in her pleased and proud way that caused a pleasant hurting in the back of his throat.

'Hello, John Lee.'

He looked up quickly. 'Hello, Mr. Cuttsanger. How are you today?' He liked Mr. Cuttsanger, a string-thin man the same age as his mother, who had seemingly permanent grease stains on his hands. He wiped at them now with a dull red rag, but it didn't help.

'I'm awfully sorry about your mother, boy. Wish I coulda gone to the funeral but I couldn't get away. We were in the same grade together all through school, you know.'

'Yes, I know. She told me.'

'What're you doin' here still dressed up?' he asked, sticking the rag in his hip pocket and looking at the box.

'I reckon I have to catch a bus, Mr. Cuttsanger.' His heart did a little flip-flop. Not the old school bus either, but a real bus.

'Where you off to, John Lee?'

'Where do your buses go, Mr. Cuttsanger?'

Mr. Cuttsanger sat on the bench beside John Lee. 'The westbound will be through here in about an hour goin' to Los Angeles.

The eastbound comes through in the mornin' headed for St. Louie. You already missed it.'

'Los Angeles. My brother, Dwayne, lives in California.' But he didn't know where. He had seen the Christmas cards in the shoe box, but he hadn't paid any attention to the return address.

Mr. Cuttsanger nodded. 'Good idea, goin' to stay with Dwayne. Nothin' for you here on this played-out old farm. Heard Grace Elizabeth say the same thing. Your father ought to sell it and go with you. But I guess I know Wash better'n that.' He arose from the bench with a little sigh. He went into the station and returned with a small red flag. He stuck it in a pipe welded at an angle to the pole supporting the Gulf sign. 'There. He'll stop when he sees that. You buy your ticket from the driver.'

'Thank you, Mr. Cuttsanger. I need to mail a letter also.' He took the letter he had carefully addressed in block printing to Delbert Washburn Peacock, Jr, Gen. Del., Norman, Okla., from his pocket and handed it to Mr. Cuttsanger. 'I don't have a stamp.'

Mr. Cuttsanger looked at the letter. 'Is Wash, Jr, still in Norman?' He said it as if he doubted it.

'I don't know. That's the only address I could find.'

Mr. Cuttsanger tapped the letter against the knuckle of his thumb. 'You leave a nickel with me and I'll get a stamp from Clayton in the mornin'. Sure was a lot simpler before they closed the post office.' He sat back on the bench in the shade of the car shed. John Lee followed his eyes as he looked at Miller's Corners evaporating under the cloudless sky. An out-of-state car blasted through doing seventy. Mr. Cuttsanger sighed and accepted a nickel from John Lee. 'They don't even have to slow down any more. Used to be thirty-five-mile speed-limit signs at each end of town. Guess they don't need 'em now. Ain't nothin' here but me and the cafe. Myrtle's been saying for nearly a year she was gonna move to Hawley or maybe even Liberal. Closed the post office in fifty-five, I think it was. That foundation across the highway is where the grocery store used to be. Don't reckon you remember the grocery store?'

'No, sir, but I remember the feed store.'

'Imagine that. You musta been about four, five years old.'

'I was born in forty-eight.'

'Closed the feed store in fifty-two. Imagine you rememberin' that far back.' He continued to ramble on in his pleasant friendly voice. John Lee asked questions and made comments to keep him going, to make the time pass faster. A whole hour before the bus would come.

But it finally did, cutting off the highway in a cloud of dust and a dragon hiss of air brakes. John Lee looked at the magic name in the little window over the windshield: LOS ANGELES. He swallowed and solemnly shook hands with Mr. Cuttsanger.

'Good-by, Mr. Cuttsanger.'

'Good-by, John Lee. You take care now.'

John Lee nodded and picked up the box and walked to the bus, his legs trembling. The door sighed open and the driver got out. He opened a big door on the side of the bus under *Continental Trailways*. He took the pasteboard box.

'Where you goin'?'

'I'd like a ticket to Los Angeles, please.' He couldn't keep from smiling when he said the name. The driver put a tag on the box, put it in with the suitcases, and closed the door. John Lee followed him into the bus. Inside it was cool like some of the stores in Liberal.

He bought his ticket and sat down in the front seat, scooting to the window as the bus lurched back onto the highway. He looked back at Miller's Corners and waved to Mr. Cuttsanger, but he was taking down the red flag and didn't see.

John Lee leaned back in the seat and hugged himself. Once more he couldn't keep from smiling. After a bit, he looked around at the other people. There weren't many and some weren't wearing Sunday clothes; so he decided it would be all right to take off his jacket. He settled back in the seat, watching the baked Kansas countryside rush past the window. Strange, he thought, it looks the same way it does from the school bus. Even though he tried to prevent it, the smile returned unbidden every once in a while.

The bus went through Hawley without stopping, past the white rococo courthouse with its high clock tower; past the school, closed for the summer; over the hump in the highway by the old depot where the railroad tracks had been taken out; across the bridge over Crooked Creek.

It stopped in Liberal and the driver called out, 'Rest stop!' John Lee didn't know what a rest stop was, and so he stayed on the bus. He noticed that some of the other passengers didn't get off either. He decided there was nothing to worry about.

He tried to see everything when the bus left Liberal, to look on both sides at once, because it was the farthest he had ever been. But Oklahoma looked just like Kansas, Texas looked just like Oklahoma, and New Mexico looked like Texas, only each seemed a little bleaker than the one before. The bus stopped in Tucumcari for supper. John Lee had forgotten to eat dinner, and his bladder felt like it would burst.

He was nervous but he managed all right. He'd eaten in a cafe before, and, by watching the others, he found out where the toilet was and how to pay for his meal. It was dark when the bus left Tucumcari. He tried to go to sleep, to make the time pass faster, the way he always did when the next day was bringing wondrous things. But, as usual, the harder he tried, the wider awake he was.

He awoke when the bus stopped for breakfast and quickly put his coat over his lap, hoping no one had noticed. He waited until everyone else had gotten off, then headed for the toilet keeping his coat in front of him. He didn't know for sure where he was, but all the cars had Arizona license plates.

It was after dark when the bus pulled into the Los Angeles terminal, though it seemed to John Lee as if they had been driving through town for hours. He had never dreamed it was so big. He watched the other passengers collect their luggage and got his pasteboard box.

Then he went out into: Los Angeles.

He walked around the street with the box clutched in his arms in total bedazzlement. Buildings, lights, cars, people, so many different kinds of people. It was the first time he had ever seen a Chinese, except in the movies, although he wasn't absolutely sure that it wasn't a Japanese. There were dozens of picture shows, lined up in rows. He liked movies and used to go nearly every Saturday afternoon, a long time ago before the picture show in Hawley closed.

And buses, with more magic names in the little windows: SUNSET BLVD; HOLLYWOOD BLVD; PASADENA; and lots of names he didn't recognize; but they were no less magic, he was sure, because of that.

He was standing on the curb, just looking, when a bus with HOLLYWOOD BLVD in the little window pulled over and opened its door right in front of him. The driver looked at him impatiently. It was amazing how the bus had stopped especially for him. He got on. There didn't seem to be anything else he could do.

'Vine!' the driver bawled sometime later. John Lee got off and stood at the corner of Hollywood and Vine grinning at the night. He walked down Hollywood Boulevard, gawking at everything, reading the names in stars on the sidewalk. He never imagined there would be so many cars or so many people at night. There were more than you would see in Liberal, even on Saturday afternoon. And the strange clothes the people wore. And men with long hair like the Beatles. Mary Ellen Walker had a colored picture of them pasted on her notebook.

He didn't know how far he had walked—the street never seemed to end—but the box was heavy. He was hungry and his Sunday shoes had rubbed a blister on his heel. He went into a cafe and sat in a booth, glad to get rid of the weight of the box. Most of the people looked at him as he came in. Several of them smiled. He smiled back. A couple of people had said hello on the street too. Hollywood was certainly a friendly place.

He told the waitress what he wanted. He looked around the cafe and met the eyes of a man at the counter who had smiled when he came in. The man smiled again. John Lee smiled back, feeling good. The man got off the stool and came to the booth carrying a cup of coffee.

'May I join you?' He seemed a little nervous.

'Sure.' The man sat down and took a quick sip of coffee. 'My name is John Lee Peacock.' He held out his hand. The man looked startled, then took it, giving it a quick shake and hurriedly breaking contact. 'I'd rather be called Johnny, though.'

The man's skin was moist. John Lee guessed he was about forty and a little bit fat. He nodded, quickly, like a turkey. 'Warren.'

'Pleased to meet you, Mr. Warren. You live in Hollywood?'

'Yes.'

The waitress brought the food and put it on the table. Warren was flustered. 'Oh . . . ah . . . put that on my ticket.'

The waitress looked at John Lee. Her mouth turned down a little at the corners. 'Sure, honey,' she said to Mr. Warren.

John Lee discarded the straw from his ice tea and put sugar in it. 'Aren't you eating?'

'Ah . . . no. No, I've already eaten.' He took another nervous sip of the coffee, and John Lee heard a smothered snicker from the booth behind him. 'You didn't have to pay for my supper. I've got money.'

'My pleasure.'

'Thank you, Mr. Warren.'

'You're welcome. Uh . . . how long you been in town?'

'Just got here a little while ago. On a Continental Trailways bus, all the way from Miller's Corners, Kansas.' John Lee still couldn't believe where he was. He had to say it out loud. 'I sure do like bein' in Los Angeles, Mr. Warren.'

'You have a place to stay yet?'

He hadn't really thought about that. 'No, sir. I guess I haven't.'

Warren smiled and seemed to relax a little. It was working out okay, but the kid was putting on the hick routine a little thick. 'Don't worry about it tonight. You can stay at my place and look for something tomorrow.'

'Thank you, Mr. Warren. Thats very nice of you.'

'My pleasure. Uh . . . what made you come to Los Angeles?'

John Lee swallowed a mouth full of food. 'My mamma died the other day. Before she died, she gave me the money to get away.'

'I want to sit on the porch a while and rest,' she had said.

'It was either Los Angeles or St. Louis, and the Los Angeles bus came by first.' He pushed the gray memories back out of the way. 'And here I am!'

Warren looked at him, no longer smiling. 'How old are you?'

'I was fifteen last January.' He wondered if he was expected to ask Mr. Warren's age.

'God!' Warren breathed. He slumped in the seat for a moment, then seemed to come to a decision. 'Look, uh . . . Johnny. I just remembered something. I won't be able to put you up for the night after all. As a matter of fact, I have to dash. I'm sorry.'

'That's all right, Mr. Warren. It was kind of you to make the offer.'

'My pleasure. So long.' He hurried away. John Lee watched him stop at the cash register. When he left, the cashier looked at John Lee and nodded.

'Nice goin' there, John Lee Peacock, sugah.' The voice whispered in his ear with a honeyed Southern accent. He turned and looked nose to nose into a grinning black face. 'Got yoself a free dinnah and didn't have to put out.'

'What,' he said, completely befuddled.

A second face, a white one, appeared over the back of the seat. It said, 'May we join you?' doing a good imitation of Mr. Warren.

'Yeah, I guess so.' They came around and sat opposite him, both of them as skinny as Mr. Cuttsanger. He thought they walked a little funny.

The black one said, 'I'm Pearl and this is Daisy Mae.'

'How ja do,' Daisy Mae said, chewing imaginary gum.

'Really?' John Lee asked, grinning.

'Really, what, sugah?' Pearl asked.

'Are those really your names?'

'Isn't he *cute?*' shrieked Daisy Mae.

Pearl patted his hand. 'Just keep your eyes and ears open and your pants shut, sugah. You'll get the hang of it.' He lit a pale blue cigarette and offered one to John Lee. John Lee shook his head. Pearl saw John Lee's bemused expression and wiggled the cigarette. 'Nieman-Marcus,' he said matter-of-factly.

'Well, if it isn't the Queen of Spades and Cotton Tail.' They all three looked up at a chubby young man, standing with his hand delicately on his hip. His fleshy lips coiled into a smirk at John Lee. He wore light eye make-up with a tiny diamond in one pierced ear. He was with a muscular young man who looked at John Lee coldly. 'You girls stage another commando raid on Romper Room?'

'Why, lawdy, Miss Scawlett, how you do talk!' Pearl did his best Butterfly McQueen imitation, and his hands were like escaping blackbirds.

'This is a cub scout meeting and we're den mothers,' Daisy Mae said in a flat voice. The muscular young man grabbed Miss Scarlett's arm and pulled him away.

'It's a den of something!' he shot back over his shoulder.

'Did you see how Miss Scarlett looked at our John Lee?' Daisy Mae rolled his eyes.

'The bitch is in heat.'

'Who was that gorgeous butch number she was with?'

'Never laid eyes on him before.'

'Your eyes aren't what you'd like to lay on him,' Daisy Mae said dryly.

Pearl quickly put his hands over John Lee's ears. 'Don't talk like that afore this sweet child! You *know* I don't like rough trade!'

John Lee laughed and they laughed with him. He didn't know what they were talking about most of the time, but he decided he liked these two strange people. 'Doesn't . . . uh . . . Miss Scarlett like you?'

'Sugah,' Pearl said seriously, taking his hands away, 'Miss Scawlett doesn't like anybody.'

'Stay away from her, John Lee,' Daisy Mae said, meaning it.

'She has a problem,' Pearl pronounced.

'A *big* problem,' Daisy Mae agreed.

'What?' John Lee asked, imagining all sorts of thing.

'She's hung like a horse.' Pearl nodded sagely.

'A *big* horse.' Daisy Mae nodded also.

John Lee could feel his ears getting red. Damnation, he thought. He laughed in embarrassment. 'What's wrong with that?' He remembered Leo Whittaker in his room at school who bragged that he had the biggest one in Kansas and would show it to you if you would go out under the bleachers.

'Sugah,' Pearl said, patting his hand again, 'Miss Scawlett is a *lady*.'

'It's a wonder it doesn't turn green and fall off the way she keeps it tied down. Makes her walk bowlegged.'

'Don't be catty, Daisy Mae. Just count your blessin's.' Daisy Mae put his chin on the heel of his hand and stared morosely at nothing, like Garbo in *Anna Christie*. 'John Lee, sugah,' Pearl continued, 'was all that malarkey you gave that score the truth?'

'Huh?' John Lee asked, completely confused.

'It was,' Daisy Mae said in his incredible but true voice.

'You really don't have a place to stay tonight?'

'Huh-uh.' He wondered why Pearl doubted him.

'And he's also really fif-*teen*,' Daisy Mae said, cocking his eyes at Pearl.

'Daisy Mae, sugah,' Pearl said with utmost patience, 'I'm only bein' a Sistuh of Mercy, tryin' to put a roof ovuh this sweet child's head, tryin' to keep him from bein' picked up by the po-leece fah vay-gran-cee.'

Daisy Mae shrugged fatalistically.

'Why does it matter that I'm fifteen?' John Lee really wanted to know what they were talking about.

'You *are* from the boonies,' Daisy Mae said in wonder.

'Sugah, you come stay with us. There's a lot you've got to learn. If we leave you runnin' around loose, you gonna get in seer-ee-us trouble. Sugah, this town is full of tiguhs and . . . you . . . are . . . a . . . juicy . . . lamb.'

'Your fangs are showing,' Daisy Mae said tonelessly.

Pearl turned to him, about to cut him dead, but instead threw up his arms and did Butterfly McQueen again. 'Lawzy, Miss Daisy Mae, you done got a spot on yo' pretty shirt!' He turned back to John Lee with a martyred expression. 'I wash and clean and iron and scrub and work my fanguhs to the bone, and this slob can get covered in spaghetti sauce eatin' *jelly beans!*'

John Lee dissolved in a fit of giggles. Pearl couldn't hold his outraged expression any longer and began to grin. Daisy Mae chuckled and said, 'Don't pay any attention to her, John Lee. She's got an Aunt Jemimah complex.'

Pearl got up. 'Let's get out of this meat market. There are too many eyes on our little rump roast.'

Daisy Mae put his hand on John Lee's. 'John Lee, if we run into a cop, *try* to look twenty-one.'

He wiped the laugh tears from his eyes. 'I'll do my best.' He got the pasteboard box and followed them out of the cafe. They cut hurriedly around the corner past a large sidewalk newsstand, then jaywalked to a parking lot. Pearl and Daisy Mae acted like a couple of cat burglars, and John Lee had to hurry to keep up.

They got into a '63 Corvair and drove west on Hollywood Boulevard until it became a residential street, then turned right on Laurel Canyon. They wound up into the Hollywood Hills, Pearl and Daisy Mae chattering constantly, making John Lee laugh a lot. He felt very good and very lucky.

Pearl pulled into a garage sitting on the edge of the pavement with no driveway. They went up a long flight of rickety wooden steps to a small two-bedroom house with a porch that went all the way around. Pearl flipped on the lights. 'It ain't Twelve Oaks, sugah, but we like it.'

John Lee stared goggle-eyed. He'd been in Aunt Rose's and Aunt Lilah's fancy houses lots of times, but they ran to beige, desert rose, and old gold. These colors were absolutely electric. The wild patterns made him dizzy, and there were pictures and statues and things hanging from the ceiling.

'Golly,' he said.

'Take a load off,' Daisy Mae said, pointing to a big reclining chair covered in what looked like purple fur. John Lee put the box on the floor and gingerly sat down. He leaned back and was surprised at how comfortable it was. Pearl put a record on the record player, but John Lee didn't recognize the music. He yawned. Daisy Mae stood over the box. 'What's in this carton you keep clutching to your bosom?'

'My things.'

'Pardon my nose,' Daisy Mae said and opened it. He pulled out some of John Lee's everyday clothes. 'You auditioning for the sixteenth road company of *Tobacco Road?*'

'Don't pay any attention,' Pearl said, sitting beside John Lee. 'She's a costumer at Paramount. Thinks she knows *every*-thing about clothes.'

'Don't knock it. I had to dress thirty bitchy starlets to buy that chair you got your black ass on. I'll hang these up for you, John Lee.'

John Lee yawned again. 'Thank you.'

Pearl threw up his hands. 'Land o' Goshen, this child is ex-*haus*-ted!'

Daisy Mae carried the box into a bedroom. 'Two days on a Continental Trailways bus would give Captain Marvel the drearies.'

Pearl took John Lee's arm and pulled him out of the chair. 'Come on, sugah. We gotta give you a nice bath and put you to *bed*, afore you co-lapse.' He led him to the bathroom, showed him where everything was, and turned on the shower for him. 'Give a holler if you need anything.'

'Thank you.' Pearl left. John Lee had never taken a shower before, although he had seen them at Aunt Rose's and Aunt Lilah's. He took off his clothes and got in.

The door opened and Pearl came in, pushing back the shower curtain. 'You all right, sugah? Oh, sugah, you are *all right!*' He leered at John Lee, but in such a way that made him laugh. His ears turned red anyway. Pearl winked and closed the curtain. 'You don't mind if I brush my teeth?'

'No. Go ahead.' He could hear Pearl sloshing and brushing. After a bit there was silence. He pulled back the shower curtain a little and peeped out. Pearl was leaning against the wash basin, a toothbrush in his hand, his head down, and his eyes closed. John Lee watched him, wondering if he should say anything.

'John Lee,' Pearl said without looking up, his voice serious and the accent totally absent.

'Yes, Pearl?' He spoke quietly and cautiously.

'John Lee, don't pay any attention when we tease you about how cute you are, or when we ogle your body. It's just the way we are. It's just the way the lousy world is.'

'I won't, Pearl.' He felt the hurting in the back of his throat, but he didn't know why.

Pearl suddenly stood up, the big grin back on his face. 'Well. Look at me. Poor Pitiful Pearl. Now. What do you sleep in? Underwear? Pee-jays? Nightshirt? Your little bare skin?'

'My pajamas are in the box, I think.'

'Good enough.' Pearl left the bathroom and returned when John Lee was drying on a big plush towel printed like the American flag. Pearl reached in and hung the pajamas on the doorknob without looking in. 'There you go, sugah.'

'Thank you, Pearl.'

He left the bathroom in his pajamas with his Sunday suit over his arm. Daisy Mae took the suit. 'I'll clean and press that for you.'

'You don't have to, Daisy Mae.' The names were beginning to sound normal to him.

Daisy Mae grinned. 'It won't hurt me.'

'Thank you.'

Pearl took his arm. 'Time for you to go to bed.' He led John Lee into the bedroom. There was an old, polished brass bed. John Lee

stared at it, then ran his hand over the turned-back sheets. Even
Aunt Rose hadn't thought about red silk sheets. He never imagined
such luxury.

'Golly,' he said.

Pearl laughed and grabbed him in a big hug and kissed him on
the forehead. 'Sugah, you are just not to be be-*lieved!*' John Lee
grinned uncomfortably and turned red. Pearl pulled the sheet up
around his neck and patted his cheek. 'Sleep tight.'

'Good night, Pearl.'

Daisy Mae stuck his head in to say good night. Pearl turned at
the door and smiled fondly at him, then went out, closing it. John
Lee wiggled around on the silk sheets. Golly, he thought, golly,
golly, golly!

Pearl walked dreamily into the living room and collapsed becomingly onto the big purple fur chair. He sighed hugely. 'Daisy Mae.
Now I know what it must feel like to be a mother.'

The next morning John Lee woke slowly and stretched until his
muscles popped. He looked at the ceiling, but there was no faded
water-stained paper, only neat white tiles with an embossed flower
in the center of each. He slid to the side of the bed and felt the silk
sheets flow like water across his skin. He went to the bathroom and
relieved himself, splashing cold water on his face and combing the
tangles out of his hair. He sure needed a haircut. He wondered if he
ought to let it grow long now that he was in Hollywood.

Hollywood.

He'd almost forgotten. He bet Miss Mahan was worried about
him. He sure liked Miss Mahan and a pang of guilt struck him. He
should have told her he wouldn't be back in school this fall,
especially after she was nice enough to come to mamma's funeral
and all. Well, there was nothing he could do now. Mr. Cuttsanger
would tell her—and everybody else—where he was.

He went back to his room and put on his best pair of blue jeans, a
white tee-shirt and his gray sneakers. He wondered where everyone
was. The house was very quiet. He guessed they had both gone to
work. He went out on the back porch—only Pearl called it a
deck—and saw Daisy Mae lying there on a blanket stark naked. He
started to go back in, but Daisy Mae looked up. 'Good morning,
slugabed, you sleep well?'

John Lee fidgeted, trying not to look at Daisy Mae. 'Yeah. Real
good. Where's Pearl?'

'She's at work. Does windows for May Company.'

'Didn't you have to work today at Paramount?'

'Got a few days off. Just finished something called *Wives and*

Lovers. Gonna be a dog. You want some breakfast, or you wanta join me?'

'Uh . . . what're you doin'?' He sure didn't seem to care if anybody saw him naked.

'Gettin' some sun, tryin' to get rid of this fish-belly white.'

'You always do it with . . . uh . . . no clothes on?' You're acting like a hick again, John Lee Peacock. Damnation, he thought.

Daisy Mae chuckled. 'Sure. Otherwise, I'd look like a two-tone Ford. If it embarrasses you, I'll put some clothes on.'

'No,' he protested quickly. 'No, of course it doesn't embarrass me. I think I *will* join you.'

'Okay.' He pointed back over his head without looking. 'There's another blanket there on the chaise.'

John Lee spread the blanket on the porch and pulled his tee-shirt over his head. He pulled off his shoes and socks. Daisy Mae wasn't paying any attention to him. He looked around. The next house up the hill overlooked them, but that was the only one. He didn't see anybody up there. He took a deep breath, slipped off his pants and his shorts, and quickly lay down on his stomach. He might as well get some sun on his back first.

Daisy Mae spoke without looking at him. 'Don't stay in one position more than five minutes, or you'll blister.'

'Okay.' He estimated five minutes had passed, swallowed, and turned over on his back. He looked straight into the eyes of a woman leaning on the railing of the next house up, watching him. He froze. The bottom dropped out of his stomach. Then he jumped up and grabbed his pants. He knew he was acting like an idiot, but he couldn't stop himself. He hopped on one foot, trying to get the pants on, but his toes kept getting in the way. They caught on the crotch and he fell flat on his butt. He managed to wiggle into them, sitting on the floor.

Daisy Mae looked up. 'You sit on a bee or something?'

'No.' He motioned with his head at the woman, afraid to look at her because he knew he was beet red all over.

Daisy Mae looked up, grinned, and waved. 'Hi, Sue.' He didn't do anything to cover himself, didn't seem to care that she saw him.

'Hello, Daisy Mae.' Her voice was husky and amused. 'Who's your bashful friend?'

'John Lee Peacock from Kansas. This is Sue. San Diego Lightfoot Sue.'

Damnation, John Lee thought, I'm acting like a fool, sitting here hunkered up against this shez, as Daisy Mae calls it. Doesn't anyone in Hollywood have a normal name? He forced himself to look up. She was still leaning on the railing, looking at him. Only now she was smiling. She was wearing a paint-stained sweat shirt and blue jeans. Her hair was tied up in a scarf but auburn strands dangled out. She wasn't wearing any make-up that he could see. She was kinda old, he thought, but really very stunning. Her smile was nice. He felt himself smiling back.

'Nothing to be bashful about, John Lee Peacock. I've seen more male privates than you could load in a boxcar.' Her voice was still amused but she wasn't putting him down.

'Maybe so,' he answered, 'but I haven't had any ladies see mine.' His boldness made him start getting red again.

She laughed and he felt goose bumps pop out on his arms. 'You could have a point there, John Lee. How would you like to make a little money?'

'Huh?'

'It's okay,' Daisy Mae said, getting up and wrapping a towel around his waist. 'Sue's an artist. She wants you to pose for her.'

John Lee looked back up at her. 'That's right,' she said. 'I'm as safe as mother's milk.'

'Well, okay, I guess. But you don't need to pay me for something like that.' He got up and kicked his underwear under the chaise.

'Of course I'll pay you. It's very hard work. Come on up.'

'Uh . . . how do I get up there?'

'Go down to the street and come up my steps. Front door's open, come on in. You'll find me.' She smiled again and went out of sight.

He looked at Daisy Mae. 'Will it be all right with Pearl?'

'Sure. We've both posed for her. She's good. Scoot.' Daisy Mae went into the house. John Lee put on his tee-shirt and shoes. He wondered if he should take off his pants and put on his underwear, but decided against it.

He opened her front door and went in as she had told him. She was right about him finding her. The whole house was one big room. A small kitchen was in one corner behind a folding screen. A day bed was against one wall between two bureaus that had been painted yellow. There was a door to a closet and another to a bathroom. There were a couple of tired but comfortable-looking easy chairs, a drafting table with a stool pushed under it, and an easel under a skylight. Pictures were everywhere; some in color, mostly black and white sketches; thumbtacked all over the walls, leaning in stacks against the bureaus, chairs, walls. A big orange cat lay curled in a chair. It opened one eye, gave John Lee the once over, and went back to sleep.

Sue was standing at the easel, frowning at the painting he couldn't see. She had a brush stuck behind one ear and was holding another like a club. 'I'm glad you showed up, John Lee. This thing is going nowhere.' She flipped a cloth over it and leaned it against the wall.

John Lee stared at the pictures. Nearly all of them were of people, most of them naked, though there were a couple of the cat. Some of the people were women but most of them seemed to be men. He spotted a sketch of Pearl and Daisy Mae, leaning against each other naked, looking like a butterfly with one black and one white wing.

She watched him look for a while. 'This is just the garbage. I sell the good stuff. That one of Pearl and Daisy Mae turned out rather well. It's hanging in a gay bar in the Valley. Got eleven hundred for it.'

'Golly.'

'You're right. It was a swindle.'

'Do you . . . ah . . . want me to . . . do you want to paint my picture with my . . . clothes off?' He waved his hand vaguely at some of the nude sketches. Damn his ears!

She didn't seem to notice. 'If you don't mind. Don't worry about it. It'll be a few days yet. Give you a chance to get used to the idea. I want to make some sketches and work on your face for a while.' She came to him and put her hand on his cheek. 'You've got something in your face, John Lee. I don't know . . . what it is. More than simple innocence. I just hope I can capture it. Hold still, I want to feel your bones.' He grinned and it made her smile. 'Makes you feel like a horse up for sale, doesn't it?' She ran her cool fingers over his face, and he didn't want her to ever stop. He closed his eyes.

Suddenly, she caught her fingers in his hair and shook him. She laughed and hugged him against her warm soft breasts. His stomach did a flip-flop. She released him quickly and crossed her arms with her hands under her armpits. She laughed a little nervously. 'You're just like Punkin. Scratch his ears and he'll go to sleep on you.'

'Punkin?'

She pointed at the cat. 'Don't you think he looks remarkably like a pumpkin when he's curled up asleep like that?'

'Yeah.' He laughed.

'Do you want to start now?'

'I guess.'

'Okay. Just sit in that chair and relax.' She pulled the stool from beneath the drafting table and put it in front of the chair. She sat on the stool with her legs crossed, a sketch pad propped on one knee. She lit a cigarette and held it in her left hand while she worked rapidly with a stick of charcoal. 'You can talk if you want to. Tell me about yourself.'

So he did. He told her about Miller's Corners, Hawley, the farm, school, Miss Mahan who also painted but only flowers, Mr. Cuttsanger, his mother, a lot about his mother, not much about his father because he didn't really know very much when you got right down to it. He made her chuckle about Aunt Rose and Aunt Lilah. She kept turning the pages of the sketch pad and starting over. He wanted to see what she was drawing, but he was afraid to move.

She seemed to read his mind. 'You don't have to sit so still, John Lee. Move when you want to.' He changed positions but he still couldn't see. Punkin suddenly leaped in his lap, making him jump. The cat walked up his chest and looked into his eyes. Then he began to purr and curled up with his head under John Lee's chin.

Sue chuckled. 'You are a charmer, John Lee. He treats most people with majestic indifference.' John Lee grinned and stroked the cat. Punkin squirmed in delicious ecstasy. Then John Lee's stomach rumbled.

Sue put the pad down and laughed. 'You poor lamb. I'm starving you to death.' She looked at her watch. 'Good grief, it's two thirty. What do you want to eat?'

'Anything.'

'Anything it is.'

He stood with Punkin curled in his arms, watching her do wonderful things with eggs, ham, green peppers, onions, and buttered toast. He said he loved scrambled eggs; and she laughed and said scrambled eggs indeed, you taste my omelets and you'll be my slave forever. She pulled down a table that folded against the wall, set out the two steaming plates with two glasses of cold milk. He was quite willing to be her slave forever, even without the omelet.

Punkin sat on the floor with his tail curled around his feet, watching them, making short, soft clarinet sounds. She laughed. 'Isn't that pitiful? The cat food's under the sink if you'd like to feed him.'

'Sure.' He tried to pour the cat food into the bowl, but Punkin kept grabbing the box with his claws and sticking his head in it. John Lee sat on the floor having a fit of giggles. God o' mighty, he thought, everything is so wonderfully, marvelously, absolutely perfectly good.

She continued sketching after they did the dishes. He sat in the chair feeling luxuriously content. He smiled.

'May I share it?' Sue asked, almost smiling herself.

'Huh? Oh, nothin'. I was just . . . feeling good.' Then he felt embarrassed. 'You . . . ah . . . been painting pictures very long?'

'Oh, I've dabbled at it quite a while, but I've only been doing it seriously for a couple of years.' She smiled in a funny, wry way. 'I'm just an aging roundheel who decided she'd better find another line of work while she could.'

He didn't know what she was talking about. 'You're not old.'

'I stood on the shore and chunked rocks at the Mayflower.' She sighed. 'I'm forty-five.'

'Golly. I thought you were about thirty.'

She laughed her throaty laugh that made him tingle. 'Honey, at your age everyone between twenty-five and fifty looks alike.'

'I think you're beautiful,' he said and wished he hadn't, but she smiled and he was glad he had.

'Thank you, little lamb. You should have seen me when I was your age.' She stopped drawing and sat with her head to one side, remembering. 'You should have seen me when I was fifteen.' Then she shifted her position on the stool and laughed. 'I was quite a dish—if I do say so myself. We were practically neighbors, you know that?' she said, changing the subject. 'I'm an old Okie from way back. Still can't bear to watch *The Grapes of Wrath*. We came to California in '33 and settled in San Diego. Practically starved to death. My father died in '35, and my mother went back to telling fortunes and having seances—among other things. My father wouldn't let her do it while he was alive.'

'Golly,' he said bug-eyed. 'A real fortune teller?'

'Well,' she said wryly, 'I never thought of it as being very real, but I don't know anymore.' She looked at him speculatively for a moment, then shrugged. 'Whether she was real or not, I don't know but I guess she was pretty good, 'cause there seemed to be plenty of money after that. Then the war started. And if you're twenty-three, in San Diego, during a war, you can make lots of money if you keep your wits about you.' She shifted again on the stool. 'Well, we won't go into that.'

'Where's your mother now?'

'Oh, she's dead . . . I imagine. It was in '45, I think. Yeah, right after V-J Day, I went over for a visit and she wasn't there. Never heard from her again. You know, her house is still there in San Diego. I get a tax bill every year. I don't know why I keep paying it. Guess I'd rather do that than go through all that junk she had accumulated. I was down there a few years ago and went by the place. Everything was still there just as it was; two feet deep in dust, of course. I'm surprised vandals haven't stripped the place, considering what the neighborhood's become. I took a few things as keepsakes, but I didn't hang around long. It's worse than it was when she was there.'

She worked a while in silence, then stopped drawing again and looked at him in a way that made his stomach feel funny. 'If I were twenty and you were twenty . . . you're gonna be a ring-tailed boomer when you're twenty, John Lee.' She suddenly laughed and began drawing. 'If I'm gonna make people older and younger, I might as well make myself fifteen—no point in wasting five years.'

He didn't know what a ring-tailed boomer was, but the way she said it made his ears turn red. Her mentioning San Diego reminded him. 'Why do they call you San Diego Lightfoot Sue?'

'Daisy Mae has a big mouth,' she said wryly. 'I'll tell you about it someday.'

'I sure like Pearl and Daisy Mae,' he said and smiled.

'So do I.'

'Pearl is awfully nice to me.'

'Some people have a cat and some people have a dog.'

He sure wished he knew what people were talking about, at least some of the time.

It seemed to him hardly any time had passed when Pearl sashayed in with a May Co. carton under his arm. 'It is I, Lady Bountiful, come to free the slaves,' he brayed and presented the box to John Lee with a flourish. 'It's a Welcome To California present.'

'Golly.' He took the box gingerly.

'Well, *open* it.' John Lee fumbled at the string while Pearl planted a kiss on Sue's cheek. 'Sugah, you look more like Lauren Bacall every *day!*'

Sue grinned. 'Hello, Pearl. How are you?'

He sighed an elaborate sigh. 'I am *worn* to a frazzle. I've been slaving over a tacky May Company window all day. If they would *only* let me be *cre-a-tive!*'

'Wilshire Boulevard would never survive it.'

John Lee stared at the contents of the box. 'How did you know what size I wore?'

'Daisy Mae has tape measures in her eyeballs.' He made fluttering motions with his hands. 'Well, try them *on.*'

John Lee grinned and hurried to the bathroom with the box. He put it on the side of the tub and went through it. There were pants, a shirt, socks, shoes, and, he was glad to see, underwear. But he had never seen gold underwear and it looked kinda skimpy. He quickly shucked off his clothes and slipped on the gold shorts. Golly, he thought. They fit like his hide, and he kept wanting to pull them up, but that's all there was to them.

The shirt was yellow and soft. He rubbed it on his face, then slipped it over his head. It fit tight around his waist, and the neck was open halfway to his navel. He looked for buttons but there weren't any. The sleeves were long and floppy and had little pearl snaps on the cuffs.

He slipped on the pants, which had alternating dark-brown and light-brown vertical stripes. He was surprised to find that they didn't come any higher than the shorts. He gave them an experimental tug and decided they wouldn't fall off. They were tight almost to the knees and got loose and floppy at the bottom.

He sat on the commode to put on the shoes but stood again to hitch the pants up in back. He slipped on the soft, fuzzy gold socks. The shoes were brown and incredibly shiny. And they didn't even have shoestrings. He stood up, gave the pants a hitch, and looked at himself in the mirror. He couldn't make himself stop grinning.

He opened the bathroom door and walked out, still grinning. Pearl made his eyes go big and round, and Sue leaned against one of the yellow bureaus with her mouth puckered up. John Lee walked nervously to them, the shoes making a thump at every step. 'The pants are a little bit too tight,' he said and didn't know what to do with his hands.

'Oh, sugah, you are *wrong* about that!'

'If he had his hair slicked down with pomade, he'd look like an adagio dancer . . . or something,' Sue said in a flat voice.

Pearl lowered his eyebrows at her, then twirled his finger at John Lee. 'Turn around.'

He turned nervously, worried because Sue didn't seemed pleased.

'John Lee, sugah,' Pearl said in awe, 'you have *got* the *Power!*'

'Pearl. Don't you think you went a little overboard?' Sue put her hand on the back of John Lee's neck. 'If he walked down Hollywood Boulevard in that, he'd have to carry a machine gun.'

'Well!' Pearl swelled up in mock outrage. 'At least they're not *lavender!*'

Sue laughed. John Lee laughed too, but he wasn't exactly sure why. They were saying things he didn't understand again. But he felt an overwhelming fondness for Pearl at that moment. He reached out and shook Pearl's hand. 'Thank you, Pearl. I think the clothes are beautiful.' Then, because he felt Pearl would be pleased, he kissed him on the cheek.

The effect was startling. Pearl's face seemed to turn to putty and went through seven distinct expression changes. His mouth worked like a goldfish and he kept blinking his eyes. Then he pulled himself together and said too loudly, 'Listen, you all. Dinner will be ready in exactly seventy-two minutes. We're having my world-famous sowbelly and chittlin lasagne.' He hurried out, walking too fast.

John Lee was up very early the next morning. Sue opened the door still in her bathrobe. 'I didn't know what time you wanted me to come over,' he said apologetically. 'Did I wake you up?'

Sue smiled and motioned him in. 'Ordinarily, I'm not coordinated enough to tie my shoes before noon, but I woke up about two hours ago ready to go to work. I didn't even take time to dress.' She indicated one wall of the room. 'Check out the gallery while I put the wreck together.'

All the old sketches had been cleared away from the wall. John Lee saw himself thumbtacked in neat rows. 'Golly,' he said, walking slowly down the rows. The sketches were all of his face: some sheets were covered with eyes, laughing, sleepy, dreamy, contemplative; others with mouths, smiling, grinning, pouting, pensive. There were noses and ears and combinations. He recognized some of the full-face sketches: this one was when he was talking about his mother; that one when he was petting Punkin; that one when he was telling of Aunt Rose and Aunt Lilah; another when he sat in rapt attention, listening to Sue.

She emerged from the bathroom dressed much as she had been the day before except that she wore a little make-up and her hair fell through the scarf, hanging long and fluffy down her back. John Lee thought she was absolutely gorgeous. 'What do you think,' she asked tentatively, not quite smiling.

He couldn't think of anything to say that wasn't obvious to the eye, and so he just grinned in extreme pleasure.

She smiled happily. 'I think I've caught you, John Lee. I really feel good about it. You're just what I've been needing.'

'What're you gonna draw today?'

She indicated a large canvas in position on the easel. 'I'm ready to start, if you are.'

Oh, Lord, he thought, just don't turn red. 'Yeah. I guess so.'

'You can keep your pants on for a while, if it'll make you more comfortable. I'll work on your head and torso.' She was businesslike, not seeming to notice his nervousness. It made him feel a little better.

He took a deep breath. 'No . . . I might as well get it over with.' She nodded and began puttering around with paints and turpentine, not looking at him, without seeming to be deliberately not looking at him. He pulled the tee-shirt over his head and wondered what to do with it. Quit stalling, he admonished, and slipped off his sneakers and socks. He looked at her but she was still ignoring him. He quickly pulled off his pants and shorts. He stood there feeling as if there were a cyclone in his stomach. 'Well,' he said, 'I'm ready.'

She turned and looked at him as if she had seen him naked every day of his life. 'You have absolutely nothing to be embarrassed about, John Lee.'

'Well,' he said, 'well . . .'

'What's the matter?'

'I don't know what to do with my *hands!*' Then he couldn't keep from laughing and she laughed with him. 'What do you want me to do?'

'Let's see . . .' She moved one of the chairs under the light. 'Lean against the chair. I want you relaxed . . .'

'I'll try,' he chuckled.

She smiled. 'I want you relaxed and completely innocent of your nudity. Sort of the *September Morn* effect.'

'You're asking a lot.' He leaned against the chair, trying to look innocent.

She gave a throaty laugh and shook her head. 'You look more like a chicken thief. Don't try too hard. Just relax and be comfortable, like you were yesterday.'

'I had my clothes on yesterday.'

'I know. You'll do okay as soon as you get used to it.'

'I still don't know what to do with my hands.'

'Don't do anything with them. Just forget 'em; let them find their own position. I know it's not easy. Just forget I'm here. Pretend you're in the woods completely alone. You've just been swimming in a little lake, and now you're relaxing in the sun, leaning against a warm rock. Try to picture it.'

'Okay, I'll try.'

'You're not thinking about anything, just resting, feeling the sun on your body.' She watched him. A pucker of concentration appeared over his nose. He shifted his hips slightly to get more comfortable, and his fidgety hands finally came to rest at his sides. His diaphragm moved slowly as his breathing became softer. The frown gradually disappeared from his face, and the quality she couldn't put a name to took its place. God, she thought, it brought back memories she had thought were put away forever. She felt like a giddy young girl.

'That's it, John Lee,' she said very softly, trying not to disturb him. She picked up a stick of charcoal and began to work rapidly. A pleased smile flickered across his lips and then disappeared. 'Beautiful, John Lee, beautiful. Don't close your eyes; watch the sun reflecting on the water.'

She got the basic form the way she wanted it in charcoal, then began squeezing paint from tubes onto a palette. She applied the base colors quickly, almost offhandedly. After about fifteen minutes she said, 'When you get tired, let me know and we'll take a break.'

'No. I'm fine.'

After another half hour she saw his thumb twitch. 'If you're not tired,' she said, putting the palette down, 'I am. Would you like some coffee?'

'Yeah,' he said without moving. 'Are you sure I can get back in the same position again?'

'I'm sure.' She tossed him her bathrobe and he put it on. 'Do a few knee bends and get the kinks out.' She poured two cups of coffee from the electric percolator. 'I told you it was hard work.'

He grinned and stretched his arms forward, rolling the muscles in his shoulders. 'I'm not tired.'

She handed him a cup. 'You've been warned.' She opened the back door when she heard a plaintive cry from outside. Punkin strolled in and looked up at her, demanding attention. She picked him up and he started purring loudly.

John Lee found it easy to keep the same position the rest of the morning. Sue had made him as comfortable as she could because of his inexperience. She worked steadily with concentration. He missed the easy chatter of the day before, but he didn't want to disturb her. They took periodic breaks, though she sometimes became so engrossed she forgot. Then she would admonish him gently for not reminding her. When they broke for lunch, she made him do knee bends and push-ups and then massaged his back and shoulders with green rubbing alcohol.

Daisy Mae strolled in with a foil-covered Pyrex dish. 'You didn't do that when Pearl and I posed for you,' he said with feigned huffiness and slipped the dish into the oven.

'Hello, Daisy Mae,' John Lee grinned, putting on the robe. 'Look at the sketches.'

'Hello, John Lee. I knew Sue would get so absorbed she'd forget to feed you. So I brought the leftover lasagne.' He looked over the sketches, critically, with his fingers theatrically stroking his chin. 'I think the girl shows some promise, though I see years of study ahead.'

Sue kissed him on the cheek and began setting the table for three. Daisy Mae sprawled in a chair like a wilting lily. 'God!' he grunted. 'I got a call from Paramount this morning. I start back to work Thursday. We're doing a *west*-ern. On lo-*ca*-tion. My *God*. In *Arizona!* Centipedes! Tarantulas! Scorpions! Rattlesnakes! Sweaty starlets! If I'm not back in five weeks, send the Ma-*rines!*'

Sue laughed. 'You can console yourself with thoughts of all those butch cowboys.'

'Darling,' he said, arching his wrist at her, 'some of those cowboys are about as butch as Pamela Tiffin. I could tell you stories . . .'

'Don't bother. I've heard most of them.'

'I haven't,' John Lee piped in brightly.

Sue started to say something, but Daisy Mae beat her to it. 'Someday, John Lee. You're much too young to lose *all* your illusions.'

When they had eaten, Sue thanked him for bringing the lasagne and shooed him out. He started to peek under the cloth covering the painting, but she slapped his hand. 'You know better than that.'

'Can John Lee bunk over here tomorrow night? I'm giving myself a going-away party before I'm exiled to the burning deserts, and it's liable to last all night.'

She stood very still for a moment. Then she nodded with a jerk of her head. 'Of course.' Daisy Mae waltzed out with his Pyrex dish. Sue looked after him for a moment, then at John Lee sitting bewildered on the day bed. She gave him a quick nervous smile. 'You ready?'

He took off the bathrobe, hardly feeling embarrassed at all, and took his place, bringing back the woods, the lake, and the warm rock, but needing them only for a moment to get started.

At four thirty she covered the painting and began washing the brushes. She had said hardly anything at all since Daisy Mae left, giving him only an occasional soft-voiced direction. He put his clothes on and went to her. 'Is it turning out the way you'd hoped?'

Her eyes met his. He saw sadness in them and something that had gotten lost. 'Yes,' she said almost unaudibly. Then she smiled. 'You're a joy to paint, John Lee. Now, run along before Pearl comes traipsing in. I'd rather not have company this evening. Be over bright and early, and I think we'll finish it tomorrow.'

Punkin stopped him on the steps, wanting to be petted. He picked up the cat and glanced back to see Sue watching him through the window. She turned away quickly.

The painting was completed at three p.m. the next afternoon. Sue stood back from it and looked at John Lee, smiling. He went to her hesitantly, almost fearfully, still naked, and looked at it. 'Golly,' he breathed. When she painted a nude, she really painted everything. He felt the heat starting at his ears and flowing downward. He was almost used to being naked in front of her, but it was an astonishing shock to *see* himself being naked.

She laughed fondly. 'John Lee, you're a regular traffic light.'

'No, I'm not,' he muttered and got even redder.

Suddenly, her arms were around him, hugging him tightly to her. He felt electricity bouncing in the bottom of his stomach. He threw his arms around her and wanted to be enveloped by her. 'John Lee, my little lamb,' she whispered in his ear, bending her head because she was an inch taller, 'do you like it?'

'Yes!' he breathed, with that peculiar pain in the back of his throat again. 'Oh, yes.'

He shifted his head slightly so he could see. The painting was done in pale sun-washed colors. He leaned against a suggestion of something white which might have been a large rock. It was everything she had said she wanted, and more. He seemed totally innocent of clothing, so completely comfortable was he in his nudity. His body was relaxed, but there was no lethargy in it. There was something slightly supernatural about the John Lee in the painting, as if perhaps he were a fawn or a wood sprite, definitely an impression of a forest creature. The various shades of pale green in the background implied a forest, and there was a dappling of leaf shadows on his shoulder and chest—but only a suggestion. However, these were unimportant. The figure dominated the painting, executed in fine detail, like a Raphael. The face was innocent, totally uncorrupted by worldly knowledge. But there was a quality in it even purer than simple innocence. The eyes were lost in a reverie.

'Do I look like that?' he asked, slightly overwhelmed.

'Well . . .' she said with a husky chuckle, 'yes, you do. Although I will have to admit I idealized you somewhat.'

'Is it okay if I bring Pearl and Daisy Mae over to see it?' he asked with growing excitement. 'Pearl was supposed to come home at noon today to help with the party. Only she . . . I mean he, calls it a Druid ritual.'

She laughed and released him. 'All right.'

He raced happily to the door then skidded to a halt. He hurried back, grinning sheepishly, and picked up his pants. He put them on, hopping on one foot, then out the door, clattering down the steps. She looked at the empty doorway for a moment, then rubbed at her eyes but was unable to stop the tears.

'Hell!' she said out loud. 'Oh, hell!'

John Lee came over from the party about ten o'clock dressed in his new clothes and carrying a Lufthansa flight bag Pearl had packed for him. He flopped into one of the chairs, grinning. Sue was in the other, reading. She looked at him speculatively. Punkin leaped lightly from her lap and stretched mightily, his rear end high in the air, his chin against the floor, and his toes splayed. Then he hopped into John Lee's lap. Stroking the cat and still grinning, he met her eyes. They both burst into a fit of giggles.

'John Lee, you have *no* staying power,' she choked out between gasps of laughter.

He got himself under control, gulping air. 'I'd much rather be over here with you.'

'I hope Pearl gave you a whip and a chair to go with those clothes.'

'No, but he warned me to stay out of corners and, above all, bedrooms.'

There was a light tap on the door. 'I've been expecting this,' she muttered. 'Come on in!'

The door opened, and a pale, slim, good-looking young man wafted in like the queen of Rumania inspecting the hog pens. 'Hello,' he sighed, not quite holding out his hand to be kissed. 'Pearl was telling us about the painting you did of John Lee. May I see it?' He looked at John Lee and smiled anemically.

'Of course.' Sue got up and turned the light on over the easel. A shriek of laughter drifted over from next door. The young man strolled to the painting and stood motionless for a full two minutes staring at it.

Then he sighed. 'Pearl is so lucky. My last one ran off with my stereo, my Polaroid, and knocked out three fillings.'

'That's . . . ah . . . too bad,' she said, valiantly not smiling.

'Yes,' he said and sighed again. 'I'd like to buy it.'

'It's not for sale.'

'I'll give you a thousand.'

She shook her head.

'Two thousand.'

'Sorry.'

He sighed again as if he expected nothing from life but an endless series of defeats. 'Oh, well. Thank you for letting me see it.'

'You're extremely welcome.'

He drifted to the door like a wisp of fog, turned, gave John Lee a wan smile, and departed. They both stared at the closed door.

'I feel as if I just played the last act of *La Traviata*,' Sue said in a stunned voice.

'If I remember correctly,' John Lee said, 'that was Cow-Cow.'

She lifted the painting from the easel. 'There's only one thing to do if we don't want a parade through here all night. Be back shortly.' She left, taking the painting with her.

When she returned half an hour later, he was dozing. 'The showing was an unqualified success. I was offered se-ven thou-sand dol-lars for it. You never saw so many erotic fantasies hanging out. It was like waving a haunch of beef at a bunch of half-starved tigers.' She put the painting back on the easel and stood looking at it. 'It *is* good, though, isn't it, John Lee?' She sounded only partially convinced. 'It really is good.' She looked at him, sprawled in the chair, half asleep, smiling happily at her. 'Well,' she laughed, 'neither the artist nor the model are qualified judges. And that crowd at Pearl's could only see a beautiful child with his privates exposed.'

She sat on the arm of the chair, putting her hand on the side of his face. He closed his eyes and moved his face against her hand the way Punkin would do. 'You're such a child, John Lee,' she said softly, feeling her eyes getting damp. 'Your body may fool people for a while, but up here,' she caught her fingers in his hair, 'up here, you're an innocent, trusting, guileless child. And I think you may break my heart.' She closed her eyes, trying to hold back the tears, afraid she was making a fool of herself.

He looked up at her, feeling things he had never felt before, wanting things he had never wanted before. Perhaps if he hadn't been floating in the dreamlike area between wakefulness and sleep, his natural shyness might have prevented him. He slipped his arms slowly around her neck and pulled her gently to him. He felt her tense as if about to pull away, then her lips were like butterfly wings against his. She lay across him with her face buried in his neck. He stroked her hair and brushed his lips against her cheek.

'Is this what you want, John Lee?' she asked, her voice unsteady. 'Is this what you really want?'

'Yes,' he answered. 'You're all I want.'

'You're sure you're not just feeling sorry for an old lady?' she said shakily, trying to sound if she were making a joke, but not succeeding completely.

He held her tighter. 'I love you, San Diego Lightfoot Sue.'

She stood up, wiping at her eyes with trembling fingers. 'Daisy Mae and his big mouth,' she said, half laughing and half crying. John Lee stood up also, giving the striped pants a hitch in the back. 'Oh, John Lee,' she said, hugging him to her, 'take off those awful clothes.'

He stood on tiptoe to kiss her because his mouth came only to her chin. He removed the clothes, feeling no embarrassment at all. She turned out the light and locked the door before undressing, feeling embarrassment herself for the first time in nearly thirty years. She turned back the cover of the day bed, and they lay in the warm night, listening to the shrieks of strained laughter from Pearl's, feeling, exploring, each trying to touch every part of the other's body with every part of his own. Then, she showed him what to do and kissed him when he was clumsy.

They lay together, drowsily. Flamenco music drifted over from the party next door. Sue had her arms around John Lee, her breasts pressed against his back, her face against his neck. 'John Lee?'

'Mmmm?'

'John Lee, when you're twenty . . . have you thought, I'll be fifty?'

'I love you, Sue. It doesn't matter to me.'

She was silent for a moment. 'Perhaps it doesn't now. You're too young to know the difference, and I still have a few vestiges of my looks left. But in a few years you'll want a girl your own age, and in a few years I'll be an old woman.' He started to protest, but she put her fingers on his lips, brushing them with feathery touches. 'Your lips are like velvet, John Lee,' she whispered. He opened his mouth slightly and touched her fingers with his tongue. Then she clamped her arms around him and began weeping on his shoulder. 'My God, John Lee! I don't want to be like your favorite aunt, or even your mother! I don't want to see you married to some empty-headed girl, some pretty *young* girl, having your babies like a brood sow, living in a tract house in Orange County. I want to be the one to have your babies, but I'm too old . . .'

He twisted in her arms to face her and stopped her words with his mouth. The second time, she showed him how to make it last longer, how to make it better, and he was very adept. He fell asleep in her arms where she held him like a teddy bear, but she lay awake for many hours, making a decision.

The next morning, he moved his things from Pearl's to Sue's.

When he had gone, Pearl began to sob, large tears rolling down his face. His hands clutched at each other like graceful black spiders. Daisy Mae put down the glass of tomato juice with the raw egg and Tabasco he had made for his hangover and took Pearl in his arms.

'Oh, Pearl, you knew it would happen. Just like it always happens,' he soothed.

'But John Lee was different from the others,' he forced out between heaving sobs.

'Yes, he was. But he's just next-door. He's still our friend. We can see him anytime.'

'But it's not the same. Sue will be taking care of him, not me! Oh, Daisy Mae,' he wailed, 'if this is what it's like to lose a child, I don't want to be a mother any more!'

Sue began a new painting that morning. 'I want you like you were last night,' she told John Lee, 'sitting all asprawl in the chair, half asleep, with Punkin in your lap, but *not* in those same clothes.' They went through his meager wardrobe. She selected a pair of khaki-colored jeans and gave him one of her short-sleeve sweat shirts. She showed him how to sit. 'Leave your shoes off. I have a foot fetish.' She ran her fingernails quickly across the bottom of his foot. His leg jerked and he grabbed her, giggling, and pulling her in his lap. She submitted happily to his kisses for a moment, then pulled away.

'Okay,' she laughed, 'calm yourself. We've got work to do.'

'Yes, ma'am,' he said primly, striking a pose and beaming at her.

Thank God, she thought, he doesn't seem to have any regrets.

'My *Gawd!*' Pearl shrieked, seeing the new painting for the first time. He bulged his eyes and hugged himself. '*Sue!* That's the most erotic thing I've seen in my *life!* It's practically porno-*graphic!*' If I look at it any longer, I'm gonna embarrass myself.' He turned away dramatically and saw John Lee grinning and blushing.

'I embarrass myself a little with that one,' Sue admitted. 'Talk about erotic fantasies.'

The painting was in dark brooding colors, but a light from somewhere fell across John Lee, sitting deep in the chair, one bare foot tucked under him and the other dangling. One hand lay on his thigh and the other negligently stroked the orange cat in his lap. His face was sleepy and sensual. His eyes looked directly at you.

They were the eyes of an innocent fawn, but they were also the eyes of a stag in rut.

'You're not . . . ah . . . gonna show it to a bunch of people, are you?' John Lee asked tentatively.

When he woke the next morning, the bed beside him was empty. He rubbed the sleep from his eyes and unfolded the note lying on her pillow. 'John Lee, my love,' it read in her masculine scrawl, 'I had to go to San Diego for the day and didn't want to wake you. I'll be back tonight late. Sue.'

He was asleep when she came in. She sat on the edge of the bed and moved her hand lightly across his chest. 'John Lee. Wake up, honey.'

He squirmed on the bed. 'Sue?' he mumbled without opening his eyes. He turned over on his stomach, burying his head, fighting wakefulness.

She pulled back the covers and slapped him lightly on his bare bottom. 'Wake up. I want to do another painting. Get dressed.'

'I'm too sleepy. Leave your number and I'll call you.'

'Okay, smarty,' she laughed, 'you've got thirty seconds before I get out the ice cubes.'

'White slaver,' he grinned, sitting up and kissing her.

'Where did you hear that?'

'I spent the day with Pearl and Daisy Mae.'

She kissed him and stood up. 'Come on, get a move on.' She put a new canvas on the easel. 'Why wasn't Pearl at work? And I thought Daisy Mae had left for, my God, Arizona.'

'Today is Saturday,' he said and went into the bathroom.

'So it is. I sorta lose track.' She began squeezing black and white paint from tubes.

John Lee washed his face and ran a comb through his hair. He came out of the bathroom and put on the same clothes he had worn for the last painting. 'These okay?' She nodded. 'Shoes or foot fetish?' he grinned.

She wrinkled her nose at him. 'Shoes.'

He put on his Sunday shoes rather than the sneakers. 'Daisy Mae doesn't leave for a couple of weeks yet. They're having fittings and things. Wardrobe gave her . . . him an 1865 lady's riding skirt with a *zipper* on the side. Any *welder* in *Duluth* would know better than that. What do you want me to do?'

'Just stand there.' Her voice was tense and hurried.

'Stand?' he groaned. 'Don't you want to do another one of me sitting down?' He snapped his fingers. 'Do one of me asleep in bed!' She didn't laugh at his joke, and so he stood where she indicated. She began, using only black and white. 'Don't artists need the northern light, or something?' he asked hopefully, pointing to the dark skylight.

She smiled. 'That's just an excuse artists have been using for the last few thousand years when they didn't feel like working. Be patient with me, John Lee. You can sleep all day tomorrow. I have to go back to San Diego.'

'Can't I go with you?'

'No, John Lee.' Her voice was so serious that he didn't say anything else.

She finished just before dawn. He was about to fall asleep standing, and so she undressed him and put him to bed. He put his arms around her and kissed her, wanting her to stay a little while. 'No,' she said, running her fingers through his hair, 'you're too sleepy. I'll be back in a few days and we can stay in bed for a week.'

He smiled and his eyelids began to droop. 'That'll be nice.'

'Yes, my little lamb, very nice.' She kissed him gently on the mouth. He was asleep before she got out the door.

He woke up late Sunday afternoon and immediately looked at the painting. It wasn't as well done as the other two, he thought. It had a hurried look. It was also in black and white. The John Lee in the painting was just standing there, his arms hanging at his sides, looking at you from beneath lowered brows. John Lee looked at the floor where he had been standing when he posed, but nothing was there. Yet, in the painting, there were lines on the floor. He was standing within a pentagram. And he looked different; he looked older, at least five years older, at least twenty.

Tuesday night Pearl and Daisy Mae took him to Graumann's Chinese where he thought the movie was great and had a wonderful time standing in the footprints, though he had never heard of most of the people who had made them. After the movie they went to a Chinese restaurant where he ate Chinese food for the first time. He didn't really like it, but he told Pearl he did because it made him happy. It was nearly midnight when he got back to Laurel Canyon. Pearl wanted him to stay in his old room, but he said he'd better not because Sue might come home during the night and he wanted to be there.

He went up the wooden steps feeling incredibly content. If Sue were only there. Punkin came down the banister like a tightrope walker, making little soft sounds of greeting. John Lee picked him up and made crooning noises. The cat butted his head against John

Lee's chin, making him chuckle. He carried Punkin into the house and turned on the light.

His head exploded. His legs wouldn't hold him up any longer, and he fell to his knees, dropping the cat. There was something white beside him, but he couldn't make his eyes focus. He thought he heard a voice, but he wasn't sure because of the wind screaming through his head. The white thing grabbed him and pulled him to his feet. It shouted more words at him, but he couldn't understand what they were. Something crashed into his face. The fog cleared a little. There was a man dressed in white, holding the front of his shirt. He could smell the sour whiskey on his breath. He slapped John Lee again and shoved him against the wall, but he managed to stay on his feet.

The wind was dying in his head. He heard the man's angry words. 'Jesus Christ!' he said, looking at the picture of John Lee sitting in the chair. He took a knife from his pocket and slashed through the canvas.

'Stop it!' John Lee croaked and took an unsteady step in the man's direction.

He whirled, pointing the knife at John Lee. 'Jesus Christ!' he said again, in amazement. 'You're just a little kid! She threw me over for a little kid!' The man's face seemed to collapse as he lunged at John Lee with the knife. John Lee grabbed his arm, but the man was far too strong. Then the man stepped on Punkin's tail. The cat screeched and sank his claws into the man's leg. He bawled and fell against John Lee. They both went to the floor, the man on top, his face beside John Lee's.

'Jesus God,' the man whispered in bewilderment. Then his breath crept out in an adenoidal whine and didn't go back in again. John Lee squirmed from beneath him. The man rolled onto his back. The knife handle stuck straight up in his chest, blood already clinging to it. John Lee tried to get to his feet but could only make it to his knees. He saw Pearl and Daisy Mae run in, but there was something very wrong with them. They floated slowly through the air, running toward him but getting farther away. Their mouths moved but only honking sounds came out. Then the floor hit him in the face.

The first thing John Lee felt was someone clutching his hand. He opened his eyes and they felt sticky. Pearl's tense and worried face leaned over him, smiling tentatively. 'Pearl?' His face hurt and his mouth wouldn't work properly. He sounded as if he were talking with a mouth full of cotton.

'Don't try to talk, John Lee, sugah,' Pearl said anxiously,

'You're in the hospital. They said you had a mild concussion. I was scared to death. You've been unconscious for ages. This is *Thursday.*'

John Lee put his hand to his face and felt bandages on his mouth and a compress under his lip. 'What happened,' he had to swallow to get the words out, 'happened to my mouth?' It hurt to talk.

'You got a split lip. It's all purple and swelled up. But don't sweat it, sugah. It makes you look ve-ry sex-y.'

John Lee grinned but stopped when it hurt too much. 'Is Sue back?'

'She sat with you all night. I made her go home and sleep. They put you in a tacky ward, but Sue had you moved to this nice private room.'

'The man . . .' He tried hard to remember what happened. 'The man . . .'

'He's dead, sugah. You never saw so many police cars and ambulances and red lights. I don't know what they're gonna do, John Lee.' Pearl was distraught.

Sue came in. 'Don't upset him Pearl. Everything will be all right.' She smiled brightly, and John Lee felt everything would be. 'How are you feeling, little lamb?'

'Awful,' he groaned and tried to laugh, but it hurt too much.

Pearl gave his arm a pat and said, 'I'd better get back to work before May Company fires my little black fanny. Bye, sugah.'

'Bye, Pearl.' Pearl left with a big grin. Sue sat in the chair he had vacated. She took John Lee's hand and held it to her face.

'I'm so sorry,' she said as if in pain.

He wanted to bring back her bright smile. 'You're looking particularly beautiful today.' He had never seen her dressed up before. She wore a silk suit in soft green, her auburn hair loose and long.

She did smile. 'Thank you—and thank Playtex, Maidenform, and Miss Clairol. You look . . . pretty awful.' But she said it as if she didn't mean it.

'Pearl said I looked ve-ry sex-y.'

She grinned and then her face was serious. 'John Lee, are you lucid enough to listen and understand what I have to say?' He nodded. 'All right. There'll be a . . . hearing . . . or something in a few days, when you're feeling better, with the juvenile authorities. You won't be in any trouble, because they know Jocko attacked you. They know it was an accident . . .'

'Who was he?' he interrupted.

She looked at him for a moment. 'Someone I used to know,' she said softly.

'Did you love him? Was he your lover?' He didn't know if he was saying it right. He wanted to know, but he also wanted her to know that he didn't care.

'They're not exactly the same thing, but, yes, to both.' She didn't look at him.

'You gave him up for me,' he said in wonder, loving her so much it hurt.

She looked at him then and smiled, but there was a funny look in her eyes. 'I'd give up most anything for you, John Lee.'

The next couple of weeks were a blur. A bunch of people talked to him: men in blue suits and tight-faced women in gray. He told them everything that happened, and they went away to be replaced by others, but none of them would let him see Sue again. There was one lady he liked, who said she was a judge. He told her that his grandfather was a judge but he died a long time ago. She asked him about everything and he told her. She had a kind voice and made the others behave the way Miss Mahan would.

'But, Your Honor,' one of the men said, 'this child has killed a drunken sailor in a knife fight over a prostitute!'

The judge laughed pleasantly. 'Really, Mr. Maley, there's no need for exaggeration. You're not addressing a jury. John was merely protecting himself when attacked. The man's death resulted when he fell on his own knife.'

'You can't deny he's been living with a known prostitute. I wouldn't be surprised if she hasn't seduced him.'

'Please, Mr. Maley,' the judge frowned, displeased, 'don't speak that way in front of the child.'

'You saw those paintings! Disgusting!'

The judge stood up and began putting on her coat. 'Artists have been painting nudes for several thousand years, Mr. Maley. You should see the collection in the Vatican. And these are very good paintings. I made the artist an offer for the nude myself. Come along, John. I'll take you to dinner. Good evening, gentlemen.'

Dwayne came to see him one day, but John Lee would never have recognized him. He hadn't seen him since he went away to the army seven years before. Dwayne was twenty-nine, big and good-looking like all the Peacock men. He shook hands with John Lee, saying little, and went away after talking to the judge.

Aunt Rose and her husband flew out from Hawley. She touched him a lot and clucked a lot. Of course, she'd *like* to take care of him, him being the youngest son of her late sister and all, but the way things were, the economy and the cost of living and all, she just didn't see how she could.

It was a terrible thing, her sister marrying into the Peacock family, such an unfortunate family. Poor Grace Elizabeth's husband had died the same day she was buried, the very day John Lee had left on the bus. He had fallen off the tractor and been run over by his own plow. He had crawled almost all the way to the house before he bled to death. Such a tragic family, the Peacocks. Her sister had lost six of her children, five of them in infancy and poor Wash, Jr.

They had tracked him down in Oklahoma because the farm was his now; or, she should say, they had tracked down his wife; or, she should say, his ex-wife. Wash, Jr., had been killed six years ago when a pipe fell off a rig and crushed his skull. His wife hadn't even notified the family. Then she married a Mexican driller from Texas and was living in Tulsa, but what could you expect from one of them trashy O'Dell girls. It was a good thing she had had none of Wash, Jr.'s children, just three stillbirths, because she had no claim on the family at all now. Of course, she had two fat brown babies by her new husband, but you know how Mexicans are: like rabbits.

Dwayne hadn't wanted the farm. He just told them to sell it and send him the money. Dwayne was the logical person to take John Lee, being his closest kin. Her sister, Lilah, was in no shape to take care of him. If Dwayne couldn't, then she didn't know what would happen to the poor thing, him living with a prostitute and all.

Aunt Rose and her husband flew back to Hawley.

The judge told him how sorry she was, but if one of his relatives didn't assume custody, as a minor he would have to be declared a ward of the state. But it wouldn't be too bad. He'd have a nice place to live, could finish school, and would have lots of other boys his own age. He asked her why he couldn't live with Sue, but she said it was out of the question and wouldn't discuss it further.

But Dwayne did assume custody, and John Lee moved into his brother's small apartment on Beachwood near Melrose. 'Half the money from the sale of the farm is rightfully yours,' Dwayne said, dressing for work. 'You'll have to go to school this fall. The judge said so. Other than that, your time is your own. But you're not supposed to see that woman again.' He showed John Lee how to turn the couch into a bed and then left for work. He was a bartender at a place on Highland and worked from six until it closed at two in the morning.

John Lee caught the bus to Melrose and Vine and rode to

Hollywood and Highland. He took a taxi to the house in Laurel Canyon. Sue wasn't at home and he couldn't find Punkin. The three paintings had been framed and were hanging. She had repaired the damaged one. No other paintings were in sight. Everything had been pushed against the walls, leaving most of the floor bare. There were blue chalk marks on the bare boards that had been hastily and inadequately rubbed out. The room smelled oddly.

He found an envelope on the kitchen table with his name on it. He removed the folded piece of notepaper. 'John Lee, my little lamb,' it read, 'I knew you would come, although they told us we mustn't see each other again. You must stay away for a while, John Lee. Only a little while, then it won't matter what they say. There'll be nothing they can do. I love you. Sue.'

Pearl wasn't at home either, and so he went back to Dwayne's apartment, watched television for a while, took a bath, and went to bed on the convertible sofa. He didn't know when Dwayne came in about two thirty.

Dwayne always slept until nearly noon. John Lee found little to talk to him about, and Dwayne seemed to prefer no conversation at all. John Lee watched television a lot, went to many movies, and waited for Sue.

He fell asleep in front of the television a few days later and was awakened by Dwayne and the man who was with him. Dwayne frowned at him and the man smiled nervously. The man said something to Dwayne, but he shook his head and led the man into the bedroom, closing the door. John Lee went to bed and didn't know when the man left.

The next morning he looked into the bedroom. Dwayne was sprawled on the bed, naked, still asleep. A twenty dollar bill lay beside him, partially under his hip. John Lee closed the door and fixed breakfast.

Dwayne came in while he was washing the dishes. He didn't say anything for a while, fixing a cup of instant coffee. He sat at the table in his underwear, sipping the coffee. John Lee continued with the dishes, not looking at him. Then he felt Dwayne's eyes on him and he turned. 'I don't want you to think I'm queer,' Dwayne said flatly. 'I don't do anything, just lay there. If those guys want to pay me good money, it's no skin off my nose.' He turned back to his coffee.

John Lee hung up the dishtowel to dry. 'I understand,' he said, but he wasn't sure that he did. 'It's all right with me.'

Dwayne didn't answer but went on sipping coffee as if John Lee weren't there. He made sure, from then on, he was asleep before Dwayne came home.

Sue called a few nights later. He had never heard her voice over the phone, but it sounded different: brighter, less throaty, younger. 'Come over, John Lee, my little lamb,' she laughed gleefully. 'I'm ready. Come over for the showing.'

The taxi had to stop a block away because of the police cars and fire trucks. John Lee ran terrified through the milling crowd, but when he reached Sue's house there was nothing to see. The rickety wooden steps went up the hill for about twenty feet and ended in midair. There was nothing beyond them, only a rectangle of bare earth where the house had been. But nothing else, not even the concrete foundation.

He felt a touch on his arm. He whirled to stare wide-eyed at Pearl. He couldn't speak, his throat was frozen. His heart was pounding too hard and he couldn't breathe. Pearl took his arm and led him into the house where he had spent his first night in Hollywood.

Pearl gave him a sip of brandy which burned his throat and released the muscles. 'What happened? Where's Sue?' he asked, afraid to get an answer.

'I don't know,' Pearl said without any trace of corn pone accent. He seemed on the verge of hysteria himself. 'There was a fire . . .'

'A fire?' he asked, uncomprehending.

'I think it was a fire . . .' Pearl nervously dropped the brandy bottle. He picked it up, ignoring the stain on the carpet.

'Where's Sue?'

'She . . . she was in the house. I heard her scream,' he said rapidly, not looking at John Lee.

John Lee didn't feel anything. His body was frozen and numb. Then, he couldn't help himself. He began to bawl like a baby. It was all slipping away. He could feel the good things escaping his fingers.

Pearl sat beside him on the purple fur chair and tried to comfort him. 'She was over there all evening, singing to herself. I could hear her, she was very happy. I went over but she wouldn't let me in. She said I knew better than to look at an artist's work before it was finished. She said anyway it was a private showing for you. I didn't hear her singing after that, and then, a little while ago, I heard a noise like thunder or an explosion. I looked over, and there was a bright green light in the house, like it was burning on the inside, but not like fire either. I heard her scream. It was an awful, terrible scream. There was another voice, a horrible gloating voice,

I couldn't understand. Then the whole house began to glow with that same green light. It got brighter and brighter, but there was no heat from it. Then it went away and the house wasn't there anymore.'

Pearl got up and handed John Lee an envelope. 'I found this on the deck. She must have tossed it down earlier.' John Lee took the envelope with his name on it. He recognized her handwriting, but it was more hurried and scrawled than usual. He opened it and read the short note.

He went back to school that fall and lived with Dwayne. He said his name was Johnny, because John Lee was home and Sue. He met a lot of girls who wanted him, but they were pallid and dull after Sue. He went with them and slept with them but was unable to feel anything for them. He never turned down any man who propositioned him either, and there were many. He didn't care about the money, he only needed someone to relieve the pressures that built up in him. It didn't make any difference, man or woman. He let lonely middle-aged women keep him, but he never found what he was looking for.

By the time he was eighteen he had grown a couple of inches and had filled out. He moved from the apartment on Beachwood and got a place of his own. He never saw Dwayne again.

The envelope with his name on it was soiled and frayed from much handling. He read it every night. 'John Lee, my little lamb,' it read. 'I tried very hard, so very hard. I thought I had succeeded but something is going wrong. I can feel it. I wish you could have seen me when I was fifteen, John Lee. I wish you could have seen me when when I was fifteen. I'm afraid.' It was unsigned.

SOONER OR LATER OR NEVER NEVER

Gary Jennings

The Anula tribe of Northern Australia associate the dollar-bird with rain, and call it the rain-bird. A man who has the bird for his totem can make rain at a certain pool. He catches a snake, puts it alive into the pool, and after holding it under water for a time takes it out, kills it, and lays it down by the side of the creek. Then he makes an arched bundle of grass stalks in imitation of a rainbow, and sets it up over the snake. After that all he has to do is to sing over the snake and the mimic rainbow; *sooner or later the rain will fall.*'

—Sir James Frazer
The Golden Bough

The Rev. Orville Dismey
Dean of Missionary Vocations
Southern Primitive Protestant Seminary
Grobian, Virginia

Most Reverend Sir:

It has been quite a long time since we parted, but the attached Frazer quotation should help you to remember me—Crispin Mobey, your erstwhile student at dear old SoPrim. Since it occurred to me that you may have heard only a sketchy account of my activities in Australia, this letter will constitute my full report.

I should especially like to refute anything you may have heard, from other Southern Primitive Protestant missionaries in the South Pacific, about my mission to the Anula tribe having been less than an unqualified success. If I helped a little to wean the Anulas away from pagan sorceries—and I did—I feel I have brought them that much closer to the True Word, and my mission was worth its cost.

It was also, for me, the realization of a lifelong dream. Even as a boy in Dreer, Virginia, I saw myself as a future missionary to the backward and unenlightened corners of the world, and comported myself in keeping with that vision. Among the rougher-hewn young men of Dreer I often heard myself referred to, in a sort of awe, as 'that Christly young Mobey.' In all humility, I deplored being set on such a pedestal.

But it was not until I entered the hallowed halls of Southern Primitive Protestant Seminary that my previously vague aspirations found their focus. It was during my senior year at dear old SoPrim that I came upon Sir James Frazer's twelve-volume anthropological epic, *The Golden Bough*, with its account of the poor deluded Anula tribe. I investigated, and discovered to my joy that there still was such a tribe in Australia, that it was just as pitiably devoid of Salvation as it had been when Frazer wrote about it, and that no SoPrim mission had ever been sent to minister to these pathetically unsaved souls. Unquestionably (I said to myself) the time, the need and the man had here conjoined. And I began campaigning for a Board of Missions assignment to the overlooked Anulas.

This did not come easily. The Regents complained that I was dismally near failing even such basic ecclesiastic subjects as Offertory Management, Histrionics and Nasal Singing. But you came to my rescue, Dean Dismey. I remember how you argued, 'Admittedly, Mobey's academic grades tend toward Z. But let us in mercy write a Z for zeal, rather than zero, and grant his application. It would be almost criminal, gentlemen, if we did *not* send Crispin Mobey to the Outback of Australia.'

(And I believe this report on my mission will demonstrate that your faith in me, Dean Dismey, was not misplaced. I will say, modestly, that during my travels Down Under, I was often referred to as 'the very picture of a missionary.')

I would have been perfectly willing to work my passage to Australia, to claw my way unaided into the Outback, and to live as primitively as my flock while I taught them the True Word. Instead, I was surprised to discover that I had at my disposal a generous allocation from the Overseas Mission Fund—over-generous, in fact, as all I intended to take with me was some beads.

'Beads!' exclaimed the Mission Board bursar, when I presented my requisition. 'You want the entire allocation in *glass beads?*'

I tried to explain to him what I had learned from my research. The Australian aborigines, I had been given to understand, are the most primitive of all the peoples living on Earth. An actual remnant of the Stone Age, these poor creatures never even got far enough up the scale of evolution to develop the bow and arrow.

'My dear boy,' the bursar said gently. 'Beads went out with Stanley and Livingstone. You'll want an electric golf cart for the chief. Lampshades for his wives. They wear them for hats, you know.'

'The Anulas never heard of golf, and they don't wear hats. They don't wear anything.'

'All the best missionaries,' the bursar said rather stiffly, 'swear by lampshades.'

'The Anulas are practically cavemen,' I insisted. 'They don't even have spoons. They have no written language. I've got to educate them from ape on up. I'm just taking the beads to catch their fancy, to show I'm a friend.'

'Snuff is always appreciated,' he tried as a last resort.

'Beads,' I said firmly.

As you have no doubt deduced from the invoices, my allocation bought a tremendous lot of colored glass beads. I really should have waited to buy them in Australia and avoided the excessive transportation bill; they filled one entire cargo hold of the ship which took me from Norfolk that June day.

Arriving at Sydney, I transferred the beads to a warehouse on the Woolloomooloo docks, and went to report immediately to SoPrim-ProPac Shagnasty (as Pacific Elder Shagnasty likes to style himself; he was a Navy Chaplain during World War II). I found that august gentleman, after some search and inquiry, at the local clubhouse of the English-Speaking Union. 'A fortress, a refuge,' he called the ESU, 'among the inarticulate Aussies. Will you join me in one of these delicious Stingarees?'

I declined the drink and launched into the story behind my visit.

'Going to the Anulas, eh? Way up in the North, eh?' He nodded judiciously. 'Excellent choice. Virgin territory. You'll find good fishing.'

A splendid metaphor, I thought. 'That's what I came for, sir,' I said enthusiastically.

'Yes,' he mused. 'I lost a Royal Coachman up there on the River Roper, three years back.'

'Mercy me!' I exclaimed, aghast. 'I had no idea the poor heathens were hostile! And one of the Queen's own chauf—!'

'No, no, no! A trout fly!' He stared at me. 'I begin to

understand,' he said after a moment, 'why SoPrim sent you to the Outback. I trust you're leaving for the North immediately.'

'I want to learn the native language before I get started,' I said. 'The Berlitz people in Richmond told me I could study Anula at their branch school here in Sydney.'

But next day, when I located the Berlitz office, I discovered to my chagrin that I would have to learn at least rudimentary German first. Their only teacher of the Anula tongue was a melancholy defrocked priest of some German Roman Catholic order—a former missionary himself—and he spoke no English.

It took me a restless and anxious three months of tutorage in the German language (while storage charges piled up on my beads) before I could start learning Anula from the ex-priest, Herr Krapp. As you can imagine, Dean Dismey, I was on guard against any subtle Papist propaganda he might try to sneak into my instruction. But the only thing I found odd was that Herr Krapp's stock of Anula seemed to consist mainly of phrases of endearment. And he frequently muttered almost heartbrokenly, in his own language, *'Ach, das liebenswerte schwarze Mädchen!'* and licked his chops.

By the end of September, Herr Krapp had taught me all he knew, and I saw no reason to delay any longer my start for the Outback. I hired two drivers and two trucks to carry my beads and myself. Besides my Missionary Kampkit (a scaled-down revival tent), my luggage consisted only of my Holy Bible, my spectacles, a one-volume abridgment of *The Golden Bough* and my textbook of the Anula language, *Die Gliederung der australischen Sprachen*.

Then I went to bid farewell to Elder Shagnasty. I found him again, or still, at the English-Speaking Union's refreshment stand.

'Back from the bush, eh?' he greeted me. 'Have a Stingaree. How are all the little blackfellows?'

I tried to explain that I hadn't gone yet, but he interrupted me to introduce a military-looking gentleman standing at the counter.

'Major Mashworm is a Deputy Protector of the Aborigines. He'll be interested to hear how you found his little black wards, as he never seems to get any farther Outback than right here.'

I shook hands with Major Mashworm and told him that I hadn't yet seen his little black wards, but expected to shortly.

'Ah, another Yank,' he said as soon as I opened my mouth.

'Sir!' I said, bridling. 'I am a *South*erner!'

'Quite so, quite so,' he said, as if it made no difference at all. 'And are you circumcised?'

'Sir!' I gasped. 'I am a *Chris*tian!'

'Too right. Well, if you expect to get anywhere with a myall abo tribe, you'll have to be circumcised or they won't accept you as a full-grown bloke. The abo witch doctor will do it for you, if necessary, but I fancy you'd rather have it done in hospital. The native ceremony also involves knocking out one or two of your teeth, and then you have to squat out in the bush, twirling a bullroarer, until you're jake again.'

Had I heard about this when I first heard of the Anulas, my zeal might have been less. But, having come this far, I saw nothing for it but to submit to the operation. Still, someone might have told me earlier; I could have been healing while I was studying languages. As it was, I couldn't defer my departure. So I had the operation done that very night at Sydney Mercy—by a slightly incredulous doctor and two sniggering nurses—and got my little caravan on the road right afterward.

The trip was sheer agony, not to say a marathon embarrassment. Convalescence involved wearing a cumbersome contraption that was a cross between a splint and a truss, and which was well-nigh impossible to conceal even beneath a mackintosh several sizes too large for me. I won't dwell on the numerous humiliations that beset me at rest stops along the way. But you can get some idea of the pain I suffered, Reverend Dismey, if you imagine yourself in my tender condition, driving in a badly sprung Vietnam War-relic truck, along a practically nonexistent road, all the way from Richmond to the Grand Canyon.

Everything in the vast interior of Australia is known roughly as the Outback. But the Northern Territory, where I was going, is even out back of the Outback, and is known to the Aussies as the Never Never. The territory is the size of Alaska, but has exactly as many people in it as my hometown of Dreer, Virginia. The Anula tribal grounds are situated in the far north of this Never Never, on the Barkly Tableland between the bush country and the tropical swamps of the Gulf of Carpentaria—a horrible 2,500 miles from my starting point at Sydney.

The *city* of Cloncurry (pop. 1,955) was our last real glimpse of humankind. By way of illustrating what I mean, the next town we touched, Dobbyn, had a population of about 0. And the last town with a name in all that Never Never wilderness, Brunette Downs, seemed to have a population of minus something.

That was where my drivers left me, as agreed from the start. It was the last possible place they might contrive to hitchhike a ride back toward civilization. They showed me the direction I should take from there, and I proceeded on my pilgrim's progress into the

Unknown, driving one of the trucks myself and parking the other in Brunette Downs for the time being.

My drivers said I would eventually come upon an Experimental Agricultural Station, where the resident agents would have the latest word on where to find the nomadic Anulas. But I arrived there late one afternoon to find the station deserted, except for a few lethargic kangaroos and one shriveled, whiskery little desert rat who came running and whooping a strange cry of welcome:

'*Cooee!* What cheer? What cheer? Gawdstrewth, it's bonzer to see a bloody newchum buggering barstid out here, dinkum it is!'

(Lest this outburst has horrified you, Dean Dismey, allow me to explain. At first, I blushed at the apparent profanities and obscenities employed by the Australians, from Mashworm on down. Then I realized that they use such locutions as casually and innocently as punctuation. And, their 'Strine' dialect being what it is, I never knew *when* to blush at their real deliberate cuss words, because I couldn't tell which they *were*. Therefore, rather than try here to censor or euphemize every utterance, I will report conversations verbatim and without comment.)

'Set your arse a spell, cobber! The billy's on the boil. We'll split a pannikin and have a real shivoo, what say?'

'How do you do?' I managed to get in.

'What-o, a Yank!' he exclaimed in surprise.

'Sir,' I said with dignity, 'I am a Virginian.'

'Strewth? Well, if yer looking to lose it, you've come to one helluva place for gash. There ain't a blooming sheila inside three hundred mile, unless yer aiming to go combo with the Black Velvet.'

This made no sense whatever, so to change the subject I introduced myself.

'Garn! A narky Bush Brother? Should of known, when you announced you was cherry. Now I'll have to bag me bloody langwidge.'

If he 'bagged' his language, it was to no noticeable degree. He repeated one obscene-sounding proposal several times before I interpreted it as an invitation to have a cup of tea ('go snacks on Betty Lee') with him. While we drank the tea, brewed over a twig fire, he told me about himself. At least I suppose that's what he told me, though all I got out of it was that his name was McCubby.

'Been doing a walkabout in the woop-woop, fossicking for wolfram. But my cuddy went bush with the brumbies and I found meself in a prebloodydicament. So I humped my bluey in here to the Speriment Station, hoping I'd strike a stock muster, a squatter, anybody, even a dingo-barstid jonnop. But no go, and I was bloody well down on my bone when you showed your dial.'

'What do you do out here?' I asked.

'I toldjer, I been fossicking for wolfram.'

'Well, you've got so many unfamiliar animals here in Australia,' I said apologetically. 'I never heard of a wolf ram.'

He peered at me suspiciously and said, 'Wolfram is tungsten ore. Fossicking is prospecting.'

'Speaking of Australian fauna,' I said, 'can you tell me what a dollar-bird is?'

(The dollar-bird, you will recall, sir, is the totem agent mentioned in Frazer's account of the rain-making ceremony. I had come this far without being able to learn just what a dollar-bird *was*.)

'It ain't no fawn, Rev,' said McCubby. 'And you can be glad it ain't. That was a dollar-bird which just took a dump on your titfer.'

'What?'

'I keep forgetting yer a newchum,' he sighed. 'Your titfer is your titfertat, your hat. A dollar-bird just flew over and let fly.'

I took off my pith helmet and wiped at it with a tuft of grass.

'The dollar-bird,' McCubby said pedantically, 'is so called because of a silvery-colored circular patch on its spread wings.'

'Thank you,' I said, and started to tell him how the bird had inspired my mission to the aborigines—

'To the abos! Strike me blind!' blurted McCubby. 'And here I thought you was out to preach at the buggering snoozers up at Darwin. I presoom the whole rest of the world is already gone Christian, then, if Gawd's scraping the barrel for blackfellow converts.'

'Why, no,' I said. 'But the abos have as much right as anybody else to learn the True Word. To learn that their pagan gods are delusive devils tempting them to Hell fire.'

'They're looking forward to Hell fire, Rev,' said McCubby, 'as an improvement on the Never Never. Ain't they got enough grief without you having to inflict religion on 'em?'

'Religion is a sap,' I said, quoting William Penn, 'to penetrate the farthest boughs of the living tree.'

'Looks to me like yer bringing the bingis a whole bloody cathedral,' he said. 'What kind of swag you got in the lorry, anyway?'

'Beads,' I said. 'Nothing but beads.'

'Beans, eh?' he said, cocking an eye at the huge truck. 'You must be more than meejum fond of flute fruit.'

Before I could correct his misapprehension, he stepped to the rear of the vehicle and unlatched the gate doors. The entire van was loaded to the ceiling with beads, dumped in loose for convenience. So of course McCubby was instantly engulfed in a seething avalanche, while several more tons of the beads inundated about two acres of the local flatlands, and rivulets and droplets of them went twinkling off to form a diminishing nimbus around the main mass. After a while, the mound behind the truck heaved and blasphemed, and McCubby's whiskery head emerged.

'Look what you've done,' I said, justifiably exasperated.

'Oh my word,' he said softly. 'First time beans ever dumped *me*.'

He picked up one of the things, tried his teeth on it and said, 'Rev, these would constipate a cassowary.' He took a closer look at it and staggered through the pile toward me, dribbling beads from every fold of his clothes. 'Somebody has give you the sweet but-all, son,' he confided. 'These ain't beans. They're glass.'

I'm afraid I snapped at him. 'I know it! They're for the natives!'

He looked at me, expressionless. He turned, still expressionless, and looked slowly around the glittering expanse that spread seemingly to the horizon in all directions. He asked cautiously:

'What religion did you say yer magging?'

I ignored him. 'Well,' I sighed. 'No sense trying to pick them all up before nightfall. Mind if I camp here until morning?'

I was awakened several times during the night by a hideous crunching noise from the perimeter of our glass desert, but, since McCubby didn't stir, I tried not to let it perturb me.

We arose at sun-up, our whole part of the world gleaming 'like the buggering Land of Hoz,' as McCubby put it. After breakfast I began the Herculean task of regathering my stock, with a rusty shovel I found in a tumbledown station outbuilding. McCubby left me for a while, to go slithering across the beads to their outer reaches. He came back beaming happily, with an armload of bloody scraps of fur.

'Dingo scalps,' he chortled. 'Worth a quid apiece in bounties. Rev, you may have spragged the curse of this whole blunny continent. Out there's just *heaped* with the carcasses of dingos, rabbits and dunnikan rats what tried to make a meal off your bijous. Oh my word!'

He was so pleased at the sudden windfall that he hunted up

another shovel and pitched in to help me scoop beads. It was night again by the time we had the truck reloaded, and, at that, half its content was topsoil. The territory around the Experiment Station still looked like Disneyland.

'Oh, well,' I said philosophically. 'Good thing I've got another truckful waiting at Brunette Downs.'

McCubby started, stared at me, and went off muttering in his beard.

The next morning I set forth on the last lap of my mission of mercy. McCubby told me he had encountered the Anula tribe on his trek in to the station. They were camped in a certain swale of acacia trees, he said, scratching for witchetty grubs and irriakura bulbs, the only available food in this dry season.

And it was there I found them, just at sundown. The whole tribe couldn't have numbered more than seventy-five souls, each of them uglier than the next. Had I not known of their crying need of me, I might have backed off. The men were great broad-shouldered fellows, coppery-black, with even blacker beards and hair brushed frizzily around their low foreheads, sullen eyes and bone-pierced flat noses. The women had more hair and no beards, and limp, empty breasts that hung down each one's front like a couple of pinned-on medals. The men wore only a horsehair rope around their middles, in which they stuck their boomerangs, music sticks, feather charms and the like. The women wore *nagas*, fig-newton-sized aprons of paperbark. The children wore drool.

They looked up dully as I brought the truck to a halt. There was no evidence either of welcome or of hostility. I climbed onto the truck hood, waved my arms and called out in their language, 'My children, come unto me! I bring tidings of great joy!'

A few of the tots crept closer and picked their noses at me. The women went on rooting around the acacias with their yamsticks. The men simply continued to do nothing. They're all bashful, I thought; nobody wants to be first.

So I strode boldly into their midst and took a gnarled, white-haired oldster by the arm. I leaned into the truck cab, opened the little hatch that gave access to the van, and plunged the old savage's resisting hand inside. It came out grasping a fistful of dirt and one green bead, at which he blinked in perplexity. As I had hoped, curiosity brought the rest of the tribe around.

'Plenty for everybody, my children!' I shouted in their language. Pulling and hauling, I forced them one by one up to the cab. They each obediently reached through the hatch, took one bead

apiece and drifted back to their occupations as if thankful the
ceremony was over.

'What's the matter?' I asked one shy young girl, the last of the
procession and the only person who had taken *two* beads. 'Doesn't
anybody like the pretty-pretties?' She flinched guiltily, put back
one of the beads and scampered away.

I was flabbergasted at the lack of enthusiasm. As of now, the
Anulas had one tiny bead apiece, and I had about six hundred
billion. Beginning to suspect what was amiss, I went and stood
among them and listened to their furtive, secretive talk. *I couldn't
understand a word!* Horrors, I thought. Unless I could communicate, I had no hope of making them accept the beads . . . or
me . . . or the Gospel. Could I have stumbled on the wrong tribe?
Or were they deliberately misunderstanding me and talking in
gibberish? There was one way to find out, and that without more
ado. I turned the truck around and drove pell-mell back for the
station, hoping mightily that McCubby hadn't left yet.

He hadn't. The wild dogs and other varmints were still com-
miting suicide en masse by dining on my leftover beads, and
McCubby wasn't about to leave until the bounty business petered
out. I reached the station at sunrise again, when he was out
collecting the night's harvest of scalps. I leaped from the truck and
blurted out my problem:

'I don't understand the Anulas' speech and they don't understand mine. You claim you know most of the abo tongues. What am
I doing wrong?' I reeled off a sentence and asked anxiously, 'Did
you understand that?'

'Too right,' he said. 'You offered me thirty pfennigs to get my
black arse in bed with you.' He added, 'Cheap barstid.'

A little rattled, I pleaded, 'Never mind what the words *said*. Is
my pronunciation bad or something?'

'Oh, no. Yer mooshing perfect Pitjantjatjara.'

'What?'

'A considerably diff'rent langwidge from Anula. Anula has nine
noun classes. Transitive werbs incorporate the object pronouns.
The werbs show many tenses and moods and also a separate
negative conjugation.'

'What?'

'On the other hand, in Pitjantjatjara, the suffixes indicating the
personal pronouns may be appended to the first inflected word in
the sentence, not merely to the werb root.'

'What?'

'I don't like to bulsh on your linguistic accomplishments, cobber, but Pitjantjatjara, although it *has* four declensions and four conjugations, is alleged to be the simplest of all the bloody Australoid langwidges.'

I was speechless.

'How much,' McCubby asked after a while, 'is thirty pfennigs in shillings and pence?'

I murmured uncertainly, 'Maybe I'd better go and minister to the Pitjantjatjara tribe instead, as long as I know their language.'

McCubby shrugged. 'They live way the Hell the other side of the Great Sandy. And they're no myall rootdiggers like these Anulas. They're all upjumped stockriders and donahs now, on the merino sheep stations around Shark Bay. Also, them boongs would prob'ly wind up converting *you*, and that's the dinkum oil. They're staunch Roman Catholics.'

Well, that figured. And I was beginning to suspect why the once-Reverend Herr Krapp had been defrocked.

My next move was obvious: to hire McCubby as my interpreter to the Anulas. At first he balked. My expense fund was so depleted by now that I couldn't offer enough money to tempt him away from his booming business here in dingo scalps. But finally I thought to offer him all the beads in the second truck—'Enough to kill every dingo in the Outback.' So he rolled up his swag and took the wheel (I was dead tired of driving), and we headed again for the Anula country.

On the way, I told McCubby how I intended to introduce the blackfellows to modern Southern Primitive Protestantism. I read aloud to him Sir James Frazer's paragraph in *The Golden Bough*, concluding, 'After that, all he does is sing over the snake and the mimic rainbow . . .'

'*All* he does!' McCubby snorted.

'Sooner or later the rain will fall.' I closed the book. 'And that's where I step in. If the rain doesn't fall, the natives can plainly see that their sorcery doesn't work, and I can turn their clearer eyes toward Christianity. If the rain *should* fall, I simply explain that they were actually praying to the true, Protestant God without realizing it, and the rain-bird had nothing to do with it.'

'And how do you cozen 'em into doing this rain-bird corroboree?'

'Heavens, they're probably doing it all the time. The good Lord knows they need rain. This whole country is burned crisp as paper.'

'If it do come on to rain,' McCubby muttered darkly, 'My

word, *I'll* fall down on me knees.' What that signified, I (unfortunately) did not grasp at the time.

The reception at the Anula camp was rather different this day. The abos swarmed to greet McCubby. Three of the younger females in particular appeared to rejoice at his arrival.

'Ah, me cheeky little blackgins,' he said affectionately. Then, after a colloquy with the tribe's elders, he said to me, 'They want to offer you a lubra too, Rev.'

A lubra is a female, and I had expected this hospitality, knowing it to be a custom of the Anulas. I instructed McCubby to explain my religious reasons for declining, and went to work to set up my KampKit tent on a knoll overlooking the native camp. As I crawled into it, McCubby asked, 'Going to plow the deep so early?'

'I just want to take off my clothes,' I said. 'When in Rome, you know. See if you can borrow one of those waist strings for me.'

'*A nood missionary?*' he said, scandalized.

'Our church teaches that the body is nothing,' I said, 'but a machine to carry the soul around. Besides, I feel a true missionary should not set himself above his flock in matters of dress and social deportment.'

'A true missionary,' McCubby said drily, 'ain't got the crocodile hide of these bingis.' But he brought me the horsehair rope. I tied it around my waist and stuck into it my Holy Bible, my pocket comb and my spectacles case.

I confess that, when I was thus attired, I hesitated at the tent flap. For one as modest and introverted as myself, it was painful to think of stepping out there—especially in view of the females—in my stark white nudity. But after all, I consoled myself, I wasn't quite as stark as my flock. On the Sydney surgeon's orders, I would have to wear my truss-and-splint contrivance for another week.

So I scrambled out of the tent and stood up, dancing delicately as the ground stubble jabbed my bare feet. My, all those white eyeballs in all those black faces! McCubby was staring just as intently and unbelievingly as everyone else. He worked his mouth for a while before he could speak.

'Crikey! No wonder yer Virginian, poor cove.'

The abos began to crowd around, and point and babble and measure the apparatus as if they contemplated getting copies to wear. Finally, a trifle annoyed, though still lightly dancing in a way that may have looked merry, I asked my goggling interpreter why everyone was making so much fuss.

'They think yer either bragging or humbugging. Dinkum, so do I.'

So, still jigging, I told him about my operation, that I had endured it because it was an age-old Anula custom. McCubby repeated this to the mob. The blackfellows nodded knowingly at each other, jabbered even more furiously, and came one by one to pat me on the head.

'Ah, they approve, do they?' I said with great satisfaction.

'They think yer crazy as a kookaburra,' McCubby said flatly. 'It's supposed to bring good luck to fondle a zany.'

'What?'

'If you'll take a pike at the men of your flock,' he suggested, 'you'll note that the custom of circumbloodycision must of went out of style some time back.'

I looked, and it was so. I found myself mentally composing some unChristian remarks to make to Major Mashworm. So, to elevate my thoughts, I proposed that we try again to distribute my gift of beads. I don't know what McCubby told the blackfellows, but the whole tribe trooped off eagerly to the truck and came back with a double handful of beads apiece. Several of them made two or more trips. I was pleased.

The very brief tropical twilight was on us now; the Anulas' cooking fires began to flicker among the acacias. I wouldn't be able to accomplish anything more today; so McCubby and I set our own billy on a fire. We had just settled down to our tucker when one of the abos came up smiling and handed me a slab of bark heaped with some kind of native food. Whatever it was, it quivered disgustingly, and, looking at it, so did I.

'Emu fat,' said McCubby. 'Their favorite delicacy. It's in return for them beads.'

I was ever so delighted by this gesture, but the dish was nauseatingly difficult to get down. It was like eating a bowlful of lips.

'I'd wolf the stuff if I was you,' McCubby advised, after a visit to the natives' fires. 'They're likely to come and take it back, when they give up on the beads.'

'What?'

'They've been boiling 'em for three hours now, and it seems they still taste gritty.'

'They're *eating* the *beads?!*'

McCubby saw my consternation and said, almost kindly, 'Rev, all that these boongs live for is to eat for to live for to eat. They don't have houses and they don't wear pockets, so they got no use for propitty. They know they're as ugly as the backside of a wombat, so they got no use for pretties. In this crook country, finding food is cruel hard. If anything new comes along, they try it for food, in hopes.'

I was too weary even to worry; I crept into my replica revival tent desiring only to 'plow the deep,' in McCubby's phrase. As it turned out, though, I got precious little sleep. I had to keep evicting a succession of young black girls who, I presume, had a childish desire to sleep under canvas for a change.

I arose quite late in the morning, to find all the Anulas still huddled, groaning, in their *wagga* rugs. 'You won't see any rain-debbil corroboree today,' McCubby told me. 'Them rumbustious beads has got 'em all just about keck-livered.'

Now I *was* worried. Suppose they all died like the dingos!

'I wouldn't do this for any ruggerlugs but you, Rev,' said McCubby, digging into his swag. 'But I'll squander some of my lollies on 'em.'

'What?'

'Chawnklit. It's what *I* use for trading and bribing the bingis. They like it a buggering sight better than beads.'

When he brought it out, I exclaimed, 'That's not chocolate, that's Ex-Lax!'

'That's what they like about it. A pleasure at both ends.'

The events of the rest of that day are indescribable. But the setting sun picked bright glints from little heaps of beads here and there throughout the rolling land in the locality. And I was having troubles of my own; I had begun to itch intolerably, all over. McCubby wasn't surprised.

'Meat ants,' he theorized, 'or sugar ants, white ants, buffalo flies, marsh flies, blowflies. We also got anopheles mosquitoes. I tell you, Rev, missionaries ain't got the hide for cavorting bare-arse out here.' Not too regretfully, I gave up my notion of living as primitively as my horny-skinned flock and went back to wearing clothes.

That day was not an entire waste, however. I reminded McCubby that we required a pool of water for the upcoming ritual, and he led me to the Anulas' tribal oasis.

'T'ain't much of a billabong in the Dry,' he admitted. The waterhole was respectably wide and deep, but it contained only a scummy, fetid expanse of mud, through which meandered a sullen, greenish trickle of water, the thickness of a lead pencil. 'But come the Wet and it'd faze Noah. Anyhow, I figger it must be the one in your Golden Bow-Wow. It's the only water inside a hunderd mile.'

I wondered how, if Frazer's hero had been desperate enough to try conjuring up a rain, he had been provided with a pool to do it at. But I muttered, 'Well, dam it, that's all.'

'Rev, I'm shocked at your intemperate bloody langwidge!'

I explained. We would throw up a temporary dam across the lower end of the billabong. By the time the Anulas recovered from their internal malfunctions, the water should have attained a level sufficient for our purpose. So that's what we did, McCubby and I: hauled and stacked up stones, and chinked their interstices with mud, which the fierce sun baked to an adobe-like cement. We knocked off at nightfall, and the water was already as high as our ankles.

I awoke the next morning to a tumult of whoops, shrills and clangor from the direction of the Anulas' camp. Ah, thought I, stretching complacently, they've discovered their new and improved waterworks and are celebrating. But then McCubby thrust his bristly head through my tent flap and announced, 'War's been declared!'

'Not with America?!' I gasped—his report had sounded rather accusatory—but he had as suddenly withdrawn. I dragged on my boots and joined him on the knoll, and realized he had meant a tribal war.

There were about twice as many blacks down there as I had remembered, and every one of them was ululating loud enough for two more. They milled about, whacking at one another with spears and yamsticks, flinging stones and boomerangs, and jabbing brands from the cooking fires into each other's frizzy hair.

'It's their neighbor tribe, the Bingbingas,' said McCubby. 'They live downstream on the creek, and this sun-up they found their water turned off. They're accusing the Anulas of trying mass murder, so as to take over their grubbing grounds. If this ain't a fair cow!'

'We must do something!'

McCubby rummaged in his swag and brought out a toy-like pistol. 'This is only a pipsqueak twenty-two,' he said. 'But they ought to nick off home when they see white-man weapons.'

We pelted together down the slope and into the fray, McCubby ferociously pop-popping his little revolver in the air, and I brandishing my Holy Bible to proclaim that Right was on our side. Sure enough, the invading Bingbingas fell back from this new onslaught. They separated out of the confusion and withdrew, carrying their wounded. We chased them to the top of a nearby hill, from which vantage they shook their fists and shouted taunts and insults for a while before retiring, defeated, in the direction of their home grounds.

McCubby circulated through the Anula camp, dusting the only medicament he carried—athlete's-foot powder—on the more seriously wounded. There were few casualties, actually, and most of those had suffered only bloody noses, lumped skulls or superficial depilations where hair or whiskers had been yanked out. I played battlefield Chaplain as best I could in dumb show, pantomiming spiritual comfort at them. One good thing. All the Anulas appeared to have recovered utterly from their bead-diet prostration. Doubtless this early-morning exercise had helped.

When things had calmed down, and after some breakfast tucker and tea, I dispatched McCubby to search through the tribe for an unoccupied male of the clan which claimed the dollar-bird for its *kobong*, or totem. He did find a young man of that persuasion and, overcoming his stubborn unwillingness, brought him to me.

'This is Yartatgurk,' said McCubby. 'Named after the bird.'

Yartatgurk walked with a limp, because of a stiff Bingbinga kick in the shin, and was bushily bearded only on the left side of his face, because of a Bingbinga firebrand. The rest of the tribe came and hunkered down expectantly around the three of us, as if eager to see what new and individual treat I had in store for their young man.

'Now we must recapitulate the procedure,' I said, and began to read *The Golden Bough*'s description of the ceremony, McCubby translating phrase by phrase. At the conclusion, young Yartatgurk stood up abruptly and, despite his limp, commenced a vigorous heel-and-toe toward the far horizon. All the other Anulas began muttering among themselves and tapping their foreheads with a forefinger.

When McCubby had fetched the struggling Yartatgurk back, I said, 'Surely they must all be familiar with the ritual.'

'They say, if yer so buggering thirsty as to go through all that taradiddle, it'd of been just as easy to lug an artesian drill in here as all them beads. Too right!'

'That's not the point,' I said. 'According to Frazer, the belief is that long ago the dollar-bird had a snake for a mate. The snake lived in a pool and used to make rain by spitting up into the sky until clouds appeared and the rain fell.'

This, translated, sent the Anulas into an absolute frenzy of chattering and head-tapping.

'They say,' McCubby interpreted, 'you show them a bird

mating with a snake and they'll gladly go and get you all the water you want, if they have to hump the bloody Carpentaria Gulf down here by hand.'

This was distressing. 'I'm quite sure a reputable anthropologist like Frazer wouldn't *lie* about their tribal beliefs.'

'If he's any kin to the Frazer I used to cobber with—old Blazer Frazer—he'd lie about which is his left and right hand.'

'Well,' I said unquenchably, 'I've come twelve thousand miles to repudiate this custom, and I won't be put off. Now tell Yartatgurk to stop that whimpering and let's get on with it.'

McCubby managed, by giving Yartatgurk a large slab of Ex-Lax, to convince him that the ceremony—idiotic as he might ignorantly think it—wasn't going to hurt him. The three of us went first to check on the billabong, and found it gratifyingly abrim with repulsive brown water, wide and deep enough to have submerged our truck. From there, we headed into the endless savannah.

'First,' I said, 'we need a snake. A live one.'

McCubby scratched in his whiskers. 'That might be a wowser, Rev. The boongs have et most of the snakes within hunting range. And they sprag 'em from a cautious distance, with boomerang or spear. The wipers out here in the Never Never, you don't want to meet 'em alive.'

'Why?'

'Well, we got the tiger snake and the death adder, which their wenom has been measured twenty times as wicked as the bloody cobra's. Then there's the taipan, and I've seen meself a horse die five minutes after a taipan nipped him. Then there's—'

He broke off to make a grab for Yartatgurk, who was trying to sneak away. McCubby pointed into the bush and sent the blackfellow horizonward with explicit instructions. Yartatgurk limped off, looking about him nervously and sucking moodily on his chunk of chocolate. McCubby didn't look any too happy himself, as we followed after the native at a distance.

'I wish it was your buggering Frazer we was sending on this chase,' he muttered.

'Oh, come,' I said encouragingly. 'There must be *some* non-poisonous variety that will serve our purpose.'

'Won't help our purpose none if we tread on one of the others first,' growled McCubby. 'If this ain't the most nincompoop—'

There was a sudden commotion out ahead of us, where we had last seen Yartatgurk creeping, hunched over, through the tussocky grass.

'He's got one!' I shouted, as the blackfellow rose up into view with a strangled cry. He was silhouetted against the sky, toiling desperately with something huge and lashing, a fearsome sight to behold.

'Dash me rags!' breathed McCubby in awed surprise. 'I ain't never seen a Queensland python this far west before.'

'A python!'

'Too bloody right,' said McCubby in unfeigned admiration. 'Twenty feet if he's a hinch.'

I gaped at the lunging, Laocoön-like tableau before us. Yartatgurk was almost invisible inside the writhing coils, but he was clearly audible. I wondered momentarily if we might not have bitten off more than we could chew, but I sternly laid that specter of uncertainty. Manifestly, the good Lord was following Frazer's scenario.

'Yartatgurk is inquiring,' McCubby said quietly, 'who we're rooting for.'

'Do you suppose we'll spoil the magic if we lend a hand?'

'We'll spoil the blackfellow if we don't. Look there.'

'Mercy on us, he's spouting blood!'

'T'ain't blood. If you'd just et a quarter-pound of Hex-Lax and then got hugged by a python, you'd spout too.'

We fought our way into the squirming tangle and finally managed to peel the creature loose from Yartatgurk. Then it took the utmost strength of all three of us to straighten it out and prevent its coiling again. Yartatgurk had turned almost as white as I, but he bravely hung onto the python's tail—being lashed and tumbled about, sometimes high off the ground—while McCubby, at its head, and I, grasping its barrel-like middle, manhandled it toward the billabong.

By the time we made it to the pool bank, all three of us were being whipped through the air, back and forth past each other, and occasionally colliding. 'Now,' I gasped out, between the snake's convulsions, 'he's got to—hold it under—*oof!*—the water . . .'

'I don't think,' said McCubby, on my left, 'he's likely to agree,' said McCubby, from behind me. 'When I yell *go*,' said McCubby, on my right, 'dowse him and the snake both,' said McCubby, from overhead. '*Cooee!—GO!!!*'

At the command, he and I simultaneously swung our portions of the python out over the water and let go. It and the wretched Yartatgurk, flapping helplessly along like the tail of a kite, disappeared with a mighty splash. Instantly the billabong was roiled into a hissing brown froth.

'Pythons,' panted McCubby, when he could get his breath, 'hates water worse'n cats do.'

The entire Anula tribe, I now noticed, had come down to cluster on the opposite side of the billabong, and were attentively following the proceedings with eyes like boiled onions.

'Was you to ask me,' said McCubby, when we had rested a while, 'I'd be hard put to say who was holding who under.'

'I reckon it's been long enough,' I decreed.

We waded waist-deep into the pool and, after being knocked about a bit, managed to grab hold of the slithery loops and haul the reptile onto the bank. Yartatgurk, we were pleased to see, came along clenched in a coil of the python's tail.

Somewhere along about here, our handmade dam collapsed. Its mud chinking had been gradually eroded as the water backed up behind it during the night and morning. Now the agitation of the billabong toppled the weakened structure, and all the collected water drained out with a swoosh. This would probably gratify the thirsty Bingbingas downstream, I reflected, if it didn't drown them all in that first grand flood-wave.

The submersion had taken some of the fight out of the snake, but not a great deal. McCubby and I sustained numerous bruises and contusions during this stage of the struggle, while we fought to immobilize the forepart of the thing. Yartatgurk was of no help to us, as he had gone quite limp and, clutched by the freely thrashing tail of the serpent, was being batted like a bludgeon against the surrounding trees and terrain.

'It's time for him to kill it!' I shouted to McCubby.

As the blackfellow whisked to and fro past us, McCubby listened to his barely audible mumblings and reported, 'He says nothing would give him greater pleasure.'

Our fantastic battle went on for a while longer, until it became obvious that Yartatgurk wasn't up to killing the monster anytime soon, and I called to McCubby to inquire what to do next.

'I'll hang on best I can,' he bellowed back, between curses and grunts. 'You run for my swag. Get my pistol. Shoot the bugger.'

I went, but with misgivings. I feared that we white men —perhaps unconsciously flaunting our superiority—were taking too much of a hand in this ceremony, and might, by our meddling, botch whatever mystical significance it held for the natives.

I came back at a run, gripping the revolver in both hands. The python appeared to have recovered entirely from its watery ordeal and was flailing more energetically than ever, occasionally keeping both men in the air at once. In all that confusing uproar, and in my own excitement, nervousness and unfamiliarity with the weapon, I took quaking aim and shot Yartatgurk in the foot.

He did not make any outright complaint (though I think he might have if he could have), but his eyes were eloquent. I could almost have wept at their glazed expression of disappointment in me. This was a chastening thing to see, but I suppose even the most divinely inspired spiritual leader encounters it at least once in his career. None of us is perfect.

Meanwhile McCubby had disengaged himself from the mêlée. He snatched the pistol from me and emptied it into the serpent's ugly head. For a long time, then, he and I leaned against each other and panted wearily, while the blackfellow and the python lay side by side and twitched.

Yartatgurk's wound, I am relieved to say, was not a serious one. Actually, he had suffered more from his stay underwater. McCubby pumped his flaccid arms up and down, and he disgorged quite an astonishing quantity of water, mud, weeds and pollywogs, while I bound up the hole in his foot with a strip torn from my crotch bandages. A .22, it seems, fires a triflingly small pellet, and this one had passed cleanly through the abo's foot without so much as nicking a tendon. As the lead did not remain in the wound, and as it bled freely, there appeared to be little cause for agonizing—though agonize is what Yartatgurk did, at great and vociferous length, when he regained consciousness.

I decided to let the fellow enjoy a short rest and the commiseration of his clucking tribemates. Besides, I was by now so implicated in the ceremony that I figured a little more intervention could do no harm. So I went myself to perform the next step in the rite: to set up the 'mimic rainbow' of grass over the defunct snake. After fumbling unsuccessfully at this project for a considerable while, I came back and said despairingly to McCubby, 'Every time I try to bend the grass into a bow it just crumbles into powder.'

'Whajjer expect,' he said with some acerbity, 'after eight buggery months of drought?'

Here was another verity, like the dried-up billabong, which I couldn't reconcile with Frazer's account. If the grass was dry enough to warrant rain-making, it was too dry to be bent.

Then I had an inspiration, and went to look at the muck of our recent dam-site pool. As I'd hoped, there was a sparse growth of grass there, nicely waterlogged by its night's immersion. I plucked all I could find and tied it into a frazzled rainbow with my boot-laces. This horseshoe-shaped object I propped up around the dead python's neck, making him look as jaunty as a racehorse in the winner's circle.

Feeling very pleased with myself, I returned to McCubby. He, like the Anulas, was sympathetically regarding Yartatgurk, who I gathered was relating the whole history of his wounded foot from the day it was born.

'Now tell him,' I said, 'all he has to do is sing.'

For the first time, McCubby seemed disinclined to relay my instructions. He gave me a long look. Then he clasped his hands behind his back and took a contemplative turn up and down the billabong bank, muttering to himself. Finally he shrugged, gave a sort of bleak little laugh, and knelt down to interrupt the nattering Yartatgurk. As McCubby outlined the next and final step, Yartatgurk's face gradually assumed the expression of a hamstrung horse being asked to perform its own *coup de grâce*. After what seemed to me an unnecessarily long colloquy between the two, McCubby said:

'Yartatgurk begs to be excused, Rev. He says he's just had too much to think about, these past few days. First he had to meditate on the nature of them beads you fed him. Then he had to mull over the Bingbingas' burning of his beard, which cost him three years to cultivate and got blazed off in three winks. Then there was being half squoze to a pulp, and then three-quarters drownded, and then nine-tenths bludged to death, and then having his hoof punctuated. He says his poor inferior black brain is just so full of material for study that it's clean druv out the words of all the songs he knows.'

'He doesn't have to sing words,' I said. 'I gather that any sprightly tune will do, crooned Heavenward in a properly beseeching manner.'

There was a short silence.

'In all this empty woop-woop,' said McCubby under his breath, 'one-eighth of a human bean to a square mile, and *you* have to be the one-eighth I cobber up with.'

'McCubby,' I said patiently, 'this is the most important part of the entire ritual.'

'Ah, well. Here goes the last of me Hex-Lax.'

He handed the chocolate to the blackfellow and launched into a long and seductive argument. At last, with a red-eyed glare at me, and so suddenly that I and the Anulas all jumped, Yartatgurk barked viciously into a clamorous chant. The other natives looked slightly uneasy and began to drift back toward their camp.

'My word,' said McCubby. 'Yer hearing something that not many white coves ever do. The age-old Anula death song.'

'Nonsense,' I said. 'He's not going to die.'

'Not him. You.'

I shook my head reprovingly. 'I've no time for levity. I must get to work on the sermon I'll preach at the conclusion of all this.'

As you can appreciate, Dean Dismey, I had set myself quite a task. I had to be ready with two versions of my sermon, depending on whether the rain-making was or was not successful. But the sermons had certain similarities—for example, in both of them I referred to Prayer as 'a Checkbook on the Bank of God.' And this, of course, posed the problem of explaining a checkbook in terms that an Outback aborigine of Stone Age intellect could comprehend.

While I worked in the seclusion of my tent, I yet kept an ear cocked to Yartatgurk's conscientious keening. As night came down, he began to get hoarse, and several times seemed on the verge of flagging in his endeavor. Each time, I would lay aside my pencil and go down to wave encouragingly at him across the billabong. And each time, this indication of my continued interest did not fail to inspire him to a redoubled output of chanting.

The rest of the Anulas remained quietly in their camp this night, without any moans of indigestion, combat fatigue or other distress. I was grateful that no extraneous clamor disturbed my concentration on the sermons, and even remarked on it to McCubby:

'The natives seem restful tonight.'

'T'ain't often the poor buggers come the bounce on a bellyful of good python meat.'

I cried, 'They've eaten the ceremonial snake?!'

'Don't matter,' he said consolingly. 'The whole skelington is still down there under your wicker wicket.'

Oh, well, I thought. There was nothing I could do about it now. And, as McCubby implied, the skeleton ought to represent as potent a symbol as the entire cadaver.

It was well after midnight, and I had just finished the notes for my next day's services, when a deputation of tribal elders came calling.

'They say you'd oblige 'em, Rev, either to hurry up and die as warranted, or else to placate Yartatgurk some way. They can't get to sleep with him caterwauling.'

'Tell them,' I said, with a magisterial wave of my hand, 'it will all soon be over.'

I knew not how truly I had spoken, until I was violently awakened some hours later by my tent's folding up like an umbrella—*thwack!*—and disappearing into the darkness.

Then, just as violently, the darkness was riven and utterly abolished by the most brilliant, writhing, forking, jagging, snarling cascade of lightning I ever hope to see. It was instantly succeeded by an even blacker darkness, the acrid odor of ozone, and a rolling cannonade of thunder that simply picked up the whole Never Never land and shook it like a blanket.

When I could hear again, I discerned McCubby's voice, whimpering in stark horror out of the darkness, 'Gawd strike me blind.' It seemed more than likely. I was admonishing him to temper his impiety with prudence, when a second cosmic uproar, even more impressive than the first, raged through the echoing dome of Heaven. I had not yet recovered from its numbing fury when a wind like a driving piston took me in the back, balled me up and sent me tumbling end over end across the countryside. I caromed painfully off numerous acacias and eucalyptuses and unidentifiable other obstacles, until I collided with another human body. We grabbed onto each other, but kept on traveling until the wind ebbed for a moment.

By great good fortune it was McCubby I had encountered —though I must say he seemed unaware of any good fortune in this. 'What in buggery have you gone and done?' he demanded, in a quaver.

'What hath *God* wrought?' I corrected him. Oh, it would make an ineradicable impression on the Anulas, when I explained that this was not really the doing of their dollar-bird. 'Now,' I couldn't help exclaiming, 'if it will only pour down rain!'

The words were no sooner spoken than McCubby and I were flattened again. The rain had come down like God's boot heel. It continued mercilessly to stamp on my back, grinding me into the solid ground so that I could barely expand my chest to breathe. This, I thought in my anguish, is really more than I meant to ask for.

After an incalculable while, I was able to inch my mouth over beside McCubby's ear and roar loud enough for him to hear, 'We've got to find my sermon notes before the rain ruins them!'

'Your bloody notes are in Fiji by now!' he bellowed back. 'And so will we be if we don't do a bleeding bunk in a bleeding hurry!'

I tried to remonstrate that we couldn't leave the Anulas now, when everything was proceeding so well, and when I had such a God-given opportunity to make a splendid conversion of the whole tribe.

'Can't you get it through your googly skull?' he shouted. 'This is the Cockeye Bob—come earlier and worse than I ever seen it! This whole land will be underwater, and us with it, *if* we don't get blew a thousand mile and tore to rags in the bush!'

'But my entire mission will have been in vain,' I protested, between the peals of thunder. 'And the poor Anulas deprived of—'

'Bugger the bloody black barstids!' he howled. 'They waved mummuk hours ago. We got to get to the lorry—if it ain't flew away. Make the high ground by the Speriment Station.'

Clinging fast together, we were just able to blunder our way through what seemed a solid wall of water. The lightning and thunder were simultaneous now, blinding and deafening us at the same time. Torn-off branches, uprooted shrubbery and trees of increasingly larger size careened like dark meteors across the Never Never land. Once we ducked the weirdest missile of all—the eerily airborne skeleton of Yartatgurk's python, still sporting its natty grass collar.

I thought it odd that we met none of the blackfellows. But we did find the truck at last, jostling anxiously on its springs and squeaking in every rivet as if crying for help. Wind-blasted water streamed *up* its weather side and smoked off its top like the spindrift from a hurricane sea. I really think that only the dead weight of the remaining beads, which still filled eight-ninths of the van, prevented the truck's having been overturned.

McCubby and I fought our way to the lee door and opened it, to have it nearly blown off the hinges as the wind clawed at it. The inside of the cab was no quieter than outdoors, what with the thunder still headsplittingly audible and the rain practically denting the metal, but the stiller air inside was easier to breathe.

When he stopped panting, McCubby wrung another minor cloudburst out of his whiskers and then started the engine. I laid a restraining hand on his arm. 'We can't abandon the Anulas to this,' I said. 'Couldn't we dump the beads and crowd in the women and pickaninnies at least?'

'I toldjer, they all took a ball of chalk hours ago!'

'Does that mean they've gone?'

'Soon as you sacked out. They were well clear of the low ground by the time the Cockeye Bob came down.'

'Hm,' I said, a little hurt. 'Rather ungrateful of them, to desert their spiritual adviser without notice.'

'Oh, they're *grateful*, Rev,' McCubby said acidly. 'That's why they waved mummuk. You made 'em wealthy. My word, they're reg'lar plutes now. Nicked off to Darwin, they did, to peddle that python skin to a shoe manufactory.'

I could only wheeze, 'God moves in a mysterious way . . .'

'Anyhow, that was the reason they guv me,' said McCubby, as the truck began to roll. 'But now I suspicion they smelled the blow coming and bunked out, like bandicoots before a bush fire.'

'Without warning us?'

'Well, that Yartatgurk *had* put the debbil-debbil on you with that death song of his.' After a moment, McCubby added darkly, 'I didn't savvy that the boong bugger had narked me too.'

With that, he headed the truck for the Experimental Station. Neither the windshield wipers nor the headlights were of any use. There was no road, and the faint track we had followed coming out here was now obliterated. The air was still thick with flying debris. The truck jolted now and then to the resounding impact of a hurtling eucalyptus bole, or chunk of rock, or kangaroo, for all I know. Miraculously, none of them came through the windshield.

Gradually we inched upward from the low country, along the gently rising slope of a plateau. When we reached its level top we knew we were safe from the rising waters. And when we nosed down its farther slope, the rackety violence of the storm abated somewhat, cut off from us by the intervening highland.

As the noise subsided behind us, I broke our silence to ask McCubby what would become of the Anulas now. I ventured the hope that they would spend their newfound wealth on implements and appliances to raise their living standards. 'Perhaps build a rustic church,' I mused, 'and engage a circuit preacher . . .'

McCubby snorted. 'Wealth to them, Rev, is a couple of quid, which is all they'll get for that skin. And they'll blow it all in one cranky shivoo. Buy a few bottles of the cheapest plonk they can find, and stay shikkered for a week. Wake up sober in the Compound calaboose, more'n likely, with the Jumping Joe Blakes for comp'ny.'

This was most discouraging. It appeared that I had accomplished nothing whatsoever by my coming, and I said so.

'Why, they'll never forget you, Rev,' McCubby said through his teeth. 'No more will every other bloke in the territory that you caught with his knickers down. Here you've brought on the Wet nearly two months early, and brought it with a vengeance. Prob'ly drownded every jumbuck in the Never Never, washed out the railroad perway, bankrupted every ringer, flooded out the peanut farmers and the cotton planters . . .'

'Please,' I implored. 'Don't go on.'

There was another long and gloomy silence. Then McCubby took pity on me. He lifted my spirits somewhat—and encapsulated my mission—with a sort of subjunctive consolation:

'If you came out here,' he said, 'mainly to break the bingis of conjuring up pagan debbil-debbils to make rain, well, you can bet your best Bible they'll never do *that* again.'

And on that optimistic note I shall hasten this report toward its happy conclusion.

Several days later, McCubby and I arrived at Brunette Downs. He had the truckloads of beads transferred into a caravan of Land Rovers and headed Outback once more. I doubt not at all that he has since become a multimillionaire 'plute' by cornering the market in dingo scalps. I was able to engage another driver, and the two of us returned the rented trucks to Sydney.

By the time I got back to the city, I was absolutely penniless, and looking picturesquely, not to say revoltingly, squalid. I hied myself at once to the English-Speaking Union in search of SoPrimProPac Shagnasty. It was my intention to apply for some temporary underling job in the Sydney SoPrim organization and to beg a small salary advance. But it became immediately apparent, when I found Elder Shagnasty, that he was in no charitable mood.

'I keep getting these *dunning* letters,' he said peevishly, 'from the Port of Sydney Authority. A freight consignment of some sort is at the docks in your name. I can't sign for it, can't even find out what it is, but they keep sending me outrageous bills for its storage.'

I said I was just as much in the dark as he, but Elder Shagnasty interrupted, 'I wouldn't advise that you hang about here, Mobey. Deputy Protector Mashworm may come in at any minute, and he's after your hide. He has already flayed a goodly portion of mine.'

'Mine, too,' I couldn't forbear muttering.

'*He* keeps getting letters of reproach from the Resident Commissioner of the Northern Territory, inquiring why in blazes you were ever let loose to corrupt the blackfellows. It seems a whole tribe descended on Darwin, got vilely intoxicated and tore up half the city before they could be corralled. When they were sober enough to be questioned, they said a new young Bush Brother— unmistakably you—had provided the money for their binge.'

I tried to bleat an explanation, but he overrode me.

'That wasn't all. One of the blacks claimed the Bush Brother had shot and wounded him. Others said that the missionary had provoked an intertribal war. Still others claim he danced naked before them and then fed them poison, but that part wasn't too clear.'

I whinnied again, and was again overridden.

'I don't know exactly *what* you did up there, Brother Mobey, and frankly I don't care to be told. I would, however, be everlastingly grateful for one word from you.'

'What's that, Reverend Shagnasty?' I asked huskily.

He stuck out his hand. 'Goodbye.'

Having not much else to do, I drifted down to the Woolloomooloo docks to inquire about that mysterious freight consignment. It turned out to have been sent by dear old SoPrim's Overseas Mission Boards, and consisted of one Westinghouse two-seater electric golf cart, seven gross of Lightolier lampshades—that's 1,008 lampshades—and a number of cartons of Old Crone Brand burley snuff.

I was too benumbed and disheartened by this time even to evince surprise. I signed a receipt and was given a voucher. I carried the voucher to the sailors' low quarter of the city, where I was approached by shifty-eyed men. One of them, the master of a rusty trawler engaged in smuggling Capitalist luxuries to the under-advantaged Communists of Red China, bought my entire consignment sight unseen. I have no doubt that I was bilked on the transaction, but I was satisfied to be able to pay off the accumulated storage fees on the stuff and have enough left over to buy steerage passage on the first tramp ship leaving for the good old USA.

The only landfall in this country was New York City, so that's where I debarked, about a fortnight ago. Hence the postmark on this letter, because I am still here. I was penniless again by the time I landed. But through serendipitous coincidence I visited the local Natural History Museum (because admission was free) at just the time they were preparing a new aborigine tableau in the Australian wing. When I mentioned my recent stay among the Anulas I was at once engaged as a technical consultant.

The salary is modest, but I managed to put away a bit each week, in hope of soon returning to Virginia and to dear old SoPrim Seminary, to find out what my next assignment might be. Just recently, however, I have discovered that a mission calls me right here.

The artist painting the backdrop of the aborigine tableau—I take him to be an Italian chap; he is called Daddio—has introduced me to what he calls his 'in-group': habitants of an homogenous village within the very confines of Manhattan Island. He led me into a dim, smoky cellar room (a 'pad') full of these people—bearded, smelly, inarticulate, in various stages of undress—and I felt almost transported back among the abos.

Daddio nudged me and whispered, 'Go on, say it. Loud, and just the way I coached you, man.'

So I declaimed to the room at large the curious introduction he had made me rehearse in advance:

'I am the Reverend Crispin Mobey, boy Bush Brother! I have just been circumcised and I learned my Pitjantjatjara from a defrocked priest named Krapp!'

The people in the room, who had been desultorily chatting among themselves, were instantly silent. Then one said, in a hushed and reverent murmur, 'This cat Mobey is so far in *we're* out . . .'

'Like all of a sudden,' breathed another, '*Howl* is the square root of Peale . . .'

A lank-haired girl arose from a yoga squat and scrawled on the wall with her green eyebrow pencil, 'Leary, no. Larry Welk, si.'

'*Naked Lunch* is, like, Easter brunch,' said someone else.

'Like, man,' said several people at once, 'our leader has been taken to *us!*'

None of this conveyed any more to me than had the arcane utterances of McCubby and Yartatgurk. But I have been accepted here as I never was among the Anulas. Nowadays these people wait with bearded lips agape for my tritest pronouncement and listen, as avidly as no other congregation I have ever known, to my most recondite sermons. The one about Prayer being a Checkbook, etc. I have recited on several occasions in the tribe's coffeehouses, to an accompaniment of tribal *sitar* music.

And so, Dean Dismey, I have been divinely guided—all unwittingly but unswervingly—to the second mission of my career. The more I learn of these villagers and their poor deluded idolatries, the more I feel certain that, soon or later, I can be of Help.

I have applied to the missions office of the local Southern Primitive Protestant branch for proper accreditation, and have taken the liberty of listing you, reverend sir, and Elder Shagnasty as references. Any good word that you may be kind enough to vouchsafe in my behalf will be more than appreciated by

> Yours for Humility Rampant,
> Crispin Mobey

JEFFTY IS FIVE

Harlan Ellison

When I was five years old, there was a little kid I played with: Jeffty. His real name was Jeff Kinzer, and everyone who played with him called him Jeffty. We were five years old together, and we had good times playing together.

When I was five, a Clark Bar was as fat around as the gripping end of a Louisville Slugger, and pretty nearly six inches long, and they used real chocolate to coat it, and it crunched very nicely when you bit into the center, and the paper it came wrapped in smelled fresh and good when you peeled off one end to hold the bar so it wouldn't melt onto your fingers. Today, a Clark Bar is as thin as a credit card, they use something artificial and awful-tasting instead of pure chocolate, the thing is soft and soggy, it costs fifteen or twenty cents instead of a decent, correct nickel, and they wrap it so you think it's the same size it was twenty years ago, only it isn't; it's slim and ugly and nasty tasting and not worth a penny, much less fifteen or twenty cents.

When I was that age, five years old, I was sent away to my Aunt Patricia's home in Buffalo, New York for two years. My father was going through 'bad times,' and Aunt Patricia was very beautiful and had married a stockbroker. They took care of me for two years. When I was seven, I came back home and went to find Jeffty, so we could play together.

I was seven. Jeffty was still five. I didn't notice any difference. I didn't know: I was only seven.

When I was seven years old I used to lie on my stomach in front of our Atwater Kent radio and listen to swell stuff. I had tied the ground wire to the radiator, and I would lie there with my coloring books and my Crayolas (when there were only sixteen colors in the big box), and listen to the NBC red network: Jack Benny on the

Jell-O Program, Amos 'n' Andy, Edgar Bergen and Charlie McCarthy on the Chase and Sanborn Program, One Man's Family, First Nighter; the NBC blue network: Easy Aces, the Jergens Program with Walter Winchell, Information Please, Death Valley Days; and best of all, the Mutual Network with The Green Hornet. The Lone Ranger, The Shadow and Quiet Please. Today, I turn on my car radio and go from one end of the dial to the other and all I get is 100 strings orchestras, banal housewives and insipid truckers discussing their kinky sex lives with arrogant talk show hosts, country and western drivel and rock music so loud it hurts my ears.

When I was ten, my grandfather died of old age and I was 'a troublesome kid,' and they sent me off to military school, so I could be 'taken in hand.'

I came back when I was fourteen. Jeffty was still five.

When I was fourteen years old, I used to go to the movies on Saturday afternoons and a matinee was ten cents and they used real butter on the popcorn and I could always be sure of seeing a western like Lash LaRue, or Wild Bill Elliott as Red Ryder with Bobby Blake as Little Beaver, or Roy Rogers, or Johnny Mack Brown; a scary picture like *House of Horrors* with Rondo Hatton as the Strangler, or *The Cat People*, or *The Mummy*, or *I Married a Witch* with Fredric March and Veronica Lake; plus an episode of a great serial like The Shadow with Victor Jory, or Dick Tracy or Flash Gordon; and three cartoons; a James Fitzpatrick Travel Talk; Movietone News; a sing-along and, if I stayed on till evening, Bingo or Keno; and free dishes. Today, I go to movies and see Clint Eastwood blowing people's heads apart like ripe cantaloupes.

At eighteen, I went to college. Jeffty was still five. I came back during the summers, to work at my Uncle Joe's jewelry store. Jeffty hadn't changed. Now I knew there was something different about him, something wrong, something weird, Jeffty was still five years old, not a day older.

At twenty-two I came home for keeps. To open a Sony television franchise in town, the first one. I saw Jeffty from time to time. He was five.

Things are better in a lot of ways. People don't die from some of the old diseases any more. Cars go faster and get you there more quickly on better roads. Skirts are softer and silkier. We have paperbacks even though they cost as much as a good hardcover used to. When I'm running short in the bank I can live off credit cards till things even out. But I still think we've lost a lot of good stuff. Did you know you can't buy linoleum any more, only vinyl floor covering? There's no such thing as oilcloth any more; you'll never again smell that special, sweet smell from your grandmother's kitchen. Furniture isn't made to last thirty years or longer because they took a survey and found that young homemakers like to throw their furniture out and bring in all new color-coded borax every seven years. Records don't feel right; they're not thick and solid like the old ones, they're thin and you can bend them . . . that doesn't seem right to me. Restaurants don't serve cream in pitchers any more, just that artificial glop in little plastic tubs, and one is never enough to get coffee the right color. Everywhere you go, all the towns look the same with Burger Kings and MacDonald's and 7-Elevens and motels and shopping centers. Things may be better, but why do I keep thinking about the past?

What I mean by five years old is not that Jeffty was retarded. I don't think that's what it was. Smart as a whip for five years old; very bright, quick, cute, a funny kid.

But he was three feet tall, small for his age, and perfectly formed, no big head, no strange jaw, none of that. A nice, normal-looking five year old kid. Except that he was the same age as I was: twenty-two.

When he spoke, it was with the squeaking, soprano voice of a five year old; when he walked it was with the little hops and shuffles of a five year old; when he talked to you, it was about the concerns of a five year old . . . comic books, playing soldier, using a clothes pin to attach a stiff piece of cardboard to the front fork of his bike so the sound it made when the spokes hit was like a motorboat, asking questions like *why does that thing do that like that*, how high is up, how old is old, why is grass green, what's an elephant look like? At twenty-two, he was five.

Jeffty's parents were a sad pair. Because I was still a friend of Jeffty's, still let him hang around with me in the store, sometimes took him to the county fair or to the miniature golf or the movies, I wound up spending time with *them*. Not that I much cared for them, because they were so awfully depressing. But then, I suppose one couldn't expect much more from the poor devils. They had an alien thing in their home, a child who had grown no older than five in twenty-two years, who provided the treasure of that special childlike state indefinitely, but who also denied them the joys of watching the child grow into a normal adult.

Five is a wonderful time of life for a little kid . . . or it *can* be, if the child is relatively free of the monstrous beastliness other children indulge in. It is a time when the eyes are wide open and the patterns are not yet set; a time when one has not yet been hammered into accepting everything as immutable and hopeless; a time when the hands can not do enough, the mind cannot learn enough, the world is infinite and colorful and filled with mysteries. Five is a special time before they take the trembling hands that want to hold everything, touch everything, figure everything out, and make them lie still on desktops. A time before people begin saying 'act your age' and 'grow up' or 'you're behaving like a baby.' It is a time when a child who acts adolescent is still cute and responsive and everyone's pet. A time of delight, of wonder, of innocence.

Jeffty had been stuck in that time, just five, just so.

But for his parents it was an ongoing nightmare from which no one—not social workers, not priests, not child psychologists, not teachers, not friends, not medical wizards, not psychiatrists, no one—could slap or shake them awake. For seventeen years their sorrow had grown through stages of parental dotage to concern, from concern to worry, from worry to fear, from fear to confusion, from confusion to anger, from anger to dislike, from dislike to naked hatred, and finally, from deepest loathing and revulsion to a stolid, depressive acceptance.

John Kinzer was a shift foreman at the Balder Tool & Die plant. He was a thirty year man. To everyone but the man living it, his was a spectacularly uneventful life. In no way was he remarkable . . . save that he had fathered a twenty-two-year-old five year old.

John Kinzer was a small man, soft, with no sharp angles, with pale eyes that never seemed to hold mine for longer than a few seconds. He continually shifted in his chair during conversations, and seemed to see things in the upper corners of the room, things no one else could see . . . or wanted to see. I suppose the word that best suited him was *haunted*. What his life had become . . . well, *haunted* suited him.

Leona Kinzer tried valiantly to compensate. No matter what hour of the day I visited, she always tried to foist food at me. And when Jeffty was in the house she was always at *him* about eating: 'Honey, would you like an orange? A nice orange? Or a tangerine? I have tangerines. I could peel a tangerine for you.' But there was clearly such fear in her, fear of her own child, that the offers of sustenance always had a faintly ominous tone.

Leona Kinzer had been a tall woman, but the years had bent her. She seemed always to be seeking some area of wallpapered wall or storage niche into which she could fade, adopt some chintz or rose-patterned protective coloration and hide forever in plain sight of the child's big brown eyes, pass her a hundred times a day and never realize she was there, holding her breath, invisible. She always had an apron tied around her waist. And her hands were red from cleaning. As if by maintaining the environment immaculately she could pay off her imagined sin: having given birth to this strange creature.

Neither of them watched television very much. The house was usually dead silent, not even the sibilant whispering of water in the pipes, the creaking of timbers settling, the humming of the refrigerator. Awfully silent, as if time itself had taken a detour around that house.

As for Jeffty, he was inoffensive. He lived in that atmosphere of gentle dead and dulled loathing, and if he understood it, he never remarked in any way. He played, as a child plays, and seemed happy. But he must have sensed, in the way of a five year old, just how alien he was in their presence.

Alien. No, that wasn't right He was *too* human, if anything. But out of phase, out of synch with the world around him, and resonating a different vibration than his parents, God knows. Nor would other children play with him. As they grew past him, they found him at first childish, then uninteresting, then simply frightening as their perceptions of aging became clear and they could see he was not affected by time as they were. Even the little ones, his own age, who might wander into the neighborhood, quickly came to shy away from him like a dog in the street when a car backfires.

Thus, I remained his only friend. A friend of many years. Five years. Twenty-two years. I liked him; more than I can say. And never knew exactly why. But I did, without reserve.

But because we spent time together, I found I was also—polite society—spending time with John and Leona Kinzer. Dinner, Saturday afternoons sometimes, an hour or so when I'd bring Jeffty back from a movie. They were grateful: slavishly so. It relieved them of the embarrassing chore of going out with him, of having to pretend before the world that they were loving parents with a perfectly normal, happy, attractive child. And their gratitude extended to hosting me. Hideous, every moment of their depression, hideous.

I felt sorry for the poor devils, but I despised them for their inability to love Jeffty, who was eminently loveable.

I never let on, even during the evenings in their company that were awkward beyond belief.

We would sit there in the darkening living room—*always* dark or darkening, as if kept in shadow to hold back what the light might reveal to the world outside through the bright eyes of the house

—we would sit and silently stare at one another. They never knew what to say to me.

'So how are things down at the plant,' I'd say to John Kinzer.

He would shrug. Neither conversation nor life suited him with any ease or grace. 'Fine, just fine,' he would say, finally.

And we would sit in silence again.

'Would you like a nice piece of coffee cake?' Leona would say. 'I made it fresh just this morning.' Or deep dish green apple pie. Or milk and toll house cookies. Or a brown betty pudding. 'No, no, thank you, Jeffty and I grabbed a couple of cheeseburgers on the way home.' And again, silence.

Then, when the stillness and the awkwardness became too much even for them (and who knew how long that total silence reigned when they were alone, with that thing they never talked about any more, hanging between them), Leona Kinzer would say, 'I think he's asleep.'

John Kinzer would say, 'I don't hear the radio playing.'

Just so, it would go on like that, until I could politely find excuse to bolt away on some flimsy pretext. Yes, that was the way it would go on, every time, just the same . . . except once.

'I don't know what to do any more.' Leona said. She began crying. 'There's no change, not one day of peace.'

Her husband managed to drag himself out of the old easy chair and went to her. He bent and tried to sooth her, but it was clear from the graceless way in which he touched her graying hair that the ability to be compassionate had been stunned in him. 'Shhh, Leona, it's all right. Shhh.' But she continued crying. Her hands scraped gently at the antimacassars on the arms of the chair.

Then she said, 'Sometimes I wish he had been stillborn.'

John looked up into the corners of the room. For the nameless shadows that were always watching him? Was it God he was seeking in those spaces? 'You don't mean that,' he said to her, softly, pathetically, urging her with body tension and trembling in his voice to recant before God took notice of the terrible thought. But she meant it; she meant it very much.

I managed to get away quickly that evening. They didn't want witnesses to their shame. I was glad to go.

And for a week I stayed away. From them, from Jeffty, from their street, even from that end of town.

I had my own life. The store, accounts, suppliers' conferences, poker with friends, pretty women I took to well-lit restaurants, my own parents, putting anti-freeze in the car, complaining to the laundry about too much starch in the collars and cuffs, working out at the gym, taxes, catching Jan or David (whichever one it was) stealing from the cash register. I had my own life.

But not even *that* evening could keep me from Jeffty. He called me at the store and asked me to take him to the rodeo. We chummed it up as best a twenty-two year old with other interests *could* . . . with a five year old. I never dwelled on what bound us together; I always thought it was simply the years. That, and affection for a kid who could have been the little brother I never had. (Except I *remembered* when we had played together, when we had both been the same age; I *remembered* that period, and Jeffty was still the same.)

I came to take him to a double feature, and things I should have noticed so many times before, I first began to notice only that afternoon.

I came walking up to the Kinzer house, expecting Jeffty to be sitting on the front porch steps, or in the porch glider, waiting for me. But he was nowhere in sight.

Going inside, into that darkness and silence, in the midst of May sunshine, was unthinkable. I stood on the front walk for a few moments, then cupped my hands around my mouth and yelled, 'Jeffty? Hey, Jeffty, come on out, let's go. We'll be late.'

His voice came faintly, as if from under the ground.

'Here I am, Donny.'

I could hear him, but I couldn't see him. It was Jeffty, no question about it: as Donald H. Horton, President and Sole Owner of The Horton TV & Sound Center, no one but Jeffty called me Donny. He had never called me anything else.

(Actually, it isn't a lie. I *am*, as far as the public is concerned, Sole Owner of the Center. The partnership with my Aunt Patricia is only to repay the loan she made me, to supplement the money I came into when I was twenty-one, left to me by my grandfather. It wasn't a very big loan, only eighteen thousand, but I asked her to be a silent partner, because of when she had taken care of me as a child.)

'Where are you, Jeffty?'

'Under the porch in my secret place.'

I walked around the side of the porch, and stooped down and pulled away the wicker grating. Back in there, on the pressed dirt, Jeffty had built himself a secret place. He had comics in orange crates, he had a little table and some pillows, it was lit by big fat candles, and we used to hide there when we were both . . . five.

'What'cha up to?' I asked, crawling in and pulling the grate closed behind me. It was cool under the porch, and the dirt smelled comfortable, the candles smelled clubby and familiar. Any kid would feel at home in such a secret place: there's never been a kid who didn't spend the happiest, most productive, most deliciously mysterious times of his life in such a secret place.

'Playin',' he said. He was holding something golden and round. It filled the palm of his little hand.

'You forget we were going to the movies?'

'Nope. I was just waitin' for you here.'

'Your mom and dad home?'

'Momma.'

I understood why he was waiting under the porch. I didn't push it any further. 'What've you got there?'

'Captain Midnight Secret Decoder Badge,' he said, showing it to me on his flattened palm.

I realized I was looking at it without comprehending what it was for a long time. Then it dawned on me what a miracle Jeffty had in his hand. A miracle that simply could *not* exist.

'Jeffty,' I said softly, with wonder in my voice, 'where'd you get that?'

'Came in the mail today. I sent away for it.'

'It must have cost a lot of money.'

'Not so much. Ten cents an' two inner wax seals from two jars of Ovaltine.'

'May I see it?' My voice was trembling, and so was the hand I extended. He gave it to me and I held the miracle in the palm of my hand. It was *wonderful*.

You remember. *Captain Midnight* went on the radio nationwide in 1940. It was sponsored by Ovaltine. And every year they issued a Secret Squadron Decoder Badge. And every day at the end of the program, they would give you a clue to the next day's installment in a code that only kids with the official badge could decipher. They stopped making those wonderful Decoder Badges in 1949. I remember the one I had in 1945; it was beautiful. It had a magnifying glass in the center of the code dial. *Captain Midnight* went off the air in 1950, and though it was a short-lived television series in the mid-Fifties, and though they issued Decoder Badges in 1955 and 1956, as far as the *real* badges were concerned, they never made one after 1949.

The Captain Midnight Code-O-Graph I held in my hand, the one Jeffty said he had gotten in the mail for ten cents *(ten cents!!!)* and two Ovaltine labels, was brand new, shiny gold metal, not a dent or a spot of rust on it like the old ones you can find at exorbitant prices in collectible shoppes from time to time . . . it was a *new* Decoder. And the date on it was *this* year.

But *Captain Midnight* no longer existed. Nothing like it existed on the radio. I'd listened to the one or two weak imitations of old-time radio the networks were currently airing, and the stories were dull, the sound effects bland, the whole feel of it wrong, out of date, cornball. Yet I held a *new* Code-O-Graph.

'Jeffty, tell me about this,' I said.

'Tell you what, Donny? It's my new Capt'n Midnight Secret Decoder Badge. I use it to figger out what's gonna happen tomorrow.'

'Tomorrow how?'

'On the program.'

'*What* program?!'

He stared at me as if I was being purposely stupid. 'On *Capt'n Midnight!* Boy!' I was being dumb.

I still couldn't get it straight. It was right there, right out in the open, and I still didn't know what was happening. 'You mean one of those records they made of the old time radio programs? Is that what you mean, Jeffty?'

'What records?' he asked. He didn't know what *I* meant.

We stared at each other, there under the porch. And then I said, very slowly, almost afraid of the answer, 'Jeffty, how do you hear *Captain Midnight?*'

'Every day. On the radio. On my radio. Every day at five-thirty.'

News. Music, dumb music, and news. That's what was on the radio every day at five-thirty. Not *Captain Midnight*. The Secret Squadron hadn't been on the air in twenty years.

'Can we hear it tonight?' I asked.

'Boy!' he said. I was being dumb. I knew it from the way he said it; but I didn't know *why*. Then it dawned on me: this was Saturday. *Captain Midnight* was on Monday through Friday. Not on Saturday or Sunday.

'We goin' to the movies?'

He had to repeat himself twice. My mind was somewhere else. Nothing definite. No conclusions. No wild assumptions leapt to. Just off somewhere trying to figure it out, and concluding—as *you* would have concluded, as *anyone* would have concluded rather than accepting the truth, the impossible and wonderful truth—just finally concluding there was a simple explanation I didn't yet perceive. Something mundane and dull, like the passage of time that steals all good, old things from us, packratting trinkets and plastic in exchange. And all in the name of Progress.

'We goin' to the movies, Donny?'

'You bet your boots we are, kiddo,' I said. And I smiled. And I handed him the Code-O-Graph. And he put it in his side pants pocket. And we crawled out from under the porch. And we went to the movies. And neither of us said anything about *Captain Midnight* all the rest of that day. And there wasn't a ten-minute stretch, all the rest of that day, that I didn't think about it.

It was inventory all that next week. I didn't see Jeffty till late Thursday. I left the store in the hands of Jan and David, told them I had some errands to run, and left early. At 4:00. I got to the Kinzer's right around 4:45. Leona answered the door, looking exhausted and distant. 'Is Jeffty around?' She said he was upstairs in his room . . .

. . . listening to the radio.

I climbed the stairs two at a time.

All right, I had finally made that impossible, illogical leap. Had the stretch of belief involved anyone but Jeffty, adult or child, I would have reasoned out more explicable answers. But it *was* Jeffty, clearly another kind of vessel of life, and what he might experience should not be expected to fit into the ordered scheme.

I admit it: I *wanted* to hear what I heard.

Even with the door closed, I recognized the program:

'*There he goes, Tennessee! Get him!*'

There was the heavy report of a rifle shot and the keening whine of the slug ricocheting, and then the same voice yelled triumphantly, '*Got him! D-e-a-a-a-d center!*'

He was listening to the American Broadcasting Company, 790 kilocycles, and he was hearing *Tennessee Jed*, one of my most favorite programs from the Forties, a western adventure I had not heard in twenty years, because it had not existed for twenty years.

I sat down on the top step of the stairs, there in the upstairs hall of the Kinzer home, and I listened to the show. It wasn't a rerun of an old program, because there were occasional references in the body of the drama to current cultural and technological developments, and phrases that had not existed in common usage in the Forties: aerosol spray cans, laseracing of tatoos, Tanzania, the word 'up-tight.'

I could not ignore the fact. Jeffty was listening to a *new* segment of *Tennessee Jed*.

I ran downstairs and out the front door to my car. Leona must have been in the kitchen. I turned the key and punched on the radio and spun the dial to 790 kilocycles. The ABC station. Rock music.

I sat there for a few moments, then ran the dial slowly from one end to the other. Music, news, talk shows. No *Tennessee Jed*. And it was a Blaupunkt, the best radio I could get. I wasn't missing some perimeter station. It simply was not there!

After a few moments I turned off the radio and the ignition and went back upstairs quietly. I sat down on the top step and listened to the entire program. It was *wonderful*.

Exciting, imaginative, filled with everything I remembered as being most innovative about radio drama. But it was modern. It wasn't an antique, re-broadcast to assuage the need of that dwindling listenership who longed for the old days. It was a new show, with all the old voices, but still young and bright. Even the commercials were for currently available products, but they weren't as loud or as insulting as the screamer ads one heard on radio these days.

And when *Tennessee Jed* went off at 5:00, I heard Jeffty spin the dial on his radio till I heard the familiar voice of the announcer Glenn Riggs proclaim, '*Presenting Hop Harrigan! America's ace of the air-waves!*' There was the sound of an airplane in flight. It was a prop plane, *not* a jet! Not the sound kids today have grown up with, but the sound *I* grew up with, the *real* sound of an airplane, the growling, revving, throaty sound of the kind of airplanes G-8 and His Battle Aces flew, the kind Hop Harrigan flew. And then I heard Hop say, '*CX-4 calling control tower. CX-4 calling control tower. Standing by!*' A pause, then, '*Okay, this is Hop Harrigan . . . coming in!*'

And Jeffty, who had the same problem all of us kids had in the Forties with programming that pitted equal favorites against one another on different stations, having paid his respects to Hop Harrigan and Tank Tinker, spun the dial and went back to ABC where I heard the stroke of a gong, the wild cacophony of nonsense Chinese Chatter, and the announcer yelled, '*T-e-e-e-rry and the Pirates!*'

I sat there on the top step and listened to Terry and Connie and Flip Corkin and, so help me God, Agnes Moorehead as The Dragon Lady, all of them in a new adventure that took place in a Red China that had not existed in the days of Milton Caniff's 1937 version of the Orient, with river pirates and Chiang Kai-shek and war-lords and the naive Imperialism of American gunboat diplomacy.

Sat, and listened to the whole show, and sat even longer to hear *Superman* and part of *Jack Armstrong, the All-American Boy*, and part of *Captain Midnight*, and John Kinzer came home and neither he nor Leona came upstairs to find out what had happened to me, or where Jeffty was, and sat longer, and found I had started crying, and could not stop, just sat there with tears running down my face, into the corners of my mouth, sitting and crying until Jeffty heard me and opened his door and saw me and came out and looked at me in childish confusion as I heard the station break for the Mutual Network and they began the theme music of *Tom Mix*, 'When it's Round-up time in Texas and the Bloom is on the Sage,' and Jeffty touched my shoulder and smiled at me and said, 'Hi, Donny. Wanna come in an' listen to the radio with me?'

Hume denied the existence of an absolute space, in which each thing has its place; Borges denies the existence of one single time, in which all events are linked.

Jeffty received radio programs from a place that could not, in logic, in the natural scheme of the space-time universe as conceived by Einstein, exist. But that wasn't all he received. He got mail order premiums that no one was manufacturing. He read comic books that had been defunct for three decades. He saw movies with actors who had been dead for twenty years. He was the receiving terminal for endless joys and pleasures of the past that the world had dropped along the way. On its headlong suicidal flight toward New Tomorrows, the world had razed its treasurehouse of simple happiness, had poured concrete over its playgrounds, had abandoned its elfin stragglers, and all of it was being impossibly, miraculously stunted back into the present through Jeffty. Revivified, updated, the traditions maintained but contemporaneous. Jeffty was the unbidding Aladdin whose very nature formed the magic lampness of his reality.

And he took me into his world.

Because he trusted me.

We had breakfast of Quaker Puffed Wheat Sparkies and warm Ovaltine we drank out of *this* year's little Orphan Annie Shake-Up Mugs. We went to the movies and while everyone else was seeing a comedy starring Goldie Hawn and Ryan O'Neal, Jeffty and I were enjoying Humphrey Bogart as the professional thief Parker in John Huston's brilliant adaptation of the Donald Westlake novel, *Slayground*. The second feature was Spencer Tracy, Carole Lombard and Laird Cregar in the Val Lewton-produced film of *Leinengen Versus the Ants*.

Twice a month we went down to the newsstand and bought the current pulp issues of *The Shadow, Doc Savage* and *Startling Stories*. Jeffty and I sat together and I read to him from the magazines. He particularly liked the new short novel by Henry Kuttner, 'The Dreams of Achilles,' and the new Stanley G. Weinbaum series of short stories set in the subatomic particle universe of Redurna. In September we enjoyed the first installment of the new Robert E. Howard Conan novel, ISLE OF THE BLACK ONES, in *Weird Tales:* and in August were only mildly disappointed by Edgar Rice Burroughs' fourth novella in the Jupiter series featuring John Carter of Barsoom—'Corsairs of Jupiter.' But the editor of *Argosy All-Story Weekly* promised there would be two more stories in the series, and it was such an unexpected revelation for Jeffty and me, that it dimmed our disappointment at the lessened quality of the current story.

We read comics together, and Jeffty and I both decided —separately, before we came together to discuss it—that our favorite characters were Doll Man, Airboy and The Heap. We also adored the George Carlson strips in *Jingle Jangle Comics*, particularly the Pie-Face Prince of old Pretzelburg stories, which we read together and laughed over, even though I had to explain some of the subtler puns to Jeffty, who was too young to have that kind of subtle wit.

How to explain it? I can't. I had enough physics in college to make some offhand guesses, but I'm more likely wrong than right. The laws of the conservation of energy occasionally break. These are laws that physicists call 'weakly violated.' Perhaps Jeffty was a catalyst for the weak violation of conservation laws we're only now beginning to realize exist. I tried doing some reading in the area—muon decay of the 'forbidden' kind: gamma decay that doesn't include the muon neutrino among its products—but nothing I encountered, not even the latest readings from the Swiss Institute for Nuclear Research near Zurich gave me an insight. I was thrown back on a vague acceptance of the philosophy that the real name for 'science' is *magic*.

No explanations, but enormous good times.

The happiest time of my life.

I had the 'real' world, the world of my store and my friends and my family, the world of profit & loss, of taxes and evenings with young women who talked about going shopping or the United Nations, of rising cost of coffee and microwave ovens. And I had

Jeffty's world, in which I existed only when I was with him. The things of the past he knew as fresh and new, I could experience only when in his company. And the membrane between the two worlds grew even thinner, more luminous and transparent. I had the best of both worlds. And knew, somehow, that I could carry nothing from one to the other.

Forgetting that, for just a moment, betraying Jeffty by forgetting, brought an end to it all.

Enjoying myself so much, I grew careless and failed to consider how fragile the relationship between Jeffty's world and my world really was. There is a reason why the present begrudges the existence of the past. I never really understood. Nowhere in the beast books, where survival is shown in battles between claw and fang, tentacle and poison sac, is there recognition of the ferocity the present always brings to bear on the past. Nowhere is there a detailed statement of how the present lies in wait for What-Was, waiting for it to become Now-This-Moment so it can shred it with its merciless jaws.

Who could know such a thing . . . at any age . . . and certainly not at my age . . . who could understand such a thing?

I'm trying to exculpate myself. I can't. It was my fault.

It was another Saturday afternoon.

'What's playing today?' I asked him, in the car, on the way downtown.

He looked up at me from the other side of the front seat and smiled one of his best smiles. 'Ken Maynard in *Bullwhip Justice* an' *The Demoloshed Man.*' He kept smiling, as if he'd really put one over on me. I looked at him with disbelief.

'You're *kidding!*' I said, delighted. 'Bester's THE DEMOL-ISHED MAN?' He nodded his head, delighted at my being delighted. He knew it was one of my favorite books. 'Oh, that's super!'

'Super *duper,*' he said.

'Who's in it?'

'Franchot Tone, Evelyn Keyes, Lionel Barrymore and Elisha Cook, Jr.' He was much more knowledgeable about movie actors than I'd ever been. He could name the character actors in any movie he'd ever seen. Even the crowd scenes.

'And cartoons?' I asked.

'Three of 'em, a *Little Lulu,* a *Donald Duck* and a *Bugs Bunny.* An' a *Pete Smith Specialty* an' a *Lew Lehr Monkeys is da C-r-r-r-aziest Peoples.*'

'Oh boy!' I said. I was grinning from ear to ear. And then I looked down and saw the pad of purchase order forms on the seat. I'd forgotten to drop it off at the store.

'Gotta stop by the Center,' I said. 'Gotta drop off something. It'll only take a minute.'

'Okay,' Jeffty said. 'But we won't be late, will we?'

'Not on your tintype, kiddo,' I said.

When I pulled into the parking lot behind the Center, he decided to come in with me and we'd walk over to the theater. It's not a large town. There are only two movie houses, the Utopia and the Lyric. We were going to the Utopia, only three blocks from the Center.

I walked into the store with the pad of forms, and it was bedlam. David and Jan were handling two customers each, and there were people standing around waiting to be helped. Jan turned a look on me and her face was a horror-mask of pleading. David was running from the stockroom to the showroom and all he could murmur as he whipped past was, 'Help!' and then he was gone.

'Jeffty,' I said, crouching down, 'listen, give me a few minutes. Jan and David are in trouble with all these people. We won't be late, I promise. Just let me get rid of a couple of these customers.' He looked nervous, but nodded okay.

I motioned to a chair and said, 'Just sit down for a while and I'll be right with you.'

He went to the chair, good as you please, though he knew what was happening, and he sat down.

I started taking care of people who wanted color television sets. This was the first really substantial batch of units we'd gotten in—color television was only now becoming reasonably priced and this was Sony's first promotion—and it was bonanza time for me. I could see paying off the loan and being out in front for the first time with the Center. It was business.

In my world, good business comes first.

Jeffty sat there and stared at the wall. Let me tell you about the wall.

Stanchion and bracket designs had been rigged from floor to within two feet of the ceiling. Television sets had been stacked artfully on the wall. Thirty-three television sets. All playing at the same time. Black and white, color, little ones, big ones, all going at the same time.

Jeffty sat and watched thirty-three television sets, on a Saturday afternoon. We can pick up a total of thirteen channels including the

UHF educational stations. Golf was on one channel; baseball was on a second; celebrity bowling was on a third; the fourth channel was a religious seminar; a teen-age dance show was on the fifth; the sixth was a rerun of a situation comedy; the seventh was a rerun of a police show; eighth was a nature program showing a man flycasting endlessly; ninth was news and conversation; tenth was a stock car race; eleventh was a man doing logarithms on a blackboard; twelfth was a woman in a leotard doing sitting-up exercises; and on the thirteenth channel was a badly-animated cartoon show in Spanish. All but six of the shows were repeated on three sets. Jeffty sat and watched that wall of television on a Saturday afternoon while I sold as fast and as hard as I could, to pay back my Aunt Patricia and stay in touch with my world. It was business.

I should have known better. I should have understood about the present and the way it kills the past. But I was selling with both hands. And when I finally glanced over at Jeffty, half an hour later, he looked like another child.

He was sweating. That terrible fever sweat when you have stomach flu. He was pale, as pasty and pale as a worm, and his little hands were gripping the arms of the chair so tightly I could see his knuckles in bold relief. I dashed over to him, excusing myself from the middle-aged couple looking at the new 21' Mediterranean model.

'Jeffty!'

He looked at me, but his eyes didn't track. He was in absolute terror. I opulled him out of the chair and started toward the front door with him, but the customers I'd deserted yelled at me, 'Hey!' The middle-aged man said, 'You wanna sell me this thing or don't you?'

I looked from him to Jeffty and back again. Jeffty was like a zombie. He had come where I'd pulled him. His legs were rubbery and his feet dragged. The past, being eaten by the present, the sound of something in pain.

I clawed some money out of my pants pocket and jammed it into Jeffty's hand. 'Kiddo . . . listen to me . . . get out of here right now!' He still couldn't focus properly. '*Jeffty*.' I said as tightly as I could, *listen* to me!' The middle-aged customer and his wife were walking toward us. 'Listen, kiddo, get out of here right this minute. Walk over to the Utopia and buy the tickets. I'll be right behind you.' The middle-aged man and his wife were almost on us. I shoved Jeffty through the door and watched him stumble away in the wrong direction, then stop as if gathering his wits, turn and go back past the front of the Center and in the direction of the Utopia. 'Yes sir,' I said, straightening up and facing them, 'Yes, ma'am, that is one terrific set with some sensational features! If you'll just step back here with me. . . .'

There was a terrible sound of something hurting but I couldn't tell from which channel, or from which set, it was coming.

Most of it I learned later, from the girl in the ticket booth, and from some people I knew who came to me to tell me what had happened. By the time I got to the Utopia, nearly twenty minutes later, Jeffty was already beaten to a pulp and had been taken to the Manager's office.

'Did you see a very little boy, about five years old, with big brown eyes and straight brown hair . . . he was waiting for me?'

'Oh, I think that's the little boy those kids beat up?'

'What!? *Where is he?*'

'They took him to the Manager's office. No one knew who he was or where to find his parents—'

A young girl wearing an usher's uniform was placing a wet paper towel on his face.

I took the towel away from her and ordered her out of the office. She looked insulted and snorted something rude, but she left. I sat on the edge of the couch and tried to swab away the blood from the lacerations without opening the wounds where the blood had caked. Both his eyes were swollen shut. His mouth was ripped badly. His hair was matted with dried blood.

He had been standing in line behind two kids in their teens. They started selling tickets at 12:30 and the show started at 1:00. The doors weren't opened till 12:45. He had been waiting, and the kids in front of him had had a portable radio. They were listening to the ballgame. Jeffty had wanted to hear some program, God knows what it might have been, *Grand Central Station, Land of the Lost,* God only knows which one it might have been.

He had asked if he could borrow their radio to hear the program for a minute, and it had been a commercial break or something, and the kids had given him the radio, probably out of some malicious kind of courtesy that would permit them to take offense and rag the little boy. He had changed the station . . . and they'd been unable to get it to go back to the ballgame. It was locked into the past, on a station that was broadcasting a program that didn't exist for anyone but Jeffty.

They had beaten him badly . . . as everyone watched.

And they had run away.

I had left him alone, left him to fight off the present without sufficient weaponry. I had betrayed him for the sale of a 21 inch Mediterranian console television, and now his face was pulped meat. He moaned something inaudible and sobbed softly.

'Shhh, it's okay, kiddo, it's Donny. I'm here. I'll get you home, it'll be okay.'

I should have taken him straight to the hospital. I don't know why I didn't. I should have. I should have done that.

When I carried him through the door, John and Leona Kinzer just stared at me. They didn't move to take him from my arms. One of his hands was hanging down. He was conscious, but just barely. They stared, there in the semi-darkness of a Saturday afternoon in the present. I looked at them. 'A couple of kids beat him up at the theatre.' I raised him a few inches in my arms and extended him. They stared at me, at both of us, with nothing in their eyes, without movement. 'Jesus Christ,' I shouted, 'He's been beaten! He's your son! Don't you even want to touch him? What the hell kind of people are you?!'

Then Leona moved toward me very slowly. She stood in front of us for a few seconds, and there was a leaden stoicism in her face that was terrible to see. It said, *I have been in this place before, many times, and I cannot bear to be in it again; but I am here now.*

So I gave him to her. God help me, I gave him over to her.

And she took him upstairs to bathe away his blood and his pain.

John Kinzer and I stood in our separate places in the dim living room of their home, and we stared at each other. He had nothing to say to me.

I shoved past him and fell into a chair. I was shaking.

I heard the bath water running upstairs.

After what seemed a very long time Leona came downstairs, wiping her hands on her apron. She sat down on the sofa and after a moment John sat down beside her. I heard the sound of rock music from upstairs.

'Would you like a piece of nice pound cake?' Leona said.

I didn't answer. I was listening to the sound of the music. Rock music. On the radio. There was a table lamp on the end table beside the sofa. It cast a dim and futile light in the shadowed living room. Rock music from the present, on a radio upstairs? I started to say something, and then *knew* . . .

I jumped up just as the sound of hideous crackling blotted out the music, and the table lamp dimmed and dimmed and flickered. I screamed something, I don't know what it was, and ran for the stairs.

Jeffty's parents did not move. They sat there with their hands folded, in that place they had been for so many years.

I fell twice rushing up the stairs.

There isn't much on television that can hold my interest. I bought an old cathedral-shaped Philco radio in a second-hand store, and I replaced all the burnt-out parts with the original tubes from old radios I could cannibalize that still worked. I don't use transistors or printed circuits. They wouldn't work. I've sat in front of that set for hours sometimes, running the dial back and forth as slowly as you can imagine, so slowly it doesn't look as if it's moving at all sometimes.

But I can't find *Captain Midnight* or *The Land of the Lost* or *The Shadow* or *Quiet Please*.

So she did love him, still a little bit, even after all those years. I can't hate them: they only wanted to live in the present world again. That isn't such a terrible thing.

It's a good world, all things considered. It's much better than it used to be, in a lot of ways. People don't die from the old diseases any more. They die from new ones, but that's Progress, isn't it?

Isn't it?

Tell me.

Somebody please tell me.

THE THIRD LEVEL

Jack Finney

The presidents of the New York Central and the New York, New Haven and Hartford railroads will swear on a stack of timetables that there are only two. But I say there are three, because I've *been* on the third level at Grand Central Station. Yes, I've taken the obvious step: I talked to a psychiatrist friend of mine, among others. I told him about the third level at Grand Central Station, and he said it was a waking-dream wish fulfillment. He said I was unhappy. That made my wife kind of mad, but he explained that he meant the modern world is full of insecurity, fear, war, worry and all the rest of it, and that I just want to escape. Well, hell, who doesn't? Everybody I know wants to escape, but they don't wander down into any third level at Grand Central Station.

But that's the reason, he said, and my friends all agreed. Everything points to it, they claimed. My stamp collecting, for example; that's a 'temporary refuge from reality.' Well, maybe, but my grandfather didn't need any refuge from reality; things were pretty nice and peaceful in his day, from all I hear, and he started my collection. It's a nice collection, too, blocks of four of practically every U.S. issue, first-day covers, and so on. President Roosevelt collected stamps, too, you know.

Anyway, here's what happened at Grand Central. One night last summer I worked late at the office. I was in a hurry to get uptown to my apartment so I decided to subway from Grand Central because it's faster than the bus.

Now, I don't know why this should have happened to me. I'm just an ordinary guy named Charley, 31 years old, and I was wearing a tan gabardine suit and a straw hat with a fancy band; I

passed a dozen men who looked just like me. And I wasn't trying to
escape from anything; I just wanted to get home to Louisa, my
wife.

I turned into Grand Central from Vanderbilt Avenue, and went
down the steps to the first level, where you take trains like the
Twentieth Century. Then I walked down another flight to the
second level, where the suburban trains leave from, ducked into
an arched doorway heading for the subway—and got lost. That's
easy to do. I've been in and out of Grand Central hundreds of
times, but I'm always bumping into new doorways and stairs
and corridors. Once I got into a tunnel about a mile long and came
out in the lobby of the Roosevelt Hotel. Another time I came
up in an office building on Forty-sixth Street, three blocks
away.

Sometimes I think Grand Central is growing like a tree, pushing
out new corridors and staircases like roots. There's probably a long
tunnel that nobody knows about feeling its way under the city right
now, on its way to Times Square, and maybe another to Central
Park. And maybe—because for so many people through the years
Grand Central *has* been an exit, a way of escape—maybe that's how
the tunnel I got into . . . But I never told my psychiatrist friend
about that idea.

The corridor I was in began angling left and slanting downward
and I thought that was wrong, but I kept on walking. All I could
hear was the empty sound of my own footsteps and I didn't pass a
soul. Then I heard that sort of hollow roar ahead that means open
space and people talking. The tunnel turned sharp left; I went
down a short flight of stairs and came out on the third level at Grand
Central Station. For just a moment I thought I was back on the
second level, but I saw the room was smaller, there were fewer
ticket windows and train gates, and the information booth in the
center was wood and old-looking. And the man in the booth wore a
green eyeshade and long black sleeve protectors. The lights were
dim and sort of flickering. Then I saw why; they were open-flame
gaslights.

There were brass spittoons on the floor, and across the station a
glint of light caught my eye; a man was pulling a gold watch from
his vest pocket. He snapped open the cover, glanced at his watch,
and frowned. He wore a dirty hat, a black four-button suit with tiny
lapels, and he had a big, black, handle-bar mustache. Then I
looked around and saw that everyone in the station was dressed like
1890 something; I never saw so many beards, sideburns and fancy

mustaches in my life. A woman walked in through the train gate; she wore a dress with leg-of-mutton sleeves and skirts to the top of her high-buttoned shoes. Back of her, out on the tracks, I caught a glimpse of a locomotive, a very small Currier & Ives locomotive with a funnel-shaped stack. And then I knew.

To make sure, I walked over to a newsboy and glanced at the stack of papers at his feet. It was the *World;* and the *World* hasn't been published for years. The lead story said something about President Cleveland. I've found that front page since, in the Public Library files, and it was printed June 11, 1894.

I turned toward the ticket windows knowing that here—on the third level at Grand Central—I could buy tickets that would take Louisa and me anywhere in the United States we wanted to go. In the year 1894. And I wanted two tickets to Galesburg, Illinois.

Have you ever been there? It's a wonderful town still, with big old frame houses, huge lawns, and tremendous trees whose branches meet overhead and roof the streets. And in 1894, summer evenings were twice as long, and people sat out on their lawns, the men smoking cigars and talking quietly, the women waving palm-leaf fans, with the fireflies all around, in a peaceful world. To be back there with the first World War still twenty years off, and World War II over 40 years in the future . . . I wanted two tickets for that.

The clerk figured the fare—he glanced at my fancy hatband, but he figured the fare—and I had enough for two coach tickets, one way. But when I counted out the money and looked up, the clerk was staring at me. He nodded at the bills. 'That ain't money, mister,' he said, 'and if you're trying to skin me you won't get very far,' and he glanced at the cash drawer beside him. Of course the money was old-style bills, half again as big as the money we use nowadays, and different-looking. I turned away and got out fast. There's nothing nice about jail, even in 1894.

And that was that. I left the same way I came, I suppose. Next day, during lunch hour, I drew $300 out of the bank, nearly all we had, and bought old-style currency (that *really* worried my psychiatrist friend). You can buy old money at almost any coin dealer's, but you have to pay a premium. My $300 bought less than $200 in old-style bills, but I didn't care; eggs were thirteen cents a dozen in 1894.

But I've never again found the corridor that leads to the third level at Grand Central Station, although I've tried often enough.

Louisa was pretty worried when I told her all this, and didn't want me to look for the third level any more, and after a while I stopped; I went back to my stamps. But now we're *both* looking, every week end, because now we have proof that the third level is still there. My friend Sam Weiner disappeared! Nobody knew where, but I sort of suspected because Sam's a city boy, and I used to tell him about Galesburg—I went to school there—and he always said he liked the sound of the place. And that's where he is, all right. In 1894.

Because one night, fussing with my stamp collection, I found —Well, do you know what a first-day cover is? When a new stamp is issued, stamp collectors buy some and use them to mail envelopes to themselves on the very first day of sale; and the postmark proves the date. The envelope is called a first-day cover. They're never opened; you just put blank paper in the envelope.

That night, among my oldest first-day covers, I found one that shouldn't have been there. But there it was. It was there because someone had mailed it to my grandfather at his home in Galesburg; that's what the address on the envelope said. And it had been there since July 18, 1894—the postmark showed that—yet I didn't remember it at all. The stamp was a six-cent, dull brown, with a picture of President Garfield. Naturally, when the envelope came to Granddad in the mail, it went right into his collection and stayed there—till I took it out and opened it.

The paper inside wasn't blank. It read:

> 941 Willard Street
> Galesburg, Illinois
> July 18, 1894

Charley:

I got to wishing that you were right. Then I got to *believing* you were right. And, Charley, it's true; I found the third level! I've been here two weeks, and right now, down the street at the Dalys', someone is playing a piano, and they're all out on the front porch singing Seeing Nellie Home. And I'm invited over for lemonade. Come on back, Charley and Louisa. Keep looking till you find the third level! It's worth it, believe me!

The note is signed SAM.

At the stamp and coin store I go to, I found out that Sam bought $800 worth of old-style currency. That ought to set him up in a nice little hay, feed and grain business; he always said that's what he really wished he could do, and he certainly can't go back to his old business. Not in Galesburg, Illinois, in 1894. His old business? Why, Sam was my psychiatrist.

THE SILKEN-SWIFT

Theodore Sturgeon

There's a village by the Bogs, and in the village is a Great House. In the Great House lived a squire who had land and treasures and, for a daughter, Rita.

In the village lived Del, whose voice was a thunder in the inn when he drank there; whose corded, cabled body was golden-skinned, and whose hair flung challenges back to the sun.

Deep in the Bogs, which were brackish, there was a pool of purest water, shaded by willows and wide-wondering aspen, cupped by banks of a moss most marvelously blue. Here grew mandrake, and there were strange pipings in midsummer. No one ever heard them but a quiet girl whose beauty was so very contained that none of it showed. Her name was Barbara.

There was a green evening, breathless with growth, when Del took his usual way down the lane beside the manor and saw a white shadow adrift inside the tall iron pickets. He stopped, and the shadow approached, and became Rita. 'Slip around to the gate,' she said, 'and I'll open it for you.'

She wore a gown like a cloud and a silver circlet round her head. Night was caught in her hair, moonlight in her face, and in her great eyes, secrets swam.

Del said, 'I have no business with the squire.'

'He's gone,' she said. 'I've sent the servants away. Come to the gate.'

'I need no gate.' He leaped and caught the top bar of the fence, and in a continuous fluid motion went high and across and down beside her. She looked at his arms, one, the other; then up at his hair. She pressed her small hands tight together and made a little laugh, and then she was gone through the tailored trees, lightly, swiftly, not looking back. He followed, one step for three of hers, keeping pace with a new pounding in the sides of his neck. They crossed a flower bed and a wide marble terrace. There was an open door, and when he passed through it he stopped, for she was nowhere in sight. Then the door clicked shut behind him and he whirled. She was there, her back to the panel, laughing up at him in the dimness. He thought she would come to him then but instead she twisted by, close, her eyes on his. She smelt of violets and sandalwood. He followed her into a great hall, quite dark but full of the subdued lights of polished wood, cloisonné, tooled leather and gold-threaded tapestry. She flung open another door, and they were in a small room with a carpet made of rosy silences, and a candle-lit table. Two places were set, each with five different crystal glasses and old silver as prodigally used as the iron pickets outside. Six teakwood steps rose to a great oval window. 'The moon,' she said, 'will rise for us there.'

She motioned him to a chair and crossed to a sideboard, where there was a rack of decanters—ruby wine and white; one with a strange brown bead; pink, and amber. She took down the first, and poured. Then she lifted the silver domes from the salvers on the table, and a magic of fragrance filled the air. There were smoking sweets and savories, rare seafood and slivers of fowl, and morsels of strange meat wrapped in flower-petals, spitted with foreign fruits and tiny soft seashells. All about were spices, each like a separate voice in the distant murmur of a crowd: saffron and sesame, cumin and marjoram and mace.

And all the while Del watched her in wonder, seeing how the candles left the moonlight in her face, and how completely she trusted her hands, which did such deftnesses without supervision . . . so composed she was, for all the silent secret laughter that tugged at her lips, for all the bright dark mysteries that swirled and swam within her.

They ate, and the oval window yellowed and darkened while the candlelight grew bright. She poured another wine, and another, and with the courses of the meal they were as May to the crocus and as frost to the apple.

Del knew it was alchemy and he yielded to it without question. That which was purposely oversweet would be piquantly cut; this induced thirst would, with exquisite timing, be quenched. He knew she was watching him; he knew she was aware of the heat in his cheeks and the tingle at his fingertips. His wonder grew, but he was not afraid.

In all this time she spoke hardly a word; but at last the feast was

over and they rose. She touched a silken rope on the wall, and
paneling slid aside. The table rolled silently into some ingenious
recess and the panel returned. She waved him to an L-shaped couch
in one corner, and as he sat close to her, she turned and took
down the lute which hung on the wall behind her. He had his moment of confusion; his arms were ready for her, but not for the
instrument as well. Her eyes sparkled, but her composure was
unshaken.

Now she spoke, while her fingers strolled and danced on the lute,
and her words marched and wandered in and about the music. She
had a thousand voices, so that he wondered which of them was truly
hers. Sometimes she sang, sometimes it was a wordless crooning.
She seemed at times remote from him, puzzled at the turn the
music was taking, and at other times she seemed to hear the pulsing
roar in his eardrums, and she played laughing syncopations to it.
She sang words which he almost understood:

> Bee to blossom, honey-dew
> Claw to mouse, and rain to tree,
> Moon to midnight, I to you;
> Sun to starlight, you to me . . .

and she sang something wordless:

> Ake ya rundefle, rundefle fye,
> Orel ya rundefle kown,
> En yea, en yea, ya bunderbee bye
> En sor, en see, en sown.

which he also almost understood.

In still another voice she told him the story of a great hairy spider
and a little pink girl who found it between the leaves of a half-open
book; and at first he was all fright and pity for the child; but then
she went on to tell of what the spider suffered, with her home
disrupted by this yawping giant, and so vividly did she tell it that at
the end he was laughing at himself and all but crying for the poor
spider.

So the hours slipped by, and suddenly, between songs, she was in
his arms; and in the instant she had twisted up and away from him,
leaving him gasping. She said, 'No, Del. We must wait for the
moon.'

His thighs ached and he realized that he had half-risen, arms out,
hands clutching and feeling the extraordinary fabric of her gown
though it was gone from them; and he sank back to the couch with

an odd, faint sound that was wrong for the room. He flexed his fingers and, reluctantly, the sensation of white gossamer left them. At last he looked across at her and she laughed and leapt high lightly, and it was as if she stopped in midair to stretch for a moment before she alighted beside him, bent and kissed his mouth, and leapt away.

The roaring in his ears was greater, and at this it seemed to acquire a tangible weight. His head bowed; he tucked his knuckles into the upper curve of his eye-sockets and rested his elbows on his knees. He could hear the sweet susurrus of Rita's gown as she moved about the room; he could sense the violets and sandalwood. She was dancing, immersed in the joy of movement and of his nearness. She made her own music, humming, sometimes whispering to the melodies in her mind.

And at length he became aware that she had stopped; he could hear nothing, though he knew she was still near. Heavily he raised his head. She was in the center of the room, balanced like a huge white moth, her eyes quite dark now with their secrets quiet. She was staring at the window, poised, waiting.

He followed her gaze. The big oval was black no longer, but dusted over with silver light. Del rose slowly. The dust was a mist, a loom, and then, at one edge, there was a shard of the moon itself creeping and growing.

Because Del stopped breathing, he could hear her breath; it was rapid and so deep it faintly strummed her versatile vocal cords.

'Rita . . .'

Without answering she ran to the sideboard and filled two small glasses. She gave him one, then, 'Wait,' she breathed, 'oh, wait!'

Spellbound, he waited while the white stain crept across the window. He understood suddenly that he must be still until the great oval was completely filled with direct moonlight, and this helped him, because it set a foreseeable limit to his waiting; and it hurt him, because nothing in life, he thought, had ever moved so slowly . . . he had a moment of rebellion, in which he damned himself for falling in with her complex pacing; but with it he realized that now the darker silver was wasting away, now it was a finger's breadth, and now a thread, and now, and *now*—

She made a brittle feline cry and sprang up the dark steps to the window. So bright was the light that her body was a jet cameo against it. So delicately wrought was her gown that he could see the epaulettes of silver light the moon gave her. She was so beautiful his eyes stung.

'Drink,' she whispered, 'drink with me, darling, darling . . .'

For an instant he did not understand her at all, and only gradually did he become aware of the little glass he held. He raised it toward her and drank. And of all the shocks and titillations of taste he had had this night, this was the most startling; for it had no taste at all, almost no substance, and a temperature almost exactly that of blood. He looked stupidly down at the glass and back up at the girl. He thought that she had turned about and was watching him, though he could not be sure, since her silhouette was the same.

And then he had his second of unbearable shock, for the light went out.

The moon was gone, the window, the room; Rita was gone.

For a stunned instant he stood taut, stretching his eyes wide. He made a sound that was not a word. He dropped the glass and pressed his palms to his eyes, feeling them blink, feeling the stiff silk of his lashes against them. Then he snatched the hands away, and it was still dark, and more than dark; this was not a blackness. This was like trying to see with an elbow or with a tongue; it was not black, it was *nothingness*.

He fell to his knees.

Rita laughed.

An odd, alert part of his mind seized on the laugh and understood it, and horror and fury spread through his whole being; for this was the laugh which had been tugging at her lips all evening, and it was a hard, cruel, self assured laugh. And at the same time, because of the anger or in spite of it, desire exploded whitely within him. He moved toward the sound, groping, mouthing. There was a quick, faint series of rustling sounds from the steps, and then a light, strong web fell around him. He struck out at it, and recognized it for the unforgettable thing it was—her robe. He caught at it, ripped it, stamped upon it. He heard her bare feet run lightly down and past him, and lunged, and caught nothing. He stood, gasping painfully.

She laughed again.

'I'm blind,' he said hoarsely. 'Rita, I'm blind!'

'I know,' she said coolly, close beside him. And again she laughed.

'What have you done to me?'

'I've watched you be a dirty animal of a man,' she said.

He grunted and lunged again. His knees struck something—a chair, a cabinet—and he fell heavily. He thought he touched her foot.

'Here, lover, here!' she taunted.

He fumbled about for the thing which had tripped him, found it, used it to help him upright again. He peered uselessly about.

'Here, lover!'

He leaped, and crashed into the door-jamb: cheekbone, collar-bone, hipbone, ankle were one straight blaze of pain. He clung to the polished wood.

After a time he said, in agony, 'Why?'

'No man has ever touched me and none ever will,' she sang. Her breath was on his cheek. He reached and touched nothing, and then he heard her leap from her perch on a statue's pedestal by the door, where she had stood high and leaned over to speak.

No pain, no blindness, and not even the understanding that it was her witch's brew working in him could quell the wild desire he felt at her nearness. Nothing could tame the fury that shook him as she laughed. He staggered after her, bellowing.

She danced around him, laughing. Once she pushed him into a clattering rack of fire-irons. Once she caught his elbow from behind and spun him. And once, incredibly, she sprang past him and, in midair, kissed him again on the mouth.

He descended into Hell, surrounded by the small, sure patter of bare feet and sweet cool laughter. He rushed and crashed, he crouched and bled and whimpered like a hound. His roaring and blundering took an echo, and that must have been the great hall. Then there were walls that seemed more than unyielding; they struck back. And there were panels to lean against, gasping, which became opening doors as he leaned. And always the black nothing-ness, the writhing temptation of the pat-pat of firm flesh on smooth stones, and the ravening fury.

It was cooler, and there was no echo. He became aware of the whisper of the wind through trees. The balcony, he thought; and then, right in his ear, so that he felt her warm breath, 'Come, lover . . .' and he sprang. He sprang and missed, and instead of sprawling on the terrace, there was nothing, and nothing, and then, when he least expected it, a shower of cruel thumps as he rolled down the marble steps.

He must have had a shred of consciousness left, for he was vaguely aware of the approach of her bare feet, and of the small cautious hand that touched his shoulder and moved to his mouth, and then his chest. Then it was withdrawn, and either she laughed again or the sound was still in his mind.

Deep in the Bogs, which were brackish, there was a pool of purest water, shaded by willows and wide-wondering aspens, cupped by banks of a moss most marvelously blue. Here grew mandrake, and there were strange pipings in midsummer. No one ever heard them but a quiet girl whose beauty was so very contained that none of it showed. Her name was Barbara.

No one noticed Barbara, no one lived with her, no one cared. And Barbara's life was very full, for she was born to receive. Others are born wishing to receive, so they wear bright masks and make attractive sounds like cicadas and operettas, so others will be forced, one way or another, to give to them. But Barbara's receptors were wide open, and always had been, so that she needed no substitute for sunlight through a tulip petal, or the sound of morning-glories climbing, or the tangy-sweet smell of formic acid which is the only death cry possible to an ant, or any other of the thousand things overlooked by folk who can only wish to receive.

Barbara had a garden and an orchard, and took things in to market when she cared to, and the rest of the time she spent in taking what was given. Weeds grew in her garden, but since they were welcomed, they grew only where they could keep the water-melons from being sunburned. The rabbits were welcome, so they kept to the two rows of carrots, the one of lettuce, and the one of tomato vines which were planted for them, and they left the rest alone. Goldenrod shot up beside the bean-hills to lend a hand upward, and the birds ate only the figs and peaches from the waviest top branches, and in return patrolled the lower ones for caterpillars and egg-laying flies. And if a fruit stayed green for two weeks longer until Barbara had time to go to market, or if a mole could channel moisture to the roots of the corn, why it was the least they could do.

For a brace of years Barbara had wandered more and more, impelled by a thing she could not name—if indeed she were aware of it at all. She knew only that over-the-rise was a strange and friendly place, and that it was a fine thing on arriving there to find another rise to go over. It may very well be that she now needed someone to love, for loving is a most receiving thing, as anyone can attest who has been loved without returning it. It is the one who is loved who must give and give. And she found her love, not in her wanderings, but at the market. The shape of her love, his colors and sounds, were so much with her that when she saw him first it was without surprise; and thereafter, for a very long while, it was quite enough that he lived. He gave to her by being alive, by setting the air athrum with his mighty voice, by his stride, which was, for a man afoot, the exact analog of what the horseman calls a 'perfect seat.'

After seeing him, of course, she received twice and twice again as much as ever before. A tree was straight and tall for the magnificent sake of being straight and tall, but wasn't straightness a part of him, and being tall? The oriole gave more now than song, and the hawk more than walking the wind, for had they not hearts like his, warm blood and his same striving to keep it so for tomorrow? And more and more, over-the-rise was the place for her, for only there could there be more and still more things like him.

But when she found the pure pool in the brackish Bogs, there was no more over-the-rise for her. It was a place without hardness or hate, where the aspens trembled only for wonder, and where all contentment was rewarded. Every single rabbit there was *the* champion nose-twinkler, and every waterbird could stand on one leg the longest, and proud of it. Shelf-fungi hung to the willow-trunks, making that certain, single purple of which the sunset is incapable, and a tanager and a cardinal gravely granted one another their definitions of *red*.

Here Barbara brought a heart light with happiness, large with love, and set it down on the blue moss. And since the loving heart can receive more than anything else, so it is most needed; and Barbara took the best birdsongs, and the richest colors, and the deepest peace, and all the other things which are most worth giving. The chipmunks brought her nuts when she was hungry and the prettiest stones when she was not. A green snake explained to her, in pantomime, how a river of jewels may flow uphill, and three mad otters described how a bundle of joy may slip and slide down and down and be all the more joyful for it. And there was the magic moment when a midge hovered, and then a honeybee, and then a bumblebee, and at last a hummingbird; and there they hung, playing a chord in A-sharp minor.

Then one day the pool fell silent, and Barbara learned why the water was pure.

The aspens stopped trembling.

The rabbits all came out of the thicket and clustered on the blue bank, backs straight, ears up, and all their noses as still as coral.

The waterbirds stepped backwards, like courtiers, and stopped on the brink with their heads turned sidewise, one eye closed, the better to see with the other.

The chipmunks respectfully emptied their cheek-pouches, scrubbed their paws together and tucked them out of sight; then stood still as tent-pegs.

The pressure of growth around the pool ceased: the very grass waited.

The last sound of all to be heard—and by then it was very quiet—was the soft *whick!* of an owl's eyelids, as it awoke to watch.

He came like a cloud, the earth cupping itself to take each of his golden hooves. He stopped on the bank and lowered his head, and for a brief moment his eyes met Barbara's, and she looked into a second universe of wisdom and compassion. Then there was the arch of the magnificent neck, the blinding flash of his golden horn.

And he drank, and he was gone. Everyone knows the water is pure, where the unicorn drinks.

How long had he been there? How long gone? Did time wait, too, like the grass?

'And couldn't he stay?' she wept. 'Couldn't he stay?'

To have seen the unicorn is a sad thing; one might never see him more. But then—to have seen the unicorn!

She began to make a song.

It was late when Barbara came in from the Bogs, so late the moon was bleached with cold and fleeing to the horizon. She struck the highroad just below the Great House and turned to pass it and go out to her garden house.

Near the locked main gate an animal was barking. A sick animal, a big animal . . .

Barbara could see in the dark better than most, and soon saw the creature clinging to the gate, climbing, uttering that coughing moan as it went. At the top it slipped, fell outward, dangled; then there was a ripping sound, and it fell heavily to the ground and lay still and quiet.

She ran to it, and it began to make the sound again. It was a man, and he was weeping.

It was her love, her love, who was tall and straight and so very alive—her love, battered and bleeding, puffy, broken, his clothes torn . . . crying.

Now of all times was the time for a lover to receive, to take from the loved one his pain, his trouble, his fear. 'Oh, hush, hush,' she whispered, her hands touching his bruised face like swift feathers. 'It's all over now.'

She turned him over on his back and knelt to bring him up sitting. She lifted one of his thick arms around her shoulder. He was very heavy, but she was very strong. When he was upright, gasping weakly, she looked up and down the road in the waning moonlight. Nothing, no one. The Great House was dark. Across the road, though, was a meadow with high hedgerows which might break the wind a little.

'Come, my love, my dear love,' she whispered. He trembled violently.

All but carrying him, she got him across the road, over the shallow ditch, and through a gap in the hedge. She almost fell with him there. She gritted her teeth and set him down gently. She let him lean against the hedge, and then ran and swept up great armfuls of sweet broom. She made a tight springy bundle of it and set it on the ground beside him, and put a corner of her cloak over it, and gently lowered his head until it was pillowed. She folded the rest of the cloak about him. He was very cold.

There was no water near, and she dared not leave him. With her kerchief she cleaned some of the blood from his face. He was still very cold. He said, 'You devil. You rotten little devil.'

'Shh.' She crept in beside him and cradled his head. 'You'll be warm in a minute.'

'Stand still,' he growled. 'Keep running away.'

'I won't run away,' she whispered. 'Oh, my darling, you've been hurt, so hurt. I won't leave you. I promise I won't leave you.'

He lay very still. He made the growling sound again.

'I'll tell you a lovely thing,' she said softly. 'Listen to me, think about the lovely thing,' she crooned.

'There's a place in the Bogs, a pool of pure water, where the trees live beautifully, willow and aspen and birch, where everything is peaceful, my darling, and the flowers grow without tearing their petals. The moss is blue and the water is like diamonds.'

'You tell me stories in a thousand voices,' he muttered.

'Shh. Listen, my darling. This isn't a story, it's a real place. Four miles north and a little west, and you can see the trees from the ridge with the two dwarf oaks. And I know why the water is pure!' she cried gladly. 'I know why!'

He said nothing. He took a deep breath and it hurt him, for he shuddered painfully.

'The unicorn drinks there,' she whispered. 'I *saw* him!'

Still he said nothing. She said, 'I made a song about it. Listen, this is the song I made:

"*And he—suddenly gleamed! My dazzled eyes*
Coming from outer sunshine to this green
And secret gloaming, met without surprise
The vision. Only after, when the sheen
And splendor of his going fled away,
I knew amazement, wonder and despair,
That he should come—and pass—and would not stay,

The Silken-swift—the gloriously Fair!
That he should come—and pass—and would not stay.
So that, forever after, I must go,
Take the long road that mounts against the day,
Travelling in the hope that I shall know
Again that lifted moment, high and sweet,
Somewhere—on purple moor or windy hill—
Remembering still his wild and delicate feet,
The magic and the dream—remembering still!"

His breathing was more regular. She said, 'I truly *saw* him!'

'I'm blind,' he said. 'Blind, I'm blind.'

'Oh, my dear . . .'

He fumbled for her hand, found it. For a long moment he held it. Then, slowly, he brought up his other hand and with them both he felt her hand, turned it about, squeezed it. Suddenly he grunted, half-sitting. 'You're here!'

'Of course, darling. Of course I'm here.'

'Why?' he shouted. 'Why? *Why?* Why all of this? Why blind me?' He sat up, mouthing, and put his great hand on her throat. 'Why do all that if . . .' The words ran together into an animal noise. Wine and witchery, anger and agony boiled in his veins.

Once she cried out.

Once she sobbed.

'Now,' he said, 'you'll catch no unicorns. Get away from me.' He cuffed her.

'You're mad. You're sick.' she cried.

'Get away,' he said ominously.

Terrified, she rose. He took the cloak and hurled it after her. It almost toppled her as she ran away, crying silently.

After a long time, from behind the hedge, the sick, coughing sobs began again.

Three weeks later Rita was in the market when a hard hand took her upper arm and pressed her into the angle of a cottage wall. She did not start. She flashed her eyes upward and recognized him, and then said composedly, 'Don't touch me.'

'I need you to tell me something,' he said. 'And tell me you *will!*' His voice was as hard as his hand.

'I'll tell you anything you like,' she said. 'But don't touch me.'

He hesitated, then released her. She turned to him casually. 'What is it?' Her gaze darted across his face and its almost-healed scars. The small smile tugged at one corner of her mouth.

His eyes were slits. 'I have to know this: Why did you make up all that . . . prettiness, that food, that poison . . . just for me? You could have had me for less.'

She smiled. 'Just for you? It was your turn, that's all.'

He was genuinely surprised. 'It's happened before?'

She nodded. 'Whenever it's the full of the moon—and the squire's away.'

'You're lying!'

'You forget yourself!' she said sharply. Then, smiling, 'It is the truth, though.'

'I'd've heard talk—'

'Would you now? And tell me—how many of your friends know about your humiliating adventure?'

He hung his head.

She nodded. 'You see? They go away until they're healed, and they come back and say nothing. And they always will.'

'You're a devil. . . . Why do you do it? Why?'

'I told you,' she said openly. 'I'm a woman and I act like a woman in my own way. No man will ever touch me, though. I am virgin and shall remain so.'

'You're *what?*' he roared.

She held up a restraining, ladylike glove. 'Please,' she said, pained.

'Listen,' he said, quietly now, but with such intensity that for once she stepped back a pace. He closed his eyes, thinking hard. 'You told me . . . the pool, the pool of the unicorn, and a song, wait—wait. *"The Silken-swift, the gloriously Fair . . ."* Remember? And then I—I saw to it that *you'd* never catch a unicorn!'

She shook her head, complete candor in her face. 'I like that, *"The Silken-swift."* Pretty. But believe me—no! That isn't mine.'

He put his face close to hers, and though it was barely a whisper, it came out like bullets. 'Liar! Liar! I couldn't forget. I was sick, I was hurt, I was poisoned, but I know what I did!' He turned on his heel and strode away.

She put the thumb of her glove against her upper teeth for a second, then ran after him. 'Del!'

He stopped but, rudely, would not turn. She rounded him, faced him. 'I'll not have you believing that of me . . . it's the one thing I have left,' she said tremulously.

He made no attempt to conceal his surprise. She controlled her expression with a visible effort, and said, 'Please. Tell me a little more—just about the pool, the song, whatever it was.'

'You don't remember?'

'I don't *know!*' she flashed. She was deeply agitated.

He said, with mock patience, 'You told me of a unicorn pool out in the Bogs. You said you had seen him drink there. You made a song about it. And then I—'

'Where? Where was this?'

'You forget so soon?'

'Where? Where did it happen?'

'In the meadow, across the road from your gate, where you followed me,' he said. 'Where my sight came back to me when the sun came up.'

She looked at him blankly, and slowly her face changed. First the imprisoned smile struggling to be free, and then—she was herself again, and she laughed. She laughed a great ringing peal of the laughter that had plagued him so, and she did not stop until he put one hand behind his back, then the other, and she saw his shoulders swell with the effort to keep from striking her dead.

'You animal!' she said, good-humoredly. 'Do you know what you've done? Oh, you . . . you *animal!*' She glanced around to see that there were no ears to hear her. 'I left you at the foot of the terrace steps,' she told him. Her eyes sparkled. 'Inside the gates, you understand? And you . . .'

'Don't laugh,' he said quietly.

She did not laugh. 'That was someone else out there. Who, I can't imagine. But it wasn't I.'

He paled. 'You followed me out.'

'On my soul I did not,' she said soberly. Then she quelled another laugh.

'That can't be,' he said. 'I couldn't have . . .'

'But you were blind, blind and crazy, Del-my-lover!'

'Squire's daughter, take care,' he hissed. Then he pulled his big hand through his hair. 'It can't be. It's three weeks; I'd have been accused . . .'

'There are those who wouldn't,' she smiled. 'Or—perhaps she will, in time.'

'There has never been a woman so foul,' he said evenly, looking her straight in the eye. 'You're lying—you know you're lying.'

'What must I do to prove it—aside from that which I'll have no man do?'

His lips curled. 'Catch the unicorn,' he said.

'If I did, you'd believe I was virgin?'

'I must,' he admitted. He turned away, then said, over his shoulder, 'But—*you?*'

She watched him thoughtfully until he left the marketplace. Her eyes sparkled; then she walked briskly to the goldsmith's, where she ordered a bridle of woven gold.

If the unicorn pool lay in the Bogs nearby, Rita reasoned, someone who was familiar with that brackish wasteland must know of it. And when she made a list in her mind of those few who traveled the Bogs, she knew whom to ask. With that, the other deduction came readily. Her laughter drew stares as she moved through the marketplace.

By the vegetable stall she stopped. The girl looked up patiently.

Rita stood swinging one expensive glove against the other wrist, half-smiling. 'So you're the one.' She studied the plain, inward-turning, peaceful face until Barbara had to turn her eyes away. Rita said, without further preamble, 'I want you to show me the unicorn pool in two weeks.'

Barbara looked up again, and now it was Rita who dropped her eyes. Rita said, 'I can have someone else find it, of course. If you'd rather not.' She spoke very clearly, and people turned to listen. They looked from Barbara to Rita and back again, and they waited.

'I don't mind,' said Barbara faintly. As soon as Rita had left, smiling, she packed up her things and went silently back to her house.

The goldsmith, of course, made no secret of such an extraordinary commission; and that, plus the gossips who had overheard Rita talking to Barbara, made the expedition into a cavalcade. The whole village, turned out to see; the boys kept firmly in cheek so that Rita might lead the way; the young bloods ranged behind her (some a little less carefree than they might be) and others snickering behind their hands. Behind them the girls, one or two a little pale, others eager as cats to see the squire's daughter fail, and perhaps even . . . but then, only she had the golden bridle.

She carried it casually, but casualness could not hide it, for it was not wrapped, and it swung and blazed in the sun. She wore a flowing white robe, trimmed a little short so that she might negotiate the rough bogland; she had on a golden girdle and little gold sandals, and a gold chain bound her head and hair like a coronet.

Barbara walked quietly a little behind Rita, closed in with her own thoughts. Not once did she look at Del, who strode somberly by himself.

Rita halted a moment and let Barbara catch up, then walked beside her. 'Tell me,' she said quietly, 'why did you come? It needn't have been you.'

'I'm his friend,' Barbara said. She quickly touched the bridle with her finger. 'The unicorn.'

'Oh,' said Rita. 'The unicorn.' She looked archly at the other girl. 'You wouldn't betray all your friends, would you?'

Barbara looked at her thoughtfully, without anger. 'If . . . when you catch the unicorn,' she said carefully, 'what will you do with him?'

'What an amazing question! I shall keep him, of course!'

'I thought I might persuade you to let him go.'

Rita smiled, and hung the bridle on her other arm. 'You could never do that.'

'I know,' said Barbara. 'But I thought I might, so that's why I came.' And before Rita could answer, she dropped behind again.

The last ridge, the one which overlooked the unicorn pool, saw a series of gasps as the ranks of villagers topped it, one after the other, and saw what lay below; and it was indeed beautiful.

Surprisingly, it was Del who took it upon himself to call out, in his great voice, 'Everyone wait here!' And everyone did; the top of the ridge filled slowly, from one side to the other, with craning, murmuring people. And then Del bounded after Rita and Barbara.

Barbara said, 'I'll stop here.'

'Wait,' said Rita, imperiously. Of Del she demanded, 'What are you coming for?'

'To see fair play,' he growled. 'The little I know of witchcraft makes me like none of it.'

'Very well,' she said calmly. Then she smiled her very own smile. 'Since you insist, I'd rather enjoy Barbara's company too.'

Barbara hesitated. 'Come, he won't hurt you, girl,' said Rita. 'He doesn't know you exist.'

'Oh,' said Barbara, wonderingly.

Del said gruffly, 'I do so. She has the vegetable stall.'

Rita smiled at Barbara, the secrets bright in her eyes. Barbara said nothing, but came with them.

'You should go back, you know,' Rita said silkily to Del, when she could. 'Haven't you been humiliated enough yet?'

He did not answer.

She said, 'Stubborn animal! Do you think I'd have come this far if I weren't sure?'

'Yes,' said Del, 'I think perhaps you would.'

They reached the blue moss. Rita shuffled it about with her feet and then sank gracefully down to it. Barbara stood alone in the shadows of the willow grove. Del thumped gently at an aspen with his fist. Rita, smiling, arranged the bridle to cast, and laid it across her lap.

The rabbits stayed hidden. There was an uneasiness about the grove. Barbara sank to her knees, and put out her hand. A chipmunk ran to nestle in it.

This time there was a difference. This time it was not the slow silencing of living things that warned of his approach, but a sudden babble from the people on the ridge.

Rita gathered her legs under her like a sprinter, and held the bridle poised. Her eyes were round and bright, and the tip of her tongue showed between her white teeth. Barbara was a statue. Del put his back against his tree, and became as still as Barbara.

Then from the ridge came a single, simultaneous intake of breath, and silence. One knew without looking that some stared speechless, that some buried their faces or threw an arm over their eyes.

He came.

He came slowly this time, his golden hooves choosing his paces like so many embroidery needles. He held his splendid head high. He regarded the three on the bank gravely, and then turned to look at the ridge for a moment. At last he turned again, and came round the pond by the willow grove. Just on the blue moss, he stopped to look down into the pond. It seemed that he drew one deep clear breath. He bent his head then, and drank, and lifted his head to shake away the shining drops.

He turned toward the three spellbound humans and looked at them each in turn. And it was not Rita he went to, at last, nor Barbara. He came to Del, and he drank of Del's eyes with his own just as he had partaken of the pool—deeply and at leisure. The beauty and wisdom were there, and the compassion, and what looked like a bright white point of anger. Del knew that the creature had read everything then, and that he knew all three of them in ways unknown to human beings.

There was a majestic sadness in the way he turned then, and dropped his shining head, and stepped daintily to Rita. She sighed, and rose up a little, lifting the bridle. The unicorn lowered his horn to receive it—

—and tossed his head, tore the bridle out of her grasp, sent the golden thing high in the air. It turned there in the sun, and fell into the pond.

And the instant it touched the water, the pond was a bog and the birds rose mourning from the trees. The unicorn looked up at them, and shook himself. Then he trotted to Barbara and knelt, and put his smooth stainless head in her lap.

Barbara's hands stayed on the ground by her sides. Her gaze roved over the warm white beauty, up to the tip of the golden horn and back.

The scream was frightening. Rita's hands were up like claws, and she had bitten her tongue; there was blood on her mouth. She screamed again. She threw herself off the now-withered moss toward the unicorn and Barbara. 'She can't be!' Rita shrieked. She collided with Del's broad right hand. 'It's wrong, I tell you, she, you, I . . .'

'I'm satisfied,' said Del, low in his throat. 'Keep away, squire's daughter.'

She recoiled from him, made as if to try to circle him. He stepped forward. She ground her chin into one shoulder, then the other, in a gesture of sheer frustration, turned suddenly and ran toward the ridge. 'It's mine, it's mine,' she screamed. 'I tell you, it can't be her, don't you understand? I never once, I never did, but she, but she—'

She slowed and stopped, then, and fell silent at the sound that rose from the ridge. It began like the first patter of rain on oak leaves, and it gathered voice until it was a rumble and then a roar. She stood looking up, her face working, the sound washing over her. She shrank from it.

It was laughter.

She turned once, a pleading just beginning to form on her face. Del regarded her stonily. She faced the ridge then, and squared her shoulders, and walked up the hill, to go into the laughter, to go through it, to have it follow her all the way home and all the days of her life.

Del turned to Barbara just as she bent over the beautiful head. She said, 'Silken-swift . . . go free.'

The unicorn raised its head and looked up at Del. Del's mouth opened. He took a clumsy step forward, stopped again. *'You!'*

Barbara's face was wet. 'You weren't to know,' she choked. 'You weren't ever to know. . . . I was so glad you were blind, because I thought you'd never know.'

He fell on his knees beside her. And when he did, the unicorn touched her face with his satin nose, and all the girl's pent-up beauty flooded outward. The unicorn rose from his kneeling, and whickered softly. Del looked at her, and only the unicorn was more beautiful. He put out his hand to the shining neck, and for a moment felt the incredible silk of that mane flowing across his fingers. The unicorn reared then, and wheeled, and in a great leap was across the bog, and in two more was on the crest of the farther ridge. He paused there briefly, with the sun on him, and then was gone.

Barbara said, 'For us, he lost his pool, his beautiful pool.'

And Del said, 'He will get another. He must.' With difficulty he added, 'He couldn't be . . . punished . . . for being so gloriously Fair.'

ANOTHER ORPHAN

John Kessel

'And I only am escaped alone to tell thee.'
—Job

e woke to darkness and swaying and the stink of many bodies. He tried to lift his head and reach across the bed and found he was not in his bed at all. He was in a canvas hammock that rocked back and forth in a room of other hammocks.

'Carol?' Still half-asleep, he looked around, then lay back, hoping that he might wake and find this just a dream. He felt the distance from himself he often felt in dreams. But the room did not go away, and the smell of sweat and salt water and some overwhelming stink of oil became more real. The light slanting down through a latticed grating above became brighter; he heard the sound of water and the creak of canvas, and the swaying did not stop, and the men about him began to stir. It came to him, in that same dream-like calm, that he was on a ship.

A bell sounded twice, then twice again. Most of the other men were up, grumbling, and stowing away the hammocks.

'What ails you, Fallon?' someone called. 'Up, now.'

2

His name was Patrick Fallon. He was thirty-two years old, a broker for a commission house at the Chicago Board of Trade. He played squash at an athletic club every Tuesday and Thursday night. He lived with a woman named Carol Bukaty.

The night before, he and Carol had gone to a party thrown by one of the other brokers and his wife. As sometimes happened with these parties, this one had degenerated into an exchange of sexual innuendo, none of it apparently serious, but with undertones of suspicions and the desire to hurt. Fallon had had too much wine and had said a few things to the hostess and about Carol that he had immediately wanted to retract. They'd driven back from the party in silence, but the minute they'd closed the door it had been a fight. Neither of them shouted, but his quiet statement that he did not respect her at all and hers that she was sickened by his excess, managed quite well. They had become adept in three years at getting at each other. They had, in the end, made up, and had made love.

As Fallon had lain there on the edge of sleep, he had had the idle thought that what had happened that evening was silly, but not funny. That something was wrong.

Fallon had the headache that was the residue of the wine; he could still smell Carol. He was very hungry and dazed as he stumbled into the bright sunlight on the deck of the ship. It was there. It was real. He was awake. The ocean stretched flat and empty in all directions. The ship rolled slightly as it made way with the help of a light wind, and despite the early morning it was already hot. He did not hear the sound or feel the vibration of an engine. Fallon stared, unable to collect the scattered impressions into coherence; they were all consistent with the picture of an antiquated sailing ship on a very real ocean, all insane when compared with where his mind told him he ought to be.

The men had gone to their work as soon as they'd stretched into the morning light. They wore drab shirts and canvas trousers; most were barefoot. Fallon walked unsteadily along the deck, trying to keep out of their way as they set to scrubbing the deck. The ship was unlike anything he had ever seen on Lake Michigan; he tried to ignore the salt smell that threatened to make it impossible for him to convince himself this was Lake Michigan. Yet it seemed absurd for such a small vessel to be in the middle of an ocean. He knew that the Coast Guard kept sailing ships for training its cadets, but these were no cadets.

The deck was worn, scarred and greasy with a kind of oily, clear lard-like grease. The rail around the deck was varnished black and weather-beaten, but the pins set through it to which the rigging was secured were ivory. Fallon touched one—it was some kind of tooth. More ivory was used for rigging-blocks and on the capstan around which the anchor chain was wound. The ship was a thing of black wood fading to white under the assault of water and sun, and of white ivory corroding to black under the effect of dirt and hard use. Three long boats, pointed at both ends, hung from arms of wood and metal on the left—the port—side; another such boat was slung at the rear of the deck on the starboard side, and on the raised part of the deck behind the mainmast two other boats were turned turtle and secured. Add to this the large hatch on the main deck and a massive brick structure that looked like some old-fashioned oven just behind the front mast, and there hardly seemed room for the fifteen or twenty men on deck to go about their business. There was certainly no place to hide.

'Fallon! Set your elbows to that deck or I shall have to set your nose to it!' A short, sandy-haired man accosted him. Stocky and muscular, he was some authority; there was insolence in his grin, and some seriousness. The other men looked up.

Fallon got out of the man's way. He went over to one of the groups washing down the deck with salt water, large scrub brushes, and what looked like push brooms with leather flaps instead of bristles, like large versions of the squeegees used to clean windows. The sandy-haired man watched him as he got down on his hands and knees and grabbed one of the brushes.

'There's a good lad, now. Ain't he, fellows?'

A couple of them laughed. Fallon started scrubbing, concentrating on the grain of the wood, at first fastidious about not wetting the already damp trousers he had apparently slept in, soon realizing that that was a lost cause. The warm water was sloshed over them, the men leaned on the brushes, and the oil slowly flaked up and away through the spaces in the rail into the sea. The sun rose and it became even hotter. Now and then one of the men tried to say a word or two to him, but he did not answer.

'Fallon here's got the hypos,' someone said.

'Or the cholera,' another said. 'He does look a bit bleary about the eye. Are you thirsty, Fallon? D'your legs ache? Are your bowels knotted?'

'My bowels are fine,' he said.

That brought a good laugh. 'Fine, he says! Manxman!' The sailor called to a decrepit old man leaning on his squeegee. 'Tell the King-Post that Fallon's bowels are fine, now! The scrubbing does seem to have eased them.'

'Don't ease them here, man!' the old man said seriously. The men roared again, and the next bucket of water was sloshed up between Fallon's legs.

* * *

3

In the movies men had faced similar situations. The amnesiac soldier came to on a farm in Wales. But invariably the soldier would give evidence of his confusion, challenging the farm owner, pestering his fellow workers with questions about where he was and how he got there, telling them of his persistent memory of a woman in white with golden hair. Strangely—strangely even to Fallon—he did not feel that way. Confusion, yes, dread, curiosity—but no desire to call attention to himself, to try to make the obvious reality of his situation give way to the apparent reality of his memories. He did not think this was because of any strength of character or remarkable powers of adaptation. In fact, everything he did that first day revealed his ignorance of what he was supposed to know and do on the ship. He did not feel any great presence of mind; for minutes at a time he would stop working, stunned with awe and fear at the simple alienness of what was happening. If it was a dream, it was a vivid dream. If anything was a dream, it was Carol and the Chicago Board of Trade.

The soldier in the movie always managed, despite the impediments of his amnesia and the ignorance of those around him, to find the rational answer to his mystery. That shell fragment which had grazed his forehead in Normandy had sent him back to Wessex sanitorium, from which he had wandered during an air raid, to be picked up by a local handyman driving his lorry to Llanelly, who in the course of the journey decided to turn a few quid by leasing the poor soldier to a farmer as his half-wit cousin laborer. So it had to be that some physicist at the University of Chicago, working on the modern equivalent of the Manhattan Project, had accidentally created a field of gravitational energy so intense that a vagrant vortex had broken free from it, and, in its lightning progress through the city on its way to extinction, had plucked Fallon from his bed in the suburbs, sucked him through a puncture in the fabric of space and time, to deposit him in a hammock on a mid-nineteenth-century sailing ship. Of course.

Fallon made a fool of himself ten times over during the day. Despite his small experience with fresh-water sailing, he knew next to nothing about the work he was meant to do on this ship. Besides cleaning the deck and equipment, the men scrubbed a hard, black soot from the rigging and spars. Fallon would not go up into the rigging. He was afraid, and tried to find work enough on the deck.

He did not ask where the oil and soot had come from; it was obvious the source had been the brick furnace that was now topped by a tight-fitting wooden cover. Some of the cracks in the deck were filled with what looked like dried blood, but it was only the casual remark of one of the other men that caused him to realize, shocked at his own slowness, that this was a whaling ship.

The crew was an odd mixture of types and races; there were white and black, a group of six Orientals who sat apart on the rear deck and took no part in the work, men with British and German accents, and an eclectic collection of others—Polynesians, an Indian, a huge, shaven-headed black African, and a mostly naked man covered from head to toe with purple tattoos, whorls and swirls and vortexes, images and symbols, none of them quite decipherable as a familiar object or person. After the decks had been scrubbed to a remarkable whiteness, the mate named Flask set Fallon to tarring some heavy ropes in the fore part of the ship, by himself, where he would be out of the others' way. The men seemed to realize that something was wrong with him, but said nothing and apparently did not take it amiss that one of their number should begin acting strangely.

Which brought him, hands and wrists smeared with warm tar, to the next question: how did they know who he was? He was Fallon to all of them. He had obviously been there before he awakened; he had been a regular member of the crew with a personality and role to fill. He knew nothing of that. He had the overwhelming desire to get hold of a mirror to see whether the face he wore was indeed the face he had worn in Chicago the night before. The body was the same, down to the appendix scar he'd carried since he was nine years old. His arms and hands were the same; the fatigue he felt and the rawness of his skin told him he had not been doing this type of work long. So assume he was there in his own person, his Chicago person, the *real* Fallon. Was there now some confused nineteenth-century sailor wandering around a brokerage house on Van Buren? The thought made him smile. The sailor at the Board of Trade would probably get the worst of it.

So they knew who he was, even if he didn't remember ever having been here before. There was a Patrick Fallon on the ship, and *he* had somehow been brought here to fill that role. Reasons unknown. Method unknown. Way out. . . .

Think of it as an adventure. How many times as a boy had he dreamed of similar escapes from the mundane? Here he was, the answer to a dream, twenty-five years later. It would make a tremendous story when he got back, if he could find someone he could trust enough to tell it to—if he could get back.

There was a possibility that he tried to keep himself from dwelling on. He had come here while asleep, and though this reality gave no evidence of being a dream, if there was a symmetry to insanity, then on waking the next morning, might he not be back in his familiar bed? Logic presented the possibility. He tried not to put too much faith in logic. Logic had not helped him when he was on the wrong side of the soybean market in December, 1980.

The long tropic day declined; the sunset was a travel agent's dream. They were traveling east, by the signpost of that light. Fallon waited, sitting by a coil of rope, watching the helmsman at the far end of the ship lean, dozing, on the long ivory tiller that served this ship in place of the wheel with handspikes he was familiar with from Errol Flynn movies. It had to be a bone from some long-dispatched whale, another example of the savage Yankee practicality of whoever had made this whaler. It was a queerly innocent, gruesome artistry. Fallon had watched several idle sailors in the afternoon carving pieces of bone while they ate their scrap of salt pork and hard bread.

'Fallon, you can't sleep out here tonight, unless you want the Old Man to find you lying about.' It was a tall sailor of about Fallon's age. He had come down from aloft shortly after Fallon's assignment to the tar bucket, had watched him quietly for some minutes before giving him a few pointers on how the work was done. In the falling darkness, Fallon could not make out his expression, but the voice held a quiet distance that might mask just a trace of kindness. Fallon tried to get up and found his legs had grown so stiff he failed on the first try. The sailor caught his arm and helped him to his feet. 'You're all right?'

'Yes.' Fallon was embarrassed.

'Let's get below, then.' They stepped toward the latticed hatch near the bow.

'And there he is,' the sailor said, pausing, lifting his chin aft.

'Who?' Fallon looked back with him and saw the black figure there, heavily bearded, tall, in a long coat, steadying himself by a hand in the rigging. The oil lamp above the compass slightly illuminated the dark face—and gleamed deathly white along the ivory leg that projected from beneath his black coat. Fixed, immovable, the man leaned heavily on it.

'Ahab,' the sailor said.

4

Lying in the hammock, trying to sleep, Fallon was assaulted by the feverish reality of where he was. The ship rocked him like a gentle parent in its progress through the calm sea; he heard the rush of water breaking against the hull as the *Pequod* made headway, the sighing of the breeze above, heard the steps of the nightwatch on deck, the occasional snap of canvas, the creaking of braces; he sweated in the oppressive heat below-decks; he drew heavy breaths, trying to calm himself, of air laden with the smell of mildewed canvas and what he knew to be whale oil. He held his hands before his face and in the profound darkness knew them to be his own. He touched his neck and felt the slickness of sweat beneath the beard. He ran his tongue over his lips and tasted salt. Through the open hatch he could make out stars that were unchallenged by any other light. Would the stars be the same in a book as they were in reality?

In a book. Any chance he had to sleep flew from him whenever he ran up against that thought. Any logic he brought to bear on his situation crumbled under the weight of that absurdity. A time machine he could accept, some chance cosmic displacement that sucked him into the past. But not into a book. That was insanity; that was hallucination. He knew that if he could sleep now, he would wake once more in the real world. But he had nothing to grab hold of. He lay in the darkness listening to the ship and could not sleep at all.

They had been compelled to read *Moby Dick* in the junior-year American Renaissance class he'd taken to fulfill the last of his Humanities requirements. Fallon remembered being bored to tears by most of Melville's book, struggling with his interminable sentences, his woolly speculations that had no bearing on the story; he remembered being caught up by parts of that story. He had seen the movie with Gregory Peck. Richard Basehart, king of the sci-fi flicks, had played Ishmael. Fallon had not seen anyone who looked like Richard Basehart on this ship. The mate, Flask—he remembered that name now. He remembered that all the harpooners were savages. Queequeg.

He remembered that in the end, everyone but Ishmael died.

He had to get back. Sleep, sleep, you idiot, he told himself. He could not keep from laughing; it welled up in his chest and burst through his tightly closed lips. Fallon's laugh sounded more like a man gasping for breath than one overwhelmed by humor: he barked, he chuckled, he sucked in sudden draughts of air as he

tried to control the spasms. Tears were in his eyes, and he twisted
his head from side to side as if he were strapped to a bed in
some ward. Some of the others stirred and cursed him, but
Fallon, a character in a book where everyone died on the last
page, shook with helpless laughter, crying, knowing he would not
sleep.

5

With a preternatural clarity born of the sleepless night, Fallon
saw the deck of the *Pequod* the next morning. He was a little
stunned yet, but if he kept his mind in tight check the fatigue would keep him from thinking, and he would not feel the
distress that was waiting to burst out again. Like a man carrying a balloon filled with acid, Fallon carried his knowledge
tenderly.

He observed with scientific detachment, knowing that sleep
would ultimately come, and with it perhaps escape. The day was
bright and fair, a duplicate of the previous one. The whaler was
clean and prepared for her work; all sails were set to take advantage
of the light breeze, and the mastheads were manned with lookouts.
Men loitered on deck. On the rear deck—the quarter-deck, they
called it—Ahab paced, with remarkable steadiness for a man
wearing an ivory leg, between the compass in its box and the
mainmast, stopping for seconds to stare pointedly at each end of his
path. Fallon could not take his eyes off the man. He was much older
than Fallon had imagined him from his memories of the book.
Ahab's hair and beard were still black, except for the streak of
white which ran through them as the old scar ran top to bottom
across his face, but the face itself was deeply worn, and the man's
eyes were sunken in wrinkles, hollow. Fallon remembered Tigue
who had traded in the gold pit, who had once been the best boy on
the floor—the burn-out, they called him now, talking a very good
game about shorting the market. Tigue's eyes had the same hollow
expectation of disaster waiting inevitably for him—just him—that
Ahab's held. Yet when Fallon had decided Ahab had to be the same
empty nonentity, the man would pause at the end of his pathway
and stare at the compass, or the gold coin that was nailed to the
mast, and his figure would tighten in the grip of some stiffening
passion, as if he were shot through with lightning. As if he were at
the focal point of some cosmic lens that concentrated all the power

of the sun on him, so that he might momentarily burst into spontaneous flame.

Ahab talked to himself, staring at the coin. His voice was conversational, and higher pitched than Fallon had imagined it would be. Fallon was not the only man who watched him in wonder and fear.

'There's something ever egotistical in mountain-tops and towers, and all other grand and lofty things; look here—three peaks as proud as Lucifer. The firm tower, that is Ahab; the volcano, that is Ahab; the courageous, the undaunted, and victorious fowl, that, too, is Ahab; all are Ahab; and this round globe is but the image of the rounder globe, which, like a magician's glass, to each and every man in turn but mirrors back his own mysterious self . . .'

All spoken in the tone of a man describing a minor auto accident (the brown Buick swerved to avoid the boy on the bicycle, crossed over the yellow line and hit the milk truck which was going south on Main Street). As soon as he had stopped, Ahab turned and, instead of continuing his pacing, went quietly below.

One of the ship's officers—the first mate, Fallon thought—who had been talking to the helmsman before Ahab began to speak, now advanced to look at the coin. Fallon began to remember what was going to happen. Theatrically, though there was nobody there to listen to him, the mate began to speak aloud about the Trinity and the sun, hope and despair. Next came another mate, who talked of spending it quickly, then gave a reading comparing the signs of the zodiac to a man's life. Overwritten and silly, Fallon thought.

Flask now came to the doubloon and figured out how many cigars he could buy with it. Then came the old man who had sloshed the water all over Fallon the previous morning, who gave a reading of the ship's doom under the sign of the lion. Then Queequeg, then one of the Orientals, then a black boy—the cabin boy.

The boy danced around the mast twice, crouching low, rising on his toes, and each time around stared at the doubloon with comically bugged eyes. He stopped. 'I look, you look, he looks, we look, ye look, they look.'

I look, you look, he looks, we look, ye look, they look.

They all looked at it; they all spouted their interpretations. That was what Melville had wanted them to do to prove his point. Fallon did not feel like trying to figure out what that point was. After the dramatics, the *Pequod* went back to dull routine, and he to clean up work on the deck, to tarring more ropes. They had a lot of ropes.

He took a break and walked up to the mast to look at the coin

himself. Its surface was stamped with the image of three mountains, with a flame, a tower, and a rooster at their peaks. Above
were the sun and the signs of the zodiac. REPUBLICA DEL EQUADOR:
QUITO, it said. A couple of ounces, worth maybe $1,300 on the
current gold market, according to the London fix Fallon last
remembered. It wouldn't be worth as much to these men, of
course; this was pre-inflation money. He remembered that the
doubloon had been nailed there by Ahab as a reward to whoever
spotted Moby Dick first.

I look, you look, he looks, we look, ye look, they look.

Fallon looked, and nothing changed. His tiredness grew as the
day wore through a brutally hot afternoon. When evening at last
came and the grumbling of his belly had been at least partially
assauged by the meager meal served the men, Fallon fell exhausted
into the hammock. He did not worry about not sleeping this time;
consciousness fell away as if he had been drugged. He had a vivid
dream. He was trying, under cover of darkness, to pry the
doubloon away from the mast so that he might throw it into the sea.
Anxiously trying not to let the helmsman at the tiller spot him, he
heard the step, tap, step, tap of Ahab's pacing a deck below. It was
one of those dreams where one struggles in unfocused terror to
accomplish some simple task. He was afraid he might be found any
second by Ahab. If he were caught, then he would be exposed and
vilified before the crew's indifferent gaze.

He couldn't do it. He couldn't get his fingers under the edge of
the coin, though he bruised them bloody. He heard the knocking of
Ahab's whalebone step ascending to the deck; the world contracted
to the coin welded to the mast, his broken nails, the terrible fear.
He heard the footsteps drawing nearer behind him as he frantically
tried to free the doubloon, yet he could not run, and he would not
turn around. At the last, after an eternity of anxiety, a hand fell on
his shoulder and spun him around, his heart leaping into his throat.
It was not Ahab, but Carol.

He woke breathing hard, pulse pounding. He was still in the
hammock, in the forecastle of the *Pequod*. He closed his eyes again,
dozed fretfully through the rest of the night. Morning came: he was
still there.

The next day several of the other men prodded him about not
having taken a turn at the masthead for a long time. He stuck to
mumbled answers and hoped they would not go to any of the
officers. He wanted to disappear. He wanted it to be over. The men
treated him more scornfully as the days passed. And the days
passed, and still nothing happened to free him. The doubloon

glinted in the sun each morning, the center of the ship, and Fallon
could not get away. I look, you look, he looks, we look, ye look,
they look.

6

  Fallon had assumed his sullen station by the tar bucket. There he
felt at least some defense from his confusion. He could concentrate
on the smell and feel of the tar; he remembered the summers on the
tarred road in front of his grandparents' house in Elmira, how the
sun would raise shining bubbles of tar at the edges of the
re-surfaced country road, how the tar would stick to your sneakers
and get you a licking if you tracked it into grandmother's immaculate kitchen. He and his cousin Seth had broken the bubbles with
sticks and watched them slowly subside into themselves. The tar
bucket on the *Pequod* was something Fallon could focus on. The tar
was real; the air he breathed was real—Fallon himself was real.
  Stubb, the second mate, stood in front of him, arms akimbo. He
stared at Fallon; Fallon lifted his head and saw the man's small
smile. There was no charity in it.
  'Time to go aloft, Fallon. You've been missing your turn, and we
won't have any slackers aboard.'
  Fallon couldn't think of anything to say. He stumbled to his feet,
wiping his hands on a piece of burlap. A couple of the other sailors
were watching, waiting for Fallon to shy off or for Stubb to take
him.
  'Up with ye!' Stubb shoved Fallon's shoulder, and he turned,
fumbling for the rigging. Fallon looked momentarily over the side
of the ship to the sea that slid calmly by them; the gentle rolling of
the deck that he had in so short a time become accustomed to now
returned to him with frightening force. Stubb was still behind him.
Taking a good breath, he pulled himself up and stepped barefoot
onto the rail. Facing inward now, he tried to climb the rigging.
Stubb watched him with dispassion, waiting, it seemed, for his
failure. Expecting it. It was like trying to climb one of those rope
ladders at the county fair: each rung he took twisted the ladder in
the direction of his weight, and the rocking of the ship, magnified
as he went higher, made it hard for his feet to find the next step. He
had never been a particularly self-conscious man, but felt he was
being watched by them all now, and was acutely conscious of how
strange he must seem. How touched with idiocy and fear.

Nausea rose, the deck seemed farther below than it had any reason to be, the air was stifling, the wind was without freshness and did not cool the sweat from his brow and neck. He clutched the ropes desperately; he tried to take another step, but the strength seemed drained from his legs. Humiliated, burning with shame yet at the same time mortally afraid of falling—and of more than that, of the whole thing, of the fact that here he was where he ought not to be, cheated, abused, mystified—he wrapped his arms around the rigging, knees wobbly, sickness in his gut, bile threatening to heave itself up the back of his throat. Crying, eyes clenched tight, he wished it would all go away.

'Fallon! Fallon, you dog, you dog-*fish*, why don't you climb! You had better climb, weak-liver, for I don't want you down on my deck again if you won't!' Stubb roared his rage. Fallon opened his eyes, saw the red-faced man staring furiously up at him. Perhaps he'll have a stroke, Fallon thought.

He hung there, half-up, half-down, unable to move. I want to go home, he thought. Let me go home. Stubb raged and ridiculed him; others gathered to laugh and watch. Fallon closed his eyes and tried to go away. He heard a sound like the wooden mallet of the carpenter.

'What is the problem here, Mr. Stubb?' A calm voice. Fallon looked down again. Ahab stood with his hand on the mainmast to steady himself, looking up. His thumb was touching the doubloon.

Stubb was taken by surprise, as if Ahab were some apparition that had been called up by an entirely inappropriate spell. He jerked his head upward to indicate Fallon.

Squinting against the sun, Ahab studied Fallon for some time. His face was unnaturally pale in comparison to the tanned faces of the others turned up to look at him. Yet against the pallor, the white scar ran, a death-like sign, down the side of his face. His dark hair was disarrayed in the hot breeze. He was an old man; he swayed in the attempt to steady himself.

'Why don't ye go up?' Ahab called to Fallon.

Fallon shook his head. He tried to step up another rung, but though his foot found the rope, he didn't seem to have the strength he needed to pull himself up.

Ahab continued to look at him. He did not seem impatient or angry, only curious, as if Fallon were an animal sitting frozen on a traffic mall, afraid of the cars that passed. He seemed content to stand watching Fallon indefinitely. Stubb shifted nervously from foot to foot, his anger displaced and negated. The crewmen simply watched. Some of them looked above Fallon in the rigging; the ropes he clung to jerked, and he looked up himself to see that the man who had been standing at the masthead was coming down to help him.

'Bulkington!' Ahab cried, waving to the man to stop, 'Let him be!' The sailor retreated upward and swung himself onto the yardarm above the mainsail. The *Pequod* waited. If there were whales to be hunted, they waited too.

Very distinctly, so that Fallon heard every word, Ahab said, 'You must go up. You have taken the vow with the rest, and I will not have you go back on it. Would you go back on it? You must go up, or else you must come down, and show yourself for the coward and weakling you would then be.'

Fallon clung to the rigging. He had taken no vow. It was all a story. What difference did it make what he did in a story? If he was to be a character in a book, why couldn't he defy it, do what he wanted instead of following the path they indicated? By coming down he could show himself as himself.

'Have faith!' Ahab called.

Above him, Bulkington hawked and spat, timing it so that with the wind and the rocking of the *Pequod*, he hit the sea and not the deck. Fallon bent his head back and looked up at him. It was the kind sailor who had helped him below on that first night. He hung suspended. He looked down and watched Ahab sway with the rolling of the deck, his eyes still fixed on Fallon. The man was crazy. Melville was crazy for inventing him.

Fallon clenched his teeth, pulled on the ropes and pushed himself up another step toward the masthead. He was midway up the mainsail, thirty feet above the deck. He concentrated on one rung at a time, breathing steadily, and pulled himself up. When he reached the level of the mainyard, Bulkington swung himself below Fallon and helped him along. The complicated motion that came when the sailor stepped onto the ropes had Fallon clinging once again, but this time he was out of it fairly quickly. They ascended, step by dizzying step, to the masthead. The sailor got onto the port masthead hoop, helping Fallon into the starboard. The *Pequod*'s flag snapped in the wind a couple of feet above their heads.

'And here we are, Fallon,' Bulkington said. Immediately he dropped himself down into the rigging again, so nimbly and suddenly that Fallon's breath was stopped in fear for the man's fall.

Way below, the men were once more stirring. Ahab exchanged some words with Stubb; then, moving out to the rail and steadying himself by a hand on one of the stays, a foreshortened black puppet far below, he turned his white face up to Fallon once again.

Cupping his hand to his mouth, he shouted, 'Keep a steady eye, now! If ye see fin or flank of him, call away!'

Call away. Fallon was far above it all now, alone. He had made it. He had taken no vow and was not obligated to do anything he did not wish to. He had ascended to the masthead of his own free will, but, if he was to become a whaler, then what harm would there be in calling out whales—normal whales? Not literary ones. Not white ones.

He looked out to the horizon. The sea stretched out to the utmost ends of the world, covering it all, every secret, clear and blue and a little choppy under the innocent sky.

7

Fallon became used to the smell of the *Pequod*. He became accustomed to feeling sweaty and dirty, to the musty smell of mildew and the tang of brine trying to push away the stench of the packing plant.

He had not always been fastidious in his other life. In the late sixties, after he had dropped out of Northwestern, he had lived in an old house in a rundown neighborhood with three other men and a woman. They had called it 'The Big House,' and to the outside observer they must have been hippies. 'Hair men.' 'Freaks.' 'Dropouts.' It was a vocabulary that seemed quaint now. The perpetual pile of dirty dishes in the sink, the Fillmore West posters, the black light, the hot and cold running roaches, the early-fifties furniture with corners shredded to tatters by the three cats. Fallon realized that that life had been as different from his world at the Board of Trade as the deck of the *Pequod* was now.

Fallon had dropped out because, he'd told himself, there was nothing he wanted from the university that he couldn't get from its library, or by hanging around the student union. It was hard for him to believe how much he had read then: Skinner's behaviorism, Spengler's history, pop physics and Thomas Kuhn, Friedman and Galbraith, Shaw, Conrad, Nabokov, and all he could find of Hammett, Chandler, Macdonald and their imitators. Later he had not been able to figure out just why he had forsaken a degree so easily; he didn't know if he was too irresponsible to do the work, or too slow, or above it all and following his own path. Certainly he had not seen himself as a rebel, and the revolutionary fervor his peers affected (it had seemed affectation ninety percent of the time) never took hold of Fallon completely. He had observed, but not taken part in, the melee at the Democratic Convention. But he put in his time in the back bedroom listening to the Doors and blowing dope until the world seemed no more than a slightly bigger version of the Big House and his circle of friends. He read *The Way of Zen*. He knew Hesse and Kerouac. He hated Richard Nixon and laughed at Spiro Agnew. Aloft in the rigging of the *Pequod*, those years came back to Fallon as they never had in his last five years at the CBT. What a different person he had been at twenty. What a strange person, he realized, he had become at twenty-eight. What a marvelous—and frightening—metamorphosis.

He had gotten sick of stagnating, he told himself. He had seen one or another of his friends smoke himself into passivity. He had seen through the self-delusions of the other cripples in the Big House: cripples was what he had called them when he'd had the argument with Marty Solokov and had stalked out. Because he broke from that way of living did not mean he was selling out, he'd told them. He could work any kind of job; he didn't want money or a house in the suburbs. He had wanted to give himself the feeling of getting started again, of moving, of putting meaning to each day. He had quit washing dishes for the university, moved into a dingy flat closer to the center of the city, and scanned the help-wanted columns. He still saw his friends often and got stoned maybe not quite so often, and listened to music and read. But he had had enough of 'finding himself,' and he recognized in the others how finding yourself became an excuse for doing nothing.

Marty's cousin was a runner for Pearson Joel Chones on the Chicago Mercantile Exchange who had occasionaly come by the house, gotten high and gone to concerts. Fallon had slept with her once. He called her up, and she asked around, and eventually he cut his hair short—not too short—and became a runner for Pearson, too. He became marginally better groomed. He took a shower and changed his underwear every day. He bought three ties and wore one of them on the trading floor because that was one of the rules of the exchange.

It occurred to Fallon to find Ishmael, if only to see the man who would live while he died. He listened and watched; he learned the name of every man on the ship—he knew Flask and Stubb and Starbuck and Bulkington, Tashtego, Dagoo and Queequeg, identified Fedallah, the lead Philippine boatsman. There *was* no Ishmael. At first Fallon was puzzled, then came the beginnings of hope. If the reality he was living in could be found to differ from the reality of Melville's book in such an important particular, then could it not differ in some other way—some way that would at least lead to his survival? Maybe this Ahab caught his white whale. Maybe Starbuck would steel himself to the point where he could defy the madman and take over the ship. Perhaps they would never sight Moby Dick.

Then an unsettling realization smothered the hope before it could come fully to bloom: there was not necessarily an Ishmael in the book. '*Call* me Ishmael,' it started. Ishmael was a pseudonym for some other man, and there would be no one by that name on the *Pequod*. Fallon congratulated himself on a clever bit of literary detective work.

Yet the hope refused to remain dead. Yes, there was no Ishmael on the *Pequod;* or anyone on the ship not specifically named in the book might be Ishmael, any one of the anonymous sailors, within certain broad parameters of age and character—and Fallon wracked his brain trying to remember what the narrator said of himself —might be Ishmael. He grabbed at that; he breathed in the possibility and tried on the suit for size. Why not? If absurdity were to rule to the extent that he had to be there in the first place, then why couldn't he be the one who lived? More than that, why couldn't he make himself that man? No one else knew what Fallon knew. He had the advantage over them. Do the things that Ishmael did, and you may be him. If you have to be a character in a book, why not be the hero?

Fallon's first contact with the heart of capitalism at the CME had been frightening and amusing. Frightening when he screwed up and delivered a May buy-order to a July trader and cost the company 10,000 dollars. It was only through the grace of God and his own guts in facing it out that he had made it through the disaster. He had, he discovered, the ability to hide himself behind a facade which, to the self-interested observer, would appear to be whatever that observer wished it to be. If his superior expected him to be respectful and curious, then Fallon was respectfully curious. He did it without having to compromise his inner self. He was not a hypocrite.

The amusing part came after he had it all down and he began to watch the market like an observer at a very complex monopoly game. Or, more accurately, like a baseball fan during a pennant race. There were at least as many statistics as in a good baseball season, enough personalities, strategies, great plays, blunders, risk and luck. Fallon would walk onto the floor at the beginning of the day—the huge room with its concert-hall atmosphere, the banks of price boards around the walls, the twilight, the conditioned air, the hundreds of bright-coated traders and agents—and think of half time at homecoming. The floor at the end of the day, as he walked across the hardwood scattered with mounds of paper scraps like so much confetti, was a basketball court after the NCAA finals. Topping it all off, giving it that last significant twist that was necessary to all good jokes, was the fact that this was all supposed to mean something; it was real money they were playing with, and one tick of the board in Treasury Bills cost somebody eleven-hundred dollars. This was serious stuff, kid. The lifeblood of the nation—of the free world. Fallon could hardly hold in his laughter, could not stop his fascination.

Fallon's first contact with the whale—his first lowering—was in Stubb's boat. The man at the forward masthead cried out, 'There she blows! Three points off starboard! There she blows! Three —no, four of 'em!'

The men sprang to the longboats and swung them away over the side. Fallon did his best to look as if he was helping. Stubb's crew leapt into the boat as it was dropped into the swelling sea, heedless to the possibility of broken bones or sprained ankles. Fallon hesitated a second at the rail, then threw himself off with the feeling of a man leaping off the World Trade Center. He landed clumsily and half-bowled over one of the men. He took his place at a center oar and pulled away. Like the man falling off the building, counting off the stories as they flew past him, Fallon thought, 'So far, so good.' And waited for the crash.

'Stop snoring, ye sleepers, and pull!' Stubb called, halfway between jest and anger. 'Pull, Fallon! Why don't you pull? Have you never seen an oar before? Don't look over your shoulder, lad, *pull!* That's better. Don't be in a hurry, men—softly, softly now—but damn ye, pull until you break something! Tashtego! Can't you harpoon me some men with backs to them? *Pull!'*

Fallon pulled until he thought the muscles in his arms would snap, until the small of his back spasmed as if he were indeed being harpooned by the black-haired Indian behind him in the bow. The sea was rough, and they were soon soaked with spray. After a few minutes Fallon forgot the whales they pursued, merged into the rhythm of the work, fell in with the cunning flow of Stubb's curses and pleas, the crazy sermon, now whispered, now shouted. He concentrated on the oar in his hands, the bite of the blade into the water, the simple mechanism his body had become, the working of his lungs, the dry rawness of the breath dragged in and out in time to their rocking, back-breaking work. Fallon closed his eyes, heard the pulse in his ears, felt the cool spray and the hot sun, saw the rose fog of the blood in his eyelids as he faced into the bright and brutal day.

At twenty-five, Fallon was offered a position in the office upstairs. At twenty-seven, he had an offer from DCB International to become a broker. By that time he was living with Carol. Why not? He was still outside it all, still safe within. Let them think what they would of him; he was protected, in the final analysis, by that great indifference he held to his breast the way he held Carol close at night. He was not a hypocrite. He said nothing he did not believe in. Let them project upon him whatever fantasies they might hold dear to themselves. He was outside and above it all, analyzing futures for DCB International. Clearly, in every contract that crossed his desk, it was stated that DCB and its brokers were not responsible for reverses that might be suffered as a result of suggestions they made.

So he had spent the next four years, apart from it, pursuing his interests, which, with the money he was making, he found were many. Fallon saw very little of the old friends now. Solokov's cousin told him he was now in New York, cadging money from strangers in Times Square. Solokov, she said, claimed it was a pretty good living. He claimed he was still beating the system. Fallon had grown up enough to realize that no one really beat any system—as if there were a system. There was only buying and selling, subject to the forces of the market and the infirmities of the players. Fallon was on the edges of it, could watch quietly, taking part as necessary (he had to eat), but still stay safe. He was no hypocrite.

'To the devil with ye, boys, will ye be outdone by Ahab's heathens? Pull, spring it, my children, my fine hearts-alive, smoothly, smoothly, bend it hard starboard! Aye, Fallon, let me see you sweat, lad, can you sweat for me?'

They rose on the swell, and it was like rowing uphill; they slid down the other side, still rowing, whooping like children on a toboggan ride, all the time Stubb calling on them. Fallon saw Starbuck's boat off to his right; he heard the rush of water beneath them, and the rush of something faster and greater than their boat.

Tashtego grunted behind him.

'A hit, a hit!' Stubb shouted, and beside Fallon the whaleline was running out with such speed that it sang and hummed and smoked. One of the men sloshed water over the place where it slid taut as a wire over the gunnel. Then the boat jerked forward so suddenly that Fallon was nearly knocked overboard when his oar, still trailing in the water, slammed into his chest. Gasping at the pain, he managed to get the oar up into the air. Stubb had half-risen from his seat in the stern.

They flew through the water. The whaleboat bucked as it slapped the surface of every swell the whale pulled them through. Fallon held on for dear life, not sure whether he ought to be grateful he hadn't been pitched out when the ride began. He tried to twist around to see the monster that was towing them, but able to turn only half way, all he could see for the spray and the violent motion was the swell and rush of white water ahead of them. Tashtego, crouched in the bow, grinned wickedly as he tossed out wooden blocks tied to the whaleline in order to tire the whale with their drag. You might as well try to tire a road grader.

Yet he could not help but feel exhilarated, and he saw that the others in the boat, hanging on or trying to draw the line in, were flushed and breathing as hard as he.

He turned again and saw the whale.

Fallon had been a good swimmer in high school. He met Carol Bukaty at a swimming pool about a year after he had gone to work at the CME. Fallon first noticed her in the pool, swimming laps. She was the best swimmer there, better than he, though he might have been stronger than she in the short run. She gave herself over to the water and did not fight it; the kick of her long legs was steady and strong. She breathed easily and her strokes were relaxed, yet powerful. She did not swim for speed, but she looked as if she could swim for days, so comfortable did she seem in the water. Fallon sat on the steps at the pool's edge and watched her for half an hour without once getting bored. He found her grace in the water arousing. He knew he had to speak to her. He slid into the pool and swam laps behind her.

At last she stopped. Holding onto the trough at the end of the pool, she pushed her goggles up onto her forehead and brushed the wet brown hair away from her eyes. He drew up beside her.

'You swim very well,' he said.

She was out of breath. 'Thank you.'

'You look as if you wouldn't ever need to come out of the water. Like anything else might be a comedown after swimming.' It was a strange thing for him to say, it was not what he wanted to say, but he did not know what he wanted, besides her.

She looked puzzled, smiled briefly, and pulled herself onto the side of the pool, letting her legs dangle in the water. 'Sometimes I feel that way,' she said. 'I'm Carol Bukaty.' She stuck out her hand, very businesslike.

'Pat Fallon.'

She wore a grey tank suit; she was slender and small-breasted, tall, with a pointed chin and brown eyes. Fallon later discovered that she was an excellent dancer, that she purchased women's clothing for one of the major Chicago department stores, that she traveled a great deal, wrote lousy poetry, disliked cooking, liked children, and liked him. At first he was merely interested in her sexually, though the first few times they slept together it was not very good at all. Gradually the sex got better, and in the meantime Fallon fell in love.

She would meet him at the athletic club after work; they would play racquet ball in the late afternoon, go out to dinner and take in a movie, then spend the night at his or her apartment. He met her alcoholic father, a retired policeman who told endless stories about ward politics and the Daley machine, and Carol spent a Christmas with him at his parents. After they moved in together, they settled into a comfortable routine. He felt secure in her affection for him. He did not want her, after a while, as much as he had that first day, those first months, but he still needed her. It still mattered to him what she was doing and what she thought of him. Sometimes it mattered to him too much, he thought. Sometimes he wanted to be without her at all, not because he had anything he could only do without her, but only because he wanted to *be* without her.

He would watch her getting dressed in the morning and wonder what creature she might be, and what that creature was doing in the same room with him. He would lie beside her as she slept, stroking the short brown hair at her temple with his fingertips, and be overwhelmed with the desire to possess her, to hold her head between his hands and know everything that she was; he would shake with the sudden frustration of its impossibility until it was all he could do to keep from striking her. Something was wrong with him, or with her. He had fantasies of how much she would miss him if he died, of what clothes she would wear to the funeral, of what stories she would tell her lovers in the future after he was gone.

If Carol felt any of the same things about him, she did not tell him. For Fallon's part, he did not try to explain what he felt in any but the most oblique ways. She should know how he felt, but of course she did not. So when things went badly, and they began to

do so more and more, it was not possible for him to explain to her
what was wrong, because he could not say it himself, and the pieces
of his discontent were things that he was too embarrassed to admit.
Yet he could not deny that sometimes he felt as if it was all over
between them, that he felt nothing—and at others he would smile
just to have her walk into the room.

Remarkable creature though the whale was, it was not so hard to
kill one after all. It tired, just as a man would tire under the attack
of a group of strangers. It slowed in the water, no longer able so
effortlessly to drag them after it. They pulled close, and Stubb
drove home the iron, jerked it back and forth, drew it out and drove
it home again, fist over fist on the hilt, booted foot over the gunnel
braced against the creature's flesh, sweating, searching for the
whale's hidden life. At last he found it, and the whale shuddered
and thrashed a last time, spouting pink mist, then dark
blood, where once it spouted feathery white spray. Like a man,
helpless in the end, it rolled over and died. Stubb was jolly, and
the men were methodical; they tied their lines around the
great tail and, as shadows grew long and the sun fell perpendicularly toward the horizon, drew the dead whale to the
Pequod.

8

During the cutting up and boiling down of the whale that night,
Fallon, perhaps in recognition of his return to normality as
indicated by his return to the masthead, was given a real job: slicing
the chunks of blubber that a couple of other sailors were hewing out
of the great strips that were hauled over the side into 'bible leaves.'
Fallon got the hang of it pretty quickly, though he was not fast, and
Staley, the British sailor who was cutting beside him, kept poking
at him to do more. 'I'm doing all the work, Fallon,' he said, as if his
ambition in life were to make sure that he did no more than his own
share of the work.
    Using a sharp blade like a long cleaver, Fallon would position the
chunk of blubber, skin side down on the cutting table, and
imitating Staley, cut the piece into slices like the pages of a book,
with the skin as its spine. The blubber leaves flopped outward or
stuck to each other, and the table became slick with grease. Fallon
was at first careful about avoiding his hands, but the blubber would

slide around the table as he tried to cut it if he didn't hold it still. Staley pushed him on, working with dexterity, though Fallon noted that the man's hands were scarred, with the top joint of the middle finger of his left hand missing.

His back and shoulders ached with fatigue, and the smoke from the try-works stung his eyes. When he tried to wipe the tears away, he only smeared his face with grease. But he did a creditable job, cursing all the time. The cursing helped, and the other men seemed to accept him more for it. When finally they were done, and the deck was clean the next day, they were issued a tot of grog and allowed to swim within the lee of the stationary ship. The men were more real to him than when he had sat and watched from the outcast's station of the tar bucket. He was able to speak to them more naturally than he had ever done. But he did not forget his predicament.

'Ye are too serious, Fallon,' Staley told him, offering Fallon some of his grog. 'I can see you brooding there, and look how it set you into a funk. Ye are better now, perhaps, but mind you stick to your work and ye may survive this voyage.'

'I won't survive it. Neither will you—unless we can do something about Captain Ahab.'

Bulkington, who had been watching them, came by. 'What of Captain Ahab?'

Fallon saw a chance in this. 'Does his seeking after this white whale seem right to you?'

'The whale took his leg,' Staley said.

'Some say it unmanned him,' the other said, lower. 'That's two legs you'd not like to lose yourself, I'll daresay.'

Fallon drew them aside, more earnest now. 'We will lose more than our balls if we do nothing about this situation. The man is out of his mind. He will drag us all down with him, and this ship with all of us, if we can't convince Starbuck to do something. Believe me, I know.'

Friendly Bulkington did not look so friendly. 'You do talk strange, Fallon. We took an oath, and we signed the papers before we even sailed a cable from shore. A captain is a captain. You are talking mutiny.'

He had to go carefully.

'No, wait. Listen to me. Why are we sent on this trip? Think of the—the stockholders, or whatever you call them. The owners. They sent us out to hunt whales.'

'The white whale is a whale,' Staley looked petulant.

'Yes, of course, it's a whale. But there are hundreds of whales to be caught and killed. We don't need to hunt that one. Hasn't he set his sights on just Moby Dick? What about that oath? That gold piece on the mast? That says he's just out for vengeance. There was nothing about vengeance in the papers we signed. What do you think the owners would say if they knew about what he plans? Do you think they would approve of this wild goose chase?'

Staley was lost. 'Goose chase?'

Bulkington was interested. 'Go on.'

Fallon had his foot in the door; he marshaled the arguments he had rehearsed over and over again. 'There's no more oil in Moby Dick than in another whale. . . .'

'They say he's monstrous big,' Staley interjected.

Fallon looked pained. 'Not so big as any two whales, then. Ahab is not after any oil you can boil out of the whale's flesh. If the owners knew what he intended, the way I do, if they knew how sick he was the week before he came out of that hole of a cabin he lives in, if they saw that light in his eye and the charts he keeps in his cabinet. . . .'

'Charts? What charts? Have you been in his cabin?'

'No, not exactly,' Fallon said. 'Look, I know some things, but that's just because I keep my eyes open and I have some sources.'

'Fallon, where do you hail from? I swear that I cannot half the time make out what you are saying. Sources? What do you mean by that?'

'Oh, Jesus!' He had hoped for better from Bulkington.

Staley darkened. 'Don't blaspheme, man! I'll not take the word of a blasphemer.'

Fallon saw another opening. 'You're right! I'm sorry. But look, didn't the old man himself blaspheme more seriously than I ever could the night of that oath? If you are a God-fearing man, Staley, you'll know that that is true. Would you give your obedience to such a man? Moby Dick is just another of God's creatures, a dumb animal. Is it right to seek vengeance on an animal? Do you want to be responsible for that? God would not approve.'

Staley looked troubled, but stubborn. 'Do not tell me what the Almighty approves. That is not for the likes of you to know. And Ahab is the captain.' With that he walked to the opposite side of the deck and stood there watching them as if he wanted to separate himself as much as possible from the conversation, yet still know what was going on.

Fallon was exasperated and tired.

'Why don't you go with Staley, Bulkington? You don't have to

stick around with me, you know. I'm not going to do your
reputation any good.'

Bulkington eyed him steadily. 'You are a strange one, Fallon. I
did not think anything of you when I first saw you on the *Pequod*.
But you may be talking some sense.'

'Staley doesn't think so.'

Bulkington took a pull on his grog. 'Why did you try to persuade
Staley of Ahab's madness? You should have known that you
couldn't convince such a man that the sky is blue, if it were written
in the articles he signed that it was green. Starbuck perhaps, or me.
Not Staley. Don't you listen to the man you are talking to?'

Fallon looked at Bulkington; the tall sailor looked calmly back at
him, patient, waiting.

'Okay, you're right,' Fallon said. 'I have the feeling I would not
have a hard time convincing you, anyway. You know Ahab's insane,
don't you?'

'It's not for me to say. Ahab has better reasons than those you
give to him.' He drew a deep breath, looked up at the sky, down at
the men who swam in the shadow of the ship. He smiled. 'They
should be more wary of sharks,' he said.

'The world does look a garden today, Fallon. But it may be that
the old man's eyes are better than ours.'

'You know he's mad, and you won't do anything?'

'The matter will not bear too deep a looking into.' Bulkington
was silent for a moment. 'You know the story about the man born
with a silver screw in his navel? How it tasked him, until one day he
unscrewed it to divine its purpose?'

Fallon had heard the joke in grade school on the South Side. 'His
ass fell off.'

'You and Ahab are too much like that man.'

They both laughed. 'I don't have to unscrew my navel,' Fallon
said. 'We're all going to lose our asses anyway.'

They laughed again. Bulkington put his arm around his shoulders, and they toasted Moby Dick.

9

There came a morning when, on pumping out the bilge, someone
noticed that considerable whale oil was coming up with the water.
Starbuck was summoned and, after descending into the hold

himself, emerged and went aft and below to speak with Ahab.
Fallon asked one of the others what was going on.

'The casks are leaking. We're going to have to lay up and break
them out. If we don't, we stand to lose a lot of oil.'

Some time later Starbuck reappeared. His face was red to the
point of apoplexy, and he paced around the quarter-deck with his
hands knotted behind his back. They waited for him to tell them
what to do; he stared at the crewmen, stopped, and told them to be
about their business. 'Keep pumping,' he told the others. 'Maintain
the lookout.' He then spoke briefly to the helmsman leaning on the
whalebone tiller, and retreated to the corner of the quarter-deck to
watch the wake of the ship. After a while Ahab himself staggered
up onto the deck, found Starbuck, and spoke to him. He then
turned to the men on deck.

'Furl the t'gallantsails,' he called, 'and close reef the topsails, fore
and aft; back the main-yard; up Burtons, and break out in the main
hold.'

Fallon joined the others around the hold. Once the work had
commenced, he concentrated on lifting, hauling, and not straining
his back. The Manxman told them that he had been outside Ahab's
cabin during the conference and that Ahab had threatened to shoot
Starbuck dead on the spot when the mate demanded they stop
chasing the whale to break out the hold. Fallon thought about the
anger in Starbuck's face when he'd come up again. It struck him
that the Starbuck of Melville's book was pretty ineffectual; he had
to be to let that madman go on with the chase. But this Starbuck
—whether like the one in the book or not—did not like the way
things were going. There was no reason why Fallon had to sit
around and wait for things to happen. It was worth a shot.

But not that afternoon.

Racism assured that the hardest work in the dank hold was done
by the colored men—Dagoo, Tashtego, and Queequeg. They did
not complain. Up to their knees in the bilge, clambering awkwardly
over and about the barrels of oil in the murderous heat and
unbreathable air of the hold, they did their jobs.

It was evening before the three harpooners were told they could
halt for the day and they emerged, sweaty, covered with slime, and
bruised. Fallon collapsed against the side of the try-works; others
sat beside him. Tall Queequeg was taken by a coughing fit, then
went below to his hammock. Fallon gathered his strength, felt the
sweat drying stickily on his arms and neck. There were few clouds,
and the moon was waxing full. He saw Starbuck then, standing at

the rear of the quarter-deck, face toward the mast. Was he looking at the doubloon?

Fallon got shakily to his feet; his legs were rubbery. The first mate did not notice him until he was close. He looked up.

'Yes?'

'Mr. Starbuck, I need to speak to you.'

Starbuck looked at him as if he saw him for the first time. Fallon tried to look self-confident, serious. He'd gotten that one down well at DCB.

'Yes?'

Fallon turned so that he was facing inward toward the deck and Starbuck had his back to it to face him. He could see what was happening away from them and would know if anyone came near.

'I could not help but see that you were angry this morning after speaking to Captain Ahab.'

Starbuck looked puzzled.

'I assume that you must have told Ahab about the leaking oil, and he didn't want to stop his hunt of the whale long enough to break out the hold. Am I right?'

The mate watched him guardedly. 'What passed between Captain Ahab and me was none of your affair, or of the crew's. Is that what you've come to trouble me with?'

'It is a matter that concerns me,' Fallon said. 'It concerns the rest of the crew, and it ought to concern you. We are being bound by his orders, and what kind of orders is he giving? I know what you've been thinking; I know that this personal vengeance he seeks frightens and repulses you. I *know* what you're thinking. I could see what was in your mind when you stood at this rail this afternoon. He is not going to stop until he kills us all.'

Starbuck seemed to draw back within himself. Fallon saw how beaten the man's eyes were; he did not think the mate was a drinker, but he looked like someone who had just surfaced after a long weekend. He could almost see the clockwork turning within Starbuck, a beat too slow, with the belligerence of the drunk being told the truth about himself that he did not want to admit. Fallon's last fight with Stein Jr at the brokerage had started that way.

'Get back to your work,' Starbuck said. He started to turn away.

Fallon put his hand on his shoulder. 'You have to—'

Starbuck whirled with surprising violence and pushed Fallon away so that he nearly stumbled and fell. The man at the tiller was watching them.

'To work! You do not know what I am thinking! I'll have you flogged if you say anything more! A man with a three-hundreth lay has nothing to tell me. Go on, now.'

Fallon was hot. 'God damn you. You stupid—'

'Enough!' Starbuck slapped him with the back of his hand, the way Stein had tried to slap Fallon. Stein had missed. It appeared that Mr. Starbuck was more effectual than Stein Jr Fallon felt his bruised cheek. The thing that hurt the most was the way he must have looked, like a hangdog insubordinate who had been shown his place. As Fallon stumbled away, Starbuck said, in a steadier voice, 'Tend to your own conscience, man. Let me tend to mine.'

10

Lightning flashed again.

'I now know that thy right worship is defiance. To neither love nor reverence wilt thou be kind; and even for hate thou canst but kill, and all are killed!'

Ahab had sailed them into the heart of a typhoon. The sails were in tatters, and the men ran across the deck shouting against the wind and trying to lash the boats down tighter before they were washed away or smashed. Stubb had gotten his left hand caught between one of the boats and the rail; he now held it with his right and grimaced. The mastheads were touched with St. Elmo's fire. Ahab stood with the lightning rod in his right hand and his right foot planted on the neck of Fedallah, declaiming at the lightning. Fallon held tightly to a shroud to keep from being thrown off his feet. The scene was ludicrous; it was horrible.

'No fearless fool now fronts thee!' Ahab shouted at the storm. 'I own thy speechless, placeless power; but to the last gasp of my earthquake life will dispute its unconditional, unintegral mastery in me! In the midst of the personified impersonal, a personality stands here!'

Terrific, Fallon thought. Psychobabble. Melville writes in a storm so Ahab can have a backdrop against which to define himself. They must not have gone in for realism much in Melville's day. He turned and tried to lash the rear quarter boat tighter; its stern had already been smashed in by a wave that had just about swept three men, including Fallon, overboard. Lightning flashed, followed a split-second later by the rolling thunder. Fallon recalled that five-seconds' count meant the lightning was a mile away; by that measure the last bolt must have hit them in the ass. Most of the crew were staring open-mouthed at Ahab and the glowing, eerie flames that touched the masts. The light had the bluish tinge of mercury vapor lamps in a parking lot. It sucked the color out of things; the faces of the frightened men were the sickly hue of fish bellies.

'Thou canst blind, but I can then grope. Thou canst consume, but I can then be ashes!' You bet. 'Take the homage of these poor eyes, and shutter-hands. I would not take it. . . .' Ahab ranted on. Fallon hardly gave a damn anymore. The book was too much. Ahab talked to the storm and the God behind it; the storm answered him back, lightning flash for curse. It was dramatic, stagy; it was real: Melville's universe was created so that such dialogues could take place; the howling gale and the tons of water, the crashing waves, flapping canvas, the sweating, frightened men, the blood and seawater—all were created to have a particular effect, to be sure, but it was the real universe, and it would work that way because that was the way it was set up to work by a frustrated, mystified man chasing his own obsessions, creating the world as a warped mirror of his distorted vision.

'There is some unsuffusing thing beyond thee, thou clear spirit, to whom all thy eternity is but time, all thy creativeness mechanical. . . .'

There is an ex-sailor on a farm in Massachusetts trying to make ends meet while his puzzled wife tries to explain him to the relatives.

'The boat! The boat!' cried Starbuck. 'Look at thy boat, old man!'

Fallon looked, and backed away. A couple of feet from him the harpoon that was lashed into the bow was tipped with the same fire that illuminated the masts. Silently within the howling storm, from its barbed end twin streamers of electricity writhed. Fallon backed away to the rail, heart beating quickly, and clutched the slick whalebone.

Ahab staggered toward the boat; Starbuck grabbed his arm. 'God! God is against thee, old man! Forbear! It's an ill voyage! Ill begun, ill continued; let me square the yards while we may, old man, and make a fair wind of it homewards, to go on a better voyage than this.'

Yes, yes, at last Starbuck had said it! Fallon grabbed one of the braces; he saw others of the crew move to the rigging as if to follow Starbuck's order before it was given. They cried, some of them in relief, others in fear, others as if ready at last to mutiny. Yes!

Ahab threw down the last links of the lightning rod. He grabbed
the harpoon from the boat and waved it like a torch about his head;
he lurched toward Fallon.

'You!' he shouted, staggering to maintain his balance under the
tossing deck, hoisting the flaming harpoon to his shoulder as if he
meant to impale Fallon on the spot. 'But cast loose that rope's end
and you will be transfixed—by this clear spirit!' The electricity at
the barb hummed inches before him; Fallon could feel his skin
prickling and smelled ozone. He felt the rail at the small of his
back, cold. The other sailors fell away from the ropes; Starbuck
looked momentarily sick. Fallon let go of the brace.

Ahab grinned at him. He turned and held the glowing steel
before him with both hands like a priest holding a candle at mass on
a feast day.

'All your oaths to hunt the white whale are as binding as mine;
and heart, soul, and body, lung and life, old Ahab is bound. And
that you may know to what tune this heart beats; look ye here!
Thus I blow out the last fear!'

He blew out the flame.

They ran out the night without letting the anchors over the side,
heading due into the gale instead of riding with the wind at their
backs, with tarpaulins and deck truck blown or washed overboard,
with the lightning rod shipped instead of trailing in the sea as it
ought to, with the man at the tiller beaten raw about the ribs trying
to keep the ship straight, with the compass spinning round like a
top, with the torn remains of the sails not cut away until long after
midnight.

By morning the storm had much abated, the wind had come
around, and they ran before it in heavy seas. Fallon and most of the
other common sailors, exhausted, were allowed to sleep.

11

The argument with Starbuck and his attempts to rouse others to
defy Ahab had made Fallon something of a pariah. He was now as
isolated as he had been when he'd first come to himself aboard the
Pequod. Only Bulkington did not treat him with contempt or fear,
but Bulkington would do nothing about the situation. He would
rather talk, and they often discussed what a sane man would do in
their situation, given the conflicting demands of reason and duty.

Fallon's ability to remain detached always failed him somewhere in the middle of these talks.

So Fallon came to look upon his stints at the masthead as escape of a sort. It was there that he had first realized that he could rise above the deck of the *Pequod*, both literally and figuratively, for some moments; it was there that he had first asserted his will after days of stunned debility. He would not sing out for the white whale, if it should be his fortune to sight it, but he did sing out more than once for lesser whales. The leap of his heart at the sight of them was not feigned.

They were sailing the calm Pacific east and south of Japan. They had met the *Rachel,* and a thrill had run through the crew at the news that she had encountered Moby Dick and had failed to get him, losing several boats, and the captain's son, in the process. Fallon's memory was jogged. The *Rachel* would pick up Ishmael at the end of the book, when all the others were dead.

They met the *Delight,* on which a funeral was in progress. From the mainmast lookout, Fallon heard the shouted talk between Ahab and her captain about another failed attempt at the white whale. He watched as the dead man, sewn up in his hammock, was dropped into the sea.

It was a clear, steel-blue day. The sea rolled in long, quiet swells; the *Pequod* moved briskly ahead before a fair breeze, until the *Delight* was lost in the distance astern. The air was fresh and clear out to the rim of the world, where it seemed to merge with the darker sea. It was as fair a day as they had seen since Fallon had first stood a watch at the masthead.

Up above the ship, almost out of the world of men entirely, rolling at the tip of the mast in rhythm to the rolling of the sea swells, which moved in time with his own easy breathing, Fallon lost his fear. He seemed to lose even himself. Who was he? Patrick Fallon, analyst for a commodities firm. Perhaps that had been some delusion; perhaps that world had been created somewhere inside of him, pressed upon him in a vision. He was a sailor on the *Pequod.* He thought that this was part of some book, but he had not been a reader for many years.

Memories of his other life persisted. He remembered the first time he had ever made love to a woman—to Sally Torrance, in the living room of her parents' house while they were away skiing in Minnesota. He remembered cutting his palm playing baseball when the bat had shattered in his hand. The scar in the middle of his hand could not be denied.

Who denied it? He watched an albatross swoop down from above him to skim a few feet above the water, trying to snag some high-leaping fish. It turned away, unsuccessful, beating its wings slowly as it climbed the air. There was rhythm to its unconscious dance. Fallon had never seen anything more beautiful. He hung his arms over the hoop that surrounded him, felt the hot sun beating on his back, the band of metal supporting him.

This was the real world; he accepted it. He accepted the memories that contradicted it. I look, you look, he looks. Could his mind and heart hold two contradictory things? What would happen to him then? He accepted the albatross, the fish, the sharks he could see below the water's surface from his high vantage point. He accepted the grace of the sea, its embrace on this gentlest of days, and he accepted the storm that had tried to kill them only days before. The *Delight*, reason told him—let reason be; he could strain reason no further than he had—the *Delight* might perhaps have been a ship from a story he had read, but he had no doubt that the man who had been dropped to his watery grave as Fallon watched had been a real man.

The blue of sky and sea, the sound of the flag snapping above him, the taste of the salt air, the motion of the sea and earth itself as they swung Fallon at the tip of the mast, the memories and speculations, the feel of warm sun and warm iron—all the sensual world flowed together for Fallon then. He could not say what he felt. Joy that he could hardly contain swelled in his chest. He was at one with all his perceptions, with all he knew and remembered, with Carol, wherever or whatever she might be, with Bulkington and Dagoo and Starbuck and Stein Jr. and the Big House and Queequeg and the CBT and Ahab. Ahab.

Why had Fallon struggled so long against it? He was alive. What thing had driven him to fight so hard? What had happened to him was absurd, but what thing was not absurd? What thing had made him change from the student to the dropout to the analyst to the sailor? Who might Patrick Fallon be? He stretched out his right arm and turned his hand in the sun.

'Is it I, or God, or who, that lifts this arm?' Fallon heard the words quite distinctly, as if they were spoken only for him, as if they were not spoken at all but were only thoughts. God perhaps did lift Fallon's arm, and if that were so, then who was Fallon to question the wisdom or purpose of the motion? It was his only to move.

A disturbance in the blue of the day.

Why should he not have a choice? Why should that God give him the feeling of freedom if in fact He was directing Fallon's every breath? Did the Fates weave this trance-like calm blue day to lead Fallon to these particular conclusions, so that not even his thoughts in the end were his own, but only the promptings of some force beyond him? And what force could that be if not the force that created this world, and who created this world but Herman Melville, a man who had been dead for a very long time, a man who had no possible connection with Fallon? And what could be the reason for the motion? If this was the real world, then why had Fallon been given the life he had lived before, tangled himself in, felt trapped within, only to be snatched away and clumsily inserted into a different fantasy? What purpose did it serve? Whose satisfaction was being sought?

The moment of wholeness died; the world dissolved into its disparate elements. The sea rolled on. The ship fought it. The wind was opposed by straining canvas. The albatross dove once again, and skimming over the surface so fast it was a white blur, snatched a gleam of silver—a flying fish—from midflight. It settled to the ocean's surface, tearing at its prey.

The day was not so bright as it had been. Fallon tried to accept it still. He did not know if there was a malign force behind the motion of the earth in its long journey, or a beneficent one whose purpose was merely veiled to men such as himself—or no force at all. Such knowledge would not be his. He was a sailor on the *Pequod*.

Upon descending, Fallon heard from Bulkington that Starbuck and Ahab had had a conversation about turning back to Nantucket, that the mate had seemed almost to persuade the captain to give up the hunt, but that he had failed.

Fallon knew then that they must be coming to the end of the story. It would not be long before they spotted the white whale, and three days after that *Pequod* would go down with all hands not previously killed in the encounter with the whale—save one. But Fallon had given up the idea that he might be that one. He did not, despite his problems, qualify as an Ishmael. That would be overstating his importance, he thought.

12

He woke suddenly to the imperative buzzing of his alarm clock. His heart beat very fast. He tried to slow it by breathing deeply. Carol stirred beside him, then slept again.

He felt disoriented. He walked into the bathroom, staring, as if he had never seen it before. He slid open the mirrored door of the medicine chest and looked inside at the almost-empty tube of toothpaste, the old safety razor, the pack of double-edged blades, the darvon and tetracycline capsules, the foundation make-up. When he slid the door shut again, his tanned face looked back at him.

He was slow getting started that morning; when Carol got up, he was still drinking his coffee, with the radio playing an old Doors song in the background. Carol leaned over him, kissed the top of his head. It appeared that she loved him.

'You'd better get going,' she said. 'You'll be late.'

He hadn't worried about being late, and it hit him for the first time what he had to do. He had to get to the Board of Trade. He'd have to talk to Stein Jr, and there would be a sheaf of notes on his desk asking him to return calls to various clients who would have rung him up while he was gone. He pulled on the jacket of his pinstriped suit, brushed back his hair, and left.

Waiting for the train, he realized that he hadn't gone anywhere to return from.

He had missed his normal train and arrived late. The streets were nowhere near as crowded as they would have been an hour earlier. He walked north on LaSalle Avenue between the staid, dark old buildings. The sky that showed between them was bright, and already the temperature was rising; it would be a hot one. He wished it were the weekend. Was it Thursday? It couldn't still be Wednesday. He was embarrassed to realize he wasn't sure what day it was.

He saw a very pretty girl in the lobby of the Board of Trade as he entered through the revolving doors. She was much prettier than Carol, and had that unself-conscious way of walking. But she was around the corner before he had taken more than a few steps inside. He ran into Joe Wendelstadt in the elevator, and Joe began to tell him a story about Raoul Lark from Brazil who worked for Cacex in Chicago, and how Lark had tried to pick up some feminist the other night. And succeeded. Those Brazilians.

Fallon got off before Joe could reach the climax. In his office Molly, the receptionist, said Stein wanted to see him. Stein smelled of cigarettes, and Fallon suddenly became self-conscious. He had not brushed his own teeth. When did he ever forget that? Stein had an incipient zit on the end of his nose. He didn't really have anything to talk to Fallon about; he was just wasting time as usual.

Tigue was sick or on vacation.

Fallon worked through the morning on various customer accounts. He had trouble remembering where the market had closed the day before. He had always had a trick memory for such figures, and it had given him the ability to impress a lot of people who knew just as much about the markets as he did. He spent what was left of the morning on the phone to his clients, with a quick trip down to the trading floor to talk to Parsons in the soybean pit.

Carol called and asked him if he could join her for lunch. He remembered he had a date with Kim, a woman from the CME he had met just a week before. He made his excuses to Carol and took off for the Merc.

Walking briskly west on Jackson, coming up on the bridge across the river, he realized he had been rushing around all day and yet could hardly remember what he'd done since he had woken up. He still couldn't remember whether it was Wednesday or Thursday.

As he crossed the bridge with the crowds of lunch-hour office workers, the noontime sun glared brightly for a second from the oily water of the river. Fallon's eyes did not immediately recover. He stopped walking and somebody bumped into him.

'Excuse me,' he said unconsciously.

There was a moment of silence, then the noise of the city resumed, and he could see again. He stood at the side of the bridge and looked down at the water. The oil on the surface made rainbow-colored black swirls. Fallon shook his head and went on.

Kim stood him up at the restaurant. She did not arrive to meet him, and he waited a long time by the cashier. Finally he made the woman seat him at a table for two. He looked at his watch but had some trouble reading the time. Was he due back at the office?

Just then someone sat down opposite him. It was an old man in a dark suit who had obviously undergone some great ordeal. His face held a look of great pain or sorrow—with hate burning just beneath it. Though his hair was black (and quite unforgivably unkempt for midtown Chicago, as was his rough suit), a shock of white fell across his forehead, and a scar ran from the roots of that white hair straight down the man's face, leaping the brow and eye to continue across the left cheek, sinewing down the jaw and neck to disappear beneath his shirt collar.

He looked strangely familiar.

'It won't work,' the man said. 'You cannot get away. You have signed the articles, like the rest, and are in for a three-hundreth lay.'

'Three-hundreth lay?' Fallon was bewildered.

'A three-hundreth part of the general catastrophe is yours. Don't thank me. It isn't necessary.' The old man looked even more sorrowful and more wild, if it were possible to combine those seemingly incompatible emotions.

'To tell you the truth,' he said, 'I wouldn't hold you to the contract if it were strictly up to me.' He shrugged his shoulders and opened his palms before him. 'But it isn't.'

Fallon's heart was beating fast again. 'I don't remember any contract. You're not one of my clients. I don't trade for you. I've been in this business for a long time, mister, and I know better than to sign. . . .'

The wildness swelled in the man. There was something burning in him, and he looked about to scream, or cry.

'*I* have been in the business longer than *you!*' He swung his leg out from beneath the table and rapped it loudly with his knuckle. Fallon saw that the leg was of white bone. 'And *I* can tell *you* that you signed the contract when you signed aboard this ship—there's no other way to get aboard—and you must serve until you strike land again or it sinks beneath you!'

The diners in the restaurant dined on, oblivious. Fallon looked toward the plate glass at the front of the room and saw the water rising rapidly up it, sea-green and turbid, as the restaurant and the city fell to the bottom of the sea.

13

Once again he was jerked awake, this time by the din of someone beating the deck of the forecastle above them with a club. The other sleepers were as startled as Fallon. He rolled out of the hammock with the mists of his dream still clinging to him, pulled on his shirt and scrambled up to the deck.

Ahab was stalking the quarter-deck in a frenzy of impatience. 'Man the mastheads!' he shouted.

The men who had risen with Fallon did just that, some of them only half-dressed. Fallon was one of the first up and gained one of the hoops at the main masthead. Three others stood on the mainyard below him. Fallon scanned the horizon and saw off to starboard and about a mile ahead of them the jet of mist that indicated a whale. As it rose and fell in its course through the rolling seas, Fallon saw that it was white.

'What do you see?' Ahab called from far below. Had he noticed Fallon's gaze fixed on the spot in front of them?

'Nothing! Nothing, sir!' Fallon called. Ahab and the men on deck looked helpless so far below him. Fallon did not know if his lying would work, but there was the chance that the other men in the rigging, not being as high as he, would not be able to make out Moby Dick from their lower vantage points. He turned away from the whale and made a good show of scanning the empty horizon.

'Top gallant sails!—stunsails! Alow and aloft, and on both sides!' Ahab ordered. The men fixed a line from the mainmast to the deck, looped its lower end around Ahab's rigid leg. Ahab wound the rope around his shoulders and arm, and they hoisted him aloft, twisting with the pressure on the hemp, toward the masthead. He twirled slowly as they raised him up, and his line of sight was obscured by the rigging and sails he had to peer through.

Before they had lifted him two-thirds of the way up, he began to shout.

'There she blows!—there she blows! A hump like a snowhill! It is Moby Dick!'

Fallon knew enough to begin shouting and pointing immediately, and the men at the other two masts did the same. Within a minute everyone who had remained on the deck was in the rigging trying to catch a glimpse of the creature they had sought, half of them doubting his existence, for so many months.

Fallon looked down toward the helmsman, who stood on his toes, the whalebone tiller under his arm, arching his neck trying to see the whale.

The others in the rigging were now arguing about who had spotted Moby Dick first, with Ahab the eventual victor. It was his fate, he said, to be the one to first spot the whale. Fallon couldn't argue with that.

Ahab was lowered to the deck, giving orders all the way, and three boats were swung outboard in preparation for the chase. Starbuck was ordered to stay behind and keep the ship.

As they chased the whale, the sea became calmer, so the rowing became easier—though just as back-breaking—and they knifed through the water, here as placid as a farm pond, faster than ever. Accompanying the sound of their own wake, Fallon heard the wake of the whale they must be approaching. He strained arms, back, and legs, pulling harder in time to Stubb's cajoling chant, and the rushing grew. He snatched a glance over his shoulder, turned to the rowing, then looked again.

The white whale glided through the sea smoothly, giving the impression of immeasurable strength. The wake he left was as steady as that of a schooner; the bow waves created by the progress of his broad, blank brow through the water fanned away in precise lines whose angle with respect to the massive body did not change. The three whaleboats rocked gently as they broke closer through these successive waves; the foam of Moby Dick's wake was abreast of them now, and Fallon saw how quickly it subsided into itself, giving the sea back its calm face, innocent of knowledge of the creature that had passed. Attendant white birds circled above their heads, now and then falling to or rising from the surface in busy flutterings of wings and awkward beaks. One of them had landed on the broken shaft of a harpoon that protruded from the snow-white whale's humped back; it bobbed up and down with the slight rocking of the whale in its long, muscular surging through the sea. Oblivious. Strangely quiet. Fallon felt as if they had entered a magic circle.

He knew Ahab's boat, manned by the absurd Filipinos, was ahead of them and no doubt preparing to strike first. Fallon closed his eyes, pulled on his oar, and wished for it not to happen. For it to stop now, or just continue without any change. He felt as if he could row a very long time; he was no longer tired or afraid. He just wanted to keep rowing, feeling the rhythm of the work, hearing the low and insistent voice of Stubb telling them to break their backs. Fallon wanted to listen to the rushing white sound of the whale's wake in the water, to know that they were perhaps keeping pace with it, to know that, if he should tire, he could look for a second over his shoulder and find Moby Dick there still. Let the monomaniac stand in the bow of his boat—if he was meant to stand there, if it was an unavoidable necessity—let him stand there with the raised lance and concentrate his hate into one purified moment of will. Let him send that will into the tip of that lance so that it might physically glow with the frustrated obtuseness of it. Let him stand there until he froze from the suspended desire, and let the whale swim on.

Fallon heard a sudden increase in the rushing of the water, several inarticulate cries. He stopped pulling, as did the others, and turned to look in time to see the whale lift itself out of the water, exposing flanks and flukes the bluish white of cemetery marble, and flip its huge tail upward to dive perpendicularly into the sea. Spray drenched them, and sound returned with the crash of the waves coming together to fill the vacuum left by the departure of the creature that had seconds before given weight and direction, place, to the placeless expanse of level waters. The birds circled above the subsiding foam.

They lifted their oars. They waited.

'An hour,' Ahab said.

They waited. It was another beautiful day. The sky was hard and blue as the floor of the swimming pool where he had met Carol. Fallon wondered again if she missed him, if he had indeed disappeared from that other life when he had taken up residence in this one—but he thrust those thoughts away. They were meaningless. There was no time in that world after his leaving it; that world did not exist, or if it existed, the order of its existence was not of the order of the existence of the rough wood he sat on, the raw flesh of his hands and the air he breathed. Time was the time between the breaths he drew. Time was the duration of the dream he had had about being back in Chicago, and he could not say how long that had been, even if it had begun or ended. He might be dreaming still. The word 'dream' was meaningless, and 'awake.' And 'real,' and 'insane,' and 'known,' and all those other interesting words he had once known. Time was waiting for Moby Dick to surface again.

The breeze freshened. The sea began to swell.

'The birds!—the birds!' Tashtego shouted, so close behind Fallon's ear that he winced. The Indian half-stood, rocking the whaleboat as he pointed to the sea birds, which had risen and were flying toward Ahab's boat twenty yards away.

'The whale will breach there,' Stubb said.

Ahab was up immediately. Peering into the water, he leaned on the steering oar and reversed the orientation of his boat. He then exchanged places with Fedallah, the other men reaching up to help him through the rocking boat. He picked up the harpoon, and the oarsmen stood ready to row.

Fallon looked down into the sea, trying to make out what Ahab saw. Nothing, until a sudden explosion of white as the whale, rocketing upward, turned over as it finally hit the surface. In a moment Ahab's boat was in the whale's jaws, Ahab in the bows almost between them. Stubb was shouting and gesturing, and Fallon's fellows fell to the oars in a disorganized rush. The Filipinos in the lead boat crowded into the stern while Ahab, like a man trying to open a recalcitrant garage door, tugged and shoved at Moby Dick's jaw, trying insanely to dislodge the whale's grip. Within seconds filled with crashing water, cries and confusion, Moby Dick had bitten the boat in two, and Ahab had belly-flopped over the side like a swimming-class novice.

Moby Dick then began to swim tight circles around the smashed boat and its crew. Ahab struggled to keep his head above water. Neither Stubb nor Flask could bring his boat close enough to pick him up. The *Pequod* was drawing nearer, and finally Ahab was able to shout loudly enough to be heard, 'Sail on the whale—drive him off!'

It worked. The *Pequod* picked up the remnants of the whaleboat while Fallon and the others dragged its crew and Ahab into their own boat.

The old man collapsed in the bottom of the boat, gasping for breath, broken and exhausted. He moaned and shook. Fallon was sure he was finished whale chasing, that Stubb and the others would see the man was used up, that Starbuck would take over and sail them home. But in a minute or two Ahab was leaning on his elbow asking after his boat's crew, and a few minutes after that they had resumed the chase with double oarsmen in Stubb's boat.

Moby Dick drew steadily away as exhaustion wore them down. Fallon did not feel he could row any more after all. The *Pequod* picked them up and they gave chase in vain under all sail until dark.

14

On the second day's chase all three boats were smashed in. Many suffered sprains and contusions, and one was bitten by a shark. Ahab's whale-bone leg was shattered, with a splinter driven into his own flesh. Fedallah, who had been the captain's second shadow, was tangled in the line Ahab had shot into the white whale, dragged out of the boat, and drowned. Moby Dick escaped.

15

It came down to what Fallon had known it would come down to eventually.

In the middle of that night he went to talk to Ahab, who slept in one of the hatchways as he had the night before. The carpenter was making him another leg, wooden this time, and Ahab was curled sullenly in the dark lee of the after scuttle. Fallon did not know whether he was waiting or asleep.

He started down the stairs, hesitated on the second step. Ahab lifted his head. 'What do you need?' he asked.

Fallon wondered what he wanted to say. He looked at the man huddled in the darkness and tried to imagine what moved him, tried to see him as a man instead of a thing. Was it possible he was only a man, or had Fallon himself become stylized and distorted by living in the book of Melville's imagination?

'You said—talking to Starbuck today—you said that everything that happens is fixed, decreed. You said it was rehearsed a billion years before any of it took place. Is it true?'

Ahab straightened and leaned toward Fallon, bringing his face into the dim light thrown by the lamps on deck. He looked at him for a moment in silence.

'I don't know. So it seemed as the words left my lips. The Parsee is dead before me, as he fortold. I don't know.'

'That is why you're hunting the whale.'

'That is why I'm hunting the whale.'

'How can this hunt, how can killing an animal tell you anything? How can it justify your life? What satisfaction can it give you in the end, even if you boil it all down to oil, even if you cut Moby Dick into bible-leaves and eat him? I don't understand it.'

The captain looked at him earnestly. He seemed to be listening, and leaping ahead of the questions. It was very dark in the scuttle, and they could hardly see each other. Fallon kept his hands folded tightly behind him. The blade of the cleaver he had shoved into his belt lay cool against the skin at the small of his back; it was the same knife he used to butcher the whale.

'If it is immutably fixed, then it does not matter what I do. The purpose and meaning are out of my hands, and thine. We have only to take our parts, to be the thing that it is written for us to be. Better to live that role given us than to struggle against it or play the coward, when the actions must be the same nonetheless. Some say I am mad to chase the whale. Perhaps I am mad. But if it is my destiny to seek him, to tear, to burn and kill those things that stand in my path—then the matter of my madness is not relevant, do you see?'

He was not speaking in character.

'If these things are not fixed, and it was not my destiny to have my leg taken by the whale, to have my hopes blasted in this chase, then how cruel a world it is. No mercy, no power but its own controls it; it blights our lives out of merest whim. No, not whim, for there would then be no will behind it, no builder of this Bedlam hospital, and in the madhouse, when the keeper is gone, what is to stop the inmates from doing as they please? In a universe of cannibals, where all creatures have preyed upon each other, carrying on an eternal war since the world began, why should I not exert my will in whatever direction I choose? Why should I not bend others to my will?' The voice was reasonable, and tired. 'Have I answered your question?'

Fallon felt the time drawing near. He felt light, as if the next breeze might lift him from the deck and carry him away. 'I have an idea,' he said. 'My idea is—and it is an idea I have had for some time now, and despite everything that has happened, and what you say, I can't give it up—my idea is that all that is happening . . .' Fallon waved his hand at the world, '. . . is a story. It is a book written by a man named Herman Melville and told by a character named Ishmael. You are the main character in the book. All the things that have happened are events in the book.

'My idea also is that I am not from the book, or at least I wasn't originally. Originally I lived a different life in another time and place, a life in the real world and not in a book. It was not ordered and plotted like a book, and. . . .'

Ahab interrupted in a quiet voice: 'You call this an ordered book? I see no order. If it were so orderly, why would the whale task me so?'

Fallon knotted his fingers tighter behind him. Ahab was going to make him do it. He felt the threads of the situation weaving together to create only that bloody alternative, of all the alternatives that might be. In the open market, the price for the future and price for the physical reality converged on delivery day.

'The order's not an easy thing to see, I'll admit,' Fallon said. He laughed nervously.

Ahab laughed louder. 'It certainly is not. And how do you know this other life you speak of was not a play? A different kind of play. How do you know your thoughts are your own? How do you know that this dark little scene was not prepared just for us, or perhaps for someone who is reading about us at this very moment and wondering about the point of the drama just as much as we wonder at the pointlessness of our lives?' Ahab's voice rose, gaining an edge of compulsion. 'How do we know anything?' He grabbed his left wrist, pinched the flesh and shook it.

'How do we know what lies behind this matter? This flesh is a wall, the painting over the canvas, the mask drawn over the player's face, the snow fallen over the fertile field, or perhaps the scorched earth. I know there is something there; there must be something, but it cannot be touched because we are smothered in this flesh, this life. How do we know—'

'Stop it! Stop it!' Fallon shouted. 'Please stop asking things! You should not be able to say things like that to me! Ahab does not talk to me!'

'Isn't this what I am supposed to say?'

Fallon shuddered.

'Isn't this scene in your book?'

He was dizzy, sick. 'No! Of course not!'

'Then why does that disturb you? Doesn't this prove that we are not pieces of a larger dream, that this is a real world, that the blood that flows within our veins is real blood, that the pain we feel has meaning, that the things we do have consequence? We break the mold of existence by existing. Isn't that reassurance enough?' Ahab was shouting now, and the men awake on deck trying to get the boats in shape for the last day's chase and the *Pequod's* ultimate destruction put aside their hammers and rope and listened to his justification.

It was time. Fallon, shaking with anger and fear, drew the knife from behind him and leapt at the old man. In bringing up the blade for the attack he hit it against the side of the narrow hatchway. His grip loosened. Ahab threw up his hands, and despite the difference in age and mobility between them, managed to grab Fallon's wrist before he could strike the killing blow. Instead, the deflected cleaver struck the beam beside Ahab's head and stuck there. As Fallon tried to free it, Ahab brought his forearm up and smashed him beneath the jaw. Fallon fell backward, striking his head with stunning force against the opposite side of the scuttle. He momentarily lost consciousness.

When he came to himself again, Ahab was sitting before him with his strong hands on Fallon's shoulders, supporting him, not allowing him to move.

'Good, Fallon, good,' he said. 'You've done well. But now, no more games, no more dramas, no easy way out. Admit that this is not the tale you think it is! Admit that you do not know what will happen to you in the next second, let alone the next day or year! Admit that we are both free and unfree, alone and crowded in by circumstance in this world that we indeed did not make, but indeed have the power to affect! Put aside those notions that there is another life somehow more real than the life you live now, another air to breathe somehow more pure, another love or hate somehow more vital than the love or hate you bear me. Put aside your fantasy and admit that you are alive, and thus may momentarily die. Do you hear me, Fallon?'

Fallon heard, and saw, and felt and touched, but he did not know. The *Pequod*, freighted with savages and isolatoes, sailed into the night, and the great shroud of the sea rolled on as it rolled five thousand years ago.

THE MANOR OF ROSES

Thomas Burnett Swann

1

I am thirty-five, a woman of middle years, and yet in this time of pox and plague, of early death and the dying of beauty before the body dies, it is said that I am still as beautiful as a Byzantine Madonna, poised in the heaven of a gold mosaic and wearing sorrow like a robe of white petals. But sorrow is not a gown. It is a nakedness to the searching eye of the curious, to the magpie-tongued who love to pry out grief: She grieves too long . . . The Manor demands an heir . . . Who will defend us from the encroaching forest, the thieves and the Mandrake People?

It was eleven years ago, in the year 1202 of Our Lord, that my husband's comrade-in-arms, Edmund-the-Wolf, rode to me with the news of my husband's death and, as if for compensation, the riches captured before he had died in battle. Captured? Pillaged, I should say, in the sack of Constantinople. You see, it is a time when men are boys, rapacious and cruel, as ready to kill a Jew, a Hungarian, a Greek as an Infidel; happy so long as they wield a sword and claim to serve God. A time when boys who have not yet grown to their fathers' pride—Crusading, it is called—are the only true men.

And yet I loved my husband, a red-haired Norman, gay as the men of the South, and not like most of our stern northern people. I loved him for his gaiety, his hair the color of Roman bricks, and because he left me a son.

But the Crusader's code, like an evil demon of pox, also possesses children. Only last year in France and Germany, Stephen proclaimed his message from Christ, Nicholas piped his irresistible flute, and the children yearned to them as tides to the moon and flowed in a sea of white immaculate robes toward the shores of that greater sea, the Mediterranean.

Little of the madness crossed to England. Perhaps our children are not inclined to visions, perhaps they prefer the hunt to the drafty halls of a church and talks with God. But the madness, missing the thousands, somehow touched my son. He rode to London, astride his roan palfrey and dressed in a jerkin of sheepskin dyed to the yellow of gorse, with a leather belt at his waist and a fawn-colored pouch a-jingle with new-minted pennies. Ready to board a ship for Marseilles and join Stephen! But Stephen and most of his army were sold as slaves to the Infidel; Nicholas died of the plague before he reached the sea; and my son of fifteen summers, reaching London, stood on the banks of the Thames to choose what twin-castled ship would bear him across the channel, and fell to the blade of a common cutpurse. The Devil, I think, possessed the children, a jest to fling like a gauntlet in the teeth of God.

God is not blind however. In less than a year, he sent me those other children, struck with the same madness: John, a dark-haired Norman; Stephen, a Saxon but named like the boy of France; and Ruth, whom they called their guardian angel (but no one knew if she came from Heaven or Hell). God, I felt, had made me His instrument to preserve them from my own son's ruin. Was He wrong to trust me with so precious and difficult a task? I tried, Mother of God I tried! I sheltered them from the Mandrakes of the forest. Loved them, hurt them, and then at the last—But you shall judge me. . . .

He ran blinded by tears across the heath, startling birds into flight, pheasants and grouse enough to feast a king. Conies peered from their nests and submerged like frogs in a pond with a dull, simultaneous plop. Didn't they know that he, timorous John, who had lost his bow in the woods and scattered the arrows out of his quiver, was not a creature to fear? He had come from the hunt with his father, lord of Goshawk Castle, and the knights Robert, Arthur, Edgar, and the rest. The names of the knights were different, their features almost identical. Rough hands, calloused from wielding swords against the Infidel—and their fellow Englishmen. Cheeks ruddy with mead and not with the English climate. Odorous bodies enveloped by furlined surcoats which they pridefully wore even in the flush of summer, instead of imitating the villeins with their

simple breechclouts or their trousers without tunics. Lank, sweat-
dampened hair, long in the back and cut in a fringe across their
foreheads.

John, the Baron's son, had been allowed the first shot at a stag
beleaguered by hounds. He was not a good bowman, but the stag
had been much too close to miss except by design. He had missed
by design. Once, gathering chestnuts with his friend Stephen, the
shepherd, he had seen the same animal, a splendid beast with horns
like wind-beaten trees along the North Sea.

'He isn't afraid of us,' Stephen had whispered.

'Nor has he reason to be,' said John. 'We would never harm him.
He's much too beautiful.'

Now, the animal had turned and looked at him with recognition,
it seemed, and resignation; harried by hounds; bemused in a clump
of bracken. John had fired his arrow above the antlers. The stag had
escaped, bursting out of the bracken as if the coarse ferns were
blades of grass and leveling three dogs with his adamantine hooves.

'Girl!' his father had shouted, hoarse with rage at losing a feast
and a pair of antlers to grace his barren hall. 'I should get you a
distaff instead of a bow!'

For punishment John was bladed. After the knights had downed
a smaller animal, a young doe, they had stretched him across the
warm, bloody carcass and each man had struck him with the flat of
his sword. Most of the knights had softened their blows. After all,
he was their liege-lord's son. But his father's blow had left him
bleeding and biting his tongue to hold back shameful tears.

Then they had left him.

'Go to the kennels and get your friend Stephen to dry your tears,'
his father had sneered. A coarse guffaw greeted the taunt. Stephen
was said to have lain with every villein's daughter between twelve
and twenty, and men without daughters liked to jest: 'Girls weep
till Stephen dries their tears.'

Alone in the woods, John forgot his shame; he was too frightened. Just turned twelve, he knew of desperate thieves, sentenced
to die by the rope, who had taken refuge among the syca-mores
which remembered the Romans, and the oaks which had drunk the
blood of Druid sacrifices. As for animals, there were wolves and
bears and long-tusked boars, and amphisbaenas too, the twin-
headed serpents, and griffins with scaly wings. Worst of all, there
were the Mandrake People who, grown like roots, clambered out of
the ground to join their kin in acts of cannibalism.

Where could he go? Not to the castle, certainly, where the huntes had doubtless climbed in a broad wooden tub to scrape the grime of weeks from each other's backs, while kitchen wenches doused them with buckets of steaming water and ogled their naked brawn. Once, the castle had held his mother. Its darkness had shone with the whiteness of her samite; its odors were masked with the cloves and the cinnamon, the mace and the musk of her kitchen; its bailey had bloomed with a damson tree whose seeds had come from the Holy Land, and delicate shallots, the 'Onions of Ascalon,' had reared their tender shoots around the tree, like little guardian gnomes.

'If there must be fruits of war,' she had said, 'we must see that they are living things, not dead, sweet things, not bitter, soft things, not hard. The verdure of earth and not the gold from dead men's coffers.'

Six years ago she had died of the pox. Now, when he knelt on the stone floor of the chapel, he prayed to Father, Son, and Mary, but Mary was Mother.

No, he could not go to the castle. He could but he did not wish to visit the Abbot's cottage and face another lesson in logic and astrology, Lucan and Aristotle. He was a willing, indeed a brilliant scholar. But there were times to study and times to look for Stephen. In spite of his father's taunt, it was time to look for Stephen. It was not that his friend was soft or womanish like a sister. He was, in fact, as rough-swearing, ready-to-fight a boy as ever tumbled a girl in the hay. But he curbed his roughness with John, respected his learning, and ignored his weaknesses.

Stephen was a Saxon villein three years older than John. His forebears, he rightly claimed, had once been powerful earls. But the conquering Normans had reduced them to the status of serfs and attached them to their own former lands, which had once held a wooden hall surrounded by a palisade, but now a castle built by John's grandfather, a square stone keep encircled by curtain walls whose gatehouse was toothed with a rusty portcullis and guarded by archers in hidden embrasures. Stephen's parents were dead, killed by the Mandrake People in one of their swift forays out of the forest to steal sheep and hogs. It was on that very day, two years ago, that he and Stephen had become inseparable friends. John had found him crouching above his mother's body. John, who did not even know his name, had laid a tentative arm around his shoulders—an act of extraordinary boldness for one so shy—and half expected a snarled rebuff or even a blow. But Stephen had buried his head in the arms of his master's son and sobbed convulsively without tears.

It was not long before they agreed to adopt each other as brothers and, cutting their forearms with a hunting knife, mingled their blood to cement the bond.

From that time till now, Stephen had lived in a loft above the kennels, dog-boy, shepherd, farmer, fighter with fists and cudgel second to none. He could not read English, much less French and Latin, but the wolves feared his cudgel and grown men his fists. How could you best describe him? Angry, sometimes, but angry *for* things and not against them. For the serfs and the squalor in which they lived; the dogs which were run too hard in the hunt and gored by wild boars; the animals killed for sport and not for food. Sometimes, too, he was glad: loudly, radiantly, exuberantly keen on things—drawing a bow, feeding his dogs, swinging a scythe.

At other times he was neither angry nor glad, but beyond anger and gladness; enraptured by dreams: of meeting an angel or finding Excalibur or, best of all, buying his freedom and becoming a Knight Hospitaler to succor pilgrims and slaughter Infidels ('But you would have to take an oath of chastity,' John reminded him. 'I'll think about that when the time comes,' said Stephen). Furthermore, he was one of those rarest of rarities, a dreamer who acts on his dreams, and lately he had talked about the ill-fated Children's Crusade, and how it was time for other Stephens, other Nicholases, to follow the first children and, armed with swords instead of crosses, succeed where they had failed.

It was John's unspeakable fear that Stephen would leave for Jerusalem without him, and yet he did not know if he had the courage for such a journey, through the dark Weald to London and then by ship to Marseilles and the ports of Outre-Mer, the Outer Land, the Saracen Land. Now, he quickened his pace and thought of arguments with which to dissuade his friend. He met old Edward scything in the Common Meadow; a tattered breechclout around his loins, his face and shoulders as coarse and brown as a saddle ridden from London to Edinburgh. Edward did not look up from his task, nor miss a stroke of the scythe. 'Why look at the sky?' he liked to mutter. 'It belongs to angels, not to serfs.'

'Have you seen Stephen?' John asked.

Swish, swish, swish went the scythe, and the weeds collapsed as if they had caught the plague.

'HAVE YOU SEEN STEPHEN?'

'I'm not deaf,' the old man growled. 'Your father's taken my youth, my pigs, and my corn, but not my ears. Not yet, anyway. Your friend'll be losing his, though, 'less he does his work. He oughta be here in the Meadow right now.'

'But where *is* he?' cried John in desperation.

'Making for the Roman Place with that look in his eyes. That's where he hides, you know. Daydreams. Didn't even speak to me.'

The Roman Place. The ruin where the Romans had worshipped their sun-god, Mithras, in an underground vault. Later, by way of apology to the Christian God, the Saxons had built a timber church to conceal the spot and turned the vault into a crypt for their dead. During the Norman Conquest, women and children had hidden in the church, and the Normans had set a torch to the roof and burned the building with all of its occupants. The charred and misshapen remnants were almost concealed—healed, as it were—by flowering gorse, and a few blackened timbers, which thrust like seeking hands from the yellow flowers, summoned no worshippers to the buried gods.

A stranger would not suspect a vault beneath the gorse, but John parted the spiny branches and climbed through a narrow hole to a flight of stairs. A sacredness clung to the place, a sense of time, like that of a Druid stone which lichen had aged to a muted, mottled orange and which thrust at the stars as if to commune with them in cosmic loneliness. Here, the worshippers of Mithras had bathed themselves in the blood of the sacrificial bull and climbed through the seven stages of initiation to commune with the sun instead of the stars. A nasty pagan rite, said the Abbot, and John had asked him why Jehovah had ordered Abraham to sacrifice Isaac. 'It was only a test,' snapped the Abbot.

'But what about Jephthah's daughter? *She* wasn't a test.' The Abbot had changed the subject.

Already, at twelve, John had begun to ask questions about the Bible, God, Christ, and the Holy Ghost. To Stephen, religion was feeling and not thought. God was a patriarch with a flowing beard, and angels were almost as real as the dogs in his kennel. With John it was different. Only the Virgin Mary was not a subject for doubts, arguments, but a beautiful, ageless woman robed in samite, dwelling in the high places of the air or almost at hand, outshining the sun and yet as simple as bread, grass, birds, and Stephen's love; invisible but never unreachable.

At the foot of the stairs he faced a long, narrow cave with earthen walls which contained the loculi of Christians buried in their cerements and which converged to the semi-circle of an apse. Now, the apse was empty of Mithras slaying the sacred bull and Mary holding the infant Christ. Stephen knelt in their place. He held a waxen candle which lit the frescoed roof: Jesus walking on water;

multiplying loaves and fish; bidding the blind to see and the lame to walk.

'John,' he gasped, 'I have found—'

'A Madonna!'

She lay in a nest of bindweed shaped to a simple pallet. Her face was an ivory mask in the light of the candle. A carved Madonna, thought John, from the transept of a French cathedral, but flushed with the unmistakable ardors of life. No, he saw with a disappointment which approached dismay, she was much too young for the Virgin; a mere girl.

'An angel,' said Stephen.

'An angel,' sighed John, resenting her youthfulness. What did he need with a second angel, a girl at that? God (or the Virgin Mary) had sent him Stephen, angelic but not female and certainly not effeminate, his hair a riot instead of an aureole, his face more ruddy than pink: a Michael or Gabriel fit for sounding a trumpet instead of strumming a lyre.

The angel stirred and opened her eyes with a pretty fluttering; not with surprise or fright, but almost, thought John, with artful calculation, like some of the rustic lasses who flocked to Stephen's loft. Her teeth were as white as her linen robe, which was bound at the waist by a cord of cerulean silk. Her pointed slippers, unicorn leather trimmed with blue velvet, were such as might be worn in the soft pastures of heaven. She lacked only wings. Or had she concealed them under her robe? John was tempted to ask.

Stephen forestalled him. 'Greet her,' he whispered. 'Welcome her!'

'In what language?' asked John sensibly. 'I don't know the tongues of angels.'

'Latin, I should think. She must know that, with all the priests muttering their Benedicites.'

Stephen had a point. Rude English was out of the question, and also the French of the Normans, who, after all, had descended from barbarous Vikings.

'Quo Vadis?' asked John none too politely.

Her smile, though delectable, no doubt, to Stephen, did not answer the question.

'What are you doing here?' he repeated in Norman French.

Stephen, who understood some French, frantically nudged him. 'You shouldn't question an angel. Welcome her! Worship her! Quote her a psalm or a proverb.'

'We aren't sure she's an angel. She hasn't told us, has she?'

At last she spoke. 'I do not know how I came here,' she said in flawless Latin and, seeing the blankness on Stephen's face, repeated the words in English, but with a grave dignity which softened the rough tongue. At the same time, John noticed the crucifix which she held or rather clutched in her hands: a small Greek cross with arms of equal length, wrought of gold and encrusted with stones which he knew from his studies, though not from his father's castle, were the fabulous pearls of the East. 'I remember only a darkness, and a falling, and a great forest. I wandered until I found the passage to this cave, and took shelter against the night. I must have been very tired. I feel as if I have slept for a long time.' She lifted the cross and then, as if its weight had exhausted her slender hands, allowed it to sink becomingly against her breast.

'I suppose,' said John with annoyance, 'you're hungry.'

Stephen sprang to his feet. 'But angels don't eat! Can't you see, John? God has sent her to us as a sign! To lead us to the Holy Land! Stephen of France had his message from Christ. We have our angel.'

'But look what happened to Stephen of France. Sold as a slave or drowned in the sea. Only the sharks know which.'

'I don't think he's dead. And if he is, then he listened to the Devil's voice and not to God's. But we can *see* our angel.'

'Indeed, you can see me,' she said, 'and you ought to see that I am famished. Angels do eat, I assure you—at least when they travel—and something more substantial than nectar and dew. Have you venison perhaps? Mead?'

'You must take her to the castle,' said Stephen, clearly reluctant to part with his new-found angel. 'I've nothing so fine in the kennels.'

'No,' said John. 'I'm not taking anyone to the castle. I've decided to stay with you in the kennels.'

'Because of your father?'

'Yes. He bladed me before all of his men, and then he called me a—' He could not bring himself to repeat the taunt, especially to Stephen. 'He called me a churl. Because I missed a stag. *Our* stag. The one we promised never to harm.'

Stephen nodded with understanding. 'I'm glad you missed him. They say he's the oldest stag in the forest. They say'—and here he lowered his voice—'that he isn't a stag at all, but Merlin turned to a beast by Vivian. But John, how can you live with me in the kennels? It would wound your father's pride. A baron's son sharing a loft with a dog-boy! He'd give you more than a blading, and as for me! You mayn't remember he cut off my father's ears because he broke a scythe. And now with an angel on our hands, the only thing to do is—'

'Get the angel off our hands?'

'Leave at once for the Holy Land. I have a little food in the kennels, a change of wear. You needn't go back to the castle at all. We've only to follow the Roman road through the Weald to London, and take ship to Marseilles, and from thence proceed to Outre-Mer.'

'But Marseilles was where the French Stephen fell in the hands of slavers.'

'But we have a guide!'

'If she isn't really an angel—'

'At least we'll have made our escape from the castle.'

'You mean we should leave the castle *forever?*' The prospect of leaving his father exhilarated him; he would feel like a falcon with its hood removed. But the castle held all of his possessions, his codex, *The Kings of Britain,* written on the finest vellum and bound between ivory covers; and the parchment containing his favorite poem, 'The Owl and the Nightingale,' copied laboriously by his own precise hand. Much more important, it held his mother's ghost, his sum of remembering: stairs she had climbed, tapestries woven, garments mended; his mother living in song what she could not live in life and singing of noble warriors and deathless loves:

> See, he who carved this wood
>   commands me to ask
> You to remember, oh treasure-
>   adorned one,
> The pledge of old . . .

'Leave my father's castle,' he repeated, 'and not come back? Ever?'

Stephen's face turned as red as the Oriflamme, the fiery banner of the French kings. '*Your father's castle?* This land belonged to my ancestors when yours were scurvy Vikings! You think I'll stay here forever as dog-boy and shepherd? Serving a man who blades his own son? Giving him what I grow and what I hunt, and asking his leave to take a wife? John, John, there's nothing for either of us here. Ahead of us lies Jerusalem!'

To Stephen, the name was a trumpet blast; to John, a death knell.

'But a forest stands in the way, and then a channel, and a rough sea swarming with Infidels. They have ships too, you know, swifter than ours and armed with Greek Fire.'

But Stephen had gripped his shoulders and fixed him with his blue, relentless gaze. 'You know I can't leave you.'

'You know you won't have to,' sighed John.

The angel interrupted them, looking a little peeved that in their exchange of pleas and protestations, of male endearments, they were neglecting their quest and their inspiration. 'As for leading you to the Holy Land, I don't even know this forest through which you say we must pass. But here in the ground it is damp, and before I came here, I did not like the look of the castle. It seemed to me dark and fierce, with a dry ditch and a gloomy keep, and narrow windows without a pane of glass. A fortress and not a home. If indeed I am an angel, I hope to find dwellings more pleasant here on earth. Or else I shall quickly return to the sky. In the meantime, let us set off for London, and you shall lead *me* until I begin to remember.'

The angel between them, they climbed the stairs to the sun and, skirting old Edward, who was still busily scything in the Common Meadow, came at last to the kennels. It was mid-day. The Baron and his knights had remained in the castle since the hunt. His villeins, trudging out of the fields, had gathered in the shade of the water-mill to enjoy their gruel and bread. Had anyone noticed the quick, furtive passage of the would-be Crusaders, he would have thought them engaged in childish sports, or supposed that Stephen had found a young wench to share with his master's son and probably muttered, 'It's high time.'

While Stephen's greyhounds lapped at their heels, they climbed to his loft above the kennels to get his few belongings: two clover-green tunics with hoods for wintry days; wooden clogs and a pair of blue stockings which reached to the calf of the leg; a leather pouch bulging with wheaten bread and rounds of cheese; a flask of beer; and a knotted shepherd's crook.

'For wolves,' said Stephen, pointing to the crook. 'I've used it often.'

'And Mandrakes,' added John wickedly, hoping to frighten the angel.

'But we have no change of clothes for a girl,' said Stephen.

'Never mind,' she smiled, guzzling Stephen's beer and munching his bread till she threatened to exhaust the supply before they began their journey. 'When my robe grows soiled, I shall wash it in a stream and,' she added archly, 'the two of you may see if I am truly an angel.'

The remark struck John as unangelic if not indelicate. As if they would spy on her while she bathed!

But Stephen reassured her. 'We never doubted you were. And now—' A catch entered his voice. Quickly he turned his head and seemed to be setting the loft in order.

'We must leave him alone with his hounds,' whispered John to the angel, leading her down the ladder.

A silent Stephen rejoined them in the Heath. His tunic was damp from friendly tongues and his face was wet, but whether from tongues or tears, it was hard to say.

'You don't suppose,' he said, 'we could take one or two of them with us? The little greyhound without any tail?'

'No,' said John. 'My father will stomp and shout when he finds us gone, but then he'll shrug: "Worthless boys, both of them, and no loss to the castle." But steal one of his hounds, and he'll have his knights on our trail.'

'But our angel has no name,' cried Stephen suddenly and angrily, as if to say: 'As long as she's come to take me from my hounds, she might at least have brought a name.'

'I *had* a name, I'm sure. It seems to have slipped my mind. What would you like to call me?'

'Why not Ruth?' said Stephen. 'She was always going on journeys in the Bible, leading cousins and such, wasn't she?'

'A mother-in-law,' corrected John, who felt that, what with a Crusade ahead of them, Stephen should know the Scriptures.

'Leading and *being* led,' observed the angel, whose memory, it seemed, had begun to return. 'By two strapping husbands. Though,' she hurried to explain, 'not at the same time. Yes, I think you should call me Ruth.'

She is much too young for Ruth, thought John, who guessed her to be about fifteen (though of course as an angel she might be fifteen thousand). The same age as Stephen, whose thoughts were attuned to angelic visions but whose bodily urges were not in the least celestial. Unlike a Knight Templar, he had made no vow of chastity. The situation was not propitious for a crusade in the name of God.

But once they had entered the Weald, the largest forest in southern England, he thought of Mandrakes and griffins instead of Ruth. It was true that the Stane, an old Roman highway, crossed the Weald to join London and Chichester—they would meet it within the hour—but even the Stane was not immune to the forest.

2

At Ruth's suggestion, they carefully skirted the grounds of a neighboring castle, the Boar's Lair.

'Someone might recognize John,' she said. 'Send word to his father.'

'Yes,' John agreed, staring at the Norman tower, one of the black wooden keeps built by William the Conqueror to enforce his conquest. 'My father and Philip the Boar were once friends. Philip used to dine with us on Michaelmas and other feast days, and I played the kettledrums for him. Since then, he and my father have fallen out about their boundaries. They both claim a certain grove of beechnut trees—pannage for their swine. Philip wouldn't be hospitable, I'm sure.'

Deviously, circuitously, by way of a placid stream and an old water wheel whose power no longer turned mill-stones and ground wheat into flour, they reached the Roman Stane. Once a proud thoroughfare for unconquerable legions, it had since resounded to Saxon, Viking, and Norman, who had used it for commerce and war but, unlike the conscientious Romans, never repaired the ravages of wheels and weather. Now, it had shrunk in places to the width of a peasant's cart, but the smooth Roman blocks, set in concrete, still provided a path for riders and walkers and great ladies in litters between two horses.

'I feel like the Stane,' sighed Ruth, 'much-trodden and a trifle weedy.' She had torn the edge of her robe on prickly sedges and muddied the white linen. She had lost the circlet which haloed her head, and her silken tresses, gold as the throats of convolvulus flowers, had spilled like their trailing leafage over her shoulders. As for John, he was hot, breathless, and moist with sweat, and wishing that like a serf he dared to remove his long-sleeved tunic and revel in his breechclout.

'Stephen,' Ruth sighed, 'now that we've found the road, can't we rest a little?' Her speech, though still melodious, had relaxed into easy, informal English.

'We've just begun!' he laughed. 'London lies days away. We want to be leagues down the road before night.'

'But it's already mid-afternoon. Why not rest till it gets a little cooler?'

'Very well,' he smiled, reaching out to touch her in good-humored acquiescence. Stephen, who found difficulty with words, spoke with his hands, which were nests to warm a bird, balms to heal a dog, bows to extract the music from swinging a scythe, wielding an ax, gathering branches to build a fire. He could gesture or point or touch with the exquisite eloquence of a man who was deaf, dumb, and blind. When you said good morning to him, he clapped you on the shoulder. When you walked with him, he brushed against you or caught you by the arm. He liked to climb trees for the rough feel of the bark or swim in a winter stream and slap the icy currents until he warmed his body. But he saved his touch for the things or the people he loved. Neither ugly things nor unkind people.

'We'll rest as long as you like,' he said.

Ruth smiled. 'I think I should borrow one of your tunics. You see how my robe keeps dragging the ground.'

With a flutter of modesty she withdrew to a clump of bracken and changed to a tunic.

'Watch out for basilisks,' John called after her. 'Their bite is fatal, you know.' He muttered under his breath to Stephen: 'First she ate your food, and now she wears your clothes.'

'*Our* food and clothes,' reproved Stephen. 'Remember, we're Crusaders together.'

John was shamed into silence. He had to listen to Ruth as she bent branches, snapped twigs, and rustled cloth, almost as if she wished to advertise the various stages of her change. He thought of the wenches—ten? twenty?—who had disrobed for Stephen. The subject of sexual love confused him. The Aristotelian processes of his brain refused to sift, clarify, and evaluate the problem; in fact, they crumpled like windmills caught in a forest fire. He had loved his mother—what was the word?—filially; Stephen he loved fraternally. But as for the other thing, well, he had not been able to reconcile the courtly code as sung by the troubadours—roses and guerdons and troths of deathless fidelity—and the sight of Stephen, surprised last year in his loft with a naked wench and not in the least embarrassed. Stephen had grinned and said: 'In a year or so, John, we can wench together!' The girl, snickering and making no effort to hide her nakedness, had seemed to him one of those Biblical harlots who ought to be shorn, or stoned. Who could blame poor Stephen for yielding to such allurements! As for himself, however, he had sworn the chivalric oath to practice poverty, chastity, and obedience to God. He had thought of a monastery but rather than part with Stephen, who was not in the least monastic, he was willing to try a life of action.

'Has a crow got your tongue?' smiled Stephen. 'I didn't mean to scold.' He encircled John's shoulder with his arm. 'You smell like cloves.'

John stiffened, not at the touch but at what appeared to be an insinuation. He had not forgotten his father's taunt: 'Girl!' According to custom, it was girls and women who packed their gowns in clove-scented chests, while the men of a castle hung their robes in the room called the *garderobe*, another name for the lavatory cut in the wall beside the stairs, with a round shaft dropping to the moat. The stench of the shaft protected the room—and the robes—from moths.

'They belonged to my mother,' he stammered. 'The cloves, I mean. I still use her chest.'

'My mother put flowering mint with her clothes,' said Stephen. 'All two gowns! I like the cloves better, though. Maybe the scent will rub off on me. I haven't bathed for a week.' He gave John's shoulder a squeeze, and John knew that his manhood had not been belittled. But then, Stephen had never belittled him, had he? Teased him, yes; hurt him in play; once knocked him down for stepping on the tail of a dog; but never made light of his manliness.

'It's not a dangerous road,' Stephen continued, talkative for once, perhaps because John was silent. 'The abbots of Chichester patrol it for brigands. They don't carry swords, but Gabriel help the thief who falls afoul of their staves!'

'But the forest,' John said. 'It's all around us like a pride of griffins. With green, scaly wings. They look as if they're going to eat up the road. They've already nibbled away the edges, and'—he lowered his voice—'she came out of the forest, didn't she?'

Stephen laughed. 'She came out of the sky, simpleton! Didn't you hear her say she don't know nothing about the forest?'

Before John could lecture Stephen on his lapse in grammar, Ruth exploded between them, as green as a down in the tenderness of spring. She blazed in Stephen's tunic, its hood drawn over her head. She had bound her waist with the gold sash from her robe and, discarding her velvet slippers, donned his wooden clogs, whose very ugliness emphasized the delicacy of her bare feet. She had bundled her linen robe around her slippers and crucifix.

'No one would ever guess that I'm an angel,' she smiled. 'Or even a girl.'

'Not an angel,' said Stephen appreciatively. 'But a girl, yes.

You'd have to roughen your hands and hide your curls to pass for a
boy.'

She made a pretence of hiding her hair, but furtively shook
additional curls from her hood the moment they resumed their
journey, and began to sing a familiar song of the day:

> In a valley of this restless mind,
> I sought in mountain and in mead . . .

Though she sang about a man searching for Christ, the words
rippled from her tongue as merrily as if she were singing a carol.
John wished for his kettledrums and Stephen began to whistle.
Thus, they forgot the desolation of the road, largely untraveled at
such an hour and looking as if the griffin-scaly forest would soon
complete its meal.

Then, swinging around a bend and almost trampling them,
cantered a knight with a red cross painted on his shield—a Knight
Templar, it seemed—and after him, on a large piebald palfrey, a
lady riding pillion behind a servant who never raised his eyes from
the road. The knight frowned at them; in spite of the vows
demanded of his order, he looked more dedicated to war than to
God. But the lady smiled and asked their destination.

'I live in a castle up the road,' said John quickly in Norman
French. Unlike his friends, he was dressed in the mode of a young
gentleman, with a tunic of plum-colored linen instead of cheap
muslin, and a samite belt brocaded with silver threads. Thus, he
must be their spokesman. 'I have come with my friends to search
for chestnuts in the woods, and now we are going home.'

The knight darkened his frown to a baleful glare and reined his
steed, as if he suspected John of stealing a fine tunic to masquerade
as the son of a gentleman. Boys of noble birth, even of twelve, did
not as a rule go nutting with villeins whom they called their friends,
and not at such an hour.

'We have passed no castle for many miles,' he growled, laying a
thick-veined hand on the hilt of his sword.

'My father's is well off the road, and the keep is low,' answered
John without hesitation. 'In fact, it is called the Tortoise, and
it is *very* hard to break, like a tortoise shell. Many a baron has
tried!'

'Mind you get back to the Tortoise before dark,' the lady
admonished. 'You haven't a shell yourself, and the Stane is
dangerous after nightfall. My protector and I are bound for the
castle of our friend, Philip the Boar. Is it far, do you know?'

'About two leagues,' said John, and he gave her explicit

directions in French so assured and polished that no one, not even
the glowering knight, could doubt his Norman blood and his noble
birth. It was always true of him that he was only frightened in
anticipation. Now, with a wave and a courtly bow, he bade them
Godspeed to the castle of the Boar, received a smile from the lady,
and led his friends toward the mythical Tortoise.

'Such a handsome lad,' he heard the lady exclaim, 'and manly as
well.'

'If I hadn't been so scared,' said Stephen, once a comfortable
distance separated them from the knight, his lady, and the unre-
sponsive servant, 'I'd have split my tunic when you said your castle
was named the Tortoise. There isn't a castle for the next ten miles!
It's the first fib I ever heard you tell.'

'You were scared too?' asked John, surprised at such an admission.

'You can bet your belt I was! They were lovers, you know. Bound
for a tryst at the castle of the Boar. He winks at such things, I hear.
Runs a regular brothel for the gentry, including himself. That lady
has a husband somewhere, and the Knight Templar might just have
run us through to keep us from carrying tales.'

With the fall of darkness, they selected a broad and voluminous oak
tree, rather like a thicket set on the mast of a ship, and between
them the boys helped Ruth to climb the trunk. With nimble hands,
she prepared a nest of leaves and moss in the crook of the tree and,
having removed her clogs and hidden them, along with her crucifix,
settled herself with the comfort of perfect familiarity. She seemed
to have a talent for nests, above or below the ground. After she had
eaten some bread and cheese and drunk some beer, she returned to
the ground, stubbornly refusing assistance from either boy, and
showed herself a more than adept climber.

'Is she angry with us?' asked John.

'She drank all that beer,' explained Stephen, 'and while she's
gone—'

They scrambled to the edge of the nest and, bracing themselves
against a limb, aimed at the next oak. Gleefully, John pretended
that Ruth was crouching under the branches.

He was sorry to see her emerge from an elm instead of the
inundated oak and rejoin them in the nest.

'I was looking for rushes to keep us warm,' she said. 'But I didn't
find a single one. We'll have to lie close together.' She chose the
middle of the nest, anticipating, no doubt, a boy to warm her on
either side, and Stephen obligingly stretched on her left.

With the speed and deftness of Lucifer disguised as a serpent, John wriggled between them, forcing Ruth to the far side of the nest. Much to his disappointment, she accepted the arrangement without protest and leaned against him with a fragrance of galangal, the aromatic plant imported from Outre-Mer and used as a base for perfume by the ladies of England.

'The stars are bright tonight,' she said. 'See, John, there's Arcturus peeping through the leaves, and there's Sirius, the North Star. The Vikings called it the Lamp of the Wanderer.'

Stephen nudged him as if to say: 'You see! Only an angel knows such things.'

'Stephen,' he whispered.

'Yes?'

'I'm not afraid anymore. Of leaving the castle. Not even of the forest!'

'Aren't you, John?'

'Because I'm not alone.'

'I told you we were safe with our angel.'

'I don't mean the angel.' He made a pillow of Stephen's shoulder, and the scent of dogs and haylofts effaced Ruth's galangal.

'Go to sleep, little brother. Dream about London—and the Holy Land.'

But fear returned to John before he could dream. At an hour with the feel of midnight, chill and misty and hushed of owls, he was roused by the blast of a horn and a simultaneous shriek like that of a hundred otters caught in a mill wheel. The sounds seemed to come from a distance and yet were harsh enough to make him throw up his hands to his ears.

'Hunters have found a Mandrake!' cried Stephen, sitting up in the nest. 'It's a moonless night, and it must be just after twelve. That's when they hunt, you know. They blow on a horn to muffle the shriek. Let's see what they've caught.'

But John was not eager to leave the tree. 'If they've killed a Mandrake, they won't want to share it. Besides, they might be brigands.'

Ruth had also been roused by the shriek. 'John is right,' she said. 'You shouldn't want to see such a horrible sight. A baby torn from the earth!'

'I'll stay and keep Ruth company,' said John, but Stephen hauled him out of the nest and sent him slipping and scraping down the trunk.

'But we can't leave Ruth alone!' he groaned, picking himself up from a bed of acorns.

'Angels don't need protection. Hurry now, or we'll miss the hunters.'

They found the Mandrake hunters across the road and deep among the trees, a pair of rough woodsmen, father and son to judge from their height, build, and flaxen hair, though the elder was as bent and brown as a much-used sickle, and his son wore a patch over one of his eyes. The woodsmen were contemplating a dead Mandrake the size and shape of a new-born baby, except for the dirt-trailing tendrils, the outsized genitals, and the greenish tangle of hair which had grown above ground with purple, bell-shaped flowers. The pathetic body twitched like a hatcheted chicken. Dead at its side and bound to it by a rope lay a dog with bloody ears.

Though the night was moonless and the great stars, Arcturus and Sirius, were veiled by the mist of the forest, one of the hunters carried a lantern, and John saw the Mandrake, the dog, the blood in an eerie, flickering light which made him remember Lucifer's fall to Hell and wonder if he and Stephen had fallen after him.

One of the woodsmen saw them. 'Might have gotten yourselves killed, both of you,' he scolded, digging beeswax out of his ears with his little finger. 'Laid out like that old hound with busted eardrums.' He removed a long-bladed knife from his tunic and under his father's direction—'no, no, clean and quick . . . cut it, don't bruise it'—sliced the Mandrake into little rootlike portions, resinous rather than bloody, which he wrapped in strips of muslin and placed carefully in a sharkskin pouch.

'One less of the devils,' muttered the father, unbending himself to a rake instead of a sickle. 'Another week and it'd have climbed right out of the ground. Joined its folk in the warrens.'

'A Richard's ransom in aphro-aphro*disiacs!*' stuttered the son, completing the word with a flourish of triumph. The market for Mandrake roots was lucrative and inexhaustible: aging barons deserted by sexual powers; lovers whose love was unrequited. From Biblical times, the times of Jacob and Leah, the root had been recognized as the one infallible aphrodisiac. Yes, a Richard's ransom was hardly an overstatement. A man would pay gold and silver, land and livestock, to win his love or resurrect his lust.

When the woodsmen had finished their grisly dissection, the son smiled at the boys and offered them a fragment the size of a small pea. 'You fellows put this in a girl's gruel, and she'll climb all over you.'

'He doesn't need it,' said John, intercepting the gift. 'Girls climb over him as it is. Like ants on a crock of sugar!'

'But you need it, eh?' laughed the son, winking his single eye at John. One-eyed serfs were common in France and England, and most of them had lost their eyes to angry masters and not in fights. Perhaps the young woodsman had not been prompt to deliver firewood for the hearth in a great hall. 'Now you'll be the crock. But where's the sugar?'

'He'll have it,' said Stephen, noticing John's embarrassment. 'Sugar enough for a nest! Give him a year or two. He's only twelve.' Then he pointed to the carcass of the dog. 'Did you have to use a greyhound? Couldn't you have done it yourselves? After all, you have the wax in your ears.'

'Everyone knows a dog gives a sharper jerk. Gets the whole Mandrake at once. Like pulling a tooth, root and all. Besides, he was an old dog. Not many more years in his bones. We can buy a whole kennel with what we made from the root.'

When the men had departed, talking volubly about the sale of their treasure at the next fair, and how they would spend their money in secret and keep their lord from his customary third, the boys buried the dog.

'I wish they had put beeswax in his ears too,' said Stephen bitterly. 'And see where they whipped him to make him jump!'

'Beeswax doesn't help a dog,' said John. 'At least I read that in a bestiary. His ears are so keen that the shriek penetrates the wax and kills him anyway.'

'It's no wonder the Mandrakes eat us. The way we drag their babies from the ground and cut them up! If it weren't for my parents, I could pity the poor little brutes. Now, a lot of dirty old men will strut like coxcombs and chase after kitchen wenches.'

'I suppose,' said John, who had furtively buried the fragment of Mandrake with the dog, 'the question is, who started eating whom first.' Then he clutched Stephen's hand and said: 'I think I'm going to be sick.'

'No, you're not,' said Stephen, steadying John with his arm. 'We're going back to the tree and get some sleep.'

But Stephen was trembling too; John could feel the tremors in his arm. He's sad for the dog, he thought. I *won't* be sick. It would only make him sadder.

Ruth was waiting for them with a look which they could not read in the misted light of the stars.

'We're sorry we left you so long,' said Stephen, 'but the hunters had just killed a Mandrake, and. . . .'

'I don't want to hear about it.'

'Mandrakes can't climb trees, can they?' asked John. 'The parents might be about, you know.'

'Of course they can climb trees,' said Stephen, who was very knowledgeable about the woods and improvised what he did not know. 'They *are* trees, in a way. Roots at least.'

'Do you think they suspect we're up here? They can't see us, but can they sniff us out?'

'I wish you two would stop talking about Mandrakes,' snapped Ruth. 'You would think they surrounded us, when everyone knows the poor creatures are almost extinct.'

'Stephen's parents were killed by Mandrakes,' said John sharply. He would have liked to slap the girl. She had a genius for interruptions or improprieties. It was proper and generous for Stephen to express compassion for a Mandrake baby, but unforgivable for this ignorant girl to sympathize with the whole murderous race. Her ethereal origins now seemed about as likely to him as an angel dancing on the head of a pin, a possibility which, to John's secret amusement, his Abbot had often debated with utmost seriousness.

Ruth gave a cry. 'I didn't know.'

'How could you?' said Stephen. 'At least the ones who killed my parents fought like men. They didn't sneak up in the dark. They stormed out of the forest before dusk, waving their filthy arms and swinging clubs. We had a chance against them—except my mother, who was bringing us beer in the fields. We were haying at the time and we had our scythes for weapons. They only got one of us besides my parents, and we got four of them. It's the females who're really dangerous—the young ones who pass for human and come to live in the towns. The males can't do it; they're much too hairy right from the start, and—well, *you* know. Too well endowed. But the little girls look human, at least on the outside. Inside, it's a different matter—resin instead of blood; brown skeletons which're—what would you call them, John?'

'Fibrous.'

Ruth listened in silence and shrank herself into a little ball. Like a diadem spider, thought John, with brilliant gold patterns. Drawing in her legs and looking half her size.

'Tell her about them, John,' said Stephen, who was getting breathless from such a long speech. 'You know the whole story.' And then to Ruth: 'He knows everything. French, English, Latin. All our kings and queens from Arthur down to bad old King John.

Even those naughty pagan goddesses who went about naked and married their brothers.'

John was delighted to continue the history. He liked to deliver lectures, but nobody except Stephen ever listened to him.

'In the old days, before the Crusades,' said John, who warmed to his tale like a traveling story teller, 'in the old days the Mandrakes lived in the forest, and they were so dirty and hairy that you could never mistake them for human. They weren't particular about their diet. They liked any meat—animal or human—and they trapped hunters in nets and roasted them over hot coals and then strewed their bones on the ground as we do with drumsticks at Michaelmas.' Here, like a skilled jongleur, he paused and looked at Ruth to gauge the effect of his tale. The sight of her reassured him. If she pressed any harder against the edge of the nest, she would roll from the tree. 'But one day a little Mandrake girl wandered out of the forest, and a simple blacksmith took her for a lost human child, naked and dirty from the woods, and took her into his family. The child grew plump and beautiful, the man and his wife grew peaked, and everyone said how generous it was for a poor blacksmith to give his choicest food—and there wasn't much food that winter for anyone—to a foundling. But in the summer the girl was run down and killed by a wagon loaded with hay. The townspeople were all ready to garrot the driver—until they noticed that the girl's blood was a mixture of normal red fluid and thick, viscous resin.'

'What does "viscous" mean?' interrupted Stephen.

'Gluey. Like that stuff that comes out of a spider when she's spinning her web. Thus, it was learned that Mandrakes are vampires as well as cannibals, and that the more they feed on humans, the less resinous their blood becomes, until the resin is almost replaced, though their bones never do turn white. But they have to keep on feeding or else their blood will revert.

'Well, the Mandrakes heard about the girl—from a runaway thief, no doubt, before they ate him—and how she had "passed" until the accident. They decided to send some more of their girls into the villages, where life was easier than in the forest. Some of the Mandrakes slipped into houses at night and left their babies, well-scrubbed of course, in exchange for humans, which they carried off into the woods for you can imagine what foul purposes. The next morning the family would think that the fairies had brought them a changeling, and everyone knows that if you disown a fairy's child, you'll have bad luck for the rest of your life. It was a long time before the plan of the Mandrakes became generally known around the forest. Now, whenever a mother finds a strange baby in her crib, or a new child wanders into town, it's usually stuck with a knife. If resin flows out, the child is suffocated and burned. Still, an occasional Mandrake does manage to pass.

'You see, they aren't at all like the Crusaders in the last century who became vampires when they marched through Hungary—the Hungarian campfollowers, remember, gave them the sickness, and then the Crusaders brought it back to England. They had to break the skin to get at your blood, and they had a cadaverous look about them before they fed, and then they grew pink and bloated. It was no problem to recognize and burn them. But the Mandrake girls, by pressing their lips against your skin, can draw blood right through the pores, and the horrible thing is that they don't look like vampires and sometimes they don't even know what they are or how they were born from a seed in the ground. They feed in a kind of dream and forget everything the next morning.'

'I think it's monstrous,' said Ruth.

'They are, aren't they?' agreed John happily, satisfied that his story had been a success.

'Not *them*. I mean sticking babies with knives.'

'But how else can you tell them from roots? It's because a few people are sentimental like you that Mandrakes still manage to pass.'

'Frankly,' said Ruth, 'I don't think Mandrakes pass at all. I think they keep to themselves in the forest and eat venison and berries and *not* hunters. Now go to sleep. From what you've told me, it's a long way to London. We all need some rest.'

'Good night,' said Stephen.

'Sweet dreams,' said Ruth.

3

The next morning, the sun was a Saracen shield in the sky —Saladin's Shield, a Crusader would have said—and the forest twinkled with paths of sunlight and small white birds which spun in the air or perched on limbs and constantly flickered their tails. Ruth and Stephen stood in the crook of the tree and smiled down at John as he opened his eyes.

'We decided to let you sleep,' said Stephen. 'You grunted like a boar when I first shook you. So we followed a wagtail to find some breakfast.'

'And found you some wild strawberries,' said Ruth, her lips

becomingly red from the fruit. She gave him a deep, brimming
bowl. 'I wove it from sedges.' For one who professed an ignorance
of the forest, she possessed some remarkable skills.

Once on the ground, they finished their breakfast with three-
cornered, burry beechnuts, which required some skillful pounding
and deft fingers to extract the kernels; and Ruth, appropriating
Stephen's beer, took such a generous swallow that she drained the
flask.

'To wash down the beechnuts,' she explained.

'I don't know why the pigs like them so much,' said Stephen.
'They're not worth the trouble of shelling.'

'The pigs don't shell them,' reminded the practical John.

'Anyway,' continued Stephen, 'we hadn't much choice in this
part of the forest. We found a stream though.' Hoisting the pouch
which held their remnants of food and their few extra garments, he
said: 'Ruth, get your bundle and let's take a swim.'

'I hid it,' she reminded him, almost snappishly. 'There may be
thieves about. I'll get it after we swim.'

All that mystery about a crucifix, thought John. As if she
suspected Stephen and me of being brigands. And after she drank
our beer!

The stream idled instead of gushed, and pepperwort, shaped like
four-leafed clovers, grew in the quiet waters along the banks.
Stephen, who took a monthly bath in a tub with the stable hands
while the daughters of villeins doused him with water, hurried to
pull his tunic over his head. He was justly proud of his body and
had once remarked to John, 'The less I wear, the better I look. In a
gentleman's clothes like yours, I'd still be a yokel. But naked—!
Even gentlewomen seem to stare.'

But John was quick to restore the proprieties. In the presence of
Ruth, he had no intention of showing his thin, white body, or
allowing Stephen to show his radiant nakedness.

'You can swim first,' he said to her. 'Stephen and I will wait in
the woods.'

'No,' she laughed. 'You go first. Stephen is already down to his
breechclout, and *that* is about to fall. But I won't be far away.'

'You won't peep, will you?' John called after her, but Ruth,
striding into the forest as if she had a destination, did not answer
him.

The stream was chilly in spite of the Saracen sun. John huddled
among the pepperwort, the water as high as his knees, till Stephen
drenched him with a monumental splash, and then they frolicked

among the plants and into the current and scraped each other's
backs with sand scooped from the bottom and, as far as John was
concerned, Ruth and the road to London could wait till the Second
Coming!

When they climbed at last on the bank, they rolled in the grass to
dry their bodies. Stephen, an expert wrestler, surprised John with
what he called his amphisbaena grip; his arms snaked around
John's body like the ends of the two-headed serpent and flattened
him on the ground.

'I'm holding you for ransom,' he cried, perched on John's chest
like the seasprite Dylan astride a dolphin. 'Six flagons of beer with
roasted malt!'

'I promise—' John began, and freed himself with such a burst of
strength that Stephen sprawled in the grass beneath the lesser but
hardly less insistent weight of John. 'I promise you sixteen licks
with an abbot's rod!'

Stephen was not disgruntled. 'By Robin's bow,' he cried, 'you've
learned all my tricks!'

'I guess we had better dress,' said John, releasing his friend to
avoid another reversal. 'Ruth will want to swim too. I hope she
didn't peep,' he added, looking askance at some furiously agitated
ferns beyond the grassy bank. To his great relief, they disgorged a
white wagtail and not a girl. Still, something had frightened the
bird.

'What do you think she would see?' laughed Stephen.

'You,' said John, eyeing his friend with an admiration which was
more wistful than envious. Stephen was a boy with a man's body,
'roseate-brown from toe to crown,' to quote a popular song, and
comely enough to tempt an angel. When he shook his wet hair, a
great armful of daffodils seemed to bestrew his head. A marriage of
beauty and strength, thought John. For the hundredth time he
marveled that such a boy could have chosen him for a brother;
actually chosen, when they had no bond of blood, nor even of race.
He peered down at himself and wished for his clothes. At the castle
he never bathed in the tub with his father's friends: only with
Stephen, sometimes, in the stream of the old millwheel, or alone in
the heath from his own little bucket (even in the castle, he had no
private room, but slept with the rancid sons of his father's knights).

But Stephen said: 'You know, John, you're not so skinny now.
You've started to fill out. The bones are there. The strength too, as
you just proved. All you need is a little more meat. You'll be a man
before you know it.'

'Next year?' asked John, though such a prospect seemed as far from his grasp as a fiery-plummaged phoenix. 'You were a man at thirteen.'

'Eleven. But I'm different. I'm a villein. We grow fast. With you, I'd say two or possibly three more years. Then we can wench together for sure.'

'Who would want me when she could have you?'

Stephen led him to the bank of the stream. 'Look,' he said, and pointed to their reflections in a space of clear water between the pepperworts: the bright and the dark, side by side; the two faces of the moon. 'I have muscles, yes. But you have brains. They show in your face.'

'I don't like my face. I won't even look in those glass mirrors they bring back from the Holy Land. I always look startled.'

'Not as much as you did. Why, just since we left the castle, I've seen a change. Yesterday, when you faced down the Knight Templar, I was ready to wet my breechclout! But you never batted an eye. And you looked so *wise*. One day you'll have my muscles, but you can bet a brace of pheasants I'll never have your brains. Come on now, let's give Ruth a chance.'

At Stephen's insistence—and he had to insist vigorously—they bundled their tunics and wore only their breechclouts, the shapeless strips of cloth which every man, whether priest, baron, or peasant, twisted around his loins. Now they would look like field hands stripped for a hot day's work, and John's fine tunic would not arouse suspicion or tempt thieves.

'But my shoulders,' John began, 'they're so white.'

'They'll brown in the sun on the way to London,' he said, and then: 'RUTH, you can take your swim!'

He had to repeat her name before she answered in a thin, distant voice: 'Yes, Stephen?'

'You can swim now. You'll have the stream to yourself.' To John he smiled, 'She took you seriously about not peeping. But you know, John, *we* didn't promise.'

'You'd spy on an angel?'

Stephen slapped his back. 'Now who's calling her an angel? No, I wouldn't spy. I'd just *think* about it. I've always wondered if angels are built like girls. Let's do a bit of exploring while she bathes. I could eat another breakfast after that swim. But we mustn't stray too far from the stream.'

Beyond a coppice of young beeches, Stephen discovered a cluster of slender stalks with fragrant, wispy leaves. 'Fennels. Good for the fever you catch in London. We might pick a few, roots and all.'

But John, thinking of Mandrakes, had no use for roots and followed his nose to a bed of mint. 'This is what your mother used to sweeten her gowns, isn't it?'

'Yes, and it's also good to eat.' They knelt in the moist soil to pluck and chew the leaves, whose sweetly burning juices left them hoarse and breathless, as if they had gulped a heady muscatel.

But where was the stream, the road, the oak in which they had slept?

'The trees all look the same,' said Stephen, 'but there, that old beech. Haven't we seen it before? And there, the torn ground—'

They had wandered, it seemed, to the place of the Mandrake hunt. The hole remained in the earth, disturbingly human-shaped, with branching clefts from which the limbs had been wrenched by the hapless dog.

'Let's get away from here,' said John, as nausea slapped him like the foul air of a *garderobe*.

'Wait,' said Stephen. 'There's a second hole. It's—it's where we buried the dog. *God's bowels!*' It was his crudest oath. 'The dirty Infidels have dug him up and—'

Around the hole they saw a litter of bones . . . skull . . . femur . . . pelvis . . . stripped of their meat and scattered carelessly through the grass.

'Stephen,' said John, seizing his friend's hand. 'I know how you feel. It was cruel of them to eat the dog. But we've got to get away from here. They'll take us for the hunters!'

Something had waited for them.

At first it looked like a tree. No, a corpse exhumed from a grave with roots entwining its limbs. It wheezed; lurched; moved, swaying, toward them. It was bleached to the color of a beechnut trunk—at least, those parts of the skin (or was it bark?) which showed through the greenish forest of hair (or rootlets?). Red eyes burned in black hollows (tiny fire-dragons peering from caves, thought John). The mouth seemed a single hairlip until it split into a grin which revealed triangular teeth like those of a shark: to crush, tear, shred.

'Run!' screamed John, tugging at his friend, but proud Stephen had chosen to fight.

'Dog-eater!' He charged the Mandrake and used his head for a ram.

The creature buckled like a rotten door but flung out its limbs and enveloped Stephen into its fall; fallen, it seemed a vegetable octopus, lashing viny tentacles around its prey.

Unlike Stephen, John grew cold with anger instead of hot; blue instead of flushed; as if he had plunged in a river through broken ice. First he was stunned. Then the frost-caves of his brain functioned with crystalline clarity. He knew that he was young and relatively weak; against that bark-tough skin, his naked fists would beat in vain. A blind, weaponless charge would not avail his friend. He fell to his knees and mole-like clawed the ground. Pebbles. Pine cones. Beechnuts. Pretty, petty, useless. Then, a stone, large and jagged. With raw, bleeding hands, he wrestled the earth for his desperately needed weapon and, without regaining his feet, lunged at the fallen Mandrake. The fibrous skull cracked and splintered sickeningly beneath the stone and spewed him with resin and green vegetable matter like a cabbage crushed by a millstone.

'Stephen!' he cried, but the answer hissed above him, shrill with loathing:

'Human!'

Multitudinous fingers caught and bound him with coils of wild grapevine and dragged him, together with Stephen, over the bruising earth.

The Mandrake warrens were not so much habitations as lightless catacombs for avoiding men and animals. No one knew if the creatures had built them or found, enlarged, and connected natural caves and covered the floors with straw. John was painfully conscious as his thin body, little protected by the shreds of his breechclout, lurched and scraped down a tortuous passage like the throat of a dragon. His captors, he guessed, could see in the dark, but only the scraping of Stephen's body told him that he had not been separated from his friend.

'Mother of God,' he breathed, 'let him stay unconscious!'

For a long time he had to judge their passage from room to room by the sudden absence of straw which marked a doorway. Finally, a dim, capricious light announced their approach to a fire; a council chamber perhaps; the end of the brutal journey.

The room of the fire was a round, spacious chamber where Mandrake females were silently engaged in piling chunks of peat on a bed of coals. Neither roots nor branches were used as fuel, John saw, since that which began as a root did not use wood for any purpose. Wryly he wondered how the Mandrakes would feel if they knew that the fuel they burned had once been vegetation.

Their captors dumped them as men might deposit logs beside a hearth, and joined the women in feeding the fire. John was tightly trussed, his feet crossed, his hands behind his back, but he rolled his body to lie on his side and look at Stephen's face. His friend's cheeks were scratched; his forehead was blue with a large bruise; and the daffodils of his hair were wilted with blood and cobwebs.

'Stephen, Stephen, what have they done to you?' he whispered, biting his lip to stifle the threat of tears. His hero, fallen, moved him to tenderness transcending worship. For once he had to be strong for Stephen. He had to think of escape.

He examined the room. There were neither beds nor pallets. Apparently the Mandrakes slept in the smaller rooms and used their council chamber as a baron used his hall. It was here that they met to talk and feast. The earthen walls were blackened from many fires. Bones littered the straw, together with teeth, fur, and hair; inedible items. The stench of the refuse was overpowering and, coupled with that of excrement and urine, almost turned John's stomach. He fought nausea by wondering how his fastidious Abbot would have faced the situation: identified himself, no doubt, with Hercules in the Augean stables or Christ amid the corruptions of the Temple.

Then, across the room, he saw the crucifix. Yes, it was unmistakable, a huge stone cross. Latin, with arms of unequal length, and set in an alcove shaped like an apse. Turtle-backed stones served as seats. Between the seats the ground had been packed and brushed by the knees of suppliants. The place was clearly a chapel, and John remembered the tale—a myth, he had always supposed—that after the Christians had come to England with Augustine, a priest had visited the Mandrakes in their warrens. Once they had eaten him, they had reconsidered his words and adopted Christianity.

'Bantling-killer!'

A Mandrake slouched above him, exuding a smell of tarns stagnant with scum. His voice was gutteral and at first unintelligible. Bantling-killer. Of course. *Baby*-killer. The creature was speaking an early form of English. He went on to curse all athelings in their byrnies—knights in their mail—and to wish that the whale-road would swallow the last of them as they sailed to their wars in ring-prowed ships of wood. Then, having blasted John's people, he became specific and accused John and Stephen of having killed the bantling with their dog. *His* bantling, he growled, grown from his own seed. Though the Mandrakes copulated like men and animals, John gathered that their females gave birth to objects resembling acorns which they planted in the ground and nurtured into roots. If allowed by hunters to reach maturity, the roots burst from the ground like a turtle out of an egg, and their mothers bundled them into the warrens to join the tribe—hence, the word 'bantling' from 'bantle' or 'bundle.'

'No,' John shook his head. 'No. We did not kill your baby. Your bantling. It was hunters who killed him!'

The creature grinned. A grin, it seemed, was a Mandrake's one expression; anger or pleasure provoked the same bared teeth. Otherwise, he looked as vacant as a cabbage.

'Hunters,' he said. 'You.'

The crowded room had grown as hot as the kitchen before a feast in a castle, but the figures tending the fire, hunched as if with the weight of dirt, toil, and time, seemed impervious to the heat. They had obviously built the fire to cook their dinner, and now they began to sharpen stakes on weathered stones. Even the stakes were tin instead of wood.

The whir of the flames must have alerted the young Mandrakes in the adjacent chambers. They trooped into the room and gathered, gesticulating, around the two captives. They had not yet lapsed into the tired shuffle of their elders; they looked both energetic and intelligent. Life in the forest, it seemed, slowly stultified quick minds and supple bodies. It was not surprising that the weary elders, however they hated men, should try to pass their daughters into the villages.

The girls John saw, except for one, appeared to be adolescents, but hair had already forested their arms and thickened their lips. The one exception, a child of perhaps four, twinkled a wistful prettiness through her grime. Her eyes had not yet reddened and sunken into their sockets; her mouth was the color of wild raspberries. She could still have passed.

The children seemed to have come from the midst of a game. Dice, it appeared, from the small white objects they rattled, a little like the whale-bone cubes which delighted the knights in John's castle. But the dice of the Mandrake children were not so much cubes as irregular, bony lumps scratched with figures. The Greeks, John recalled from the Abbot's lectures, had used the knucklebones of sheep and other animals in place of cubes.

But the Mandrake children had found a livelier game. They stripped John and Stephen of their breechclouts and began to prod their flesh with fingers like sharp carrots and taunt them for the inadequacy of human loins. The Mandrake boys, naked like their parents, possessed enormous genitals; hence, the potency of the murdered, fragmented roots as aphrodisiacs. Stephen stirred fitfully but to John's relief did not awake to find himself the object of ridicule. With excellent reason, he had always taken pride in the badge of his manhood, and to find himself surpassed and taunted by boys of eight and nine would have hurt him more than blows.

Only the girl of four, staring reproachfully at her friends, took no part in the game.

A church bell chimed, eerily, impossibly it seemed to John in such a place, and a hush enthralled the room. An aged Mandrake, rather like a tree smothered by moss, hobbled among the silenced children and paused between John and Stephen. Examining. Deliberating. Choosing. He chose Stephen. When he tried to stoop, however, his back creaked like a rusty drawbridge. He will break, thought John. He will never reach the ground. But he reached the ground and gathered Stephen in his mossy arms.

'Bloody Saracen!' shouted John. 'Take your hands off my friend!' Stretching prodigiously, he managed to burst the bonds which held his ankles and drive his knee into the Mandrake's groin. The creature gave such a yelp that red-hot pokers seemed to have gouged John's ears. He writhed on the ground and raised his hands to shut out the shriek and the pain. Shadows cobwebbed his brain. When he struggled back to clarity, Stephen lay in the chapel before the crucifix. Looming above him, the aged Mandrake stood like Abraham above Isaac. The other adults, perhaps twenty of them, sat on the turtle-shaped stones, while the children sat near the fire to watch the proceedings from which their elders had barred them. The impression John caught of their faces—brief, fleeting, hazy with smoke and the dim light of the room—was not one of malice or even curiosity, but respect and fear, and the pretty child had turned her back and buried her face in the arms of an older girl.

The officiating Mandrake intoned what seemed to be a prayer and a dedication. John caught words resembling 'Father' and 'Son' and realized with horror if not surprise that just as the Christian humans burned a Yule log and decked their castles with hawthorn, holly, and mistletoe in honor of Christ, so the Christian Mandrakes were dedicating Stephen to a different conception of the same Christ. First, the offering, then the feast. The same victim would serve both purposes.

He had already burst the grapevines which held his ankles. In spite of his bound hands, he struggled to his feet and reeled toward the chapel. Once, he had killed a Mandrake with cold implacabili-ty. Now he had turned to fire: the Greek fire of the East, hurled at ships and flung from walls; asphalt and crude petroleum, sulphur and lime, leaping and licking to the incandescence of Hell. He felt as if stones and Mandrakes must yield before his advance; as if Mary, the Mother of Christ, must descend from the castles of heaven or climb from the sanctuary of his heart and help him deliver his friend.

But the Mandrakes rose in a solid palisade; and, shrunk to a boy of twelve, he hammered his impotent fists against their wood.

'No,' he sobbed, falling to his knees. 'Me. Not Stephen.'

'JOHN.'

His name tolled through the room like the clash of a mace against an iron helmet. 'John, he will be all right.' Her flaxen hair, coarsened with dirt and leaves, rioted over her shoulders like tarnished gold coins. She wore her linen robe, but the white cloth had lost its purity to stains and tears. She might have been a fallen angel, and her eyes seemed to smoulder with memories of heaven or visions of Hell.

She had entered the room accompanied, not compelled. She was not their captive. She has gained their favor, he thought, by yielding to their lust. But God will forgive her if she saves my friend, and I, John, will serve her until I die. If she saves my friend—

He saw that she held her crucifix; gripped it as if you would have to sever the hand before you could pry her fingers from its gold arms.

One of her companions called to the priest, who stood impassively between his cross of stone and his congregation, and above Stephen. He neither spoke nor gestured, but disapproval boomed in his silence.

Ruth advanced to the fire and held her crucifix in the glow of the flames, which ignited the golden arms to a sun-washed sea, milkily glinting with pearls like Saracen ships, and the Mandrakes gazed on such a rarity as they had never seen with their poor sunken eyes or fancied in their dim vegetable brains. In some pathetic, childlike way, they must have resembled the men of the First Crusade who took Jerusalem from the Seljuk Turks and gazed, for the first time, at the Holy Sepulchre; whatever ignoble motives had led them to Outre-Mer, they were purged for that one transcendent moment of pride and avarice and poised between reverence and exaltation. It was the same with the Mandrakes.

The priest nodded in grudging acquiescence. Ruth approached him through the ranks of the Mandrakes, which parted murmurously like rushes before the advancing slippers of the wind, and placed the crucifix in his hands. His fingers stroked the gold with slow, loving caresses and paused delicately on the little mounds of the pearls. She did not wait to receive his dismissal. Without hesitation and without visible fear, she walked to John and unbound his hands.

'Help me with Stephen,' she said. 'I have traded the cross for your lives.'

Once they had stooped from the shadows of the last cave and risen to face the late morning sun, the Mandrake left them without a look or a gesture, avid, it seemed, to return to the council chamber and the bartered crucifix. In the dark corridors, Stephen had regained consciousness but leaned on Ruth and John and allowed them to guide his steps, their own steps guided by the slow, creaking shuffle of the Mandrake.

'Stephen, are you all right?' John asked.

'Tired,' he gasped, stretching his battered limbs in the grass and closing his eyes.

'And you, Ruth?' John looked at her with awe and wonderment and not a little fear. He had witnessed a miracle.

She did not look miraculous as she lay beside Stephen. Once she had seemed to shrink into a spider; now she reminded him of a wet linen tunic, flung to the ground, torn, trampled, forsaken.

'What happened, Ruth?'

'They found me by the bank after my swim. I reached for a stocking and looked up to see—them.'

'And—?'

'They laid hands on me. Dragged me toward their warrens. I fought them, but the one who held me was very strong.'

'And you thought of the crucifix? How they were Christians and might value it?'

'Yes. You remember, I had hidden it in our tree. I tried to make them understand that I would give them a treasure if they let me go. You know how they talk. Like little children just learning to speak. Words and phrases all run together. But strange, old-fashioned words. I kept shouting, 'Treasure, treasure!' but they didn't understand. Finally, I remembered an old word used by our ancestors. 'Folk-hoarding,' I cried, and 'Crucifix!' and they understood. They're very devout in their way. They grinned, argued, waved their snaky arms. Then they let me go. I led them to the tree. We passed the place where you and Stephen had fought. I saw bits of your breechclouts and knew their friends had captured you. I stopped in my tracks and said I wanted your freedom as well as mine. Otherwise, no exchange. One of them said, 'If crucifix ring-bright. If time—'

'They climbed right after me up the trunk of the tree. The sight of the crucifix as I unwrapped it made them hold their breath. I held it out to them, but they shook their heads. No, they wouldn't touch it. It was for their priest. They seemed to feel their own filth and ugliness might tarnish the gold or lessen the magic. They didn't grin or look vacant anymore. They looked as if they wanted to cry. They turned their backs and let me dress in the robe—and brought me here.'

'And they kept their promise.'

'Of course. They're Christians, aren't they?'

Her story troubled him. He had heard of many Christians who failed to keep promises; Crusaders, for example, with Greeks or Saracens. 'But why—' he began, meaning to ask why the Mandrakes would feel bound by a promise to a hated human girl.

'We can't sit here all day,' she interrupted. 'They might change their minds, Christian or not. Where is the road?'

Shakily they climbed to their feet, Stephen without help at his own request ('I must get my balance back.'), and saw the trees which encircled and encaged them, great sycamores and greater oaks, looking as if they were sentient old kings in an old country, Celt, Roman, and Saxon, watchfully standing guard until the usurping Normans had felt the slow fingers of the land shape them to the lineaments of Britannia, Britain, England, as the paws and tongue of a bear sculpture her cub into her own small likeness.

'I think,' said Stephen, 'that the road lies *that* way.'

But Stephen was still befuddled by the blows to his head. They walked for a long time and did not come to the road . . . but came to the Manor of Roses.

4

I watched them as they struggled out of the forest, the stalwart boy supported by his friends, the slighter, dark-haired boy and the girl with angel hair. On a sunny morning, you see, I leave the Manor with the first twittering of sparrows and gather the white roses from the hedge which surrounds my estate, or visit the windmill, the first, I believe, in southern England, and watch the millstones, powered no longer by water, grinding grain for the bread of my kitchen. Now, it was afternoon. I had lunched in the shade of a mulberry tree (apricots, bread, and mead), returned to the hedge of roses, and seen the children. I must have gasped at the sight. They stopped and stared at me over the hedge. The girl stiffened and whispered to the boys. It was not a time when children called at strange manor houses. Startled sparrows, they seemed. Not in littleness or frailty, you understand. The girl and the older boy were more than children. It was rather their vulnerability. Something had almost broken them, and they did not know if I were hunter or friend. I had to prove my friendliness as if I were coaxing sparrows to eat from my hand.

'Follow the hedge to the right,' I smiled. 'You will see the gate. If you've come from the forest, you must be tired and hungry. I can give you food and a place to sleep.' I had made a basket of roses out of my arms. I had no fear of thorns, with my gloves of antelope leather; my long, tight sleeves buttoned at the wrist; my wimple and cap; and my blue, ankle-length skirt, brocaded with star-colored fleurs-de-lis and hanging in folds from my low-belted waist. I watched the boys, clad in breechclouts clumsily fashioned from leaves, and envied them a man's freedom to dress and ride where he will (unless he dresses in armor and rides to war).

The youngest, the dark-haired boy, still supporting his friend, addressed me with the courteous French of a gentleman:

'We are not attired for the company of a lady. You see, we have come from the forest.' His face confirmed the impression of his speech. It is said that Saladin, England's noblest enemy, had such a face as a boy: ascetic, scholar, poet. But first and last, I saw his need and that of his friend, the Saxon lad with the build of wandering Aengus, the Great Youth, whose kisses were called his birds. Even the breechclout seemed an affront to his body. Still, he needed me. His mouth, though forced to a smile, was tight with fatigue and hunger, and a wound had raked his forehead. Both were spider-webbed with scratches.

The girl, though her white gown was stained and torn, resembled an angel sculptured from ivory and set in the tympanum of a London cathedral: beautiful, aloof, expressionless. She is tired, I thought. Weariness has drained her face. Later I will read her heart.

I met them at the wicket in the hedge, a gate so small and low that my son had jumped it in a single bound when he rode for the Stane and London.

I held out my arms to greet them; my armful of roses.

They kept their ground, the dark boy straining toward me, the girl away from me, the Saxon drawn between them.

'I can offer you more than flowers,' I said, spilling the roses.

The Norman said, 'My Lady, whom have we the honor of addressing?'

'I am called the Lady Mary. You have come to the Manor of Roses.'

'I thought,' he said, 'you might be another Mary. Will you help my friend? He has suffered a blow to his head.' But it was the Norman and not his friend I helped. He swayed on his feet, leaned to my strength, and caught my outstretched hand.

'I will soil your gown.'

'With the good brown earth? It is the purest of all substances. The mother of roses.'

'But you scattered your flowers on the ground.'

'I have others.' Supporting him with my arm and followed by his friends, I drew him toward the house.

Once, a moat had surrounded the Manor, but after my husband's death I had filled the water with earth and planted mulberry trees, aflutter now with linnets and silvery filamented with the webs of silkworms; the trees formed a smaller ring within the ring of the rose hedge to island but not to isolate my house, which was built of bricks instead of the cold grey stones preferred by the neighboring barons. My husband had offered to build me a manor for my wedding gift.

'Build it of bricks,' I had said. 'The color of your hair.'

'And stoutly,' he said. But the high curtain wall with its oaken door, its rows of weathered bricks from a ruined Roman villa, and its narrow embrasures for bowmen to fire their arrows, had somehow a look of having lost its threat, like armor hung on the wall. Gabriel knows, I could not stand a siege with my poor, bedraggled retainers: gardeners, gatemen, cooks, seneschal, stable-boy—thirty in all, without a knight among them. The wasting fever had not been kind to the Manor of Roses.

The gatekeeper moved to help me with the boy. 'He will tire you, my Lady.'

I shook my head. No burden can equal the ache of emptiness.

Once we had entered the bailey, Sarah the cook, who had slipped out of the kitchen and thrown back her hood to catch some sun, tossed up her ponderous hands—I suspect it required some effort—and squealed, 'My Lady, what have you found?'

'Children, what else? Sarah, hurry to the kitchen and prepare a meal such as young boys—young men—like. Pheasant and—'

'I know, I know,' she said. 'You forget I've sons of my own, who serve you every night!' Sarah, her three sons and her two daughters, were new to the Manor, but she acted as if she had been my nurse since childhood. 'I know what young boys like. The beast of the chase and the fowl of the warren. All that flies and all that goes on hooves, and two of everything unless it's as big as a boar!' She waddled ahead of us up the stairs to the door and, laboriously genuflecting, vanished under the lintel with its wooden Madonna cradling the Holy Infant.

'It's a lovely house,' said the Saxon boy in English. 'It looks like an abbot's grange.'

'A very rich abbot,' explained the Norman, fearful no doubt that I had misunderstood his friend's compliment, since poor abbots lived in squalid cottages.

'I meant,' stammered the Saxon, 'it looks so bright and peaceful, with its Mother and Child, and its—' He waited for his friend to complete his sentence.

'Its two pointed roofs instead of battlements, and real windows instead of slits for archers, with *glass* in the windows! And Stephen, see the herb garden. Parsley, thyme, bay leaf, marjoram, mace, tarragon—'

'You know a lot about herbs,' I said.

'I've read an herbal.'

Once in the Manor, I took them to the bath. In all the Weald, I think, in all of England, no other house can claim a fountain for bathing enclosed under the roof. The mouth of a dolphin, hammered from bronze by the artisans of Constantinople, spewed a vigorous streamlet into a basin where Tritons gamboled on vari-colored tiles. For baths in the cold of winter, I stuffed the dolphin's mouth and filled the basin with kettles hot from the kitchen.

'Your friend shall bathe first,' I said to the boys. All of us now were speaking English. And to her: 'Your name is—?'

When the girl was slow to answer, the Saxon said: 'Ruth. She is our guardian angel. She rescued us.'

'From wild beasts?'

'From Mandrakes.'

I shuddered. 'They are much in the woods, poor misshapen brutes. They have never harmed me, though. You must tell me later about your escape. Now then, Ruth. You shall have the bath to yourself. After you have bathed, I shall send you clothes, and a perfume made from musk, and . . .'

She looked at me with cool, veiled eyes. 'You are very kind.' I wanted to say to her: I am more than twice your age, and far less beautiful. Trust me, my dear. Trust me!

I turned to the boys. The Norman, I learned, was John; the Saxon, Stephen. 'When Ruth has finished, it will be your turn.'

'Thank you, my lady,' said John. 'We would like to bathe with a dolphin. But—'

'You would rather eat! What about bread and cheese and pennyroyal tea to hold you till time for supper? Or,' I added quickly, 'beer instead of tea.' Pennyroyal! I had been too much with women.

'Beer,' they said in one breath. 'But,' said John, 'my brother has a wound.'

'Brother?' I asked, surprised. A Norman gentleman and a Saxon peasant!

'We adopted each other. Have you something for his head?'

'For my stomach,' grinned Stephen. 'That's where I hurt the most.'

'For both,' I said.

The hall of my manor house is hot and damp in the summer, and cold in the winter even with pine logs, as big around as a keg of beer, crackling on the hearth. It has always been a room for men; shouting, roistering, warming themselves with mead. For myself, I prefer the solar, the room of many purposes in which I sleep and dine and weave, and entertain the friends who come infrequently now to visit me. I left the boys in the solar with three loaves of bread, two enormous cheeses, and a flagon of beer, and told them to eat and afterwards to bathe themselves with cloths dipped in camphor and wrap fresh linen around their waists.

'Call me after you've finished.'

I had scarcely had time to find a gown for Ruth when I heard John's voice: 'Lady Mary, we've finished.'

I found them so fragrant with camphor that I overlooked the patches of dirt they had left on their knees and elbows. The bread, cheese, and wine had vanished as if there had been a raid by kitchen elves, denied their nightly tribute of crumbs. I tended the boys' wounds with a paste of fennel and dittany and they yielded themselves to my fingers without embarrassment, sons to a mother, and made me feel as if my hands had rediscovered their purpose.

'It doesn't burn at all,' said Stephen. 'My father used a poultice of adder's flesh pounded with wood-lice and spiders. But it burned like the devil, and stank.'

'Lady Mary's hands are like silk,' said John. 'That's why it doesn't burn.'

The boys began to dress in tunics which had belonged to my son: John in green, with a fawn-colored cape drawn through a ring-brooch and knotted at his shoulder, and *chausses* or stockings to match the cape, and black leather shoes with straps; Stephen in blue, with a pale rose cape and silver *chausses*, but looking with each additional garment as if another chain had shackled him to the wall.

'I wouldn't show myself in the forest like this,' he muttered. 'I'd be taken for a pheasant and shot on sight.'

'It's only for tonight,' I said. 'Don't you want to look the gallant for Ruth?'

'She's used to me naked. She'll take me for a jester.'

'My lady.'

Ruth had entered the room. She was dressed in a crimson gown or *cotte*, caught at the waist by a belt of gilded doeskin but falling around her feet in billows through which the toes of her slippers peeped like small green lizards. She had bound her hair in a moss-green net, and her yellow tresses twinkled like caged fireflies. (Strange, I always thought of her in terms of forest creatures: wild; unknowable; untamable.)

'My lady, the boys may have their bath. I thank you for sending me so lovely a gown.'

'We've had our bath,' said Stephen with indignation. 'Can't you see we're dressed as gallants?'

'Lady Mary put fennel and dittany on our wounds,' said John, 'and now they don't hurt any more.'

'And we're going to eat,' said Stephen.

'Again,' said John.

Ruth examined the solar and almost relaxed from her self-containment. 'Why, it's lovely,' she said, extending her arm to include the whole of the room. 'It's all made of sunlight.'

'Not entirely,' I smiled, pointing to the high, raftered ceiling with its tie-beam and king-post. 'Cobwebs collect unless I keep after Sarah's sons. They have to bring a ladder, you see, and they don't like dusting among the dark crevices. They're afraid of elves.'

'But the rest,' Ruth said. 'There's no darkness anywhere.'

The room was kindled with afternoon light from the windows: the fireplace, heaped with logs; a tall-backed chair with square sides and embroidered cushions or bankers; a huge recessed window shaped like an arch and filled with roseate panes of glass from Constantinople; and, hiding the wooden timbers of the floor, a Saracen carpet of polygons, red, yellow, and white, with a border of stylized Persian letters. My wainscotted walls, however, were purely English, their oaken panels painted the green of leaves and bordered with roses to match the carpet.

Ruth explored the room with the air of a girl familiar with

beauty, is shapes and its colors, but not without wonder. She touched my loom with loving recognition and paused at my canopied bed to exclaim: 'It's like a silken tent!'

'But the linnets,' she said, pointing to the wicker cage which hung beside the bed. 'Don't they miss the forest?'

'They are quite content. I feed them sunflower seeds and protect them from stoats and weasels. In return, they sing for me.'

'Is it true that a caged linnet changes his song?'

'Yes. His voice softens.'

'That's what I mean. The wildness goes.'

'Shouldn't it, my dear?'

'I don't know, Lady Mary.'

We sat on benches drawn to a wooden table with trestles, John and I across from Ruth and Stephen. My husband and I had been served in the great hall by nimble, soft-toed squires who received the dishes from kitchen menials. After his death, however, I began to dine in the solar instead of the hall. For the last year I had been served by Shadrach, Meshach, and Abednego, the three illegitimate sons of my cook, Sarah. As a rule, I liked to dine without ceremony, chatting with the sons—identical triplets with fiery red hair on their heads and arms, and thus their name: they seemed to have stepped out of a furnace. But tonight, for the sake of my guests, I had ordered Sarah and her two illegitimate daughters, Rahab and Magdalena, to prepare, and her sons to serve, a banquet instead of a supper. The daughters had laid the table with a rich brocade of Saracen knights astride their swift little ponies, and they had placed among the knights, as if it were under seige, a molded castle of sugar, rice-flour, and almond-paste.

After I had said the grace, the sons appeared with lavers, ewers, and napkins and passed them among my guests. Stephen lifted a laver to his mouth and started to drink, but John whispered frantically:

'It isn't soup, it's to wash your hands.'

'There'll be other things to drink,' I promised.

'I haven't felt this clean since I was baptized!' Stephen laughed, splattering the table with water from his laver.

Both Ruth and John, though neither had eaten from dishes of beaten silver, were fully at ease with knives and spoons; they cut the pheasant and duck before they used their fingers and scooped the fish-and-crab-apple pie with the spoons. But Stephen watched his friends with wry perplexity.

'I never used a knife except to hunt or fish,' he sighed. 'I'll probably cut off a finger. Then you can see if I'm a Mandrake!'

'We'd know that already,' said John. 'You'd look like a hedgehog and somebody would have chopped you up a long time ago for aphrodisiacs. You'd have brought a fortune.' His gruesome remarks, I gathered, were meant to divert me from the fact that he had furtively dropped his knife, seized a pheasant, and wrestled off a wing. His motive was as obvious as it was generous. He did not wish to shame his friend by his own polished manners.

I laughed heartily for the first time since the death of my son. 'Knives were always a nuisance. Spoons too. What are fingers for if not to eat with? So long as you don't bite yourself!' I wrenched a drumstick and thigh from the parent bird and felt the grease, warm and mouthwatering, ooze between my fingers. 'Here,' I said to Stephen. 'Take hold of the thigh and we'll divide the piece.' The bone parted, the meat split into decidedly unequal portions. Half of my drumstick accompanied John's thigh.

'It means you're destined for love,' I said.

'He's already had it,' said John. 'Hay-lofts full of it.'

'She doesn't mean that kind,' said Stephen, suddenly serious. She means caring—taking care of—don't you, Lady Mary? I've had that too, of course.' He looked at John.

'Then it means you'll always have it.'

'I know,' he said.

John smiled at Stephen and then at me, happy because the three of us were friends, but silent Ruth continued to cut her meat into snail-sized portions and lift them to her mouth with the fastidiousness of a nun (her fingers, however, made frequent trips).

Shadrach, Meshach, and Abednego scurried between the solar and the kitchen, removing and replenishing, but it looked as if John and Stephen would never satisfy their hunger. With discrete if considerable assistance from Ruth, they downed three pheasants, two ducks, two fish-and-crabapple pies, and four tumblers of mead.

'Leave some for us,' hissed Shadrach in Stephen's ear. 'This is the *last* bird.' Stephen looked surprised, then penitent, and announced himself as full as a tick on the ear of a hound. Shadrach hurried the last bird back to the kitchen.

After the feast the boys told me about their adventures, encouraging rather than interrupting each other with such comments as, 'You tell her about the stream with the pepperwort, John,' or 'Stephen, you're better about the fighting.' John talked more because he was more at ease with words; Stephen gestured as much as he talked and sometimes asked John to finish a sentence for him; and Ruth said nothing until the end of the story, when she recounted, quietly, without once meeting my gaze, the episode of her capture and bargain with the Mandrakes. I studied her while she spoke. Shy? Aloof, I would say. Mistrustful. Of me, at least. Simple jealousy was not the explanation. I was hardly a rival for the kind of love she seemed to want from Stephen. No, it was not my beauty which troubled her, but the wisdom which youth supposes to come with age; in a word, my mature perceptions. There was something about her which she did not wish perceived.

'And now for the gifts,' I said.

'Gifts?' cried John.

'Yes. The dessert of a feast is the gifts and not the pies.'

'But we have nothing to give you.'

'You have told me a wondrous and frightening story. No jongleur could have kept me more enthralled. And for you, I have—' I clapped my hands and Shadrach, Meshach, and Abednego appeared with my gifts, some musical instruments which had once belonged to my son. For Ruth, a rebec, a pear-shaped instrument from the East, three-stringed and played with a bow; for the boys, twin nakers or kettledrums which Stephen strapped to his back and John began to pound with soft-headed wooden drumsticks.

Ruth hesitated with her rebec till Stephen turned and said, 'Play for us, Ruth! What are you waiting for, a harp?'

Then Ruth joined them, the boys marching round and round the solar, Stephen first, John behind him pounding on the drums and thumping the carpet with his feet, and finally Ruth, playing with evident skill and forgetting to look remote and enigmatic. Shadrach, Meshach, and Abednego had lingered in the doorway, and behind them Sarah appeared with her plump, swarthy daughters. I was not surprised when they started to sing; I was only surprised to find myself joining them in the latest popular song:

> Summer is a-comin' in,
> Loud sing cuckoo.
> Groweth seed and bloweth mead,
> And springs the wood anew.
> Sing, cuckoo!

In an hour the three musicians, their audience departed to the kitchen, had exhausted the energies which the meal had revived. Ruth sank in the chair beside the hearth. The boys, thanking me profusely for their gifts, climbed into the window seats. Stephen yawned and began to nod his head. John, in the opposite seat, gave him a warning kick.

'Come,' I said to them. 'There's a little room over the kitchen which used to belong to my son. The hall was too big, the solar too warm, he felt. I'll show you his room while Ruth prepares for bed. Ruth, we'll fix you a place in the window. You see how the boys are sitting opposite each other. I've only to join the seats with a wooden stool and add a few cushions to make a couch. Or' —and I made the offer, I fear, with visible reluctance— 'you may share my own bed under the canopy.'

'The window seats will be fine.'

I pointed to the Aumbry, a wooden cupboard aswirl with wrought-iron scroll work, almost like the illuminated page of a psalter. 'There's no lock. Open the doors and find yourself a nightdress while I show the boys their room.'

My son's room was as small as a chapel in a keep, with one little square of a window, but the bed was wide as well as canopied, and irresistible to the tired boys.

'It's just like yours!' John cried.

'Smaller. But just as soft.'

'At home I slept on a bench against the wall, in a room with eight other boys—sons of my father's knights. I got the wall bench because my father owned the castle.'

'I slept on straw,' said Stephen, touching the mattress, sitting, stretching himself at length, and uttering a huge, grateful sigh. 'It's like a nest of puppies. What makes it so soft?'

'Goose-feathers.'

'The geese we ate tonight—*their* feathers will stuff a mattress, won't they?'

'Two, I suspect.' I fetched them a silk-covered bearskin from a small, crooked cupboard which my son had built at the age of thirteen. 'And now I must see to Ruth.'

I am not a reticent person, but the sight of the boys—Stephen in bed and sleepily smiling goodnight, John respectfully standing but sneaking an envious glance at his less respectful friend—wrenched me almost to tears. I did not trust myself to say that I was very glad to offer them my son's bed for as long as they chose to stay in the Manor of Roses.

I could only say: 'Sleep as late as you like. Sarah can fix you breakfast at any hour.'

'You're very kind,' said Stephen. 'But tomorrow, I think, we must get an early start for London.'

'London!' I cried. 'But your wounds haven't healed!'

'They were just scratches really, and now you've cured them with your medicine, if we stayed, we might *never* want to go.'

'I might never want you to go.'

'But don't you see, Lady Mary, we have to fight for Jerusalem.'

'You expect to succeed where kings have failed? Frederick Barbarossa? Richard-the-Lion-Hearted? Two little boys without a weapon between them!'

'We're not little boys,' he protested. 'I'm a young swain—*fifteen winters old*—and John here is a—stripling who will grow like a bindweed. Aren't you, John?'

'Grow, anyway,' said John without enthusiasm. 'But I don't see why we have to leave in the morning.'

'Because of Ruth.'

'And Ruth is your guardian angel?' I asked with an irony lost on the boy.

'Yes. Already she's saved our lives.'

'Has she, Stephen? Has she? Sleep now. We'll talk tomorrow. I want to tell you about my own son.'

I returned to the solar heavy of foot. It was well for Ruth that she had changed to a nightdress, joined the window seats with the necessary stool, and retired to bed in a tumble of cushions. Now, she was feigning sleep but forgetting to mimic the slow, deep breaths of the true sleeper. Well, I could question her tomorrow. One thing I knew. She would lead my boys on no unholy Crusade.

A chill in the air awakened me. It was not unusual for a hot summer day to grow wintry at night. I rose, lit a candle, and found additional coverlets for myself and Ruth. Her face seemed afloat in her golden hair; decapitated, somehow; or drowned.

I thought of the boys, shivering in the draft of their glassless window. I had not remembered to draw the canopy of their bed. In my linen nightdress and my pointed satin slippers which, like all the footwear expected of English ladies, cruelly pinched my toes, I passed through the hall and then the kitchen, tiptoed among the pallets of Sarah and her children stretched near the oven, and climbed a staircase whose steepness resembled a ladder.

Lifting aside a coarse leather curtain, I stood in the doorway of my son's room and looked at the boys. They had fallen asleep without extinguishing the pewter lamp which hung from a rod beside their bed. The bearskin covered their chins, and their bodies had met for warmth in the middle of the bed. I leaned above them and started to spread my coverlet. John, who was closer to me, opened his eyes and smiled.

'Mother,' he said.

'Mary,' I said, sitting on the edge of the bed.

'That's what I meant.'

'I'm sorry I woke you.'

'I'm glad. You came to bring us a coverlet, didn't you?'

'Yes. Won't we wake your brother?'

His smile broadened; he liked my acceptance of Stephen as his brother and equal. 'Not our voices. Only if I got out of bed. Then he would feel me gone. But once he's asleep, he never hears anything, unless it's one of his hounds.'

'You're really going tomorrow?'

'I don't want to go. I don't think Stephen does either. It's Ruth's idea. She whispered to him in the solar, when you and I were talking. But I heard her just the same. She said they must get to London. She said it was why she had come, and why she had saved us from the Mandrakes.'

'Why won't she trust me, John?'

'I think she's afraid of you. Of what you might guess.'

'What is there to guess?'

There was fear in his eyes. He looked at Stephen, asleep, and then at me. 'I think that Ruth is a Mandrake. One who has passed.'

I flinched. I had thought: thief, adventuress, harlot, carrier of the plague, but nothing so terrible as Mandrake. Though fear was a brand in my chest, I spoke quietly. I did not want to judge her until he had made his case. He might be a too imaginative child, frightened by the forest and now bewildered with sleep. He was only twelve. And yet, from what I had seen, I had thought him singularly rational for his years. Stephen, one might have said, would wake in the night and babble of Mandrake girls. Never John. Not without reason, at least.

'Why do you think that, John?'

His words cascaded like farthings from a purse cut by a pickpocket: swift, confused at times, and yet with a thread of logic which made me share his suspicions. Ruth's mysterious arrival in the Mithraeum. Her vague answers and her claim to forgetfulness. Her lore of the forest. Her shock and disgust when he and Stephen had told her about the Mandrake hunters. Her strangely successful bargain with the crucifix.

'And they kept their word,' he said. 'Even when they thought

Stephen and I had killed one of their babies. It was as if they let us go so that she could *use* us.'

'It's true they're Christians,' I said. 'I've found their stone crosses in the woods around my Manor. They might have felt bound by their word. An oath to a savage, especially a Christian savage, can be a sacred thing. Far more sacred than to some of our own Crusaders, who have sacked the towns of their sworn friends. Ruth may have told you the truth about the crucifix.'

'I know,' he said. 'I know. It's wicked of me to suspect her. She's always been kind to me. She brought me strawberries in the forest once! And Stephen worships her. But I had to tell you, didn't I? She might have passed when she was a small child. Grown up in a village. But someone became suspicious. She fled to the forest. Took shelter in the Mithraeum where Stephen and I found her. You see, if I'm right—'

'We're all in danger. You and Stephen most of all. You have been exposed to her visitations. We shall have to learn the truth before you leave this house.'

'You mean we must wound her? But if she passed a long time ago, we would have to cut to the bone.'

'We wouldn't so much as scratch her. We would simply confront her with an accusation. Suppose she is a Mandrake. Either she knew already when she first met you or else her people told her in the forest. Told her with pride: "See, we have let you grow soft and beautiful in the town!" Tomorrow we shall demand proof of her innocence. Innocent, she will offer herself to the knife. The offer alone will suffice. But a true Mandrake will surely refuse such a test, and then we will know her guilt.'

'It's rather like trial by combat, isn't it?' he said at last. 'God condemns the guilty. Pricks him with conscience until he loses the fight. But this way, there won't be a combat, just a trial. God will make Ruth reveal her guilt or innocence.'

'And you and I will be His instruments. Nothing more.'

'And if she's guilty?'

'We'll send her into the forest and let her rejoin her people.'

'It will break Stephen's heart.'

'It will save his life. Save him from Ruth—and from going to London. Without his angel, do you think he'll still persist in his foolish crusade? He will stay here with you and me. The Manor of Roses has need of two fine youths.'

'You won't make him a servant because he's a villein? His ancestors were Saxon earls when mine were pirates.'

'Mine were pirates too. Bloodthirsty ones, at that. No, you and

Stephen shall both be my sons. You adopted him. Why shouldn't
I?'

'You know,' he said, 'when you first spoke to us at the hedge
—after we had come from the forest—you said we'd come to the
Manor of Roses. At first I thought you meant the *manner* of roses.
Without the capitals.'

'Did you, John?'

'Yes. And it's quite true. Of the house, I mean, and you. The
manner of roses.'

'But I have thorns to protect the ones I love. Ruth will feel them
tomorrow.' I knelt beside him and touched my lips to his cheek. It
was not as if I were kissing him for the first time, but had kissed
him every night for—how many years?—the years of my son when
he rode to London.

'You're crying,' he said.

'It's the smoke from the lamp. It has stung my eyes.'

He clung to my neck, no longer a boy; a small child I could
almost feed at my breast.

'I like your hair when it's loose,' he said. 'It's like a halo that
comes all the way to your shoulders.'

He fell asleep in my arms.

5

I woke to the strident twittering of sparrows. Their little shapes
flickered against the window panes, and for once I regretted the
glass. I would have liked them to flood the room with their
unmelodious chirpings and share in my four-walled, raftered safety.
Minikin beings, they reveled in the sun, noisily, valiantly, yet prey
to eagle and hawk from the wilderness of sky, and the more they
piped defiance, the more they invited death.

But other sparrows were not beyond my help.

I rose and dressed without assistance. I did not call Sarah's
daughters to comb my hair and exclaim, 'But it's like black samite!'
and fasten the sleeves above my wrists and burden my fingers with
jade and tourmaline. I did not wish to awaken Ruth. I dreaded the
confrontation.

Encased from the tip of my toes to the crest of my hair, amber
and green in wimple, robe, gloves, stockings, and slippers, I
walked into the courtyard and sat on a bench among my herbs,
lulled by the soft scent of lavender, but not from my hesitations;

piqued by the sharp pungency of tarragon, but not to pride in what I must ask of Ruth.

The sun was as high as a belltower before the sounds from the solar told me that the children had waked and met. Ruth and Stephen were belaboring John when I entered the room. Stephen looked liberated in his breechclout, and Ruth disported herself in his green tunic, the one he had worn reluctantly to my feast, but without the *chausses* or the cape. They were telling John that he ought to follow their example and dress for the woods.

'You're white as a sheep this morning,' chided Stephen. 'Your shoulders need the sun.'

John, engulfed by his cape and tunic, might have been ten instead of twelve. I pitied the child. He would have to side with me against his friends. He returned my smile with a slight nod of his head, as if to say, 'It must be now.'

Stephen's voice was husky with gratitude: 'Lady Mary, we must leave you and make our way to London. You've fed us and given us a roof, and we won't forget you. In a dark forest, you have been our candle. Your gifts—the drums and rebec—will help us to earn our passage to the Holy Land.'

'Knights and abbots will throw you pennies,' I said. 'Robbers will steal them. It will take you a long time to earn your passage.'

'But that's why we have to go! To start earning. And when we come back this way, we'll bring you a Saracen shield to hang above your hearth.' He kissed my hand with a rough, impulsive tenderness. An aura of camphor wreathed him from yesterday's bath. He had combed his hair in a fringe across his forehead, like jonquils above his bluer-than-larkspur eyes. I thought how the work of the comb would soon be spoiled; the petals wilted by the great forest, tangled with cobwebs, matted perhaps with blood.

'I think you should know the nature of your company.'

His eyes widened into a question. The innocence of them almost shook my resolve. 'John? But he's my friend! If you mean he's very young, you ought to have seen him fight the Mandrakes.'

'Ruth.'

'Ruth is an angel.' He made the statement as one might say, 'I believe in God.'

'You want her to be an angel. But is she, Stephen? Ask her.'

He turned to Ruth for confirmation. 'You said you came from the sky, didn't you?'

'I said I didn't remember.' She stared at the Persian carpet and seemed to be counting the polygons or reading the cryptic letters woven into the border.

'But you said you remembered falling a great distance.'

'There are other places to fall than out of the sky.'

John spoke at last. 'But you remembered things.' His voice seemed disembodied. It might have come from the vault of a deep Mithraeum. 'About the forest. Where to find wild strawberries. How to weave a cup out of rushes. How to escape from the Mandrakes.'

'Ruth,' I said. 'Tell them who you are. Tell me. We want to know.'

She began to tremble. 'I don't know. I don't know.' I was ready to pity her when she told the truth.

I walked to the Aumbry with slow, deliberate steps. In spite of my silken slippers, I placed each foot as if I were crushing a mite which threatened my roses. I opened the doors, knelt, and reached to the lowest shelf for a Saracen poniard, its ivory hilt emblazoned with sapphires in the shape of a running gazelle. The damascene blade was very sharp: steel inlaid with threads of silver.

There was steel in my voice as I said, 'You are not to leave my house till I know who you are. I accepted you as a guest and friend. Now I have reason to believe that you are dangerous. To the boys, if not to me.'

'You would harm me, Lady Mary?' She drank from the light of the window and joined the shadows near the hearth. I half expected her to dwindle into a spider and scuttle to safety among the dark rafters.

'I would ask you to undergo a test.'

She said: 'You think I am a Mandrake.'

'I think you must show us that you are not a Mandrake.' I walked toward her with the poniard. 'My husband killed the Saracen who owned this blade. Wrestled him for it. Drove it into his heart. You see, the point is familiar with blood. It will know what to do.'

'Lady Mary!' It was Stephen who stepped between us; charged, I should say, like an angry stag, and almost took the blade in his chest. 'What are you saying, Lady Mary?'

'Ask her,' I cried. 'Ask her! Why does she fear the knife? Because it will prove her guilt!'

He struck my hand and the poniard fell to the floor. He gripped my shoulders. 'Witch! You have blasphemed an angel!'

Anger had drained me; indignation; doubts. I dropped in his punishing hands. I wanted to sleep.

John awoke from his torpor and beat on his friend with desperate fists. 'It's true, it's true! You must let her go!'

Stephen unleashed a kick like a javelin hurled from an arblast. I forgot the poniard; forgot to watch the girl. All I could see was John as he struck the doors of the Aumbry and sank, winded and groaning to the floor. Twisting from Stephen's fingers, I knelt to the wounded boy and took him in my arms.

'I'm not hurt,' he gasped. 'But Ruth . . . the poniard . . .'

I saw the flash of light on the blade in Ruth's hand. Stephen swayed on his feet, a stag no longer: a bear chained in a pit, baited by some, fed by others—how can he tell his tormentors from his friends? Wildly he stared from the boy he had hurt to the girl he had championed. Ruth walked toward me with soundless feet and eyes as cold as hornstones under a stream. She might have been dead.

The poniard flashed between us. I threw up my hands for defense: of myself and John. She brought the blade down sharply against her own hand, the mount of the palm below her thumb. I heard—I actually heard—the splitting of flesh, the rasp of metal on bone. The blade must have cut through half of her hand before it lodged in the bone, and then she withdrew it without a cry, with a sharp, quick jerk, like a fisherman removing a hook, and stretched her fingers to display her wound. The flesh parted to reveal white bone, and crimson blood, not in the least resinous, swelled to fill the part. She smiled at me with triumph but without malice, a young girl who had vindicated herself before an accuser more than twice her years.

'Did you think I mean to hurt you?' she said almost playfully and then, seeing her blood as it reddened the carpet, winced and dropped the poniard.

Stephen steadied her into the chair by the hearth and pressed her palm to staunch the flow.

'You are an evil woman,' he glared at me. 'Your beauty is a lie. It hides an old heart.'

'Both of your friends are in pain,' I said. 'It isn't a time for curses.'

He looked at John in my arms and stiffened as if he would drop Ruth's hand and come to his friend.

'No. Stay with Ruth.' I helped John across the room to a seat in the window; the tinted panes ruddied his pale cheeks. 'He will be all right. Ruth is in greater need. Let me tend her, Stephen.'

'You shan't touch her.'

Ruth spoke for herself. 'The pain is very sharp. Can you ease it, Lady Mary?'

I treated the wound with a tincture of opium and powdered rose petals and swaddled her hand with linen. John rose from the window and stood behind me, in silent attendance on Ruth—and in antonement. Stephen, an active boy denied a chance to act, stammered to his friends:

'Forgive me, both of you. It was my Crusade, wasn't it? I brought you to this.'

Ruth's face was as white as chalk-rubbed parchment awaiting the quill of a monk. Her smile was illumination. 'But you see, Stephen, Lady Mary was right to a point. I am no more an angel than you are. Less, in fact. You're a dreamer. I'm a liar. I've lied to you from the start, as Lady Mary guessed. That's why I couldn't trust her—because I saw that she couldn't trust me. My name isn't Ruth, it's Madeleine. I didn't come from heaven but the Castle of the Boar, three miles from your own kennels. My father was noble of birth, brother to the Boar. But he hated the life of a knight—the hunts, the feasts, the joustings—and most of all, the Crusades without God's blessing. He left his brother's castle to live as a scholar in Chichester, above a butcher's shop. He earned his bread by copying manuscripts or reading the stars. It was he who taught me my languages—English and Norman French and Latin—and just as if I were a boy, the lore of the stars, the sea, and the forest. He also taught me to play the rebec and curtsey and use a spoon at the table. 'Someday,' he said, 'you will marry a knight, a gentle one, I hope, if such still exist, and you have to be able to talk to him about a man's interests, and also delight him with the ways of a woman. Then he won't ride off to fight in a foolish Crusade, as most men do because of ignorant wives.' He taught me well and grew as poor as a Welshman. When he died of the plague last year, he left me pennies instead of pounds, and no relatives except my uncle, the Boar, who despised my father and took me into his castle only because I was brought to him by an abbot from Chichester.

'But the Boar was recently widowed, and he had a taste for women. Soon I began to please him. I think I must have grown —how shall I say it?—riper, more womanly. He took me hawking and praised my lore of the forest. I sat beside him at banquets, drank his beer, laughed at his bawdy tales, and almost forgot my Latin. But after a feast one night he followed me to the chapel and said unspeakable things. My own uncle! I hit him with a crucifix from the altar. No one stopped me when I left the castle. No one knew the master was not at his prayers! But where could I go? Where but Chichester. Perhaps the Abbot would give me shelter.

'But John, as I passed near your father's castle I heard a rider behind me. I ducked in a thicket of gorse and tumbled down some stairs into a dark vault. You see, I did have a kind of fall, though not from heaven. I was stiff and tired and scared, and I fell asleep and woke up to hear Stephen proclaiming me an angel and talking about London and the Holy Land. London! Wasn't that better than Chichester? Further away from my uncle? Stephen, I let you think me an angel because I was tired of men and their lust. I had heard stories about you even at the castle—your way with a wench. After I knew you, though, I *wanted* your way. You weren't at all the boy in the stories, but kind and trusting. But I couldn't admit my lie and lose your respect.

'As for the crucifix you found in my hands, I had stolen it from my uncle. He owed me *something*, I felt. I had heard him say it was worth a knight's ransom. I hoped to sell it and buy a seamstress' shop and marry a fine gentleman who brought me stockings to mend. When I traded it to the Mandrakes, it was just as I said. They kept their promise for the sake of their faith. You see, they were much more honest than I have been.'

Stephen was very quiet. I had seen him pressed for words but never for gestures, the outstretched hand, the nod, the smile. I wanted to ease the silence with reassurances and apologies. But Ruth was looking to Stephen; it was he who must speak.

'Now I'm just another wench to you,' she said with infinite wistfulness. 'I should have told you the truth. Let you have your way. This way, I've nothing at all.'

He thought for a long time before he spoke, and the words he found were not an accusation. 'I think a part of me never really took you for an angel. At least, not after the first. I'm not good enough to deserve a guardian from heaven. Besides, you stirred me like a girl of flesh and blood. But I wanted a reason for running away. An excuse and a hope. I lacked courage, you see. It's a fearful thing for a villein to leave his master. John's father could have me killed, or cut off my hands and feet. So I lied to myself: An angel had come to guide me! We were both dishonest, Ruth—Madeleine.'

'Ruth. That's the name you gave me.'

'Ruth, we can still go to London. Without any lies between us.' Gestures returned to him; he clasped her shoulders with the deference of a brother (and looked to John: 'My arms are not yet filled'). 'But Lady Mary, it was cruel of you to find the truth in such a way.'

'She never meant to touch Ruth,' said John. 'Only to test her. It was things I told Lady Mary that made her suspicious.'

'John, John,' said Ruth, walking to him and placing her

swaddled hand on his arm. 'I know you've never liked me. You saw through my tale from the first. You thought I wanted your friend. You were right, of course. I wouldn't trade him for Robin Hood, if Robin were young again and Lord of the forest! But I never wished you ill. You were his chosen brother. How could I love him without loving you? I wanted to say: "Don't be afraid of losing Stephen to me. It was you he loved first. If I take a part of his heart, it won't be a part that belongs to you. Can't you see, John, that the heart is like the catacombs of the old Christians? You can open a second chamber without closing the first. Trust your friend to have chambers for both of us." But I said nothing. It would have shown me to be a girl instead of an angel.'

'You're coming with us, John?' asked Stephen doubtfully. 'I didn't mean to hurt you. It was like the time you stepped on my dog. But you forgave me then.'

'There's no reason now why any of you should go,' I said.

'There's no reason for us to stay.'

'You'll go on a Crusade without a guardian angel?'

'We'll walk to London and then—who knows? Venice, Baghdad. Cathay! Maybe it was just to run away I wanted, and not to save Jerusalem.' He pressed John between his big hands. 'You *are* coming, aren't you, brother?'

'No,' said John. 'No, Stephen. Lady Mary needs me.'

'So does Stephen,' said Ruth.

'Stephen is strong. I was never any use to him. Just the one he protected.'

'Someday,' said Ruth, 'you'll realize that needing a person is the greatest gift you can give him.'

'I need all of you,' I said. 'Stay here. Help me. Let me help you. London killed my son. It's a city forsaken by God.'

Stephen shook his head. 'We have to go, Ruth and I. The Boar might follow her here. She hurt his pride as well as his skull and stole his crucifix.'

John said: 'I'm going to stay.'

I packed them provisions of bread, beer, and salted bacon; gave them the Saracen poniard to use against thieves or sell in London; and strapped the rebec and kettledrums on their backs.

'You must have a livelihood in London,' I said, when Stephen wanted to leave the instruments with John.

I walked with Stephen and Ruth to the wicket and gave them directions for finding the road: Walk a mile to the east . . . look for the chestnut tree with a hole like a door in the trunk. . . .

But Stephen was looking over his shoulder for John.

'He stayed in the solar,' I said. 'He loves you too much to say good-bye.'

'Or too little. Why else is he staying with you?'

'The world is a harsh place, Stephen. Harsher than the forest, and without any islands like the Manor of Roses.' How could I make him understand that God had given me John in return for the son I had lost to the devil?

'I would be his island,' said Stephen, his big frame shaken with sobs.

'Never mind,' said Ruth. 'Never mind. We'll come back for him, Stephen.' And then to me: 'My lady, we thank you for your hospitality.' She curtsied and kissed my hand with surprising warmth.

I said: 'May an angel truly watch over you.'

They marched toward the forest as proud and straight as Vikings, in spite of their wounds and their burdens. No more tears for Stephen. Not a backward look. London. Baghdad. Cathay!

It was then that I saw the face in the dense foliage, a bleached moon in a dusk of tangled ivy.

'Ruth, Stephen,' I started to call. 'You are being watched!'

But she had no eye for the children. She was watching me. I had seen her several times in the forest. Something of curiosity—no, of awe—distinguished her from the gray, anonymous tribe. Perhaps it was she who had left the crosses around my estate, like charms to affright the devil. She had never threatened me. Once I had run from her. Like a wraith of mist before the onslaught of sunlight, she had wasted into the trees. I had paused and watched her with shame and pity.

Now, I walked toward her, compelled by a need which surpassed my fear. 'I won't hurt you,' I said. I was deathly afraid. Her friends could ooze from the trees and envelop me before I could cry for help. 'I won't hurt you,' I repeated. 'I only want to talk.'

The rank vegetable scent of her clogged my nostrils. I had always felt that the rose and the Mandrake represented the antitheses of the forest: grace and crookedness. Strange, though, now that I looked at her closely for the first time, she was like a crooked tree mistreated by many weathers; a natural object unanswerable to human concepts of beauty and ugliness.

Dredging archaic words from memories of old books, I spoke with soft emphasis. 'Tell me,' I said. 'Why do you watch my house—my mead-hall? Is it treasure-rich to you? Broad-gabled?'

She caught my meaning at once. 'Not mead-hall.'
'What then? The roses perhaps? You may pick some if you like.'
'Bantling.'
'Bantling? *In my house?*'
She knelt and seized my hand and pressed her hairy lips against
my knuckles.
'Here,' she said.
I flung my hands to my ears as if I had heard a Mandrake shriek
in the night. It was I who had shrieked. I fled . . . I fled. . . .

His eyes were closed, he rested against a cushion embroidered with
children playing Hoodman Blind. He rose from his seat when he
heard me enter the room.
'They're gone?'
'What? What did you say, John?'
'Stephen and Ruth are gone?'
'Yes.'
He came toward me. 'You're pale, Lady Mary. Don't be sad for
me. I wanted to stay.'
I said quietly: 'I think you should go with your friends. They
asked me to send you after them.'
He blinked his eyes. The lids looked heavy and gray. 'But I am
staying to protect you. To be your son. You said—'
'It was really Stephen I wanted. You're only a little boy. Stephen
is a young man. I would have taught him to be a gentleman and a
knight. But now that he's gone, what do I need with a skinny child
of twelve?'
'But I don't ask to be loved like Stephen!'
I caught him between my hands, and his lean, hard-muscled
shoulders, the manhood stirring within him, belied my taunts.
'Go to him,' I cried. 'Now, John. You'll lose him if you wait!'
Pallor drained from his face, like pain routed by opium. 'Lady
Mary,' he whispered. 'I think I understand. You *do* love me, don't
you? Enough to let me go. So much—'
I dropped my hands from his shoulders. I must not touch him. I
must not kiss him. 'So much. So much. . . .'

Beyond the hedge, he turned and waved to me, laughing, and ran to
catch his friends. Before he could reach the woods, Stephen blazed
from the trees.
'I waited,' he cried. 'I knew you would come!'
The boys embraced in such a swirl of color, of whirling bodies

and clattering kettle drums, that the fair might have come to London Town! Then, arm in arm with Ruth, they entered the woods:

> Summer is a-comin' in,
> Loud sing cuckoo. . . .

I, also, entered the woods. For a long time I knelt before one of the stone crosses left by the Mandrakes—set like a bulwark between enormous oaks to thwart whatever of evil, griffins, wolves, men, might threaten my house. My knees sank through the moss to ache against stone; my lips were dry of prayer. I knelt, waiting.

I did not turn when the vegetable scent of her was a palpable touch. I said: 'Would you like to live with me in the mead-hall?'

Her cry was human; anguish born of ecstasy. I might have said: 'Would you like to see the Holy Grail?'

'Serve you?'

'Help me. You and your friends. Share with me.'

I leaned to the shy, tentative fingers which loosened my hair and spread my tresses, as one spreads a fine brocade to admire its weave and the delicacy of its figures.

'Bantling,' she said. 'Madonna-beautiful.' What had John said? 'I love your hair when it's loose. It's like a halo. . . .' Roses and I have this in common: we have been judged too kindly by the softness of our petals.

'I must go now. Those in the mead-hall would not welcome you. I shall have to send them away. For your sake—and theirs. Tomorrow I will meet you here and take you back with me.'

Earth, the mother of roses, has many children.

PLEASE STAND BY

Ron Goulart

he art department secretary put her Christmas tree down and kissed Max Kearny. 'There's somebody to see you,' she said, getting her coat the rest of the way on and picking up the tree again.

Max shifted on his stool. 'On the last working day before Christmas?'

'Pile those packages in my arms,' the secretary said. 'He says it's an emergency.'

Moving away from his drawing board Max arranged the gift packages in the girl's arms. 'Who is it? A rep?'

'Somebody named Dan Padgett.'

'Oh, sure. He's a friend of mine from another agency. Tell him to come on back.'

'Will do. You'll have a nice Christmas, won't you, Max?'

'I think the Salvation Army has something nice planned.'

'No, seriously, Max. Don't sit around some cold bar. Well, Merry Christmas.'

'Same to you.' Max looked at the rough layout on his board for a moment and then Dan Padgett came in. 'Hi, Dan. What is it?'

Dan Padgett rubbed his palms together. 'You still have your hobby?'

Max shook out a cigarette from his pack. 'The ghost detective stuff? Sure.'

'But you don't specialize in ghosts only?' Dan went around the room once, then closed the door.

'No. I'm interested in most of the occult field. The last case I worked on involved a free-lance resurrectionist. Why?'

'You remember Anne Clemens, the blonde?'

'Yeah. You used to go out with her when we worked at Bryan-Josephs and Associates. Skinny girl.'

'Slender. Fashion model type.' Dan sat in the room's chair and unbuttoned his coat. 'I want to marry her.'

'Right now?'

'I asked her two weeks ago but she hasn't given me an answer yet. One reason is Kenneth Westerland.'

'The animator?'

'Yes. The guy who created Major Bowser. He's seeing Anne, too.'

'Well,' said Max, dragging his stool back from the drawing board. 'I don't do lovelorn work, Dan. Now if Westerland were a vampire or a warlock I might be able to help.'

'He's not the main problem. It's if Anne says yes.'

'What is?'

'I can't marry her.'

'Change of heart?'

'No.' Dan tilted to his feet. 'No.' He rubbed his hands together. 'No, I love her. The thing is there's something wrong with me. I hate to bother you so close to Christmas, but that's part of it.'

Max lit a fresh cigarette from the old one. 'I still don't have a clear idea of the problem, Dan.'

'I change into an elephant on all national holidays.'

Max leaned forward and squinted one eye at Dan. 'An elephant?'

'Middle sized gray elephant.'

'On national holidays?'

'More or less. It started on Halloween. It didn't happen again till Thanksgiving. Fortunately I can talk during it and I was able to explain to my folks that I wouldn't get home for our traditional Thanksgiving get-together.'

'How do you dial the phone?'

'I waited till they called me. You can pick up a phone with your trunk. I found that out.'

'Usually people change into cats or wolves.'

'I wouldn't mind that,' Dan said, sitting. 'A wolf, that's acceptable. It has a certain appeal. I'd even settle for a giant cockroach, for the symbolic value. But a middle sized gray elephant. I can't expect Anne to marry me when I do things like that.'

'You don't think,' said Max, crossing to the window and looking down at the late afternoon crowds, 'that you're simply having hallucinations?'

'If I am they're pretty authentic. Thanksgiving Day I ate a bale of hay.' Dan tapped his fingers on his knees. 'See, the first time I

changed I got hungry after a while. But I couldn't work the damned
can opener with my trunk. So I figured I'd get a bale of hay and
keep it handy if I ever changed again.'

'You seemed to stay an elephant for how long?'

'Twenty four hours. The first time—both times I've been in my
apartment, which has a nice solid floor—I got worried. I trumpeted
and stomped around. Then the guy upstairs, the queer ceramacist,
started pounding on the floor. I figured I'd better keep quiet so
nobody would call the cops and take me off to a zoo or animal
shelter. Well, I waited around and tried to figure things out and
then right on the nose at midnight I was myself again.'

Max ground his cigarette into the small metal pie plate on his
workstand. 'You're not putting me on, are you?'

'No, Max.' Dan looked up hopefully. 'Is this in your line? I don't
know anyone else to ask. I tried to forget it. Now, though,
Christmas is nearly here. Both other times I changed was on a
holiday. I'm worried.'

'Lycanthropy,' said Max. 'That can't be it. Have you been near
any elephants lately?'

'I was out at the zoo a couple years ago. None of them bit me or
even looked at me funny.'

'This is something else. Look, Dan, I've got a date with a girl
down in Palo Alto on Christmas Day. But Christmas Eve I can be
free. Do you change right on the dot?'

'If it happens I should switch over right at midnight on the
twenty-fourth. I already told my folks I was going to spend these
holidays with Anne. And I told her I'd be with them.'

'Which leaves her free to see Westerland.'

'That son of a bitch.'

'Major Bowser's not a bad cartoon show.'

'Successful anyway. That dog's voice is what makes the show. I
hate Westerland and I've laughed at it.' Dan rose. 'Maybe nothing
will happen.'

'If anything does it may give me a lead.'

'Hope so. Well, Merry Christmas, Max. See you tomorrow
night.'

Max nodded and Dan Padgett left. Leaning over his drawing
board Max wrote *Hex?* on the margin of his layout.

He listened to the piped in music play Christmas carols for a few
minutes and then started drawing again.

The bale of hay crackled as Max sat down on it. He lit a cigarette
carefully and checked his watch again. 'Half hour to go,' he said.

Dan Padgett poured some scotch into a cup marked Tom & Jerry and closed the venetian blinds. 'I felt silly carrying that bale of hay up here. People expect to see you with a tree this time of year.'

'You could have hung tinsel on it.'

'That'd hurt my fillings when I eat the hay.' Dan poured some more scotch and walked to the heater outlet. He kicked it once. 'Getting cold in here. I'm afraid to complain to the landlady. She'd probably say—'Who else would let you keep an elephant in your rooms? A little chill you shouldn't mind.''

'You know,' said Max, 'I've been reading up on lycanthropy. A friend of mine runs an occult bookshop.'

'Non-fiction seems to be doing better and better.'

'There doesn't seem to be any recorded case of were-elephants.'

'Maybe the others didn't want any publicity.'

'Maybe. It's more likely somebody has put a spell on you. In that case you could change into most anything?'

Dan frowned. 'I hadn't thought of that. What time is it?'

'Quarter to.'

'A spell, huh? Would I have to meet the person who did it? Or is it done from a distance?'

'Usually there has to be some kind of contact.'

'Say,' said Dan, lowering his head and stroking his nose, 'you'd better not sit on that bale of hay. Animals don't like people fooling with their food.' He was standing with his feet wide apart, his legs stiff.

Max carefully got up and moved back across the room. 'Something?'

'No,' said Dan. He leaned far forward, reaching for the floor with his hands. 'I just have an itch. My stomach.'

Max watched as Dan scratched his stomach with his trunk. 'Damn.'

Raising his head the middle sized grey elephant squinted at Max. 'Hell, I thought it wouldn't happen again.'

'Can I come closer?'

Dan beckoned with his trunk. 'I won't trample you.'

Max reached out and touched the side of the elephant. 'You're a real elephant sure enough.'

'I should have thought to get some cabbages, too. This stuff is pretty bland.' He was tearing trunkfuls of hay from the bale and stuffing them into his mouth.

Max remembered the cigarette in his hand and lit it. He walked twice around the elephant and said, 'Think back now, Dan. To the first time this happened. When was it?'

'I told you. Halloween.'

'But that's not really a holiday. Was it the day after Halloween? Or the night itself?'

'Wait. It was before. It was the day after the party at Eando Carawan's. In the Beach.'

'Where?'

'North Beach. There was a party. Anne knows Eando's wife. Her name is Eando, too.'

'Why?'

'His name is Ernest and hers is Olivia. E-and-O. So they both call themselves Eando. They paint those pictures of bug-eyed children you can buy in all the stores down there. You should know them, being an artist yourself.'

Max grunted. 'Ernie Carawan. Sure, he used to be a freelance artist, specializing in dogs. We stopped using him because all his dogs started having bug-eyes.'

'You ought to see Olivia.'

'What happened at the party?'

'Well,' said Dan, tearing off more hay, 'I get the idea that there was some guy at this party. A little round fat guy. About your height. Around thirty-five. Somebody said he was a stage magician or something.'

'Come on,' said Max, 'elephants are supposed to have good memories.'

'I think I was sort of drunk at the time. I can't remember all he said. Something about doing me a favor. And a flash.'

'A flash?'

'The flash came to him like that. It told him to—to do whatever he did.' Dan stopped eating the hay. 'That would be magic, though, Max. That's impossible.'

'Shut up and eat your hay. Anything is possible.'

'You're right. Who'd have thought I'd be spending Christmas as an elephant.'

'That magician for one,' said Max. 'What's his name? He may know something.'

'His name?'

'That's right.'

'I don't know. He didn't tell me.'

'Just came up and put a spell on you.'

'You know how it is at parties.'

Max found the phone on a black table near the bookshelves. 'Where's the phone book?'

'Oh, yeah.'

'What?'

'It's not here. The last time I was an elephant I ate it.'

'I'll get Carawan's number from information and see if he knows who this wizard is.'

Carawan didn't. But someone at his Christmas Eve party did. The magician ran a sandal shop in North Beach. His name was Claude Waller. As far as anyone knew he was visiting his ex-wife in Los Angeles for Christmas and wouldn't be back until Monday or Tuesday.

Max reached for the price tag on a pair of orange leather slippers. The beaded screen at the back of the shop clattered.

'You a faggot or something, buddy?' asked the heavy set man who came into the room.

'No, sir. Sorry.'

'Then you don't want that pair of slippers. That's my faggot special. Also comes in light green. Who are you?'

'Max Kearny. Are you Claude Waller?'

Waller was wearing a loose brown suit. He unbuttoned the coat and sat down on a stool in front of the counter. 'That's who I am. The little old shoemaker.'

Max nodded.

'That's a switch on the wine commercial with the little old winemaker.'

'I know.'

'My humor always bombs. It's like my life. A big bomb. What do you want?'

'I hear you're a magician.'

'No.'

'You aren't?'

'Not anymore. My ex-wife, that flat chested bitch, and I have reunited. I don't know what happened. I'm a tough guy. I don't take any crap.'

'I'd say so.'

'Then why'd I send her two hundred bucks to come up here?'

'Is there time to stop the check?'

'I sent cash.'

'You're stuck then, I guess.'

'She's not that bad.'

'Do you know a guy named Dan Padgett?'

'No.'

'How about Ernie Carawan?'

'Eando? Yeah.'

'On Halloween you met Dan Padgett and a girl named Anne Clemens at the party the Carawans gave.'

'That's a good act. Can you tell me what it says on the slip of paper in my pocket?'

'Do you remember talking to Dan? Could you have put some kind of spell on him?'

Waller slid forward off the stool. 'That guy. I'll be damned. I did do it then.'

'Do what?'

'I was whacked out of my mind. Juiced out of my skull, you know. I got this flash. Some guy was in trouble. This Padgett it was. I didn't think I'd really done anything. Did I?'

'He turns into an elephant on national holidays.'

Waller looked at his feet. Then laughed. 'He does. That's great. Why'd I do that do you suppose.'

'Tell me.'

Waller stopped laughing. 'I get these flashes all the time. It bugs my wife. She doesn't know who to sleep with. I might get a flash about it. Wait now.' He picked up a hammer from his workbench and tapped the palm of his hand. 'That girl. The blonde girl. What's her name?'

'Anne Clemens.'

'There's something. Trouble. Has it happened yet?'

'What's supposed to happen?'

'Ouch,' said Waller. He'd brought the hammer down hard enough to start a bruise. 'I can't remember. But I know I put a spell on your friend so he could save her when the time came.'

Max lit a cigarette. 'It would be simpler just to tell us what sort of trouble is coming.'

Waller reached out behind him to set the hammer down. He missed the bench and the hammer smashed through the top of a shoe box. 'Look, Kearny. I'm not a professional wizard. It's like in baseball. Sometimes a guy's just a natural. That's the way I am. A natural. I'm sorry, buddy. I can't tell you anything else. And I can't take that spell off your friend. I don't even remember how I did it.'

'There's nothing else you can remember about what kind of trouble Anne is going to have?'

Frowning, Waller said, 'Dogs. A pack of dogs. Dogs barking in the rain. No, that's not right. I can't get it. I don't know. This Dan Padgett will save her.' Waller bent to pick up the hammer. 'I'm pretty sure of that.'

'This is Tuesday. On Saturday he's due to change again. Will the trouble come on New Year's Eve?'

'Buddy, if I get another flash I'll let you know.'

At the door Max said, 'I'll give you my number.'

'Skip it,' said Waller. 'When I need it, I'll know it.'

The door of the old Victorian house buzzed and Max caught the doorknob and turned it. The stairway leading upstairs was lined with brown paintings of little girls with ponies and dogs. The light from the door opening upstairs flashed down across the bright gilt frames on which eagles and flowers twisted and curled together.

'Max Kearny?' said Anne Clemens over the stair railing.

'Hi, Anne. Are you busy?'

'Not at the moment. I'm going out later. I just got home from work a little while ago.'

This was Wednesday night. Max hadn't been able to find Anne at home until now. 'I was driving by and I thought I'd stop.'

'It's been several months since we've seen each other,' said the girl as Max reached the doorway to her apartment. 'Come in.'

She was wearing a white blouse and what looked like a pair of black leotards. She wasn't as thin as Max had remembered. Her blonde hair was held back with a thin black ribbon.

'I won't hold you up?' Max asked.

Anne shook her head. 'I won't have to start getting ready for a while yet.'

'Fine.' Max got out his cigarettes and sat down in the old sofa chair Anne gestured at.

'Is it something about Dan, Max?' The single overhead light was soft and it touched her hair gently.

'In a way.'

'Is it some trouble?' She was sitting opposite Max, straight up on the sofa bed.

'No,' said Max. 'Dan's got the idea, though, that you might be in trouble of some sort.'

The girl moistened her lips. 'Dan's too sensitive in some areas. I think I know what he means.'

Max held his pack of cigarettes to her.

'No, thanks. Dan's worried about Ken Westerland, isn't he?'

'That's part of it.'

'Max,' said Anne, 'I worked for Ken a couple of years ago. We've gone out off and on since then. Dan shouldn't worry about that.'

'Westerland isn't causing you any trouble?'

'Ken? Of course not. If I seem hesitant to Dan it's only that I don't want Ken to be hurt either.' She frowned, turning away. She turned back to Max and studied him as though he had suddenly appeared across from her. 'What was I saying? Well, never mind. I really should be getting ready.'

'If you need anything,' said Max, 'let me know.'

'What?'

'I said that—'

'Oh, yes. If I need anything. Fine. If I'm going to dinner I should get 'You studying modern dance?'

Anne opened the door. 'The leotards. No. They're comfortable. I don't have any show business leanings.' She smiled quickly. 'Thank you for dropping by, Max.'

The door closed and he was in the hall. Max stood there long enough to light a cigarette and then went downstairs and outside.

It was dark now. The street lights were on and the night cold was coming. Max got in his car and sat back, watching the front steps of Anne's building across the street. Next to his car was a narrow empty lot, high with dark grass. A house had been there once and when it was torn down the stone stairs had been left. Max's eyes went up, stopping in nothing beyond the last step. Shaking his head and lighting a new cigarette he turned to watch Anne's apartment house.

The front of the building was covered with yards and yards of white wooden gingerbread. It wound around and around the house. There was a wide porch across the building front. One with a peaked roof over it.

About an hour later Kenneth Westerland parked his grey Mercedes sedan at the corner. He was a tall thin man of about thirty-five. He had a fat man's face, too round and plumpcheeked for his body. He was carrying a small suitcase.

After Westerland had gone inside Max left his car and walked casually to the corner. He crossed the street. He stepped suddenly across a lawn and into the row of darkness alongside Anne's building. Using a garbage can to stand on Max pulled himself up onto the first landing of the fire escape without use of the noisy ladder.

Max sat on the fire escape rail and, concealing the match flame, lit a cigarette. When he'd finished smoking it he ground out the butt against the ladder. Then he swung out around the edge of the building and onto the top of the porch roof. Flat on his stomach he worked up the slight incline. In a profusion of ivy and hollyhock Max concealed himself and let his left eye look up into the window.

This was the window of her living room and he could see Anne sitting in the chair he'd been sitting in. She was wearing a black cocktail dress now and her hair was down, touching her shoulders. She was watching Westerland. The suitcase was sitting on the rug between Max and the animator.

Westerland had a silver chain held between his thumb and forefinger. On the end of the chain a bright silver medallion spun.

Max blinked and ducked back into the vines. Westerland was hypnotizing Anne. It was like an illustration from a pulp magazine.

Looking in again Max saw Westerland let the medallion drop into his suit pocket. Westerland came toward the window and Max eased down.

After a moment he looked in. Westerland had opened the suitcase. It held a tape recorder. The mike was in Anne's hand. In her other hand she held several stapled together sheets of paper.

Westerland pushed her coffee table in front of Anne and she set the papers on it. Her eyes seemed focused still on the spot where the spinning disc had been.

On his knees by the tape machine Westerland fitted on a spool of tape. After speaking a few words into the mike he gave it back to the girl. They began recording what had to be a script of some kind.

From the way Westerland used his face he was doing different voices. Anne's expression never changed as she spoke. Max couldn't hear anything.

Letting himself go flat he slid back to the edge of the old house and swung onto the fire escape. He waited to make sure no one had seen him and went to work on the window that led to the escape. It wasn't much work because there was no lock on it. It hadn't been opened for quite a while and it creaked. Max stepped into the hall and closed the window. Then he went slowly to the door of Anne's apartment and put his ear against it.

He could hear the voices faintly now. Westerland speaking as various characters. Anne using only one voice, not her own. Max sensed something behind him and turned to see the door of the next apartment opening. A big girl with black rimmed glasses was looking at him.

'What is it?' she said.

Max smiled and came up to her door. 'Nobody home I guess. Perhaps you'd like to subscribe to the Seditionist Daily. If I sell eight more subscriptions I get a stuffed panda.'

Max watched her for a second. 'It is sort of foolish. To hell with them then. It's not much of a paper anyway. No comics and only fifteen words in the crossword puzzle. Good night, miss. Sorry to bother you. You've opened my eyes.' He went down the stairs as the door closed behind him.

What he'd learned tonight gave him no clues as to Dan's problem. But it was interesting. For some reason Anne Clemens was the voice of Westerland's animated cartoon character, Major Bowser.

By Friday Max had found out that Westerland had once worked in night clubs as a hypnotist. That gave him no leads about why Dan Padgett periodically turned into an elephant.

Early in the afternoon Dan called him. 'Max. Something's wrong.'

'Have you changed already?'

'No, I'm okay. But I can't find Anne.'

'What do you mean?'

'She hasn't showed up at work today. And I can't get an answer at her place.'

'Did you tell her about Westerland? About what I found out the other night?'

'I know you said not to. But you also said I was due to save her from some trouble. I thought maybe telling her about Westerland was the way to do it.'

'You're supposed to save her while you're an elephant. Damn it. I didn't want her to know what Westerland was doing yet.'

'If it's any help Anne didn't know she was Major Bowser. And she thinks she went to dinner with Westerland on Wednesday.'

'No wonder she's so skinny. Okay. What else did she say?'

'She thought I was kidding. Then she seemed to become convinced. Even asked me how much Westerland probably made off the series.'

'Great,' said Max, making heavy lines on his memo pad. 'Now she's probably gone to him and asked him for her back salary or something.'

'Is that so bad?'

'We don't know.' Max looked at his watch. 'I can take off right now. I'll go out to her place and look around. Then check at Westerland's apartment. He lives out on California Street. I'll call you as soon as I find out anything.'

'In the meantime,' said Dan, 'I'd better see about getting another bale of hay.'

There was no lead on Anne's whereabouts at her apartment, which Max broke into. Or at Westerland's, where he came in through the skylight.

At noon on Saturday Max was wondering if he should sit back

and trust to Waller's prediction that Dan would save Anne when the time came.

He lit a new cigarette and wandered around his apartment. He looked through quite a few of the occult books he'd collected.

The phone rang.

'Yes?'

'This is Waller's Sandal Shop.'

'The magician?'

'Right, buddy. That is you, Kearny?'

'Yes. What's happening?'

'I got a flash.'

'So?'

'Go to Sausalito.'

'And?'

'That's all the flash told me. You and your friend get over to Sausalito. Today. Before midnight.'

'You haven't got any more details?'

'Sorry. My ex-wife got in last night and I've been too unsettled to get any full scale flashes.' The line went dead.

'Sausalito?' said Dan when Max called him.

'That's what Waller says.'

'Hey,' said Dan. 'Westerland's ex-wife.'

'He's got one, too?'

'His wife had a place over there. I remember going to a party with Anne there once. Before Westerland got divorced. Could Anne be there?'

'Wouldn't Mrs. Westerland complain?'

'No, she's in Europe. It was in Herb Caen and—Max! The house would be empty now. Anne must be there. And in trouble.'

The house was far back from the road that ran up through the low hills of Sausalito, the town just across the Golden Gate Bridge from San Francisco. It was a flat scattered house of redwood and glass.

Max and Dan had driven by it and parked the car. Max in the lead, they came downhill through a stretch of trees, descending toward the back of the Westerland house. It was late afternoon now and the great flat windows sparkled and went black and sparkled again as they came near. A high hedge circled the patio and when Max and Dan came close their view of the house was cut off.

'Think she's here?' Dan asked.

'We should be able to spot some signs of life,' Max said. 'I'm turning into a first class peeping tom. All I do is watch people's houses.'

'I guess detective work's like that,' said Dan. 'Even the occult stuff.'

'Hold it,' said Max. 'Listen.'

'To what?'

'I heard a dog barking.'

'In the house?'

'Yep.'

'Means there's somebody in there.'

'It means Anne's in there probably. Pretty sure that was Major Bowser.'

'Hi, pals,' said a high pitched voice.

'Hello,' said Max, turning to face the wide bald man behind them.

'Geese Louise,' the man said, pointing his police special at them, 'this sure saves me a lot of work. The boss had me out looking for you all day. And just when I was giving up and coming back here with my tail between my legs—well, here you are.'

'Who's your boss?'

'Him. Westerland. I'm a full time pro gunman. Hired to get you.'

'You got us,' said Max.

'Look, would you let me tell him I caught you over in Frisco? Makes me seem more efficient.'

'We will,' said Max, 'if you'll let us go. Tell him we used karate on you. We can even break your arm to make it look good.'

'No,' said the bald man. 'Let it pass. You guys want too many concessions. Go on inside.'

Westerland was opening the refrigerator when his gunman brought Max and Dan into the kitchen.

'You brought it off, Lloyd,' said Westerland, taking a popsicle from the freezer compartment.

'I studied those pictures you gave me.'

'Where's Anne?' Dan asked.

Westerland squeezed the wrapper off the popsicle. 'Here. We've only this minute finished a recording session. Sit down.'

When the four of them were around the white wooden table Westerland said, 'You, Mr. Kearny.'

Max took out his pack of cigarettes and put them on the table in front of him. 'Sir?'

'Your detective work will be the ruin of you.'

'All I did was look through a few windows. It's more acrobatics than detection.'

'Nevertheless, you're on to me. Your over protective attitude toward Miss Clemens has caused you to stumble on one of the most closely guarded secrets of the entertainment industry.'

'You mean Anne's being the voice of Major Bowser?'

'Exactly,' said Westerland, his round cheeks caving as he sucked the popsicle. 'But it's too late. Residuals and reruns.'

Dan tapped the tabletop. 'What's that mean?'

'What else? I've completed taping the soundtrack for episode 78 of Major Bowser. I have a new series in the works. Within a few months the major will be released to secondary markets. That means I don't need Anne Clemens anymore.'

Dan clenched his fist. 'So let her go.'

'Why did you ever need her?' Max asked, looking at Westerland.

'She's an unconscious talent,' said Westerland, catching the last fragment of popsicle off the stick. 'She first did that voice one night over two years ago. After a party I'd taken her to. She'd had too much to drink. I thought it was funny. The next day she'd forgotten about it. Couldn't even remember the voice. Instead of pressing her I used my hypnotic ability. I had a whole sketch book full of drawings of that damned dog. The voice clicked. It matched. I used it.'

'And made $100,000,' said Dan.

'The writing is mine. And quite a bit of the drawing.'

'And now?' said Max.

'She knows about it. She has thoughts of marrying and settling down. She asked me if $5,000 would be a fair share of the profits from the major.'

'Is that scale for 78 shows?' Max said.

'I could look it up,' said Westerland. He was at the refrigerator again. 'Lemon, lime, grape, watermelon. How's grape sound? Fine. Grape it is.' He stood at the head of the table and unwrapped the purple popsicle. 'I've come up with an alternative. I intend to eliminate all of you. Much cheaper way of settling things.'

'You're kidding,' said Dan.

'Animators are supposed to be lovable guys like Walt Disney,' said Max.

'I'm a businessman first. I can't use Anne Clemens anymore. We'll fix her first and you two at some later date. Lloyd, put these detectives in the cellar and lock it up.'

Lloyd grinned and pointed to a door beyond the stove. Max and

Dan were made to go down a long flight of wooden stairs and into a room that was filled with the smell of old newspapers and unused furniture. There were small dusty windows high up around the beamed ceiling.

'Not a very tough cellar,' Dan whispered to Max.

'But you won't be staying here,' said Lloyd. He kept his gun aimed at them and stepped around a fallen tricycle to a wide oak door in the cement wall. A padlock and chain hung down from a hook on the wall. Lloyd slid the bolt and opened the door. 'The wine cellar. He showed it to me this morning. No wine left, but it's homey. You'll come to like it.'

He got them inside and bolted the door. The chains rattled and the padlock snapped.

Max blinked. He lit a match and looked around the cement room. It was about twelve feet high and ten feet wide.

Dan made his way to an old cobbler's bench in the corner. 'Does your watch glow in the dark?' he asked as the match went out.

'It's five thirty.'

'The magician was right. We're in trouble.'

'I'm wondering,' said Max, striking another match.

'You're wondering what that son of a bitch is going to do to Anne.'

'Yes,' Max said, spotting an empty wine barrel. He turned it upside down and sat on it.

'And what'll he do with us?'

Max started a cigarette from the dying match flames. 'Drop gas pellets through the ceiling, fill the room with water, make the walls squeeze in.'

'Westerland's trickier than that. He'll probably hypnotize us into thinking we're pheasants and then turn us loose the day the hunting season opens.'

'Wonder how Lloyd knew what we looked like.'

'Anne's got my picture in her purse. And one I think we all took at some beach party once.'

Max leaned back against the dark wall. 'This is about a middle sized room, isn't it?'

'I don't know. The only architecture course I took at school was in water color painting.'

'In six hours you'll be a middle sized elephant.'

Dan's bench clattered. 'You think this is it?'

'Should be. How else are we going to get out of here?'

'I smash the door like a real elephant would.' He snapped his fingers. 'That's great.'

'You should be able to do it.'

'But Max?'

'Yeah?'

'Suppose I don't change?'

'You will.'

'We only have the word of an alcoholic shoemaker.'

'He knew about Sausalito.'

'He could be a fink.'

'He's a real magician. You're proof of that.'

'Max?'

'Huh?'

'Maybe Westerland hypnotized us into thinking I was an elephant.'

'How could he hypnotize me? I haven't seen him for years.'

'He could hypnotize you and then make you forget you were.'

'Dan,' said Max, 'relax. After midnight if we're still in here we can think up excuses.'

'How do we know he won't harm Anne before midnight?'

'We don't.'

'Let's try to break out now.'

Max lit a match and stood up. 'I don't think these barrel staves will do it. See anything else?'

'Legs off this bench. We can unscrew them and bang the door down.'

They got the wooden legs loose and taking one each began hammering at the bolt with them.

After a few minutes a voice echoed in. 'Stop that ruckus.'

'The hell with you,' said Dan.

'Wait now,' said Westerland's voice. 'You can't break down the door. And even if you could Lloyd would shoot you. I'm sending him down to sit guard. Last night at Playland he won four Betty Boop dolls at the shooting gallery. Be rational.'

'How come we can hear you?'

'I'm talking through an air vent.'

'Where's Anne?' shouted Dan.

'Still in a trance. If you behave I may let her bark for you before we leave.'

'You louse.'

Max found Dan in the dark and caught his arm. 'Take it easy.' Raising his voice he said, 'Westerland, how long do we stay down here?'

'Well, my ex-wife will be in Rome until next April. I hope to have a plan worked out by then. At the moment, however, I can't spare the time. I have to get ready for the party.'

'What party?'

'The New Year's Eve party at the Leversons'. It's the one where Anne Clemens will drink too much.'

'What?'

'She'll drink too much and get the idea she's an acrobat. She'll borrow a car and drive to the Golden Gate Bridge. While trying out her act on the top rail she'll discover she's not an acrobat at all and actually has a severe dread of heights. When I hear about it I'll still be at the Leversons' party. I'll be saddened that she was able to see so little of the New Year.'

'You can't make her do that. Hypnotism doesn't work that way.'

'That's what you say now, Padgett. In the morning I'll have Lloyd slip the papers under the door.'

The pipe stopped talking.

Dan slammed his fist into the cement wall. 'He can't do it.'

'Who are the Leversons?'

Dan was silent for a moment. 'Leverson. Joe and Jackie. Isn't that the art director at BBDO? He and his wife live over here. Just up from Sally Stanford's restaurant. It could be them.'

'It's a long way to midnight,' said Max. 'But I have a feeling we'll make it.'

'We have to save Anne,' said Dan, 'and there doesn't seem to be anything to do but wait.'

'What's the damn time, Max?'
'Six thirty.'

'Must be nearly eight by now.'
'Seven fifteen.'
'I think I still hear them up there.'

'Now?'
'Little after nine.'

'Only ten? Is that watch going?'
'Yeah, it's ticking.'

'Eleven yet, Max?'
'In five minutes.'

'They've gone, I'm sure.'

'Relax.'

'Look,' said Dan, when Max told him it was a quarter to twelve, 'I don't want to step on you if I change.'

'I'll duck down on the floor by your feet. Your present feet. Then when you've changed I should be under your stomach.'

'Okay. After I do you hop on my back.'

At five to twelve Max sat down on the stone floor. 'Happy New Year.'

Dan's feet shuffled, moved further apart. 'My stomach is starting to itch.'

Max ducked a little. In the darkness a darker shadow seemed to grow overhead. 'Dan?'

'I did it, Max.' Dan laughed. 'I did it right on time.'

Max edged up and climbed on top of the elephant. 'I'm aboard.'

'Hang on. I'm going to push the door with my head.'

Max hung on and waited. The door creaked and began to give.

'Watch it, you guys!' shouted Lloyd from outside.

'Trumpet at him,' said Max.

'Good idea.' Dan gave a violent angry elephant roar.

'Jesus!' Lloyd said.

The door exploded out and Dan's trunk slapped Lloyd into the side of the furnace. His gun sailed into a clothes basket. Max jumped down and retrieved it.

'Go away,' he said to Lloyd.

Lloyd blew his nose. 'What kind of prank is this?'

'If he doesn't go,' said Max, 'trample him.'

'Let's trample him no matter what,' said Dan.

Lloyd left.

'Hell,' said Dan. 'How do I get up those stairs?'

'You don't,' said Max, pointing. 'See there, behind that stack of papers. A door. I'll see if it's open.'

'Who cares. I'll push it open.'

'Okay. I'll go find a phone book and look up Leversons. Meet you in the patio.'

Dan trumpeted and Max ran up the narrow wooden stairs.

The elephant careened down the grassy hillside. All around now New Year's horns were sounding.

'Only two Leversons, huh?' Dan asked again.

'It's most likely the art director. He's nearest the bridge.'

They came out on Bridgeway, which ran along the water.

Dan trumpeted cars and people out of the way and Max ducked down, holding onto the big elephant ears.

They turned as the road curved and headed them for the Leverson home. 'It better be this one,' Dan said.

The old two story house was filled with lighted windows, the windows spotted with people. 'A party sure enough,' said Max.

In the long twisted driveway a motor started. 'A car,' said Dan, running up the gravel.

Max jumped free as Dan made himself a road block in the driveway.

Red tail lights tinted the exhaust of a small grey Jaguar convertible. Max ran to the car. Anne Clemens jerked the wheel and spun it. Max dived over the back of the car and, teetering on his stomach, jerked the ignition key off and out. Anne kept turning the wheel.

Max caught her by the shoulders, swung around off the car and pulled her up so that she was now kneeling in the driver's seat.

The girl shook her head twice, looking beyond Max.

He got the door open and helped her out. The gravel seemed to slide away from them in all directions.

'Duck,' yelled Dan, still an elephant.

Max didn't turn. He dropped, pulling the girl with him.

A shot smashed a cobweb pattern across the windshield.

'You've spoiled it for sure,' cried Westerland. 'You and your silly damn elephant have spoiled my plan for sure.'

The parking area lights were on and a circle of people was forming behind Westerland. He was standing twenty feet away from Max and Anne.

Then he fell over as Dan's trunk flipped his gun away from him. Dan caught up the fallen animator and shook him.

Max got Anne to her feet and held onto her. 'Bring her out of this, Westerland.'

'In a pig's valise.'

Dan tossed him up and caught him.

'Come on.'

'Since you're so belligerent,' said Westerland. 'Dangle me closer to her.'

Max had Lloyd's gun in his coat pocket. He took it out now and pointed it up at the swinging Westerland. 'No wise stuff.'

Westerland snapped his fingers near Anne's pale face.

She shivered once and fell against Max. He put his arms under hers and held her.

Dan suddenly dropped Westerland and, trumpeting once at the silent guests, galloped away into the night.

As his trumpet faded a siren filled the night.

'Real detectives,' said Max.

Both Anne and Westerland were out. The guests were too far away to hear him.

A bush crackled behind him and Max turned his head.

Dan, himself again, came up to them. 'Would it be okay if I held Anne?'

Max carefully transferred her. 'She should be fine when she comes to.'

'What'll we tell the law?'

'The truth. Except for the elephant.'

'How'd we get from his place here?'

'My car wouldn't start. We figured he'd tampered with it. We hailed a passing motorist who dropped us here.'

'People saw the elephant.'

'It escaped from a zoo.'

'What zoo?'

'Look,' said Max, dropping the gun back into his pocket, 'don't be so practical about this. We don't have to explain it. Okay?'

'Okay. Thanks, Max.'

Max lit a cigarette.

'I changed back in only an hour. I don't think it will happen again, Max. Do you?'

'If it would make you feel any better I'll spend the night before Lincoln's Birthday with you and Anne.'

'How about Ground Hog's Day?'

'How about what?' said Anne. She looked up at Dan. 'Dan? What is it?'

'Nothing much. A little trouble with Westerland. I'll explain.'

Max nodded at them and went up the driveway to meet the approaching police. Somewhere in the night a final New Year's horn sounded.

DOWNTOWN

Thomas M. Disch

1. The House of Buckwheat

Berna Neville came on the floor at eleven, after the breakfast rush, and left at seven-thirty, when the House of Buckwheat closed. It might as well have closed after lunch, the afternoon business was so thin, but all the downtown stores were obliged to subscribe to the illusion that their long decline had reached its nadir and that St. Paul was undergoing a renaissance. Berna didn't know anyone who really believed this, even the owner of the House of Buckwheat, who cleaned out most of the bills from the register promptly at two-thirty and disappeared for the day, just in time to miss the desolation of the moment, around three, when the Muzak suddenly became not only audible but oppressive in its relentless peppiness. Fifteen minutes might go by at a stretch without anyone spinning the revolving door. The tips didn't amount to much, but Berna lived frugally and could get by well enough on just her salary. At forty-six she didn't have the stamina for real waitressing, which was the reason she'd left the job at the hotel—aside from the fact that she could no longer abide the regular customers, bigwigs from the Chamber of Commerce and the State Capitol, who were loud, abusive, and tight-fisted. At least the people who came into the House of Buckwheat didn't think they could treat you like a dog, expecting you to come at the snap of their fingers. In any case, rumor had it that the hotel would be closing soon. Maybe someday they'd just decide to shut down the entire downtown area.

Berna first became aware of the woman in the green pantsuit during the quietest stretch of a Tuesday afternoon in April. Maybe she had come in other times earlier, but if so Berna hadn't taken her in. The detail that had made her notice the woman that day, apart from her being the only customer she had, was the fact of her coming in without a coat so early in the year—nothing but the pantsuit over a thin blouse. Berna hadn't thought it was that warm yet. She was about the same age as Berna, or a little older, with her hair knotted up into a bun that looked efficient but not quite tidy. She ordered the House of Buckwheat's basic offering, three pancakes, butter and syrup, $1.25, which included all the coffee you wanted from the Thermos jug on the table. This in itself seemed strange: usually a new customer would indulge in something more exotic—waffles or blueberry pancakes. It was generally the customers who came in every single day (and were beyond trying to pretend that pancakes were some kind of holiday) who ordered the place's unmodified Number One platter—'Stack one!' —customers like the colored man who handled the ticket booth at the porno movie house around the corner on Wabasha, or the nurse from St. Luke's who came in every Wednesday and left a fifty-cent tip.

As it developed, the woman in the pantsuit became another of these regulars, and the only one who put in her appearance during the deadest hour of the afternoon. She always sat at the same table, away from the windows and out of sight of the cashier. She ordered her pancakes after consulting the menu Berna brought her, and ate them one at a time, carefully apportioning the two butter pats among them. When she was done she would take a pack of cigarettes from her purse (a nice purse of wrinkled brown leather) and smoke a cigarette over her second cup of coffee. She never looked around at the other people in the restaurant, and she never read a book or a newspaper. She didn't tip.

Ordinarily Berna would have resented that, but something about the woman made that inappropriate. How could you grudge a dime from someone who evidently had so little herself, who never wore anything but that same pantsuit day after day, its green as basic as the green in a box of color crayons, with the same off-white blouse, the same scuffed low heels? How could you feel anything but sorry? She was so thin, and so pale, and her hands were so fumbly that almost every time she left the booth there'd be a small puddle of coffee to wipe off the Formica. She never acknowledged Berna as a familiar daily presence, and Berna, who had to wear a button on her uniform saying, 'Hi! My name is Berna,' regarded this as a civility rather than as coldness. Having to act friendly with customers was a strain she was glad to be spared. And anyhow Berna had a feeling that there was some connection between herself and the woman that went deeper than hellos and talk about the weather. But it was just a feeling, and Berna didn't have much use for feelings.

Even so, toward the end of May, Berna began to be concerned for the woman. From her station near the service pass-through to the kitchen she could watch the woman eating her three pancakes with such stolid, mechanical chewing and swallowing, chewing and swallowing, that Berna could tell that the act involved neither appetite nor pleasure but only the duty of supplying her body with calories. Berna felt similarly toward the process of eating, but for that very reason she ate a rational, balanced diet. She never touched the junk they served at the House of Buckwheat (even the bacon was not to be trusted, because of its nitrates), and she wanted to convey to the woman she served that *she* should not either. Could it be that this meal at three o'clock was the *only* meal the woman ate each day? Could she be that poor? Or that foolish? No one could stay healthy long on a diet of sugar, starch, and caffeine. It amounted to suicide. Did she know what she was doing? Indeed, *was* that what she was doing——or did the pancakes just represent, as they did for most of the House of Buckwheat's afternoon customers, an extra midday dessert? Berna didn't dare approach the woman and ask, and there was no other way to find out short of hiring detectives or acting in that capacity herself, which she never could have done. All she could do, and all she did, was to take the woman's order and bring her her pancakes and leave her a check for $1.25.

But she couldn't keep from wondering, and wondering led to noticing of a more particular order than Berna customarily was given to. She noticed that the woman's hair was very infrequently shampooed, and then not quite sufficiently. Similarly, her blouse went for weeks at a time without laundering. Berna noticed that the woman's hands seemed permanently soiled with a light pumice of ash, the dribbling of her cigarettes. She noticed that the seam down the side of her jacket had come unraveled, leaving a three-inch gap that winked open and shut as the woman lifted and lowered her fork, or her coffee cup, or her cigarette. She noticed the smell she gave off, a sour pungency unlike any other human smell that Berna knew.

Where would it stop? she wondered. At what point would the woman's dereliction become so pronounced that she would not be allowed into the restaurant? (For the owner was insistent that the House of Buckwheat was not going to become a haven for undesirables, whatever might happen to the rest of downtown St.

Paul.) Berna couldn't bear such thoughts. She had managed, over the last many and painful years, to establish a day-to-day routine that protected her from emotional disequilibriums. In a crisis she could get Valium. On the whole it was a life she hated, but at least she was able to keep her sanity. She didn't want this stranger coming in every afternoon and upsetting her? At least she might have sat at one of the other waitress's tables sometimes.

With this in mind Berna had once or twice kept the woman waiting, menuless, for inexcusable lengths of time, but the woman had just sat in the booth, seeming not to take offense, showing no signs of impatience. Eventually Berna had to go over and take her order for three pancakes, butter, and syrup. She always mentioned the butter and syrup, as though Berna might conceivably forget to include them in the order.

Sometimes she was able to persuade herself that she was overracting to the situation, that the woman wore this single change of clothing not from destitution but as a kind of badge of defiance (as Berna felt she wore the House of Buckwheat's uniform of black Dacron), a declaration that she would conceal her everyday despair no more than was absolutely required of her. But each day this became harder to believe, and Berna came round at last to the idea that the woman, simply, was dying, or rather was waiting for death to take hold.

Berna never discussed the woman's plight with the other waitresses, though ordinarily they all came to know each other's regular customers and to speculate more or less freely as to where they worked and how they lived. As far as she could tell they weren't even aware of the woman (who did not act in any way that would have drawn attention to herself). Even the cashier who took her money each day (always the exact amount in change, a stack of five quarters, never a bill) never accorded her any sign of special recognition, as she did to the other regulars. But then neither did Berna. It was as though the woman was able to compel whomever she dealt with to mimic her own subdued and denatured plausibility.

In July the summer's first full-scale heat wave settled over St. Paul, and business at the House of Buckwheat slackened to a trickle even at lunchtime. No one wants pancakes, in whatever combination with eggs, bacon, ice cream or fruit sauce, once the temperature has climbed above ninety. The younger and less able of the other two afternoon waitresses was laid off, and Berna became responsible for the two window tables to the left of the cash register. But even these tables were seldom occupied.

On the Friday of the second week of the heat wave, the woman came in as usual to order her invariable three pancakes, butter, and syrup, but when Berna brought them to her she didn't seem to notice. She sat there touching the edge of the wood-patterned Formica with her fingertips for so long that Berna considered going back to the booth and asking if something was wrong with the order. Then the woman slid sideways into the corner of the padded seat—not suddenly, or even alarmingly, but almost as though she'd fallen asleep. Her eyes closed and her mouth dropped open. Her arms hung limp at her sides.

No one else had noticed. The cashier and the other waitresses were taking a coffee break at the window table on the far side of the register. The Muzak was playing a xylophone rendition of 'The Fool on the Hill.'

Berna was sure the woman was dead, but she could not bring herself to go over to the booth and make certain. She would have had to touch the woman, to try and rouse her on the assumption that she had only fainted, which was entirely possible in such weather. Berna couldn't think which would be worse, knowing positively that she was dead or seeing her eyes opening, her lips forming some confused apology. Berna knew, in any case, that the woman *was* dead, so there was no point in going through the ordeal. She refused to.

Instead she went back, through the kitchen, to the windowless changing room, changed out of her uniform, and left the restaurant by the side door. She didn't excuse or explain her departure to anyone, even the cook, who was watching.

2. Butterworth's

Once on the street, in that muggy heat, Berna realized there was nowhere she could go. She turned east so as to avoid passing in front of the restaurant windows, and when she came to the entrance to Butterworth's she went inside for the sake of the air-conditioning. The department store was almost as deserted as the House of Buckwheat had been. A girl in heavy eye makeup with bruises painted on her cheekbones stood, idly glowering, before a display of L'Air du Temps.

Berna hurried through Cosmetics and past counters draped with costume jewelry. In her haste she almost knocked over a bin of purses on sale for $24.95. Each of the purses in the bin was identical to the purse of wrinkled brown leather carried by the woman in the green pantsuit.

A bell rang and a disembodied voice announced the closing of the store in another fifteen minutes. The voice asked people to take their purchases to a cashier.

Berna got on the Up escalator and awaited the moment, so lovely and so fleeting, when she would rise above all the counters and partitions and could look out across the whole sales floor as though from a low-flying helicopter. The moment came and went. On 2 she walked quickly through Menswear and past the trellised entrance to Junior Miss, festooned this month with swimsuits and beach toys, to the unencumbered expanse of Sportswear and Casuals. For some reason there was never any sales help in evidence in Sportswear and Casuals. For that reason it was Berna's favorite department, and she had come here often to enjoy at its full the store's sense of peace and protectiveness.

She ran her hand luxuriously along a rack of separates, all the same shimmery polyester-jersey blend. The prettiest of the lot was a deep plum color, though there was also a cream-colored blouse nearly as nice. Not that it mattered—Berna would never have bought such a blouse for herself. To have bought anything the store offered would have seemed somehow to diminish its dignity. Butterworth's was the oldest department store in St. Paul and beginning to show its years, but it was still the most respectable environment Berna knew of. You always felt *safe* in Butterworth's, partly because things were so expensive, partly because its few customers tended to be Berna's age or older. You never saw the riffraff here that sometimes came to the House of Buckwheat.

Another bell rang, and Berna retreated from the threat of eviction by fleeing two floors higher to Furniture. In past years Butterworth's had had six sales floors, but competition with the new St. Paul branch of Dayton's and the general decline of the downtown had made retrenchment necessary, and 4 was now the highest sales floor.

It was also the most beautiful, because the most unchanging. Berna always felt on 4 as though she'd returned to some long-forgotten family home. Here were the same ranks and files of armchairs, rockers, and recliners in Herculon and flowering chintz; the same array of sofas, coffee tables, and gigantic ceramic lamps; the same shining expanse of mahogany veneer and oak that had been here before Christmas, that would be here always. Berna negotiated the sea of tables, sideboards and wardrobes and came to the row of little rooms that ringed the elevator bank. Each little alcove featured a different style or texture. Here was a bedroom done all in butcher block, where large cubes of foam rubber were covered with a fabric their tags declared to be Pecan Illusion. In another alcove an eye-blinding breakfast nook had been created, all in white. In the next a single bookcase, innocent of books, loomed over an upright piano. The piano's cover was lowered chastely over the keyboard and supported a discreet cardboard sign:

> Please refrain from
> playing pianos and
> organs.
> Our sales staff will
> be happy to assist you.

'Miss Neville?' a voice asked—the same voice, though now unamplified, that had announced the closing of the store. She turned round to confront the floor manager, as the badge on the breast pocket of his gray pinstripe suit proclaimed him. None of his other features—the neatly trimmed hair, the eyes shadowed by the frames of his glasses, the pleasant but perfunctory smile—told anything more of him than his badge.

'Yes?' she said, deferring at once to his authority, not questioning that he should know her name.

'Would you follow me, please?'

He led her along a dim-lighted corridor of blind windows displaying various styles of curtains and draperies. At the end of the corridor was a narrow escalator with wooden treads barred by a small chain. The floor manager removed the chain and began climbing the steps of the motionless escalator. Berna hesitated before following him to the higher floor, but for a moment only.

Berna, if she had thought about it, would have expected 5 to be a jumble of stacked boxes and naked, dusty mannequins, but it presented, on the contrary, an even cheerier and more homelike atmosphere than the floor below, though its arrangement was, at first glance, not so orderly. A four-poster bed loomed up from a welter of enormous African Baskets. A long modular couch wound riverlike past console TVs and waterfall racks of carpet samples, past wooden cradles filled with magazines and a sideboard bustling with china figurines, coming to rest at last beside an oak rolltop desk, sale-priced for $959.95.

The floor manager pulled up a rush-bottomed chair to the desk, one of a set of four that sold for $125, and gestured to Berna to be seated in another.

'Well, this is where we live.'

'I beg your pardon,' said Berna, unconsciously imitating the floor manager's formal manner.

'This is where we live,' he repeated a little impatiently. 'Here and on 6.'

Berna looked about the sprawling space of the abandoned sales floor for some clue to the floor manager's riddle.

'At first it may seem . . . oh, not very private. But each of us has his or her own *private* space tucked away out of sight in addition to the sales floor proper. And at night, of course, we have the run of the store. Though there especially we must exercise discretion.'

'You mean *all* of the people who work at Butterworth's . . . ?'

The floor manager allowed himself a small laugh. 'Goodness no, Miss Neville. Most of the employees have no idea, would even say it were impossible. Only a select few—myself, the two night watchmen, Mr. Richardson, who (I should warn you) has something of a drinking problem, and a number of ladies, like yourself and Joan, who can be trusted to, how shall I say, live quietly.'

'Joan?'

'That's to say, Miss Emering. Among ourselves we tend to be informal. Joan, of course, is a special case, having lived here longest. She'd been in charge of Toy World—oh, for years and years—but when Toy World was moved to the basement and the upper floors were closed, Miss Emering was terminated. Only a few months short of her retirement.' He swiveled his head once to the left and once to the right in stiff-necked reprobation.

'Miss Emering,' he continued, 'had few resources. She lived in a residence hotel and spent her entire salary on keeping herself looking smart. One must, you know, in this business, take great care of one's *appearance*.'

Berna nodded.

'So what was to be done? She'd been thrown virtually into the streets. She was not in the best health (though she never complained). She was too old to find other employment. Toys had been her entire life. Something had to be done—and here, in the very building that was her second home, were two entire floors standing empty.'

'So she moved here?'

'Would you like to meet her?' he asked in a bright salesman-like tone that could only be answered in the affirmative. He pushed his chair back and rose, offering his hand to Berna. She followed him back along the stream of the modular sofa and around a stack of imported goatskin accent rugs and through a dense cluster of lawn furniture. There the sales floor angled round the elevator bank to become, as on the floor below, a concourse of individual rooms.

In the first of these rooms, a kind of boudoir, or bedless bedroom, the woman in the green pantsuit stood beside the gauzy curtains covering a cardboard window. She seemed, in the dim light of the alcove, much younger, even, in a subdued way, attractive.

'Miss Emering,' said the floor manager, 'this is Miss Neville. Miss Neville may be joining us.'

Miss Emering smiled at Berna. 'We've met,' she said. Her voice seemed completely different than it had in the House of Buckwheat when she would give her order—lower, clearer, authoritative. 'But we've never gotten to know each other, really. Though I knew, without our ever speaking, that you were meant to be one of us. Isn't that strange? I knew.'

'Well, if you two ladies will excuse me . . . ' said the floor manager, backing off into the shadows.

When he was gone, Miss Emering asked Berna if she smoked. She said she didn't. 'You'll excuse me if I do,' said Miss Emering and took a package of cigarettes from her purse, which lay on the black glass surface of a vanity table.

'I thought. . . . ' Berna began.

'Yes?' said Miss Emering, lifting one eyebrow ironically as she touched the tip of her cigarette with the lighter's flame.

But Berna could not bring herself to say that she had thought Miss Emering was dead. It would have seemed both ridiculous and impolite. So instead she asked: 'How did you know I'd come here?'

Miss Emering considered this, and asked in turn, 'Why *did* you?'

'For no reason. It was . . . instinctive. I've always *liked* it here. . . . '

Miss Emering nodded. 'Yes, there's something quite special about Butterworth's. We all feel that.'

'There's no one who'll miss me,' Berna declared, startling herself by her own boldness. 'No one at all, out there. And I won't miss them!'

Without really laughing, Miss Emering made a face expressive of laughter. 'Look,' she said, lifting her hand, 'I have something here that's just for you.'

She went to the rosewood armoire that stood in the corner and opened it. On the back of the door was a mirror, and inside the armoire, on a hanger, was the blouse with the ruffled collar.

'Do you like it?'

'It's beautiful.'

'Let me,' said Miss Emering, taking the blouse from the armoire and undoing its mother-of-pearl buttons.

Berna undid her blouse and let it slip to the floor. She turned her back to Miss Emering and lifted her arms. Miss Emering slipped the blouse over her arms and onto her shoulders in a single deft motion. Then, smiling, she adjusted the door of the armoire so that Berna could see herself in its mirror, and Berna, returning her smile—vacuous, melancholy, the immemorial smile of all mannequins—raised her delicately jointed fingers to touch the topmost button of the plum-colored blouse, amazed by her own changeless beauty.

MAN OVERBOARD

John Collier

Glenway Morgan Abbott had the sort of face that is associated with New England by those who like New England. It was so boney, so toothy even, so modest, so extremely serious and so nearly flinchingly unflinching, that one hardly noticed that he was actually a very good-looking man.

He also had the yacht *Zenobia*, which was handsome enough to take one's breath away at the very first glance; it showed its seriousness only on a closer inspection. Once in a very great while, I used to go on a long cruise with Glenway. I was his best, and his only intimate, friend.

Those who have seen the *Zenobia*, or seen even its picture in books on sailing, may be impolite enough to wonder how I came to be so specially friendly with the owner of a three-masted schooner which is certainly among the dozen, perhaps among the half dozen, most famous of the great yachts of the world.

Such people should realize that, though I may lack wealth and grace and charm, I do so in a special and superior way. Moreover, in spite of the glorious *Zenobia* and the impressive associations of his name, Glenway's way of life was far from being sophisticated or luxurious. His income, though still very large, was only just large enough to pay for her enormous upkeep and her numerous crew. When he wanted to get a piece of research done, he had to dip into his capital.

The fact is, Glenway had at one time been married, and to a film star, and in highly romantic circumstances. As if this wasn't enough, he had at once got divorced. The star in question was Thora Vyborg, whose beauty and personality are among the legends, or the myths, of our time. All this happened before I met him, but I had gathered, though not from Glenway, that the divorce had been distinguished by a settlement such as can only result from the cruellest heartbreak, the bitterest injury and the most efficient lawyers on the one side, and honest eyes and rather prominent front teeth on the other.

Therefore if the word yacht suggests music, ladies, awnings, white-jacketed stewards, caviar and champagne, the suggestion is altogether misleading. The only music was the wind in the rigging; there were no ladies; the solitary steward wore no jacket, and the crew wore no shirts either. They were all natives of different parts of the Pacific with different complexions and different tongues. The language used on board was a sort of sub-basic English, adequate for work, expressive in song, but not very suitable for conversation. Glenway might have had an American or a British captain or mate; however, he did not.

Anyway, every man on board knew his job. It was a pity that the cook's job was all too often only the opening of cans of frankfurters or baked beans. This was not so much due to New English frugality as to that gastronomical absent-mindedness which is so often found linked with honesty, teeth and devotion to a cause.

Glenway was devoted to a cause, and so was the *Zenobia*. All these great yachts are, of course, capable of ocean cruising; this one was used for it, and for nothing else at all. She was used and hard-used, and, though as clean as a pin, she was by no means as shiny. On the horizon, she looked like a cloud; at her mooring like a swan to the poetically minded, or to the materialistic, like a floating palace. But as soon as you stepped aboard she had more the appearance of something sent out by an oceanographical institute. All manner of oddly shaped nets and trawls and scoops were hung, or spread or stowed around her deck. On either side of the foremast there were two objects on pedestals, shoulder high, and made of that ugly, grey, rust-resisting alloy which was used everywhere on this boat in place of brass or chromium. These objects were not ventilators. They had rotating tops; these tops were hooded or cowled, or whatever you'd call it, and closely shuttered against the salty spray. If you turned one of the tops towards you, and slid open the shutter, and looked inside, you would find yourself being looked back at, quietly, by the darkly gleaming eye of a movie camera.

Up in the bow there was a bulky object lashed down under quickly removable canvas. This was a searchlight. Long chests, seated high, almost as high as the low gunwale into which they were built, contained rockets and flares. Glenway was hoping to photograph something which he believed might be nocturnal in its habits. He thought that otherwise, being a very large, noticeable creature, and being a reptile, and breathing air, it would have been seen more often by daylight.

Glenway, in a word, was looking for the sea-serpent. As he detested the sensational newspaper stories and the tiresome jokes associated with the term, he preferred to think of it as a *large marine saurian*. For short, we called it, not inaptly, *it*.

People all over the Pacific knew of Glenway's quest. They were, though tactful about it, rather too obviously so. Something about Glenway caused them to refrain from guffaws; but they put on leaky masks of politeness over their grins, or, if they took the matter seriously, they seriously sought to reclaim him from his folly. Either way, they made it all too clear that they thought him a crank and perhaps a zany because he believed in such a creature. For this reason he avoided ports as far as possible, and when taking in supplies or docked for overhaul he avoided the society of his kind. Now it so happens that, though I am of sceptical nature in most matters, I am strongly inclined to suspend disbelief when it comes to a large marine saurian. Without at least the possibility of such a creature, it seems to me that the world would be a poor and a narrow place. Glenway perceived this at our very first meeting, and it was the reason for at least the beginning of our friendship. I was forced to tell him I thought the chances were a million to one against him ever seeing his quarry, and I thought he was crazy to waste his time and his lovely money on hunting for it. This didn't worry him in the least.

'I shall find it sooner or later,' said he, when first we debated the question, 'because I know where to look.'

His theory was a simple one, and made sense up to a point. If you know how an animal is constructed you can deduce a great deal as to how it lives, and especially as to what it lives on. When you know what it eats, and where that particular food abounds, you have already a very good clue as to where to look for it.

Glenway had taken all the best authenticated reports, and he had an outline drawn up from each of them. Almost all these reports, from whatever corner of the world they may come, describe more or less the same sort of creature, so he had no trouble in getting a composite picture made by an expert hand. This, of course, showed a reptile of the plesiosaur type, but very much larger than any of the fossil plesiosaurs, being only a few inches under eighty feet in length. But here there was a snag.

Glenway had every reason to know what each extra foot on the length of a yacht adds to its maintenance bills, and he knew that an eighty foot plesiosaur is not a practicable proposition. It was not hard to calculate what its weight would be, or the size of its bite, or how large a fish could pass down its narrow gullet. 'It would spend more energy just picking up fish of that size one by one,' said Glenway, 'than it would gain by eating them. Also, schools of herrings, mackerel, haddock and so forth are mostly found in coastal waters, and fishermen have been after them by day and by night ever since fishermen existed. An airbreathing creature has to show itself on the surface fairly often; if it followed fish of that sort it would be as familiar to us as the barking shark. And finally, it would be extinct, because with those jaws it couldn't defend itself against killer whales, or threshers, and certainly not against the big sharks of the late Pleistocene.'

'Glenway, if all this is correct, you've slain your own goddam Jabberwock.'

'I was afraid I had,' said he. 'It depressed the hell out of me. But one day it struck me that people who see something very surprising, in bad visibility and so forth, will naturally tend to exaggerate the most surprising aspect of whatever it is they see. Thus an astonishingly long, snakey neck will look longer and snakier than it actually is, a small head smaller, and so forth. So I had a couple of young chaps from uncle Fred's Institute of Industrial Psychology do a series of tests. They found a deviation running up to about twenty five percent. Then I told them what I wanted it for, and asked them to modify this outline accordingly. We got this.' He handed me a second sheet. 'We can take it this is what was actually seen.'

'Why, this damned thing's only sixty feet long!' said I rather discontentedly. 'It seems to me you're correcting eye-witness reports on pure speculation.'

'No, I'm not,' said he. 'I double-checked it. I hired a reptile man and an icthyologist, and I asked them to work out what the nearest thing to a sixty-foot plesiosaur would be like if it were to be a practical proposition in terms of food, energy, defence and all that. They came up with two or three alternatives; the one that interested me was this.' He pulled out a third outline. 'If you put this on top of the psychologists' version,' said he, 'you'll see they correspond in everything essential.'

'All the same, if I'm going to believe in a large marine saurian, I'd rather have an eighty footer.'

'This one weighs more than an eighty footer,' said Glenway, 'and he's probably ten times as powerful. Those jaws have a bite of over three feet. This fellow could swallow a barracuda at a gulp. He might have to make two snaps at a porpoise. He'll follow schools of tuna, albacore, any sort of fish ranging from fifty to a hundred and fifty pounds. Not cod, of course.'

'And why not cod?'

'Fishermen. He'd have been seen.'

'Oh!'

'So evidently he doesn't follow cod.'

'And evidently you can sweat a positive out of a couple of demolished negatives. Even so, it may make some sort of sense.'

Glenway accepted this, which at least was better than he got from other people. He eagerly showed me innumerable charts he had drawn up, and had amended by his own observation. These showed the seasonal movements of deep sea fish in the east Pacific, and where these movements weren't known he had what data there was on the smaller fish that the larger ones preyed on. He went on down through the food chains, and down to plankton drifts and current temperatures and so forth, and with all these, modified by all sorts of other factors, he had marked out a great oval, with dates put in here and there, which tilted through those immense solitudes of ocean which stretch from the coast of Chili up to the Aleutians.

This was his beat, and two or three times I sailed it with him. There were almost no islands, almost no shipping lanes. I used to take a regular spell in the crow's nest; two hours in the morning and two more in the late afternoon. You can't sit day after day looking for something without an admission, deep in your mind, of the possibility of seeing it. Anyway, I was extremely fond of Glenway, and it would have given me great pleasure to have been the one who sighted his saurian for him somewhere far out on the flat green or the rolling blue. The very wish lent a sinewy twist to every water-logged palm trunk that drifted across our bows, and every distant dolphin leap offered the arc of a black, wet and leathery neck.

At the first sight of such things, my hand, more wishful even than my thoughts, would move towards the red button on the rail of the crow's nest. This, like another in the bow, and a third by the wheel, was connected with a loud buzzer in Glenway's cabin. However, the buzzer remained silent; the immense horizon, day after day, was empty.

Glenway was an excellent navigator. One morning when I was aloft he called up to ask if I could see anything ahead. I told him there was nothing, but I had no sooner raised my glasses again than I discerned a thickening, a long hump gathering itself in the infinitely faint pencil line that marked the juncture of sky and sea. 'There's something. It's land! Land ahead!'

'That's Paumoy.'

He had not bothered to mention that he was going to touch at Paumoy, the main island of an isolated group north-east of the Marquesas. I had heard of the place; there were eight or ten Americans there, and someone had said that since the war they almost never got their mail. Glenway's boat took him within fifty miles of the island, and he now told me he had agreed to touch there as he passed. Sensitive as he was to crude jokes about the sea serpent, he was still a New Englander, and he felt that people should have their mail.

The island, as we drew nearer, revealed itself as several miles of whale-back, covered with that hot froth of green which suggests coconut palms and boredom. I put down the light binoculars I was using and took up the telescope, which had a much greater range. I could see the harbour, the white bungalows spaced out around it, and I could even see the people quite clearly. Before long I saw a man catch sight of the yacht. He stared under his hand, and waved and pointed; another man came out of a bungalow with a pair of glasses. I saw the two of them go off at a run to where a jeep was standing. The jeep crawled off round the harbour, stopped at another bungalow; someone got out, someone got in. The jeep moved off again, disappeared into a grove, came out on the other side, and went toiling up a little thread-like track until it went out of sight over the ridge.

By this time other people on the shore level had turned out to look at us. They had plenty of time to do so, for the breeze fell off almost to nothing as we stood in towards the island. It was already late afternoon when the *Zenobia*, with every sail set, floated as softly as an enormous thistledown to her anchorage in the harbour of Paumoy.

'What a dreary-looking dump!' I said. 'What do they do here? Copra?'

'That, and shell. One fellow dries a sort of sea-slug and sells it to Chinese dealers all over the world. There was a Gauguin from San Francisco, but he didn't stay very long.'

'You'd think they'd cut each other's throats out of sheer boredom.'

'Well, they play poker every night of their lives, and I guess they've developed a technique of not getting on each other's nerves.'

'They must need it.' There seemed to be nothing on the island but coconut palms, which I don't like, and the blistering bungalows, all of which might have been prefabricated by the same mail-order house. What I had taken from a greater distance to be banks of vari-coloured flowers beside the bungalows, were now recognizable as heaps of tin cans, some rusty, some with their labels still on.

But I had no more time to look about me; we were on the quay, and being greeted by men in shorts and old-fashioned sun helmets, and the greeting was hearty.

'Now listen to me,' said Victor Brewer, 'we've got two new guys here who've been in Java. We've had them working like dogs ever since we sighted you, fixing a *rikstafel*. So you've got to stay to dinner. Or those guys are going to be hurt. Hell, you're not going to insult a couple of fellows who are slaving over a hot stove, fixing you a dinner.'

Glenway wanted nothing but to pick up the outgoing mail bag and be gone. On the other hand he hated the idea of hurting anyone. He looked at me as if in the faint hope that I might step in and do it for him. It was at such moments, very rare with Glenway, that I felt Fitzgerald was right about the rich being different, or half right, or a quarter right, and the thought of this, and the thought of the *rikstafel*, prevented me from obliging him. Instead, I pointed out there'd probably be no wind till nightfall, so we'd be losing hardly any time. Glenway at once surrendered, and we settled down to drinks and chat.

Listening to the chat, I remembered Glenway's remark about the technique of not getting on each other's nerves. It seemed to me that this technique was being exercised, and especially for Glenway's benefit. At the end of almost every remark our hosts made I felt myself dropping in the air pocket of a pulled punch; I experienced that disconcerting absence of impact which is the concomitant of velvet paws. It was clear they knew what Glenway was after, and they even referred to it, but with such collective tact that if one of them seemed likely to dwell on it for more than a few seconds he would be steam-rolled out of the conversation, generally by Mr. Brewer. It was he who asked, very casually, when we had been sitting some time at dinner, if Glenway was sailing the same course as usual; if he was going to pass, give or take a hundred miles, the northern extremity of Japan.

Glenway having replied that he always followed the same course: 'You know,' said Vic Brewer, letting the words fall as casually as one lets fall the poker chips when the hands are high and the stakes are higher, 'You know, you could do the hell of a good turn to a guy. If you felt like it, that is.'

'What sort of a turn?' asked Glenway. 'And which guy?'

'You don't know him,' said the man on Brewer's left. 'He's a fellow called Geisecker. He's Charlie's brother-in-law's brother-in-law, if you can work that one out.'

'He dropped in here to say hello,' said the next man. 'He came on the copra boat and he didn't know the mailboat doesn't call any more. So he's stuck.'

'The point is, this poor guy is going to be in big trouble if he doesn't get to Tokyo in the next few weeks.'

'When you get up in those latitudes you're certain to sight some boat or other bound for Japan.'

'Any little tramp; a crab fisher or anything. He'll be tickled to death.'

They spoke one after another all the way round the table, and remembering that Glenway had said they played poker every night of their lives, I was irresistibly reminded of the process of doubling up.

'We hate to see him go,' said Brewer, collecting the whole matter into his hands with the genial authority of the dealer. 'He's wonderful company, Bob Geisecker. But it's almost life or death for him, poor fellow! Look, he'll pay for his passage—anything you like—if *that's* the obstacle.'

'It isn't that,' said Glenway. 'But I haven't seen him yet.'

'He's over on the other side of the island,' said Brewer. 'He went off with Johnny Ray in the jeep less than half an hour before we sighted you.'

'That's funny,' said I, thinking of what I'd seen through the telescope.

'Damned funny,' said Brewer, 'If going off to give Johnny a hand makes him miss his chance of a passage.' And turning to Glenway, he added. 'If you'd only seen old Bob I know you'd have been glad to help him.'

'I'll take him,' said Glenway, 'If he's back in time. But the wind's been failing us, and we're behind schedule, and . . . '

'Fair enough,' said Brewer. 'If he's back in time you'll take him. If he isn't, that's his hard luck. More rice? More chicken? More shrimp? Boy, fill up that glass for Mr. Abbott.'

The dinner went on and on, and not another word was said about Mr. Geisecker. At last the heavy frondage above the table drew a deep breath and began to live and move. The wind was up, and

Glenway said we could wait no longer. We all walked together down to the quay. Glenway and I were just stepping into the dinghy when someone pointed, and looking back, as people were rightly warned not to do in the old stories, we saw, like a moonrise, the glow of headlights in the sky. The jeep was coming up on the far side of the ridge. 'That's Bob,' said Brewer. 'But don't wait. We'll get him packed up in no time, and bring him out in the launch before you can up anchor.'

Sure enough, just as we were ready to move out, the launch came alongside with Mr. Bob Geisecker and his bags. The latter had pieces of pajamas hanging out at their sides like the tongues of panting dogs. Geisecker himself seemed a little breathless. His face, as he came up the steps into the light hanging above, had something strange about it. At first I thought it was just the flustered and confused expression of a man who had to pack and get off in such a hurry; then I thought it was the fact that, after weeks and months under an equatorial sun, this considerable face still peeled and glowed as if fresh from a week-end at Atlantic City. Finally, still unsatisfied, I thought of that massive, opulently curved, wide-mouthed instrument which is included in every brass band, and which, when it is not playing at full blast, looks as if it ought to be, or at least is about to be. Mr. Geisecker greatly resembled this instrument, but he was very silent, and it was this that was strange.

There was a quick introduction, a brief welcome from Glenway, who was busy, an uncertain mumble of thanks from our guest, and a very hasty farewell from Brewer. Glenway had to give all his attention to taking the yacht out, and Geisecker stood neglected on deck, staring after the launch, his mouth open, looking something worse than lost. I took him down to his cabin, told him we breakfasted at seven, and asked him if there was anything he wanted before turning in. He seemed only vaguely aware that I was talking to him.

'Those guys,' said he, speaking like a man in a state of shock, 'I kept them in stitches. In stitches—all the time!'

'Good night,' I said. 'I'll see you in the morning.'

Next morning Geisecker joined us at breakfast. He acknowledged our greeting soberly, sat down and looked at his plate. Glenway apologized for having been so much occupied overnight and began to discuss where and when we might hope to encounter a boat headed for Tokyo or Yokohama. Geisecker lifted a face on which dawning enlightenment made me think of the rapid change from the blue-grey hush of the tropic night to the full glare and blare of tropic day; light, warmth, life and laughter all came flooding in faster than one would think believable or even desirable.

'I knew it all the time!' said he exultantly. 'Only I just didn't happen to think of it. I knew it was a gag. When those guys hustled me aboard this lugger I got the idea they were—you know—giving me the brush-off. They just about had me fooled. Now I get it. Anything for a laugh! They swore to me last night you were heading for Lima, Peru.'

'They told me very definitely,' said Glenway, staring, 'that it was of the greatest importance that you should get to Tokyo.'

Geisecker slapped his plump and crimson thigh with startling effect. 'Those guys,' said he, 'they'd ship a fellow to the moon on one of those goddam spaceships if they could get a laugh out of it. And that's what they've done to me! Tokyo's where I came from. Lima, Peru is where I was going to move on to. *That's* why they kept me all day over on the other side of the island. So I shouldn't hear which way you were going.'

'We're short of time,' said Glenway, 'but I'll put about and take you back to Paumoy if you want me to.'

'Not on your life,' said Geisecker. 'It's a good gag and I'll be goddamned if I spoil it. All I'm doing is just going around the world saying hello to people, and to tell you the truth there's a little kimono lady back in Tokyo I shan't mind saying hello to once again.' With that he obliged us with a few bars of *Madame Butterfly*.

'Glenway,' said I, 'it's just on eight. I think I'll be getting up aloft.'

'Aloft?' cried Geisecker. 'That sounds like the real salt water stuff. I've never been on one of these wind-jammers before. You've got to give me the dope on marlin-spikes, splicing the main-brace and all the rest of the crap. I tell you, boys, I'm going to learn to be a sailor. Now what's all this about going up aloft?'

'I'm just going up to the crow's nest for a couple of hours.'

'What for? Looking for something?' Even as he asked the question he turned, first on me and then on Glenway, a face which now resembled a Thespian as well as a porcine ham, it so overacted the simple feat of putting two and two together. Fixing his eyes on Glenway, he slowly raised and extended an index finger of great substance. The lower joint of this finger was adorned with curving hairs, very strong and serviceable and of a ruddy gold which glinted in the morning sun. The finger stopped about a foot short of Glenway's ribs, but its quality was so potent that it seemed to make itself felt here. In fact, I even felt it in my own.

'Abbott!' cried Geisecker triumphantly. 'Now that shows you how miffed I was last night when I thought those guys had given me the brush—it didn't ring any sort of a bell. Glenway Morgan Abbott! Christ, I've heard about you, pal. Those birds told me all sorts of yarns. *You're* the guy who goes around looking for the sea serpent!'

At this point he became aware of Glenway's regard, which was, for one naked moment at least, quite deadly. Geisecker drew back a little. 'But maybe' said he, 'maybe they were pulling my leg. I ought to have seen it right away. A fellow with your education wouldn't fall for that cheesy old bit of hokum.'

By this time Glenway had recovered himself, which is to say that he was once more subject to his customary inhibitions and compulsions. These forbade him to be discourteous to a guest; and forced him to bear witness like a zealot in favour of his large marine saurian. 'Perhaps,' said he, after a painful swallow or two, 'you haven't considered the evidence.'

He went on to summarize the affidavits of numbers of worthy citizens, all describing what was obviously the same sort of creature, seen at widely dispersed times and places. He stressed especially the sworn evidence of naval officers and sea captains, and crowned the list with a reference to the reptile clearly seen by the bearded and impeccable gentlemen in charge of Queen Victoria's own yacht, the *Osborne*.

Geisecker who had been listening with a widening smile, here heartily slapped Glenway on the back. 'You know what it was *they* saw, brother? They saw the old girl herself, flopped overboard for a dip. What do you say, boys?' said he, addressing the question to me and to the man who was clearing the table. 'That's about the size of it, believe you me! *Splash me, Albert!*'

He accompanied this last sentence with a flapping mimicry of regal and natatory gambols, which, considering he was neither on a throne nor in the water, seemed to me to show talent. Glenway, liked the august personage represented, was not amused. There was such a contest between displeasure and hospitality visible on his face that it looked for a moment like a wrestling match seen on television, only, of course, the pain was genuine.

This, and the thought that I had rather let him down over the dinner on Paumoy, moved me to an unwonted self-sacrifice. 'Glenway,' said I 'you take my spell in the crow's nest, and I'll take the wheel this morning.'

Glenway, being one of nature's martyrs, refused this handsome offer, and elected to stay down in the arena. As I went aloft I

realized how those particians must have felt, who, though inclined
to early Christian sympathies, were nevertheless pressured into
taking a box in the Colosseum on a gala night in Nero's Rome.

Every now and then I heard a roar below me, and it was not
merely that of a lion; it was that of Geisecker's laughter. Before long
I saw Glenway come forward, and pretend to busy himself with the
little nets that were used for taking up plankton and algae. In a very
few minutes Geisecker came after him, smiling, and spoke with
jovial camaraderie to the two sailors who were spreading the nets.
These men looked uneasily at Glenway before they laughed; it was
sufficiently obvious that the jests were concerned with the sea-
serpent. Glenway then dropped his work and went aft, and below.
Geisecker went bellowing along the deck, and getting no response,
he went down after Glenway. There was a period of calm; deceptive
calm, which is calmer than the other sort. Then Glenway burst up
out of the forward hatch and looked around him as if for refuge. But
there was no refuge on a yacht, not even on a yacht like the *Zenobia*.
I realized that he must have slipped through the pantry, into the
galley and thence into the men's quarters, leaving Geisecker
ditched in the saloon. Geisecker was, of all men, the least likely to
remain ditched more than three minutes. At the expiration of that
time I leaned far out and looked back, and saw his mighty, sweating
torso emerge from the companionway.

There are certain big fat men who, when they joke with you,
seem almost to enfold you in a physical embrace. This caused me to
wish we were farther from the equator, but it did not prevent me
going down to try to run a little interference for Glenway.

I soon found that it was next door to impossible to draw
Geisecker away from Glenway. There are certain people who, if
they become dimly aware they are offensive to another, will fasten
on that unfortunate with all the persistence of a cat which seeks out
the one cat-hater in a crowded room. They can't believe it; they
think you really love them; they are tickled and fascinated and
awesomely thrilled by the fantastic improbability of your dislike.
They'll pluck at your attention and finger your very flesh for the
unbelievable spectacle of your recoil, and they'll press yet closer for
the marvel of your shudder, for all the world as if recoil and
shudder were rapturous spasms induced by some novel form of love
making, to be evoked in wonder and in triumph again and again
and again.

'Good old Glen!' said Geisecker, one afternoon when Glenway
had jumped up with what I can call a muttered exclamation, and
sought refuge in his cabin. 'I love that guy. I love the way he takes

a bit of ribbing. You know—straight, dead pan, and yet you can tell that underneath he just loves it.'

'Not on that subject,' I said. 'He detests it. And so do I. It's making him miserable. It's driving him just about crazy.'

'Ah, don't give me that baloney!' said he with a good-humoured flap of his hand. Geisecker was not in the least interested in what I said about my own reaction. Sensitive to nothing else on earth, he had, unconsciously of course, better than a dog's nose for the exact nature of the feeling he inspired. This keen sense told him that I am of a type not offended by his sort of humour, and that my mounting anger was entirely on behalf of Glenway. To him, therefore, it was vicarious, second-hand, and as flavourless as a duenna's kiss. It gave him no sort of thrill, and he had no itch to increase it. I felt quite rejected.

I went down to see if I could be more effective with Glenway. I said, 'if you had the least sense of humour, you'd enjoy this monster. After all, he's the sort of thing you're looking for. He belongs to a species thought to be extinct.'

'I wish to God he was,' said Glenway.

'He may not come from the Pleistocene, but he's at least a survival from the Joke Book Age. He's a human coelacanth. He's a specimen of Comic Picture Postcard Man. He's a living Babbitt. You ought to turn your cameras on him. People'll think you're making it all up.'

It was like trying to skip and run over soft sand. Each new sentence got off to a worse start and sank deeper into Glenway's depression. At last I was altogether bogged down, and we sat there just looking at each other. Then, like the last trump, there arose an urgent, heart-stopping stridulation in the buzzer box on the wall over the bed. Glenway was out of his depression, out of his chair, into the doorway and up the companion so quickly that one felt certain intervening movements must have been left out. I followed as fast as I could; after all, it was either the sea serpent or Geisecker, and in either case I thought I'd better be there.

It was Geisecker. He was standing by the wheel, hooting with laughter, pointing out over the ocean, shouting, 'Thar she blows! Flukes on the starboard bow!'

Then the laughter doubled him up completely. I noticed that it can be true about people getting purple in the face. I noticed also that, even doubled up, Geisecker seemed bigger; there seemed to be more of him, than at other times.

Sadder still, there seemed to be less of Glenway. He seemed to be shrunken and concentrated into a narrower and grayer column of tissue than was natural. I had time to think, 'He'll be driven completely out of his mind if this continues,' and then he turned and went down the companion out of sight.

I went over to Geisecker, wondering on the way what sort of words could possibly pierce his thick hide. 'Jesus Christ!' said he. 'I knew it was true. When those boys on Paumoy told me, I knew it was true, but I just felt I had to check up on it.'

'What the hell are you talking about?' I asked.

'About old Glen and Thora Vyberg,' replied Geisecker, still gasping with mirth. 'Don't you know about Glen and Thora Vyberg?'

I knew they had been married. I vaguely remembered something about a dramatic love-at-first-sight encounter in Honolulu. I had some sort of a picture in my mind of the more-than-famous film star; of her unfathomable personality, her unknowable beauty, and the fact that she talked to no one and travelled with no one and dined with no one except her Svengali, her current director, and her publicity man. I had a fairly clear idea of what these types were like, and I could imagine that Glenway, younger then, tall, angular, already dedicated, with the ocean behind him, winged with sail and haloed with sun and money, must have seemed to offer her a part in a rather better production.

I remembered, too, that the marriage had been extremely short lived. Someone had said something about them sailing away with the sunset and returning with the dawn. No statement had been made by either party. There had been rumours, as there always are, but these were weak, uncertain; they had been drowned in a flood of better authenticated adulteries long before I ever knew Glenway. Now it seemed that some of them had been washed ashore, horribly disfigured, swollen and salty, on the ultimate beaches of Paumoy.

'You know what the boys there told me?' said Geisecker watching me closely. 'Seems they got married in no time flat and started out on this very same boat, on a big, front-page honeymoon. Believe it or not, the very first night out—round about eleven o'clock, if you get what I mean, pal—some fellow on deck sees something or other, maybe porpoises or kelp or any damn thing you like, and he gets the idea it's the old brontosaurus in person. So he presses the buzzer, and Glen comes rushing up on deck in ten seconds flat. Don't ask me any questions, pal; all I know is that first thing next morning the lugger was turned right around, and it's full steam ahead back to Honolulu, and Reno, and points in opposite directions.'

I realized at once that this was true, and had a certain beauty.

However, that was for my private contemplation and had nothing to do with Geisecker. He was regarding me with a sort of arrested gloat, his eye triumphant and his nose tilted up ready to join in the expected peal of laughter. 'Geisecker,' I said, and for the first time I heard, and he heard, a note of my direct and personal hatred in my voice, 'Geisecker, I'm not going to discuss the whys and where-fores, but from now on you're going to stay right away from Glenway. You can come on deck; you can have a chair on the port side there, between the masts. But if you step one inch . . . '

'Hold it!' said Geisecker. 'Who's talking? The owner? Skipper? First mate? Or what the hell else do you think you are? I'd like to hear what old Glen's got to say.'

I am no good at all at a row. When my first damp squib of wrath has exploded I am always overwhelmed by an immense weariness and blankness. At that moment I had neither the will nor the power to go on. But Geisecker obligingly came to my assistance. I could never decide whether he was a sadist, avid for the discomfort of his victim, or a masochist, indecently eager for the wound of being disliked. Whichever it was, he watched me with his little eye, and he actually passed his tongue over his lips. 'Anyway,' said he, 'I'm going down to ask him if there's any truth in that yarn.'

The lip-licking was so crude and so banal that it transposed everything into a different key. There was a sailor of great good nature and phenomenal size, a man called Wiggam, a native of Hawaii, who was mending a net a little way along the deck. I called him and told him, in phrases which normally appear only in balloons in comic strips, to take his net and work on it outside Abbott's door, and, in the event of Geisecker approaching that door, to cut his belly open.

I gave these deplorable instructions in a rather cold, stacatto tone, assumed in order to overcome a tendency to squeakiness, and I was reminded, even as I heard myself speak, of a small boy's imitation of a tommy gun. Had Geisecker laughed, or had the sailor looked surprised or reluctant, I should have been in a very ludicrous situation. However, it seems that sailors are simple folk; this one showed alacrity, his teeth, and a spring knife that seemed all the more purposeful for being of very moderate dimensions. He glanced at Geisecker, or rather at the belly in question, as if making certain precise and workmanlike calculations, and then he went and gathered up the long net and carried it below. Geisecker watched all this with growing seriousness.

'Look,' said he, 'maybe I got things wrong somehow, but . . . '

'Listen, Fatso,' said I, 'if you get anything else wrong you're going to be put on a little Jap crabfisher boat, see? And the name of that boat's going to be screwed up when we write it down in the log. 'Cause it'll be a Japanese name that means *the boat that never returned*. Or never existed. Work that one out next time you feel like kidding.'

I went down and found Glenway lying on his bed, not reading. I said, 'I've fixed him. I can't believe it, but I have.'

'How?' said Glenway.

When I had told him, he said, 'He won't stay fixed, not by that sort of thing.'

I said, 'You think so because I've related it with a twinkle. When I spoke to Geisecker my voice was cold and dead, like steel, and I let my eyelids drop a little. Like this.'

'He certainly won't stay fixed,' said Glenway.

'In that case his belly will be cut open,' said I. Because to Hill Wiggam, who is sitting right out there in the passage, this is his moment of fulfillment. Or it will be if Geisecker tries to get past him. It's a case of a man suddenly finding his vocation.'

'I don't want Wiggam getting into trouble,' said Glenway.

'Nor,' said I, 'does Geisecker.' With that I went up and did my afternoon spell in the crow's nest, and later I had a drink with Geisecker, to whom I said as little as possible, not knowing what to say nor how to say it. I then dined with Glenway, in his cabin, and then had a smoke with Geisecker on the port deck, and at about ten o'clock, I went to spend the last hour of the evening with Glenway, who was still extremely tense.

'What's the night like?' he asked.

I said, 'It's the most wonderful night of the whole cruise. The moon's just on full, and someone's let it down on an invisible wire, and you can see the curve of the stars going up behind it. The wind's light, but there's a hell of a big swell rolling in from somewhere. She's still got everything on but her balloon jib, and she's riding it like a steeplechaser. Why don't you go up and take the wheel for a bit?'

'Where's Geisecker?' asked Glenway.

'Amidships, on the port side, fenced in invisibly by threats,' I said with some pride.

'I'll stay down here,' said Glenway.

'Glenway,' said I, 'you're making altogether too much of this. The fact is, you've led a sheltered life; people like Geisecker have always treated you with far too much respect. It sets you apart, and I find it rather offensive. Remember what Fitzgerald said about the rich. He said you are different. Think of that! It's almost worse than being the same.'

'You forget what Hemingway said,' replied Glenway, who perhaps found little attraction in either alternative.

'The Hemingway rebuttal,' said I, 'Proves only what it was intended to prove. That is, that Hemingway is a fine, upstanding, independent citizen, and probably with a magnificent growth of hair on his chest. All the same, Fitzgerald had a point. Just because your iniquitous old grandfather happened to build a few railways—

'First of all,' interrupted Glenway, 'it was not my grandfather but my great grandfather. What's more—'

And at that moment, just as I was exulting in having induced him to unclench his hands, and look out of his eyes, and stick his neck out, the buzzer sounded again. I had forgotten to have it disconnected.

What was quite pathetic was that Glenway couldn't control an instinctive movement towards leaping off the bed. He arched up like a tetanus victim, and then collapsed as flat as an empty sack. The buzzer went on. I had a panicky feeling that he might arch up again at any moment. I lost my head and picked up a stool that stood in front of the dressing table and pounded that rattle-snake box into silence.

The silence, once achieved, seemed deep and complete. This was an illusion; we soon noticed that there were all sorts of noises here and there in the large emptiness left by the death of the outrageous buzzer. We could hear the patter of running feet on deck, and voices, and especially Geisecker's voice, spouting large jets of urgent sound.

I opened the door and the words came rushing in. 'Glen! Glen! Come up, for God's sake! Can't you hear me? Come quick!'

'My God!' I said. 'Maybe they *are* cutting his belly open.'

With that, I ran up. Geisecker was at the head of the companionway. He turned his head briefly to send another shout down the stairs; then he turned it back again to stare out over the sea. I barged into him. He blindly clutched at my arm and dragged me to the side of the boat, and pointed.

I saw something already disappearing into the great smooth side of one of the enormous waves. It was black, wet, shining, and very large. These words can be applied to a whale or a whale-shark, and maybe to two or three other things. I can summon up with absolute precision the way Geisecker's face was turning as I came up the companionway; I can remember exactly how his shout went on a

little after he had turned his head back to look over the sea again.
But I haven't the same perfect mental photograph of what I saw
disappearing into the wave. To the very best of my recollection I
saw the hinder half of an enormous back and, following on a curve,
already half lost in the black and moon-glitter, a monstrous tail.

The men who had run up were standing three or four paces away.
I looked at them, and they nodded. As they did so I heard
Glenway's voice speaking to the men. 'You saw it?' He had come up
after all, and had seen my look and their response as he came
towards us. One of them said, 'Yes, but he shout,' pointing to
Geisecker. 'He shout, shout, shout, and it go under.'

Glenway stepped towards Geisecker, thus turning his back on the
men. They couldn't see his face, but I could see it, and so could
Geisecker. I don't think Glenway even raised his hand. Geisecker
stepped backwards, which brought him, at what I would have
thought a very slight and harmless angle, against the low gunwale.
His big, fat, heavy torso went on and over; his feet went up, and he
was gone. He was overboard.

I don't remember putting my hand on the life-belt, but I can
remember flinging it, skimming it almost parallel with the side of
the boat, and feeling sure it hit the water within a very few feet of
Geisecker. Then the boat, whose six knots or so had been like
nothing at all a moment earlier, seemed to be racing ahead faster
than any boat had ever gone before.

Glenway shouted; the helmsman put the helm over and spilled
the wind out of her sails. There was always a boat ready to be
lowered at record speed. Two men were at the oars, Glenway took
the tiller, and I stood in the bows looking out for Geisecker who
could be no more than two or three hundred yards away.

The night was clear beyond all description. The enormous,
smooth swells gleamed and flashed under the moon. The yacht,
when we had drawn away from it, stood up like a snowy alp on the
water, and when, at the top of each swell, the men lifted their oars
for a moment, it was a moment of unbelievable silence, as if some
tremendous creature was holding its breath.

Then I saw Geisecker. We were lifted high on one of the great
glassy hills of sea, and he was beginning to slide down the slope of
another. He had the lifebelt. I couldn't see his real features at that
distance, but the white moonlight gave him such great hollow black
eyes, and made such a crater of his open mouth, that I got the
picture of a clown in comic distress. Then he went down, and we
went down, and two or three ridges twenty feet high humped
themselves between us.

I said, 'He's ahead of us; a couple of hundred feet. You'll see him from the top of the next one.'

But we didn't. I began to wonder if a man and a lifebelt rise and fall faster or slower on a rolling sea than does a fourteen foot boat. Before I could work out the answer we had gone up and down again and had arrived at a spot which certainly was extremely close to where I had seen him.

'You misjudged the distance,' said Glenway after perhaps half a puzzled minute.

'I must have. Anyway, he's got the lifebuoy. He'll be all right. Let's row around in a circle.'

One of the men put out a bailing can as a marker. The giant swells were so smooth that, ballasted with a couple of inches of water, the can floated up and down without shipping another drop. We went round it on a hundred foot radius and then at a hundred and fifty feet. Geisecker was not to be seen. And we could see, at one time or another, every square foot of water where he could possibly be.

'He's sunk!' said Glenway. 'A cramp . . . a shark . . . '

'No shark would have taken the life-belt down. It'd be floating right here. We'd see it.'

The words were scarcely out of my mouth when we saw it. It breached up, right out of the water—it must have come up from God knows how many fathoms—and it fell back with a splash just a boat's length ahead of us. Next moment it was beside our bow and I reached out and lifted it aboard. I turned, holding it in my hands, and showed it to Glenway. It was easier than speaking, and not so silly. We both knew perfectly well that no known creature, except possibly a sperm whale, could have taken Geisecker and the lifebelt down to that sort of depth. And we knew that what I had seen, and what the men had seen, was not a sperm whale.

We rowed around in circles for a little longer, and then we pulled back to the yacht. When we were aboard again, I said to Glenway, 'You didn't as much as touch him. You didn't even mean to touch him. You didn't even raise your hand.'

'And some of the men were watching,' said Glenway with the utmost calm. 'They can testify to that.'

If not the railway tycoon, his great grandfather, it might certainly have been his grandfather, the banker, speaking. He saw my surprise, and smiled. 'From the most scrupulous legal point of view,' said he, 'it was a pure accident. And we'll make a report accordingly. Of course, I killed the man.'

'Now wait a minute,' said I.

'Excuse me,' said he. We were near the wheel. He took it from the man who was steering, and said something to him, and the man ran forward calling to the rest of the crew who were still on deck. Next minute the helm went up, the booms swung over, the sails bellied out on the other side, and the great boat was jibed and sweeping round on to a new course.

'Where are we heading now?' said I to Glenway.

'Due east,' said he. 'To San Francisco.'

'To make the report? Can't you . . . ?'

'To put the boat up for sale.'

I said, 'Glenway, you're upset. You've got to see this business in proportion.'

He said, 'He was alive and enjoying himself, and now he's dead. I didn't like him; I detested him, but that's got nothing to do with it.'

I said, 'Don't be completely psychologically illiterate. It's got everything in the world to do with it. You hated his guts, a little too intensely, perhaps, but very understandably. You wished he was dead. In fact, you more or less said so. Now you've got guilt feelings; you're going to take the blame for it. Glenway, you're an obsessive type; you're a Puritan, a New Englander, any early Christian. Be reasonable. Be moderate.'

'Suppose you were driving a car,' said Glenway, 'and you knocked a man down and killed him?'

'I'd be very sorry, but I think I'd go on driving.'

'If you were a speed demon, and it was because of that? Or a drunk? Or if you were mentally unfit to handle a car?'

'Well . . . ' I said.

But Glenway wasn't listening. He beckoned the man who had been steering, and turned the wheel over to him. He gave him the course and told him who was to relieve him in each watch. Then he turned away and walked forward. He walked like a passenger. He walked like a man walking on a street. He was walking away from his mania, and in the very hour of its justification.

I followed him, eager to bring him back to himself, but he walked away from me too.

I said to him considerably later, 'I've found out something very interesting, talking to the men. Shall I tell you?'

'Please do,' said he.

I said, 'I thought they rather liked Geisecker because he made them laugh. But they didn't. Not a bit. Are you listening?'

'Of course,' said he as politely as a banker who has already decided not to make a loan.

I said, 'They hated him almost as much as you did, and for the same reason for making fun of it. They believed in it, all the time. They've all got different names for it, according to where they come from. Almost every man's got an uncle who's seen it, or a wife's grandfather, or someone. And it's quite clear it's the same sort of beast.'

Glenway said, 'I've decided I'm going to buy a farm or a ranch as far from the ocean as I can get. I'll breed cattle or hybridize corn or something.'

I said, 'You've been over seven years on this boat with these men, or most of them. Did you know they believed in it?'

'No,' said he. 'Or I might go in for soil biology. There's still a tremendous amount to be discovered in that field.'

This made me feel very sick. I felt Glenway was indeed different; different from me, different from himself. The beautiful *Zenobia* had to be sold, the crew disbanded and the large marine saurian left to dwindle into a figure on an old map, distant and disregarded in its watery solitude. As for myself, all my friendship with Glenway had been aboard the boat; I was part of it; I was one of these things. I had been nothing but the accomplice of his obsession, and now he was, in a way I didn't like, cured. I felt that I too was up for sale, and we talked amiably and politely and quite meaninglessly all the way back to San Francisco, and there we said goodbye to each other and promised to write.

We didn't write in over three years. One can't write to the ghost of a banker, nor expect a letter from one. But this summer, when I was in New York, I got home one night and found a letter awaiting me. The postmark was Gregory, South Dakota, which is about as far from either ocean as you can get.

He was there; he wondered if I knew those parts; he wondered if I was likely to be free; there were some interesting things to talk about. The lines were extremely few but there was all the more space to read between them. I took up the telephone.

It was nearly midnight, but of course it was two hours earlier in South Dakota. All the same Glenway was a very long time coming to the phone. 'I hope I didn't get you out of bed,' I told him.

'Heavens, no!' said he. 'I was on the roof. We get wonderful nights here; as clear as Arizona.'

I remembered that clear night in the Pacific, and the flash and glitter of the enormous glassy waves, and the silence, and the boat rising and falling so high and so low, and the yacht like a hill of snow in the distance, and the little bailing can visible at over a hundred feet. I said, 'I'd like to come out right away.'

'I rather hoped you would,' said Glenway, and began to tell me about planes and trains.

I asked him if there was anything he wanted from New York.

'There most certainly is,' said he. 'There's a man called Emil Schroeder; you'll find his address in the book; he's out in Brooklyn; he's the best lens grinder that ever got out of Germany, and he's got a package for me that I don't want sent through the mail because it's fragile.'

'What is it?' I asked. 'A microscope? Did you go in for soil biology after all?'

'Well, I did for a time,' said Glenway. 'But this is something different. It's lenses for a binocular telescope a fellow's designed for me. You see, a single eye piece is no good for following anything that moves at all fast. But this binocular thing will be perfect. I can use it on the roof, or I can set it in a mounting I've had built into the plane.'

'Glenway, do you mind telling me what the hell you're talking about?'

'Haven't you read the government report on unidentified flying objects? . . . Hello! Are you there?'

'Yes, I'm here, Glenway. And you're there. You're there, sure enough!'

'Listen, if you haven't read that report, do please get hold of it first thing tomorrow, and read it on the way out here. I don't want to hear you talking like that unfortunate Geisecker. Will you read it?'

'All right, Glenway, I will. I most certainly will.'

ONE ORDINARY DAY, WITH PEANUTS

Shirley Jackson

Mr John Philip Johnson shut his front door behind him and came down his front steps into the bright morning with a feeling that all was well with the world on this best of all days, and wasn't the sun warm and good, and didn't his shoes feel comfortable after the resoling, and he knew that he had undoubtedly chosen the precise very tie which belonged with the day and the sun and his comfortable feet, and, after all, wasn't the world just a wonderful place? In spite of the fact that he was a small man, and the tie was perhaps a shade vivid, Mr. Johnson irradiated this feeling of well-being as he came down the steps and onto the dirty sidewalk, and he smiled at people who passed him, and some of them even smiled back. He stopped at the newsstand on the corner and bought his paper, saying '*Good morning*' with real conviction to the man who sold him the paper and the two or three other people who were lucky enough to be buying papers when Mr. Johnson skipped up. He remembered to fill his pockets with candy and peanuts, and then he set out to get himself uptown. He stopped in a flower shop and bought a carnation for his buttonhole, and stopped almost immediately afterward to give the carnation to a small child in a carriage, who looked at him dumbly, and then smiled, and Mr. Johnson smiled, and the child's mother looked at Mr. Johnson for a minute and then smiled too.

When he had gone several blocks uptown, Mr. Johnson cut across the avenue and went along a side street, chosen at random; he did not follow the same route every morning, but preferred to pursue his eventful way in wide detours, more like a puppy than a man intent upon business. It happened this morning that halfway down the block a moving van was parked, and the furniture from an upstairs apartment stood half on the sidewalk, half on the steps, while an amused group of people loitered, examining the scratches on the tables and the worn spots on the chairs, and a harassed woman, trying to watch a young child and the movers and the furniture all at the same time, gave the clear impression of endeavoring to shelter her private life from the people staring at her belongings. Mr. Johnson stopped, and for a moment joined the crowd, and then he came forward and, touching his hat civilly, said, 'Perhaps I can keep an eye on your little boy for you?'

The woman turned and glared at him distrustfully, and Mr. Johnson added hastily, 'We'll sit right here on the steps.' He beckoned to the little boy, who hesitated and then responded agreeably to Mr. Johnson's genial smile. Mr. Johnson brought out a handful of peanuts from his pocket and sat on the steps with the boy, who at first refused the peanuts on the grounds that his mother did not allow him to accept food from strangers; Mr. Johnson said that probably his mother had not intended peanuts to be included, since elephants at the circus ate them, and the boy considered, and then agreed solemnly. They sat on the steps cracking peanuts in a comradely fashion, and Mr. Johnson said, 'So you're moving?'

'Yep,' said the boy.

'Where you going?'

'Vermont.'

'Nice place. Plenty of snow there. Maple sugar, too; you like maple sugar?'

'Sure.'

'Plenty of maple sugar in Vermont. You going to live on a farm?'

'Going to live with Grandpa.'

'Grandpa like peanuts?'

'Sure.'

'Ought to take him some,' said Mr. Johnson, reaching into his pocket. 'Just you and Mommy going?'

'Yep.'

'Tell you what,' Mr. Johnson said. 'You take some peanuts to eat on the train.'

The boy's mother, after glancing at them frequently, had seemingly decided that Mr. Johnson was trustworthy, because she had devoted herself whole-heartedly to seeing that the movers did not—what movers rarely do, but every housewife believes they will—crack a leg from her good table, or set a kitchen chair down on a lamp. Most of the furniture was loaded by now, and she was deep in that nervous stage when she knew there was something she had forgotten to pack—hidden away in the back of a closet somewhere, or left at a neighbor's and forgotten, or on the clothesline—and was trying to remember under stress what it was.

'This all lady?' the chief mover said, completing her dismay.

Uncertainly, she nodded.

'Want to go on the truck with the furniture, sonny?' the mover asked the boy, and laughed. The boy laughed too and said to Mr. Johnson, 'I guess I'll have a good time at Vermont.'

'Fine time,' said Mr. Johnson, and stood up. 'Have one more peanut before you go,' he said to the boy.

The boy's mother said to Mr. Johnson, 'Thank you so much; it was a great help to me.'

'Nothing at all,' said Mr. Johnson gallantly. 'Where in Vermont are you going?'

The mother looked at the little boy accusingly, as though he had given away a secret of some importance, and said unwillingly, 'Greenwich.'

'Lovely town,' said Mr. Johnson. He took out a card, and wrote a name on the back. 'Very good friend of mine lives in Greenwich,' he said. 'Call on him for anything you need. His wife makes the best doughnuts in town,' he added soberly to the little boy.

'Swell,' said the little boy.

'Goodbye,' said Mr. Johnson.

He went on, stepping happily with his new-shod feet, feeling the warm sun on his back and on the top of his head. Halfway down the block he met a stray dog and fed him a peanut.

At the corner, where another wide avenue faced him, Mr. Johnson decided to go on uptown again. Moving with comparative laziness, he was passed on either side by people hurrying and frowning, and people brushed past him going the other way, clattering along to get somewhere quickly. Mr. Johnson stopped on every corner and waited patiently for the light to change, and he stepped out of the way of anyone who seemed to be in any particular hurry, but one young lady came too fast for him, and crashed wildly into him when he stooped to pat a kitten which had run out onto the sidewalk from an apartment house and was now unable to get back through the rushing feet.

'Excuse me,' said the young lady, trying frantically to pick up Mr. Johnson and hurry on at the same time, 'terribly sorry.'

The kitten, regardless now of danger, raced back to its home. 'Perfectly all right,' said Mr. Johnson, adjusting himself carefully. 'You seem to be in a hurry.'

'Of course I'm in a hurry,' said the young lady. 'I'm late.'

She was extremely cross and the frown between her eyes seemed well on its way to becoming permanent. She had obviously awakened late, because she had not spent any extra time in making herself look pretty, and her dress was plain and unadorned with collar or brooch, and her lipstick was noticeably crooked. She tried to brush past Mr. Johnson, but, risking her suspicious displeasure, he took her arm and said, 'Please wait.'

'Look,' she said ominously, 'I ran into you and your lawyer can see my lawyer and I will gladly pay all damages and all inconveniences suffered therefrom but please this minute let me go because *I am late.*'

'Late for what?' said Mr. Johnson; he tried his winning smile on her but it did no more than keep her, he suspected, from knocking him down again.

'Late for work,' she said between her teeth. 'Late for my employment. I have a job and if I am late I lose exactly so much an hour and I cannot really afford what your pleasant conversation is costing me, be it *ever* so pleasant.'

'I'll pay for it,' said Mr. Johnson. Now these were magic words, not necessarily because they were true, or because she seriously expected Mr. Johnson to pay for anything, but because Mr. Johnson's flat statement, obviously innocent of irony, could not be, coming from Mr. Johnson, anything but the statement of a responsible and truthful and respectable man.

'What *do* you mean?' she asked.

'I said that since I am obviously responsible for your being late I shall certainly pay for it.'

'Don't be silly,' she said, and for the first time the frown disappeared. '*I* wouldn't expect you to pay for anything—a few minutes ago I was offering to pay *you*. Anyway,' she added, almost smiling, 'it *was* my fault.'

'What happens if you don't go to work?'

She stared. 'I don't get paid.'

'Precisely,' said Mr. Johnson.

'What do you mean, precisely? If I don't show up at the office exactly twenty minutes ago I lose a dollar and twenty cents an hour, or two cents a minute or . . .' She thought. '. . . Almost a dime for the time I've spent talking to you.'

Mr. Johnson laughed, and finally she laughed, too. 'You're late already,' he pointed out. 'Will you give me another four cents worth?'

'I don't understand why.'

'You'll see,' Mr. Johnson promised. He led her over to the side of the walk, next to the buildings, and said, 'Stand here,' and went out into the rush of people going both ways. Selecting and considering, as one who must make a choice involving perhaps whole years of lives, he estimated the people going by. Once he almost moved, and then at the last minute thought better of it and drew back. Finally, from half a block away, he saw what he wanted, and moved out into the center of the traffic to intercept a young man, who was hurrying, and dressed as though he had awakened late, and frowning.

'Oof,' said the young man, because Mr. Johnson had thought of no better way to intercept anyone than the one the young woman had unwittingly used upon him. 'Where do you think you're going?' the young man demanded from the sidewalk.

'I want to speak to you,' said Mr. Johnson ominously.

The young man got up nervously, dusting himself and eyeing Mr. Johnson. 'What for?' he said. 'What'd *I* do?'

'That's what bothers me most about people nowadays,' Mr. Johnson complained broadly to the people passing. 'No matter whether they've done anything or not, they always figure someone's after them. About what you're going to do,' he told the young man.

'Listen,' said the young man, trying to brush past him, 'I'm late, and I don't have any time to listen. Here's a dime, now get going.'

'Thank you,' said Mr. Johnson, pocketing the dime. 'Look,' he said, 'what happens if you stop running?'

'I'm late,' said the young man, still trying to get past Mr. Johnson, who was unexpectedly clinging.

'How much you make an hour?' Mr. Johnson demanded.

'A communist, are you?' said the young man. 'Now will you please let me—'

'No,' said Mr. Johnson insistently, '*how* much?'

'Dollar fifty,' said the young man. 'And *now* will you—'

'You like adventure?'

The young man stared, and, staring, found himself caught and held by Mr. Johnson's genial smile; he almost smiled back and then repressed it and made an effort to tear away. 'I got to *hurry*,' he said.

'Mystery? Like surprises? Unusual and exciting events?'

'You selling something?'

'Sure,' said Mr. Johnson. 'You want to take a chance?'

The young man hesitated, looked longingly up the avenue toward what might have been his destination and then, when Mr. Johnson said, 'I'll pay for it,' with his own peculiar convincing emphasis, turned and said, 'Well, okay. But I got to *see* it first, what I'm buying.'

Mr. Johnson, breathing hard, led the young man over to the side where the girl was standing; she had been watching with interest Mr. Johnson's capture of the young man and now, smiling timidly, she looked at Mr. Johnson as though prepared to be surprised at nothing.

Mr. Johnson reached into his pocket and took out his wallet. 'Here,' he said, and handed a bill to the girl. 'This about equals your day's pay.'

'But no,' she said, surprised in spite of herself. 'I mean, I *couldn't*.'

'Please do not interrupt,' Mr. Johnson told her. 'And *here*,' he said to the young man, 'this will take care of *you*.' The young man accepted the bill dazedly, but said, 'Probably counterfeit,' to the young woman out of the side of his mouth. 'Now,' Mr. Johnson went on, disregarding the young man, 'what is your name, miss?'

'Kent,' she said helplessly. 'Mildred Kent.'

'Fine,' said Mr. Johnson. 'And you, sir?'

'Arthur Adams,' said the young man stiffly.

'Splendid,' said Mr. Johnson. 'Now, Miss Kent, I would like you to meet Mr. Adams. Mr. Adams, Miss Kent.'

Miss Kent stared, wet her lips nervously, made a gesture as though she might run, and said, 'How do you do?'

Mr. Adams straightened his shoulders, scowled at Mr. Johnson, made a gesture as though he might run, and said, 'How do you do?'

'Now *this*,' said Mr. Johnson, taking several bills from his wallet, 'should be enough for the day for both of you. I would suggest, perhaps, Coney Island—although I personally am not fond of the place—or perhaps a nice lunch somewhere, and dancing, or a matinee, or even a movie, although take care to choose a really *good* one; there are *so* many bad movies these days. You might,' he said, struck with an inspiration, 'visit the Bronx Zoo, or the Planetarium. Anywhere, as a matter of fact,' he concluded, 'that you would like to go. Have a nice time.'

As he started to move away, Arthur Adams, creaking from his dumfounded stare, said, 'But see here, mister, you *can't* do this. Why—how do you know—I mean, *we* don't even know—I mean, how do you know we won't just take the money and not do what you said?'

'You've taken the money,' Mr. Johnson said. 'You don't have

to follow any of my suggestions. You may know something you prefer to do—perhaps a museum, or something.'

'But suppose I just run away with it and leave her here?'

'I know you won't,' said Mr. Johnson gently, 'because you remembered to ask *me* that. Goodbye,' he added, and went on.

As he stepped up the street, conscious of the sun on his head and his good shoes, he heard from somewhere behind him the young man saying. 'Look, you know you don't *have* to if you don't want to,' and the girl saying, 'But unless *you* don't want to . . .' Mr. Johnson smiled to himself and then thought that he had better hurry along; when he wanted to he could move very quickly, and before the young woman had gotten around to saying, 'Well, *I* will if *you* will,' Mr. Johnson was several blocks away and had already stopped twice, once to help a lady lift several large packages into a taxi and once to hand a peanut to a seagull. By this time he was in an area of large stores and many more people and he was buffeted constantly from either side by people hurrying and cross and late and sullen. Once he offered a peanut to a man who asked him for a dime, and once he offered a peanut to a bus driver who had stopped his bus at an intersection and had opened the window next to his seat and put out his head as though longing for fresh air and the comparative quiet of the traffic. The man wanting a dime took the peanut because Mr. Johnson had wrapped a dollar bill around it, but the bus driver took the peanut and asked ironically, 'You want a transfer, Jack?'

On a busy corner Mr. Johnson encountered two young people —for one minute he thought they might be Mildred Kent and Arthur Adams—who were eagerly scanning a newspaper, their backs pressed against a storefront to avoid the people passing, their heads bent together. Mr. Johnson, whose curiosity was insatiable, leaned onto the storefront next to them and peeked over the man's shoulder; they were scanning the 'Apartments Vacant' columns.

Mr. Johnson remembered the street where the woman and her little boy were going to Vermont and he tapped the man on the shoulder and said amiably, 'Try down on West Seventeen. About the middle of the block, people moved out this morning.'

'Say, what do you—' said the man, and then, seeing Mr. Johnson clearly, 'Well, thanks. Where did you say?'

'West Seventeen,' said Mr. Johnson. 'About the middle of the block.' He smiled again and said, 'Good luck.'

'Thanks,' said the man.

'Thanks,' said the girl, as they moved off.

'Goodbye,' said Mr. Johnson.

He lunched alone in a pleasant restaurant, where the food was rich, and only Mr. Johnson's excellent digestion could encompass two of their whipped-cream-and-chocolate-and-rum-cake pastries for dessert. He had three cups of coffee, tipped the waiter largely, and went out into the street again into the wonderful sunlight, his shoes still comfortable and fresh on his feet. Outside he found a beggar staring into the windows of the restaurant he had left and, carefully looking through the money in his pocket, Mr. Johnson approached the beggar and pressed some coins and a couple of bills into his hand. 'It's the price of the veal cutlet lunch plus tip,' said Mr. Johnson. 'Goodbye.'

After his lunch he rested; he walked into the nearest park and fed peanuts to the pigeons. It was late afternoon by the time he was ready to start back downtown, and he had refereed two checker games and watched a small boy and girl whose mother had fallen asleep and awakened with surprise and fear which turned to amusement when she saw Mr. Johnson. He had given away almost all of his candy, and had fed all the rest of his peanuts to the pigeons, and it was time to go home. Although the late afternoon sun was pleasant, and his shoes were still entirely comfortable, he decided to take a taxi downtown.

He had a difficult time catching a taxi, because he gave up the first three or four empty ones to people who seemed to need them more; finally, however, he stood alone on the corner and—almost like netting a frisky fish—he hailed desperately until he succeeded in catching a cab which had been proceeding with haste uptown and seemed to draw in towards Mr. Johnson against its own will.

'Mister,' the cab driver said as Mr. Johnson climbed in, 'I figured you was an omen, like. I wasn't going to pick you up at all.'

'Kind of you,' said Mr. Johnson ambiguously.

'If I'd of let you go it would of cost me ten bucks,' said the driver.

'Really?' said Mr. Johnson.

'Yeah,' said the driver. 'Guy just got out of the cab, he turned around and give me ten bucks, said take this and bet it in a hurry on a horse named Vulcan, right away.'

'Vulcan?' said Mr. Johnson, horrified. 'A fire sign on a Wednesday?'

'What?' said the driver. 'Anyway, I said to myself if I got no fare between here and there I'd bet the ten, but if anyone looked like they needed the cab I'd take it as an omen and I'd take the ten home to the wife.'

'You were very right,' said Mr. Johnson heartily. 'This is

Wednesday, you would have lost your money. Monday, yes, or even Saturday. But never never never a fire sign on a Wednesday. Sunday would have been good, now.'

'Vulcan don't run on Sunday,' said the driver.

'You wait till another day,' said Mr. Johnson. 'Down this street, please. I'll get off on the next corner.'

'He *told* me Vulcan, though,' said the driver.

'I'll tell you,' said Mr. Johnson, hesitating with the door of the cab half open. 'You take that ten dollars and I'll give you another ten dollars to go with it, and you go right ahead and bet that money on any Thursday on any horse that has a name indicating . . . let me see, Thursday . . . well, grain. Or any growing food.'

'Grain?' said the driver. 'You mean a horse named, like, Wheat or something?'

'Certainly,' said Mr. Johnson. 'Or, as a matter of fact, to make it even easier, any horse whose name includes the letters C, R, L. Perfectly simple.'

'Tall corn?' said the driver, a light in his eye. 'You mean a horse named, like, Tall Corn?'

'Absolutely,' said Mr. Johnson. 'Here's your money.'

'Tall Corn,' said the driver. 'Thank *you*, mister.'

'Goodbye,' said Mr. Johnson.

He was on his own corner and went straight up to his apartment. He let himself in and called 'Hello?' and Mrs. Johnson answered from the kitchen, 'Hello, dear, aren't you early?'

'Took a taxi home,' Mr. Johnson said. 'I remembered the cheesecake, too. What's for dinner?'

Mrs. Johnson came out of the kitchen and kissed him; she was a comfortable woman, and smiling as Mr. Johnson smiled. 'Hard day?' she asked.

'Not very,' said Mr. Johnson, hanging his coat in the closet. 'How about you?'

'So-so,' she said. She stood in the kitchen doorway while he settled into his easy chair and took off his good shoes and took out the paper he had bought that morning. 'Here and there,' she said.

'I didn't do so badly,' Mr. Johnson said. 'Couple young people.'

'Fine,' she said. 'I had a little nap this afternoon, took it easy most of the day. Went into a department store this morning and accused the woman next to me of shoplifting, and had the store detective pick her up. Sent three dogs to the pound—*you* know, the usual thing. Oh, and listen,' she added, remembering.

'What?' asked Mr. Johnson.

'Well,' she said, 'I got onto a bus and asked the driver for a transfer, and when he helped someone else first I said that he was impertinent, and quarreled with him. And then I said why wasn't he in the army, and I said it loud enough for everyone to hear, and I took his number and I turned in a complaint. Probably got him fired.'

'Fine,' said Mr. Johnson. 'But you do look tired. Want to change over tomorrow?'

'I *would* like to,' she said. 'I could do with a change.'

'Right,' said Mr. Johnson. 'What's for dinner?'

'Veal cutlet.'

'Had it for lunch,' said Mr. Johnson.

YES, WE HAVE NO RITCHARD

Bruce Jay Friedman

Since Mr. Dalton had seen many films and plays and read a good deal on the subject, he expected, after he died, to find himself before a Cyril Ritchard-type clerk, wearing white and seated at a desk. Wings were optional. Droll remarks would follow, in British accent, such as, 'We've got your records right here. What took you so long?' There would be a file cabinet and much shuffling of papers and talk about 'bringing your records up to date.' The 'front office' would be mentioned and sooner or later the 'boss,' in such lines as, 'The boss is sure going to be riled up when he sees these typing errors.' Plenty of white figured in Mr. Dalton's thoughts, too, cloaks and clouds and harps and floating things and subordinate people, too, all with such amusing comments as, 'I've got to get my wings fixed.'

What actually happened is that Mr. Dalton didn't get Ritchard. He didn't get E. G. Marshall either or, for that matter, anyone whose personality he could really nail down. The man did not wear a white robe, and Mr. Dalton, later on, could not recall what he wore. Something kind of vague and watery, if he wore anything at all. He certainly didn't have flip, or even impatient, things to say, and he sat at something that wasn't a desk, and maybe he wasn't even sitting. He seemed to be a little lower than Mr. Dalton and may have been sitting on a rock, although Mr. Dalton could not even be sure of that. Mr. Dalton himself could not remember whether he felt light and airy or whether there were clouds around and none of the Hollywood things had happened at all. Except perhaps one. He seemed to be wearing a pair of sandals he had once purchased at Vic Tanny's Gym and Health Club so as not to get athlete's foot when working out in the gym. What else he was wearing he couldn't say, or even if he *was* wearing something.

What was most disconcerting to Mr. Dalton was that he could not remember any elevator ride. It was the one thing he counted on most of all, and he was *certain* there would be one in there somewhere, a ride upward, and then, when they were finished with him, the decision as to whether to send him up or down. Mr. Dalton did not know whether to speak or wait to be spoken to, but he was so upset, he said to the man with the nebulous face and no distinctive personality, 'Look, I don't remember any elevator ride. Oh, you know what I mean. I don't really mean an elevator ride. Maybe you use a Volkswagen or a coal car, but I've got to know whether you've got a good side and a bad side here. Just tell me that, and anything you say from here on in is all right with me.'

'We have a good side and a bad side,' the man said, and this relaxed Mr. Dalton and he felt at least there was a little something to the movie ideas he'd gotten.

'But I'll bet you don't even have it the Hollywood way,' Mr. Dalton said. 'Up and down is the way they do it. I'll bet you have it left side and right.'

The nebulous man, if he was a man, said, 'That's correct.'

The reason Mr. Dalton was glad about this was that, however unsophisticated and *Reader's Digest* it may have sounded, he was quite certain that he had been a nice man during his life. He knew many people probably felt that way about themselves, but he was certain, at the very heart of himself, that he really *had* been nice and wasn't feeling this way just to buoy his spirits. If you stacked up his good deeds against his bad ones, the good ones wouldn't just outweigh the bad ones, but the goods would win ridiculously and overwhelmingly, no contest. And it wasn't that there was one sneaky thing he'd been trying to cover up and atone for by piling up millions of good deeds. There were no sneakies at all, and even if he *had* a sneaky (he hadn't), well, by God, he was still nice. He'd say that to anyone, whether he was dead or alive or whatever the hell condition he was in now.

'Did you know I've been nice?' he asked the man. 'I'm probably still nice, too, but I guess you're not concerned about me now, although, by God, I'm nice now, too, even if I'm dead. I'm just always going to be nice. But did you *know* that?'

'I know,' the man said.

'You probably have records and you're going to pull out a sheet on me. You have everybody's file, don't you? You have a file cabinet somewhere.'

'No,' the man said.

'It's not at all the way I'd imagined it,' Mr. Dalton said, or thought he said. 'But just so long as you know I've been nice. When do we get started?'

The man said, 'We could have started a little while ago, before you started talking. Or now, later, anytime.'

'Do I get a say in when we get started?' Mr. Dalton asked.

The man looked through him, and Mr. Dalton thought, 'He isn't saying anything because a little personality was beginning to come through. He clammed up just in time. A little more and I could have nailed him down, pinned him down and found out whether he was a Ritchard or a Marshall or a goddamned Wendell Willkie. He shut up like a clam though.'

And then Mr. Dalton wondered whether you were allowed to think things to yourself when you were dead. He turned off his mind for a while, just to be on the safe side. He thought of water, which was like not thinking at all to him. Maybe when you were dead, if you began thinking things, they counted it against you. Maybe a few interior thoughts at this moment wiped out forty-nine years of being nice. By God, he thought, I don't know any other way to be but nice, so I'll keep thinking. They'll be nice thoughts and even if they're baddies, they'll be nicely motivated.

'We'll go now,' the man said.

'Say some more so I can get the hang of you,' Mr. Dalton said. Mr. Dalton felt he was good at pinning personalities down, packaging people. If the man said just a little more, Mr. Dalton would have him and perhaps be able to do a routine on him, one as good as his Jack Paar imitation. Mr. Dalton could not remember whether he himself had been in advertising or not. The only thing he could remember was that somehow, somewhere, at some time, he had been at Vic Tanny's.

They seemed to walk somewhere and, try as he might, Mr. Dalton, although he'd promised to check the guy's outfit, what he looked like, his walk and mannerisms, forgot to do these things. He remembered only that the man had seemed to be a little lower than him. Mr. Dalton brought up *Green Pastures* as something he'd liked and then said, 'I'll bet you think I'm just trying to butter you up, to say I like your racket, know about it and some of my best friends are heavenly clerks or whatever you are.'

They passed a Danish modern sofa with shiny wood, and Mr. Dalton thought, 'Now there are two things I know. The Tanny slippers and the sofa. I wonder if there'll be any more. Maybe there are only two things you recognize in this whole trip or maybe twelve. I wonder how many.' He asked the man. 'I know I'm wearing Tanny slippers and I recognized a Danish modern sofa. That's all that's tangible. Will there be anything else? Anything else I can recognize or touch or sort of make reference to?'

'One more,' the man said. 'Air conditioning.'

'I've got him now,' Mr. Dalton thought. 'Now I can tell what kind of person he is. From that last line of dialogue.' And yet for the life of him, Mr. Dalton could not pinpoint what kind of man he was, although Mr. Dalton himself seemed to recall once being in advertising or at least being good at packaging people.

They stopped walking, if they had been walking. Mr. Dalton knew only that they sure as hell weren't standing still.

'Are we here?' Mr. Dalton asked. 'I mean where I'm going to be?' Then he added, 'Forever, that is,' feeling a little silly, as though he were in one of those heaven movies again.

The man nodded.

'I can't remember,' Mr. Dalton asked, 'whether you took me to the left or to the right. Let me get one thing straight. I hate to be a bore, but you do know I'm nice, don't you?'

The man nodded.

'And left is your nice side and right is your bad side?'

'Yes,' said the man.

'Then you took me to the left, right?' said Mr. Dalton, not without apprehension.

'No,' said the nebulous man. 'To the right.'

Mr. Dalton, rattled, and feeling he had every right to be rattled, said, 'But why? You're probably not convinced that I'm nice, correct?'

'No,' said the man.

'I know then,' said Mr. Dalton, quite convinced he had the answer. 'You have a reverse sort of logic up here. You put the nice guys on the bad side and the bad guys on the nice side. There's a perverse someone at work up here. Isn't that it? It's foolish, you know, because all us nice ones will know, even while we're on the bad side, that we're still nice. You're just being perverse for its own sake. Why do you have to knock yourselves out so much? Just to be different? Listen, do I get to punch you if I don't like something here?'

Mr. Dalton took a look at the man and for a brief second thought he could actually see him and size him up and guessed he had forty pounds on the man.

'Look, I mean no disrespect,' said Mr. Dalton. 'A week from

now, if I see you again, and I suppose I do (Hollywood again), I'll probably feel silly. But you must take an awful lot of abuse.'

The man said, 'I've got to go now.'

'Don't go,' said Mr. Dalton. 'I've got to get straightened out. I'm nice. You know I'm nice. Why do you put me on the bad side?'

Mr. Dalton tried to grab the man and hold onto him, looking around furiously, thinking, Christ, I'm backed against the wall. If only I could get one of those breaks you're supposed to get when you're on your ass and supposedly at an all-time low. He looked up and down the right side, where he was to be, and got the break. He saw a Bloomingdale's print, pretty good for Bloomingdale's, and a man he knew as Mr. Sydel. Mr. Sydel was engaged in doing something to the ground or whatever it was beneath him. 'Look,' said Mr. Dalton, 'I know him. I don't care what in the hell he told you, and maybe this is the first un-nice thing I've ever done, but he is not a nice man. He stole paper from some kind of a crazy company I used to work for with him, and even if he was never caught, he really was a crook. He's still a crook. And it wasn't the only bad thing he did. I can't document any others, but believe me, there were others. How in the hell can we be put on the same side? You know he's bad, don't you?'

'So I understand,' the man said. 'That is, I don't really know, but one of my colleagues so informs me.'

'He's slipping,' Mr. Dalton thought. 'By that statement he told me something that will enable me to package him, pin down his personality. He has colleagues, means he's classy, has studied . . . But, still, I'll have to know more.'

'If you both know he's bad, how come he's down here? Don't tell me. You've got the bad side divided up into sections. On one side you put baddies, like Mr. Sydel, on the other, people like me? Correct?'

'No,' the man said.

The air conditioning went on, and Mr. Dalton felt himself relax, in spite of himself.

'Look, for Christ's sake, what's the deal? I'll talk down to earth now, because nothing can hurt me. You have a good side and a bad side, right?'

The man nodded, but looked a little impatient. 'I really have to go.'

'Two more minutes won't kill you,' said Mr. Dalton. 'Who the hell do you put over on the good side? People who are nicer than me? You have some sort of score, and I didn't score high enough, is that it? The place is crowded up with people who got higher scores, right?'

The man began edging away, and Mr. Dalton said, 'You stay right here. I never punched people as much as I should, but by God, I'll punch you if I have to.' But then Mr. Dalton felt demolished and said, 'Stay with me another minute, will you? Maybe I'll never see you again, and there won't be anyone to tell me what to do. How to get along here. What the hell the rules are. The machinery of the place. I mean even if it's forever, I have to know, don't I?'

'I do have a schedule, Mr. Dalton,' the man said kindly.

'Can you call me Phillip?' Mr. Dalton asked. For a second he felt a joke coming on, like, 'If I get friendly with you, can you fix traffic tickets?' but decided not to ask it. When the joke went out of his mind, the panic started again.

'What I started to ask is how in the hell do I get over on the good side? I've been nice, you say you know I've been nice, but what the hell good has it done me? Can you name me one person who's over there so I can get an idea of what you've got to have, where I missed out?'

'I can't do that,' the man said.

'Why, for Christ's sake? I'm a dying man. I'm dead and I'm dying all over again. I need some help.'

'All right then. I'd rather not go into this, but we don't have anyone over there. There is no one on our good side.'

'It's for the staff?'

'No, even the staff doesn't use it. For a while we had women with enormous bosoms over there, for a very short while, but everyone saw the fallacy in that, and so now no one gets in.'

'There's no one on the good side,' Mr. Dalton said. 'That means we're all over here, right?'

'Yes,' the man said.

'What's it like on the good side? Can anyone see it?'

'There's no point,' the man said. 'In an extreme case, if it will make someone feel very good, we take him or her over, but it isn't such a hot idea.'

'I don't have to see it,' Mr. Dalton said. 'Maybe I'm a little curious, but that's all. Naturally, what bugs me—I'm talking calmly but I'm really stirred up about this—is that Mr. Sydel and all the Mr. Sydels have to be in the same side as me. I mean you say you know I was nice and you say you know he was a louse. How do you square it? Does he do another kind of thing up here? This is going to sound corny, but does he do harder work?'

'No,' said the man. 'Now I really have to go. I'm getting, frankly, very irritated.'

'I don't care about that,' Mr. Dalton said. The man looked at him sternly and Mr. Dalton said, 'Of course, I care, but you've got to tell me. Do I get better food? That's silly,' he added quickly. 'I'm dead and I don't eat. I don't, do I?'

'If it's necessary,' the man said, 'we bring food in.'

'Would you bring food in for Mr. Sydel if it was necessary? For all the Mr. Sydels? That's it, isn't it? You'd bring it in for me and you wouldn't for him . . .'

'No,' the man said.

'What then? There has to be something. I get to go out and have sex once a million years and he doesn't, right? That's how you get him.'

'No,' the man said. 'You both do. The figure is wrong. It's once a fortnight.'

'I get prettier girls?'

'Sometimes. And sometimes he does.'

'Then what—what? I've been nice. *He's been a bastard! What? What? What?*'

The man seemed to make a note on a piece of paper or something. 'I'll see that you get some medication,' the man said.

'I don't want any. You'd give it to Sydel, too, wouldn't you? Keep your medicine,' said Mr. Dalton, weeping, demolished.

Then he stopped crying and blocked what seemed to be the man's way. 'The air conditioning. That's it, isn't it? I get to feel it and he doesn't. I should have known. For an eternity, Sydel sits there knowing there's air conditioning and he can't feel it and I can. That's his punishment. That's my reward.'

'He feels it, too,' said the man employing a snotty tone.

'I beg you,' said Mr. Dalton on his knees. 'Look, I have no shame. I cry in front of you. I cry, I scream, I beg, I have no pride. Tell me, please tell me. Please.'

And then Mr. Dalton glanced down at his own sandals. 'Tanny's,' he said. 'That's it. I have these slippers and he doesn't. He walks barefoot for an eternity, a million eternities, and you give me, us, slippers from Tanny's and we feel nothing in our feet and he feels every bump, every splinter, every whatever the hell you've got here. I have you now, you stubborn sonofabitch. I do, you know. I defy you to tell me Sydel has Tanny slippers on, too.'

'Al Roon's Athletic Club on Eighth Avenue in New York City,' said the man, and he seemed to have lost his composure the slightest bit. Mr. Dalton waited now, waited for *him* to speak.

'We, uh, couldn't get Tanny's so we got Roon's. There really isn't any difference. It's purely administrative. If we'd gotten Tanny's we certainly wouldn't have used Roon's. You're really making a big thing out of nothing. Tanny's, Roon's, the spirit is the same, I assure you.'

'But, by God, *we've* got the Tanny's, and the Sydels have the Roon's, and never mind the administrative stuff. That's it and you know in your black heart that's it, and don't you sit there and tell me it isn't it.'

'No, no, no,' said the man. 'You've got it all wrong, Mr. Dalton.'

'Phillip,' said Mr. Dalton, sitting on something, possibly a chair, and folding his arms. 'And you can go now.'

THE BALLAD OF THE FLEXIBLE BULLET

Stephen King

The barbecue was over. It had been a good one: drinks; charcoaled T-bones, rare; a green salad and Meg's special dressing. They had started at five. Now it was 8:30 and almost dusk—the time when a big party is just starting to get rowdy. But they weren't a big party. There were just the five of them: the agent and his wife; the celebrated young writer and *his* wife; and the magazine editor, who was in his early sixties and looked older. The editor stuck to Fresca. The agent had told the young writer before the editor arrived that there had once been a drinking problem there. It was gone now, and so was the editor's wife . . . which was why they were five instead of six.

Instead of getting rowdy, an introspective mood fell over them as it started to get dark in the young writer's backyard, which fronted the lake. The young writer's first novel had been well reviewed and had sold a lot of copies. He was a lucky young man, and to his credit, he knew it.

The conversation had turned with playful gruesomeness from the young writer's early success to other writers who had made their marks early and had then committed suicide. Ross Lockridge was touched upon, and Tom Hagen. The agent's wife mentioned Sylvia Plath and Anne Sexton, and the young writer said that he didn't think Plath qualified as a *successful* writer. She had not committed suicide because of success, he said; she had gained success because she had committed suicide. The agent smiled.

'Please, couldn't we talk about something else?' the young writer's wife asked, a little nervously.

Ignoring her, the agent said, 'And madness. There have been those who have gone mad because of success.' The agent had the mild but nonetheless rolling tones of an actor offstage.

The writer's wife was about to protest again—she knew that her husband liked to talk about these things only so he could joke about them, and he wanted to joke about them because he thought about them too much—when the magazine editor spoke up. What he said was so odd she forgot to protest.

'Madness is a flexible bullet.'

The agent's wife looked startled. The young writer leaned forward quizzically. He said, 'That sounds familiar—'

'Sure,' the editor said. 'That phrase, the image, 'flexible bullet' is Marianne Moore's. She used it to describe some car or other. I've always thought it described the condition of madness very well. Madness is a kind of mental suicide. Don't the doctors say now that the only way to truly measure death is by the death of the mind? Madness is a kind of flexible bullet to the brain.'

The young writer's wife hopped up. 'Anybody want another drink?'

She had no takers.

'Well, I do, if we're going to talk about this,' she said, and went off to make herself one.

The editor said: 'I had a story submitted to me once, when I was working over at *Logan's*. Of course it's gone the way of *Collier's* and the *Saturday Evening Post* now, but we outlasted both of them.' He said this with a trace of pride. 'We published thirty-six short stories a year, or more, and every year four or five of them would be in somebody's collection of the year's best. And people *read* them. Anyway, the name of this story was 'The Ballad of the Flexible Bullet,' and it was written by a man named Reg Thorpe. A young man about this young man's age, and about as successful.'

'He wrote *Underworld Figures*, didn't he?' the agent's wife asked.

'Yes. Amazing track record for a first novel. Great reviews, lovely sales in hardcover and paperback, Literary Guild, everything. Even the movie was pretty good, although not as good as the book. Nowhere near.'

'I loved that book,' the author's wife said, lured back into the conversation against her better judgment. 'Has he written anything since then? I read *Underworld Figures* back in college, and that was . . . well, too long ago to think about.'

'You haven't aged a day since then,' the agent's wife said warmly, although privately she thought the young writer's wife was wearing a too-small halter and a too-tight pair of shorts.

'No, he hasn't written anything since then,' the editor said. 'Except for this one short story I was telling you about. He killed himself. Went crazy and killed himself.'

'Oh,' the young writer's wife said limply. Back to *that*.

'Was the short story published?' the young writer asked.

'No, but not because the author went crazy and killed himself. It never got into print because the *editor* went crazy and *almost* killed himself.'

The agent suddenly got up to freshen his own drink, which hardly needed freshening. He knew that the editor had had a nervous breakdown in the summer of 1969, not long before *Logan's* had drowned in a sea of red ink.

'I was the editor,' the editor informed the rest of them. 'In a sense we went crazy together. Reg Thorpe and I, even though I was in New York, he was out in Omaha, and we never even met. His book had been out about six months, and he had moved out there 'to get his head together,' as the phrase was then. And I happen to know this side of the story because I see his wife occasionally when she's in New York. She paints, and quite well. She's a lucky girl. He almost took her with him.'

The agent came back and sat down. 'I'm starting to remember some of this now,' he said. 'It wasn't just his wife, was it? He shot a couple of other people, one of them a kid.'

'That's right,' the editor said. 'It was the kid that finally set him off.'

'The *kid* set him off?' the agent's wife asked a little shrilly. 'What do you mean?'

But the editor's face said he would not be drawn.

'I know my side of the story because I lived it,' the magazine editor said. 'I'm lucky, too. Damned lucky. It's an interesting thing about those who try to kill themselves by pointing a gun at their heads and pulling the trigger. You'd think it would be the foolproof method, better than pills or slashing the wrists, but it isn't. When you shoot yourself in the head, you just can't tell what's going to happen. The slug may ricochet off the skull and kill someone else. It may follow the skull's curve all the way around and come out on the other side. It may lodge in the brain and blind you and leave you alive. One man may shoot himself in the temple with a .38 and wake up in the hospital. Another may shoot himself in the forehead with a .22 and wake up in hell . . . if there is such a place. I tend to believe it's here on earth, possibly in New Jersey.'

The writer's wife laughed rather shrilly.

'The only foolproof suicide method is to step off a very high building, and that's so damned messy, isn't it?

'But my point is simply this: When you shoot yourself with a flexible bullet, you really don't know what the outcome is going to be. In my case, I went off a bridge and woke up on a trash-littered embankment with a trucker whapping me on the back and pumping my arms up and down like he had only twenty-four hours to get in shape and he had mistaken me for a rowing machine. For Reg, the bullet was lethal. He . . . but I'm telling you a story I have no idea if you want to hear.'

He looked around at them questioningly in the gathering gloom. The agent and the agent's wife glanced at each other uncertainly, and the writer's wife was about to say she thought they'd had enough gloomy talk when her husband said, 'I'd like to hear it. If you don't mind telling it for personal reasons, I mean.'

'I never have told it,' the editor said, 'but not for personal reasons. Perhaps I never had the correct listeners.'

'Then tell away,' the writer said.

'Paul—' His wife put her hand on his shoulder. 'Don't you think—'

'Not now, Meg.'

The editor said:

'The story came in over the transom, and at that time *Logan's* no longer read unsolicited scripts. When they came in, a girl would just put them into return envelopes with a note that said 'Due to increasing costs and the increasing inability of the editorial staff to cope with a steadily increasing number of submissions, *Logan's* no longer reads unsolicited manuscripts. We wish you the best of luck in placing your work elsewhere.' Isn't that a lovely bunch of gobbledygook? It's not easy to use the word *increasing* three times in one sentence, but they did it.'

'And if there was no return postage, the story went into the wastebasket,' the writer said. 'Right?'

'Oh, absolutely. No pity in the naked city.'

An odd expression of unease flitted across the writer's face. It was the expression of a man who is in a tiger pit where dozens of better men have been clawed to pieces. So far this man hasn't seen a single tiger. But he has a feeling that they are there, and that their claws are still sharp.

'Anyway,' the editor said, taking out his cigarette case, 'this story came in, and the girl in the mailroom took it out, paper-clipped the form rejection to the first page, and was getting ready to put it in the return envelope when she glanced at the author's name. Well, she had read *Underworld Figures*. That fall everybody had read it, or was reading it, or was on the library waiting list, or checking the drugstore racks for the paperback.'

The writer's wife, who had seen the momentary unease on her

husband's face, took his hand. He smiled at her. The editor snapped a gold Ronson to his cigarette, and in the growing dark they could all see how haggard his face was—the loose, crocodile-skinned pouches under the eyes, the runneled cheeks, the old man's jut of chin emerging out of that late-middle-aged face like the prow of a ship. That ship, the writer thought, is called old age. No one particularly wants to cruise on it, but the staterooms are full. The gangholds, too, for that matter.

The lighter winked out, and the editor puffed his cigarette meditatively.

'The girl in the mailroom who read that story and passed it on instead of sending it back is now a full editor at G. P. Putnam's Sons. Her name doesn't matter; what matters is that on the great graph of life, this girl's vector crossed Reg Thorpe's in the mailroom of *Logan's* magazine. Hers was going up, and his was going down. She sent the story to her boss, and her boss sent it to me. I read it and loved it. It was really too long, but I could see where he could pare five hundred words off it with no sweat. And that would be plenty.'

'What was it about?' the writer asked.

'You shouldn't even have to ask,' the editor said. 'It fits so beautifully into the total context.'

'About going crazy?'

'Yes, indeed. What's the first thing they teach you in your first college creative writing course? Write about what you know. Reg Thorpe knew about going crazy, because he was engaged in going there. The story probably appealed to me because I was also going there. Now you could say—if you were an editor—that the one thing the American reading public doesn't need foisted on them is another story about Going Mad Stylishly in America, subtopic A, Nobody Talks to Each Other Anymore. A popular theme in twentieth-century literature. All the greats have taken a hack at it, and all the hacks have taken an ax to it. But this story was funny. I mean, it was really hilarious.

'I haven't read anything like it before and I haven't since. The closest would be some of F. Scott Fitzgerald's stories . . . and *Gatsby*. The fellow in Thorpe's story was going crazy, but he was doing it in a very funny way. You kept grinning, and there were a couple of places in this story—the place where the hero dumps the lime Jell-O on the fat girl's head is the best—where you laugh right out loud. But they're jittery laughs, you know. You laugh and then you want to look over your shoulder to see what heard you. The opposing lines of tension in that story were really extraordinary.

The more you laughed, the more nervous you got. And the more nervous you got, the more you laughed . . . right up to the point where the hero goes home from the party given in his honor and kills his wife and baby daughter.'

'What's the plot?' the agent asked.

'No,' the editor said, 'that doesn't matter. It was just a story about a young man gradually losing his struggle to cope with success. It's better left vague. A detailed plot synopsis would only be boring. They always are.

'Anyway, I wrote him a letter. It said this: "Dear Reg Thorpe, I've just read 'The Ballad of the Flexible Bullet' and I think it's great. I'd like to publish it in *Logan's* early next year, if that fits. Does eight hundred dollars sound O.K.? Payment on acceptance. More or less." New paragraph.'

The editor indented the evening air with his cigarette.

' "The story runs a little long, and I'd like you to shorten it by about five hundred words, if you could. I would settle for a two-hundred-word cut, if it comes to that. We can always drop a cartoon." Paragraph. "Call, if you want." My signature. And off the letter went, to Omaha.'

'And you remember it, word for word like that?' the writer's wife asked.

'I kept all the correspondence in a special file,' the editor said. 'His letters, carbons of mine back. There was quite a stack of it by the end, including three or four pieces of correspondence from Jane Thorpe, his wife. I've read the file over quite often. No good, of course. Trying to understand the flexible bullet is like trying to understand how a Möbius strip can have only one side. That's just the way things are in this best of all possible worlds. Yes, I know it all word for word, or almost. Some people know the Declaration of Independence by heart.'

'Bet he called you the next day,' the agent said, grinning. 'Collect.'

'No, he didn't call. Shortly after *Underworld Figures*, Thorpe stopped using the telephone altogether. His wife told me that. When they moved to Omaha from New York, they didn't even have a phone put in the new house. He had decided, you see, that the telephone system didn't really run on electricity but on radium. He thought this was one of the two or three best-kept secrets in the history of the modern world. He claimed—to his wife—that all that radium was responsible for the growing cancer rate, not cigarettes or automobile emissions or industrial pollution. Each telephone had a small radium crystal in the handset, and every time you used the phone, you shot your head full of radiation.'

'Yuh, he was crazy,' the writer said. They all laughed.

'He wrote instead,' the editor said, flicking his cigarette in the direction of the lake. His letter said this: "Dear Henry Wilson (or just Henry, if I may), Your letter was both exciting and gratifying. My wife was, if anything, more pleased than I. The money is fine . . . although in all honesty I must say that the idea of being published in *Logan's* at all seems like more than adequate compensation (but I'll take it, I'll take it). I've looked over your cuts, and they seem fine. I think they'll improve the story as well as clear space for those cartoons. All best wishes, Reg Thorpe."

'Under his signature was a funny little drawing . . . more like a doodle. An eye in a pyramid, like the one on the back of the dollar bill. But instead of *Novus Ordo Seclorum* on the banner beneath, there were these words: *Fornit Some Fornus.*'

'Either Latin or Groucho Marx,' the agent's wife said.

'Just part of Reg Thorpe's growing eccentricity,' the editor said. 'His wife told me that Reg had come to believe in "little people," sort of like elves or fairies. The Fornits. They were luck-elves, and he thought one of them lived in his typewriter.'

'Oh, my Lord,' the writer's wife said.

'According to Thorpe, each Fornit has a small device, like a flit-gun, full of . . . good-luck dust, I guess you'd call it. And the good-luck dust—'

'—is called fornus,' the writer finished. He was grinning broadly.

'Yes. And his wife thought it quite funny, too. At first, in fact, she thought at first—Thorpe had conceived the Fornits two years before, while he was drafting *Underworld Figures*—that it was just Reg, having her on. And maybe at first he was. It seems to have progressed from a whimsy to a superstition to an outright belief. It was . . . a flexible fantasy. But hard in the end. Very hard.'

They were all silent. The grins had faded.

'The Fornits had their funny side,' the editor said. 'Thorpe's typewriter started going to the shop a lot near the end of their stay in New York, and it was even a more frequent thing when they moved to Omaha. He had a loaner while it was being fixed for the first time out there. The dealership manager called a few days after Reg got his own machine back to tell him he was going to send a bill for cleaning the loaner as well as Thorpe's own machine.'

'What was the trouble?' the agent's wife asked.

'I think I know,' the writer's wife said.

'It was full of food,' the editor said. 'Tiny bits of cake and cookies. There was peanut butter smeared on the platens of the keys themselves. Reg was feeding the Fornit in his typewriter. He also "fed" the loaner, on the off chance that the Fornit had made the switch.'

'Boy,' the writer said.

'I knew none of these things then, you understand. For the nonce, I wrote back to him and told him how pleased I was. My secretary typed the letter and brought it in for my signature, and then she had to go out for something. I signed it and she wasn't back. And then—for no real reason at all—I put the same doodle below my name. Pyramid. Eye. And *"Fornit Some Fornus."* Crazy. The secretary saw it and asked me if I wanted it sent out that way. I shrugged and told her to go ahead.

'Two days later Jane Thorpe called me. She told me that my letter had excited Reg a great deal. Reg thought he had found a kindred soul . . . someone else who knew about the Fornits. You see what a crazy situation it was getting to be? As far as I knew at that point, a Fornit could have been anything from a left-handed monkey wrench to a Polish steak knife. Ditto fornus. I explained to Jane that I had merely copied Reg's own design. She wanted to know why. I slipped the question, although the answer would have been because I was very drunk when I signed the letter.'

He paused, and an uncomfortable silence fell on the back lawn area. People looked at the sky, the lake, the trees, although they were no more interesting now than they had been a minute or two before.

'I had been drinking all my adult life, and it's impossible for me to say when it began to get out of control. In the professional sense I was on top of the bottle until nearly the very end. I would begin drinking at lunch and come back to the office *el blotto*. I functioned perfectly well there, however. It was the drinks after work—first on the train, then at home—that pushed me over the functional point.

'My wife and I had been having problems that were unrelated to the drinking, but the drinking made the other problems worse. For a long time she had been preparing to leave, and a week before the Reg Thorpe story came in, she did it.

'I was trying to deal with that when the Thorpe story came in. I was drinking too much. And to top it all off, I was having—well, I guess now it's fashionable to call it a mid-life crisis. All I knew at the time was that I was as depressed about my professional life as I was about my personal one. I was coming to grips—or trying to—with a growing feeling that editing mass-market stories that would end up being read by nervous dental patients, housewives at lunchtime, and an occasional bored college student was not exactly a noble occupation. I was coming to grips—again, trying to, all of us at *Logan's* were at that time—with the idea that in another six months, or ten, or fourteen, there might not be any *Logan's*.

'Into this dull autumnal landscape of middle-aged angst comes a very good story by a very good writer, a funny, energetic look at the mechanics of going crazy. It was like a bright ray of sun. I know it sounds strange to say that about a story that ends with the protagonist killing his wife and infant child, but you ask any editor what real joy is, and he'll tell you it's the great story or novel you didn't expect, landing on your desk like a big Christmas present. Look, you all know that Shirley Jackson story, "The Lottery." It ends on one of the most downbeat notes you can imagine. I mean, they take a nice lady out and stone her to death. Her son and daughter participate in her murder, for Christ's sake. But was that a piece of storytelling . . . and I bet the editor at *The New Yorker* who read the story first went home that night whistling.

'What I'm trying to say is the Thorpe story was the best thing in my life right then. The one good thing. And from what his wife told me on the phone that day, my acceptance of that story was the one good thing that had happened to him lately. The author-editor relationship is always mutual parasitism, but in the case of Reg and me, that parasitism was heightened to an unnatural degree.'

'Let's go back to Jane Thorpe,' the writer's wife said.

'Yes, I did sort of leave her on a side-track, didn't I? She was angry about the Fornit business. At first, I told her I had simply doodled that eye-and-pyramid symbol under my signature, with no knowledge of what it might be, and apologized for whatever I'd done.

'She got over her anger and spilled everything to me. She'd been getting more and more anxious, and she had no one to call at all to talk to. Her folks were dead, and all her friends were back in New York. Reg wouldn't allow anyone at all in the house. They were tax people, he said, or FBI, or CIA. Not long after they moved to Omaha, a little girl came to the door selling Girl Scout cookies. Reg yelled at her, told her to get the hell out, he knew why she was there, and so on. Jane tried to reason with him. She pointed out that the girl had only been ten years old. Reg told her that the tax people had no souls, no consciences. And besides, he said, the little girl might have been an android. Androids wouldn't be subject to the child labor laws. He wouldn't put it past the tax people to send an

android Girl Scout full of radium crystals to find out if he was
keeping any secrets . . . and to shoot him full of cancer rays in the
meantime.'

'Good Lord,' the agent's wife said.

'She'd been waiting for a friendly voice, and mine was the first. I
got the Girl Scout story, I found out about the care and feding of
Fornits, about fornus, about how Reg refused to use a telephone.
She was talking to me from a pay booth in a drugstore five blocks
over. She told me that she was afraid it wasn't really tax men or FBI
or CIA Reg was worried about. She thought he was really afraid
that *They*—some hulking, anonymous group that hated Reg, was
jealous of Reg, would stop at nothing to get Reg—had found out
about his Fornit and wanted to kill it. If the Fornit was dead, there
would be no more novels, no more short stories, nothing. You see?
The essence of insanity. *They* were out to get him. In the end, not
even the IRS, which had been given him the very devil of a time
over the income *Underworld Figures* generated. In the end it was
just *They*. The perfect paranoid fantasy. *They* wanted to kill his
Fornit.'

'My God, what did you say to her?' the agent asked.

'I tried to reassure her,' the editor said. 'There I was, freshly
returned from a five-martini lunch, talking to this terrified woman
who was standing in a drugstore phone booth in Omaha, trying to
tell her it was all right, not to worry that her husband believed that
the phones were full of radium crystals, that a bunch of anonymous
people were sending android Girl Scouts to get the goods on him,
not to worry that her husband had disconnected his talent from his
mentality to such a degree that he could believe there was an elf
living in his typewriter.

'I don't believe I was very convincing.

'She asked me—no, begged me—to work with Reg on his story,
to see that it got published. She did everything but come out and
say that "The Flexible Bullet" was Reg's last contact to what we
laughingly call reality.

'I asked her what I should do if Reg mentioned Fornits again.
"Humor him," she said. Her exact words—humor him. And then
she hung up.

'There was a letter in the mail from Reg the next day—five
pages, typed, single-spaced. The first paragraph was about the
story. The second draft was getting on well, he said. He thought he
would be able to shave seven hundred words from the original ten
thousand five hundred, bringing the final down to a tight nine
thousand eight.

'The rest of the letter was about Fornits and fornus. His own observations, and questions . . . dozens of questions.'

'Observations?' The writer leaned forward. 'He was actually seeing them, then?'

'No,' the editor said. 'Not seeing them in an actual sense, but in another way . . . I suppose he was. You know, astronomers knew Pluto was there long before they had a telescope powerful enough to see it. They knew all about it by studying the planet Neptune's orbit. Reg was observing the Fornits in that way. They liked to eat at night, he said; had I noticed that? He fed them at all hours of the day, but he noticed that most of it disappeared after 8 P.M.'

'Hallucination?' the writer asked.

'No,' the editor said. 'His wife simply cleared as much of the food out of the typewriter as she could when Reg went out for his evening walk, and he went out every evening at nine o'clock.'

'I'd say she had quite a nerve getting after you,' the agent grunted. He shifted his large bulk in the lawn chair. 'She was feeding the man's fantasy herself.'

'You don't understand why she called and why she was so upset,' the editor said quietly. He looked at the writer's wife. 'But I'll bet you do, Meg.'

'Maybe,' she said, and gave her husband an uncomfortable, sideways look. 'She wasn't mad because you were feeding his fantasy. She was afraid you might upset it.'

'Bravo.' The editor lit a fresh cigarette. 'And she removed the food for the same reason. If the food continued to accumulate in the typewriter, Reg would make the logial assumption, proceding directly from his own decidedly illogical premise. Namely, that is Fornit had either died or left. Hence, no more fornus. Hence, no more writing. Hence. . . .'

The editor let the word drift away on cigarette smoke and then resumed:

'He thought that Fornits were probably nocturnal. They didn't like loud noises—he had noticed that he hadn't been able to write on mornings after noisy parties—they hated TV, they hated free electricity, they hated radium. Reg sold their TV set to Goodwill for twenty dollars, he said, and his wristwatch with the radium dial was long gone. Then the questions: How did I know about the Fornits? Was it possible that I had one in residence? If so, what did I think about this, this, and that? I don't need to be more specific, I think. If you've ever gotten a dog of a particular breed and can recollect the questions you asked about its care and feeding, you'll know most of the questions Reg asked me. One little doodle below my signature was all it took to open Pandora's box.'

'What did you write back?' the agent asked.

The editor said slowly. 'That's where the trouble really began. For both of us. Jane had said, 'Humor him,' so that's what I did. Unfortunately, I rather overdid it. I answered his letter at home, and I was very drunk. The apartment seemed much too empty. It had a stale smell—cigarette smoke, not enough airing. Things were going to seed with Sandra gone. The drop cloth on the couch all wrinkled. Dirty dishes in the sink, that sort of thing. The middle-aged man unprepared for domesticity.

'I sat there with a sheet of my personal stationery rolled into the typewriter and I thought: *I need a Fornit. In fact, I need a dozen of them to dust this damn lonely house with fornus from end to end.* In that instant I was drunk enough to envy Reg Thorpe his delusion.

'I said I had a Fornit, of course. I told Reg that mine was remarkably similar to his in its characteristics. Nocturnal. Hated loud noise, but seemed to enjoy Bach and Brahms . . . I often did my best work after an evening of listening to them, I said. I had found that my Fornit had a decided taste for Kirschner's bologna . . . had Reg ever tried it? I simply left little scraps of it near the Scripto I always carried—my editorial blue pencil, if you like—and it was almost always gone in the morning. Unless, as Reg said, it had been noisy the night before. I told him I was glad to know about radium, even though I didn't have a glow-in-the-dark wristwatch. I told him my Fornit had been with me since college. I got so carried away with my own invention that I wrote nearly six pages. At the end I added a paragraph about the story, a very perfunctory thing, and signed it.'

'And below your signature—?' the agent's wife asked.

'Sure. *Fornit some Fornus.*' He paused. 'You can't see it in the dark, but I'm blushing. I was so goddamned drunk, so goddamned *smug* . . . I might have had second thoughts in the cold light of dawn, but by then it was too late.'

'You'd mailed it the night before?' the writer murmured.

'So I did. And then, for a week and a half, I held my breath and waited. One day the manuscript came in, addressed to me, no covering letter. The cuts were as we had discussed them, and I thought that the story was letter perfect, but the manuscript was . . . well, I put it in my briefcase, took it home, and retyped it myself. It was covered with weird yellow stains. I thought . . .'

'Urine?' the agent's wife asked.

'Yes, that's what I thought. But it wasn't. And when I got home, there was a letter in my mailbox from Reg. Ten pages this time. In the course of the letter the yellow stains were accounted for. He hadn't been able to find Kirschner's bologna, so had tried Jordan's.

'He said they loved it. Especially with mustard.

'I had been quite sober that day. But his letter, combined with those pitiful mustard stains ground right into the pages of his manuscript, sent me directly to the liquor cabinet. Do not pass go, do not collect two hundred dollars. Go directly to Drunk.'

'What else did the letter say?' the agent's wife asked. She had grown more and more fascinated with the tale, and was now leaning over her not-inconsiderable belly in a posture that reminded the writer's wife of Snoopy standing on his doghouse and pretending to be a vulture.

'Only two lines about the story this time. All credit thrown to the Fornit . . . and to me. The bologna had really been a fantastic idea. Rackne loved it, and a consequence—'

'Rackne?' the author asked.

'That was the Fornit's name,' the editor said. 'Rackne. As a consequence of the bologna, Rackne had really gotten behind in the rewrite. The rest of the letter was a paranoid chant. You have never seen such stuff in your life.'

'Reg and Rackne . . . a marriage made in heaven,' the writer's wife said, and giggled nervously.

'Oh, not at all,' the editor said. 'Theirs was a working relationship. And Rackne was male.'

'Well, tell us about the letter.'

'That's one I don't have by heart. It's just as well for you that I don't. Even abnormality grows tiresome after a while. The mailman was CIA. The paperboy was FBI; Reg had seen a silenced revolver in his sack of papers. The people next door were spies of some sort; they had surveillance equipment in their van. He no longer dared to go down to the corner store for supplies because the proprietor was an android. He had suspected it before, he said, but now he was sure. He had seen the wires crisscrossing under the man's scalp, where he was beginning to go bald. And the radium count in his house was way up; at night he could see a dull, greenish glow in the rooms.

'His letter finished this way: 'I hope you'll write back and apprise me of your own situation (and that of your Fornit) as regards *enemies*, Henry. I believe that reaching you has been an occurrence that transcends coincidence. I would call it a life ring—from (God? Providence? Fate? Supply your own term)—at the last possible instant.

' "It is not possible for a man to stand alone for long against a thousand *enemies*. And to discover, at last, that one is *not* alone . . . is it too much to say that the commonality of our experience stands between myself and total destruction? Perhaps not. I must know: Are the *enemies* after your Fornit as they are after Rackne? If so, how are you coping? If not, do you have any idea *why not?* I repeat, *I must know.*"

'The letter was signed with the *Fornit Some Fornus* doodle beneath, and then a P.S. just one sentence. But lethal. The P.S. said: 'Sometimes I wonder about my wife.'

'I read the letter through three times. In the process, I killed an entire bottle of Black Velvet. I began to consider options on how to answer his letter. It was a cry for help from a drowning man—that was pretty obvious. The story had held him together for a while, but now the story was done. Now he was depending on me to hold him together. Which was perfectly reasonable, since I'd brought the whole thing on myself.

'I walked up and down the house, through all the empty rooms. And I started to unplug things. I was very drunk, remember, and heavy drinking opens unexpected avenues of suggestibility. Which is why editors and lawyers are willing to spring for three drinks before talking contract at lunch.'

The agent brayed laughter, but the mood remained tight and tense and uncomfortable.

'And, please keep in mind that Reg Thorpe was one hell of a writer. He was absolutely convinced of the things he was saying. FBI. CIA. IRS. *They. The enemies.* Some writers possess a very rare gift for cooling their prose the more passionately they feel their subject. Steinbeck had it, so did Hemingway, and Reg Thorpe had the same talent. When you entered his world, everything began to seem very logical. You began to think it very likely, once you accepted the basic Fornit premises, that the paperboy *did* have a silenced .38 in his bag of papers. That the college kids next door with the van might indeed be KGB agents with death-capsules in wax molars, on a do-or-die mission to kill or capture Rackne.

'Of course, I didn't accept the basic premise. But it seemed so hard to think. And I unplugged things. First the color TV, because everybody knows that they really do give off radiation. At *Logan's* we had published an article by a perfectly reputable scientist suggesting that the radiation given off by the household color television was interrupting human brain waves just enough to alter them minutely but permanently. This scientist suggested that it might be the reason for declining college board scores, literacy tests, and grammar school development of arithmetical skills. After all, who sits closer to the TV than a little kid?

'So I unplugged the TV, and it really did seem to clarify my thoughts. In fact, it made it so much better that I unplugged the radio, the toaster, the washing machine, the dryer. Then I remembered the microwave oven, and I unplugged that. I felt a real sense of relief when that fucking thing's teeth were pulled. It was one of the early ones, about the size of a house, and it probably really *was* dangerous. Shielding on them's better these days.

'It occurred to me just how many things we have in any ordinary middleclass house that plug into the wall. An image occurred to me of this nasty electrical octopus, its tentacles consisting of electrical cables, all snaking into the walls, all connected with wires outside, and all wires leading to power stations run by the government.

'There was a curious doubling in my mind as I did those things,' the editor went on, after pausing for a sip of his Fresca. 'Essentially, I was responding to a superstitious impulse. There are plenty of people who won't walk under ladders or open a umbrella in the house. There are basketball players who cross themselves before taking foul shots, and baseball players who change their socks when they're in a slump. I think it's the rational mind playing a bad stereo accompaniment with the irrational subconscious. Forced to define "irrational subconscious," I would say that it is a small padded room inside all of us, where the only furnishing is a small card table, and the only thing on the card table is a revolver loaded with flexible bullets.

'When you change course on the sidewalk to avoid the ladder or step out of your apartment into the rain with your furled umbrella, part of your integrated self peels off and steps into that room and picks the gun up off the table. You may be aware of two conflicting thoughts: *Walking under a ladder is harmless,* and *Not walking under a ladder is also harmless.* But as soon as the ladder is behind you—or as soon as the umbrella is open—you're back together again.'

The writer said, 'That's very interesting. Take it a step further for me, if you don't mind. When does that irrational part actually stop fooling with the gun and put it up to its temple?'

The editor said, 'When the person in a question starts writing letters to the op-ed page of the paper demanding that all the ladders be taken down because walking under them is dangerous.'

There was a laugh.

'Having taken it that far, I suppose we ought to finish. The irrational self has actually fired the flexible bullet into the brain when the person begins tearing around town, knocking ladders over and maybe injuring the people who were working on them. It is not certifiable behavior to walk around ladders rather than under them. It is not certifiable behavior to write letters to the paper saying that New York City went broke because of all the people callously walking under workmen's ladders. But it is certifiable to start knocking over ladders.'

'Because it's overt,' the writer muttered.

The agent said, 'You know, you've got something there, Henry. I've got this thing about not lighting three cigarettes on a match. I don't know how I got it, but I did. Then I read somewhere that it came from the trench warfare in World War I. It seems that the German sharpshooters would wait for the Tommies to start lighting each other's cigarettes. On the first light you got the range. On the second one you got the windage. And on the third one you blew the guy's head off. But knowing all that didn't make any difference. I still can't light three on a match. One part of me says it doesn't matter if I light a dozen cigarettes on one match. But the other part—this very ominous voice, like an interior Boris Karloff—says *"ohhh, if you doooo. . . ."'*

'But all madness isn't superstitious, is it?' the writer's wife asked timidly.

'Isn't it?' the editor replied. 'Jeanne d'Arc heard voices from heaven. Some people think they are possessed by demons. Others see gremlins . . . or devils . . . or Fornits. The terms we use for madness suggest superstition in some form or other. Mania . . . abnormality . . . irrationality . . . lunacy . . . insanity. For the mad person, reality has skewed. The whole person begins to reintegrate in that small room where the pistol is.

'But the rational part of me was still very much there. Bloody, bruised, indignant, and rather frightened, but still on the job. Saying: "Oh, that's all right. Tomorrow when you sober up, you can plug everything back in, thank God. Play your games if you have to. But no more than this. No further than this."

'That rational voice was right to be frightened. There's something in us that is very much attracted to madness. Everyone who looks off the edge of a tall building has felt at least a faint, morbid urge to jump. And anyone who has ever put a loaded pistol up to his head. . . .'

'Ugh, don't,' the writer's wife said. 'Please.'

'All right,' the editor said. 'My point is just this: Even the most well-adjusted person is holding onto his or her sanity by a greased rope. I really believe that. The rationality circuits are shoddily built into the human animal.

'With the plugs pulled, I went into my study, wrote Reg Thorpe a letter, put it in an envelope, stamped it, took it out, and mailed it. I don't actually remember doing any of these things. I was too drunk. But I deduce that I did them because when I got up the next morning, the carbon was still by my typewriter, along with the stamps and the box of envelopes. The letter was about what you'd expect from a drunk. What it boiled down to was this: The enemies were drawn by electricity as well as by the Fornits themselves. Get rid of the electricity and you got rid of the enemies. At the bottom I had written, "the electricity is fucking up your thinking about these things, Reg. Interference with brain waves. Does your wife have a blender?"'

'In effect, you had started writing letters to the paper,' the writer said.

'Yes, I wrote that letter on a Friday night. On Saturday morning I got up around eleven, hung over and only blurrily aware of what sort of mischief I'd been up to the night before. Great pangs of shame as I plugged everything back in. Greater pangs of shame —and fear—when I saw what I'd written to Reg. I looked all over the house for the original to that letter, hoping like hell I hadn't mailed it. But I had. And the way I got through the day was by making a resolution to take my lumps like a man and go on the wagon. Sure I was.

'The following Wednesday there was a letter from Reg. One page, handwritten. *Fornit Some Fornus* doodles all over it. In the center, just this: "You were right. Thank you, thank you, thank you. Reg. You were right. Everything is fine now. Reg. Thanks a lot. Fornit is fine. Reg. Thanks. Reg."'

'Oh, my,' the writer's wife said.

'Bet his wife was mad,' the agent's wife said.

'But she wasn't. Because it worked.'

'Worked?' the agent said.

'He got my letter in the Monday morning post. Monday afternoon he went down to the local power company office and told them to cut his power off. Jane Thorpe, of course, was hysterical. Her range ran on electricity; she did indeed have a blender, a sewing machine, a washer-dryer combination . . . well, you understand. On Monday evening I'm sure she was ready to have my head on a plate.

'But it was Reg's behavior that made her decide I was a miracle worker instead of a lunatic. He sat her down in the living room and talked to her quite rationally. He said that he knew he'd been acting in a peculiar fashion. He knew that she'd been worried. He told her that he felt much better with the power off, and that he would be glad to help her through any inconvenience that it caused. And then he suggested that they go next door and say hello.'

'Not to the KGB agents with the radium in their van?' the writer asked.

'Yes, to them. Jane was totally floored. She agreed to go over with him, but she told me that she was girding herself up for a really nasty scene. Accusations, threats, hysteria. She had begun to consider leaving Reg if he wouldn't get help for his problem. She told me that Wednesday morning on the phone that she had made herself a promise: the power was the next-to-the-last straw. One more thing, and she was going to leave for New York. She was becoming afraid, you see. The thing had worsened by such degrees as to be nearly imperceptible, and she loved him, but even for her, it had gotten as far as it could go. She had decided that if Reg said one strange word to the students next door, she was going to break up housekeeping. I found out much later that she had already asked some very circumspect questions about the procedure in Nebraska to effect an involuntary committal.'

'The poor woman,' the writer's wife murmured.

'But the evening was a smashing success,' the editor said. 'Reg was at his most charming . . . and according to Jane, that was very charming indeed. She hadn't seen him so much on in three years. The sullenness, the secretiveness, they were gone. The nervous tics. The involuntary jump and look over his shoulder when ever a door opened. He had a beer and talked about all the topics that were current back in those dim, dead days: the war, the possibilities of a volunteer army, the riots in the cities, the pot laws.

'The fact that he had written *Underworld Figures* came up, and they were . . . "author struck" was the way Jane put it. Three of the four had read it, and you can bet the odd one wasn't going to linger any on his way to the library.'

The writer laughed and nodded. He knew about that bit.

'So,' the editor said, 'we leave Reg Thorpe and his wife for just a little while, without electrical power but happier than they've been in a good long time—'

'Good thing he didn't have an IBM typewriter,' the agent said.

'—and return to Ye Editor. Two weeks have gone by. Summer is ending. Ye Editor has, of course, fallen off the wagon any number of times, but has managed on the whole to remain pretty respectable. The days have gone their appointed rounds. At Cape Kennedy they are getting ready to put a man on the moon. The new issue of *Logan's,* with John Lindsay on the cover, is out on the stands, and selling miserably, as usual. I had put in a purchase order for a short story called "The Ballad of the Flexible Bullet," by Reg Thorpe, first serial rights, proposed publication January 1970, proposed purchase price eight hundred dollars, which was standard then for a *Logan's* lead story.

'I got a buzz from my superior, Jim Dohegan. Could I come up and see him? I trotted into his office at ten in the morning, looking and feeling my very best. It didn't occur to me until later that Janey Morrison, his secretary, looked like a wake in progress.

'I sat down and asked Jim what I could do for him, or vise versa. I won't say the Reg Thorpe name hadn't entered my mind; having the story was a tremendous coup for *Logan's,* and I suspected a few congratulations were in order. So you can imagine how dumbfounded I was when he slid two purchase orders across the desk at me. The Thorpe story, and a John Updike novella we had scheduled as the February fiction lead. RETURN stamped across both.

'I looked at the revoked purchase orders. I looked at Jimmy. I couldn't make any sense out of it. I really couldn't get my brains to work over what it meant. There was a block in there. I looked around and I saw his hotplate. Janey brought it in for him every morning when she came to work and plugged it in so he could have fresh coffee when he wanted it. That had been the drill at *Logan's* for three years or more. And that morning all I could think of was, *if that thing were unplugged, I could think. I know if that thing were unplugged, I could put this together.*

'I said, "What is this, Jim?"

' "I'm sorry as hell to have to be the one to tell you this, Henry," he said. *"Logan's* isn't going to be publishing any more fiction as of January 1970." '

The editor paused to get a cigarette, but his pack was empty. 'Does anyone have a cigarette?'

The writer's wife gave him a Salem.

'Thank you, Meg.'

He lit it, shook out the match, and dragged deep. The coal glowed mellowly in the dark.

'Well,' he said, 'I'm sure Jim thought I was crazy. I said, "Do you mind?" and leaned over and pulled the plug on his hotplate.

'His mouth dropped open and he said, "What the hell, Henry?"

' "It's hard for me to think with things like that going," I said. "Interference." And it really seemed to be true, because with the plug pulled, I was able to see the situation a great deal more clearly. "Does this mean I'm pinked?" I asked him.

' "I don't know," he said, "That's up to Sam and the board. I just don't know, Henry."

'There were a lot of things I could have said. I guess what Jimmy was expecting was a passionate plea for my job. You know that saying, "he had his ass out to the wind?" . . . I maintain that you don't understand the meaning of that phrase until you're the head of a suddenly nonexistent department.

'But I didn't plead my cause or the cause of fiction at *Logan's*. I pleaded for Reg Thorpe's story. First, I said that we could move it up over the deadline—put it in the December issue.

'Jimmy said, "Come on, Henry, the December ish is locked up. You know that. And we're talking ten thousand words here."

' "Nine thousand eight," I said.

' "And a full-page illo," he said. "Forget it."

' "Well, we'll scrap the art," I said. 'Listen, Jimmy, it's a great story, maybe the best fiction we've had in the last five years.'

'Jimmy said, "I read it, Henry. I know it's a great story. But we just can't do it. Not in December. It's Christmas, for God's sake, and you want to put a story about a guy who kills his wife and kid under the Christmas trees of America? You must be"—He stopped right there, but I saw him glance over to his hotplate. He might as well have said it out loud, you know?'

The writer nodded slowly, his eyes never leaving the dark shadow that was the editor's face.

'I started to get a headache. A very small headache at first. It was getting hard to think again. I remembered that Janey Morrison had an electric pencil sharpener on her desk. There were all those fluorescents in Jim's office. The heaters. The vending machines in the concession down the hall. When you stopped to think of it, the whole fucking building ran on electricity; it was a wonder that anyone could get anything done. That was when the idea began to creep in, I think. The idea that *Logan's* was going broke because no one could think straight. And the reason no one could think straight was because we were all cooped up in this high-rise building that ran on electricity. Our brain waves were completely messed up. I remember thinking that if you could have gotten a doctor in there with one of those EEG machines, they'd get some awfully weird graphs. Full of those big, spiky alpha waves that characterize malignant tumors in the forebrain. 'Just thinking about those things made my headache worse. But I gave it one more try. I asked him if he would at least ask Sam Vadar, the editor in chief, to let the story stand in the January issue. As *Logan's* fiction valedictory, if necessary. The final *Logan's* story.

'Jimmy was fiddling with a pencil and nodding. He said, "I'll bring it up, but you know it's not going to fly. We've got a story by a one-shot novelist and we've got a story by John Updike that's just as good . . . maybe better . . . and—"

' "*The Updike story is not better!*" I said.

' "Well, Jesus, Henry, you don't have to shout—"

' "*I am not shouting!*" I shouted.

'He looked at me for a long time. My headache was quite bad by then. I could hear the fluorescents buzzing away. They sounded like a bunch of flies caught in a bottle. It was a really hateful sound. And I thought I could hear Janey running her electrical pencil sharpener. *They're doing it on purpose*, I thought. *They want to mess me up. They know I can't think of the right things to say while those things are running, so . . . so. . . .*

'Jim was saying something about bringing it up at the next editorial meeting, suggesting that instead of an arbitrary cutoff date, they publish all the stories I had verbally contracted for . . . although . . .

'I got up, went across the room, and shut off the lights.

' "What did you do that for?" Jimmy asked.

' "You know why I did it," I said. "You ought to get out of here, Jimmy, before there's nothing left of you."

'He got up and came over to me. "I think you ought to take the rest of the day off, Henry," he said. "Go home. Rest. I know you've been under a strain lately. I want you to know I'll do the best I can on this. I feel as strongly as you do . . . well, almost as strongly. But you ought to just go home and put your feet up and watch some TV."

' "TV," I said, and laughed. It was the funniest thing I'd ever heard. "Jimmy," I said, "you tell Sam Vadar something else for me."

' "What's that, Henry?"

' "Tell him he needs a Fornit. This whole outfit. One Fornit? A dozen of them."

' "A Fornit," he said, nodding. "O.K., Henry. I'll be sure to tell him that."

'My headache was very bad. I could hardly even see. Somewhere in the back of my mind I was already wondering how I was going to tell Reg and wondering how Reg was going to take it.

' "I'll put in the purchase order myself, if I can find out whom to send it to," I said. "Reg might have some ideas. A dozen Fornits. Get them to dust this place with fornus from end to end. Shut off the fucking power, all of it." I was walking around his office, and

Jimmy was staring at me with his mouth open. "Shut off all the power, Jimmy, you tell them that. Tell Sam that. No one can think with all that electrical interference, am I right?'

' "You're right. Henry, 100 percent. You just go on home and get some rest. OK? Take a nap or something."

' "And Fornits. They don't like all that interference. Radium, electricity, it's all the same thing. Feed them bologna. Cake. Peanut butter. Can we get requisitions for that stuff?" My headache was this black ball of pain behind my eyes. I was seeing two of Jimmy, two of everything. All of a sudden I needed a drink. If there was no fornus—and the rational side of my mind assured me there was not—then a drink was the only thing in the world that would get me right.

' "Sure, we can get the requisitions," he said.

' "You don't believe any of this, do you, Jimmy?" I asked.

' "Sure I do. It's OK You just want to go home and rest a little while."

' "You don't believe it now," I said, "but maybe you will when this rag goes into bankruptcy. How in the name of God can you believe you're making rational decisions when you're sitting less than fifteen yards from a bunch of Coke machines and candy machines and sandwich machines?" Then I really had a terrible thought. *"And a microwave oven!"* I screamed at him. *"They got a microwave oven to heat the sandwiches up in!"*

'He started to say something, but I didn't pay any attention. I ran out. Thinking of that microwave oven explained everything. I had to get away from it. That was what made the headache so bad. I remember seeing Janey and Kate Younger from the ad department and Mert Strong from publicity in the outer office, all of them staring at me. They must have heard me shouting.

'My office was on the floor just below. I took the stairs. I went into my office, turned off all the lights, and got my briefcase. I took the elevator down to the lobby, but I put my briefcase between my feet and poked my fingers in my ears. I also remember the other three or four people in the elevator looking at me rather strangely.' The editor uttered a dry chuckle. 'They were scared. So to speak. Cooped up in a little moving box with an obvious madman, you would have been scared, too.'

'Oh, surely, *that's* a little strong,' the writer's wife said.

'Not at all. Madness has to start *somewhere*. If this story's *about* anything—if events in one's own life can ever be said to be *about* anything—then this is a story about the genesis of insanity. Madness has to start somewhere, and it has to go somewhere. Like a road. Or a bullet from the barrel of a gun. I was still miles behind Reg Thorpe, but I was over the line. You bet.

'I had to go somewhere, so I went to Four Fathers, a bar on 49th. I remember picking that bar specifically because there was no juke and no color TV and not many lights. I remember ordering the first drink. After that I don't remember anything until I woke up the next day in my bed at home. There was puke on the floor and a very large cigarette burn in the sheet over me. In my stupor I had apparently escaped dying in one of two extremely nasty ways —choking or burning. Not that I probably would have felt either.'

'Jesus,' the agent said, almost respectfully.

'It was a blackout,' the editor said. 'The first real bona fide blackout of my life—but they're always a sign of the end, and you never have very many. One way or the other, you never have very many. But any alcoholic will tell you that a blackout isn't the same as *passing* out. It would save a lot of trouble if it were. No, when an alky blacks out, he keeps *doing* things. An alky in a blackout is a busy little devil. Sort of like a malign Fornit. He'll call up his ex-wife and abuse her over the phone, or drive his car the wrong way on the turnpike and wipe out a carload of kids. He'll quit his job, rob a market, give away his wedding ring. Busy little devils.

'What *I* had done, apparently, was to come home and write a letter. Only this one wasn't to Reg. It was to me. And *I* didn't write it—at least, according to the *letter,* I didn't.'

'Who did?' the writer's wife asked.

'Bellis.'

'Who's Bellis?'

'His Fornit,' the writer said almost absently. His eyes were shadowy and far away.

'Yes, that's right,' the editor said, not looking a bit surprised. He made the letter in the sweet night air for them again, indenting at the proper points with his finger.

'"Hello from Bellis. I am sorry for your problems, my friend, but would like to point out at the start that you are not the only one with problems. This is no easy job for me. I can dust your damned machine with fornus from now unto forever, but moving the KEYS is supposed to be your job. That's what God made big people FOR. So I sympathize, but that's all the sympathy you get.

'"I understand your worry about Reg Thorpe. I worry not about Thorpe but my brother, Rackne. Thorpe worries about what will happen to him if Rackne leaves, but only because he is selfish. The curse of serving writers is that they are *all* selfish. He worries not

about what will happen to Rackne if THORPE leaves. Or goes *el
bonzo seco*. Those things have apparently never crossed his oh-so-
sensitive mind. But, luckily for us, all our unfortunate problems
have the same short-term solution, and so I strain my arms and my
tiny body to give it to you, my drunken friend. YOU may wonder
about long-term solutions; I assure you there are none. All wounds
are mortal. Take what's given. You sometimes get a little slack in
the rope, but the rope always has an end. So what. Bless the slack
and don't waste breath cursing the drop. A grateful heart knows
that in the end we all swing.

'You must pay him for the story yourself. But not with a personal
check. Thorpe's mental problems are severe and perhaps dangerous, but this in no way indicates stupiddity.'' The editor stopped
here and spelled: *S-T-U-P-I-D-D-I-T-Y*. Then he went on. ''If
you give him a personal check, he'll crack wise in about nine
seconds.

'Withdraw eight hundred and some few-odd dollars from your
personal account and have your bank open a new account for you in
the name of Arvin Publishing, Inc. Make sure they understand you
want checks that look businesslike—nothing with cute dogs or
canyon vistas on them. Find a friend, someone you can trust, and
list him as co-drawer. When the checks arrive, make one for eight
hundred dollars and have the co-drawer sign the check. Send the
check to Reg Thorpe. That will cover your ass for the time being.

'Over and out.' It was signed ''Bellis,'' Not in holograph. In
type.'

'Whew,' the writer said again.

'When I got up the first thing I noticed was the typewriter. It
looked like somebody had made it up as a ghost-typewriter in a
cheap movie. The day before, it was an old black office Underwood.
When I got up—with a head that felt about the size of North
Dakota—it was a sort of gray. The last few sentences of the letter
were clumped up and faded. I took one look and figured my faithful
old Underwood was probably finished. I took a taste and went out
into the kitchen. There was an open bag of confectioners' sugar on
the counter with a scoop in it. There was confectioners' sugar
everywhere between the kitchen and the little den where I did my
work in those days.'

'Feeding your Fornit,' the writer said. 'Bellis had a sweet tooth.
You thought so anyway.'

'Yes. But even as sick and hungover as I was, I knew perfectly
well who the Fornit was.'

He ticked off the points on his fingers.

'First, Bellis was my mother's maiden name.

'Second, that phrase *el bonzo seco*. It was a private phrase my brother and I used to use to mean crazy. Back when we were kids.

'Third, and in a way most damning, was that spelling of the word *stupidity*. It's one of those words I habitually misspell. I had an almost screamingly literate writer once who used to spell *refrigerator* with a *d*—*refridgerator*—no matter how many times the copy editors blooped it. And for this guy, who had a doctoral degree from Princeton, *ugly* was always going to be *ughly*.'

The writer's wife uttered a sudden laugh—it was both embarrassed and cheerful. 'I do that.'

'All I'm saying is that a man's misspellings—or a woman's—are his literary fingerprints. Ask any copy editor who has done the same writer a few times.

'No, Bellis was I and I was Bellis. Yet the advice was damned good advice. In fact, I thought it was *great* advice. But here's something else—the subconscious leaves its fingerprints, but there's a stranger down there, too. A hell of a weird guy who knows a hell of a lot. I'd never seen that phrase *co-drawer* in my life, to the best of my knowledge . . . but there it was, and it was a good one, and I found out some time later that banks actually use it.

'I picked up the phone to call a friend of mine, and this bolt of pain—incredible!—went through my head. I thought of Reg Thorpe and his radium and put the phone down in a hurry. I went to see the friend in person after I'd taken a shower and gotten a shave and had checked myself about nine times in the mirror to make sure my appearance approximated how a rational human being is supposed to look. Even so, he asked me a lot of questions and looked me over pretty closely. So I guess there must have been a few signs that a shower, a shave, and a good dose of Listerine couldn't hide. He wasn't in the biz, and that was a help. News has a way of traveling, you know. In the biz. So to speak. Also, if he'd been in the biz, he would have known Arvin Publishing, Inc. was responsible for *Logan's* and would have wondered just what sort of scam I was trying to pull. But he wasn't, he didn't, and I was able to tell him it was a self-publishing venture I was interested in since *Logan's* had apparently decided to deep-six the fiction department.'

'Did he ask you why you were calling it Arvin Publishing?' the writer asked.

'Yes.'

'What did you tell him?'

'I told him,' the editor said, smiling a wintry smile, 'that Arvin was my mother's maiden name.'

There was a little pause, and then the editor resumed; he spoke almost uninterrupted to the end.

'So I began waiting for the printed checks, of which I wanted exactly one. I exercised to pass the time. You know—pick up the glass, flex the elbow, empty the glass, flex the elbow again. Until all the exercise wears you out and you just sort of fall forward with your head on the table. Other things happened, but those were the ones that really occupied my mind—the waiting and the flexing. As I remember. I have to reiterate that, because I was drunk a lot of the time, and for every single thing I remember, there are probably fifty or sixty I don't.

'I quit my job—that caused a sigh of relief all around, I'm sure. From them because they didn't have to perform the existential task of firing me for craziness from a department that was no longer in existence; from me because I didn't think I could ever face that building again—the elevator, the fluorescents, the phones, the thought of all that waiting electricity.

'I wrote Reg Thorpe and his wife a couple of letters each during that three-week period. I remember doing hers, but not his—like the letter from Bellis. I wrote those letters in blackout periods. But I hewed to my old work-habits when I was blotto, just as I hewed to my old misspellings. I never failed to use a carbon . . . and when I came to the next morning, the carbons were lying around. It was like reading letters from a stranger.

'Not that the letters were crazy. Not at all. The one where I finished up with the P.S. about the blender was a lot worse. These letters seemed . . . almost reasonable.'

He stopped and shook his head, slowly and wearily.

'Poor Jane Thorpe. Not that things *appeared* to be all that bad at their end. It must have seemed to her that her husband's editor was doing a very skillfull—and humane—job of humoring him out of his deepening depression. The question of whether or not it's a good idea to humor a person who has been entertaining all sorts of paranoid fantasies—fantasies that almost led in one case to an actual assault on a little girl—probably occurred to her; if so, she chose to ignore the negative aspects, because she was humoring him, too. Nor have I ever blamed her for it—he wasn't just a meal ticket, some nag that was to be worked and humored, humored and worked until he was ready for the rendering plant; she loved the guy. In her own special way, Jane Thorpe was a great lady. And after living with Reg from the Early Times to the High Times and finally to the Crazy Times, I think she would have agreed with Bellis about blessing the slack and not wasting your breath cursing the drop. Of course, the more slack you get, the harder the snap when you finally fetch up at the end . . . but even that quick snap can be a blessing, I reckon—who wants to strangle?

'I had return letters from both of them in that short period —remarkably sunny letters . . . although there was a strange, almost final quality to that sunlight. It seemed as if . . . well, never mind the cheap philosophy. If I can think of what I mean, I'll say it. Let it go for now.

'He was playing hearts with the kids next door every night, and by the time the leaves started to fall, they thought Reg Thorpe was just about God come down to earth. When they weren't playing cards or tossing a Frisbee, they were talking literature, with Reg gently rallying them through their paces. He'd gotten a puppy from the local animal shelter and walked it every morning and night, meeting other people on the block the way you do when you walk your mutt. People who'd decided the Thorpes were really very peculiar people now began to change their minds. When Jane suggested that without electrical appliances, she could really use a little house help, Reg agreed at once. She was flabbergasted by his cheery acceptance of the idea. It wasn't a question of money—after *Underworld Figures* they were rolling in dough—it was a question, Jane figured, of *they*. *They* were everywhere, that was Reg's scripture, and what better agent for *they* than a cleaning woman that went everywhere in your house, looked under beds and in closets and probably in desk drawers as well, if they weren't locked and then nailed shut for good measure.

'But he told her to go right ahead, told her he felt like an insensitive clod not to've thought of it earlier, even though—she made a point of telling me this—he was doing most of the heavy chores, such as handwashing, himself. He made only one small request: that the woman not be allowed to come into his study.

'Best of all, most encouraging of all from Jane's standpoint, was the fact that Reg had gone back to work, this time on a new novel. She had read the first three chapters and thought they were marvelous. All of this, she said, had begun when I had accepted "The Ballad of the Flexible Bullet" for *Logan's*—the period before that had been dead low ebb. And she blessed me for it.

'I am sure she really meant that last, but her blessing seemed to have no great warmth, and the sunniness of her letter was marred somehow—here we are, back to *that*. The sunshine in her letter was like sunshine on a day when you see those mackerel-scale clouds that mean it's going to rain like hell soon.

'All this good news—hearts and dog and cleaning woman and new novel—and she was too intelligent to really believe he was getting well again . . . or so I believed, even in my own fog. Reg had been exhibiting symptoms of psychosis. Psychosis is like lung cancer in one way—neither one of them clears up on its own, although both cancer patients and lunatics may have their good days.

'May I borrow another cigarette, dear?'

The writer's wife gave him one.

'After all,' he resumed, bringing out the Ronson, 'the signs of his *idée fixe* were all around her. No phone; no electricity. He'd put Reynolds Wrap over all the switch plates. He was putting food in his typewriter as regularly as he put it into the new puppy's dish. The students next door thought he was a great guy, but the students next door didn't see Reg putting on rubber gloves to pick up the newspaper off the front stoop in the morning because of his radiation fears. They didn't hear him moaning in his sleep, or have to soothe him when he woke up screaming with dreadful night-mares he couldn't remember.

'You, my dear'—he turned toward the writer's wife—'have been wondering why she stuck with him. Although you haven't said as much, it's been on your mind. Am I right?'

She nodded.

'Yes. And I'm not going to offer a long motivational thesis—the convenient thing about stories that are true is that you need only say *this is what happened* and let people worry for themselves about why. Generally, nobody ever knows why things happen anyway . . . particularly the ones who say they do.

'But in terms of Jane Thorpe's own selective perception, things *had* gotten one hell of a lot better. She interviewed a middle-aged black woman about the cleaning job, and brought herself to speak as frankly as she could about her husband's idiosyncracies. The woman, Gertrude Rulin by name, laughed and said she'd done for people who were a whole lot stranger. Jane spent the first week of the Rulin woman's employ pretty much the way she'd spent that first visit with the young people next door—waiting for some crazy outburst. But Reg charmed Gertrude as completely as he'd charmed the kids, talking to her about her church work, her husband, and her youngest son, Jimmy, who according to Gert-rude, made Dennis the Menace look like the biggest bore in the first grade. She'd had eleven children in all, but there was a nine-year gap between Jimmy and his next oldest sib. He made things hard on her.

'Reg seemed to be getting well . . . at least, if you looked at things a certain way, he did. But he was just as crazy as ever, of course, and so was I. Madness may well be a sort of flexible bullet, but any ballistics expert worth his salt will tell you no two bullets are exactly the same. Reg's one letter to me talked a little bit about his new novel, and then passed directly to Fornits. Fornits in general, Rackne in particular. He speculated on whether *they* actually wanted to kill Fornits, or—he thought this more likely —capture them alive and study them. He closed by saying, "both my appetite and my outlook on life have improved immeasurably since we began our correspondence, Henry. Appreciate it all. Affectionately yours, Reg." And a P.S. below, inquiring casually if an illustrator had been assigned to do his story. That caused a guilty pang or two and a quick trip to the liquor cabinet on my part.

'Reg was into Fornits; I was into wires.

'My answering letter mentioned Fornits only in passing—by then I really *was* humoring the man, at least on that subject; an elf with my mother's maiden name and my own bad spelling habits didn't interest me a whole hell of a lot.

'What had come to interest me more and more was the subject of electricity, and microwaves, and RF waves, and RF interference from small appliances, and low-level radiation, and Christ knows what else. I went to the library and took out books on the subject; I bought books on the subject. There was a lot of scary stuff in them . . . and of course that was just the sort of stuff I was looking for.

'I had my phone taken out and my electricity turned off. It helped for a while, but one night when I was staggering in the door drunk with a bottle of Black Velvet in my hand and another one in my topcoat pocket, I saw this little red eye peeping down at me from the ceiling. God, for a minute I thought I was going to have a heart attack. It looked like a bug up there at first . . . a great big dark bug with one glowing eye.

'I had a Coleman gas lantern and I lit it. Saw what it was at once. Only instead of relieving me, it made me feel worse. As soon as I got a good look at it, it seemed I could feel large, clear bursts of pain going through my head—like radio waves. For a moment it was as if my eyes had rotated in their sockets and I could look into my own brain and see cells in there smoking, going black, dying. It was a smoke detector—a gadget that was even newer than microwave ovens back in 1969.

'I bolted out of the apartment and went downstairs—I was on the fifth floor, but by then I was always taking the stairs—and hammered on the super's door. I told him I wanted that thing out of there, wanted it out of there *right away*, wanted it out of there *tonight*, wanted it out of there *within the hour*. He looked at me as though I had gone completely—you should pardon the expression —bonzo seco, and I can understand that now. That smoke detector was supposed to make me feel *good*, it was supposed to make me *safe*. Now, of course, they're the law, but back then it was a Great Leap Forward, paid for by the building tenants' association.

'He removed it—it didn't take long—but the look in his eyes was not lost upon me, and I could, in some limited way, understand his feelings. I needed a shave, I stank of whiskey, my hair was sticking up all over my head, my topcoat was dirty. He would know I no longer went to work; that I'd had my television taken away; that my phone and electrical service had been voluntarily interrupted. He thought I was crazy.

'I may have been crazy, but—like Reg—I was not stupid. I turned on the charm. Editors have got to have a certain amount, you know. And I greased the skids with a ten-dollar bill. Finally, I was able to smooth things over, but I knew from the way people were looking at me in the next couple of weeks—my last two weeks in the building, as things turned out—that the story had traveled. The fact that no member of the tenants' association approached me to make wounded noises about my ingratitude was particularly telling. I suppose they thought I might take after them with a steak knife.

'All of that was very secondary in my thoughts that evening, however. I sat in the glow of the Coleman lantern, the only light in the three rooms except for all the electricity in Manhattan that came through the windows. I sat with a bottle in one hand, a cigarette in the other, looking at the plate in the ceiling where the smoke detector with its single red eye—an eye that was so unobtrusive in the daytime that I had never even noticed it—had been. I thought of the undeniable fact that, although I'd had all the electricity turned off in my place, there had been that one live item . . . and where there was one, there might be more.

'Even if there wasn't, the whole building was rotten with wires—it was filled with wires the way a man dying of cancer is filled with evil cells and rotting organs. Closing my eyes, I could see all those wires in the darkness of their conduits, glowing with a sort of green nether light. And beyond them, the entire city. One wire, almost harmless in itself, running to a switch plate . . . the wire behind the switch plate a little thicker, leading down through a conduit to the basement, where it joined a still thicker wire . . . that one leading down under the street to a whole *bundle* of wires, only those wires so thick that they were really cables.

'When I got Jane Thorpe's letter mentioning the tinfoil, part of my mind recognized that she saw it as a sign of Reg's craziness, and that part knew I would have to respond as if my *whole* mind thought she was right. The other part of my mind—by far the larger part now—thought: "What a marvelous idea!" And I covered my own switch plate in identical fashion the very next day. I was the man, remember, that was supposed to be helping Reg Thorpe. In a desperate sort of way, it's actually quite funny.

'I determined that night to leave Manhattan. There was an old family place in the Adirondacks I could go to, and that sounded fine to me. The one thing keeping me in the city was Reg Thorpe's story. If "The Ballad of the Flexible Bullet" was Reg's life ring in a sea of madness, it was mine, too—I wanted to place it in a good magazine. With that done, I could get the hell out.

'So that's where the not-so-famous Wilson-Thorpe correspondence stood just before the shit hit the fan. We were like a couple of dying drug addicts comparing the relative merits of heroin and 'ludes. Reg had Fornits in his typewriter, I had Fornits in the walls, and both of us had Fornits in our heads.

'And there was *they*. Don't forget *they*. I hadn't been flogging the story around for long before deciding *they* included every magazine fiction editor in New York—not that there were many by the fall of 1969. If you'd grouped them together, you could have killed the whole bunch of them with one shotgun shell, and before long I started to feel that was a damned good idea.

'It took about five years before I could see it from their perspective. I'd upset the super, and he was just a guy who saw me when the heat screwed up and when it was time for his Christmas tip. These other guys . . . well, the irony was just that a lot of them really *were* my friends. Jared Baker was the assistant fiction editor at *Esquire* in those days, and Jared and I had been in the same rifle company during World War II, for instance. These guys weren't just uneasy after sampling the new improved Henry Wilson. They were appalled. If I'd just sent the story around with a pleasant covering letter explaining the situation—my version of it, anyway —I probably would have sold the Thorpe story almost right away. But oh, no, that wasn't good enough. Not for this story. I was going to see that this story got the *personal treatment*. So I went from door to door with it, a stinking, grizzled ex-editor with shaking hands and red eyes and a big old bruise on his left cheekbone from where he had run into the bathroom door on the way to the can in the dark two nights before. I might as well have been wearing a sign reading BELLVUE BOUND.

Nor did I want to talk to these guys in their offices. In fact, I could not. The time had long since passed when I could get into an elevator and ride it up forty floors. So I met them like pushers meet junkies—in parks, on steps, or in the case of Jared Baker, in a Burger Heaven on 49th Street. Jared at least would have been delighted to buy me a decent meal, but the time had passed, you understand, when any self-respecting maître d' would have let me in a restaurant where they serve business-people.

The agent winced.

'I got perfunctory promises to read the story, followed by concerned questions about how I was, how much I was drinking. I remember—hazily—trying to tell a couple of them about how electricity and radiation leaks were fucking up everyone's thinking, and when Andy Rivers, who edited fiction for *American Crossings*, suggested I ought to get some help, I told him *he* was the one who ought to get some help.

' "You see those people out there on the street?" I said. We were standing in Washington Square Park. 'Half of them, maybe even three-quarters of them, have got brain tumors. I wouldn't sell you Thorpe's story on a bet, Andy. Hell, you couldn't understand it in this city. Your brain's in the electric chair, and you don't even know it.'

'I had a copy of the story in my hand, rolled up like a newspaper. I whacked him on the nose with it, the way you'd whack a dog for piddling in the corner. Then I walked off. I remember him yelling for me to come back, something about having a cup of coffee and talking it over some more, and then I passed a discount record store with loudspeakers blasting heavy metal onto the sidewalk and banks of snowy-cold fluorescent lights inside, and I lost his voice in a kind of deep buzzing sound inside my head. I remember thinking two things—I had to get out of the city soon, very soon, or I would be nursing a brain tumor of my own, and I had to get a drink right away.

'That night when I got back to my apartment, I found a note under the door. It said, *"We want you out of here, you crazy-bird."* I threw it away without so much as a second thought. We veteran crazy-birds have more important things to worry about than anonymous notes from fellow tenants.

'I was thinking over what I'd said to Andy Rivers about Reg's

story. The more I thought about it—and the more drinks I
had—the more sense it made. "Flexible Bullet" was funny, and on
the surface it was easy to follow . . . but below that surface level it
was surprisingly complex. Did I really think another editor in the
city could grasp the story on all levels? Maybe once, but did I still
think so now that my eyes had been opened? Did I really think
there was room for appreciation and understanding in a place that
was wired up like a terrorist's bomb? God, loose volts were leaking
out everywhere.

'I read the paper while there was still enough daylight to do so,
trying to forget the whole wretched business for a while, and there
on page one of the *Times* was a story about how radioactive material
from nuclear power plants kept disappearing—the article went on
to theorize that enough of that stuff in the right hands could quite
easily be used to make a very dirty nuclear weapon.

'I sat there at the kitchen table as the sun went down, and in my
mind's eye I could see *them* panning for plutonium dust like 1849
miners panning for gold. Only *they* didn't want to blow up the city
with it, oh, no. *They* just wanted to sprinkle it around and fuck up
everyone's minds. They were the bad Fornits, and all that radioactive dust was bad-luck fornus. The worst bad-luck fornus of all
time.

'I decided I didn't want to sell Reg's story after all—at least, not
in New York. I'd get out of the city just as soon as the checks I'd
ordered arrived. When I was upstate, I could start sending it
around to the out-of-town literary magazines. *Sewanee Review*
would be a good place to start, I reckoned, or maybe *Iowa Review*. I
could explain to Reg later. Reg would understand. That seemed to
solve the whole problem, so I took a drink to celebrate. And then
the drink took a drink. And then the drink took the man. So to
speak. I blacked out. I had only one more blackout left in me, as it
happened.

'The next day my Arvin Publishing checks came. I typed one of
them up and went to see my friend, the "co-drawer." There was
another one of those tiresome cross-examinations, but this time I
kept my temper. I wanted that signature. Finally, I got it. I went to
a business supply store and had them make up a Arvin Publishing
letter-stamp while I waited. I stamped a return address on a
business envelope, typed Reg's address (the confectioners' sugar
was out of my machine, but the keys still had a tendency to stick),
and added a brief personal note, saying that no check to an author
had ever given me more personal pleasure . . . and that was true.
Still is. It was almost an hour before I could bring myself to mail

it—I just couldn't get over how *official* it looked. You never would have known that a smelly drunk who hadn't changed his underwear in days had put *that* one together.'

He paused, crushed out his cigarette, looked at his watch. Then, oddly like a conductor announcing a train's arrival in some city of importance, he said, 'We have reached the inexplicable.

'This is the point in my story that most interested the two psychiatrists and various mental caseworkers with whom I was associated over the next thirty months of my life. It was the only part of it they really wanted me to recant, as a sign that I was getting well again. As one of them put it, "This is the only part of your story that cannot be exposed as no more than faulty induction . . . once, that is, your sense of logic has been mended." Finally, I *did* recant, because I knew—even if they didn't—that I *was* getting well, and I was damned anxious to get out of the sanatorium. I thought if I didn't get out fairly soon, I'd go crazy all over again. So I recanted—Galileo did, too, when they held his feet to the fire—but I have never recanted in my own mind. I don't say that what I'm about to tell you really happened; I say only that I still *believe* it happened. That's a small qualification, but to me it's crucial.

'So, my friends, the inexplicable:

'I spent the next two days preparing to move upstate. The idea of driving the car didn't disturb me at all, by the way, I had read as a kid that the inside of a car is one of the safest places to be during an electrical storm, because the rubber tires serve as near-perfect insulators. I was actually looking forward to getting in my old Chevrolet, cranking up all the windows, and driving out of the city, which I had begun to see as a sink of lightning. Nevertheless, part of my preparations included removing the bulb in the dome light, and taping over the socket, turning the headlight knob all the way to the left to kill the dash lights, and cutting the radio cable.

'When I came in on the last night I meant to spend in the apartment, the place was empty except for the kitchen table, the bed, and my typewriter in the den. The typewriter was sitting on the floor. I had no intentions of taking it with me—it had too many bad associations, and besides, the key were going to stick forever. Let the next tenant have it, I thought—it, and Bellis, too.

'It was just sunset, and the place was a funny color. I was pretty drunk, and I had another bottle in my topcoat pocket against the watches of the night. I started across the den, meaning to go into the bedroom, I suppose. There I would sit on the bed and think about wires and electricity and free radiation and drink until I was drunk enough to go to sleep.

'What I called the den was really the living room. I made it my workplace because it had the nicest light in the whole apartment—a big westward-facing window that looked all the way to the horizon. That's something close to the Miracle of the Loaves and Fishes in a fifth-floor Manhattan apartment, but the line of sight was there. I didn't question it; I just enjoyed it. That room was filled with a clear, lovely light even on rainy days.

'But the quality of the light that evening was eerie. The sunset had filled the room with a red glow. Furnace light. Empty, the room seemed too big. My heels made flat echoes on the hardwood floor.

'The typewriter sat in the middle of the floor, and I was just going around it when I saw there was a ragged scrap of paper stuck under the roller—that gave me a start, because I knew there had been no paper in the machine when I went out for the last time to get the fresh bottle.

'I looked around, wondering if there was someone—some intruder—in the place with me. Except it wasn't really intruders, or burglars, or junkies, I was thinking of . . . it was ghosts.

'I saw a ragged blank place on the wall to the left of the bedroom door. I at least understood where the paper in the typewriter had come from. Someone had simply torn off a ragged piece of the old wallpaper.

'I was still looking at this when I heard a single small clear noise—*clack!*—from behind me. I jumped and whirled around with my heart knocking in my throat. I was terrified, but I knew what that sound was just the same—there was no question at all. You work with words all your life and you know the sound of a typewriter platen hitting paper, even in a deserted room at dusk, where there is no one to strike the key.'

They looked at him in the dark, their faces blurred white circles, saying nothing, slightly huddled together now. The writer's wife was holding one of the writer's hand tightly in both of her own.

'I felt . . . outside myself. Unreal. Perhaps this is always the way one feels when one arrives at the point of the inexplicable. I walked slowly over to the typewriter. My heart was pounding madly up there in my throat, but I felt mentally calm . . . icy, even.

'*Clack!* Another platen popped up. I saw it this time—the key was in the third row from the top, on the left.

'I got down on my knees very slowly, and then all the muscles in my legs seemed to go slack, and I half-swooned the rest of the way down until I was sitting there in front of the typewriter with my dirty London Fog topcoat spread around me like the skirt of a girl who has made her very deepest curtsy. The typewriter clacked twice more, fast, paused, then clacked again. Each *clack* made the same kind of flat echo my footfalls had made on the floor.

'The wallpaper had been rolled into the machine so that the side with the dried glue on it was facing out. The letters were ripply and bumpy, but I could read them, *rackn*, it said. Then it clacked again and the word was *rackne*.

'Then—' He cleared his throat and grinned a little. 'Even all these years later this is hard to tell . . . to just say right out. O.K. The simple fact, with no icing on it, is this. I saw a hand come out of the typewriter. An incredibly tiny hand. It came out from between the keys *B* and *N* in the bottom row, curled itself into a fist, and hammered down on the spacer bar. The machine jumped a space—very fast, like a hiccup—and the hand drew back down inside.'

The agent's wife giggled shrilly.

'Can it, Marsha,' the agent said softly, and she did.

'The clacks began to come a little faster,' the editor went on, 'and after a while I fancied I could hear the creature that was shoving the key arms up gasping, the way anyone will gasp when he is working hard, closer and closer to his physical limit. After a while the machine was hardly printing at all, and most of the keys were filled with that old gluey stuff, but I could read the impressions. It got out *rackne* is *d* and then the *y* key stuck to the glue. I looked at it for a moment, and then I reached out one finger and freed it. I don't know if it—Bellis—could have freed it himself. I think not. But I didn't want to see it . . . him . . . try. Just the fist was enough to have me tottering on the brink. If I saw the elf entire, so to speak, I think I really would have gone crazy. And there was no question of getting up to run. All the strength had gone out of my legs.

'*Clack-clack-clack*, those tiny grunts and sobs of effort, and after every word that pallid ink- and dirt-streaked fist would come out between the *B* and the *N* and hammer down on the space bar. I don't know exactly how long it went on. Seven minutes, maybe. Maybe ten. Or maybe forever.

'Finally, the clacks stopped, and I realized I couldn't hear him breathing anymore. Maybe he had fainted . . . maybe he had just given up and gone away . . . or maybe he had died. Had a heart attack or something. All I really know for sure is that the message was not finished. It read, completely in lower case: *rackne is dying its*

*the little boy jimmy thorpe doesn't know tell thorpe rackne is dying the
little boy jimmy is killing rachne bel* . . . and that was all.

'I found the strength to get to my feet then, and I left the room. I
walked in great big tippy-toe steps, as if I thought it had gone to
sleep and if I made any of those flat echoey noises on the bare wood,
it would wake up and the typing would start again . . . and I
thought if it did, the first *clack* would start me screaming. And then
I would just go on until my heart or my head burst.

'My Chevvy was in the parking lot down the street, all gassed
and loaded and ready to go. I got in behind the wheel and remembered the bottle in my topcoat pocket. My hands were shaking
so badly that I dropped it, but it landed on the seat and didn't
break.

'I remembered the blackouts, and my friends, right then a
blackout was exactly what I wanted, and exactly what I got. I
remember taking the first drink from the neck of the bottle, and the
second. I remember turning over the accessory and getting Frank
Sinatra on the radio singing "That Old Black Magic," which
seemed fitting enough. Under the circumstances. So to speak. I
remember singing along, and having a few more drinks. I was in the
back row of the lot, and I could see the traffic light on the corner
going through its paces. I kept thinking of those flat clacking
sounds in the empty room, and the fading red light in the den. I
kept thinking of those puffing sounds, as if some body-building elf
had hung fishing sinkers on the ends of a Q-Tip and was doing
bench presses inside my old typewriter. I kept seeing the pebbly
surface on the back side of that torn scrap of wallpaper. My mind
kept wanting to examine what must have gone on before I came
back to the apartment . . . kept wanting to see it—him—Bellis
—jumping up, grabbing the loose edge of the wallpaper by the door
to the bedroom because it was the only thing left in the room
approximating paper—hanging on—finally tearing it loose and
carrying it back to the typewriter on its—on *his*—head like the leaf
of a nipa palm. I kept trying to imagine how he—it—could ever
have run it into the typewriter. And none of that was blacking out,
so I kept drinking and Frank Sinatra stopped and there was an ad
for Crazy Eddie's and then Sarah Vaughn came on singing "I'm
Gonna Sit Right Down and Write Myself a Letter"—and that was
something *else* I could relate to since I'd done just that recently, or
at least I'd *thought* I had up until tonight when something happened
to give me cause to rethink my position on that matter, so to
speak—and I sang along with good old Sarah Soul, and right about
then I must have achieved escape velocity because in the middle of

the second chorus with no lag at all I was puking my guts out while somebody first thumped my back with his palms and then lifted my elbows behind me and put them down and then thumped my back with his palms again. That was the trucker. Every time he thumped I'd feel a great clot of liquid rise up in my throat and get ready to go back down except then he'd lift my elbows, and every time he lifted my elbows I'd puke again, and most of it wasn't even Black Velvet but river water. When I was able to lift my head enough to look around, it was six o'clock in the evening three days later and I was lying on the bank of the Jackson River in western Pennsylvania, about sixty miles north of Pittsburgh. My Chevvy was sticking out of the river, rear end up. I could still read the McCarthy sticker on the bumper.

'Is there another Fresca, love? My throat's dry as hell.'

The writer's wife fetched him one silently, and when she handed it to him, she impulsively bent and kissed his wrinkled, alligator-hide cheek. He smiled, and his eyes sparkled in the dim light. She was, however, a good and kindly woman, and the sparkle did not in any way fool her. It was merriness that made eyes sparkle that way.

'Thank you, Meg.'

He drank deeply, coughed, waved away the offer of a cigarette.

'I've had enough of those for the evening. I'm going to quit them entirely. In my next incarnation. So to speak.

'The rest of my own tale really needs no telling. It would have against it the only sin that any tale can ever really be guilty of—it's predictable. They fished something like forty bottles of Black Velvet out of my car, a good many of them empty. I was babbling about elves, and electricity, and Fornits, and plutonium miners, and fornus, and I seemed utterly insane to them, and that of course is exactly what I was.

'Now here's what happened in Omaha while I was driving around—according to the gas credit slips in the Chevvy's glove compartment—five northeastern states. All of this, you understand, was information I obtained from Jane Thorpe over a long and painful period of correspondence, which culminated in a face-to-face meeting in New Haven, where she now lives, shortly after I was dismissed from the sanatorium as a reward for finally recanting. At the end of that meeting we wept in each other's arms, and that was when I began to believe that there could be a real life for me—perhaps even happiness—again.

'That day, around three o'clock in the afternoon, there was a knock at the door of the Thorpe home. It was a telegraph boy. The telegram was from me—the last item of our unfortunate correspondence. It read: REG HAVE INFORMATION THAT RACKNE IS DYING IT'S THE LITTLE BOY ACCORDING TO BELLISBELLIS SAYS THE BOY'S NAME IS JIMMY FORNIT SOME FORNUS HENRY.

'In case that marvelous Howard Baker question of *What did he know and when did he know it* has gone through your mind, I can tell you that I knew Jane had hired a cleaning woman; I didn't know—except through Bellis—that she had a l'il devil son named Jimmy. I suppose you'll have to take my word for that, although in all fairness I have to add that the shrinks who worked on my case over the next two and a half years never did.

'When the telegram came, Jane was at the grocery store. She found it after Reg was dead, in one of his back pockets. The time of transmission and delivery were both noted on it, along with the added line *No telephone/Deliver original.* Jane said that although the telegram was only a day old, it had been so much handled that it looked as if he'd had it for a month.

'In a way, that telegram, those twenty-six words, was the real flexible bullet, and I fired it directly into Reg Thorpe's brain all the way from Patterson, New Jersey, and I was so fucking drunk I don't even remember doing it.

'During the last two weeks of his life, Reg had fallen into a pattern that seemed normality itself. He got up at six, made breakfast for himself and his wife, then wrote for an hour. Around eight o'clock he would lock his study and take the dog for a long, leisurely walk around the neighborhood. He was very forthcoming on these walks, stopping to chat with anyone who wanted to chat with him, tying the pooch outside a nearby café to have a midmorning cup of coffee, then rambling on again. He rarely got back to the house before noon. On many days it was twelve-thirty or one o'clock. Part of this was an effort to escape the garrulous Gertrude Rulin, Jane believed, because his pattern hadn't really begun to solidify until a couple of days after she started working for them.

'He would eat a light lunch, lie down for an hour or so, then get up and write for two or three hours. In the evenings he would sometimes go next door to visit with the young people, either with Jane or alone; sometimes he and Jane took in a movie, or just sat in the living room and read. They turned in early, Reg usually awhile before Jane. She wrote there was very little sex, and what there was of it was unsuccessful for both of them. "But sex isn't as important for most women," she said, "and Reg was working full-out again, and that was a reasonable substitute for him. I would say that, under the circumstances, those last two weeks were the happiest in the last five years." I damn near cried when I read that.

'I didn't know anything about Jimmy, but Reg did. Reg knew everything except for the most important fact—that Jimmy had started coming to work with his mother.

'How furious he must have been when he got my telegram and began to realize! Here *they* were, after all. And apparently his own wife was one of *them*, because *she* was in the house when Gertrude and Jimmy were there, and she had never said a thing to Reg about Jimmy. What was it he had written to me in that earliest letter? "Sometimes I wonder about my wife."

'When she arrived home on the day the telegram came, she found Reg gone. There was a note on the kitchen table that said: "Love—I've gone down to the bookstore. Back by suppertime." This seemed perfectly fine to Jane . . . but if Jane had known about my telegram, the very normality of that note would have scared the hell out of her. I think. She would have understood that Reg believed she had changed sides.

'Reg didn't go near any bookstore. He went to Littlejohn's Gun Emporium downtown. He bought a .45 automatic and two thousand rounds of ammunition. He would have bought an AK-70 if Littlejohn's had been allowed to sell them. He meant to protect his Fornit, you see. From Jimmy, from Gertrude, from Jane. From *them*.

'Everything went according to established routine the next morning. She remembered thinking he was wearing an awfully heavy sweater for such a warm fall day, but that was all. The sweater, of course, was because of the gun. He went out to walk the dog with the .45 stuffed into the waistband of his chinos.

'Except the restaurant where he usually got his morning coffee was as far as he went, and he went directly there, with no lingering or conversation along the way. He took the pup around to the loading area, tied its leash to a railing, and then went back toward his house by way of backyards.

'He knew the schedule of the young people next door very well; knew they would all be out. He knew where they kept their spare key. He let himself in, went upstairs, and watched his own house.

'At eight-forty he saw Gertrude Rulin arrive. And Gertrude wasn't alone. There was indeed a small boy with her. Jimmy Rulin's boisterous first-grade behavior convinced the teacher and the school guidance counselor almost at once that everyone (except maybe Jimmy's mother, who could have used a rest from Jimmy) would be better off if he waited another year. Jimmy was stuck with repeating kindergarten, and he had afternoon sessions for the first half of the year. The two day-care centers in her area were full, and she couldn't change to afternoons for the Thorpe's because she had another cleaning job on the other side of town from two to four.

'The upshot of everything was Jane's reluctant agreement that Gertrude could bring Jimmy with her until she was able to make other arrangements. Or until Reg found out, as he was sure to do.

'She thought Reg *might* not mind—he had been so sweetly reasonable about everything lately. On the other hand, he might have a fit. If that happened, other arrangements would *have* to be made. Gertrude said she understood. And for heaven's sake, Jane added, the boy was not to touch any of Reg's things. Gertrude said for sure not; the mister's study door was locked and would stay locked.

'Thorpe must have crossed between the two yards like a sniper crossing no-man's-land. He saw Gertrude and Jane washing bed linen in the kitchen. He didn't see the boy. He moved along the side of the house. No one in the dining room. No one in the bedroom. And then, in the study, where Reg had morbidly expected to see him, there Jimmy was. The kid's face was hot with excitement, and Reg surely must have believed that here was a bona fide agent of *them* at last.

'The boy was holding some sort of death ray in his hand, it was pointed at the desk . . . and from inside his typewriter, Reg could hear Rackne screaming.

'You may think I'm attributing subjective data to a man who's not dead—or, to be more blunt, making stuff up. But I'm not. In the kitchen both Jane and Gertrude heard the distinctive warbling sounds of Jimmy's plastic space blaster . . . he'd been shooting it around the house ever since he started coming with his mother, and Jane hoped daily that its batteries would go dead. There was no mistaking the sound. No mistaking the place it was coming from, either—Reg's study.

'The kid really *was* Dennis the Menace material, you know—if there was a room in the house he wasn't supposed to go, that was the one place he *had* to go, or die of curiosity. It didn't take him long to discover that Jane kept a key to Reg's study on the dining room mantel, either. Had he been in there before? I think so. Jane said she remembered giving the boy an orange three or four days before, and later, when she was clearing out the house, she found orange peels under the little studio sofa in that room. Reg didn't eat oranges—claimed he was allergic to them.

'Jane dropped the sheet she was washing back into the sink and rushed into the bedroom. She heard the loud *wah-wah-wah* of the space blaster, and she heard Jimmy, yelling: *'I'll getcha! You can't run! I can seeya through the GLASS!'* And . . . she said . . . she said that she heard something screaming. A high, despairing sound, she said, so full of pain it was almost insupportable.

' "When I heard that," she said, "I knew that I would have to leave Reg no matter *what* happened, because all the old wives' tales were true . . . madness was catching. Because it was Rackne I was hearing; somehow that rotten little kid was shooting Rackne, killing it with a two-dollar space gun from Kresge's.

' "The study door was standing open, the key in it. Later on that day I saw one of the dining room chairs standing by the mantel, with Jimmy's sneaker prints all over the seat. He was bent over Reg's typewriter table. He—Reg—had an old office model with glass inserts in the sides. Jimmy had the muzzle of his blaster pressed against one of those and was shooting it into the typewriter. *Wah-wah-wah-wah*, was purple pulses of light shooting out of the typewriter, and suddenly I could understand everything Reg had ever said about electricity, because although that thing ran on nothing more than harmless old C or D cells, it really did feel as if there were waves of poison coming out of that gun and rolling through my head and frying my brains.

' "*I seeya in there!*' Jimmy was screaming, and his face was filled with a small boy's glee—it was both beautiful and somehow gruesome. *'You can't run away from Captain Future! You're dead, alien!'* And that screaming . . . getting weaker . . . smaller . . .

' "*Jimmy, you stop it!*' I yelled.

' "He jumped. I'd startled him. He turned around . . . looked at me . . . stuck out his tongue . . . and then pushed the blaster against the glass panel and started shooting again. *Wah-wah-wah*, and that rotten purple light.

' "Gertrude was coming down the hall, yelling for him to stop, to get out of there, that he was going to get the whipping of his life . . . and then the front door burst open and Reg came up the hall, bellowing. I got one good look at him and understood that he was insane. The gun was in his hand.

' "*Don't you shoot my baby!*' Gertrude screamed when she saw him, and reached out to grapple with him. Reg simply clubbed her aside.

' "Jimmy didn't even seem to realize any of this was going on—he just went on shooting the space blaster into the typewriter. I could see that purple light pulsing in the blackness between the keys, and it looked like one of those electrical arcs they tell you not to look at without a pair of special goggles because otherwise it might boil your retinas and make you blind.

' "Reg came in, shoving past me, knocking me over.

' "*RACKNE!*' he screamed. *'YOU'RE KILLING RACKNE.'*

' "And even as Reg was rushing across the room, apparently planning to kill that child," Jane told me, "I had time to wonder just how many times he *had* been in that room, shooting that gun into the typewriter when his mother and I were maybe upstairs changing beds or in the backyard hanging clothes where we couldn't hear the *wah-wah-wah* . . . where we couldn't hear that thing . . . the Fornit . . . inside, screaming.

' "Jimmy didn't stop even when Reg came bursting in—just kept shooting into the typewriter as if he knew it was his last chance, and since then I have wondered if perhaps Reg wasn't right about *they*, too—only maybe *they* just sort of float around, and every now and then *they* dive into a person's head like someone doing a double-gainer into a swimming pool, and *they* get that somebody to do the dirty work and then check out again, and the guy *they* were in says, 'Huh? Me? Did *what?'*

' "And in the second before Reg got there, the screaming from inside the typewriter turned into a brief, drilling shriek—and I saw blood splatter all over the inside of that glass insert, as if whatever was in there had finally just exploded, the way they say a live animal will explode if you put it in a microwave oven. I know how crazy it sounds, but I *saw* that blood—it hit the glass in a blot and then started to run.

' " 'Got it,' Jimmy said, highly satisfied. 'Got—'

' "Then Reg threw him all the way across the room. He hit the wall. The gun was jarred out of his hand, hit the floor, and broke. It was nothing but plastic and Eveready batteries, of course.

' "Reg looked into the typewriter, and he screamed. Not a scream of pain or fury, although there was fury in it—mostly it was a scream of grief. He turned toward the boy then. Jimmy had fallen to the floor, and whatever he *had* been—if he ever *was* anything more than just a mischievous little boy—now he was just a six-year-old in terror. Reg pointed the gun at him, and that's all I remember." '

The editor finished his soda and put the can carefully aside.

'Gertrude Rulin and Jimmy Rulin remember enough to make up for the lack,' he said. 'Jane called out, "Reg, *No!*" and when he looked around at her, she got to her feet and grappled with him. He shot her, shattering her left elbow, but she didn't let go. As she continued to grapple with him, Gertrude called to her son, and Jimmy ran to her.

'Reg pushed Jane away and shot her again. This bullet tore along the left side of her skull. Even an eighth of an inch to the right and he would have killed her. There is little doubt of that, and none at all that, if not for Jane Thorpe's intervention, he would have surely killed Jimmy Rulin and quite possibly the boy's mother as well.

'He *did* shoot the boy—as Jimmy ran into his mother's arms just outside the door. The bullet entered Jimmy's left buttock on a downward course. It exited from his left thigh, missing the bone, and passed through Gertrude Rulin's shin. There was a lot of blood, but no major damage done to either.

'Gertrude slammed the study door and carried her screaming bleeding son down the hallway and out the front door.' The editor paused again, thoughtfully.

'Jane was either unconscious by that time or she has deliberately chosen to forget what happened next. Reg sat down in his office chair and put the muzzle of the .45 against the center of his forehead. He pulled the trigger. The bullet did not pass through his brain and leave him a living vegetable, nor did it travel in a semicircle around his skull and exit harmlessly on the far side. The fantasy was flexible, but the final bullet was as hard as it could be. He fell forward across the typewriter, dead.

'When the police broke in, they found him that way; Jane was sitting in a far corner, semiconscious.

'The typewriter was covered with blood, presumably filled with blood as well; head wounds are very, very messy.

'All of the blood was Type O.

'Reg Thorpe's type.

'And that, ladies and gentlemen, is my story; I can tell no more.' Indeed, the editor's voice had been reduced to little more than a husky whisper.

There was none of the usual post-party chatter, or even the awkwardly bright conversation people sometimes use to cover a cocktail party indiscretion, or to at least disguise the fact that things had at some point become much more serious than a dinner-party situation usually warranted.

But as the writer saw the editor to his car, he was unable to forbear one final question. 'The story,' he said. 'What happened to the story?'

'You mean Reg's—'

' "The Ballad of the Flexible Bullet," that's right. The story that caused it all. *That* was the real flexible bullet—for you, if not for him. What in the hell happened to this story that was so goddam great?'

The editor opened the door of his car; it was a small blue Chevette with a sticker on the back bumper that read FRIENDS DON'T LET FRIENDS DRIVE DRUNK. 'No, it was never published. If Reg had a carbon copy, he destroyed it following my receipt and acceptance of the tale—considering his paranoid feelings about *they*, that would have been very much in character.

'I had his original plus three photocopies with me when I went into the Jackson River. All four in a cardboard carton. If I'd put that carton in the trunk, I would have the story now, because the rear end of my car never went under—even if it had, the pages could have been dried out. But I wanted it close to me, so I put it in the front, on the driver's side. The windows were open when I went into the water. The pages . . . I assume they just floated away and were carried out to sea. I'd rather believe that than believe they rotted along with the rest of the trash at the bottom of that river, or were eaten by catfish, or something even less aesthetically pleasing. To believe they were carried out to sea is more romantic, and slightly more unlikely, but in matters of what I choose to believe, I find I can still be flexible.

'So to speak.'

The editor got into his small car and drove away. The writer stood and watched until the taillights had winked out, and then turned around. Meg was there standing in the darkness, smiling a little tentatively at him. Her arms were crossed tightly across her bosom, although the night was warm.

'We're the last two,' she said. 'Want to go in?'

'Sure.'

Halfway up the walk she stopped and said: 'There are no Fornits in your typewriter, are there, Paul?'

And the writer, who had sometimes—often—wondered exactly where the words *did* come from, said bravely: 'Absolutely not.'

They went inside arm in arm and closed the door against the night.

THAT HELL-BOUND TRAIN

Robert Bloch

When Martin was a little boy, his daddy was a railroad man. Daddy never rode the high iron, but he walked the tracks for the CB&Q, and he was proud of his job. And every night when he got drunk, he sang this old song about 'That Hell-Bound Train.'

Martin didn't quite remember any of the words, but he couldn't forget the way his daddy sang them out. And when Daddy made the mistake of getting drunk in the afternoon and got squeezed between a Pennsy tank car and an AT&SF gondola, Martin sort of wondered why the Brotherhood didn't sing the song at his funeral.

After that, things didn't go so good for Martin, but somehow he always recalled Daddy's song. When Mom up and ran off with a traveling salesman from Keokuk (Daddy must have turned over in his grave, knowing she'd done such a thing, and with a *passenger*, too!), Martin hummed the tune to himself every night in the Orphan Home. And after Martin himself ran away, he used to whistle the song softly at night in the jungles, after the other bindle stiffs were asleep.

Martin was on the road for four or five years before he realized he wasn't getting anyplace. Of course he'd tried his hand at a lot of things—picking fruit in Oregon, washing dishes in a Montana hash house, stealing hubcaps in Denver and tires in Oklahoma City —but by the time he'd put in six months on the chain gang down in Alabama he knew he had no future drifting around this way on his own.

So he tried to get on the railroad like his daddy had, and they told him that times were bad.

But Martin couldn't keep away from the railroads. Wherever he traveled, he rode the rods; he'd rather hop a freight heading north in sub-zero weather than lift his thumb to hitch a ride with a

Cadillac headed for Florida. Whenever he managed to get hold of a can of Sterno, he'd sit there under a nice warm culvert, think about the old days, and often as not he'd hum the song about 'That Hell-Bound Train.' That was the train the drunks and the sinners rode—the gambling men and the grifters, the big-time spenders, the skirt chasers, and all the jolly crew. It would be really fine to take a trip in such good company, but Martin didn't like to think of what happened when that train finally pulled into the Depot Way Down Yonder. He didn't figure on spending eternity stoking boilers in hell, without even a company union to protect him. Still, it would be a lovely ride. If there was *such* a thing as a hell-bound train. Which, of course, there wasn't.

At least Martin didn't *think* there was, until that evening when he found himself walking the tracks heading south, just outside of Appleton Junction. The night was cold and dark, the way November nights are in the Fox River Valley, and he knew he'd have to work his way down to New Orleans for the winter, or maybe even Texas. Somehow he didn't much feel like going, even though he'd heard tell that a lot of those Texas automobiles had solid-gold hubcaps.

No sir, he just wasn't cut out for petty larceny. It was worse than a sin—it was unprofitable, too. Bad enough to do the devil's work, but then to get such miserable pay on top of it! Maybe he'd better let the Salvation Army convert him.

Martin trudged along humming Daddy's song, waiting for a rattler to pull out of the Junction behind him. He'd have to catch it—there was nothing else for him to do.

But the first train to come along came from the other direction, roaring toward him along the track from the south.

Martin peered ahead, but his eyes couldn't match his ears, and so far all he could recognize was the sound. It *was* a train, though; he felt the steel shudder and sing beneath his feet.

And yet, how could it be? The next station south was Neenah-Menasha, and there was nothing due out of there for hours.

The clouds were thick overhead, and the field mists rolled like a cold fog in a November midnight. Even so, Martin should have been able to see the headlight as the train rushed on. But there was only the whistle, screaming out of the black throat of the night. Martin could recognize the equipment of just about any locomotive ever built, but he'd never heard a whistle that sounded like this one. It wasn't signaling; it was screaming like a lost soul.

He stepped to one side, for the train was almost on top of him now. And suddenly there it was, looming along the tracks and grinding to a stop in less time than he'd believed possible. The wheels hadn't been oiled, because they screamed too, screamed like the damned. But the train slid to a halt, and the screams died away into a series of low, groaning sounds, and Martin looked up and saw that this was a passenger train. It was big and black, without a single light shining in the engine cab or any of the long string of cars; Martin couldn't read any lettering on the sides, but he was pretty sure this train didn't belong on the Northwestern Road.

He was even more sure when he saw the man clamber down out of the forward car. There was something wrong about the way he walked, as though one of his feet dragged, and about the lantern he carried. The lantern was dark, and the man held it up to his mouth and blew, and instantly it glowed redly. You don't have to be a member of the Railway Brotherhood to know that this is a mighty peculiar way of lighting a lantern.

As the figure approached, Martin recognized the conductor's cap perched on his head, and this made him feel a little better for a moment—until he noticed that it was worn a bit too high, as though there might be something sticking up on the forehead underneath it.

Still, Martin knew his manners, and when the man smiled at him, he said, 'Good evening, Mr. Conductor.'

'Good evening, Martin.'

'How did you know my name?'

The man shrugged. 'How did you know I was the conductor?'

'You *are*, aren't you?'

'To you, yes. Although other people, in other walks of life, may recognize me in different roles. For instance, you ought to see what I look like to the folks out in Hollywood.' The man grinned. 'I travel a great deal,' he explained.

'What brings you here?' Martin asked.

'Why, you ought to know the answer to that, Martin. I came because you needed me. Tonight, I suddenly realized you were backsliding. Thinking of joining the Salvation Army, weren't you?'

'Well—' Martin hesitated.

'Don't be ashamed. To err is human, as somebody-or-other once said. *Reader's Digest*, wasn't it? Never mind. The point is, I felt you needed me. So I switched over and came your way.'

'What for?'

'Why, to offer you a ride, of course. Isn't it better to travel comfortably by train than to march along the cold streets behind a

Salvation Army band? Hard on the feet, they tell me, and even harder on the eardrums.'

'I'm not sure I'd care to ride your train, sir,' Martin said. 'Considering where I'm likely to end up.'

'Ah, yes. The old argument.' The Conductor sighed. 'I suppose you'd prefer some sort of bargain, is that it?'

'Exactly,' Martin answered.

'Well, I'm afraid I'm all through with that sort of thing. There's no shortage of prospective passengers anymore. Why should I offer you any special inducements?'

'You must want me, or else you wouldn't have bothered to go out of your way to find me.'

The Conductor sighed again. 'There you have a point. Pride was always my besetting weakness, I admit. And somehow I'd hate to lose you to the competition, after thinking of you as my own all these years.' He hesitated. 'Yes, I'm prepared to deal with you on your own terms, if you insist.'

'The terms?' Martin asked.

'Standard proposition. Anything you want.'

'Ah,' said Martin.

'But I warn you in advance, there'll be no tricks. I'll grant you anywish you can name—but in return, you must promise to ride the train when the time comes.'

'Suppose it never comes?'

'It will.'

'Suppose I've got the kind of wish that will keep me off forever?'

'There is no such wish.'

'Don't be too sure.'

'Let me worry about that,' the Conductor told him. 'No matter what you have in mind, I warn you that I'll collect in the end. And there'll be none of this last-minute hocus-pocus, either. No last-hour repentances, no blonde *fräuleins* or fancy lawyers showing up to get you off. I offer a clean deal. That is to say, you'll get what you want, and I'll get what I want.'

'I've heard you trick people. They say you're worse than a used-car salesman.'

'Now, wait a minute—'

'I apologize,' Martin said hastily. 'But it *is* supposed to be a fact that you can't be trusted.'

'I admit it. On the other hand, you seem to think you have found a way out.'

'A sure-fire proposition.'

'Sure-fire? Very funny!' The man began to chuckle, then halted. 'But we waste valuable time, Martin. Let's get down to cases. What do you want from me?'

Martin took a deep breath. 'I want to be able to stop time.'

'Right now?'

'No. Not yet. And not for everybody. I realize that would be impossible, of course. But I want to be able to stop time for myself. Just once, in the future. Whenever I get to a point where I know I'm happy and contented, that's where I'd like to stop. So I can just keep on being happy forever.'

'That's quite a proposition,' the Conductor mused. 'I've got to admit I've never heard anything just like it before—and believe me, I've listened to some lulus in my day.' He grinned at Martin. 'You've really been thinking about this, haven't you?'

'For years,' Martin admitted. Then he coughed. 'Well, what do you say?'

'It's not impossible, in terms of your own *subjective* time sense,' the Conductor murmured. 'Yes, I think it could be arranged.'

'But I mean *really* to stop. Not for me just to *imagine* it.'

'I understand. And it can be done.'

'Then you'll agree?'

'Why not? I promised you, didn't I? Give me your hand.'

Martin hesitated. 'Will it hurt very much? I mean, I don't like the sight of blood and—'

'Nonsense! You've been listening to a lot of poppycock. We already have made our bargain, my boy. I merely intend to put something into your hand. The ways and means of fulfilling your wish. After all, there's no telling at just what moment you may decide to exercise the agreement, and I can't drop everything and come running. So it's better if you can regulate matters for yourself.'

'You're going to give me a time stopper?'

'That's the general idea. As soon as I can decide what would be practical.' The Conductor hesitated. 'Ah, the very thing! Here, take my watch.'

He pulled it out of his vest pocket; a railroad watch in a silver case. He opened the back and made a delicate adjustment; Martin tried to see just exactly what he was doing, but the fingers moved in a blinding blur.

'There we are,' the Conductor smiled. 'It's all set, now. When you finally decide where you'd like to call a halt, merely turn the stem in reverse and unwind the watch until it stops. When it stops, time stops, for you. Simple enough?' And the Conductor dropped the watch into Martin's hand.

The young man closed his fingers tightly around the case. 'That's all there is to it, eh?'

'Absolutely. But remember—you can stop the watch only once. So you'd better make sure that you're satisfied with the moment you choose to prolong. I caution you in all fairness; make very certain of your choice.'

'I will.' Martin grinned. 'And since you've been so fair about it, I'll be fair, too. There's one thing you seem to have forgotten. It doesn't really matter *what* moment I choose. Because once I stop time for myself, that means I stay where I am forever. I'll never have to get any older. And if I don't get any older, I'll never die. And if I never die, then I'll never have to take a ride on your train.'

The Conductor turned away. His shoulders shook convulsively, and he may have been crying. 'And you said *I* was worse than a used-car salesman,' he gasped, in a strangled voice.

Then he wandered off into the fog, and the train whistle gave an impatient shriek, and all at once it was moving swiftly down the track, rumbling out of sight in the darkness.

Martin stood there, blinking down at the silver watch in his hand. If it wasn't that he could actually see it and feel it there, and if he couldn't smell that peculiar odor, he might have thought he'd imagined the whole thing from start to finish—train, Conductor, bargain, and all.

But he had the watch, and he could recognize the scent left by the train as it departed, even though there aren't many locomotives around that use sulfur and brimstone as fuel.

And he had no doubts about his bargain. That's what came of thinking things through to a logical conclusion. Some fools would have settled for wealth, or power, or Kim Novak. Daddy might have sold out for a fifth of whiskey.

Martin knew that he'd made a better deal. Better? It was foolproof. All he needed to do now was choose his moment.

He put the watch in his pocket and started back down the railroad track. He hadn't really had a destination in mind before, but he did now. He was going to find a moment of happiness. . . .

Now young Martin wasn't altogether a ninny. He realized perfectly well that happiness is a relative thing; there are conditions and degrees of contentment, and they vary with one's lot in life. As a hobo, he was often satisfied with a warm handout, a double-length bench in the park, or a can of Sterno made in 1957 (a vintage year).

Many a time he had reached a state of momentary bliss through such simple agencies, but he was aware that there were better things. Martin determined to seek them out.

Within two days he was in the great city of Chicago. Quite naturally, he drifted over to West Madison Street, and there he took steps to elevate his role in life. He became a city bum, a panhandler, a moocher. Within a week he had risen to the point where happiness was a meal in a regular one-arm luncheon joint, a two-bit flop on a real army cot in a real flophouse, and a full fifth of muscatel.

There was a night, after enjoying all three of these luxuries to the full, when Martin thought of unwinding his watch at the pinnacle of intoxication. But he also thought of the faces of the honest johns he'd braced for a handout today. Sure, they were squares, but they were prosperous. They wore good clothes, held good jobs, drove nice cars. And for them, happiness was even more ecstatic—they ate dinner in fine hotels, they slept on innerspring mattresses, they drank blended whiskey.

Squares or no, they had something there. Martin fingered his watch, put aside the temptation to hock it for another bottle of muscatel, and went to sleep determined to get himself a job and improve his happiness quotient.

When he awoke he had a hangover, but the determination was still with him. Before the month was out Martin was working for a general contractor over on the South Side, at one of the big rehabilitation projects. He hated the grind, but the pay was good, and pretty soon he got himself a one-room apartment out on Blue Island Avenue. He was accustomed to eating in decent restaurants now, and he bought himself a comfortable bed, and every Saturday night he went down to the corner tavern. It was all very pleasant, but—

The foreman liked his work and promised him a raise in a month. If he waited around, the raise would mean that he could afford a second-hand car. With a car, he could even start picking up a girl for a date now and then. Other fellows on the job did, and they seemed pretty happy.

So Martin kept on working, and the raise came through and the car came through and pretty soon a couple of girls came through.

The first time it happened, he wanted to unwind his watch immediately. Until he got to thinking about what some of the older men always said. There was a guy named Charlie, for example, who worked alongside him on the hoist. 'When you're young and don't know the score, maybe you get a kick out of running around with those pigs. But after awhile, you want something better. A nice girl of your own. That's the ticket.'

Martin felt he owed it to himself to find out. If he didn't like it better, he could always go back to what he had.

Almost six months went by before Martin met Lillian Gillis. By that time he'd had another promotion and was working inside, in the office. They made him go to night school to learn how to do simple bookkeeping, but it meant another fifteen bucks extra a week, and it was nicer working indoors.

And Lillian *was* a lot of fun. When she told him she'd marry him, Martin was almost sure that the time was now. Except that she was sort of—well, she was a *nice* girl, and she said they'd have to wait until they were married. Of course, Martin couldn't expect to marry her until he had a little more money saved up, and another raise would help, too.

That took a year. Martin was patient, because he knew it was going to be worth it. Every time he had any doubts, he took out his watch and looked at it. But he never showed it to Lillian, or anybody else. Most of the other men wore expensive wristwatches and the old silver railroad watch looked just a little cheap.

Martin smiled as he gazed at the stem. Just a few twists and he'd have something none of these other poor working slobs would ever have. Permanent satisfaction, with his blushing bride—

Only getting married turned out to be just the beginning. Sure, it was wonderful, but Lillian told him how much better things would be if they could move into a new place and fix it up. Martin wanted decent furniture, a TV set, a nice car.

So he started taking night courses and got a promotion to the front office. With the baby coming, he wanted to stick around and see his son arrive. And when it came, he realized he'd have to wait until it got a little older, started to walk and talk and develop a personality of its own.

About this time the company sent him out on the road as a troubleshooter on some of those other jobs, and now he *was* eating at those good hotels, living high on the hog and the expense account. More than once he was tempted to unwind his watch. This was the good life . . . Of course, it would be even better if he just didn't have to *work*. Sooner or later, if he could cut in on one of the company deals, he could make a pile and retire. Then everything would be ideal.

It happened, but it took time. Martin's son was going to high school before he really got up there into the chips. Martin got a strong hunch that it was now or never, because he wasn't exactly a kid anymore.

But right about then he met Sherry Westcott, and she didn't seem to think he was middle-aged at all, in spite of the way he was losing hair and adding stomach. She taught him that a toupee could cover the bald spot and a cumberbund could cover the pot gut. In fact, she taught him quite a lot and he so enjoyed learning that he actually took out his watch and prepared to unwind it.

Unfortunately, he chose the very moment that the private detectives broke down the door of the hotel room, and then there was a long stretch of time when Martin was so busy fighting the divorce action that he couldn't honestly say he was enjoying any given moment.

When he made the final settlement with Lil he was broke again, and Sherry didn't seem to think he was so young, after all. So he squared his shoulders and went back to work.

He made his pile eventually, but it took longer this time, and there wasn't much chance to have fun along the way. The fancy dames in the fancy cocktail lounges didn't seem to interest him anymore, and neither did the liquor. Besides, the Doc had warned him off that.

But there were other pleasures for a rich man to investigate. Travel, for instance—and not riding the rods from one hick burg to another, either. Martin went around the world by plane and luxury liner. For a while it seemed as though he would find his moment after all, visiting the Taj Mahal by moonlight. Martin pulled out the battered old watch case, and got ready to unwind it. Nobody else was there to watch him—

And that's why he hesitated. Sure, this was an enjoyable moment, but he was alone. Lil and the kid were gone, Sherry was gone, and somehow he'd never had time to make any friends. Maybe if he found new congenial people, he'd have the ultimate happiness. That must be the answer—it wasn't just money or power or sex or seeing beautiful things. The real satisfaction lay in friendship.

So on the boat trip home, Martin tried to strike up a few acquaintances at the ship's bar. But all these people were much younger, and Martin had nothing in common with them. Also they wanted to dance and drink, and Martin wasn't in condition to appreciate such pastimes. Nevertheless, he tried.

Perhaps that's why he had the little accident the day before they docked in San Francisco. 'Little accident' was the ship's doctor's way of describing it, but Martin noticed he looked very grave when he told him to stay in bed, and he'd called an ambulance to meet the liner at the dock and take the patient right to the hospital.

At the hospital, all the expensive treatment and the expensive smiles and the expensive words didn't fool Martin any. He was an old man with a bad heart, and they thought he was going to die.

But he could fool them. He still had the watch. He found it in his coat when he put on his clothes and sneaked out of the hospital.

He didn't have to die. He could cheat death with a single gesture—and he intended to do it as a free man, out there under a free sky.

That was the real secret of happiness. He understood it now. Not even friendship meant as much as freedom. This was the best thing of all—to be free of friends or family or the furies of the flesh.

Martin walked slowly beside the embankment under the night sky. Come to think of it, he was just about back where he'd started, so many years ago. But the moment was good, good enough to prolong forever. Once a bum, always a bum.

He smiled as he thought about it, and then the smile twisted sharply and suddenly, like the pain twisting sharply and suddenly in his chest. The world began to spin, and he fell down on the side of the embankment.

He couldn't see very well, but he was still conscious, and he knew what had happened. Another stroke, and a bad one. Maybe this was it. Except that he wouldn't be a fool any longer. He wouldn't wait to see what was still around the corner.

Right now was his chance to use his power and save his life. And he was going to do it. He could still move; nothing could stop him.

He groped in his pocket and pulled out the old silver watch, fumbling with the stem. A few twists and he'd cheat death, he'd never have to ride that Hell-Bound Train. He could go on forever. *Forever.*

Martin had never really considered the word before. To go on forever—but *now?* Did he *want* to go on forever, like this; a sick old man, lying helplessly here in the grass?

No. He couldn't do it. He wouldn't do it. And suddenly he wanted very much to cry, because he knew that somewhere along the line he'd outsmarted himself. And now it was too late. His eyes dimmed, there was a roaring in his ears. . . .

He recognized the roaring, of course, and he wasn't at all surprised to see the train come rushing out of the fog up there on the embankment. He wasn't surprised when it stopped, either, or when the Conductor climbed off and walked slowly toward him.

The Conductor hadn't changed a bit. Even his grin was still the same.

'Hello, Martin,' he said. 'All aboard.'

'I know,' Martin whispered. 'But you'll have to carry me. I can't walk. I'm not even really talking anymore, am I?'

'Yes, you are,' the Conductor said. 'I can hear you fine. And you can walk, too.' He leaned down and placed his hand on Martin's chest. There was a moment of icy numbness, and then, sure enough, Martin could walk after all.

He got up and followed the Conductor along the slope, moving to the side of the train.

'In here?' he asked.

'No, the next car,' the Conductor murmured. 'I guess you're entitled to ride Pullman. After all, you're quite a successful man. You've tasted the joys of wealth and position and prestige. You've known the pleasures of marriage and fatherhood. You've sampled the delights of dining and drinking and debauchery, too, and you traveled high, wide and handsome. So let's not have any last-minute recriminations.'

'All right,' Martin sighed. 'I can't blame you for my mistakes. On the other hand, you can't take credit for what happened, either. I worked for everything I got. I did it all on my own. I didn't even need your watch.'

'So you didn't,' the Conductor said, smiling. 'But would you mind giving it back to me now?'

'Need it for the next sucker, eh?' Martin muttered.

'Perhaps.'

Something about the way he said it made Martin look up. He tried to see the Conductor's eyes, but the brim of his cap cast a shadow. So Martin looked down at the watch instead.

'Tell me something,' he said softly. 'If I give you the watch, what will you do with it?'

'Why, throw it into the ditch,' the Conductor told him. 'That's all I'll do with it.' And he held out his hand.

'What if somebody comes along and finds it? And twists the stem backward, and stops time?'

'Nobody would do that,' the Conductor murmured. 'Even if they knew.'

'You mean, it was all a trick? This is only an ordinary, cheap watch?'

'I didn't say that,' whispered the Conductor. 'I only said that no one has ever twisted the stem backward. They've all been like you, Martin—looking ahead to find that perfect happiness. Waiting for the moment that never comes.'

The Conductor held out his hand again.

Martin sighed and shook his head. 'You cheated me after all.'

'You cheated yourself, Martin. And now you're going to ride that Hell-Bound Train.'

He pushed Martin up the steps and into the car ahead. As he entered, the train began to move, and the whistle screamed. And Martin stood there in the swaying Pullman, gazing down the aisle at the other passengers. He could see them sitting there, and somehow it didn't seem strange at all.

Here they were; the drunks and the sinners, the gambling men and the grifters, the big-time spenders, the skirt chasers, and all the jolly crew. They knew where they were going, of course, but they didn't seem to give a damn. The blinds were drawn on the windows, yet it was light inside, and they were all living it up—singing and passing the bottle and roaring with laughter, throwing the dice and telling their jokes and bragging their big brags, just the way Daddy used to sing about them in the old song.

'Mighty nice traveling companions,' Martin said. 'Why, I've never seen such a pleasant bunch of people. I mean, they seem to be really enjoying themselves!'

The Conductor shrugged. 'I'm afraid things won't be quite so jazzy when we pull into that Depot Way Down Yonder.'

For the third time, he held out his hand. 'Now, before you sit down, if you'll just give me that watch. A bargain's a bargain—'

Martin smiled. 'A bargain's a bargain,' he echoed. 'I agreed to ride your train if I could stop time when I found the right moment of happiness. And I think I'm about as happy right here as I've ever been.'

Very slowly, Martin took hold of the silver watch stem.

'No!' gasped the Conductor. 'No!'

But the watch stem turned.

'Do you realize what you've done?' the Conductor yelled. 'Now we'll never reach the Depot! We'll just go on riding, all of us—forever!'

Martin grinned. 'I know,' he said. 'But the fun is in the trip, not the destination. You taught me that. And I'm looking forward to a wonderful trip. Look, maybe I can even help. If you were to find me another one of those caps, now, and let me keep this watch—'

And that's the way it finally worked out. Wearing his cap and carrying his battered old silver watch, there's no happier person in or out of this world now and forever—than Martin. Martin, the new brakeman on that Hell-Bound Train.

WILL YOU WAIT?

Alfred Bester

They keep writing those antiquated stories about bargains with the Devil. You know . . . sulphur, spells and pentagrams; tricks, snares and delusions. They don't know what they're talking about. Twentieth Century diabolism is slick and streamlined, like jukeboxes and automatic elevators and television and all the other modern efficiencies that leave you helpless and infuriated.

A year ago I got fired from an agency job for the third time in ten months. I had to face the fact that I was a failure. I was also dead broke. I decided to sell my soul to the Devil, but the problem was how to find him. I went down to the main reference room of the library and read everything on demonology and devil-lore. Like I said, it was all just talk. Anyway, if I could have afforded the expensive ingredients which they claimed could raise the Devil, I wouldn't have had to deal with him in the first place.

I was stumped, so I did the obvious thing; I called Celebrity Service. A delicate young man answered.

I asked, 'Can you tell me where the Devil is?'

'Are you a subscriber to Celebrity Service?'

'No.'

'Then I can give you no information.'

'I can afford to pay a small fee for one item.'

'You wish limited service?'

'Yes.'

'Who is the celebrity, please?'

'The Devil.'

'Who?'

'The Devil . . . Satan, Lucifer, Scratch, Old Nick . . . The Devil.'

'One moment, please.' In five minutes he was back, extremely annoyed. 'Veddy soddy. The Devil is no longer a celebrity.'

He hung up. I did the sensible thing and looked through the telephone directory. On a page decorated with ads for Sardi's Restaurant I found Satan, Shaitan, Carnage & Bael, 477 Madison Avenue, Judson 3-1900. I called them. A bright young woman answered.

'SSC&B. Good morning.'

'May I speak to Mr. Satan, please?'

'The lines are busy. Will you wait?'

I waited and lost my dime. I wrangled with the operator and lost another dime but got the promise of a refund in postage stamps. I called Satan, Shaitan, Carnage & Bael again.

'SSC&B. Good morning.'

'May I speak to Mr. Satan? And please don't leave me hanging on the phone. I'm calling from a—'

The switchboard cut me off and buzzed. I waited. The coin-box gave a warning click. At last a line opened.

'Miss Hogan's office.'

'May I speak to Mr. Satan?'

'Who's calling?'

'He doesn't know me. It's a personal matter.'

'I'm sorry. Mr. Satan is no longer with our organization.'

'Can you tell me where I can find him?'

There was muffled discussion in broad Brooklyn and then Miss Hogan spoke in crisp Secretary: 'Mr. Satan is now with Beëlzebub, Belial, Devil & Orgy.'

I looked them up in the phone directory. 383 Madison Avenue, Plaza 6-1900. I dialed. The phone rang once and then chocked. A metallic voice spoke in sing-song: 'The number you are dialing is not a working number. Kindly consult your directory for the correct number. This a recorded message.' I consulted my directory. It said Plaza 6-1900. I dialed again and got the same recorded message.

I finally broke through to a live operator who was persuaded to give me the new number of Beëlzebub, Belial, Devil & Orgy. I called them. A bright young woman answered.

'B.B.D.O. Good morning.'

'May I speak to Mr. Satan, please?'

'Who?'

'Mr. Satan.'

'I'm sorry. There is no such person with our organization.'

'Then give me Beëlzebub or the Devil.'

'One moment, please.'

I waited. Every half minute she opened my wire long enough to gasp: 'Still ringing the Dev—' and then cut off before I had a chance to answer. At last a bright young woman spoke. 'Mr. Devil's office.'

'May I speak to him?'

'Who's calling?'

I gave her my name.

'He's on another line. Will you wait?'

I waited. I was fortified with a dwindling reserve of nickels and dimes. After twenty minutes, the bright young woman spoke again: 'He's just gone into an emergency meeting. Can he call you back?'

'No. I'll try again.'

Nine days later I finally got him.

'Yes, sir? What can I do for you?'

I took a breath. 'I want to sell you my soul.'

'Have you got anything on paper?'

'What do you mean, anything on paper?'

'The Property, my boy. The Sell. You can't expect B.B.D.O. to buy a pig in a poke. We may drink out of dixie cups up here, but the sauce has got to be a hundred proof. Bring in your Presentation. My girl'll set up an appointment.'

I prepared a Presentation of my soul with plenty of Sell. Then I called his girl.

'I'm sorry, he's on the Coast. Call back in two weeks.'

Five weeks later she gave me an appointment. I went up and sat in the photo-montage reception room of B.B.D.O. for two hours, balancing my Sell on my knees. Finally I was ushered into a corner office decorated with Texas brands in glowing neon. The Devil was lounging on his contour chair, dictating to an Iron Maiden. He was a tall man with the phoney voice of a sales manager; the kind that talks loud in elevators. He gave me a Sincere handshake and immediately looked through my Presentation.

'Not bad,' he said. 'Not bad at all. I think we can do business. No what did you have in mind? The usual?'

'Money, success, happiness.'

He nodded. 'The usual. Now we're square shooters in this shop. B.B.D.O. doesn't dry-gulch. We'll guarantee money, success and happiness.'

'For how long?'

'Normal life-span. No tricks, my boy. We take our estimates from the Actuary Tables. Offhand I'd say you're good for another forty, forty-five years. We can pin-point that in the contract later.'

'No tricks?'

He gestured impatiently. 'That's all bad public relations, what you're thinking. I promise you, no tricks.'

'Guaranteed?'

'Not only do we guarantee service; we *insist* on giving service. B.B.D.O. doesn't want any beefs going up to the Fair Practice Committee. You'll have to call on us for service at least twice a year or the contract will be terminated.'

'What kind of service?'

He shrugged. 'Any kind. Shine your shoes; empty ashtrays; bring you dancing girls. That can be pin-pointed later. We just insist that you use us at least twice a year. We've got to give you a quid for your quo. *Quid pro quo.* Check?'

'But no tricks?'

'No tricks. I'll have our legal department draw up the contract. Who's representing you?'

'You mean an agent? I haven't got one.'

He was startled. 'Haven't got an agent? My boy, you're living dangerously. Why, we could skin you alive. Get yourself an agent and tell him to call me.'

'Yes, sir. M-May I . . . Could I ask a question?'

'Shoot. Everything is open and above-board at B.B.D.O.'

'What will it be like for me . . . wh-when the contract terminates?'

'You really want to know?'

'Yes.'

'I don't advise it.'

'I want to know.'

He showed me. It was like a hideous session with a psychoanalyst, in perpetuity . . . an eternal, agonizing self-indictment. It was hell. I was shaken.

'I'd rather have inhuman fiends torturing me,' I said.

He laughed. 'They can't compare to man's inhumanity to himself. Well . . . changed your mind, or is it a deal?'

'It's a deal.'

We shook hands and he ushered me out. 'Don't forget,' he warned. 'Protect yourself. Get an agent. Get the best.'

I signed with Sibyl & Sphinx. That was on March 3rd. I called S&S on March 15th. Mrs. Sphinx said: 'Oh yes, there's been a hitch. Miss Sibyl was negotiating with B.B.D.O. for you, but she had to fly to Sheol. I've taken over for her.'

I called April 1st. Miss Sibyl said: 'Oh yes, there's been a slight delay. Mrs. Sphinx had to go to Salem for a try-out. A witch-burning. She'll be back next week.'

I called April 15th. Miss Sibyl's bright young secretary told me that there was some delay getting the contracts typed. It seemed that B.B.D.O. was re-organizing its legal department. On May 1st Sibyl & Sphinx told me that the contracts had arrived and that *their* legal department was looking them over.

I had to take a menial job in June to keep body and soul together. I worked in the stencil department of a network. At least once a week a script would come in about a bargain with the Devil which was signed, sealed and delivered before the opening commercial. I used to laugh at them. After four months of negotiation I was still threadbare.

I saw the Devil once, bustling down Park Avenue. He was running for Congress and was very busy being jolly and hearty with the electorate. He addressed every cop and doorman by first name. When I spoke to him he got a little frightened; thinking I was a Communist or worse. He didn't remember me at all.

In July, all negotiations stopped; everybody was away on vacation. In August everybody was overseas for some Black Mass Festival. In September Sibyl & Sphinx called me to their office to sign the contract. It was thirty-seven pages long, and fluttered with pasted-in corrections and additions. There were half a dozen tiny boxes stamped on the margin of every page.

'If you only knew the work that went into this contract,' Sibyl & Sphinx told me with satisfaction.

'It's kind of long, isn't it?'

'It's the short contracts that make all the trouble. Initial every box, and sign on the last page. All six copies.'

I initialled and signed. When I was finished I didn't feel and different. I'd expected to start tingling with money, success and happiness.

'Is it a deal now?' I asked.

'Not until *he's* signed it.'

'I can't hold out much longer.'

'We'll send it over by messenger.'

I waited a week and then called.

'You forgot to initial one of the boxes,' they told me.

I went to the office and initialed. After another week I called.

'*He* forgot to initial one of the boxes,' they told me that time.

On October 1st I received a special delivery parcel. I also received a registered letter. The parcel contained the signed, sealed and delivered contract between me and the Devil. I could at last be rich, successful and happy. The registered letter was from B.B.D.O. and informed me that in view of my failure to comply with Clause 27-A of the contract, it was considered terminated, and I was due for collection at their convenience. I rushed down to Sibyl & Sphinx.

'What's Clause 27-A?' they asked.

We looked it up. It was the clause that required me to use the services of the Devil at least once every six months.

'What's the date of the contract?' Sibyl & Sphinx asked.

We looked it up. The contract was dated March 1st, the day I'd had my first talk with the Devil in his office.

'March, April, May . . .' Miss Sibyl counted on her fingers. 'That's right. Seven months have elapsed. Are you sure you didn't ask for *any* service?'

'How could I? I didn't have a contract.'

'We'll see about this,' Miss Sphinx said grimly. She called B.B.D.O. and had a spirited argument with the Devil and his legal department. Then she hung up. 'He says you shook hands on the deal March 1st,' she reported. 'He was prepared in good faith to go ahead with his side of the bargain.'

'How could I know? I didn't have a contract.'

'Didn't you ask for anything?'

'No. I was waiting for the contract.'

Sibyl & Sphinx called in their legal department and presented the case.

'You'll have to arbitrate,' the legal department said, and explained that agents are forbidden to act as their client's attorney.

I hired the legal firm of Wizard, Warlock, Voodoo, Dowser & Hag (99 Wall Street, Exchange 3–1900), to represent me before the Arbitration Board (479 Madison Avenue, Lexington 5–1900). They asked for a $200 retainer plus twenty percent of the contract's benefits. I'd managed to save $34 during the four months I was working in the stencil department. They waived the retainer and went ahead with the Arbitration preliminaries.

On November 15th the network demoted me to the mail room, and I seriously contemplated suicide. Only the fact that my soul was in jeopardy in an arbitration stopped me.

The case came up December 12th. It was tried before a panel of three impartial Arbitrators and took all day. I was told they'd mail me their decision. I waited a week and called Wizard, Warlock, Voodoo, Dowser & Hag.

'They've recessed for the Christmas holidays,' they told me.

I called January 2nd.

'One of them's out of town.'

I called January 10th.

'He's back, but the other two are out of town.'

'When will I get a decision?'

'It could take months.'

'How do you think my chances look?'

'Well, we've never lost an arbitration.'

'That sounds pretty good.'

'But there can always be a first time.'

That sounded pretty bad. I got scared and figured I'd better copper my bets. I did the sensible thing and hunted through the telephone directory until I found Seraphim, Cherubim and Angel, 666 Fifth Avenue, Templeton 6–1900. I called them. A bright young woman answered.

'Seraphim, Cherubim and Angel. Good morning.'

'May I speak to Mr. Angel, please?'

'He's on another line. Will you wait?'

I'm still waiting.

SULE SKERRY

Jane Yolen

Mairi rowed the coracle with quick, angry strokes, watching the rocky shoreline and the little town of Caith perched on its edge recede. She wished she could make her anger disappear as easily. She was sixteen, after all, and no longer a child. The soldiers whistled at her, even in her school uniform, when she walked to and from the Academy. And wasn't Harry Stones, who was five years older than she and a lieutenant in the RAF, a tail gunner, mad about her? She knew he would have asked her Dad for her hand, though she was too young yet, a school girl. Whenever he came to visit, he brought her something. Once even a box of chocolates, though they were very dear.

But to be sent away from London, to her Gran's house, to this desolate, isolated Scottish sea town because of a few German raids when she could have helped, could have at least cooked and taken care of the flat for her father because the help had all gone off to war jobs. To be there in case a bomb *did* fall, so she could race out and help evacuate all the poor unfortunates, maybe even win a medal, and wouldn't Jenny Eivensley look green then. But he had sent her off, her Dad, and Harry had agreed, even though it meant they couldn't see each other very often. It was not in the least fair.

She pulled again on the oars. The little skin boat tended to wallow and needed extra bullying. It wasn't built like a proper British rowboat. It was roundish, shaped more like a turtle shell than a ship. Mairi hated it. Hated all of the things in Caith. She knew she should have been in London helping rather than wallowing in a coracle. She pulled on the oars and the boat shot ahead.

The thing about rowing, she reminded herself, was that you watched where you had been, not where you were heading. She could see the town, with its crown of mewing seabirds, disappear from sight. Her destination did not matter. It was all ocean anyway—cold, uninviting, opaque; a dark green mirror that reflected nothing. And now there was ocean behind as well as ahead, for the shore had thinned out to an invisible line.

Suddenly, without warning, the coracle fetched up against a rock, a series of water-smoothed amphibious mounds, that loomed up out of the sea. Only at the bump did Mairi turn and look. Out of the corner of her eye she saw a quick scurry of something large and grey and furry on the far side of the rocks. She heard a splash.

'Oh,' she said out loud. 'A seal!'

The prospect of having come upon a seal rockery was enough to make her leap incautiously from the coracle onto the rock, almost losing the boat in her eagerness. But her anger was forgotten. She leaned over and pulled the little boat out of the water, scrapping its hull along the grey granite. Then she upended the coracle and let it dry, looking for all the world like a great dozing tortoise drying in the hazy sun.

Mairi shrugged out of her mackintosh and draped it on the rock next to the boat. Then snuggling the watchcap down over her curls and pulling the bulky fisherman's sweater over her slim hips, she began her ascent.

The rocks were covered with a strange purple-grey lichen that was both soft and slippery. Mairi fell once, bruising her right knee without ripping her trousers. She cursed softly, trying out swear words that she had never been allowed to use at home or in Gran's great house back on shore. Then she started up again, on her hands and knees, more carefully now, and at last gained the high point on the rocks after a furious minute of climbing that went backwards and sideways as often as it went up.

The top of the gray rocks was free of the lichen and she was able to stand up, feeling safe, and look around.

She could not see Caith, with its little watchful wind-scored houses lined up like a homefront army to face the oncoming tides in the firth, with Gran's grand house standing on one side, the sergeant major. She could not even see the hills behind, where cliffs hunched like the bleached fossils of some enormous prehistoric ocean beast washed ashore. All that she could see was the unbroken sea, blue and black and green and gray, with patterns of color that shifted as quickly as the pieces in a child's kaleidoscope. Grey-white foam skipped across wave tops, then tumbled down and fractured into bubbles that popped erratically, leaving nothing but a greyish scum that soon became dark water again. She thought she saw one or two dark seal heads in the troughs of the waves, but they never came close enough for her to count. And overhead the sky was lowering, a color so dirty, it would have made even the bravest sailor long for shore. There was a storm coming, and Mairi guessed she should leave.

She shivered, and suddenly knew where she was. These rocks were the infamous Sule Skerry rocks that Gran's cook had told her about.

'Some may call it a rookery,' Cook had said one morning when Mairi had visited with her in the dark kitchen. Cook's cooking was awful—dry, bland, and unvaried. But at least she knew stories and always imparted them with an intensity that made even the strangest of them seem real. 'Aye, some may call it a rookery. But us from Caith, we know. It be the home of the selchies who are men on land and seals in the sea. And the Great Selchie himself lives on that rock. Tall he is. And covered with a sealskin when he tumbles in the waves. But he is a man for all that. And no maiden who goes to Sule Skerry returns the same.'

She had hummed a bit of an old song, then, with a haunting melody that Mairi, for all her music training at school, could not repeat. But the words of the song, some of them, had stuck with her:

> An earthly nourrice sits and sings,
> And aye she sings, 'Ba, lily wean!
> Little ken I my bairn's father,
> Far less the land that he staps in.'
>
> Then ane arose at her bed-fit,
> An a grumly guest I'm sure was he:
> 'Here am I, thy bairn's father,
> Although I be not comelie.
>
> I am a man upon the land,
> I am a selchie in the sea
> And when I'm far frae ev'ry strand
> My dwelling is in Sule Skerry.'

A warning tale, Mairi thought. A boogeyman story to keep foolish girls safe at home. She smiled. She was a Londoner, after all, not a silly Scots maid.

And then she heard a strange sound, almost like an echo of the music of Cook's song, from the backside of the rocks. At first she thought it was the sound of wind against water, the sound she heard continuously at Gran's home where every room rustled with the music of the sea. But this was different somehow, a sweet, low throbbing, part moan and part chant. Without knowing the why of it, only feeling a longing brought on by the wordless song, and excusing it as solving a mystery, she went looking for the source of the song. The rockface was smooth on this side, dry, without the slippery, somber lichen; and the water was calmer so it did not splash up spray. Mairi continued down the side, the tune reeling her in effortlessly.

Near the waterline was a cave opening into the west face of the rock, a man-sized opening as black and uninviting as a collier's pit. But she took a deep, quick breath, and went in.

Much to her surprise, the inside of the cave glowed with an incandescent blue-green light that seemed to come from the cave walls themselves. Darker pockets of light illuminated the concave sections of the wall. Pieces of seaweed caught in these niches gave the appearance of household goods.

Mairi could scarcely breathe. Any loud sound seemed sacrilegious. Her breath itself was a violation.

And then she heard the moan-song again, so loud that it seemed to fill the entire cave. It swelled upward like a wave, then broke off in a bubbling sigh.

Mairi walked slowly in, not daring to touch the cave walls in case she should mar the perfection of the color, yet fearing that she might fall for the floor of the cave was littered with puddles of water. Slowly, one foot in front of another, she explored the cave. In the blue green light, her sweater and skin seemed to take on an underwater tinge as if she had been transformed into a mermaid.

And then the cave ended, tapering off to a rounded apse with a kind of stone altar the height of a bed. There was something dark lying on the rock slab. Fearfully, Mairi inched towards it and when she got close, the dark thing heaved up slightly and spoke to her in a strange guttural tongue. At first Mairi thought it was a seal, a wounded seal, but then she saw it was a man huddled under a sealskin coat. He suddenly lay back, feverish and shuddering, old blood beading his head like a crown.

Without thinking, Mairi moved closer and put her hand on his forehead expecting it to burn with temperature, but he was cold and damp and slippery to the touch. Then he opened his eyes and they were the same blue-green color as the walls, as the underside of a wave. She wondered for a moment if he were blind, for there seemed to be no pupil in those eyes. Then he closed the lids and smiled at her, whispering in that same unknown tongue.

'Never mind, never mind, I'll get help,' whispered Mairi. He might be a fisherman from the town or an RAF man shot down on a mission. She looked at his closed-down face. Here, at last, was her way to aid the war effort. 'Lie still. First I'll see to your wounds. They taught us first aid at school.'

She examined his forehead under the slate-grey hair, but whatever wound had been there was now closed and seamed with scabs. And when she started to slip the sealskin coat down to examine him for other wounds, she was shocked to discover he had no clothes on under it. No clothes at all.

She hesitated then. Except for the statues in the museum she had never seen a man naked. Not even in the first aid books. But what if he were *hurt unto death*. The fearsome poetry of the old phrase decided her. She inched back the sealskin covering as gently as she could.

He did not move except for the rise and fall of his chest. His body was covered with fine hairs, gray as the hair on his head. He had broad, powerful shoulders and slim, tapering hips. The skin on his hands was strangely wrinkled as if he had been underwater too long. She realized with a start that he was quite, quite beautiful —but alien. As her grandmother often said, 'Men are queer creatures, so different from us, child. And someday you will know it.'

Then his eyes opened again and she could not look away from them. He smiled, opened his mouth, and began to speak, to chant really. Mairi bent down over him and he opened his arms to her, the grey webbing between his fingers pulsing strongly. And without willing it, she covered his mouth with hers. All the sea was in that kiss, cold and vast, and perilous. It drew her in till she thought she would faint with it, with his tongue darting around hers as quick as a minnow. And then his arms encircled her and he was as strong as the tide.

She felt only the briefest of pain, and drowning in her love for him, she let the land go.

When Mairi awoke, she was sitting on the stone floor and cold, bone-chilling cold. She shivered and pushed her hand across her cheeks. They were wet, though whether with tears or from the damp air she could not say.

Above her, on the stone bed, the wounded man breathed raggedly. Occasionally he let out a moan. Mairi stood and looked down at him. His flesh was pale, wan, almost translucent. She put her hand on his shoulder but he did not move. She wondered if she had fallen and hit her head, if she had dreamed what had happened.

'Help, I must get help for him,' she thought. She covered him again with the coat and made her way back to the cave mouth. Her entire body ached and she decided she must have fallen and blacked out.

The threatening storm had not yet struck, but the dark slant of rain against the horizon was closer still. Mairi scrambled along the rocks to where the coracle waited. She put on her mac, then heaved the boat over and into the water and slipped in, getting only her boots wet.

It was more difficult rowing back, rowing against the tide. Waves broke over the bow of the little boat, and by the time she was within sight of the town, she was soaked to the skin. The stones of Sule Skerry were little more than grey wave tops then, and with one pull on the oar, they disappeared from sight. The port enfolded her, drew her in. She felt safe and lonely at once.

When Mairi reached the shore there was a knot of fishermen drawing in their boats. A few were still at work on the bright orange nets, folding them carefully in that quick, intricate pattern that only they seemed to know. One man, in a blue watch cap, held up a large piece of tattered white cloth, an awning of silk. It seemed to draw the other men to him. He gestured with the silk and it billowed out as if capturing the coming storm.

Suddenly Mairi was horribly afraid. She broke into the circle of men. 'Oh please, please,' she cried out, hearing the growing wail of wind in her voice. 'There's a man on the rocks. He's hurt.'

'The rocks?' The man with the silk stuffed it into his pocket, but a large fold of it hung down his side. 'Which rocks.'

'Out there. Beyond the sight-line. Where the seals stay,' Mairi said.

'Whose child is she?' asked a man who still carried an orange net. He spoke as if she were too young to understand him, or were a foreigner.

'Old Mrs. Goodleigh's grandchild. The one with the English father,' came an answer.

'Mavis' daughter, the one who became a nurse in London.'

'Too good for Caith, then?'

Mairi was swirled about in their conversation.

'Please,' she tried again.

'Suppose'n she means The Rocks?'

'Yes,' begged Mairi. 'The rocks out there. Sule Skerry.'

'Hush, child. Must na say the name in sight of the sea,' said the blue cap man.

'Toss it a coin, Jock,' said the white silk man. The man called Jock reached into his pocket and flung a coin out to the ocean. It skipped across the waves twice, then sank.

'That should quieten. Now then, The Rocks you say?'

Mairi turned to the questioner. He had a face like a map, wrinkles marking the boundries of nose and cheek. 'Yes, sir,' she said breathily.

'Aye, he might have fetched up there,' said the white silk man, drawing it out of his pocket again for the others to see.

Did they know him, then, Mairi wondered.

'Should we leave him to the storm?' asked Jock.

'He might be one of ours,' the map-faced man said.

They all nodded at that.

'He's sheltered.' Mairi spoke suddenly. 'In a cave. A grotto, like. It's all cast over with a blue and green light.'

'Teched, she is. There's no grotto there,' said the blue cap.

'No blue and green light either,' said the map-faced man, turning from her and speaking earnestly with his companions. 'Even if he's one of them, he might tell us what we need. Our boys could use the knowledge. From that bit of silk, it's hard to say which side he's on.' He reached out and touched the white cloth with a gnarled finger.

'Aye, we'd best look for him.'

'He won't be hard to find,' Mairi said. 'He's sick. Hurt, I touched him.'

'What was he wearing then?' asked blue cap.

The wind had picked up and Mairi couldn't hear the question. 'What?' she shouted.

'Wearing. What was the fellow wearing?'

Suddenly remembering that the man had been naked under the coat, she was silent.

'She doesn't know. Probably too scared to go close. Come on,' said Jock.

The men pushed past her and dragged along two of the large six-men boats that fished the haaf banks. The waves were slapping angrily at the shore, gobbling up pieces of the sand and churning out pebbles at each retreat. Twelve men scrambled into the boats and headed out to sea, their oars flashing together.

Three men were left on shore, including the one holding the white silk. They stood staring out over the cold waters, their eyes squinted almost shut against the strange bright light that was running before the storm.

Mairi stood near them, but apart.

No one spoke.

It was a long half hour before the first of the boats leapt back towards them, across a wave, just seconds ahead of the rain.

The second boat beached just as the storm broke, the men jumping out onto the sand and drawing the boat up behind them. A dark form was huddled against the stern.

Mairi tried to push through to get a close glimpse of the man, but blue cap spoke softly to her.

'Nay, nay girl, don't look. He's not what you would call a pretty sight. He pulled a gun on Jock and Jock took a rock to him.'

But Mairi had seen enough. The man was dressed in a flier's suit, and a leather jacket with zippers. His blonde hair was matted with blood.

'That's not the one I saw,' she murmured. 'Not the one I. . . .'

'Found him lying on the rocks, just as the girl said. Down by the west side of the rocks,' said Jock. 'We threw his coins to the sea and bought our way home. Though I don't know that German coins buy much around here. Bloody Huns.'

'What's a German flier doing this far west, I'd like to know,' said map-face.

'Maybe he was trying for America,' Jock answered, laughing sourly.

'Ask him. When he's fit to talk,' said blue cap.

The man with the white silk wrapped it around the German's neck. The parachute shroud lines hung down the man's back. Head down, the German was marched between Jock and blue cap up the strand and onto the Main Street. The other men trailed behind.

With the rain soaking through her cap and running down her cheeks, Mairi took a step towards them. Then she turned away. She kicked slowly along the water's edge till she found the stone steps that led up to her Gran's house. The sea pounded a steady reminder on her left, a bass continuo to the song that ran around in her head. The last three verses came to her slowly.

> Now he has ta'en a purse of goud
> And he has put it upon her knee

> Sayin' 'Gie to me my little young son
> An tak ye up thy nourrice-fee.'

She had already started to put her hands in her pockets to keep them warm. It did not surprise her to find a coin in one of the mac's deep pockets. Reluctantly she drew it out. It was green and gold, slightly crusted, as if it had lain on the ocean bottom for some time. She had never seen it before and could only guess how it had gotten into her coat. She closed her hand around the coin, so tightly a second coin was imprinted on her palm.

> An it shall pass on a summer's day
> when the sun shines het on every stane
> That I will take my little young son
> And teach him for to swim his lane.

> An thu sall marry a proud gunner
> An a right proud gunner I'm sure he'll be
> An the very first shot that ere he shoots
> He'll kill baith my young son and me.'

If it were true, and not some dream brought on by a fall (she felt again those cold, compelling hand on her, the movement of the webbings pulsing on her breasts, the briney smell of his breath) then Harry Stones would have to marry her after all. Her father could not deny them that.

Only what would the doctor say, she wondered. 'A fine little boy, Mrs. Stones. Only one problem, I'm afraid, he's covered all over with grey hair and he looks rather like a seal.'

And laughing and crying at the same time, Mairi began to run up the stone steps. The sound of the sea followed her all the way home, part melody and part unending moan.

LA RONDE

Damon Knight

He felt that he was gone a long time, and when he came back from wherever it was, he found himself sitting on a stone, gazing at a wrecked automobile that was tilted upside down against a tree. One of the front wheels was lazily turning. The door on the driver's side hung open; below it the whole top of the car had been crushed flat, and it seemed to him a miracle that anyone had got out alive.

There was a buzzing in his head, but he stood up and went closer to the wreck to see if anyone needed help. The car was empty. What could have become of the driver?

For that matter, what was he himself doing here? Perhaps it would come back to him in a minute, when he was rested. He went all around the car with a kind of dumb obstinacy, through brush that whipped his legs under his coat. No one was there.

Above him there was a broad muddy swath, littered with glass, bits of chrome, and more incongruous things—scattered pieces of white tissue, sunglasses, a pack of cigarettes. He climbed, helping himself up from one sapling to another, until he reached the highway, where he stood looking uncertainly around him. There were long black skid marks on the macadam. The road made a curve here, and on the opposite side the slope resumed, rising another hundred feet against the gray sky. It was very cold.

He peered down the slope again, thinking that from this elevation he might be able to see the body of the driver, but he could barely make out the wreck itself through the screen of branches.

Although he could not think very clearly because of the continuous dull buzzing in his head, he knew that he ought to report the accident, and he trudged out around the curve in the direction the car had been going. The road straightened here for a distance of half a mile or so; it was empty and gray under the sky, with the gloomy forested slope on one side and the ravine on the other. There were no highway signs, no billboards, nothing to tell him where he might be.

The road ran on, empty and cold under the gray sky. The forested hill was behind him now and on either side were bare fields. A few flakes of snow came drifting along; they melted at once on the highway. Then the snow came more thickly and made a white film in which he left a trail of glistening footprints. For some reason this alarmed him, but when he looked back after a few minutes, he saw that the prints were rapidly being covered.

He went on, with the snow whipping into his eyes, until he came to a private road with a chain across it. He ducked under the chain. The road went up steeply, covered with dead leaves and fallen branches. Over the crest of the rise, it ran straight between fields grown up with tall weeds to a white house on a hill. While he was climbing the slope he had been sheltered a little from the wind-driven snow, but now it flew at him again. As he approached the house he could see that the windows were boarded up. The big front door had a padlock on it. He went around the house and found the back door padlocked too.

As he stood under the eaves to get out of the wind, he noticed an oblong pit covered by a framework of metal bars next to the foundation. He crouched over it and tugged at the framework; the metal was rusted and heavy, but it came up. He laid it aside. When he had cleared out the dead leaves and spruce needles underneath, he found, as he had guessed, that the pit was a light-well for a cellar window. He pulled up the hinged window, crawled through and dropped into musty darkness.

The light from the cobwebbed glass was water-gray, but it was enough to show him the wooden steps that led up to a trap-door. When he raised the trap, he found himself in a long gray room illuminated only by a watery glow at one of the windows. It was cold—colder, it seemed, than the outdoors. His ghostly breath rose in the air.

There was firewood and kindling in a box beside the old-fashioned cook-stove, but not a scrap of paper, though he opened one drawer after another and lighted matches to look in. In one of the drawers he found the stub of a candle, and with this in his shivering hand he went through a pantry into a dining room, and from there into a library. Even here there was no newspapers, only the moldy-apricot-colored leather books in the glass-fronted book-cases. He retreated into the kitchen, and this time opened the doors of cabinets, where he found brittle shelf paper under the heavy old plates and tumblers. He pulled out a few pieces of this, and presently had a fire going in the stove.

The tall wooden icebox was empty, but he found peaches in a glass jar in the pantry. The jar was like none he had ever seen; it had a glass top held down by two jointed handles, and a red rubber gasket between jar and lid. He stood beside the stove, which was now radiating an almost imperceptible warmth, and ate the peaches with a cold metallic-tasting spoon.

There was a kerosene lamp on the kitchen table; he filled it from a can he found in the pantry and lighted it. It smoked at first, blackening the inside of the glass chimney, until he found out how to adjust and trim the wick. Carrying the lamp, he mounted the back stairway and found two bedrooms. The beds had been stripped, but the mattresses, covered with coarse gray-striped twill, remained. He dragged one of them down the stairs to the kitchen; there, in front of the stove, he stretched out in his clothes and fell asleep.

The cold woke him early in the morning; the fire had gone out. He built it up again, ate the rest of the peaches for breakfast, and then set out to explore the house. All the furniture was Victorian, even the pieces that looked almost new. Under the high cross-beamed ceiling hung a black wrought iron chandelier with candles in it. Kerosene lamps with painted china shades were on all the tables. The living room, dining room, and library had fireplaces, red brick in the living room, green tile in the other two; there were fireplaces in two of the upstairs bedrooms as well. Two other upstairs rooms had doors which he could not open.

He went down again to forage in the pantry. He found sacks of flour and cornmeal, cans of condensed milk, oil and lard, and jar after jar of preserved fruit and vegetables. There was plenty of wood stacked on the porch and in the yard.

With tools he found in the cellar he pried loose the staple that held the padlock on the back door, so that he could go in and out freely while leaving the door apparently still locked. Gray smoke ascended from the kitchen chimney; he could not help that, but the sky was so overcast, although it was no longer snowing, that he thought the smoke would not be seen.

With flour, water and condensed milk he mixed a batter and made pancakes. There was even a whole cheese, not very moldy; he cut off the bad part and ate a wedge with his pancakes.

Afterward he made fires in all the fireplaces downstairs. He fed them until they roared in the chimneys, but the stubborn cold of the house yielded slowly. Even when he sat in a wing chair with his feet on the hearth, he could feel the insistent chill probing at his back.

All through the house, the firelight sent shadows racing up the walls. These shadows disturbed him, and he went to work filling the oil lamps, trimming and adjusting their wicks.

Nowhere in the house was there any electrical appliance: no lights, no television, not even a radio. There were no newspapers, and no magazines except for the bound volumes of *Harper's* and *The Century* in the library. Even the bathroom fixtures were old; the shower (which did not work) was a vast sunflower-head of metal suspended on a stalk over the claw-footed bathtub. In the mahogany medicine cabinet he found bone toothbrushes with black hog-bristles, and medicines in plain brown bottles with paper labels: ipecac, calamine. Yet he knew that the house could not have been abandoned for more than a year of two; there was dust everywhere, but only a light film, not the accumulation of a century. Moreover, it was curious, in a house with so much food in it, that there was no sign of rats.

He was reluctant to damage anything in the house, but in the end his curiousity won out, and he forced the two locked doors upstairs. Behind one of them was a lumber room, choked with bedsteads, sofas, chairs, all dusty and soiled, but modern in appearance. The second room had been fitted out as an office, with an oak desk, a leather armchair, and an ancient Royal typewriter, the kind with a little glass window in the side through which part of the works could be seen.

Beside the typewriter lay a sheaf of manuscript. The first few words caught his eye, and he sat down to read.

My maternal great-grandfather built his house on a terrace at the foot of a wooded hill in Potamos Township, near the New York and New Jersey borders of Pennsylvania in what they now call the 'Tri-States' area. Behind the house there are seven Norway spruces, of which the tallest is about eighty feet; the ground beneath them is carpeted with brown needles, and the wind moves quietly through their branches. Farther up the hill are Scotch pines, native spruces and firs, maples, and birch. Still farther up, a mile or so above the house, there is an old logging road, now grown up in maple saplings, and above that the foundations of a settler's cabin, the stones barely visible in the underbrush. Except for these, and a power line that crosses the hill, there is no sign of human habitation.

The house itself is of white-painted frame and shiplap construction, three stories tall, with dormers, a veranda and an Italian slate roof. Over the years it has settled, having been built without footings, as the custom then was, but the frame is sturdy; I remember that an electrician who was called in to wire the house, when I was a boy, complained that he had to drill through innumerable 'cats,' diagonal framing members which united the studs.

The downstairs rooms are paneled in golden oak; the floors are parquet. All the rooms, even the old servants' quarters on the third floor, are ample in size; the living room ceiling is eighteen feet high, and the rest fifteen. These high ceilings make the house 'hard to heat,' as the local expression has it, but they give a sense of spaciousness and a quality of sound entirely different from that in 'modern' cheap-jack houses. It is a soothing and relaxing ambience, a feeling of permanence and safety, which must be experienced to be appreciated.

When I saw the house again, after the death of my aunt Margaret in 1978, the silences of the vast rooms seemed to speak of boyhood pleasures. I am half-convinced that houses somehow soak up the psychic experiences of their inhabitants; there are certain houses that have a mean-spirited or discouraged air, and there are city apartments which seem to radiate a sense of irritability, as if the walls still contained the last echoes of an angry shout.

My aunt Margaret, who had lived in this house since I was a boy, and to whom my parents willed the possession and use of the property during her lifetime, was, I now think, a kindred soul; we were alike at least in that each of us was happiest in a state of nonmatrimony. When I was a child, however, I disliked and feared her, because she sometimes seemed aware of my existence and sometimes not.

It was she who had redecorated the house and covered all the sofas with chintz, hung 'modern' pictures and strewn the coffee tables with cigarette boxes and French novels. Yet even her old age and illness seemed to have left no psychic traces in this house. The walls, the cornices, the mantelpieces seemed to say, 'Here we are, as we have always been. Why have you stayed away so long?'

I must add that although there were no ghosts in the house itself, the cellar was another matter. It was irregular and low, angling around a huge stone that had been too big for the excavators to remove; to reach it, one went down through a trap in the kitchen and then had to walk stooping along a sort of cobwebbed passageway to reach the farther room where the furnace was. In this chamber, so long as the light was on, I felt no uneasiness, but in the stifling dark something was there, some malevolent and incoherent impulse that was older than the house.

Against the well-meant advice of my friends, I settled my affairs in New York, retired from my practice, sold most of my furniture, and disposed of my lease. In September I moved into the old house. A local woman, Mrs. Beveridge, helped me set the place to rights. I gathered that she was a recent widow, in straitened circumstances; I asked her to stay on as my housekeeper, and she agreed.

Mrs. Beveridge was a woman of perhaps fifty, sturdily built, with pale skin and dark hair which she wore in an old-fashioned bun. Her husband, whom she rarely mentioned, had been a carpenter or roofer or something of that sort; she herself had had little education, but she had a high degree of native intelligence and had formed her mind by reading. I felt myself lucky to have her, not only because of her efficiency in caring for the house, but because there was no suggestion on either side of any sexual innuendo between us. She spoke little, in a quiet voice, and adapted her habits perfectly to mine. When I wanted her for any reason she was there; when I wished to be alone she effaced herself. In the evenings she retired to her room on the third floor, where I sometimes heard her radio playing softly.

In November an early storm knocked down power lines and left us without light or heat. Mrs. Beveridge kindled fires in the fireplaces and kept the wood range going in the kitchen; I got out the kerosene lamps which were kept for such emergencies, and we ate by candlelight. During the four days of the storm, I became accustomed to the soft light of lamps and candles and grew to like it. When the power came on again, I discovered that I was actually disappointed. The electric lights seemed cold and impersonal; they revealed too much; I preferred the warm brown darkness, the mystery. I continued to use the lamps; Mrs. Beveridge appeared to have no objection.

With her help, I carried down some pieces of furniture abandoned years ago in the attic. The marble-topped dressers and tables were as sound as ever; the chairs and love seats, of course, were upholstered in horsehair, impossibly hard to sit on, and the leather was cracked and peeling. As soon as I was able, I got an upholsterer in Stroudsburg to come out and take these pieces away for refinishing. I had them done in rose and blue plush, or rather mohair, a deep-piled fabric. When they were brought back and arranged in the living room, the remaining modern pieces looked all the more out of place. One by one I got rid of them. At the Auction

Barn, so-called, on the Port Jervis road I found a huge icebox and two large copper washtubs. I consulted Mrs. Beveridge about each of these changes, half-expecting her to demur since they involved more labor for her, but she expressed her entire satisfaction, and indeed, I often heard her singing quietly at her work. At last, more than nine months after I had begun, I was able to look about me and see nothing whatever that had been made later than the year 1910. I had, of course, canceled my subscriptions to all newspapers and magazines. Our supplies were delivered in bulk by a Mr. Thomas and stored by Mrs. Beveridge.

From a dealer in Stroudsburg I acquired a parlor organ in fair condition. It had not been converted to motorized operation, as so many old organs have; the bellows was cracked, however, and some of the padding under the keys was worn away. When it was restored, it functioned perfectly. The organ had a keyboard of two and a half octaves, and with the use of various stops ('Tremolo,' 'Celeste,' 'Vox Humana,' and the like) it could produce an astonishing variety of pleasant sounds. I made some effort to learn this instrument, and amused myself with it sometimes when Mrs. Beveridge was at her work, but she was so much better at it than I that in the evenings I merely sat and listened to her play. We had a music book, published in the 1880s, which contained some charming things of Schubert's, as well as some sacred music and even a few popular songs.

I discovered in myself an insatiable appetite for Victorian literature—novels, miscellanies, journals. That spring I haunted the antique shops and secondhand stores around Potamos. One of my prizes was a leather-bound set of Dickens, published in 1878, with the original illustrations; another was a work entitled *Dr. Hood's Plain Talks and Common Sense Medical Adviser*, a quaint heavy volume which recommended prussic acid for stomach ulcers, and cocaine for heroin addiction. As for health care, I knew quite well that if I became seriously ill, I should have to seek modern medical treatment, but my health was good as long as I took care not to overstrain my heart, and Mrs. Beveridge was never ill.

I was aware that the Victorian life I was attempting to re-create within these walls was not the reality. The songs of Victorian men and women were not all decorous, nor were all their habits nice. A real Victorian bachelor in my situation would long before now, in all probability, have undone the laces of his housekeeper's underwear. No, it was not the real Victorian world that I was attempting to re-create, but my boyhood's imaginary world of safety, serenity, and gentleness.

I confess that I was as much alarmed as pleased by the alacrity with which Mrs. Beveridge fell in with my scheme. Never once did she suggest even by a smile or a gesture that what we were doing was absurd. She seemed to take it all as perfectly normal, and it was this that alarmed me. Either we were falling together into a folie á deux, or she was humoring me, with consummate skill, for some motive of her own which I could not guess.

At any rate, the life we now began to lead was so pleasant that I ceased to question it. In the mornings, in fine weather, I tended my garden; in the afternoons I worked in my study, and in the evenings Mrs. Beveridge and I decorously diverted ourselves. On fair days the house was sunny, and the porch pillars, which I could see through the glass pane of the door at the far end of the living room, gave back the pure essence of light. But it is the winter evenings that I remember with more pleasure, when the whole world was shut out in darkness, and the lamps were surrounded by a brown gloom.

With the aid of an old book of parlor tricks and games, Mrs. Beveridge and I relearned the art of the cat's cradle, forming more and more intricate figures with a loop of string. Beginning with the Cat's Cradle, we went on to the Calm Sea; the Upturned Cradle, the Mattress Turned Over, the Cat's Eye, the Pig on the Pegs. We also played at making hand shadows on the wall: the Bird in Flight, the Tortoise, The Goose a Prisoner (in which one hand grips the wrist of the other which forms the goose), and so on; we played word games, at which Mrs. Beveridge was very good, and sometimes Anagrams, Scat, or Old Maid.

I counted, I say, on the fact that I was completely aware of my own deepening obsession, but this belief was shaken one morning, when, arising earlier than usual, I went down to the kitchen to see if there was any coffee. It was about seven o'clock; the day was clear, and the sunlight reflecting from the white snow gave a shimmer to the atmosphere. Mrs. Beveridge was nowhere in sight, but a man in a long coat was carrying a sack up the steps of the back porch to the pantry. At first I thought he was Mr. Thomas; then I saw that he was an older and stouter man, and when he shifted his burden I noticed that he was wearing a long brown apron under his coat. He turned and stumped down the stairs again, and as I went to another window to watch him, I distinctly saw him get up on the driver's seat of a wagon drawn by two massive horses. I saw the wagon move off down the driveway; then it was gone.

When Mrs. Beveridge came in a few moments later, I asked her, 'Who was here just now?'

'Why, Mr. Thomas,' she replied, and gave me such a puzzled look that I could not say any more.

One of our evening amusements was the Ouija board. Mrs. Beveridge was very adept at this, and under her fingertips the planchette swept rapidly about the board, spelling out ambiguous communications from various defunct notables (Napoleon informed us, for instance, that he did not like fish).

I soon noticed that she could manipulate the planchette by herself, and it was not long before I discovered that she often went into light trance while doing so. This gave me the notion of trying to deepen the trance, to which she readily assented, and I found her to be an excellent subject; after a few sessions she exhibited all the classical signs of deep trance; catalepsy, glove anesthesia, amnesia, hallucination, and all the rest. I was able to suggest to her that her hand would write automatically, a procedure less tiresome than the Ouija board. While she sat with her eyes closed, the pencil in her fingers traced large, childish letters, only a dozen or so to a page. When her pencil slipped off the edge of the paper she seemed to know it, and after a moment's hesitation would begin a new line; when she reached the bottom of the paper I lifted her hand, put a fresh sheet under it, and she began where she had left off, even if it were in the middle of a word.

When I say that her writing was childish I mean to be understood literally; not only were the letters large and painfully formed, but the *t*'s were often uncrossed and there were many misspellings, 'Annd' for 'and,' for example, and 'pulleded' for 'pulled.' The lines sloped more and more downward as she wrote, and that seemed curious to me, because she was right-handed. When something agitated her, as when I asked her to describe a dream she had had the night before, her writing grew more irregular and the lines sometimes ran into each other.

These sessions were tiring to her, but she was as interested by their results as I was, and we performed them at least two or three times a week for a considerable period. We had been able to dispense with hypnotic induction entirely, by the use of posthypnotic suggestion; after having settled herself comfortably, on a word of command, she would go promptly into deep trance and begin to write. Ordinarily I would suggest a topic, but on several occasions she produced rather surprising things without any prompting from me. Her most elaborate effort was a narrative which she produced in the course of five consecutive sessions. In each case I woke her after three-quarters of an hour, and on the following evening I suggested to her that she would go on with the narrative until it was done. The transcript which follows is verbatim except for the correction of errors in spelling, the elimination of repetitions, etc.

Some people seem to be born with a taste for violence. One of these was a man named Norman Edwards, who lived with his wife Sally in a hillside house in a suburb of Newark, New Jersey. The living room and master bedroom were upstairs, the kitchen, family room, and spare bedroom were down. Edwards, who worked as an insurance underwriter in Newark, was a man in his thirties, pale, horse-faced, deceptively slender. His hands were large, and he enjoyed using them.

One Saturday morning in early October he was taking down the screens on the side of the house when he heard the water hiss in the upstairs bathroom. Sally had slept late that morning. Edwards raised the window quietly and put his head in. He saw her body moving against the blue shower curtain in the tub. He leaned in over the windowsill, stretched as far as he could, and grabbed her leg. He heard a shriek and a thump. He waited, but the water kept on running. 'Sally?' he said. She did not answer.

He climbed in the window and switched the shower curtain aside. She was lying in the tub with her yellow shower cap on. A little blood from her nose was washing away in pink trails. He turned off the water and pulled her upright. Her eyes were open, but she looked stuporous.

He had her dressed by the time the doctor came; by then her nose was beginning to swell. It was broken, as it turned out, and they kept her in the hospital overnight to see if she had a concussion. When Edwards saw her the next day there was a red and purple bruise spreading out from under the bandage, and she had two beautiful shiners. 'It was just a joke, Sally,' he said, but she turned her head away.

That afternoon her sister Wanda came over. 'Sally sent me for some things.' She walked past him up the stairs.

'They going to keep her? I thought she was getting out today.' Edwards followed her.

'That's it. Some complications,' Wanda said. She opened a suitcase on the bed and began pulling things out of bureau drawers. When she finished packing the suitcase, she started on another.

'She doesn't need all that in the hospital,' Edwards said.

'She might,' Wanda said. She lifted the two suitcases and walked past him.

He caught up with her downstairs and crowded her against the wall. 'You're lying, aren't you?' he said. 'She isn't coming home.'

'That's right,' Wanda said, 'and *listen to me*, you bastard, if you lay a hand on me, Morris will kill you. Now get out of my way.'

After a moment he stepped back, and she carried the suitcases down to her car, got in and drove off.

When he thought about the incident, Edwards realized that he was hearing in his mind the sound Sally's nose had made when it hit the water faucet, a sort of crunching *click*. He had not actually heard the sound, but it was perfectly clear to him, and he found himself playing it over and over, each time with the same little stab of pleasure.

It was not a complete surprise to him that he felt this way. Once, as a boy, he had hit his older brother Tim with a baseball bat, and he had heard the same sort of sound—a *thud*, with a sharp little *crack* in the middle of it when Tim's collarbone had broken.

Edwards called Wanda's number several times, hoping Sally would answer the phone, but it was always Wanda or Morris, and they told him Sally didn't want to talk to him. Twice he went to their house and made a nuisance of himself. On the day after the second of these visits, when Wanda had threatened to call the police, Morris Hollander came to see Edwards. Hollander, Sally's sister's husband, was a prosperous man who had business interests up and down New Jersey. He was much older than Wanda, at least sixty, but he was still trim and erect. His sleek hair was not white, not gray, but something in between, and he wore emerald cuff links.

'Hello, Morris, what do you want?' Edwards said.

'You can't invite me in? We have to talk on the doorstep?'

'All right,' said Edwards, and led the way upstairs to the living room.

Hollander laid his hat carefully on the sofa, but he did not sit down or take off his black overcoat. 'Norman,' he said, 'I'll put the whole thing in a nutshell. You're making Sally nervous, she don't want to see you, so what good is it? Save the aggravation.'

'Sally is my wife,' Edwards said.

'O.K., why not treat her like a wife? Arguments I understand, believe me, and even to hit someone I understand, but to break your wife's nose—this I don't understand.'

'It was an accident.'

'So? A woman is taking a shower, you reach through the window and grab her leg—this is an accident? If you're walking down the street, I throw a banana peel under your foot, you fall and break your hip—this is also an accident?'

The old man took a turn around the room. 'I was married to my first wife, she should rest in peace, twenty-seven years. To me a divorce is a shame. But I wouldn't say to Sally, go back to him, your place is with your husband. It's better she shouldn't have more accidents.'

He turned and gave Edwards one level look. 'So, now I said what I came to say. Don't make no more trouble. Good-bye, Norman.'

Edwards was thinking about the phrase, 'fall and break your hip,' and in the plosive of the last word he seemed to hear the faint sound of a breaking bone. As Hollander started down the stairs, he said, 'Morris.'

The old man half-turned, taking his hand off the banister. 'Yes?'

'Go to hell.' Edwards kicked him hard in the chest. The old man fell backward and clattered down the stairs. When Edwards got to him, he was lying against the wall with his neck bent, and he was dead.

Edwards knelt, got his arms under the body, hoisted it to his chest with an effort, and stood. As he carried it through the kitchen, the phone began to ring. He put his foot on a chair, steadied the body with his knee and one arm, picked up the receiver. 'Hello.'

'Norman, this is Wanda. Excuse me for calling, but is Morris there?'

'Morris? No,' he said, speaking over the dead man's face. 'Why would he be here?'

'Well, he said he was going to stop by on his way home from Sparta. Anyway, if he comes over there, would you please ask him to call me?'

'Sure. 'Bye.'

He put the receiver down, hoisted the body chest-high again, and went out to the driveway where Morris's big blue Lincoln was parked. He toppled the body gently into the trunk headfirst, moved the heavy arm that seemed to want to cling to him, then folded the legs. He explored the pockets gingerly for car keys, found them, and stepped back.

The body lay on its side, one arm underneath. By the time he got where he was going, it would be stiff; it might be harder to get out of the trunk. He bent the legs upward as far as he could, folded the arm. The other one was too hard to get at; this would have to do. What else? The hat. Where was the hat?

Edwards went back through the kitchen, glancing at the phone, but it did not ring. He found Morris's hat under the little table at the foot of the stairs, hiding there like a black animal. He put it on top of the body in the trunk, closed the lid, and went back inside for his jacket and topcoat. When he pulled out onto the street, it was just after two o'clock.

The day was cold and bright, the road clear; most of the traffic was coming the other way. According to the map, there were three or four lakes and reservoirs not far from U.S. Route 206. Edwards drove steadily north, keeping just under the speed limit. The car handled well. At Netcong he turned northeast to have a look at Lake Hopatcong. The approaches were too shallow, and there were too many trailers parked on the shore. He kept going around the lake, then northwest again to Lake Mohawk, but it did not suit him, either. He drove through Newton, Lafayette, and Augusta. North of Branchville there was a turnoff marked 'Culvers Lake.' Edwards kept on going. He realized now that the Jersey lakes would not do. He was close to the state line already; somewhere along the Delaware there would be a private place where he could tip the car down into the deep water. Then he would walk or hitchhike to the nearest town, stay in a motel overnight, and take the bus home in the morning.

North of Dingmans Ferry the map showed the highway running close to the river, and he glimpsed it, or thought he did, occasionally through the trees, but there was no good approach. The sky had turned gray; there were a few flakes of snow. He turned on his headlights. A curve came up, too fast. As he swung around it, braking, two yellow-white eyes leaped into view, the headlights of another car. He turned frantically, saw the lights blaze up, felt a hammering jolt. Then things began to become very queer.

NARROW VALLEY

R. A. Lafferty

*I*n the year 1893, land allotments in severalty were made to the remaining eight hundred and twenty-one Pawnee Indians. Each would receive one hundred and sixty acres of land and no more, and thereafter the Pawnees would be expected to pay taxes on their land, the same as the White-Eyes did.

'Kitkehahke!' Clarence Big-Saddle cussed. 'You can't kick a dog around proper on a hundred and sixty acres. And I sure am not hear before about this pay taxes on land.'

Clarence Big-Saddle selected a nice green valley for his allotment. It was one of the half dozen plots he had always regarded as his own. He sodded around the summer lodge that he had there and made it an all-season home. But he sure didn't intend to pay taxes on it.

So he burned leaves and bark and made a speech:

'That my valley be always wide and flourish and green and such stuff as that!' he orated in Pawnee chant style, 'but that it be narrow if an intruder come.'

He didn't have any balsam bark to burn. He threw on a little cedar bark instead. He didn't have any elder leaves. He used a handful of jack-oak leaves. And he forgot the word. How you going to work it if you forget the word?

'Petahauerat!' he howled out with the confidence he hoped would fool the fates.

'That's about the same long of a word,' he said in a low aside to himself. But he was doubtful. 'What am I, a White Man, a burr-tailed jack, a new kind of nut to think it will work?' he asked. 'I have to laugh at me. Oh well, we see.'

He threw the rest of the bark and the leaves on the fire, and he hollered the wrong word out again.

And he was answered by a dazzling sheet of summer lightning.

'Skidi!' Clarence Big-Saddle swore. 'It worked. I didn't think it would.'

Clarence Big-Saddle lived on his land for many years, and he paid no taxes. Intruders were unable to come down to his place. The land was sold for taxes three times, but nobody ever came down to claim it. Finally, it was carried as open land on the books. Homesteaders filed on it several times, but none of them fulfilled the qualification of living on the land.

Half a century went by. Clarence Big-Saddle called his son.

'I've had it, boy,' he said. 'I think I'll just go in the house and die.'

'OK dad,' the son Clarence Little-Saddle said. 'I'm going in to town to shoot a few games of pool with the boys. I'll bury you when I get back this evening.'

So the son Clarence Little-Saddle inherited. He also lived on the land for many years without paying taxes.

There was a disturbance in the courthouse one day. The place seemed to be invaded in force, but actually there were but one man, one woman, and five children. 'I'm Robert Rampart,' said the man, 'and we want the Land Office.'

'I'm Robert Rampart Junior,' said a nine year old gangler, 'and we want it pretty blamed quick.'

'I don't think we have anything like that,' the girl at the desk said. 'Isn't that something they had a long time ago?'

'Ignorance is no excuse for inefficiency, my dear,' said Mary Mabel Rampart, an eight year old who could easily pass for eight and a half. 'After I make my report, I wonder who will be sitting at your desk tomorrow?'

'You people are either in the wrong state or the wrong century,' the girl said.

'The Homestead Act still obtains,' Robert Rampart insisted. 'There is one tract of land carried as open in this county. I want to file on it.'

Cecilia Rampart answered the knowing wink of a beefy man at a distant desk. 'Hi,' she breathed as she slinked over. 'I'm Cecilia Rampart, but my stage name is Cecilia San Juan. Do you think that seven is too young to play ingenue roles?'

'Not for you,' the man said. 'Tell your folks to come over here.'

'Do you know where the Land Office is?' Cecilia asked.

'Sure. It's the fourth left-hand drawer of my desk. The smallest office we got in the whole courthouse. We don't use it much any more.'

The Ramparts gathered around. The beefy man started to make out the papers.

'This is the land description—' Robert Rampart began, '—why, you've got it down already. How did you know?'

'I've been around here a long time,' the man answered.

They did the paper work, and Robert Rampart filed on the land.

'You won't be able to come onto the land itself, though,' the man said.

'Why won't I?' Rampart demanded. 'Isn't the land description accurate?'

'Oh, I suppose so. But nobody's ever been able to get to the land. It's become a sort of joke.'

'Well, I intend to get to the bottom of that joke,' Rampart insisted. 'I will occupy the land, or I will find out why not.'

'I'm not sure about that,' the beefy man said. 'The last man to file on the land, about a dozen years ago, wasn't able to occupy the land. And he wasn't able to say why he couldn't. It's kind of interesting, the look on their faces after they try it for a day or two, and then give it up.'

The Ramparts left the courthouse, loaded into their camper, and drove out to find their land. They stopped at the house of a cattle and wheat farmer named Charley Dublin. Dublin met them with a grin which indicated he had been tipped off.

'Come along if you want to, folks,' Dublin said. 'The easiest way is on foot across my short pasture here. Your land's directly west of mine.'

They walked the short distance to the border.

'My name is Tom Rampart, Mr. Dublin.' Six year old Tom made conversation as they walked. 'But my name is really Ramires, and not Tom. I am the issue of an indiscretion of my mother in Mexico several years ago.'

'The boy is a kidder, Mr. Dublin,' said the mother Nina Rampart, defending herself. 'I have never been in Mexico, but sometimes I have the urge to disappear there forever.'

'Ah yes, Mrs. Rampart. And what is the name of the youngest boy here?' Charles Dublin asked.

'Fatty,' said Fatty Rampart.

'But surely that is not your given name?'

'Audifax,' said five year old Fatty.

'Ah well, Audifax, Fatty, are you a kidder too?'

'He's getting better at it, Mr. Dublin,' Mary Mabel said. 'He was a twin till last week. His twin was named Skinny. Mama left Skinny unguarded while she was out tippling, and there were wild dogs in the neighborhood. When mama got back, do you know what was left of Skinny? Two neck bones and an ankle bone. That was all.'

'Poor Skinny,' Dublin said. 'Well, Rampart, this is the fence and the end of my land. Yours is just beyond.'

'Is that ditch on my land?' Rampart asked.

'That ditch *is* your land.'

'I'll have it filled in. It's a dangerous deep cut even if it is narrow. And the other fence looks like a good one, and I sure have a pretty plot of land beyond it.'

'No, Rampart, the land beyond the second fence belongs to Holister Hyde,' Charley Dublin said. 'That second fence is the *end* of your land.'

'Now, just wait a minute, Dublin! There's something wrong here. My land is one hundred and sixty acres, which would be a half mile on a side. Where's my half mile width?'

'Between the two fences.'

'That's not eight feet.'

'Doesn't look like it, does it, Rampart? Tell you what—there's plenty of throwing-sized rocks around. Try to throw one across it.'

'I'm not interested in any such boys' games,' Rampart exploded. 'I want my land.'

But the Rampart children *were* interested in such games. They got with it with those throwing rocks. They winged them out over the little gully. The stones acted funny. They hung in the air, as it were, and diminished in size. And they were small as pebbles when they dropped down, down into the gully. None of them could throw a stone across that ditch, and they were throwing kids.

'You and your neighbor have conspired to fence open land for your own use,' Rampart charged.

'No such thing, Rampart,' Dublin said cheerfully. 'My land checks perfectly. So does Hyde's. So does yours, if we knew how to check it. It's like one of those trick topological drawings. It really is a half mile from here to there, but the eye gets lost somewhere. It's your land. Crawl through the fence and figure it out.'

Rampart crawled through the fence, and drew himself up to jump the gully. Then he hesitated. He got a glimpse of just how deep that gully was. Still, it wasn't five feet across.

There was a heavy fence post on the ground, designed for use as a corner post. Rampart up-ended it with some effort. Then he shoved it to fall and bridge the gully. But it fell short, and it shouldn't have. An eight foot post should bridge a five foot gully.

The post fell into the gully, and rolled and rolled and rolled. It spun as though it were rolling outward, but it made no progress except vertically. The post came to rest on a ledge of the gully, so close that Rampart could almost reach out and touch it, but it now appeared no bigger than a match stick.

'There is something wrong with that fence post, or with the world, or with my eyes,' Robert Rampart said. 'I wish I felt dizzy so I could blame it on that.'

'There's a little game that I sometimes play with my neighbor Hyde when we're both out,' Dublin said. 'I've a heavy rifle and I train it on the middle of his forehead as he stands on the other side of the ditch apparently eight feet away. I fire it off then (I'm a good shot), and I hear it whine across. It'd kill him dead if things were as they seem. But Hyde's in no danger. The shot always bangs into that little scuff of rocks and boulders about thirty feet below him. I can see it kick up the rock dust there, and the sound of it rattling into those little boulders comes back to me in about two and a half seconds.'

A bull-bat (poor people call it the night-hawk) raveled around in the air and zoomed out over the narrow ditch, but it did not reach the other side. The bird dropped below ground level and could be seen against the background of the other side of the ditch. It grew smaller and hazier as though at a distance of three or four hundred yards. The white bars on its wings could no longer be discerned; then the bird itself could hardly be discerned; but it was far short of the other side of the five foot ditch.

A man identified by Charley Dublin as the neighbor Hollister Hyde had appeared on the other side of the little ditch. Hyde grinned and waved. He shouted something, but could not be heard.

'Hyde and I both read mouth,' Dublin said, 'so we can talk across the ditch easy enough. Which kid wants to play chicken? Hyde will barrel a good-sized rock right at your head, and if you duck or flinch you're chicken.'

'Me! Me!' Audifax Rampart challenged. And Hyde, a big man with big hands, did barrel a fearsome jagged rock right at the head of the boy. It would have killed him if things had been as they appeared. But the rock diminished to nothing and disappeared into the ditch. Here was a phenomenon—things seemed real-sized on either side of the ditch, but they diminished coming out over the ditch either way.

'Everybody game for it?' Robert Rampart Junior asked.

'We won't get down there by standing here,' Mary Mabel said.

'Nothing wenchered, nothing gained,' said Cecilia. 'I got that from an add for a sex comedy.'

Then the five Rampart kids ran down into the gully. Ran *down* is right. It was almost as if they ran down the vertical face of a cliff. They couldn't do that. The gully was no wider than the stride of the biggest kids. But the gully diminished those children, it ate them alive. They were doll-sized. They were acorn-sized. They were running for minute after minute across a ditch that was only five feet across. They were going deeper in it, and getting smaller. Robert Rampart was roaring his alarm, and his wife Nina was screaming. Then she stopped. 'What am I carrying on so loud about?' she asked herself. 'It looks like fun. I'll do it too.'

She plunged into the gully, diminished in size as the children had done, and ran at a pace to carry her a hundred yards away across a gully only five feet wide.

That Robert Rampart stirred things up for a while then. He got the sheriff there, and the highway patrolmen. A ditch had stolen his wife and five children, he said, and maybe had killed them. And if anybody laughs, there may be another killing. He got the colonel of the State National Guard there, and a command post set up. He got a couple of airplane pilots. Robert Rampart had one quality: when he hollered, people came.

He got the newsmen out from T-Town, and the eminent scientists, Dr. Velikof Vonk, Arpad Arkabaranan, and Willy McGilly. That bunch turns up every time you get on a good one. They just happen to be in that part of the country where something interesting is going on.

They attacked the thing from all four sides and the top, and by inner and outer theory. If a thing measures a half mile on each side, and the sides are straight, there just has to be something in the middle of it. They took pictures from the air, and they turned out perfect. They proved that Robert Rampart had the prettiest hundred and sixty acres in the country, the larger part of it being a lush green valley, and all of it being a half mile on a side, and situated just where it should be. They took ground-level photos then, and it showed a beautiful half mile stretch of land between the boundaries of Charley Dublin and Holister Hyde. But a man isn't a camera. None of them could see that beautiful spread with the eyes in their heads. Where was it?

Down in the valley itself everything was normal. It really was a half mile wide and no more than eighty feet deep with a very gentle slope. It was warm and sweet, and beautiful with grass and grain.

Nina and the kids loved it, and they rushed to see what squatter had built that little house on their land. A house, or a shack. It had never known paint, but paint would have spoiled it. It was built of split timbers dressed near smooth with axe and draw knife, chinked with white clay, and sodded up to about half its height. And there was an interloper standing by the little lodge.

'Here, here what are you doing on our land?' Robert Rampart Junior demanded of the man. 'Now you just shamble off again wherever you came from. I'll bet you're a thief too, and those cattle are stolen.'

'Only the black-and-white calf,' Clarence Little-Saddle said. 'I couldn't resist him, but the rest are mine. I guess I'll just stay around and see that you folks get settled all right.'

'Is there any wild Indians around here?' Fatty Rampart asked.

'No, not really. I go on a bender about every three months and get a little bit wild, and there's a couple Osage boys from Gray Horse that get noisy sometimes, but that's about all,' Clarence Little-Saddle said.

'You certainly don't intend to palm yourself off on us as an Indian.' Mary Mabel challenged. 'You'll find us a little too knowledgeable for that.'

'Little girl, you as well tell this cow there's no room for her to be a cow since you're so knowledgeable. She thinks she's a short-horn cow named Sweet Virginia. I think I'm a Pawnee Indian named Clarence. Break it to us real gentle if we're not.'

'If you're an Indian where's your war bonnet? There's not a feather on you anywhere.'

'How you be sure? There's a story that we got feathers instead of hair on—Aw, I can't tell a joke like that to a little girl! How come you're not wearing the Iron Crown of Lombardy if you're a white girl? How you expect me to believe you're a little white girl and your folks came from Europe a couple hundred years ago if you don't wear it? There were six hundred tribes, and only one of them, the Oglala Sioux, had the war bonnet, and only the big leaders, never more than two or three of them alive at one time, wore it.'

'Your analogy is a little strained,' Mary Mabel said. 'Those Indians we saw in Florida and the ones at Atlantic City had war bonnets, and they couldn't very well have been the kind of Sioux you said. And just last night on the TV in the motel, those Massachusetts Indians put a war bonnet on the President and called him the Great White Father. You mean to tell me that they were all phonies? Hey, who's laughing at who here?'

'If you're an Indian where's your bow and arrow?' Tom Rampart interrupted. 'I bet you can't even shoot one.'

'You're sure right there,' Clarence admitted. 'I never shot one of those things but once in my life. They used to have an archery range in Boulder Park over in T-Town, and you could rent the things and shoot at targets tied to hay bales. Hey, I barked my whole forearm and nearly broke my thumb when the bow-string thwacked home. I couldn't shoot that thing at all. I don't see how anybody ever could shoot one of them.'

'OK kids,' Nina Rampart called to her brood. 'Let's start pitching this junk out of the shack so we can move in. Is there any way we can drive our camper down here, Clarence?'

'Sure, there's a pretty good dirt road, and it's a lot wider than it looks from the top. I got a bunch of green bills in an old night charley in the shack. Let me get them, and then I'll clear out for a while. The shack hasn't been cleaned out for seven years, since the last time this happened. I'll show you the road to the top, and you can bring your car down it.'

'Hey you old Indian, you lied!' Cecilia Rampart shrilled from the doorway of the shack. 'You *do* have a war bonnet. Can I have it?'

'I didn't mean to lie, I forgot about that thing,' Clarence Little-Saddle said. 'My son Clarence Bare-Back sent that to me from Japan for a joke a long time ago. Sure, you can have it.'

All the children were assigned tasks carrying the junk out of the shack and setting fire to it. Nina Rampart and Clarence Little-Saddle ambled up to the rim of the valley by the vehicle road that was wider than it looked from the top.

'Nina, you're back! I thought you were gone forever,' Robert Rampart jittered at seeing her again. 'What—where are the children?'

'Why, I left them down in the valley, Robert. That is, ah, down in that little ditch right there. Now you've got me worried again. I'm going to drive the camper down there and unload it. You'd better go on down and lend a hand too, Robert, and quit talking to all these funny-looking men here.'

And Nina went back to Dublin's place for the camper.

'It would be easier for a camel to go through the eye of a needle than for that intrepid woman to drive a car down into that narrow ditch,' the eminent scientist Dr. Velikof Vonk said.

'You know how that camel does it?' Clarence Little-Saddle offered, appearing of a sudden from nowhere. 'He just closes one of his own eyes and flops back his ears and plunges right through. A camel is mighty narrow when he closes one eye and flops back his ears. Besides, they use a big-eyed needle in the act.'

'Where'd this crazy man come from?' Robert Rampart demanded, jumping three feet in the air. 'Things are coming out of the ground now. I want my land! I want my children! I want my wife! Whoops, here she comes driving it. Nina you can't drive a loaded camper into a little ditch like that! You'll be killed or collapsed!'

Nina Rampart drove the loaded camper into the little ditch at a pretty good rate of speed. The best of belief is that she just closed one eye and plunged right through. The car diminished and dropped, and it was smaller than a toy car. But it raised a pretty good cloud of dust as it bumped for several hundred yards across a ditch that was only five feet wide.

'Rampart, it's akin to the phenomenon known as looming, only in reverse,' the eminent scientist Arpad Arkabaranan explained as he attempted to throw a rock across the narrow ditch. The rock rose very high in the air, seemed to hang at its apex while it diminished to the size of a grain of sand, and then fell into the ditch not six inches of the way across. There isn't anybody going to throw across a half mile valley even if it looks five feet. 'Look at a rising moon sometime, Rampart. It appears very large, as though covering a great sector of the horizon, but it only covers one half of a degree. It is hard to believe that you could set seven hundred and twenty of such large moons side by side around the horizon, or that it would take one hundred and eighty of the big things to reach from the horizon to a point overhead. It is also hard to believe that your valley is five hundred times as wide as it appears, but it has been surveyed, and it is.'

'I want my land. I want my children. I want my wife,' Robert chanted dully. 'Damn, I let her get away again.'

'I tell you, Rampy,' Clarence Little-Saddle squared on him, 'a man that lets his wife get away twice doesn't deserve to keep her. I give you till nightfall; then you forfeit. I've taken a liking to the brood. One of us is going to be down there tonight.'

After a while a bunch of them were off in that little tavern on the road between Cleveland and Osage. It was only a half mile away. If the valley had run in the other direction, it would have been only six feet away.

'It is a psychic nexus in the form of an elongated dome,' said the eminent scientist Dr. Velikof Vonk. 'It is maintained subconsciously by the concatenation of at least two minds, the stronger of them belonging to a man dead for many years, and in another hundred years it will be considerably weakened. We know from our checking out of folk tales of Europe as well as Cambodia that these ensorceled areas seldom survive for more than two hundred and fifty years. The person who first set such a thing in being will usually lose interest in it, and in all worldly things, within a hundred years of his own death. This is a simple thanato-psychic limitation. As a short-term device, the thing has been used several times as a military tactic.

'This psychic nexus, as long as it maintains itself, causes group illusion, but it is really a simple thing. It doesn't fool birds or rabbits or cattle or cameras, only humans. There is nothing meteorological about it. It is strictly psychological. I'm glad I was able to give a scientific explanation to it or it would have worried me.'

'It is continental fault coinciding with a noospheric fault,' said the eminent scientist Arpad Arkabaranan. 'The valley really is a half mile wide, and at the same time it really is only five feet wide. If we measured correctly, we would get these dual measurements. Of course it is meteorological! Everything including dreams is meteorological. It is the animals and cameras which are fooled, as lacking a true dimension; it is only humans who see the true duality. The phenomenon should be common along the whole continental fault where the earth gains or loses a half mile that has to go somewhere. Likely it extends through the whole sweep of the Cross Timbers. Many of those trees appear twice, and many do not appear at all. A man in the proper state of mind could farm that land or raise cattle on it, but it doesn't really exist. There is a clear parallel in the Luftspiegelungthal sector in the Black Forest of Germany which exists, or does not exist, according to the circumstances and to the attitude of the beholder. Then we have the case of Mad Mountain in Morgan County, Tennessee, which isn't there all the time, and also the Little Lobo Mirage south of Presidio, Texas, from which twenty thousand barrels of water were pumped in one two-and-a-half hour period before the mirage reverted to mirage status. I'm glad I was able to give a scientific explanation to this or it would have worried me.'

'I just don't understand how he worked it,' said the eminent scientist Willy McGilly. 'Cedar bark, jack-oak leaves, and the word "Petahauerat." The thing's impossible! When I was a boy and we wanted to make a hide-out, we used bark from the skunk-spruce tree, the leaves of a box-elder, and the word was "Boadicea". All three elements are wrong here. I cannot find a scientific explanation for it, and it does worry me.'

They went back to Narrow Valley. Robert Rampart was still chanting dully: 'I want my land. I want my children. I want my wife.'

Nina Rampart came chugging up out of the narrow ditch in the camper and emerged through that little gate a few yards down the fence row.

'Supper's ready and we're tired of waiting for you, Robert,' she said. 'A fine homesteader you are! Afraid to come onto your own land! Come along now, I'm tired of waiting for you.'

'I want my land! I want my children! I want my wife!' Robert Rampart still chanted. 'Oh, there you are, Nina. You stay here this time. I want my land! I want my children! I want an answer to this terrible thing.'

'It is time we decided who wears the pants in this family,' Nina said stoutly. She picked up her husband, slung him over her shoulder, carried him to the camper and dumped him in, slammed (as it seemed) a dozen doors at once, and drove furiously down into Narrow Valley, which already seemed wider.

Why, that place was getting normaler and normaler by the minute! Pretty soon it looked almost as wide as it was supposed to be. The psychic nexus in the form of an elongated dome had collapsed. The continental fault that coincided with the noospheric fault had faced facts and decided to conform. The Ramparts were in effective possession of their homestead, and Narrow Valley was as normal as any place anywhere.

'I have lost my land,' Clarence Little-Saddle moaned. 'It was the land of my father Clarence Big-Saddle, and I meant it to be the land of my son Clarence Bare-Back. It looked so narrow that people did not notice how wide it was, and people did not try to enter it. Now I have lost it.'

Clarence Little-Saddle and the eminent scientist Willy McGilly were standing on the edge of Narrow Valley, which now appeared its true half-mile extent. The moon was just rising, so big that it filled a third of the sky. Who would have imagined that it would take a hundred and eighty of such monstrous things to reach from the horizon to a point overhead, and yet you could sight it with sighters and figure it so.

'I had the little bear-cat by the tail and I let go,' Clarence groaned. 'I had a fine valley for free, and I have lost it. I am like that hard-luck guy in the funny-paper or Job in the Bible. Destitution is my lot.'

Willy McGilly looked around furtively. They were alone on the edge of the half mile wide valley.

'Let's give it a booster shot,' Willy McGilly said.

Hey, those two got with it! They started a snapping fire and began to throw the stuff onto it. Bark from the dog-elm tree—how do you know it won't work?

It *was* working! Already the other side of the valley seemed a hundred yards closer, and there were alarmed noises coming up from the people in the valley.

Leaves from a black locust tree—and the valley narrowed still more! There was, moreover, terrified screaming of both children and big people from the depths of Narrow Valley, and the happy voice of Mary Mabel Rampart chanting 'Earthquake! Earthquake!'

'That my valley be always wide and flourish and such stuff, and green with money and grass!' Clarence Little-Saddle orated in Pawnee chant style, 'but that it be narrow if intruders come, smash them like bugs!'

People, that valley wasn't over a hundred feet wide now, and the screaming of the people in the bottom of the valley had been joined by the hysterical coughing of the camper car starting up.

Willy and Clarence threw everything that was left on the fire. But the word? The word? Who remembers the word?

'Corsicanatexas!' Clarence Little-Saddle howled out with confidence he hoped would fool the fates.

He was answered, not only by a dazzling sheet of summer lightning, but also by thunder and rain drops.

'Chahiksi!' Clarence Little-Saddle swore. 'It worked. I didn't think it would. It will be all right now. I can use the rain.'

The valley was again a ditch only five feet wide.

The camper car struggled out of narrow valley through the little gate. It was smashed flat as a sheet of paper, and the screaming kids and people in it had only one dimension.

'It's closing in! It's closing in!' Robert Rampart roared, and he was no thicker than if he had been made out of cardboard.

'We're smashed like bugs,' the Rampart boys intoned. 'We're thin like paper.'

Mort, ruine, ecrasement!' spoke-acted Cecilia Rampart like the great tragedienne she was.

'Help! Help!' Nina Rampart croaked, but she winked at Willy

and Clarence as they rolled by. 'This homesteading jag always did leave me a little flat.'

'Don't throw those paper dolls away. They might be the Ramparts,' Mary Mabel called.

The camper car coughed again and bumped along on level ground. This couldn't last forever. The car was widening out as it bumped along.

'Did we overdo it, Clarence?' Willy McGilly asked. 'What did one flat-lander say to the other?'

'Dimension of us never got around,' Clarence said. 'No, I don't think we overdid it, Willy. That car must be eighteen inches wide already, and they all ought to be normal by the time they reach the main road. The next time I do it, I think I'll throw wood-grain plastic on the fire to see who's kidding who.'

NOT LONG BEFORE THE END

Larry Niven

A swordsman battled a sorcerer, once upon a time.

In that age such battles were frequent. A natural antipathy exists between swordsmen and sorcerers, as between cats and small birds, or between rats and men. Usually the swordsman lost, and humanity's average intelligence rose some trifling fraction. Sometimes the swordsman won, and again the species was improved; for a sorcerer who cannot kill one miserable swordsman is a poor excuse for a sorcerer.

But this battle differed from the others. On one side, the sword itself was enchanted. On the other, the sorcerer knew a great and terrible truth.

We will call him the Warlock, as his name is both forgotten and impossible to pronounce. His parents had known what they were about. He who knows your name has power over you, but he must speak your name to use it.

The Warlock had found his terrible truth in middle age.

By that time he had traveled widely. It was not from choice. It was simply that he was a powerful magician, and he used his power, and he needed friends.

He knew spells to make people love a magician. The Warlock had tried these, but he did not like the side effects. So he commonly used his great power to help those around him, that they might love him without coercion.

He found that when he had been ten to fifteen years in a place, using his magic as whim dictated, his powers would weaken. If he moved away, they returned. Twice he had had to move, and twice he had settled in a new land, learned new customs, made new friends. It happened a third time, and he prepared to move again. But something set him to wondering.

Why should a man's powers be so unfairly drained out of him?

It happened to nations too. Throughout history, those lands which had been richest in magic had been overrun by barbarians carrying swords and clubs. It was a sad truth, and one that did not bear thinking about, but the Warlock's curiosity was strong.

So he wondered, and he stayed to perform certain experiments.

His last experiment involved a simple kinetic sorcery set to spin a metal disc in midair. And when that magic was done, he knew a truth he could never forget.

So he departed. In succeeding decades he moved again and again. Time changed his personality, if not his body, and his magic became more dependable, if less showy. He had discovered a great and terrible truth, and if he kept it secret, it was through compassion. His truth spelled the end of civilization, yet it was of no earthly use to anyone.

So he thought. But some five decades later (the date was on the order of 12,000 B.C.) it occurred to him that all truths find a use somewhere, sometime. And so he built another disc and recited spells over it, so that (like a telephone number already dialed but for one digit) the disc would be ready if ever he needed it.

The name of the sword was Glirendree. It was several hundred years old, and quite famous.

As for the swordsman, his name is no secret. It was Belhap Sattlestone Wirldess ag Miracloat roo Cononson. His friends, who tended to be temporary, called him Hap. He was a barbarian, of course. A civilized man would have had more sense than to touch Glirendree, and better morals than to stab a sleeping woman. Which was how Hap had acquired his sword. Or vice versa.

The Warlock recognized it long before he saw it. He was at work in the cavern he had carved beneath a hill, when an alarm went off. The hair rose up, tingling, along the back of his neck. 'Visitors,' he said.

'I don't hear anything,' said Sharla, but there was an uneasiness to her tone. Sharla was a girl of the village who had come to live with the Warlock. That day she had persuaded the Warlock to teach her some of his simpler spells.

'Don't you feel the hair rising on the back of your neck? I set the alarm to do that. Let me just check . . .' He used a sensor like a silver hula hoop set on edge. 'There's trouble coming. Sharla, we've got to get you out of here.'

'But . . .' Sharla waved protestingly at the table where they had been working.

'Oh, that. We can quit in the middle. That spell isn't dangerous.' It was a charm against lovespells, rather messy to work, but safe and tame and effective. The Warlock pointed at the spear of light glaring through the hoop-sensor. 'That's dangerous. An enormously powerful focus of mana power is moving up the west side of the hill. You go down the east side.'

'Can I help? You've taught me *some* magic.'

The magician laughed a little nervously. 'Against that? That's Glirendree. Look at the size of the image, the color, the shape. No. You get out of here, and right now. The hill's clear on the eastern slope.'

'Come with me.'

'I can't. Not with Glirendree loose. Not when it's already got hold of some idiot. There are obligations.'

They came out of the cavern together, into the mansion they shared. Sharla, still protesting, donned a robe and started down the hill. The Warlock hastily selected an armload of paraphernalia and went outside.

The intruder was halfway up the hill: a large but apparently human being carrying something long and glittering. He was still a quarter of an hour downslope. The Warlock set up the silver hula hoop and looked through it.

The sword was a flame of mana discharge, an eye-hurting needle of white light. Glirendree, right enough. He knew of other, equally powerful mana foci, but none were portable, and none would show as a sword to the unaided eye.

He should have told Sharla to inform the Brotherhood. She had that much magic. Too late now.

There was no colored borderline to the spear of light.

No green fringe effect meant no protective spells. The swordsman had not tried to guard himself against what he carried. Certainly the intruder was no magician, and he had not the intelligence to get the help of a magician. Did he know *nothing* about Glirendree?

Not that that would help the Warlock. He who carries Glirendree was invulnerable to any power save Glirendree itself. Or so it was said.

'Let's test that,' said the Warlock to himself. He dipped into his armload of equipment and came up with something wooden, shaped like an ocarina. He blew the dust off it, raised it in his fist and pointed it down the mountain. But he hesitated.

The loyalty spell was simple and safe, but it did have side effects. It lowered its victim's intelligence.

'Self-defense,' the Warlock reminded himself, and blew into the ocarina.

The swordsman did not break stride. Glirendree didn't even glow; it had absorbed the spell that easily.

In minutes the swordsman would be here. The Warlock hurriedly set up a simple prognostics spell. At least he could learn who would win the coming battle.

No picture formed before him. The scenery did not even waver.

'Well, now,' said the Warlock. '*Well*, now!' And he reached into his clutter of sorcerous tools and found a metal disc. Another instant's rummaging produced a double-edged knife, profusely inscribed in no known language, and very sharp.

At the top of the Warlock's hill was a spring, and the stream from that spring ran past the Warlock's house. The swordsman stood leaning on his sword, facing the Warlock across that stream. He breathed deeply, for it had been a hard climb.

He was powerfully muscled and profusely scarred. To the Warlock it seemed strange that so young a man should have found time to acquire so many scars. But none of his wounds had impaired motor functions. The Warlock had watched him coming up the hill. The swordsman was in top physical shape.

His eyes were deep blue and brilliant, and half an inch too close together for the Warlock's taste.

'I am Hap,' he called across the stream. 'Where is she?'

'You mean Sharla, of course. But why is that your concern?'

'I have come to free her from her shameful bondage, old man. Too long have you—'

'Hey, hey, hey. Sharla's my *wife*.'

'Too long have you used her for your vile and lecherous purposes. Too—'

'She stays of her own free will, you nit!'

'You expect me to believe that? As lovely a woman as Sharla, could she love an old and feeble warlock?'

'Do I look feeble?'

The Warlock did not look like an old man. He seemed Hap's age, some twenty years old, and his frame and his musculature were the equal of Hap's. He had not bothered to dress as he left the cavern. In place of Hap's scars, his back bore a tattoo in red and green and gold, an elaborately curlicued pentagramic design, almost hypnotic in its extradimensional involutions.

'Everyone in the village knows your age,' said Hap. 'You're two hundred years old, if not more.'

'Hap,' said the Warlock. 'Belhap something-or-other roo Cononson. Now I remember. Sharla told me you tried to bother her last time she went to the village. I should have done something about it then.'

'Old man, you lie. Sharla is under a spell. Everybody knows the power of a warlock's loyalty spell.'

'I don't use them. I don't like the side effects. Who wants to be surrounded by friendly morons?' The Warlock pointed to Glirendree. 'Do you know what you carry?'

Hap nodded ominously.

'Then you ought to know better. Maybe it's not too late. See if you can transfer it to your left hand.'

'I tried that. I can't let go of it.' Hap cut at the air, restlessly, with his sixty pounds of sword. 'I have to sleep with the damned thing clutched in my hand.'

'Well, it's too late then.'

'It's worth it,' Hap said grimly. 'For now I can kill you. Too long has an innocent woman been subjected to your lecherous—'

'I know, I know.' The Warlock changed languages suddenly, speaking high and fast. He spoke thus for almost a minute, then switched back to Rynaldese. 'Do you feel any pain?'

'Not a twinge,' said Hap. He had not moved. He stood with his remarkable sword at the ready, glowering at the magician across the stream.

'No sudden urge to travel? Attacks of remorse? Change of body temperature?' But Hap was grinning now, not at all nicely. 'I thought not. Well, it had to be tried.'

There was an instant of blinding light.

When it reached the vicinity of the hill, the meteorite had dwindled to the size of a baseball. It should have finished its journey at the back of Hap's head. Instead, it exploded a millisecond too soon. When the light had died, Hap stood within a ring of craterlets.

The swordsman's unsymmetrical jaw dropped, and then he closed his mouth and started forward. The sword hummed faintly.

The Warlock turned his back.

Hap curled his lip at the Warlock's cowardice. Then he jumped three feet backward from a standing start. A shadow had pulled itself from the Warlock's back.

In a lunar cave with the sun glaring into its mouth, a man's shadow on the wall might have looked that sharp and black. The shadow dropped to the ground and stood up, a humanoid outline that was less a shape than a window view of the ultimate blackness beyond the death of the universe. Then it leapt.

Glirendree seemed to move of its own accord. It hacked the demon once lengthwise and once across, while the demon seemed to batter against an invisible shield, trying to reach Hap even as it died.

'Clever,' Hap panted. 'A pentagram on your back, a demon trapped inside.'

'That's clever,' said the Warlock, 'but it didn't work. Carrying Glirendree works, but it's not clever. I ask you again, do you know what you carry?'

'The most powerful sword ever forged.' Hap raised the weapon high. His right arm was more heavily muscled than his left, and inches longer, as if Glirendree had been at work on it. 'A sword to make me the equal of any warlock or sorceress, and without the help of demons, either. I had to kill a woman who loved me to get it, but I paid that price gladly. When I have sent you to your just reward, Sharla will come to me—'

'She'll spit in your eye. Now will you listen to me? Glirendree *is* a demon. If you had an ounce of sense, you'd cut your arm off at the elbow.'

Hap looked startled. 'You mean there's a demon imprisoned in the metal?'

'Get it through your head. *There is no metal.* It's a demon, a bound demon, and it's a parasite. It'll age you to death in a year unless you cut it loose. A warlock of the northlands imprisoned it in its present form, then gave it to one of his bastards, Jeery of Something-or-other. Jeery conquered half this continent before he died on the battlefield, of senile decay. It was given into the charge of the Rainbow Witch a year before I was born, because there never was a woman who had less use for people, especially men.'

'That happens to have been untrue.'

'Probably Glirendree's doing. Started her glands up again, did it? She should have guarded against that.'

'A year,' said Hap. 'One year.'

But the sword stirred restlessly in his hand. 'It will be a glorious year,' said Hap, and he came forward.

The Warlock picked up a copper disc. 'Four,' he said, and the disc spun in midair.

By the time Hap had sloshed through the stream, the disc was a blur of motion. The Warlock moved to keep it between himself and Hap, and Hap dared not touch it, for it would have sheared through anything at all. He crossed around it, but again the Warlock had darted to the other side. In the pause he snatched up something else: a silvery knife, profusely inscribed.

'Whatever that is,' said Hap, 'it can't hurt me. No magic can affect me while I carry Glirendree.'

'True enough,' said the Warlock. 'The disc will lose its force in a minute anyway. In the meantime, I know a secret that I would like to tell, one I could never tell to a friend.'

Hap raised Glirendree above his head and, two-handed, swung it down on the disc. The sword stopped jarringly at the disc's rim.

'It's protecting you,' said the Warlock. 'If Glirendree hit the rim now, the recoil would knock you clear down to the village. Can't you hear the hum?'

Hap heard the whine as the disc cut the air. The tone was going up and up the scale.

'You're stalling,' he said.

'That's true. So? Can it hurt you?'

'No. You were saying you knew a secret.' Hap braced himself, sword raised, on one side of the disc, which now glowed red at the edge.

'I've wanted to tell someone for such a long time. A hundred and fifty years. Even Sharla doesn't know.' The Warlock still stood ready to run if the swordsman should come after him. 'I'd learned a little magic in those days, not much compared to what I know now, but big, showy stuff. Castles floating in the air. Dragons with golden scales. Armies turned to stone, or wiped out by lightning, instead of simple death spells. Stuff like that takes a lot of power, you know?'

'I've heard of such things.'

'I did it all the time, for myself, for friends, for whoever happened to be king, or whomever I happened to be in love with. And I found that after I'd been settled for a while, the power would leave me. I'd have to move elsewhere to get it back.'

The copper disc glowed bright orange with the heat of its spin. It should have fragmented, or melted, long ago.

'Then there are the dead places, the places where a warlock

dares not go. Places where magic doesn't work. They tend to be rural areas, farmlands and sheep ranges, but you can find the old cities, the castles built to float which now lie tilted on their sides, the unnaturally aged bones of dragons, like huge lizards from another age.

'So I started wondering.'

Hap stepped back a bit from the heat of the disc. It glowed pure white now, and it was like a sun brought to earth. Through the glare Hap had lost sight of the Warlock.

'So I built a disc like this one and set it spinning. Just a simple kinetic sorcery, but with a constant acceleration and no limit point. You know what mana is?'

'What's happening to your voice?'

'Mana is the name we give to the power behind magic.' The Warlock's voice had gone weak and high.

A horrible suspicion came to Hap. The Warlock had slipped down the hill, leaving his voice behind! Hap trotted around the disc, shading his eyes from its heat.

An old man sat on the other side of the disc. His arthritic fingers, half-crippled with swollen joints, played with a rune-inscribed knife. 'What I found out—oh, there you are. Well, it's too late now.'

Hap raised his sword, and his sword changed.

It was a massive red demon, horned and hooved, and its teeth were in Hap's right hand. It paused, deliberately, for the few seconds it took Hap to realize what had happened and to try to jerk away. Then it bit down, and the swordsman's hand was off at the wrist.

The demon reached out, slowly enough, but Hap in his surprise was unable to move. He felt the taloned fingers close his windpipe.

He felt the strength leak out of the taloned hand, and he saw surprise and dismay spread across the demon's face.

The disc exploded. All at once and nothing first, it disintegrated into a flat cloud of metallic particles and was gone, flashing away as so much meteorite dust. The light was as lightning striking at one's feet. The sound was its thunder. The smell was vaporized copper.

The demon faded, as a chameleon fades against its background. Fading, the demon slumped to the ground in slow motion, and faded further, and was gone. When Hap reached out with his foot, he touched only dirt.

Behind Hap was a trench of burnt earth.

The spring had stopped. The rocky bottom of the stream was drying in the sun.

The Warlock's cavern had collapsed. The furnishings of the Warlock's mansion had gone crashing down into that vast pit, but the mansion itself was gone without trace.

Hap clutched his messily severed wrist, and he said, 'But what happened?'

'Mana,' the Warlock mumbled. He spat out a complete set of blackened teeth. 'Mana. What I discovered was that the power behind magic is a natural resource, like the fertility of the soil. When you use it up, it's gone.'

'But—'

'Can you see why I kept it a secret? One day all the wide world's mana will be used up. No more mana, no more magic. Do you know that Atlantis is tectonically unstable? Succeeding sorcerer-kings renew the spells each generation to keep the whole continent from sliding into the sea. What happens when the spells don't work any more? They couldn't possibly evacuate the whole continent in time. Kinder not to let them know.'

'But . . . that disc.'

The Warlock grinned with his empty mouth and ran his hands through snowy hair. All the hair came off in his fingers, leaving his scalp bare and mottled. 'Senility is like being drunk. The disc? I told you. A kinetic sorcery with no upper limit. The disc keeps accelerating until all the mana in the locality has been used up.'

Hap moved a step forward. Shock had drained half his strength. His foot came down jarringly, as if all the spring were out of his muscles.

'You tried to kill me.'

The Warlock nodded. 'I figured if the disc didn't explode and kill you while you were trying to go around it, Glirendree would strangle you when the constraint wore off. What are you complaining about? It cost you a hand, but you're free of Gilirendree.'

Hap took another step, and another. His hand was beginning to hurt, and the pain gave him strength. 'Old man,' he said thickly. 'Two hundred years old. I can break your neck with the hand you left me. And I will.

The Warlock raised the inscribed knife.

'That won't work. No more magic.' Hap slapped the Warlock's hand away and took the Warlock by his bony throat.

The Warlock's hand brushed easily aside, and came back, and up. Hap wrapped his arms around his belly and backed away with his eyes and mouth wide open. He sat down hard.

'A knife always works.' said the Warlock.

'Oh,' said Hap.

'I worked the metal myself, with ordinary blacksmith's tools, so the knife wouldn't crumble when the magic was gone. The runes aren't magic. They only say—'

'Oh,' said Hap. 'Oh.' He toppled sideways.

The Warlock lowered himself onto his back. He held the knife up and read the markings, in a language only the Brotherhood remembered.

AND THIS, TOO, SHALL PASS AWAY. It was a very old platitude, even then.

He dropped his arm back and lay looking at the sky.

Presently the blue was blotted by a shadow.

'I told you to get out of here,' he whispered.

'You should have known better. What's *happened* to you?'

'No more youth spells. I knew I'd have to do it when the prognostics spell showed blank.' He drew a ragged breath. 'It was worth it. I killed Glirendree.'

'Playing hero, at your age! What can I do? How can I help?'

'Get me down the hill before my heart stops. I never told you my true age—'

'I knew. The whole village knows.' She pulled him to sitting position, pulled one of his arms around her neck. It felt dead. She shuddered, but she wrapped her own arm around his waist and gathered herself for the effort. 'You're so thin! Come on, love. We're going to stand up.' She took most of his weight onto her, and they stood up.

'Go slow. I can hear my heart trying to take off.'

'How far do we have to go?'

'Just to the foot of the hill, I think. Then the spells will work again, and we can rest.' He stumbled. 'I'm going blind,' he said.

'It's a smooth path, and all downhill.'

'That's why I picked this place. I knew I'd have to use the disc someday. You can't throw away knowledge. Always the time comes when you use it, because you have to, because it's there.'

'You've changed so. So—so ugly. And you smell.'

The pulse fluttered in his neck, like a hummingbird's wings. 'Maybe you won't want me, after seeing me like this.'

'You can change back, can't you?'

'Sure. I can change to anything you like. What color eyes do you want?'

'I'll be like this myself someday,' she said. Her voice held cool horror. And it was fading; he was going deaf.

'I'll teach you the proper spells, when you're ready. They're dangerous. Blackly dangerous.'

She was silent for a time. Then: 'What color were *his* eyes? You know, Belhap Sattlestone whatever.'

'Forget it,' said the Warlock, with a touch of pique.

And suddenly his sight was back.

But not forever, thought the Warlock as they stumbled through the sudden daylight. When the mana runs out, I'll go like a blown candle flame, and civilization will follow. No more magic, no more magic-based industries. Then the whole world will be barbarian until men learn a new way to coerce nature, and the swordsmen, the damned stupid swordsmen will win after all.

Arthur Porges

T hat morning Will Howard was taking a Sunday stroll through the woods, a pleasure which lately had been shared and intensified by Rita Henry. Not even the bright sun, the bracing air, the unique song of a canyon wren, could lighten Will's dark thoughts. Right now she was out riding with Harley Thompson at an exclusive country club. Will couldn't blame her. Harley was six feet two, a former Princeton tackle; ruggedly handsome, full of pleasant small talk; the young-executive-with-a-big-future. And he, Will Howard, a skinny, tongue-tied fellow—

At that moment he felt something tug feebly at one trouser cuff, and looked down to see a tiny field mouse pawing frantically at the cloth. Gaping, Will studied the palpitating animal, completely baffled by such strange behavior on the part of so timid a creature. Then the springy, leaping form of a weasel, implacable, fearless even of man, appeared on the trail.

Quickly Will scooped the terrified rodent into one palm. The weasel stopped, making a nasty, chikkering sound, eyes red in the triangular mask of ferocity that was its face. For a heartbeat it seemed about to attack its giant opponent, but as Will stepped forward, shouting, the beast, chattering with rage, undulated off the path.

'You poor little devil,' Will addressed the bright-eyed bit of fur in his hand. A crooked smile touched his lips. 'You didn't have a chance—just like me and Thompson!' Stooping, he deposited it gently in the underbrush. Then he stared, his jaw dropping. In place of the mouse, there appeared suddenly a chubby, Buddha-like being, some two inches tall. Actually, as measurement would have revealed, it stood precisely one and ninety-eight hundreth inches.

In a voice which although faint was surprisingly resonant, the figure said: 'Accept, O kindly mortal, the grateful thanks of Eep, the God. How can I reward you for saving me from that rapacious monster?'

Will gulped, but being an assiduous reader of Dunsany and Collier, he recovered promptly. 'You—you're a god!' he stammered.

'I am indeed a god,' the being replied complacently. 'Once every hundred years, as a punishment for cheating in chess, I become a mouse briefly—but no doubt you've read similar accounts to the point of excessive boredom. Suffice it to say, you intervened just in time. Now I'm safe for another century—unless, of course, I succumb to temptation again and change a pawn to a bishop. It's hard to resist,' he confided, 'and helps one's end game immensely.'

Will thought of Harley Thompson, the heel that walked like a man. The fellow who laughed at fantasy, who ribbed him for reading the *Magazine of Not-Yet but Could-Be*. Well he knew that behind Thompson's personable exterior was a ruthless, self-seeking, egotistical brute. Rita could never be happy with a man like that. Here was a chance to gain his first advantage over Harley. With the help of a grateful god, much could be achieved. That Dunsany knew the score, all right. Maybe three wishes—but that was tricky. Better let the god himself choose. . . .

'You mentioned a—a reward,' he said diffidently.

'I certainly did,' the god assured him, swinging on a dandelion stem and kicking minute bare feet luxuriously. 'But, alas, only a small one. I am, as you see, a very small god.'

'Oh,' Will said, rather crestfallen. Then brightening: 'May I suggest that a *small* fortune—?' Truly the presence of an immortal was sharpening his wits.

'Of course. But it would have to be exceedingly small. I couldn't go above $1.98.'

'Is that all?' Will's voice was heavy with disappointment.

'I'm afraid it is. We minor gods are always pinched for funds. Perhaps a different sort of gift—'

'Say,' Will interrupted. 'How about a diamond? After all, one the size of a walnut is actually a small object, and—'

'I'm sorry,' the god said regretfully. 'It would have to be tiny even for a diamond. One worth, in fact, $1.98.'

'Curse it!' Will groaned. 'There must be something small—'

'There should be,' the little god agreed good-naturedly. 'Anything I can do, up to $1.98, just ask me.'

'Maybe a small earthquake,' Will suggested, without much enthusiasm. 'I could predict it in advance. Then perhaps Rita—'

'A small earthquake, yes,' Eep replied. 'I could manage that. But it would be the merest trembler. Doing, I remind you, damage only to the amount of $1.98.'

Will sighed. 'You sound like a bargain basement,' he protested.

'Of course,' the god mused aloud, as if sincerely seeking a solution, 'by taking the money in a different currency—say lira—it would *seem* like more; but the value would actually be the same.'

'I give up,' Will said. Then, in a more kindly voice, as Eep looked embarrassed, 'Don't feel too bad. I know you'd like to help. It's not your fault that money's so tight.' Glumly he added 'Maybe you'll think of something yet. I'm selling now, or trying to. I'm not much of a salesman. Once the client sold *me* his office furniture. But if you could arrange a good sale—'

'It would bring in only $1.98.'

'That wouldn't be easy,' Will told him, smiling wryly. 'Right now I'm handling diesel locomotives, office buildings and abandoned mines. And I'm vice-president in charge of dry oil wells.'

'Any luck so far?' the little god demanded, kicking a grasshopper, which soared off indignantly.

'I almost sold an abandoned copper mine to a wealthy Californian for an air-raid shelter, but Thompson nosed me out—again. He showed him how one gallery in another mine could be made into the longest—and safest—bar in the world. It killed my sale; the man bought Thompson's mine for $67,000. That infernal Harley!' he exclaimed. 'I wouldn't mind his getting the supervisor's job instead of me; I'm no good at giving orders, anyhow. Or his stealing my best customers. Even his lousy practical jokes. But when it comes to Rita—! Just when she was beginning to know I'm alive,' he added bitterly.

'Rita?' the god queried.

'Rita Henry—she works in our office. A wonderful girl. So sweet, so—alive, and with the most marvelous greenish eyes—'

'I see,' Eep said, thumbing his nose at a hovering dragonfly.

'That's why I could use a little help. So do what you can, although it can't help much with a ceiling of—'

'—$1.98,' the god completed his sentence firmly. 'I shall spend the afternoon and evening here contemplating the place where my navel would be if I were not supernatural. Trust the Great (although small) God Eep. Farewell.' He walked into the grass.

Much too depressed for any amusement, Will spent the evening at home, and at eleven went gloomily to bed, convinced that a mere $1.98 worth of assistance, even from a god, was unlikely to solve his problem.

In spite of such forebodings, he was tired enough from nervous strain to fall asleep at once, only to be awakened half an hour later by a timid rapping at the apartment door.

Blearily, a robe over his pajamas, he answered it, to find Rita standing on the threshold. She gave him a warm smile that was bright with promise.

'Rita!' he gasped. 'Wha—?'

One finger on her lips, she slipped in, closing the door softly behind her. Then she was in his arms, her lips urgent, her body melting.

'Rita,' Will murmured, 'at last . . .'

She gazed up at him. Was there just a hint of puzzlement, of bewilderment in those green eyes? 'Something just seemed to force me . . . I had to come . . .' She took his hand and led him to the bedroom. There, in the warm darkness, he heard the whispery rustle of silk. 'I had to come,' Rita said again. 'We're right for each other . . . I know . . .'

The bed creaked and, on reaching out one yearning hand, Will touched skin like sun-warmed satin.

The next morning, when she picked up the wispy panties from the floor where they had been tossed in flattering haste, a scrap of paper dropped from the black nylon.

Wondering, Will picked it up. It was a newspaper clipping. Someone had written in the margin in a tiny, flowing script: 'A gratuity from the grateful (up to $1.98) God Eep.'

The clipping itself, a mere filler, read: 'At present prices, the value of the chemical compounds which make up the human body is only $1.98.'

THE TEHAMA

Bob Leman

*I*n an old house, late one night, a quantity of brick was suddenly pushed out of a cellar wall from behind, and the entrance of a tunnel was exposed. Two creatures hopped from the tunnel into the room. They were human in form, in a general way, but their legs as well as their arms terminated in hands with heavy claws, and there was something strongly canine about the heads and faces. Their doggish mouths were full of enormous yellow teeth, as pointed and sharp as needles. They were absolutely hairless, and covered with yellow mud. Here and there on the squat bodies mudless patches exposed skin as white as chalk.

They could speak. One of them said, 'Soon food.'

'Long time no food,' said the other. They spoke in whines and growls and snuffles.

'How long time?' said the first. They stared at each other with dull curiosity.

'Long time,' said the other. '*Long* time! *Long* time!' They did not possess very many words. He snapped ferocious teeth at the questioner to bring home his point.

The first snuffled agreement. In a dim, vague way, he could feel that it had been a very long time indeed. 'Hungry,' he said.

They had always been hungry, of course; hunger was their natural state, a perpetual thing. They hungered for flesh, preferably in an advanced state of natural decomposition, but also acceptable bloody and alive. They had been hungry when the medicine man's spell shut off their consciousness (such as it was), and the hunger continued—even though unfelt—during all the centuries they had lain encysted deep in the yellow clay. When consciousness returned, it was first as awareness of hunger.

'Find food,' the first one said. They looked about them. They could see very well in the dark. There was an open door on the other side of the room. They went to it and tried to pass through the doorway together. Each individual was almost as wide as the opening, and they became involved in a clumsy slapstick tussle in the doorway, chewing and clawing each other with great ferocity, leaving splotches of yellow blood on the floor.

Once they were through, however, the altercation was instantly forgotten, and they went snuffling down the passageway with their talons clicking on the stone floor. It was a very large house, and the cellars were extensive. The passage turned and twisted, and brought them at last to the foot of an iron spiral staircase, which they climbed, after some confusion and bloodletting over their order of precedence in the necessary single file. At the top of the staircase was a landing with a door. They pushed and pulled at the door, and growled at it, and bit each other out of frustration. At last one of them struck it a vindictive blow; it flew open, its lock shattered.

They had reached the kitchen. There was food here, a great deal of it, but they had no way of knowing. It was food that lay cold and odorless behind refrigerator doors, or was sealed in cans, or was boxed dry stuff that would no more have seemed food to them than the door they had just smashed. They stared about with dull wonder at the gleam of chrome and the shine of enamel, at a hundred incomprehensible artifacts.

One of them gave a noisy sniff; the other became instantly alert and joined him in testing the air. The first said, 'Food.' They moved off in the direction of the smell's source. They went through a dining room and down a hallway and into the main living room of the house, where there was indeed food.

It was in the form of two men and a German shepherd dog. The dog was large and fierce, and he had been aware of the intruders long before they became aware of him. Because he was a highly intelligent animal, and supremely well trained, he had obeyed a command to stand fast and be silent; but he quivered like a taut wire under the tension of restraining himself, and his chest trembled with a deep, subvocal growl of the utmost malignity. He was crouching to spring, a powerful engine of destruction caught up in a frenzy of rage and loathing.

When the creatures entered the room, he attacked. A voice shouted, '*Stay!*' but the dog was beyond control; he was suddenly a blur of movement, a flashing passage of great savage teeth launched at the foremost of the intruders.

The creature did not shift its position, nor did it appear to move hastily when it swung its stubby arm; but the blow was timed with exquisite precision, and in it was enormous strength. The dog's rib cage was instantly shattered and splintered, and his heart pulped; he was dead in midair. Before he could drop to the floor, the second creature hooked him at the neck with its talons and pulled. The talons of the first were sunk deep in the body, and it resisted the pull. The head separated from the body; there was a sudden, copious spout of blood.

With importunate, single-minded greed they tore the dog to pieces and began to feed noisily, cramming huge chunks into their terrible mouths, devouring flesh, bones, hide, and offal indiscriminately, crunching and snuffling and slobbering. In less than a minute nothing of the dog remained but his blood soaking into the carpet and a terrible stench in the air.

The two men were standing at the other end of the room. 'Oh, my God,' one of them said. 'Oh, my God. Oh, my God. Oh, my God.' Both of them were pale and trembling. They were slender men dressed in youthful clothing of gaudy color and design, but they were twenty years older than their clothing indicated. One of them was quite gray; the other had dyed his hair yellow. The hair of both was arranged with extreme care.

'Oh, my carpet, my carpet!' the gray one cried. 'Dennis, look at my carpet!'

'Your *carpet?*—your carpet! Look at those things! How are we going to get out of here? Oh, my God, they see us! Oh, my God!'

The dog had been no more than an appetizer for the pair. The two men promised a filling, if not particularly tasty, meal. Snuffling, the creatures moved toward them.

'Gordon, do something!' Dennis cried. 'For God's sake, do something!' His voice rose to a thin, terrified piping. 'Do something, do something.' He had wet his trousers.

'Oh, Jesus,' Gordon said. 'Yeah. Do something. I've got to—I've got to—'

'The *spell*, Gordon! The spell!'

'Yeah, the spell. I've got to—the *spell!*'

Gordon seemed to make a partial escape from his trance of terror. He snatched up two painted gourds that lay on the table. They were rattles. He began to shake them in an odd rhythm and to chant in a minor key.

The creatures halted their advance. Their snuffling ceased. They stood without motion. Gordon continued to shake his rattles, and his chanting became louder and more assured. The creatures shivered suddenly and became as rigid as stone. Then, in a ponderous and almost stately manner, they tipped and crashed stiffly to the floor, where they lay like toppled idols.

The men collapsed into chairs and sat trembling for a time. At length Gordon said, 'Well, it works. I raised them and I put them down.' He thought about it for a moment. 'It works. I did it. It really works.' He began to laugh. Dennis joined him, tentatively at first, and then with equal abandon. They were caught up in an hysteria of relief from their terror, and it was some time before they could gain control of themselves. Then, as their giggles gradually subsided, they began to stare with mounting horror at the recumbent monsters. At last Dennis said, 'We almost got killed.'

'And eaten,' Gordon said. 'Poor old Rex.'

'Oh, Jesus,' Dennis said. Both looked sick.

'The thing is,' Gordon said, 'is what do we do now? What do we do with these things?'

'You should have thought about that beforehand. 'Let's try it, let's try it,' you said. Now you've got 'em. My God, look at 'em.'

They looked at the comatose creatures with fear and revulsion. Gordon rose and edged toward them, timid and tentative, ready to take flight if they showed signs of life. They remained totally inert, their eyes closed, the feral muzzles slackly agape, revealing bits of dog clinging to the frightful teeth. Gordon reached out with a finger and, after a couple of hesitant withdrawals, poked at one of them. It had no effect.

'They're out, all right,' he said. 'Back in suspended animation, or whatever it is. The spell works okay.' He thought about that for a moment. '*Both* spells work. Everything's going according to the plan. Right?'

Dennis had cautiously come up to join him. ' "According to the plan" ' he said with scorn. ' "According to the plan." What's the matter with you? The plan was to invoke something to kill your aunt for you. How the hell are you going to get these—*things* to do that—to do *anything?*'

'I can control them. You saw that,' Gordon said defensively.

'Control?' Dennis said. 'You can raise them up and put them back to sleep, that's all. In between you've got about as much control as Rex had.'

Gordon winced. 'Well, yeah. I suppose that's right. We'll have to figure something out. But what do we do right now? These things can't stay here.'

'We'll have to hide them,' Dennis said. 'They came up from the basement. They must have been buried someplace down there. We'll find their hole and put them back.'

'And how do you suppose we'll do that? Look at the size of them. And they're as hard as a piece of wood. They must weigh three hundred pounds apiece. There's no way in the world we could carry them down to the basement—or anywhere.'

'All *right*. Leave them there, then. Use them for decoration. Just the thing to complete the decor. Hose off the mud and they'll be exactly the right color.' The room was, in fact, painted and furnished in subtle gradations of near-white.

'Oh, shut up, Dennis,' Gordon said. 'I guess there's no way out of it. I'll have to call Pokatewa for help.'

'It's not according to the plan at all. He knows too much already. We're going to get caught. I know we're going to get caught.'

'We haven't broken any laws yet. And he already knows we're up to something. Anyhow, who the hell else can help?' He went to the telephone and dialed. After a time he said, 'No answer.'

As he hung up, the doorbell rang. The two stared at each other in panic. 'What—?' Gordon said. 'Who—?'

'Oh, my God, they've got us!' Dennis said.

'The window,' said Gordon. 'You can see the front door from the bay window. See who it is.'

Dennis peered through the curtain and turned with relief on his face. 'It's him,' he said. 'The Indian. Smithers.'

'Native American,' Gordon corrected automatically. 'And don't use his paleface name. Call him Pokatewa.'

'Whatever,' Dennis said. He went out of the room, and there was the sound of the opening and closing of a door. He re-entered with a companion, a thickset man dressed in what is sometimes called 'Full Cleveland'—maroon polyester trousers, a green blazer of the same material, a black shirt with no tie, and white patent leather shoes and belt. He raised his hand to shoulder height, palm outward, and without visible irony said, 'How.'

'Smithers!' Gordon said. 'I mean Pokatewa! Am I glad to see you! I was just trying to call.'

'Well, well, well,' Smithers said. 'What have we here?' His eyes had widened for a moment at the sight of the monsters, but he showed no other sign of alarm or amazement. 'So these are what you got.'

'They're what I got,' Gordon said, 'and they're not what I wanted. What on earth am I going to do with them? What are they, anyhow? They killed my dog.'

'Ate him,' Dennis said.

Smithers was examining the teeth and talons. 'Why, I think they're what's called Ne-dake-ne-kevis,' he said. 'At least they're kind of like what the old man described. Of course he had only tradition for the description. Look at the size of 'em. They look mean.'

Gordon shuddered. 'Oh, they are, they are. But *what* are they?'

'The name means "Eaters of those whose ghosts have departed,"' Smithers said. 'What you have here is your basic ghoul. My people never did think very well of them. Where'd they come from?'

'They came up from the basement.'

'Yeah, that figures. I've heard that this area through here was put off-limits by the medicine men in the olden times. They thought the white men were crazy to live around here. When you woke 'em, they must have started burrowing and came out in your cellar.'

'Well, they can't stay here,' Gordon said. 'How do we get rid of them?'

'Gordon,' Smithers said, 'I think we'd better have a little talk. You want to fix me a drink?'

The sun was rising when Smithers left the house. He descended the broad stone stairway to his car, a huge, unabashed gas-guzzler, and drove off down the long driveway. The land on both sides of the driveway belonged to real estate speculators, now; all that remained of the old Alfred Evans estate was the house Smithers had just left, with two acres of land and a right-of-way from the highway.

The house was a very large and very ugly one, built at the turn of the century by a rich man to flaunt his wealth. The Evans brothers, Alfred and Frank, had been coal barons, rapacious cold men who pulled themselves out of the pit and into opulence in the space of a decade, leaving a debris of broken businesses and broken men at the stages of their climb, and making their name a synonym for merciless greed. They lived austere bachelor lives in the grimy house where they had been born until long after they became millionaires, when at last both built ostentatious and very similar mansions on adjoining large estates located at a decent remove from the mines. Alfred never married, but Frank had a son, and then a grandson and granddaughter, and, finally, a great-grandson. This was Gordon, who was clearly destined to be without issue and the last of the line. Gordon had inherited the Alfred Evans place when he came of age and had supported himself ever since by selling off the land, piece by piece, until only the house was left.

The other house, the Frank Evans place, was now the property of Gordon's aunt, Helena Slade, old Frank's granddaughter. Smithers parked in front of it and climbed a set of steps very like those he had just descended. He rang the bell. After a long wait, the door opened slightly. Smithers said, briskly, 'Morning, Signe. Helena in?'

'You crazy?' the old woman said. 'You know what time it is? Helena's in bed. So was I, until you come ringin'. Come back at a decent hour. This is no time to be ringin' people's doorbells.'

A distant voice called out, 'What is it, Signe?'

'It's Eddie Smithers,' the old woman shouted. 'Wants to come in. Don't know what time it is, I guess.'

'Let him in, Signe,' the voice said. 'Give him some coffee. I'll be down in a little while.'

'All right,' the old woman said, and, to Smithers, 'Well, come in, Eddie. She's as crazy as you are.'

She left him in a morning room, to which she at length brought coffee. He had drunk two cups by the time Helena Slade entered, a trim, white-haired woman wearing twin sweaters and a tweed skirt. She said, 'Good morning, Eddie. I'm sure Signe has already called your attention to the time.'

'Morning, Helena. Yes, she did. I thought what I have couldn't wait.'

'Yes. Well, tell me.' She sat and took coffee.

'Gordon's planning to kill you,' Smithers said.

The hand raising the cup may have paused for a fraction of a second; otherwise she did not visibly react. She drank and then said, in an ordinary voice, 'I wondered when he'd think of it. It's that damned idiotic will.'

'He's just about at the end of his rope,' Smithers said. 'He hasn't got anything left to sell, except his house.'

'You ought to know, Eddie. You were broker for every acre he sold, weren't you?'

'I'm a businessman,' Smithers said. 'He wanted to sell, there were buyers, somebody was going to get the commissions. Anyhow, he's broke, now. And of course when you die he gets the money you hold as trustee for him. I think you made a big mistake, there, Helena. You've refused to let him have a nickel—and it was wholly at your discretion how much of the money he was to have as income—so that now he's totally certain that your death is the only way he'll get his hands on the money. And it *is* his, after all. He's serious about this, dead serious. Even if you give him the money now, I'm not sure you'll be safe. He really hates you. You turned him down once too often when he asked for some of his money. But you'd better hand it over right away. Today, say.'

'But he could never get away with it. If he—if something

happens to me, he's the only one with a motive. And now you know what he's planning.'

'If he's caught after he does it, it won't help you a bit, will it? Give him his money.'

'Eddie,' she said, 'I can't.'

'Why not?'

There isn't any.'

'Ah,' Smithers said. 'I see. Slade cleaned you out entirely, then.' Helena had married in her youth a charming, remorseless confidence man who was known to have enriched himself greatly out of the Evans fortune before he deserted Helena and fled to the Riviera. 'And you've been using Gordon's money ever since. But how the hell could you have spent it all? There must have been anyhow a million?'

'Closer to two. Slade got some, and I went into some unfortunate speculations in trying to make up deficits. It's all gone, Eddie, every cent of it, and nothing to show for it. I'll go to prison, I suppose. Or Gordon will kill me. I knew it would come eventually.'

'Helena,' Smithers said, 'do you think I'm going to let anything like that happen to you? We've been friends for forty years and, for a while there, considerably more than just friends. Don't worry. I'll get you out of it.'

'I don't see how,' she said. 'If Gordon finds out the money's gone, he'll prosecute, and if he doesn't find out, he'll kill me to end the trust. And he's stubborn. I don't think anything will make him drop it. Not ever in his life.'

'Right!' Smithers said heartily.

She looked at him. 'Oh,' she said. 'Yes. Yes, that would do it, if Gordon died, wouldn't it? But how could we—how would you do that?'

'Why, I think I can turn his own little scheme around so he'll be the victim, not you. I'm going to give it a shot, anyhow. It'll be tricky. He's fooling around with things he doesn't understand at all. I don't either, to tell the truth. But I know a lot more than he does.'

'What is it, Eddie? What is it that he's doing?'

'Some old Indian stuff,' Smithers said. 'Witchcraft, I guess you'd say, except that I never heard the word used for the Indian version. He was trying to call up a supernatural creature to kill you.'

Helena laughed. 'No, really.'

'Oh, I'm perfectly serious. The fact is, he's already done it.

Called up his creature, that is. He didn't get quite what he was after, of course.'

She stopped laughing. 'You *are* serious.'

'I am indeed. It's my doing, really.'

'What does that mean?'

'Helena, I'm a Sangimee Indian. Everybody knows that, but nobody ever stops to think about it, because all they see is a one-hundred-percent-go-getter realtor and City Councilman and Rotarian. Sometimes I forget it myself. But I'm Sangimee, and my grandfather taught me Sangimee medicine when I was a boy. You remember his house way out on Donley Street?'

'Yes,' Helena said.

'It was still all woods behind his house then, and starting when I was about five, he began to take me to a secret place he had in there, and he taught me the lore. That's how it works—the medicine man always teaches it to his grandson, not his son. For better or worse, long before any of the other tribes, the Sangimee joined 'em when they saw they couldn't lick 'em, and for two hundred and fifty years now we've lived just like our neighbors. But during all that time the medicine men passed on the lore to their grandsons, or to boys adopted as grandsons for that purpose. And it's not just superstition. Sangimee medicine has some very real powers, and the lore recounts a good many things that sound like fairy tales, but are hard, simple truth. I know.

'During the last ten years or so, I've seen quite a lot of Gordon, selling off his land for him. You know Gordon. He goes for anything trendy, especially young people's fads. Goes all out for a while, until something else takes his attention. Disco dancing, anti-draft, cocaine, anti-nuke—he has his little fling at whatever is 'in.' Most of 'em seem kind of nasty to me, but then I'm a bourgeois flag-waver.'

'He calls me a fascist,' Helena said.

'Oh, sure. He'd call me one too, except that I'm an Oppressed Minority. I bother him because I don't behave the way his stereotype says I should. When the Indian Rights thing was the big fad with the trendy people, he jumped in with both feet, of course; and while he was still enthusiastic about it, he pestered me a lot for information about what he called Tribal Customs of Native Americans. I let it slip that I was trained as a medicine man, and he zeroed in on that. It fascinated him. I ended up telling him about the Festamatis.'

'Festamatis?'

'According to the legend, a malign spirit that lives in a dead tree.

It can be invoked by an appropriate spell, and it will do your dirty work for you, at a price. The price is one human life. It's described as a bitterly cold black mist that surrounds its victim and then passes on, leaving a stone-cold corpse. But the life it contracts to take won't do for its fee; there has to be another. In most of the stories you can guess how it came out: the person who invoked the Festamatis was himself killed as the payment. Of course, in some of the tales the Festamatis was out-smarted.

'Gordon wouldn't give me any peace until I taught him the spell. I didn't see any harm in it. I'd tried it myself a few times, and I couldn't make it work. Oh, once I got a bunch of little blind flying balls of fur that were kind of scary, but harmless. These incantations are pretty complex: a mispronounced word, or one pitched wrong, can invalidate the whole thing, or maybe change it to another spell entirely. If I couldn't get the thing right, it was certain Gordon couldn't. So I gave him a set of rattles and taught him the spell and counterspell. I was trying just then to get another point on my commission and wanted to do him a favor.

'He tried it out, he told me, and when nothing happened he wasn't surprised—I don't suppose he ever really believed it—and he put the rattles in a drawer and forgot about it. But recently, when he finally decided that the only way out of his difficulties was to do you in, Helena, he thought about the Festamatis and decided to give it another try.

'About two this morning I woke up suddenly, knowing that somewhere not too far off a spell had just been successful, and that it had to be Gordon's work. I was a little scared, to tell the truth; if there is such a thing as the Festamatis, and he'd managed to raise it, he might just be pointing it at me. We've had our share of quarrels, in the course of our deals. I got my rattles ready, just in case.

'After a couple of hours I concluded that I was safe, and I thought I'd better investigate. I got dressed and went out to Gordon's. He'd raised something, all right, but not the Festamatis; what he has are two of the ugliest monsters you ever saw, and damned dangerous ones, in the bargain. But I don't think they're supernatural; probably the last of a species that's extinct, except for them. They'd been in some kind of suspended animation since God-knows-when. Gordon's screwed-up spell woke them, and by the greatest of damn-fool luck, the counterspell put them back under. I found Gordon and his little friend scared out of their wits—the things had eaten Gordon's big dog like a pretzel—and the monsters were laid out stiff on that white carpet he's so fond of.

'Gordon and I had a nice little chat. He wanted my help, and I wormed the whole story out of him while Dennis was off changing his jeans. His mind is absolutely made up that you've got to die; when he tried to invoke the Festamatis, it was a last desperate effort to get the job done cheap. (He was going to give Dennis to the Festamatis as the payment.) If that failed, then he'd go ahead with a professional contract on your life, but that was going to be extremely expensive, and to raise the money he'd have to sell his house, the last thing in the world he wanted to do.

'So he was looking for a way to use the critters on the carpet to take care of you, since they were conveniently at hand, and, he figured, would come cheaper than the Festamatis, and he'd get to keep Dennis. He wanted me to figure out how to sic the monsters on you. He dropped hints about all the dandy commissions that would fall to me once he came into his money.

'I told him I'd try to figure something out, and that meanwhile he was to do absolutely nothing about the sleeping beauties in his living room, and that he should let absolutely no one at all into his house. I told him I'd let him know what to do sometime today. Then I came over here to advise you to hand over the money without delay. Which you now tell me you can't do.'

Helena had sat quietly as he talked. Now she said. 'That's pretty strange stuff, Eddie. Is it honest and truly the truth?'

He looked at her soberly. 'It's the truth.'

'Well,' she said. 'Well, then. I'll do whatever you say. Imagine, planning to hand poor little Dennis over to that Festis thing. Shameful. Now, how are we going to kill Gordon?'

'Not *we*,' Smithers said. 'The Ne-dake-ne-kevis. *They*'ll kill him. And in front of witnesses, just to make sure no suspicion attaches to you—or me. I've got the place picked out, and the witnesses.'

'Where, Eddie? Who?'

'Oh, I've worked up a slick little scheme. You see, Gordon will have to believe that the witnesses are for *his* benefit, to give him an alibi for the time your death is supposed to be taking place. And because there's simply no way to schedule matters with any kind of precise timing, it has to be at a place where the witnesses will be on hand at whatever time it takes place. On top of that, it has to be reasonably close to both Gordon's house and yours. It works out to just one area: somewhere close to that commune on Gore's Survey. It's located right, and there are always enough people around to make it certain that someone will see Gordon being killed by, uh, individuals that in no way resemble you or me. But just to be safe, you'd better have some guests in tonight. The descriptions of the

killers are going to sound pretty strange to the police, and they
might decide that what's being described came out of something the
witnesses smoked or dropped.'

'Very clever,' Helena said, 'but what makes you think your
'individuals' will be in the right place at the right time?'

'Your local medicine man has a method. I've got grandpa's *freese*.
A sort of musical instrument, a very primitive recorder, I guess
you'd call it. What comes out of it isn't exactly music—it only has
three notes—but by blowing on it you can control all sorts of
creatures. I imagine the Pied Piper legend grew out of something of
the kind. I think I can use it to manipulate Gordon's ghouls, the
way the Pied Piper led the rats and the children. Of course, up to
now I've only used it for a game call. Works fine on geese and wild
turkeys.'

Helena rose from her chair, walked to the window, and stared
out of it for a time. 'Eddie,' she said, 'I can hardly believe this. Do
you realize what we're doing? We're conspiring to murder.'

'Well, I don't know,' Smithers said. 'More like self-defense,
really. Or maybe extermination. Gordon's a pretty nasty article,
when you come right down to it. He really believes I'd help him kill
you for the sake of a few commissions. But we don't have to do it.'

'That's the trouble,' she said. 'I'm afraid we do.'

Gordon said much the same thing. He and Smithers were sitting in
the dining room drinking tea. He said, 'There's no use talking
about it, Smithers. I'm going to do it. Are you going to help me or
not? There's a lot of money at stake, you know. And you're already
in pretty deep.'

'Oh, sure, Gordon, I'll help you,' Smithers said. 'I just thought
you might have changed your mind. The main thing is, it's got to
be done as soon as possible. Those things can't be left in there a
minute longer than absolutely necessary.'

'Amen!' Gordon said.

'So we'll do it tonight. Okay?'

'Tonight? Well—well, sure. Sure. Uh . . . what are we going to
do, exactly?'

'Why, you'll cast the spell to wake them, and I'll Pied-Piper them
over to your aunt's house. After they've done the job, I'll pipe them
back here again and then back into their tunnel, and you'll put
them back to sleep—for the next thousand years, I hope. The
important thing is your alibi. You'll need witnesses to your
whereabouts for at least a couple of hours, to give you plenty of
coverage both before and after the act. That means you'll have to do

the wake-up incantation right in front of your witnesses. So here's what you're going to do. You'll go over somewhere close to that commune on Gore's Survey and put on a big Red-Indian act, Hollywood style. Put on some war paint. Build a fire and have Dennis beat a drum. Dance around and whoop and holler. When the communards ask what you're up to, say you're propitiating the Nature Gods, or something. When you cast the spell, it'll just seem to be part of the general carrying on. How does that sound?'

'It sounds okay. Like fun, even. Those people will dig it. Probably try and join in. It's their kind of thing.'

'I wouldn't be surprised. Now, the timing. It'll be getting dark by six thirty, and full dark a half hour after that. Have your fire built, and start your act at seven. Cast the spell at seven thirty. And be sure you time it right, because I'm going to be here with your sleeping friends, and I don't want to be caught by surprise when they wake up. Knock off the theatricals at nine sharp, say good-bye to the hippies (don't forget to mention the time) and get back here as fast as you can. And now I'm going home and get some sleep. You'd better do the same. I'll be back to see you off.'

At a little after six Gordon and Dennis took their departure, Dennis fluttering apprehensively, and Gordon alternating between fits of elation and funk. After the station wagon had disappeared down the driveway, Smithers entered the living room. The two creatures lay as they had fallen. The blood on the carpet had turned black, and only a trace of the stench remained in the air. Smithers was carrying a canvas gymnasium bag. From it he took a pair of rattles like those he had given Gordon, and a crude small wind instrument. He blew tentatively into the instrument a few times, eliciting a mournful honking, and then put it into his pocket. He took up the rattles. 'Okay, pals,' he said, 'the beauty sleep's over. Time to wake up and go to work.'

He moved into the doorway, where there was a clear line of flight behind him, and began to shake the rattles and chant. After a time the leg of one of the creatures jerked, and the other one made a movement of its head. Smithers dropped the rattles and pulled the *freese* from his pocket. As the pair rose ponderously to their feet, he began to pipe.

It was an unpleasant sound, monotonous in pitch and irritating in its lack of identifiable rhythm. For a time the creatures paid no heed, but snuffled and grunted to each other and peered about in slow bewilderment, until the effect of the *freese* at last penetrated the dim minds; then, as one creature, they turned and looked at Smithers.

Sweat appeared on his face, and he held himself ready to bolt, but there was no hesitation in the flow of sound. He blew a long, irregularly interrupted note, a sound not unlike slow Morse code, and glared at the creatures with furious concentration. Suddenly, and in unison, they swung up their right arms in a Roman salute.

Smithers took the *freese* from his mouth and wiped his face. He said, 'Well. Okay. Gotcha. Now we'll practice a little.' They were standing without motion, frozen in the salute. He put the pipe to his mouth and again blew the note, concentrating his stare upon the creatures as before. They began to move, at first in absolute unison, and then, as Smithers' skill and confidence grew, as individuals. He marched them up and down the room, clumsily in the beginning, with a consequent breakage of a number of Gordon's possessions, but in the end with precision, so that they threaded their way among the furniture with scarcely a collision. Smithers said at last, 'Right. We're ready, I guess. Forward, *march!*' He blew again.

In single file they marched out of the room, through the open front door, and down the steps, with Smithers following. They crossed the lawn, passed through a gateway in a low stone wall, and set out through the woods. It was growing dark, but there was still enough light for the creatures to be seen, and Smithers kept at a distance, moving in the deepest shadows. Once launched into motion, the pair continued to plod without further instruction; Smithers blew the *freese* only to change their direction from time to time.

Gore's Survey was a wasteland, a tract of fifteen or twenty acres that still retained the name of an old three-thousand-acre grant to a pioneer named Gore, who had parceled it out in estates and farms in the middle of the eighteenth century. It had been highly desirable land at the time Gore took it, and during the next two centuries its value increased continuously, so that over the years most of the tracts changed hands many times. Along the way, a great many were divided into smaller farms, and as early as the nineteen thirties some of these were being further subdivided into residential building lots. Any large tracts that remained intact acquired enormous value. The two Evans estates had been in that category.

It was rolling countryside, topographically varying from gentle slopes to moderate hillsides. A good deal of the aboriginal forest remained, mingled with prosperous farms. Clean small streams ran through it; there was an abundance of game. It was green and golden in the summer, and in autumn a carnival of reds and yellows. The winters were cold and white, but they spoke more of fat hibernation than of frozen hunger. Nature was kind, here.

Except to the tract of acreage that still kept the old name; that had been blighted, somehow. Nothing grew there except a flaky dry lichen, and that only in spots. The land lay amid the greenery like a gray sore, an irregular blotch of sterility. From time to time down the years, someone would buy it from the county for a trifling price and spend a few years and a good deal of money on one scheme or another—complex drainage systems, irrigation, sophisticated fertilizers and chemicals—to make it productive. The schemes always failed, and in due course the county would take it for taxes again.

In 1925 one of the hopeful entrepreneurs built a house on the tract, an undistinguished wooden farmhouse which, after its abandonment, sheltered squatters from time to time. Its current occupants were relics of the decade of drugs and violence, aging debris of the storms of the time. They lived in the past, still vaguely convinced that cooking their brains with chemicals and living in squalor revenged them somehow on a world that had passed them by and that found their existence irrelevant to its concerns. Their livelihood came from a regular cash remittance of mysterious origins, which was paid in consideration of their harboring and hiding a fugitive left over from the stormy past, a zealot who had once planted a bomb in the history stacks of a university library and managed to blow up an elderly night watchman along with the books.

These were Smithers' witnesses, not the most credible, perhaps, but in the right place at the right time. They were assembled on the rotting porch of the house as he and his monstrous puppets reached the edge of the woods. The war dance had quite successfully engaged their attention, and they watched with dreamy approval as Gordon capered around a great bonfire to Dennis's erratic thumping on a set of bongo drums.

Smithers blew a honk that froze his charges in place behind a dense thicket, and cautiously approached through the shadows for a clear view. Gordon was speaking to Dennis, who stopped drumming. Gordon took up the rattles. He began the incantation.

'Dead on time,' Smithers said. 'Get set, fellas.' He waited. After a time he said, 'Go,' and blew. The creatures stumped out of the bushes and moved ponderously toward Gordon's fire.

A fog lay upon Gore's Survey, a fog that had not been there before the incantation began. It coiled and eddied sluggishly along the ground, thickening gradually as the chant proceeded, rising no higher than a man's waist. It ended abruptly at the border of the dead land. Smithers eyed it with apprehension; he kept the *freese* close to his mouth.

Gordon's incantation ended with a truncated, minor-key drone and an elaborate flourish of the rattles. There was a moment of utter stillness. Then something came from under the earth.

The dry, ashen soil shifted, heaved, and split; through the opening rose the figure of a man, an Indian warrior in deerskins. He seemed to be unfolding himself from a doubled-up position, stretching slowly to his full height. As he did so, the sporadic red glare of the bonfire showed his arms to be bound tight to his sides. On his face was an expression of unutterable pain, of an agony beyond any nightmare of agony. He stood for a long moment, his head thrown back, seeming to stare at the black sky. And then, between one flicker of the fire and the next, his face changed: the black gape of his silent scream was erased, the knotted contortion of the facial muscles softened and relaxed; an old suffering had ended, and its marks were wiped away. On the face at that instant of deliverance was an expression of serenity and peace.

But only for that instant; then there was no face, there was no warrior. There was only a fine dust that floated and swirled gently for a moment and was dispersed by the eddies of the mist.

'A Tehama!' Smithers said. 'Oh, Jesus, Mary and Joseph.'

Suddenly there were things in the fog, fitfully visible through the slow coilings. They were a host, a swarm: foot-high stick-figures with heads like the skulls of toothed reptiles, deep grinning mouths wide in soundless shrieks of hate. They were in furious motion, making for the fire, the small limbs like flailing black wires.

They reached Dennis first, where he sat frozen with the drums in his lap. They were over him like locusts, razor teeth tearing and ripping, little black talons clawing in a frenzy. In a moment they dropped away. Dennis toppled to the ground, quite dead. There was not a mark on his body.

Smithers' puppets had almost reached the fire, now, plodding along mechanically, not to be stopped or turned except by the pipe that had set them in motion. The swarm boiled and swirled and raced at them, and up and over them, enveloping both as it had enveloped Dennis. The thick bodies continued to plod. Teeth and claws without number tore at them with insenate ferocity; their pace did not vary. The swarm dropped off them; they were dead. And still the bodies marched for a few more steps before they dropped. They were no more marked by the savage rending than Dennis had been.

All of this had taken no more than two minutes, and Smithers had not moved a muscle. Now he broke free of his paralysis. 'Run!' he bawled to the group on the porch. 'Run! Run!'

They paid no attention. Perhaps in their chemical trances they had often watched even stranger things and perceived this as nothing very different. One or two applauded, and one said, '*Yeah!*' And then the swarm was upon them.

It left them sprawled in death on the decayed planks, and surged into the house and out again, and violently boiled about on the gray earth. The movement was perceptibly slower than it had been in the beginning, and they could be made out individually, the hard thin limbs and small terrible heads, the feral little mouths wide in their soundless shrieks. Smithers was shuddering and sweating copiously in the chilly night air. He put the pipe to his mouth and once again blew.

The movement slowed further as he piped, and little by little the swarm coalesced into a dense pack, a shifting, flickering blanket of predatory small horrors covering several square yards of the dead soil. Smithers turned and entered the forest. They followed.

It was dawn again when Smithers rang Helena's bell. He said, 'Don't talk, Signe. Just get me some whiskey and call Helena.' She took one look at him and obeyed without a word.

When Helena entered the room, she found him slumped in a chair, drinking the whiskey. He said, 'Well, it's done. You're rid of Gordon. And Dennis and the hippies, too. And damn near me.' He had the look of a soldier who has been too long under fire.

She said, 'Signe's making breakfast. Eat something, and then you can tell me about it. Come along.' Smithers carried the bottle with him.

The dining room was airy and sunny, and a canary sang in a cage. Smithers had eaten bacon and eggs and reduced the bottle's level by several inches. His eyes had lost some of their wildness, and the tension on his face was softening into simple weariness. 'Gordon got the spell a little wrong, again,' he said. 'It shouldn't have mattered, because I'd already activated the corpse-eaters, and what he was doing—even though he didn't know it—was just window-dressing. But it worked, and worked wrong, and he set free a Tehama that had been set to restrain a nest of—I guess 'Biters' would be the best translation. I'd better explain what those things are.

'The Biters are just about the worst things the legends tell about, little horrors so thoroughly evil that they were loathed by even the wickedest of the spirits. The myth has it that long ago the Great Good Spirit, Gitche-Manito, prevailed in single combat over his opposite, Hake-Manito, and struck him such a blow that Hake-Manito was shattered into a million pieces. But each of the pieces retained life, and each had only one aim: to kill. To kill anything and everything, animal and vegetable, fish, fowl, and corn.

'Gitche-Manito buried them in various places all over the world. But of course simple burial wouldn't hold them, and so he put a safeguard at each burial place: a Tehama. The Biters could be confined only if they could kill. So he gave them something to kill. He took the bad medicine men, the ones who had served Hake-Manito, and buried one with each clutch of Biters. Buried them alive, for the Biters to kill. And ever since, they have been killed by the Biters ten thousand times a day, every day, suffering agonizing death endlessly repeated, and yet they cannot die. And for so long as they do not die, the Biters can continue to kill them, and so somewhat slake their thirst for killing, and will remain in restraint.

'But Gordon's spell released the Tehama; he died at last, was delivered from his long agony. When he died, the Biters were no longer confined to the grave, and they came out. They came out and killed, did enough killing to take the edge off their appetite, so I could control them, more or less, with the *freese*. I piped them over to Gordon's house and down into the tunnel the ghouls came out of, and bricked up the tunnel. And then I came down with the worst case of the shakes you ever saw. Those things are awful, Helena. You can't imagine how awful.

'I stopped by Gore's Survey on my way back here. It's pretty clear, now, what made it a desert, why nothing ever grew there. That'll be changing. But it doesn't look so good this morning. Enough corpses for a small battlefield. The things from the tunnel aren't there, though; just a couple of wet spots on the ground. They must have totally decomposed, bones and all. Odd chemistry there. Somebody'll be finding the bodies pretty soon now, and calling the sheriff. I wonder what the autopsies'll show. The bodies aren't marked. It seems the Biters don't actually bite. It may be that they don't even have any physical being. But they kill, all right. They do kill.'

Smithers gulped the rest of his whiskey and stared out the window. Helena said, 'It's all pretty strange, Eddie. And pretty awful. And very hard to believe, to tell the truth. Did it really happen?'

'Oh, it happened. You'll be hearing all about the bodies they'll find at Gore's Survey. I expect they'll end up calling it some kind of dope poisoning. . . . There's about fifteen hundred dollars back taxes on that land. I can get it for that plus costs. I think I'd better do it today. It's going to be getting green, now. Going to be good land. Be worth something.'

'Like what?'

'I don't know. Half a million, maybe.'

'If it's true. If it's not true, it's not worth the back taxes. Nothing ever grew there—ever.'

'It will now,' Smithers said, confidently.

'Well, then. We both gain something, don't we?'

'I'm a businessman,' Smithers said. 'If an opportunity comes up, I try to take advantage of it. You should, too. Gordon's house will be yours, now. You'd better sell it as quick as you can. I have a notion the blight will be hitting that area pretty soon.'

'All right, I will. I can use the money. . . . We're pretty cold-blooded, aren't we?'

'Nothing wrong with taking advantage of something that's already happened. A little hard on the hippies, I admit. Best think of it as a natural disaster, something that couldn't be helped.'

'Yes,' Helena said. 'That's what I'll do.'

In the afternoon Smithers drove his gas-guzzler up the mountain to the end of a derelict road. When it became impossible to drive any further, he left the car and proceeded on foot through the trees to a clearing. He was dressed in old khakis and a leather jacket and moccasins. He gathered wood and built a small fire; when the fire had burnt itself down to bright coals and a tiny column of white smoke was rising vertically from it into the still air, he began softly to chant. From the pocket of his jacket he took a handful of something which he dropped onto the coals.

Dense smoke rose and spread and began to churn and eddy, although there was no wind. In a few minutes the movement ceased, and it hung in a motionless small cloud around the bed of coals. It had thinned enough to permit a certain murky visibility, except for a clot of considerable density across the fire from Smithers. Smithers spoke to the clot: 'Is it you, ghost of my grandfather?'

He heard a reply, or thought he heard one, and he said, 'To tell you how things go with me, Grandfather. To tell you that I have contended with the Biters and have prevailed over them.' He paused, listening. He said, 'A Tehama was released through bungling, and the Biters came forth and killed. When their first frenzy was over, I could control them with the *freese*, and now they are as they were before. They are—I think this will make you laugh, Grandfather—they are in a tunnel under a house. The tunnel was formerly the burial place of two corpse-eaters that are now destroyed.'

He listened again and said, 'They are safely confined. I have given them a new Tehama. They will feed on him perpetually, and for so long as they do, they cannot escape. The Great Spirit's arrangement has been restored.' He paused. 'A man named Gordon Evans. A bad man, Grandfather. As bad as any of those medicine men who once served the evil spirit. The religion of this man's fathers preaches a hell. He has something worse, now. The eternal fires he was taught to fear must seem to him today like a cool oasis, a place to be longed for. And what he is suffering now, he must suffer forever. Or so we should hope. His deliverance would free the Biters again, and that must not happen. He released the old Tehama through his efforts to do murder. It is only just that he serve as the new Tehama.'

Another pause. He said, 'Oh, pretty good, Grandfather. The game laws keep getting worse. I'm only allowed to shoot one deer a year, but I usually poach a couple more. My wife died a few years ago. I have a grandson, six months old now. I don't know whether I'll teach him the lore or not. I'm not sure it wouldn't be an impediment to him. He's going to be pretty busy with his regular education. I've already entered him for his prep school, and he'll be going to Harvard or Princeton in due course. He'll have a lot of money when I finally join you over there, Grandfather. I want to prepare him to be a rich man . . . Grandfather? Grandfather?'

A faint breeze had come up, and the smoke had dispersed. Smithers scooped dirt over the remains of his fire and trod on it. He returned through the woods to his car, performed the complicated maneuvers necessary to turn it around in the narrow roadway, and drove down the mountain.

The mountain road led to a blacktop, and that to the highway. He pulled off the highway at Gore's Survey and parked for a long time, staring reflectively out at the landscape. The dead fields rolled away to the distant tree line as they had always done, lying sterile and gray in the fading light. There was no sign yet of the green future. But it was only the first day.

He drove on and at the Alfred Evans place turned in at the driveway. Nothing had changed here, either, except that around the house the flowers were just beginning to droop.

GHOST OF A CROWN

Sterling E. Lanier

Ghost stories are *passé* in some circles, I suppose,' said a new member. I didn't know his name, but he was a younger man, of what, I guess, could be called a bookish type. He had rather thick glasses and a thin, angular face. He was drinking Madeira, which is not much in vogue with most of my acquaintances, but I didn't hold that against him either.

It was a cold spring night, and the club library had a fire lit at one end of the long room. A group of us were sitting in one of the big bay window alcoves overlooking Fifth Avenue, and the park looked rather gloomy in the drifting mist below. Personally, I'd rather hit Omaha Beach alone than go into it at night.

'I like them myself,' said Bryce. He was something important in the Bank of New York. 'I read them in my office, that is, when my secretary is busy.' This raised a mild laugh. 'In fact,' he went on, unperturbed, 'I have a standing order with Blackwells, in England, to send me any new ones that look good. And I even put myself on the lists of some of these jobbers that deal in science fiction, horror stories, and such things, in case some of the old ones come in that sound good.' He sipped his drink. 'Actually, I've found that some of the best are long out of print, and damned hard to get hold of.'

Perhaps a banker was needed to break the ice, the image of bankers being so stuffy and conventional, even to those of us who knew better. It turned out that a whole lot of us read ghost stories, horror stories, wild fantasy, and so on. In no time an argument was raging over who wrote what, who wrote best (and worst!), and various schools of opinion began to get sorted out. For the library it was a pretty noisy scene. Two old gentlemen drowsing by the fire got up and left, muttering about seeing someone on the house committee, but we paid them no attention, being busy attacking H. P. Lovecraft or someone similar.

During a lull, the younger guy who had started the whole thing suddenly asked, 'But *why* do you all enjoy these things? Is it because your lives are so dull today? Or is it that you'd really *like* to believe that there are things beyond our level of knowledge, powers of darkness, say, that still can reach us at times and in certain places? In other words, friends, what grabs you about all this, as the kids say now?' He was quite excited.

We all thought for a minute. Frankly, I don't think any of us had ever given a hell of a lot of thinking time to why we enjoyed being frightened or whatever.

The young guy, whose name turned out to be Simmons, went on. 'Is it the same reason children ride roller coasters? Or do you think it may be something deeper, such as a feeling that the ancients, perhaps, knew more than we do, that a deep well of lost knowledge underlies all the broomstick and Halloween nonsense? And that by reading the stuff, you both acknowledge its reality and in a subconscious way, well, pay it a sort of respect?'

Well, the argument started afresh. Some of us admitted we liked being scared (I was one), especially if we knew we could always close the book! But a few others picked up Simmons' idea of a racial memory of the ancient past, and started telling of strange things that had happened to them or to people they knew. I noticed the really strange things were always those that had happened to someone else, while the ones that they had experienced in person sounded pretty flat.

I think almost everyone present must have had the same sequence of thoughts simultaneously. They ran: Yes, these experiences *are* dull and banal-sounding, and next—Ffellowes!.

And, of course, there he was. Leaning against the end bookcase in the alcove, just as if he'd been there all evening, and none of us, as usual, had even seen him come in! God knows how long he had been there, or how much he had heard. He was smoking a long thin cigar, very pale in color, and sipping brandy, which he took, incidently, in a tumbler.

We introduced him to Simmons, who had never met the brigadier before, and rather confusedly explained what we had been talking about, then more or less sat back, not quite panting, but pretty obvious.

Our English member smiled politely around at us. His pink face was bland, but the bright blue eyes were amused. Oh, he knew what we wanted, all right! If anyone in the room could lay claim to knowing the strange and the inexplicable, the man who had served the Empire all over the world, who had encountered more weird things in person than we had ever read about, was surely the man. And he knew we wanted a story. He teased us a little.

'I just had a nice brisk walk through the park. You chaps ought to get out more. You're all simply getting fat, sitting around here.'

I ask you! A nice brisk walk, at 38 F, through Central Park at eleven at night! That was Ffellowes, all right. If a gang of muggers jumped him he probably became invisible! Yet none of us doubted he had come that way.

He turned to look at Simmons for a moment, in a reflective way, and I rang a bell for a waiter to bring us a fresh round. I had learned the signs by now.

'You postulate, Mr.—er—ah, Simmons,' he was saying when I looked back, 'that we are subconsciously aware of older things, or past, well, unpleasantnesses, which once had power, and might still, under certain circumstances? May I ask if those are in any way your own beliefs or are simply put forward as the basis of a discussion?'

Simmons kind of drew back a little. 'It is a theory, I believe, that some people hold: that some places, and some persons even, are influenced by the ancient past, and that certain things can allegedly be summoned by the right people, in the right place, and even at the right time. Personally, I have no views on the matter.' His face turned a little pink. 'I should say,' he added, 'no views that I care to give at the present time or verbally.' He retired into his glass of Madeira, leaving us a little puzzled.

'I see,' said Ffellowes, and I had the idea he *did* see, though what it was he saw, I was damned if I knew.

A waiter had drawn up another chair, and the brigadier sat down and took a sip of his brandy. The room was suddenly very quiet.

'Many years ago,' came the clipped English tones, 'I had a friend who was Cornish. I don't mean he lived in Cornwall; I mean rather that he *was* Cornwall. His family, and, yes, he had a title, had lived there since time immemorial. They owned a ruined castle, and I mean a really frightful ruin, all tumbled stones, and also a delightful manor house, called Avalon House. Goodness knows how old the castle was, but the house was 18th century, a lovely thing of aged brick, surrounded by wild gardens and overlooking the Atlantic. It could be most windswept but was very wonderful even in winter. There were great tangled hedges, which had been planted strategically, to keep off the worst of the wind, you know, but it still could howl about the eaves in a full gale. The family were not of great wealth, but not poor either. Occasional judicious marriages with nabob's daughters and city merchants, I expect. A very normal county custom and a very normal county family, of no particular note, with a fat paragraph in Debrett's Peerage.

'We'll call my friend the Earl of Penruddock, which sounds right and was neither his name nor his title. He and I had known each other since childhood, having gone to what we call a 'little school' together, what you fellows call a grade school, I think. We were not the closest of chums, but rang each other up at times when one or another was in London, for a lunch or a drink. He was quite a normal specimen of his class, had served in the Grenadier Guards before succeeding to the title. He hunted with the Quorn and grew prize roses. When he married, I was an usher, and his wife was equally suitable, a distant cousin with some money of her own, a jolly girl, who loved the country as he did.

'I was startled one day, therefore, to get a wire from James (that was his real given name) asking me down in a curiously urgent way, down for a visit to Avalon House. There was a sort of appeal in the wire, you know, something such as "your advice most necessary" and "would be extremely grateful if you could see your way," and so on. All very peculiar from one of the most composed men I ever knew. I was doing odd jobs for the War Office already, and I found out James knew this, through what might be called the 'old boy's circuit." Still, I couldn't imagine what had made him think of me in particular.

I arranged a leave, ten days or so, with my chief, wired James to have me met and set off by train. It was late April, and as I changed to the small local train, a sort of Rowland Emmett affair with a staff all ninety in appearance, the countryside was really lovely. We went through a number of sleepy little towns and green valleys, until in late afternoon the creaky old car attendant warned me that Tolferry was next.

'James was there to meet me and I was shocked at his appearance. He was a big blond chap, like me in his late twenties, with a Guards mustache and normally a genial grin. Now, though, he looked both pale and harassed, as if some overpowering worry, some strain of overwhelming proportions were eating at his vitals. He tried to smile as he seized my bags, but it was a poor effort. Yet there was nothing in the least false about his relief at seeing me.

' "My dear man!" he said. "This is really awfully good of you. I'm at my wit's end. I had heard . . ." and here he paused in some confusion, "not to put too fine a point of it, that, well—hm—you sometimes do very strange things for your department. Not that you ever say anything but . . ." By this time we were in the car, and I quietly told him that he was not under suspicion of betraying official secrets.' Ffellowes paused and sighed. 'This was long before types like Philby had appeared, thank God. One's friends were still trustworthy.

'"I came to pick you up myself so we could talk privately," he went on. "I think I'm about to go mad at times, Donald, and you know what a slow-and-solid I've always been. I'm afraid I'll be up for commitment if anyone finds out what's going on down here, and, damnit, I'm a J.P."'

'I almost laughed, since madness may as well affect justices as any one else, but it was obvious that James had no humor left in him. In fact, to my not-untrained eye, he appeared on the verge of hysteria. So, I simply tried to soothe him as we slowly drove along the cliff road in his lumbering Diamler. And as the grey Atlantic foamed about the cliffs far below, the gist of his story began to emerge.

'"It all began with Lionel." That was how he started. And I was surprised. For I had not known that his younger (and only) brother, Lord Lionel Penruddock, was even in England. And yet Lionel Penruddock had a way of making his presence known. Nor was he one to hide his light under a bushel.

'Lionel Penruddock, at this juncture, was one of the most brilliant and also most controversial members of the younger school of archaeology. He was also, in the opinion of many, a complete swine. He used women as if they were cattle, and at least one girl was known to have committed suicide over him. As a young man, he was asked to leave Italy, at roughly the same time as Aleister Crowley and his Coven, and for the same reasons, or worse. He could now no longer dig in Egypt; even the easy-going Egyptians having had enough of his treatment of native labor, which had culminated in the deaths of three experienced men whom he had run afoul of, or the reverse. The verdict was 'loss of life due to a sandstorm,' but no one believed it. There was much more which I will not go into, and not all of it was this personal. The Foreign Office, as we knew, was beginning to take an interest in Lord Lionel, who had many strange and quite un-archaeological friends in many countries, including both Russia and Germany.

'When all this has been said, it has to be added that he was also a master of his chosen profession. He was that rare thing, a truly, all-round expert. One year he was astonishing the world with the work he did at Gohklat, and its amazing revelations of the Sarmatian Migrations. The next, he discovered the Codex Panamensis, extending the Old Empire Maya hundreds of miles beyond their previously known southern boundaries. And his fantastic recovery of a Gokstad type of Viking ship from the Namib Desert of Southwest Africa made even his most bitter professional rivals admit that he had genius.

'I had thought him to be in the Far East, but he was not. And as we drove, my poor friend attempted to tell me why his brother's appearance had so upset him and his household.

' "He simply popped up here, Donald, about a month ago. Had a couple of chaps, very rum ones, too, with him and asked if he could use the cliff cottage. Well, Isobel can't stand him, you know, and if he wanted to stay, this way he was at least out of the house. I've never got on with him, and he makes it plain he thinks, and always has, that I'm a complete ass. But, well, he *is* my only brother and he's never asked me for anything before. He's got his own money, you know, and lots of it. Mother left him a packet and he is no fool at business. So, the long and the short of it is. . . ."

'The long and the short of it was, of course, that James, good fellow that *he* was, had told his brother to use the cliff cottage as long as he liked, assuming not unnaturally that Lord Lionel sought no more than a quiet vacation. This building was a comfortable house made of stone and perched on the edge of the cliffs not far from the ruined castle of the ancestral Penruddocks. They did not use it, and it was usually to let, often to artists of some means. It was a mile from Avalon House, and that was a million miles too close for my friend's wife. Lionel's wedding present (he did not attend at St. Margarets, Westminster, needless to say) to James and Isobel had been a Tantric image of such startling and revolting obscenity that James, noting it to be covered with jewels of undoubted worth, instantly sent it under seal to the British Museum, where no doubt it still reposes in some obscure vault. It certainly could never be exhibited. That incident may give you all some small idea of Lionel, by the bye.

'Lionel, however, reappeared at the house during breakfast the following day, making his brother and sister-in-law extremely nervous, since they had expected (and hoped) to see nothing further of him during his stay. But he was perfectly polite in his sardonic way, and he could be charming when he chose. What he wanted, it seemed, was something quite simple. He had a little time on his hands, and noting and remembering the old ruined pile of stone, the aforesaid "castle," he had come to ask his brother for permission to dig around and about it. His two "assistants" would be all the help he needed. I'll have occasion to speak further of these two.

'James could see no reason why his brother should not pursue his excavations if he wished. The castle was even further from Avalon than the cottage, which may have played some part in his decision. And the place was not much visited. It had an ill-omened name throughout the countryside, and the children did not play near it, while adults mumbled about "pookahs" (the local "good folk") if the site was mentioned. It crouched on a black fang of rock which thrust out into the ocean far below and was really nothing but a gigantic jumble of stones, some of them, including the foundation, of absolutely enormous size and all laid without mortar. It had not been occupied, so far as anyone could tell, since early Plantagenet times, and some said it was far older. No roads led to it, and it had escaped the attention of any serious researchers up to that point.

'Lionel left with his brother's permission and did not reappear. He got his supplies sent in by truck, and one of the two assistants barrowed them over the hills on a cart to the cliff cottage. Lionel had a shooting brake, an early form of the American station wagon, but it was not much used, save for a rare trip to London once in a while.

'At this point, my friend stopped the car, or rather pulled off of the road to one side. His hands were actually shaking and frankly, I was just as happy he had them off the wheel. The road, as I have said, often ran very close to the cliff.

'One week after permission had been given to dig, the phenomena, for want of a better word, commenced. And they began, appropriately, at night.'

Ffellowes put his cigar out and rang the bell for another brandy. He stared at the books opposite him, but no one spoke, and the crackle of dying coals in the fireplace was quite audible. Then he went on.

'Now what I am going to tell you next is not my own information, but second-hand. Nor was it as clear and sorted out as you chaps will hear it. James was a fine fellow, but a good specimen of *Anglensus inarticulatis*. I had to keep making him stop and go back over things, and also to keep him from interrupting himself or simply mumbling. The fact was, he was so terribly embarrassed about the whole thing, even with me, and also so frightened (and ashamed of that) that he simply couldn't tell a coherent story. But what I heard finally was roughly this:

'On the night I mentioned, everyone had gone to bed early, as country folk tend to. Around two in the morning, James was awakened by a sound, or rather, two sounds. The first was the sound of a horn, a brassy, echoing bawl, not the clear note of a hunting horn. As he sat up in bed, the horn fell silent, and the night was broken by a hideous screaming, as if, as he put it, "a thousand pigs were being killed all at once!" Then, there was silence, except that all the dogs on the place, a half dozen setters, retrievers, and such, all started to howl in unison. These in turn fell silent, but a great wind began to sweep in from the Atlantic, and all the house shutters and doors rattled while slates were dislodged from the roof. This sudden gale lasted about fifteen minutes and then died away as suddenly as it had started.

'That was the first incident. Of course the whole household was roused at this one, maids scurrying about and squawking, grooms rushing about, gardeners in an uproar, lights blazing and general confusion. James took over with a few Guards bellows and managed to restore something like order, but it wasn't easy. Those screams particularly, had been appalling. Isobel got the house staff in shape finally, while James led a force of the younger men out with lights and shotguns to see what they could find.

'They found nothing, I may say, either then or the next day, nothing at all. And when they got to the cliff cottage, Lionel appeared and, on being questioned, denied hearing a sound. James informed the police, and a local bobby came out, poked about and went away, managing to convey without words that the gentry should have better things to do than bother the police with utter nonsense.

'For three days nothing further occurred. That is, nothing tangible. Yet, there was a feeling of oppression in the atmosphere, very odd in March, to be sure. The servants were nervous, and one London maid gave notice and left at once. On the third night, James was roused from an uneasy sleep by more screams, but this time plainly human and emanating from his own house, from the servants' wing in fact. Rushing to investigate, he found the butler trying to control the cook and the maids, one of whom had fainted while the others were simply hysterical. When the unconscious one was revived and the others quietened, the girl told the following story:

'She had been sewing in her bedroom when she happened to look at her window, which incidently was shut. Pressed against the glass was a face, and she almost fainted again attempting to describe it. It was very pale, she said, and the eyes were black and burning.

The hair was long and black also, and so were the beard and mustache. A great weal or scar ran across the forehead. She had screamed and her friends had run in from their adjoining rooms. The first in had seen movement at the window also, though no more than that, just as the room's occupant had fainted. Now even as they all stood in the girl's room, they were all suddenly aware that the wind had risen again from out of the west and was roaring at full blast about the house. And James felt a strange tingling of his skin, as if, he put it, he were somehow in the center of an electric discharge. He did then not ask if the others felt anything, not wishing to add to the panic, but he did ask the butler alone the following day, and the man, an old soldier, said that he at least had not noticed it.

'The wind dropped again and they all got back to bed, all the servants now sleeping two to a room.' Ffellowes smiled at us as he continued.

'What I have omitted from my account is that the servant in question, the maid, lived on the *third* floor. When James examined the room both from the inside and from the lawn on the following morning, he grew very upset indeed. The house, you see, was covered with an immense and hoary canopy of ivy, and it was clear that this had been disturbed in more than one place. Some of the stems of this plant were over two inches thick, you know. Whatever the girl had seen, and she was a local lass of an unimaginative nature, it was clearly material.

'My friend and his wife decided to face the matter in the open. They called in all the staff, from outside as well as the house people, and told them they could leave, that they were not expected to face whatever was going on, and that the Penruddocks would think none the less of them if they did, though they themselves would stay. It was their home and their responsibility. And here, I may say, James interjected something that interested me greatly. "I felt somehow, Donald, that whatever happened, I *had* to stay, was *compelled* to stay, what?" he told me.

'Well, he and his wife had a surprise coming, and a very pleasant one. The staff had had its own conference earlier, and they were *not* leaving, not even the girl who had fainted. They were all Cornish men and women, and the Penruddocks were *their* responsibility, as well as the other way, you see? Remember the loyalty of Cornwall to Charles the First when all else was lost? Under the sometimes stolid Saxon exterior, there burns often the ancient stubborness of the Celt.

'This display of loyalty heartened Isobel and James immensely, and Isobel even wept. Then they all got down to business. No one, when asked, thought that calling the police again would serve any purpose save to embarrass all concerned. On this they were all agreed. James issued all the shotguns and sporting rifles that he owned, and most of the men were veterans of the Great War. They arranged watches and made sure all doors and windows were locked after dark. Then they waited.

'James did one further thing. He went to call on Lord Lionel. He found him in the yard of the cliff cottage, issuing some instructions to one of his assistants, a short dark man with a most unpleasant face. As it happened, he approached without either of them seeing him at first and heard Lionel addressing the other in a foreign language, or rather, he thought, a very local one. Few in those days spoke Cornish, the original tongue of the land, which like Gaelic and Erse, was even then dying out, leaving only Welsh as the surviving British Celtic. But my friend had once had an old nanny who spoke it, and he thought he recognized it, though, as he put it to me, "It didn't sound quite right, but foreign somehow."

'When Lionel saw his brother, he seemed irritated and waved his helper away. "What now, noble Earl?" he said in an unpleasant manner, "more of your bogles frightening the tweenies?"

'James kept his temper and simply told his brother what had happened and asked him to keep his eyes open. The response was a jeering laugh. "Good God, James, I think you've all gone round the bend up there. Faces at the window! I should think you would keep this to yourselves. Well, I'll say nothing. I don't want to be known as the brother of a lunatic, infected by the hysterics of a still-room slut. But don't expect me to join your witch hunts. I have better things to do." And with that he had stalked into the cottage. This was the help he offered his only brother, who had never done him anything but kindness.

'James had expected little else. Lionel had been as hateful and unfriendly as a child as he was as a man. So this display was nothing new. But, as he told me about it, a thought began to stir in my own mind. All of this peculiar business had started when Lord Lionel appeared. Was there a direct connection?

'My friend went on with his tale, less disjointed now and easier to follow as he became somewhat more relaxed. It appeared that he and his household were living under siege, in a way, and a strange siege it was. The apparition of the face had not reappeared, but other things had. For one there was the smell.

'It had first been noticed in the cellars, by the butler, who was looking through the wine bins. It was a rank stench, which seemed to seep through the floor; and although they had bolted the cellar doors and stuffed rags around the cracks, it still got into the house, though far more faintly or the place would have been unlivable entirely. I smelled it myself later on, and I can assure you it was awful, a reek of graveyard mold, mixed with other, less describable things. Further, it seemed to ebb and flow, being weak at times and billowing up at others.

'The house had always kept a few sheep in a paddock, and also a small herd of dairy cows. One night, two sheep and a cow were found slaughtered, and not simply slaughtered but frightfully mangled, as if by a pack of wolves. No one had heard a sound, but the wind had been going through one of its sudden western gales, and it would have taken an artillery discharge to penetrate that. Indeed, this strange new wind, which always blew from the west when it came, was another mystery. It came at the same time or sometimes a bit beyond one of the other outrageous happenings, as if they summoned it; and though it did no direct harm, the Avalon folk were learning to dread its coming, for it always seemed to presage some appalling happening, or at least the imminent discovery of one.

'James had pulled the car back onto the road and we again resumed our slow way over the hills and gulleys. As he drove, he continued the sequence of events at what had once been the happiest of homes.

'"Thank God, Isobel and I have no kids yet,' he went on. "We were sorry before, but, by the Eternal, we're not now. They'd have gone off their chumps at half of what we've been through in the past fortnight." And this remark also set me thinking, though in a quite other direction to his.

'Now we were winding up the long drive to Avalon House, leaving the sea cliffs at our backs. As we pulled up to the entry, we saw two figures on the stairs. One was Isobel, whom I knew and loved, but with her face pallid and haunted-looking, and lines no woman her age should have possessed around her eyes and mouth. She seemed particularly glad to see us both.

'There was no welcome in the eyes of the other figure, and I knew who he was long before James made the introduction. I had seen Lord Lionel's picture on many occasions, but I should have known him anywhere, I think.

'He was middle-sized, far below his brother's blond bulk in height, and as dark and pale as James was fair and ruddy. He was by no means ugly, his long black hair framing a white clean-shaved face of considerable good looks. Nor was he a weakling, for his shoulders were immense for his stature, and his grip was that of an athlete. Yet I disliked him on sight, the instant I saw the cold jet eyes, and should have done so even had I not known of his past record.

'His voice was rather high and strident as he turned to speak to his brother. "You'll have to call off those peasants of yours, James," he said in an arrogant way. "Damned if I can afford to have these taradiddles of yours mucking up a site I am working on. That fool of a gardener was staring at my men the other day for an hour while they worked. They are highly trained and I can't afford to have them upset, d'you hear!'

'His tone was quite insufferable, and his brother flushed to the eyebrows. I was expecting trouble right then and there, but James controlled himself admirably. I expect he had had plenty of practice in his youth.

'"I shall see no one bothers you," he answered coldly. "You know why the men are looking about even though you profess to believe none of it. Since you have neither help nor advice to offer, I suggest that you, in turn, stay out of *my* hair!'

'It was a funny little scene, or rather odd. Lionel actually took a step backward, and Isobel looked at her husband in puzzlement. I don't think either of them had expected the icy tone or the rebuke from my gentle friend. I must say it took me by surprise as well.

'Lionel left abruptly and we went into the house. The butler, Traheal, was an old acquaintance of mine from the Penruddock townhouse, and he took me up to my room. "His Lordship told me why he had asked you, Captain, if I may be so bold," he said. "We badly need some help, sir." His voice dropped as he went on. "The Powers of Darkness, sir, that's what we're facing. In my opinion, we need a priest. If this goes on we'll all have to leave."

'He had been a sergeant on the Western Front and was no chicken. I bathed and got ready for dinner in a state of some perturbation.

'Dinner passed quietly, but conversation was strained, and there were long periods of silence as each of us fell into our own thoughts. We went early to bed.

'I awoke suddenly about three a.m. with a sense that something was about to happen. On impulse, I moved to the window and looked out. A red half-moon was partly hid by racing clouds, and the wind seemed to be rising. The stunted trees down toward the cliff face were bending toward the house. For some reason I felt that something was racing to the land from far, far out on the deeps.

'Then there came a sound. It seemed to come from a long way

away, but it was very loud. It did have a direction, which seemed to me to be down the coast to my left. I was on the second floor, in a room facing the front drive and hence the sea. As to the sound, it was really several sounds, a medley, so to say. Overriding the rest were what sounded like the blaring of several immense trumpets, echoing and challenging, a brazen uproar. Under this ran a strange susurration of what sounded like shouting, or perhaps screams, with an occasional ringing noise, as of metal being struck. All this ran perhaps twenty seconds and then was cut off suddenly. There was a pause and I could hear the west wind gathering strength.

'Across that in turn broke out the horrible squealing cry, or cries, which James had described to me in the car as the sound of pigs being killed. But in me they produced a different reaction. I felt I was listening to something with a note of triumph, as if something foul beyond endurance, and not only foul but alien, was rejoicing and reveling in victory. It made my flesh creep, and my hands went white as I pressed the window ledge.

'This, too, was suddenly cut off, and now the wind was making all the noise needed, tearing and raging in from the ocean and buffeting the house with great fury. The clouds were blasted away from the moon, and far out at sea I could see the white spume of great waves.

'On impulse, I opened the window, which, like all in the house, had been both shut and bolted. The wind tore into the room, making the heavy drapes stand out, and actually pushed me back a bit! As it did so, I had the most extraordinary sensation. I smelt apple blossoms! And not just smelt them, I felt drenched in the scent, delicious and exhilarating. Now early April may produce this scent in southern England, but hardly at night on a sea cliff in the midst of a gale! Time seemed to stand still as I inhaled the delicious odor, and I could hear nothing over the roar of the great winds.

'Then, that too was gone, after some few minutes, perhaps ten. The wind dropped to a gentle breeze, the clouds gathered, and a light rain began to fall. I was suddenly conscious that my room door was open, that I was wearing silk pajamas and was getting awfully cold. I slammed the window shut and turned to find James standing in the doorway.

'He was wearing a dressing gown and slippers over his night clothes. And he was staring at the window and the night sky over my shoulder, a strange look of pain on his face. His face had lost any trace of its normal amiability and looked hard and set. He spoke softly, as if to himself.

'"Too late, too late!" he said. "Ever the cycle repeats and there is no escape." His voice dropped and he said two more words I could hardly catch at all. One sounded like "curse" while the other might have been "migraine" or something that sounded like it.

'Then his face cleared and it was as if he had seen me for the first time. "Well, Donald," he said in his normal tones, "what do you think of a month of things on that nature? A pretty noise to have around one's home, eh, quite apart from all else. D'you wonder I fear for Isobel's sanity?"

'"Why don't you leave?" I said on impulse. "Or at least, send her away while you and I try to puzzle this out."

'"Because she won't go." His voice was inexpressibly tired. "Not unless I go and I *can't!* I must stay and face this thing down and I don't know why. I just know I *must.* My God, what have we done to be afflicted with this?"

'I did not refer to the earlier words he had spoken, then or later. I was sure, you see, that he had no memory of them and would have been further upset by the conviction that his mind was going, and this was the last thing I wanted. We were going to need clear heads before this business was over, of that I was sure. But the words had started a train of thought in my mind, though I hardly dared voice my thoughts, even to myself. They were too monstrous and incredible.

'The next morning I spent some time in the library, a vast old place in which my host and hostess seldom entered, neither being bookworms. It had many rare volumes, collected by ancestral Penruddocks no doubt, but modern things, too, and I had no trouble finding the reference I sought. I still could not quite face what I was thinking, for if I was right, a tragedy as old as time was building up before my very eyes, and I was powerless to interfere.

'The morning passed quietly enough. None of us referred to the previous night, by common and unspoken agreement, but the faces of all of us were haggard and full of strain. The servants were very quiet, but their faces were set and grim. Their's was loyalty indeed. I honor them.

'After lunch I asked James if he thought Lionel would mind if I strolled down to look at his site. The castle lay a mile or so south on the coast, and for reasons of my own I wished very much to see it, as well as to find out exactly how it could be reached in the most expeditious manner.

'"Can't think why he should object," said my host. "But you've seen what he can be like, damn him. He's always been like that, you know. A word and blow, that's Lionel since birth. No one but

mother could stick him at all, and he even frightened her at times.''
His face hardened in thought.

' ''I can't think why you shouldn't be allowed to look at his work.
It's my own castle, when all's said and done, not his. Go ahead.
He'll hardly be likely to treat you as he does the servants, after all.
But you can be prepared for some piece of rudeness, all the same. I
wish to goodness he'd take it into his head to go away! I don't think
he has a friend in this country, even among his fellow pot hunters.'

'Back in my room I put on heavy shoes, for the track to the castle
was a rough one, I had been warned. I also borrowed a stout stick,
of blackthorn, from the cane holder downstairs, and thus equipped,
I set out.

'It was a still afternoon and fog lay in the hollows. I had excellent
directions and a pocket compass as well, for there were bogs and
ghylls as well as the sea cliffs, of course. But I swung somewhat
inland. I did not want to be observed as I went from the cliff
cottage, and the road ran past the drive to Avalon and stopped
there. I saw the roof of the cottage as well before I got to it and was
able to avoid it by going even further east until I was well past. The
going was not bad, and though I saw no bogs close by, I caught
glimpses of livid green in the distance, but way off my line of
march. Now I angled back toward the coast, and after another half
mile or so, I saw the castle in front of me. I had studied pictures of
the thing in the house, but the reality was something else.

'A great point of dark rock jutted out over the sea, perhaps a
hundred yards square. In the center of this, on a flat area, lay a huge
pile of tumbled blocks, as black or blacker than the weathered cliff
on which they rested. The foundation layers were intact, to double
the height of a man, but above that, all was destroyed. The huge
blocks of stone looked as if some giant had reached down and
crushed the upper courses into ruin, like jackstraws turned over by
a child. I do not think modern explosives could have done a more
thorough job, even today. I had no idea that engines of destruction
had reached such a level in medieval times, or even earlier, if some
of the rumors about this place were correct.

'The area looked truly desolate, for I could see none of the white
streaks that would indicate that sea birds nested there. But as I
worked my way closer, down a bracken-covered slope, I began to
feel uncomfortable. There was an atmosphere I did not like about
this pile of time-worn rock. I could see why the locals disliked the
place. I felt an air of something menacing, as if somewhere around
me something old and strange were brooding over its wrongs, with
silent hate emanating from every fiber of its being. I raised my

glance and saw the smoke of a steamer far out on the wave-tossed horizon. Around the cliff foot, hundreds of feet below, the sea beat endlessly with a constant roar. But this view of normal things did not dispel the feelings that had been aroused by the pile of shattered stones before me. Almost, they seemed to increase them, by making the place itself even more of an intruder, something which had no habitation here in the normal world.

'I was not very close to the foundation, no more than a few feet, and suddenly, out of a hole I had not even seen in the rocks, a little to my right, a man's head popped out, making me start back. We stared at each other for a second in silence, and then the man whisked down into the cavity from which he had emerged so silently. Now, I could hear movement below, and the dark visage of the person whom I sought appeared. Lord Lionel climbed out easily, and I now noticed the very tip of a ladder protruding from the black hole behind him. Two other men followed him, and the three stood watching me attentively for a moment.

'Lord Lionel was the first to break the chilly atmosphere, though he did not sound particularly friendly.

'"Ffellowes, eh? Come to look over the dig? Didn't know you chaps at the War Office ever got outdoors these days, let alone took an interest in archaeology."

'Now this was a bad mistake, and if I were right in my gathering suspicion, the first man had made. That I was attached to the War Office and not doing regular duty in my own branch of service was not all that well-known a fact. James knew it because he had asked very high up indeed. That much I had checked. But this meant that Lord Lionel had also been asking questions about me. I let none of this show in my face but looked casually about, while very conscious of his intent gaze. And I managed to get my first good look at his two helpers. They were interesting, too.

'They might have been brothers and perhaps were. Both were short massive men, very swarthy, unshaven and dirty-looking in soiled work clothes. They had high cheekbones and narrow black eyes, eyes in which I read contempt and dislike as they watched me impassively.

'Lionel must have noticed something, since he suddenly spoke harshly to them in a language I had never before heard, a tongue both lilting and harsh at the same time. I suppose it might have been Cornish, as James thought, but these two looked like nothing I had ever seen in Cornwall, or anywhere in the British Isles, for that matter.

'Both men ducked back down the ladder, and as they vanished

into the depths, something stirred in my memory. Men like these and piles of black stones somehow went together, as if belonging! Now, what was that memory?

' "Not much to see, I'm afraid, Ffellowes. I'm still trying to clear a lower passage. There have been a number of rock falls. It's a bad place and only for experts. Can't ask you down, I fear, since the risk is mine should you happen to be hurt." Under this show of concern lay an almost open sneer. I was not to be allowed down, whatever the pretext, that was plain.

' "Shouldn't dream of troubling you," I answered, keeping my face as blank as I could. "I'm sure you and these chaps of yours know how to work in safety. Never cared for scrambling about in holes, myself." I dared not be too much the silly ass, but I could hint at it. "What was that jabber you were giving them? Some Wog or Gyppo language?"

'His dark eyes narrowed as he studied me. I hoped I had not overdone the Pukka Sahib image. The wind soughed and wailed around us as he answered slowly.

' "Yes, it's an Arab dialect. My helpers were trained in the field by my own methods, in the Near East. This way they don't gossip. I don't like gossip, Ffellowes, or prying either." He took a step closer to me. "Now, my dear captain, I have work to do. I suggest you finish your Cook's tour elsewhere. Perhaps," he added, "you can go back and hold my brother's hand. He seems to need it, now that he's taken to believing in bogey men." The malice was naked and so was something else. James had told me that his brother held him in contempt. But this was not contempt that I saw, but pure hatred, a very different thing.

' "I say, that's a bit raw," I mumbled. "Still, if you have things to do, I'll push on." What I should have liked to do was push in his nasty face, or have a good stab at it. I had determined not to lose my control, and I turned away still mumbling inaudibly.

'I thought that was to be the end of the encounter, but I was wrong. I had underestimated the depths of Lord Lionel's anger. His temper, always evil under the surface, now flared up. I felt a heavy hand on my shoulder, and I was spun around to find him glaring at me from a foot away, his face bone-white with passion.

' "You can tell my brother to stay out of *my* hair!' he hissed at me, his voice actually shaking. "Tell him to stay away from here and keep his damned house pets out of my business, too, or, by heaven, I'll give him something to really moan about! Now, get out!"

'This was too much, even for my role of chartered idiot. I chopped his hand aside with the edge of mine, a blow that really hurt, and had the satisfaction of seeing him wince. "I think, sir," I said coldly, "that you have been in too many primitive places recently. You forget yourself. This *is* England, you know."

'I meant to infuriate him further, in the hope of learning more, but I was only partly successful. His face contorted in fresh rage, but suddenly changed. Over it instead, stole a most malignant and evil smile.

'"Yes," he said in quiet tones. "Now how could I have forgot that? We are in Merry Old England." And he began to *laugh!* Still chuckling, he stalked over to the gap in his ruin and lowered himself down, without giving me the benefit of another glance.

'I walked back toward the house over the main track, having no reason to conceal myself any longer. As I walked I tried to puzzle out all the mixed and convoluted things and impressions that swam about my mind. One of them was the realization that whatever tongue his lordship had used to his men, it was nothing out of the Near East. I knew something of those languages even as a young man, and the inflections were totally different. So, why had he lied? Because the real truth would have meant something, would have given some clue as to what he was doing? I concentrated. James thought the language to Cornish or something like that. It was not Gaelic or even Welsh. I did not speak either, but had heard both often enough. Could it be the soft Celtic of Ireland (though that was a rare speech even back then). No, the consonants were far too harsh and clipped, and those two stunted giants looked like no Sons of Erin in my experience. The answer lay elsewhere, and as I thought, the vision of those two and the great black stones came unbidden to my mind, and with the vision came the solution. There was *another* Gaelic, or rather Celtic tongue still in use in Europe! I saw in my mind the great menhirs and dolmens of Brittany, the stones of mist-shrouded Carnac, lost in antiquity, about which dark legends still circulated among the peasants. Those two were Bretons!

'Now why should the employment of Bretons be a secret? I racked my brain as I strode along past the cliff cottage, paying the place no heed, since I knew it to be empty. I think I later paid for this piece of egregrious stupidity, since I might possibly have had a very useful look around. But, meanwhile, I was turning over in my mind what I knew of Brittany, ancient and modern, which was damned little, actually. I knew, and don't ask me why, that they had a dismal separatist movement from France and even a "national anthem," whose name sounded like "Bro Goz Ma Zadou." This meant nothing. I surmised that it was the past of Brittany, the last

Celtic stronghold on the continent, that was important. And of that I knew little. No one seemed to know who had built Carnac. The whole peninsula had always been a hotbed of legends and folktales, even before medieval times. Among other things, King John, Richard the Lion Heart's most unpleasant brother, had murdered his nephew, Duke Arthur of Brittany, who had a better claim to the Plantagenet throne than he. And what else? Something was just out of reach in my mind! Legends, cults, Carnac, Prince Arthur (why that name?), Celtic mysticism, black stones, west winds, apples, all of this mishmash meant something, if only I could think of *what!*

'By this time, I was at the house and I hurried in to tell James what I had seen. We sat in the old drawing room, and I related my afternoon to both of them. Isobel, after pouring tea, told me that none of it, save for one thing, conveyed anything much to her.

'"You've seen what he's like, Donald," she said. "You have no idea, really, what poor James has had to put up with, even going back to childhood. Many of the stories are family secrets. No, James, I simply won't be silent any longer, not to Donald. Why was he asked here, if not to help?" James subsided into a chair, muttering "dirty linen" into his tea cup.

'"I think you are quite correct," she went on to me, "about this hatred, I mean. Yes, he has pretended to find James silly and stupid, but I have seen him look at James when he thought no one else was watching. He hates you, darling, and always has." She turned back to me, her tired face still glowing with love.

'"When they were still little, Donald, still in the nursery, Lionel tried to kill James. They are only two years apart, apart in age. He packed a fruit cake, or rather James' portion, with ground *glass!* I don't think he could have been eight years old!"

'My friend looked at me after she had spoken. "I'm afraid it's true, you know. Had a good old nanny, who didn't take to Lionel, and she saw him do it. Told dad, and we were sent off to separate schools. If it hadn't been for an open scandal and mother's weeping, I think it might have come out in the open. As it was, dad made him see some alienist or something: they were just coming in then. I've seen the medical reports. Chap said he could do nothing with Lionel, nothing at all, and would be afraid to try. Fact is, I've never felt quite safe while he was nearby. Sounds silly, but Isobel and I have no kids, which makes him heir. Rotten thing to suspect your own brother, but he's been such an all-round bloody piece of work. . . . " His voice trailed off.

'"That's the oldest of all crimes," I said in a tight voice, "murder for a throne or title. If you get away with it, it's called *rebellion.* One thing is clear to me, and that is that all your present troubles have started since your brother came on the scene. To my knowledge, and I'd like this confirmed, there has never been any trouble of any even vaguely supernatural nature in this house, or around it, until recently?"

'Isobel looked at James. After all, it was *his* house. He shook his head, finally. "No," he said, "I can think of nothing. I expect I would have heard, too. I used to be awfully put down about it as a kid at school, come to think of it. All the others had places with Anne Boleyn or someone walking, and Cavaliers on the battlements. When they asked me, I had nothing to tell them, not even a monk or headless serf, or whatever. No, Donald, there has never been anything of the kind here."

'I could only take refuge in silence. Poor devil, if my slowly coalescing ideas were correct, he was about to get an overabundance of all the things he had treated so lightly!

'We dined early. There was little conversation, and that was of a nature which omitted any discussion of what we were awaiting. Traheal came up the stairs with me, and I knew that, on his part, it was no accident. "Well, sir," he said hoarsely, "have you got some idea now of what we are going through?"

'I stared at him, not out of any class consciousness, I assure you, but simply because my thoughts were elsewhere. Then, I realized that a good man was asking for information.

'"Yes," I answered bluntly. "I think the whole thing centers around his lordship's brother. What do you think?"

'The blaze of anger on his face surprised me, though it should not have done so had I thought. After all, Lord Lionel had grown up in these parts.

'"I knew it," he said. "Just what I've been telling the rest of them. There's black evil, and he's the man to bring it. Sir, when he was even a little child, he was *wrong*. We all knew this! The Earl, God bless him, never could see what his brother was like . . . but we could! My father was of the opinion that he was mad! All the servants used to watch him when he was young, so that he was never unobserved. We all felt that he would do his lordship an evil. And he tried, sir." He looked at me in a questioning way, as if debating what else he could tell me.

'"I know about the ground glass," I said in answer to his look. "I shall do my utmost to protect the Earl and Countess, yes, and you all as well. But I may need help. If I am right, there is a most ancient malignancy gathering around this house, yes, and one which seems to be gaining strength." Looking back from this distant point in time, it seems the maddest conversation ever held between a guest at an English country house and its dignified butler! But, you know, after what we had seen it seemed quite normal, in the context.

'I continued: "By the way, Traheal, did you know the two men Lord Lionel employs were Bretons? I am told that their language is very close to the original Cornish. And I think Lord Lionel doesn't want this known. Do you make anything of that?"

'He paused in the act of opening my door, his face thoughtful. "We used, back in the old smuggling days, sir, to have a lot to do with the Bretons. Long before my time of course, but I've heard many tales from the older folk. There was a lot of intermarriage among the sailors, back in Napoleon's day and earlier, my granny used to say. Most of us have some Breton blood in us, if you can believe the stories. And they do say, too, that a Cornishman could understand them, and vice versa, those of us who used the old talk, mind you. But there's none of them left now that speaks it any longer." He paused, still thinking, or rather, trying to recall some thought. "I don't know, Captain, that we have much in common any longer. This is King Arthur's land, you know, sir, and I do seem to remember somewhere that the Bretons lay some claim to him, too, some old stories about him living there or something. Maybe that's how the languages got to be the same? They tell us now, Captain, that there was no such King and that the whole thing was a made-up tale of some old writer." He laughed, his rosy countryman's face clearing. "You'll never get a Cornish man or woman to believe that, now. Why, to us the King over there in London, and a fine man he is, meaning no disrespect, I assure you, he's a new chum compared to *our* king." His face sobered as he turned to go back downstairs. "Those two rogues may be Bretons, though I'd hate to claim kinship to such ill-looking scoundrels. But I'll leave you with this, Captain. If those two are Lord Lionel's men, then they're also black evil. None but the worst would willingly do *his* bidding!"

'He left me with a good deal more than he thought to mull over. A missing piece had dropped onto my puzzle table, though one I could not yet fully assess. The Pendragon! The great king of legend, and the savior of what was last and best in Celtic Britain! Arthur, the most towering shape in the mist of legend, the greatest of folk heroes in Western Europe! Was he a last Roman, as some have postulated, an inspired commander of heavy cavalry? One theory I had read made him *Dux Brittanorum*, the British war leader left behind by the last Roman garrison to save what vestige of civilization he could from the barbarism reaching out of the north and west. Another school thought him to be *Comes Littorae Saxoni*, the Count of the Saxon Shore, and thus the guardian of the east coast against the migrating hordes from the dark German forests, pagans and sacrifices to the blood-stained idols of the vast Hercynian forest.

'All accounts agree on a few points, though many of them have become cause for laughter in our present state of so-called enlightenment. Arthur was a Christian, and he fought the sorcery of his enemies with spiritual powers of his own. He was aided by at least one white wizard, usually called Merlin, but sometimes Blaize, or other names. Discounting the Round Table, Galahad, the Sword in the Stone, and other such trimmings, one was left with a series of desperate battles, against diverse foes, such as that of Mount Badon, and final defeat at the hands of. . . . !

'I opened my window and leaned against the shutter, staring out into the swirling mist. Could this be the solution to my riddle? If it was, Avalon House was a nexus, a focal point for an historic crime, a crime of the immemorial and incredibly antique past. Was it now in the process of re-creation? What was Lord Lionel Penruddock, a man of the foulest antecedents, with a limitless potential for evil, doing in that slag heap without a name out there on the cliff? What was he *digging* for?

'I stared out into the dark, my eyes trying to pierce the wraiths of mist and fog, down to the nameless castle on the rock promontory of that ocean-bound crag. The night was silent, save for the distant murmur of the Atlantic surges against the Cornish shore. Yet I felt, somehow, that far to the west something was stirring, out beyond human sight or the reach of human kind at all. I looked absently at my watch. It was eleven thirty. More time had gone on than I had realized, as I had stood there trying to see light where there was none to see, trying to read sense into a matter so strange that a mention of it in most places would have been grounds for accusations of insanity! It was well for us that no one at Avalon House had returned a second time for help from the police! This battle, for that was how I saw it, had to be fought by us alone, and our antagonist was a man with strange weapons at his command. If I were right, they might be weapons against which we would find ourselves powerless.

'I was about to close and bar the windows when I heard the sound in the night. Far off, to the south, I felt sure, echoing through the mist, came the high, shrill whinnying of a horse. Now, all the horses, the some half-dozen there were, belonging to the estate, were stabled and shut in tight at sundown. So too, with the sheep and cattle. And nothing lay to the south but miles of empty cliff and moor, with no habitations or roads. Save for the cliff cottage.

'And the castle, if that were truly ever a habitation. And anything that issued from that gloomy pile meant this house and all in it no good. Whatever was coming, and I knew in my bones that it *was* coming, was advancing from there. I knew this also, just as I knew that midnight was fast approaching.

'Then I heard it again, a high-pitched neighing, which got all through my bones, nearer that last time and coming fast. That nickering cry was *wrong* in some way I could not define. No normal horse would have made such a sound, nor indeed, could have done so.

'At the same time the mist began to swirl and part. It was a cloudy night, and the stars and moon were still hidden. But the ground mist was being shredded, and I heard, far off, the first faint moan of a wind, off in the uttermost west. And almost, so faint I could hardly catch the tremor of a scent in my nostrils, I seemed to smell the delicate perfume of apples. It seemed to give me hope, though why I did not know, and it also spurred me to action.

'I hurled myself out the door and raced down the corridor toward James' and Isobel's bedroom. They had to be roused at once.

'The door was opening as I arrived, and James stood there, fully clothed, with his wife behind him. Like myself, they had not undressed, but on his feet he now wore boots, instead of the evening slippers he had worn with his dinner clothes.

'Her face was pale and frightened, though she was striving hard to conceal it. But his? The quiet, placid face of the country squire that I knew was utterly gone. He was a big man, and suddenly a most formidable one as well. His face was set like flint, in a brooding but awesome expression, one I had never seen before and I expect no one else had either. He looked steady as a rock and just as hard to move, but it was more than that. Above all, the impression was regal, in the old sense of the word, that of a great ruler and master of men, one who controlled destiny and was never its plaything.

'And as I stared transfixed at this new and mighty visage, there came from outside in the night the sound of the rising wind and over it the neighing of whatever it was out there masquerading as a horse!

'James turned and gently, without a word, pushed his wife back into the room. I caught one glimpse of her white face before the door closed. Then he turned back to me and stared hard at me for a second, as if in assessment.

'"He has loosed the Hunter upon us," he said. "Do you dare face him, and perhaps worse?" His voice was as strange as his expression had been to me, being deep and sonorous, with each word carefully chosen, as if he were speaking a language which was somehow not his, but a recently acquired tongue.

'I could only nod, for somehow speech seemed out of place, or else my tongue simply would not function in my dry mouth.

'He seemed to understand and laid on hand on my shoulder. "Then come," he said, "Follow and ask no questions for there is no longer time: We must go and face this thing at its lair. What has been summoned must be laid to rest or it will come again and that must not be."

'In silence, I followed him down the dark stairs and into the great silent hall. The clouds had parted outside, and through a mullioned window came just enough fitful moonlight to show us the way. The moaning of the wind had risen once more to gale force, but over it we could hear the neighing bray of whatever ranged the night, and ever and anon the sound of its hooves, beating a sinister tattoo as they galloped to and fro in the dark and storm.

'A patch of moonlight rested on one wall, and one could see the glimmer as it lighted on the various ancestral weapons which hung there. They ranged from trophies of foreign wars in the East, to mementos of Cavalier and Roundhead, and even older things, Lochaber axes, Scottish broadswords and claymores, with naval cutlasses of various times interwoven in the pattern.

'James moved to the wall and studied it for a moment, then reached up and unhooked a great Scottish broadsword, a thing most men would have needed two hands to swing, though he held it lightly enough in one.

'He turned to me, his face as grave as before and said, very simply, "Choose."

'As I hesitated, he added in the same slow, stately way, "We must use fire or steel. The newer things will not help against that which walks the night. The servants and the woman sleep. They cannot face what we must. Choose!'

'This last was in a tone I could not resist. Nor did the mention of his beloved wife as "the woman" rouse me to rebellion. Someone else had taken over command, and my business was to obey.

'I stepped over and peered up at the great wall. My hand went out to a blade as if led, and d'you know, the thing I had grasped almost seemed to leap into my hand. The minute I felt the hilt, I knew what I had, for I had handled the weapon in admiration a day or so earlier. It was a long, straight cut-and-thrust, with a basket hilt, made for some remote Elizabethan ancestor by the great Andrea Ferrara himself. I had been handy enough with the saber at Woolwich and later at Oxford. I could have chosen nothing better.

'"A good choice," rang out the deep voice at my side. "A noble sword indeed, though lighter than is my use to wield. Now, let us on to the contest. We face the first challenge and perhaps not the lightest!"

'Grasping the great weapon in his right hand, he strode down the hall and, freeing the bolts, flung open the great oak doors to the storm of wind and to whatever it was I knew waited for us in the night. Out beyond the portico we went, with me three paces behind.

'Facing the darkness, he called above the storm in a voice like roll-thunder. "Come and do battle, Hunter! You have no place here now! You and your kind were banished to the hills and under them, far back in the lost ages. You have no power over men of trust. I speak for Christ and defy you and all your pack. No longer should you roam the land and bring fear to the lost and the helpless in the dark! Come out, I command, on that horse I overthrew once and shall again!"

'And over the storm and the moaning winds, came an answer! Out of the night came a wild cry, a long rising sound, which pierced the noise of the wind as if it were not there. I could distinguish no words, but the tone was enough. In it, I heard defiance and anger, and something else, a kind of emptiness, as if whatever spoke were wracked with lost hopes and challenged us from bleak despair as well as dreadful hate.

'The moon had vanished for a second or two behind a cloud, and we stood in the dark, facing nothingness. In front of us and quite close, I heard the sound of a hoof, then another. Something was advancing on us and we were sightless!

'The Earl stood, his sword in the guard position, solid as one of his own great gnarled oaks. I raised my own blade, though I could see no target. I felt a sudden chill, which seemed to cut through me like a knife. Then the clouds parted and the pale moon burst through and gave us light. At the same time, the gale from the west seemed to stiffen, and I caught again the sweet scent of apples.

'In front of us, no more than ten yards off, was the outline of a great horse. Its color was a white, an opaque, shifting shade, so that it seemed almost without color at all. Its eyes were the same shade and showed no glint or light. And on its back, saddleless, it bore a rider.

'He was as dark as the horse was light, and seemed clothed in furs of a tight fit, which caught the fitful moonlight and trapped it, giving nothing back. His head was bare, with shaggy hair, and rising from it were two forked projections, as if somehow he had made a cap from the upper cranium of some strange deer. I could not see his face at all, but the flicker of red points came from the place where his eyes should have been. In one hand he held a great barbed spear, and this he now raised to shoulder height.

'I sprang forward as fast as I could for I knew I was not the target, but I was too slow for the cast.

'The feeling of cold sharpened suddenly and terribly, and something long and lightless flew toward my companion's breast. His long sword flashed in the moon gleam, and there was a crash, as of riven metal. A nimbus of flame curved about his great blade and was gone.

'The light died as the racing clouds once more covered the white moon. Out of the pitch-black air in front of us came that wild cry again, despairing and lost now, its defiance gone, leaving only loneliness and utter wildness.

' "Begone!" shouted James in that great roar. "Seek the under hills and lie quiet! On the earth your time is done and your power gone from the world. I command you, get hence and never return!" He held the great sword in both hands with the cross guard facing out.

'The moon came through the clouds again. Before us was . . . emptiness! The twin shapes of the strange steed and its night-gaunt of a rider had vanished as if they had never been. And around us the mighty winds raged as if in salute, roaring in bursts that sounded like my friend's new voice when he gave commands.

' "Come," said James, his call sounding clear over the storm. "We need mounts, so to the stables. The Hunter has lost his power, save against the frightened, and he and his were put down long ago. But this raising of the long-gone is an evil thing and perhaps not the worst. We must go and seek out our enemy in his lair. We must ride to the Caer Dhub, the Fortress of the Dark, and our time is short!"

'I had no argument, indeed I was eager to obey. I was not master here, and I had no purpose of my own any longer, except to serve as best I could. But if I were no more than a pawn, at least I was a willing one, and I raced behind James at my best speed.

'The horses were wild with excitement when we reached the stables, plunging and rearing in their stalls. But James gentled two down in a most marvelous manner, speaking to them in some language I had never heard before. Where he had learned it, I had no idea. But this new James was not the man I knew, and strange tongues were a part of this whole nightmare.

'We saddled up quickly and in a few minutes had ridden out into the full force of the wind. We took the track which led south to the cottage on the cliff, our way marked out by the intermittent moonlight. James galloped in front, an extraordinary figure in his black dinner clothes with trousers stuffed into hunting boots. I wished that I had had time to get some, but my patent leathers were better on horseback than they would have been to walk in. Like him, I carried my sword across the saddle.

'We thundered on through the night, often in sight of the sea, which was beaten to a fury by the wild and howling wind. The gale actually seemed to be still rising, and had we wished to speak, it would have been quite impossible through its shrieking and raging. It tore at us, too, so that we had to crouch over the horses' necks, and they, poor beasts, had to angle themselves against it. But they bore us nobly and never faltered.

'Now on our right I glimpsed a single light. It was one of the windows of the cottage, gleaming through the dark. But our way did not lie there, I sensed, and James never drew rein. Our path was south, south to the grim ruin on the headland, which James had called the Fortress of the Dark. It was from this that all the portents had come, the threats and the wickedness had been unleashed. It was in that nighted wreckage that some foul sorcery had been revived, and it was there that we must seek its sources, yes, and destroy them.

'I had lost my sense of direction by now, but James cantered on through the bracken and heath, and I simply followed him. Suddenly he put up his left hand, at the same time checking his mount. He gestured to me to draw rein beside him. When I came up, he leaned so close that his mouth was almost on my ear.

' "We are very close now," he shouted over the wind's howl. "We must leave the horses and go to battle on foot. They are of no use to us and they have carried us bravely. We shall let them go and they will take no hurt. Dismount now and follow."

'I did as he bade and gave my beast a pat on the flank, dismissing it. Both of them cantered back the way we had come, and we were left alone in the night and the storm. In silence we advanced, with me once more backing James. We angled into a gentle downward slope, and now the bellowing of the sea grew louder in front of us as we approached the coast. It had not yet rained through all this storm of wind, but now my face grew damp and I tasted salt. The spray of the Atlantic was being flung hundreds of feet up through the sheer force of the driven air.

'The moon broke through another cloud, and there, downslope, was the ancient fortalice, exposed in all its shattered and titanic wreckage before us. Nor was this all. Two squat shapes were crouched not a hundred feet away, staring in our direction as if awaiting us. As we stood mutually exposed, they rose to their feet and with wild cries in their harsh speech, rushed at us. One carried a great ax, like a woodsman's but larger, while the other had a stranger weapon, a thing like a great rounded hammer, large enough to need the strength of both arms to wield. Lord Lionel might have expected no danger, but he had, nonetheless, left his two guardians.

'It was over in seconds. James took the one on the right with a great sweeping blow, a blow which shore through his ax shaft like paper and drove deep into the fellow's chest. He crumpled up like a felled tree.

'The other swung his huge maul, or hammer, at my head, a swing that would have spattered my brains to pulp had it landed. I ducked under it, though I felt the air move in my hair, and extending my body, left hand on the ground, drove the Ferrara point straight through his heart. He stood for one instant, his face contorted, then fell transfixed to lie by his mate. I wrenched loose the blade and stood up. James was facing me, a look of stern approval on his face. "A good stroke," he said briefly. "Now follow, once more. The last test is to come and it will be far more dangerous than what has gone before. Be silent and keep watch, especially to the rear. We go into the dark, the true dark now, to speak with the master of these creatures.'

'We were both damp with our exertions and the wind-driven spray, up-welling from far below. But I felt no sensation of cold as I walked behind James in the direction of the fortress. Instead, I felt, despite the storm and the bleak surroundings, a sense of high resolve, almost of exhilaration. I felt myself part of a crusade, and yet certainly a stranger one never existed, consisting of two Englishmen in dinner clothes, armed with swords unused for many centuries!

'We crossed the bare wet rock around the site, and James headed unerringly for the spot where I had seen the cavity and its protruding ladder the previous day.

'In the flashes of moonlight we had no trouble picking our way over the rubble and soon the black cavity lay before us. The ladder was still in place.

'"Listen," said my friend, pausing above the opening, one hand uplifted. Faintly, above the great noise of the wind and the raging sea, I seemed to hear a far-off throbbing, a beating pulse, as if from some mighty drum deep in the earth. I had no need to ask whence it came.

'"He is there. Still he works his crimes, still conspires with things that never see the light of day. So be it. He has found that which should not have been disturbed until the end of time. And from it he gains power even now. If we wait longer, matters will grow worse."

'We two stood now in the lee of a broken wall, whose vast slabs cut off some of the force of the gale. His face was very grave, as he seemed to muse on things beyond my comprehension, leaning on the pommel of that giant sword.

'Then he looked up at me, strangely as if in doubt, not of me, I thought, but of something else, perhaps even of himself. "We must go down. But my strength is less in the shadows under the earth, and his will be more. Let us go now, before I weaken further, from doubt and lack of faith. I will go first. Remember, have an eye to the rear and to the sides!"

'With no more ado he seized the first rungs of the ladder and began to go down. I waited and, when I could no longer see his hands, began my own descent, gripping the sword with two fingers and using the rest to cling to the ladder.

'The ladder was a long one, perhaps twenty feet. When my shoes touched rock, I was glad to stand up and look about. James was next to me, peering down the long tunnel in which we now stood. For there was light. Ten paces off, set in a niche in the wall of undressed stone, a kerosene lantern burnt with a dim glow. It was as if the light were changed down here in some way, for the color was odd, a pale light, like marsh fire in a summer bog. Far down the long shallow slope of the tunnel, another spot of similar hue shone in the distance.

'Remembering his warnings, I turned and looked back the other way. Here, the rock floor leveled off, as if we stood at the top of a slope; but here were no lights. Yet I had the feeling that the tunnel did not end near us at all but ran on for unguessable distances through the heart of the hills.

'Raising a finger to his lips, James led off down the gentle slope, his huge blade at the ready. I came behind in equal silence, listening as hard as I was able. Down here, out of the sound of the storm, the silence seemed muffled, but also echoing, so that the faint scuff of our feet rang abnormally loud in my ears. The faint throbbing beat we had heard on the surface had fallen silent as we had come down the ladder, but now it resumed again, louder and louder as we progressed. Then it halted once more, and the silence closed in upon us. We were now some few paces past the second lantern, still descending, and in the remote distance was the glowworm flicker of yet another light.

'All at once, on our left, there loomed up the opening of a huge passage, whose arch was far larger than the one we trod. We listened tensely, but I could hear nothing at first except the faint sound of dripping water some way off in the distance. Concentrating hard, I began to hear something else, or thought that I did. It was a sliding sound, as if something like wet hose were being dragged over a rock. It stopped, and I could only hear the drip of moisture again, but from James' taut face I fancied I had not been mistaken.

' "If we go on," he whispered, "we will have things behind us as well as before. Be twice vigilant." He turned and moved off again, with me still in his wake.

'As we reached the third of the lights, a distance I estimated of some hundred of yards, I began to be conscious of yet another sound. This was a faint roaring, more of a vibration to be *felt*, rather than something caught by one's ears. It was not loud, but constant, as if it were coming through the rocks all around us, and it, too, seemed to emanate from in front, the direction in which we were advancing. James heard it also and turned to face me.

' "We are almost under the sea face," he whispered in my ear. "You hear the ocean as it strikes the cliff. There may be a chance still. I had hoped for this."

'What he hoped for escaped me. This whole episode had taken on the quality of a waking dream in which I felt myself a spectator as well as an actor. I could do nothing except follow and await events, in some world of which I knew nothing, except that it, and James as well, had taken over control of my actions, shaping them to suit themselves.

'We had passed the last light long since, but now ahead of us we saw something new. The tunnel took a sharp bend to the right, and the rock floor no longer sloped at all. From around this bend came a lurid glare, far stronger than the lantern gleam. As we halted to watch, the throbbing boom we had first heard burst out once more, but this time far closer. If it were not some sort of drum, then I had never heard one.

'James motioned me on and led the way cautiously. As we approached, I saw the mouth of still another tunnel opening on our left, just before the bend. It had been hidden from us as we approached by a shallow buttress or stone, which thrust from the tunnel wall. We listened as before, but could hear nothing. But from its mouth came a vile reek, a stench of decay which turned the stomach. It was the awful smell which had so sickened the people at the Avalon House, and I felt sure this was its origin. We moved slowly past the hole and more slowly still to the turn of the passage. Reaching this, we halted and peered around it. I dropped to one knee, with James over me so that we offered as little of a target as possible to any observer.

'What we saw was this: we were staring into a cave or vault, which arched to a high point in the center. It was roughly oval in shape, but appeared to be man-made rather than natural, for its proportions seemed shaped and fairly symmetrical, if rough. It was perhaps three hundred feet in circumference.

'Around the walls were dark alcoves at regular intervals, and between the alcoves rough stone benches had been hacked out of the wall material itself. In the center was a great rectangular block of smooth black stone, unadorned but polished to a glossy sheen, from which the evil light glanced back and glimmered on the walls about. The light itself came from a fire which had been lit just in front of the block itself and on our side. It seemed to be of ordinary logs, but the flame burned with a greenish glow and not the orange of a normal blaze. Smoke swirled about the place, but most of it was carried upward as if by some draught, and I thought there must be a chimney of some sort up above in the viewless center, out of our sight. Between us and the fire, with his back to us, stood a man.

'He seemed to wear a long dark robe and was bareheaded. In the light of the fire I could just see that the robe had reddish symbols or shapes of some sort on its back, but what they were I could not make out. The figure rose to its full height, arms extended over its head, and made some signs in the smoky air. The drum beat sounded louder as if in answer. But where was the drum?

'The sound seemed to come from off to my right someplace. I could not see into the black pits of the alcoves, which the firelight did not reach, and the drumbeat apparently came from one of these.

'Now the figure which postured before us began to chant, a long singsong, in some speech unknown to me. The voice was high and strident, and the sound cut through the drum song and seemed to reach a long way as if carrying to unguessable reaches of space and time. The drumming halted for a second and then resumed, louder and more menacing than before.

'James lowered his head to where I crouched. "Watch here, as I have told you. I must face what comes alone. Your task is to ward my back, unless I call. God give us strength, and His Son as well!"

'He rose, head erect, and while I watched in awe, he marched straight down into that ghastly chamber, his boots ringing on the rock, his sword loose in his great right hand.

'The figure in front of that grim altar, if that was what it was, whirled as it caught the sound, holding out its hands as if to hold off danger. And a strange sight he was.

'It was Lord Lionel, of course. What we had thought was a robe, was a long cloak, fastened about his neck with a jeweled clasp. Under it he wore a shirt of some coarse stuff that looked like frieze, and below that again a kilt of dark material, falling to just above his knees. On his legs were cross-garters, and his feet bore soft leather shoes, laceless and reaching to the ankles. He might have been garbed to play Hamlet on the stage, even to the curved dagger thrust into a gem-studded belt.

'But there was no playacting here. Even I, who loathed the man, had to admit he looked magnificent. It was as if these were his true clothes, the ones for which he had been born. His lank hair was bound back by a fillet of dull purple, and under it his eyes blazed in his chalk-white face. I read surprise, but that faded and was replaced by the raging hatred I had seen before, the fury of a demon unleashed. As he glared, the drum faltered and fell silent, and once more I heard about us the muffled roar of the Western Ocean. There was an atmosphere of waiting. I felt a wave of cold, alien and charged with malice, coming from the right of the room where the unseen drummer must lurk in the shadow of one of the niches.

'It was James who broke the silence. He took three more steps, which placed him to the left of the fire, forcing his brother to turn also and giving to me full view of both their profiles. The Earl's was calm, with the brooding calm of majesty which I had earlier noted. His strange garb in no way detracted from his towering good looks, and I felt that any clothes would have meant nothing. He was what he was now, and clothes were extraneous.

' "I have come to end it," his voice rumbled out. "I know why you are here and what you have summoned. The Hunter has been sent back to the hills, from whence only your vile arts could have roused him. Your servants, the spawn of ancient and black sorcery in the dolmens and monoliths of the lost, sunken lands of Brittany, lie dead over your head. I know, too, who seeks to be free, with his night wandering and frightening of the countryside. I know, too, how he is to be freed and what a price you will pay for it. Not even a thing like you, with your years of foreign delving into that which should have been long forgot, I say, not even you can fully know what it would cost you, and the world as well, if what sleeps here would once more come into full life!"

'The hatred left Lionel's face for a moment to be replaced by wonder. It was a shock to hear his despised brother, I think, whom he had held in such contempt for years, challenging him on his own ground and, yes, with such a wealth of apparent knowledge. Then his face hardened.

'"You think to defy me?" he shouted incredulously, "*me*, with that stupid sword? You break in here, to this place of the most ancient mystery in the aisles, the cavern of the Dark Prince, where lies his tomb? You bring that cretin in the door to attack *me*, who have sought for the knowledge of this place the world over? It is you who are mad! In the name of the Lost One who lies here, I defy you! You have a sword, have you! Well, look on this then, you whom all the world call my brother! Look on the ax of him who lies here, laid in his tomb by the faithful, when he was cheated of his rights by the Christ-worshipers in that last battle, when dying he took with him the enemy of all his hopes!" He rattled out a string of uncouth syllables, and once more that horrid drum began to pulse from its hiding place.

'Lionel had crouched at the base of the great ebon block, which I had thought an altar but which now appeared in its true light. It was a mighty catafalque. I could barely make out the faint, time-scored line of the massive lid.

'When Lionel rose, he had thrown off his cloak and in his left hand carried a great ax, double-headed, with lunate curves, its somber blades giving back no more light than the tomb at whose marge it had lain. On his right forearm hung a small round shield, of apparently the same metal with a spiked boss in the center. A grim and dangerous figure he looked as he circled the black, basalt-hued block and moved in, seeking an opening. I strained to join in, for the shield gave him a deadly advantage, and James had no such defense.

'But I had been given a charge, and I knew I could not yield to impulse. As the drumming rose in volume, I stole a glance over my shoulder to the tunnel at my back. It was well I did.

'Something as pale as white bone was creeping up on me, indistinct in the fire's murky light. I caught a glimpse of long thin arms, the fingers ending in huge claws, a face like a starved baboon's skull, all bone and yellowed fangs, with two eyes of opaque flame, pupilless and blinking. That I had turned at the last moment was luck, if anything was due to luck on that mad night. I think even the dim glow of the evil fire slowed the monster down, for whatever cavern it had stolen from must have been utterly without light.

'As it snarled hideously and rose from a crouch, I turned and lunged straight at that countenance of hell, between the orbs of pale phosphorescence it used for eyes.

'The blade bent, as the good steel struck something hard, and a shock ran up my stiffened arm to my shoulder. Even as I struck, I heard the clash of steel behind me and knew that James fought his enemy even as I.

'The foulness in front of me screamed, a high whining note which hurt my eardrums, and drew back in a scuttling lope, deeper into the dark of the tunnel. I thought I had struck its skull and knew that I had hurt but not killed it. I, too, drew back to the entrance of the huge cavern. I could not win a fight with that lurker in the shadows without light of my own, protecting James' back came first in any case.

'The thing screamed again and once more came at me in that queer scrabbling way, low to the ground. I had backed almost out of the tunnel now, and the thud-thud of the devilish drums rang in my ears, mixed with the clatter of blows as ax met sword. Now, I had room for a cut and I used it.

'Once more, that unclean head came into the light. The spider-like arms covered with pallid hairs groped for me. The fangs slavered and it crouched for a spring.

'I cut down and hard, the sweep beginning over my shoulder, and my aim was true. This sword was no courtier's rapier, but the long heavy blade of a soldier, and it bit into that bone, if bone it was, high on that unnatural head, and further yet, with a crunch I could feel down to my toes!

'For the last time I heard that eldritch cry, and as my blade came back to guard, stained with foul blood, the battle ended. Limping and swaying, the thing lurched back up the slope, clutching its mangled skull and wailing hideously, and vanished into the dark above. If I had not given it a death wound, then I had at least removed it from the board. It would make no more mischief that night.

'The ring of arms renewed made me wheel and look below. Here the war still raged and it was not going well. The dark man in the archaic dress was untouched and handling his ax and shield like a master as he circled and struck through the veils of smoke and the uncertain gleam of the fire. James was bleeding from a wound high on one shoulder, though his face was still calm and serene. But his sword was another matter. As he swerved in my direction, I saw that the broad blade was sorely battered, with many notches gouged into the edge. Even as I watched, he struck a terrible blow, which his brother took full on the blade of that grim ax. The weapons clashed together and neither gave an inch. But when James fell back into a guard position, holding the sword in both hands, point up, I saw a fresh notch, while Lionel's ax was untouched. The black metal of ax and shield had some awful power in them, perhaps a trick of forging long gone from the world.

'And he sensed his advantage. Over the rising, battering cry of that damned drum, he called out. "This ax and shield were made with blood and torment under the hills, brother. Long the owner bargained for them and none could prevail against them! Yield now and I may show mercy!"

'"One weapon prevailed against them!" came the deep-throated answer. "They were not victor at the last!"

'Circling again, Lord Lionel sneered. "Seek in the Hesperides for that weapon, dear brother. It is gone long ages from the earth, as well you know!"

'The drum beat higher still, and the Earl's eyes blazed with blue fury. Lifting high his immense sword, he fell upon his brother's shorter shape and with a series of battering blows began to drive him about the cavern, from one side of the fire to the other. And this was his undoing.

'As Lionel retreated, giving ground but protecting himself beautifully, James slipped and with a tremendous stroke drove his sword down on the stone top of that forgotten tomb. There was a rending crack and three things happened. The sword shattered, close to the cross hilt. The slab of midnight stone also cracked in two, straight across the top, and the drum suddenly ceased. Lionel leapt back, confronting his defenseless enemy in triumph, and, shaking the ax, howled something in that unknown language.

'And the sound of the sea outside on the rocks burst into a shrieking bellow such as I have never heard even in the worst of Pacific typhoons. There was another crash, like thunder, but far harder, and then yet another. High on one wall of the cavern, across the tomb, there appeared a great crack. For an instant, light came through it and a great burst of spray. Another horrendous crash shook the room and the gap doubled in size. A gout of storm-tossed sea poured in with this blow and with something else.'

Ffellowes looked around at all of us before he continued speaking, but we were as silent as the grave. The library fire had long since gone out, and we sat, intent, lit only by a small lamp in a corner of the bay.

'It was long and glittered,' he said at length. 'I could not really undertake to say what it was, even to this day. James stooped, groping on the floor, now inches deep. The next wave poured down through the gap, and the fire spat and went out. Only dim moonlight and that only at intervals now lit the vault.

'When I could see again, James was advancing on his brother, and high above his head gleamed something which caught the light with a blue flame.

'The light dimmed again, and Lionel screamed. There was another tremendous crash, but this time it appeared to come from *inside* the cave.

'For a second there was silence, save for the wind and the water, which was now sloshing about my ankles. The next surge broke through the shattered wall of the place, and as it did, in the dim light something glittering flashed through it and vanished into the wild night outside.

'"James," I called uncertainly, "are you all right?" I could see nothing and hear nothing but the elements pounding on and through the rock. The moon must have been behind a cloud. Suddenly his voice was in my ear, his huge hand under my elbow. "Quick," he shouted. "We must run for it. The cliff is falling! Let me help you!"

'We ran. My God, how we ran. James must have been exhausted, but he was supporting me and wouldn't let go either. Before we reached the first lantern, rock was falling from the tunnel roof, and vast grindings were echoing down its length. I looked back as we passed and already the light was gone in a shower of stone and sand. Ahead of us, the next lamp gleamed faintly in the gloom, but rock was already crashing down between us and its flicker. The surging water would have caught us, I'm sure, had not the tunnel sloped up ever so gently, but I could hear that raging in the rear as well.

'Tripping and stumbling, we passed the second light. The groaning of the rocks was really something now, and cracks began to appear in the tunnel's floor. We had to vault a few but somehow always managed to keep staggering on.

'The next light was close now. As we passed it, a boulder the size of my head crashed down just behind us. An idea full of terror crossed my mind. Would we be able to see the tunnel entrance, the gap in its roof, should the moon not be shining? As it turned out we couldn't, but it didn't matter.

'I simply ran into the ladder, almost knocking my addled brains out. James made me go first, and I didn't argue. You know, I still had the Ferrara sword in one hand, dumb stubbornness, I guess, but I carried it out of that hellhole and later put it back on the wall myself.

'As I climbed out, the moon came out again and flooded the landscape with pale light. But the groaning and cracking in the earth hadn't halted for a minute, and I was damned glad to see my friend's head appear at the top of the ladder. His face was pale and his eyes were half shut. It was I who grabbed him this time and hauled away until he was out of the hole. I got one arm under his shoulder and we lurched off away from the castle toward the east. One moment we were on the slippery rock of the point, the next we were on soft turf, and I never felt gladder of common dirt in my life.

'"Go on," he gasped. "We are not safe yet. I know!"

'Up the slope we went, more at a crawl than a walk, I may say, until neither one of us could go a step further, and we simply collapsed into the moist verdure of the hills.

'Behind us, the grandfather of all breaking noises cut loose and we sat up and stared. The whole great finger of stone on which the castle sat was separating from the land!

'Slowly, inexorably in the moonlight, the cliff leaned out and away. There were rending and screeching noises deep down in the earth, and even where we crouched, the ground shook as though with an earthquake.

'James stood up, and that stern look of majesty was never clearer in the moonlight. "Accursed be thy stones forever!" he shouted over the shattering noise of the cliff fall. "Lie in the sea bottom until the end of time and never trouble the world again!" As he spoke the whole promontory point, fortress and all, vanished, and a splash roared up like some vast water spout and left us drenched. When the water had left our eyes, a ragged cliff edge ran some dozen yards away from us. Beyond this there was . . . nothing.

'"So passes *Caer Dhub*," said James in a strange voice. "So passes the last of an evil lost in time. And I too pass, yet I will . . ." He never finished telling me what he would do because he had fainted. I was nigh on doing so myself, being exhausted as well as dripping wet. But someone had to get back to Avalon House, or else we would both die of exposure.

'I covered him with my jacket and in my soaked, boiled shirt, or the remnants of one, began to stumble over the faint trace Lionel's people had left on the slope. I don't know how long I had been putting one foot down after the other when I saw lights ahead and heard voices. I called out in a croak like that of an asthmatic frog and they heard me. I remember hands holding me up, but nothing more. Apparently I managed to tell them about James before I passed out, but I remember none of it, not until I woke up in my own bedroom at Avalon.

'I lost a whole day there, I later discovered. They found us at about four a.m., and I woke to an afternoon sun going down *two* days after that! That's what I call needing a rest, eh?

'Well, I got myself up and dressed and wandered downstairs. And here are James and Isobel having tea! You would have thought I'd slipped away five minutes earlier to visit the w.c. With my head full of the last time I had seen James, I could hardly believe my own eyes!

'Of course they leapt up, James spilling his tea in the process, and fell on my neck. Isobel, I was glad to note, looked ten years younger already, her eyes shining and her cheeks with some at least of the old bloom.

'But James! Here was the man I had left three-quarters dead on a cliff after the damndest struggle in my memory, beaming at me in his old tongue-tied way, trying to get out something that made sense in terms of speech!

'"Can't thank you enough, old chap. I mean, dash it, you've been a trump to help us out this way! The lads on the place tell me you pulled me out of that damned landslide, the one that got old Lionel in the bravest way. I say, really, it was awfully decent of you. I can hardly recall a thing, must have been hit by a rock or something, what?" I was speechless.

'Even the old familiar voice was back, and the deep sonorous tones I had heard on that fatal night were gone forever. The clear boy's gaze which met mine was as untouched by trouble as a three-year-old's. Whatever had ruled my friend on that cliff and in that vault had left forever. From appearance, he might never have done anything rougher than a day's guard mount in front of Buck House.

'As I tried to think of something to say, a discreet cough came from the door. I looked up and there met Traheal's steady eyes. "Very nice to see you up and about, Captain, speaking for myself and the staff. A very gallant thing you did, sir, saving his lordship like that. We all regret that poor Lord Lionel was lost in that tragic fashion, of course. No doubt he was trying to save them poor helpless men of his down below."

'"Mmh, well, thank you, Traheal," I said. So this was to be the pattern was it? "I suppose, James, they were all down below? No hope of rescue? This awful weather of late, no doubt, loosened the cliff, eh?" No one can say *I* can't pick up a cue! I went on. "Sorry as the devil about your brother. Hardly knew him, of course. Still wish to express regrets and all that."

'But now the ball had moved to another court. It was Isobel who fixed her gaze on me.

'"Such a pity. Lionel was a very peculiar man, there's no denying it, but he *was* family. I've always said that all this digging about in odd places must make one morbid. I understand they often use dynamite or some awful explosive in these excavations. They must have been careless, that's all." She paused, her blue orbs politely holding mine. "At least, that's what the police think, isn't it, James?"

'"Ah, well, yes, I expect so," mumbled her spouse. He turned to me, as if in appeal. "You know, Donald, I honestly couldn't stand him, I mean frankly, but I do feel bad about all this. I should never have let him dig down there. The whole cliff must have been as rotten as cheese." He sighed. "At least that bloody old castle is gone with the slip up there, and that's a blessing." He looked thoughtful, then turned to me again. "Isobel thinks I must have had a premonition or something the other night when we rushed out there. I'll be blowed if I can recall it, but that's what she says and she's usually right about these things. But, I'll say this. Ever since I was a kid, I've had that old pile of slag on my mind, sort of hanging over me, what? I used to go miles to even avoid looking at it. At least that's gone for good, eh, my dear?"

'"Yes," she replied very softly, "that's gone for good. It's *all* gone and it won't be back. Why even that most unpleasant smell has left the cellars. And the weather is perfect again." Cornflower-blue fixed me with the same level gaze.'

Ffellowes paused and we all drew a long breath. He lit a cigar and I leaned back in my chair for the first time in half an hour. But another figure bounced up across from me. It was this guy Simmons, and if the signs were right, he was mad as hell.

'General Ffellowes!' he exploded. 'I have never heard in my life a more preposterous farrago of fables! Do you expect me to believe this absolute tissue of—of fabrications? Are we all expected to believe that this monstrous melange of Tennyson, Geoffrey of Monmouth and Malory happened to *you*? *In person*?' He turned on his heel. 'I believe, sir, that you have done your best to ridicule me, to make me a figure of fun for some obscure purpose of your own!

This piece of senseless vulgarity is beyond belief! I shall never set foot in this institution again! Never!' He stormed out, leaving the rest of us flabbergasted.

'Well, for Pete's sake,' said someone. 'Who was that nut, anyway? And why did he blow up like that? I sure hope he keeps his word about not coming back!'

'I don't get it,' remarked Bryce. 'He was the one who brought up ghost stories in the first place. Brigadier, that's one of the best stories I ever heard, and if you say it happened, it happened, at least in my book. But what got that character so stirred up? Any ideas?'

'Well,' said Ffellowes, 'yes, I rather think I do. His name is Simmons. I have been hearing for the past year or so about one Professor Elwyn Simmons at Columbia or somewhere who is about to release the definitive work on the psychosis of witchcraft. It's supposed to be the latest word in debunking any belief in things nonmaterial, you know.' He pulled on his cigar.

Bryce chuckled. 'No wonder he got steamed up. Think he'll revise the book, sir?'

'I doubt it,' said Ffellowes, 'but I wish he'd stayed for the list of my friend's names. Like many very old families, the heir always gets handed a bundle.'

'Such as?' I cut in.

'In James' case, aside from James, of course, he drew the following: Arthur, Geraint, Percival, Bedivere and Tristram.' The ruddy face smiled at us.

For once my brain worked and back came a school English class on poetry. 'And Lionel had only one initial, which might just have been M, right?' I asked.

'You have just won the coconut, as we say in Merry England,' said the brigadier.

PAGES FROM A YOUNG GIRL'S JOURNAL

Robert Aickman

3rd October. Padua—Ferrara—Ravenna. We've reached Ravenna only four days after leaving that horrid Venice. And all in a hired carriage! I feel sore and badly bitten too. It was the same yesterday, and the day before, and the day before that. I wish I had someone to talk to. This evening, Mamma did not appear for dinner at all. Papa just sat there saying nothing and looking at least two hundred years old instead of only one hundred, as he usually does. I wonder how old he *really* is? But it's no good wondering. We shall never know, or at least I shan't. I often think Mamma *does* know, or very nearly. I wish Mamma were someone I could talk to, like Caroline's Mamma. I often used to think that Caroline and her Mamma were more like sisters together, though of course I could never say such a thing. But then Caroline is pretty and gay, whereas I am pale and quiet. When I came up here to my room after dinner, I just sat in front of the long glass and stared and stared. I must have done it for half an hour or perhaps an hour. I only rose to my feet when it had become quite dark outside.

I don't like my room. It's much too big and there are only two wooden chairs, painted in greeny-blue with gold lines, or once painted like that. I hate having to lie on my bed when I should prefer to sit, and everyone knows how bad it is for the back. Besides, this bed, though it's enormous, seems to be as hard as when the earth's dried up in Summer. Not that the earth's like that here. Far from it. The rain has never stopped since we left Venice. Never once. Quite unlike what Miss Gisborne said before we set out from my dear, dear Derbyshire. This bed really is *huge*. It would take at least eight people my size. I don't like to think about it. I've just remembered: it's the third of the month so that we've been gone exactly half a year. What a lot of places I have been to in that time—or been through! Already I've quite forgotten some of them. I never properly saw them in any case. Papa has his own ideas, and one thing I'm sure of is that they are quite unlike other people's ideas. To me the whole of Padua is just a man on a horse—stone or bronze, I suppose, but I don't even know which. The whole of Ferrara is a huge palace—castle—fortress that simply frightened me, so that I didn't *want* to look. It was as big as this bed—in its own way, of course. And those were two large, famous towns I have visited this very week. Let alone where I was perhaps two months ago! What a farce! as Caroline's Mamma always says. I wish she were here now and Caroline too. No one has ever hugged and kissed me and made things happy as they do.

The Contessa has at least provided me with no fewer than twelve candles. I found them in one of the drawers. I suppose there's nothing else to do but read—except perhaps to say one's prayers. Unfortunately, I finished all the books I brought with me long ago, and it's so difficult to buy any new ones, especially in English. However, I managed to purchase two very long ones by Mrs. Radcliffe before we left Venice. Unfortunately, though there are twelve candles, there are only two candlesticks, both broken, like everything else. Two candles *should* be enough, but all they seem to do is make the room look even larger and darker. Perhaps they are not-very-good foreign candles. I noticed that they seemed very dirty and discolored in the drawer. In fact, one of them looked quite black. That one must have lain in the drawer a very long time. By the way, there is a framework hanging from the ceiling in the middle of the room. I cannot truthfully describe it as a chandelier: perhaps as a ghost of a chandelier. In any case, it is a long way from even the foot of the bed. They do have the most enormous rooms in these foreign houses where we stay. Just as if it were very warm the whole time, which it certainly is not. What a farce!

As a matter of fact, I'm feeling quite cold at this moment, even though I'm wearing my dark-green woolen dress that in Derbyshire saw me through the whole of last winter. I wonder if I should be any warmer *in* bed? It is something I can never make up my mind about. Miss Gisborne always calls me 'such a chilly mortal.' I see I have used the present tense. I wonder if that is appropriate in the case of Miss Gisborne? Shall I ever see Miss Gisborne again? I mean in *this* life, of course.

Now that six days have passed since I have made an entry in this journal, I find that I am putting down *everything*, as I always do once I made a start. It is almost as if nothing horrid could happen to me as long as I keep on writing. That is simply silly, but I sometimes wonder whether the silliest things are not often the truest.

I write down words on the page, but what do I say? Before we started, everyone told me that, whatever else I did, I *must* keep a journal, a travel journal. I do not think this is a travel journal at all. I find that when I am traveling with Papa and Mamma, I seem hardly to look at the outside world. Either we are lumbering along, with Papa and Mamma naturally in the places from which something can be seen, or at least from which things can be best seen; or I find that I am alone in some great vault of a bedroom for hours and hours and hours, usually quite unable to go to sleep, sometimes for the whole night. I should see so much more if I could sometimes walk about the different cities on my own—naturally, I do not mean at night. I wish that were possible. Sometimes I really hate being a girl. Even Papa cannot hate my being a girl more than I do sometimes.

And when there *is* something to put down, it always seems to be the same thing! For example, here we are in still another of these households to which Papa always seems to have an entree. Plainly it is very wicked of me, but I sometimes wonder *why* so many people should want to know Papa, who is usually so silent and disagreeable, and always so old! Perhaps the answer is simple enough: it is that they never meet him—or Mamma—or me. We drive up, Papa gives us all over to the major-domo or someone, and the family never sets eyes on us, because the family is never at home. These foreign families seem to have terribly many houses and always to be living in another of them. And when one of the family *does* appear, he or she usually seems to be almost as old as Papa and hardly able to speak a word of English. I think I have a pretty voice, though it's difficult to be quite sure, but I deeply wish I had worked harder at learning foreign languages. At least—the trouble is that Miss Gisborne is so bad at teaching them. I must say *that* in my own defense, but it doesn't help much now. I wonder how Miss Gisborne would be faring if she were in this room with me? Not much better than I am, if you ask me.

I have forgotten to say, though, that this is one of the times when we *are* supposed to be meeting the precious family; though, apparently, it consists only of two people, the Contessa and her daughter. Sometimes I feel that I have already seen enough women without particularly wanting to meet any new ones, whatever their ages. There's something rather monotonous about women—unless, of course, they're like Caroline and her Mamma, which none of them are, or could be. So far the Contessa and her daughter have not appeared. I don't know why not, though no doubt Papa knows. I am told that we are to meet them both tomorrow. I expect very little. I wonder if it will be warm enough for me to wear my green satin dress instead of my green woolen dress? Probably not. ·

And this is the town where the great, the immortal Lord Byron lives in sin and wildness! Even Mamma has spoken of it several times. Not that this melancholy house is actually *in* the town. It is a villa at some little distance away from it, though I do not know in which direction, and I am sure that Mamma neither knows nor cares. It seemed to me that after we passed through the town this afternoon, we traveled on for fifteen or twenty minutes. Still, to be even in the same *region* as Lord Byron must somewhat move even the hardest heart; and my heart, I am very sure, is not hard in the least.

I find that I have been scribbling away for nearly an hour. Miss Gisborne keeps on saying that I am too prone to the insertion of unnecessary hyphens, and that it is a weakness. If a weakness it is, I intend to cherish it.

I know that an hour has passed because there is a huge clock somewhere that sounds every quarter. It must be a *huge* clock because of the noise it makes, and because everything abroad *is* huge.

I am colder than ever and my arms are quite stiff. But I must drag off my clothes somehow, blow out the candles and insinuate my tiny self into this enormous, frightening bed. I do hate the lumps you get all over your body when you travel abroad, and so much hope I don't get many more during the night. Also I hope I don't start feeling thirsty, as there's no water of any kind, let alone water safe to drink.

Ah, Lord Byron, living out there in riot and wickedness! It is impossible to forget him. I wonder what he would think of me? I do hope there are not too many biting things in this room.

4th October. What a surprise! The Contessa has said it will be quite in order for me to go for short walks in the town, provided I have my maid with me; and when Mamma at once pointed out that I had no maid, offered the services of her own! To think of this happening the very day after I wrote down in this very journal that it could never happen! I am now quite certain that it would have been perfectly correct for me to walk about the other towns too. I daresay that Papa and Mamma suggested otherwise only because of the difficulty about the maid. Of course I *should* have a maid, just as

Mamma should have a maid too and Papa a man, and just as we should all have a proper carriage of our own, with our crest on the doors! If it was that we were too poor, it would be humiliating. As we are not too poor (I am sure we are not), it is farcical. In any case, Papa and Mamma went on making a fuss, but the Contessa said we had now entered the States of the Church and were, therefore, all living under the special beneficence of God. The Contessa speaks English very well and even knows the English *idioms*, as Miss Gisborne calls them.

Papa screwed up his face when the Contessa mentioned the States of the Church, as I knew he would. Papa remarked several times while we were on the way here, that the Papal States, as he calls them, are the most misgoverned in Europe and that it was not only as a Protestant that he said so. I wonder. When Papa expresses opinions of that kind, they often seem to me to be just notions of his own, like his notions of the best way to travel. After the Contessa had spoken as she did, I felt—very strongly—that it must be rather beautiful to be ruled directly by the Pope and his cardinals. Of course, the cardinals and even the Pope are subject to error, as are our own Bishops and Rectors, all being but men, as Mr. Biggs-Hartley continually emphasizes at home; but, all the same, they simply *must* be nearer to God than the sort of people who rule us in England. I do not think Papa can be depended upon to judge such a question.

I am determined to act upon the Contessa's kind offer. Miss Gisborne says that though I am a pale little thing, I have very much a will of my own. Here will be an opportunity to prove it. There may be certain difficulties because the Contessa's maid can only speak Italian; but when the two of us shall be alone together, it is I who shall be mistress and she who will be maid, and nothing can change that. I have seen the girl. She is a pretty creature, apart from the size of her nose.

Today it has been wet, as usual. This afternoon we drove round Ravenna in the Contessa's carriage: a proper carriage for once, with arms on the doors and a footman as well as the coachman. Papa has paid off our hired coach. I suppose it has lumbered away back to Fusina, opposite to Venice. I expect I can count upon our remaining in Ravenna for a week. That seems to be Papa's usual sojourn in one of our major stopping places. It is not very long, but often it is quite long enough, the way we live.

This afternoon we saw Dante's Tomb, which is simply by the side of the street, and went into a big church with the Throne of

Neptune in it, and then into the Tomb of Galla Placidia, which is blue inside, and very beautiful. I was on the alert for any hint of where Lord Byron might reside, but it was quite unnecessary to speculate, because the Contessa almost shouted it out as we rumbled along one of the streets: 'The Palazzo Guiccioli. See the netting across the bottom of the door to prevent Lord Byron's animals from straying.' 'Indeed, indeed,' said Papa, looking out more keenly than he had at Dante's Tomb. No more was said, because, though both Papa and Mamma had more than once alluded to Lord Byron's present way of life so that I should be able to understand things that might come up in conversation, yet neither the Contessa nor Papa and Mamma knew how much I might really understand. Moreover, the little Contessina was in the carriage, sitting upon a cushion on the floor at her Mamma's feet, making five of us in all, foreign carriages being as large as everything else foreign; and I daresay *she* knew nothing at all, sweet little innocent.

'Contessina' is only a kind of nickname or *sobriquet*, used by the family and the servants. The Contessina is really a Contessa: in foreign noble families, if one person is a Duke, then all the other men seem to be Dukes also, and all the women Duchesses. It is very confusing and nothing like such a good arrangement as ours, where there is only one Duke and one Duchess to each family. I do not know the little Contessina's age. Most foreign girls look far older than they really are, whereas most of our girls look younger. The Contessina is *very* slender, a veritable slyph. She has an olive complexion, with no blemish of any kind. People often write about 'olive complexions': the Contessina really has one. She has absolutely enormous eyes, the shape of broad beans, and not far off that in color; but she never uses them to look at anyone. She speaks so little and often has such an empty, lost expression that one might think her more than slightly simple; but I do not think she is. Foreign girls are raised quite differently from the way our girls are raised. Mamma frequently refers to this, pursing her lips. I must admit that I cannot see myself finding in the Contessina a friend, pretty though she is in her own way, with feet about half the size of mine or Caroline's.

When foreign girls grow up to become women, they usually continue, poor things, to look older than they are. I am sure this applies to the Contessa. The Contessa has been very kind to me—in the few hours that I have so far known her—and even seems to be a little sorry for me—as, indeed, I am for her. But I do not understand the Contessa. Where was she last night? Is the little Contessina her only child? What has become of her husband? Is it because he is dead that she seems—and looks—so sad? Why does she want to live in such a big house—it is called a Villa, but one might think it a Palazzo—when it is all falling to bits, and much of it barely even furnished? I should like to ask Mamma these questions, but I doubt whether she would have the right answers, or perhaps any answers.

The Contessa did appear for dinner this evening, and even the little Contessina. Mamma was there too, in that frock I dislike. It really is the wrong kind of red—especially for Italy, where *dark* colors seem to be so much worn. The evening was better than last evening; but then it could hardly have been worse. (Mr. Biggs-Hartley says we should never say that: things can *always* be worse.) It was not a *good* evening. The Contessa was trying to be quite gay, despite her own obvious trouble, whatever that is; but neither Papa nor Mamma know how to respond, and I know all too well that I myself am better at thinking about things than at casting a spell in company. What I like most is just a few friends I know really well and whom I can truly trust and love. Alas, it is long since I have had even one such to clasp by the hand. Even letters seem mostly to lose themselves en route, and I can hardly wonder; supposing people are still bothering to write them in the first place, needless to say, which it is difficult to see why they should be after all this time. When dinner was over, Papa and Mamma and the Contessa played an Italian game with both playing cards and dice. The servants had lighted a fire in the Salone and the Contessina sat by it doing nothing and saying nothing. If given a chance, Mamma would have remarked that 'the child should have been in bed long ago,' and I am sure she should. The Contessa wanted to teach me the game, but Papa said at once that I was too young, which is absolutely farcical. Later in the evening, the Contessa, after playing a quite long time with Papa and Mamma, said that tomorrow she would put her foot down (the Contessa knows so many such expressions that one would swear she must have lived in England) and would *insist* on my learning. Papa screwed his face up and Mamma pursed her lips in the usual way. I had been doing needlework, which I shall never like nor see any point in when servants can always do it for us; and I found that I was thinking many deep thoughts. And then I noticed that a small tear was slowly falling down the Contessa's face. Without thinking, I sprang up; but then the Contessa smiled, and I sat down. One of my deep thoughts was that it is not so much particular disasters that make people cry, but something always there in life itself, something that a light falls on when we are trying to enjoy ourselves in the company of others.

I must admit that the horrid lumps are going down. I certainly do not seem to have acquired any more, which is an advantage when compared with what happened every night in Dijon, that smelly place. But I wish I had a more cheerful room, with better furniture, though tonight I have succeeded in bringing to bed one of our bottles of Mineral Water and even a glass from which to drink it. It is only the Italian Mineral Water, of course, which Mamma says may be very little safer than the ordinary water; but as all the ordinary water seems to come from the dirty wells one sees down the side streets, I think that Mamma exaggerates. I admit, however, that it is not like the bottled water one buys in France. How farcical to have to buy water in a bottle, anyway! All the same, there are some things that I have grown to *like* about foreign countries; perhaps even to prefer. It would never do to let Papa and Mamma hear me talk in such a way. I often wish I were not so sensitive, so that the rooms I am given and things of that kind, did not matter so much. And yet Mamma is more sensitive about the water than I am! I am sure it is not so *important*. It can't be. To me it is *obvious* that Mamma is *less* sensitive than I am, where *important* things are concerned. My entire life is based on that obvious fact! My real life, that is.

I rather wish the Contessa would invite me to share *her* room, because I think she is sensitive in the same way that I am. But perhaps the little girl sleeps in the Contessa's room. I should not really mind that. I do not *hate* or even dislike the little Contessina. I expect she already has troubles herself. But Papa and Mamma would never agree to it anyway, and now I have written all there is to write about this perfectly ordinary, but somehow rather odd, day. In this big cold room, I can hardly move with chilliness.

5th October. When I went in to greet Mamma this morning, Mamma had the most singular news. She told me to sit down (Mamma and Papa have more chairs in their rooms than I have, and more of other things too), and then said that there was to be a party! Mamma spoke as though it would be a dreadful ordeal, which it was impossible for us to avoid; and she seemed to take it for granted that I should receive the announcement in the same way. I do not know what I really thought about it. It is true that I have never enjoyed a party yet (not that I have been present at many of them); but all day I have been aware of feeling different inside myself, lighter and swifter in some way, and by this evening I cannot but think it is owing to the knowledge that a party lies before me. After all, foreign parties may be different from parties at home, and probably are. I keep pointing that out to myself. This particular party will be given by the Contessa, who, I feel sure, knows more about it than does Mamma. If she does, it will not be the only thing that the Contessa knows more about than Mamma.

The party is to be the day after tomorrow. While we were drinking our coffee and eating our panini (always very flaky and powdery in Italy), Mamma asked the Contessa whether she was sure there would be time enough for the preparations. But the Contessa only smiled—in a very polite way, of course. It is probably easier to do things quickly in Italy (when one really wants to, that is), because everyone has so many servants. It is hard to believe that the Contessa has much money, but she seems to keep more servants than we do, and, what is more, they behave more like slaves than like servants, quite unlike our Derbyshire keel-the-pots. Perhaps it is simply that everyone is so fond of the Contessa. That I should entirely understand. Anyway, preparations for the party have been at a high pitch all day, with people hanging up banners, and funny smells from the kitchen quarters. Even the Bath House at the far end of the formal garden (it is said to have been built by the Byzantines) has had the spiders swept out and been populated with cooks, perpetrating I know not what. The transformation is quite bewildering. I wonder when Mamma first knew of what lay ahead? Surely it must at least have been before we went to bed last night?

I feel I should be vexed that a new dress is so impracticable. A train of seamstresses would have to work day and night for forty-eight hours, as in the fairy tales. I should like that (who would not?), but I am not at all sure that *I* should be provided with a new dress even if whole weeks were available in which to make it. Papa and Mamma would probably still agree that I had quite enough dresses already even if it were the Pope and his cardinals who were going to entertain me. All the same, I am not really vexed. I sometimes think that I am deficient in a proper interest in clothes, as Caroline's Mamma calls it. Anyway, I have learned from experience that new dresses are more often than not thoroughly disappointing. I keep reminding myself of that.

The other important thing today is that I have been out for my first walk in the town with the Contessa's maid, Emilia. I just swept through what Papa had to say on the subject, as I had promised myself. Mamma was lying down at the time, and the Contessa simply smiled her sweet smile and sent for Emilia to accompany me.

I must admit that the walk was not a *complete* success. I took with me our copy of Mr. Grubb's 'Handbook to Ravenna and Its Antiquities' (Papa could hardly say No, lest I do something far worse), and began looking places up on the map with a view to visiting them. I felt that this was the best way to start, and that, once started, I could wait to see what life would lay before me. I am often quite resolute when there is a specific situation to be confronted. The first difficulty was the quite long walk into Ravenna itself. Though it was nothing at all to me, and though it was not raining, Emilia soon made it clear that she was unaccustomed to walking a step. This could only have been an affection, or rather pretense, because everyone knows that girls of that kind come from peasant families, where I am quite sure they have to walk about all day, and much more than merely walk about. Therefore, I took no notice at all, which was made easier by my hardly understanding a word that Emilia actually said. I simply pushed and dragged her forward. Sure enough, she soon gave up all her pretenses and made the best of the situation. There were some rough carters on the road and large numbers of horrid children, but for the most part they stopped annoying us as soon as they saw who we were, and in any case it was as nothing to the roads into Derby, where they have lately taken to throwing stones at the passing carriages.

The next trouble was that Emilia was not in the least accustomed to what I had in mind when we reached Ravenna. Of course people do not go again and again to look at their own local antiquities, however old they may be; and least of all, I suspect, Italian people. When she was not accompanying her mistress, Emilia was used to going to town only for some precise purpose: to buy something, to sell something, or to deliver a letter. There was that in her attitude which made me think of the saucy girls in the old comedies: whose only work is to fetch and carry billets-doux, and sometimes to take the places of their mistresses, with their mistresses' knowledge or otherwise. I did succeed in visiting another of these Bath Houses, this one a public spectacle and called the Baptistry of the Orthodox, because it fell into Christian hands after the last days of the Romans, who built it. It was, of course, far larger than the Bath House in the Contessa's garden, but in the interior rather dark and with a floor so uneven that it was difficult not to fall. There was also a horrible dead animal inside. Emilia began laughing, and it was quite plain what she was laughing at. She was striding about as if she were back on her mountains, and the kind of thing she seemed to be suggesting was that if I proposed to walk all the way to the very heel or toe of Italy she was quite prepared to walk with me, and perhaps to walk ahead of me. As an English girl, I did not care for this, nor for the complete reversal of Emilia's original attitude, almost suggesting that she has a deliberate and impertinent policy of keeping the situation between us under her own control. So, as I have said, the walk was not a complete success. All the same, I have made a start. It is obvious that the world has more to offer than would be likely to come my way if I were to spend my whole life creeping about with Papa at one side of me and Mamma at the other. I shall think about how best to deal with Emilia now that I better understand her ways. I was not in the least tired when we had walked back to the Villa. I despised girls who get tired, quite as much as Caroline despises them.

Believe it or not, Mamma was still lying down. When I went in, she said that she was resting in preparation for the party. But the party is not until the day after tomorrow. Poor dear Mamma might have done better not to have left England in the first place! I must take great care that I am not like that when I reach the same time of life and am married, as I suppose I shall be. Looking at Mamma in repose, it struck me that she would still be quite pretty if she did not always look so tired and worried. Of course she was once far prettier than I am now. I know that well. I, alas, am not really pretty at all. I have to cultivate other graces, as Miss Gisborne puts it.

I saw something unexpected when I was going upstairs to bed. The little Contessina had left the Salone before the rest of us and, as usual, without a word. Possibly it was only I who saw her slip out, she went so quietly. I noticed that she did not return and supposed that, at her age, she was quite worn out. Assuredly, Mamma would have said so. But then when I myself was going upstairs, holding my candle, I saw for myself what had really happened. At the landing, as we in England should call it, there is in one of the corners an odd little closet or cabinet, from which two doors lead off, both locked, as I know because I have cautiously turned the handles for myself. In this corner, by the light of my candle, I saw the Contessina, and she was being hugged by a man. I think it could only have been one of the servants, though I was not really able to tell. Perhaps I am wrong about that, but I am not wrong about it being the Contessina. They had been there in complete darkness, and, what is more, they never moved a muscle as I came up the stairs and walked calmly along the passage in the opposite direction. I suppose they hoped I should fail to see them in the dimness.

They must have supposed that no one would be coming to bed just yet. Or perhaps they were lost to all sense of time, as Mrs. Radcliff expresses it. I have very little notion of the Contessina's age, but she often looks about twelve or even less. Of course I shall say nothing to anybody.

6th October. I have been thinking on and off all day about the differences between the ways we are supposed to behave and the ways we actually do behave. And both are different from the ways in which God calls upon us to behave, and which we can never achieve whatever we do and however hard we apply ourselves, as Mr. Biggs-Hartley always emphasizes. We seem, every one of us, to be at least three different people. And that's just to start with.

I am disappointed by the results of my little excursion yesterday with Emilia. I had thought that there was so much of which I was deprived by being a girl and so being unable to go about on my own, but now I am not sure that I have been missing anything. It is almost as if the nearer one approaches to a thing, the less it proves to be there, to exist at all. Apart, of course, from the bad smells and bad words and horrid rough creatures from which and from whom we women are supposed to be 'shielded.' But I am waxing metaphysical; against which Mr. Biggs-Hartley regularly cautions us. I wish Caroline were with us. I believe I might feel quite differently about things if she were here to go about with me, just the two of us. Though, needless to say, it would make no difference to us what the things truly were—or were not. It is curious that things should seem not to exist when visited with one person, and then to exist after all if visited with another person. Of course it is all just fancy, but what (I think at moments like this) is not?

I am so friendless and alone in this alien land. It occurs to me that I must have great inner strength to bear up as I do and to fulfill my duties with so little complaint. The Contessa has very kindly given me a book of Dante's verses, with the Italian on one side and an English translation on the page opposite. She remarked that it would aid me to learn more of her language. I am not sure that it will. I have dutifully read through several pages of the book, and there is nothing in this world that I like more than reading, but Dante's ideas are so gloomy and complicated that I suspect he is no writer for a woman, certainly not for an English woman. Also his face frightens me, so critical and severe. After looking at his portrait, beautifully engraved at the beginning of the book, I begin to fear that I shall see that face looking over my shoulder as I sit gazing into the looking glass. No wonder Beatrice would have nothing to do with him. I feel that he was quite deficient in the graces that appeal to our sex. Of course one must not even hint such a thing to an Italian, such as the Contessa, for to all Italians Dante is as sacred as Shakespeare or Dr. Johnson is to us.

For once I am writing this during the afternoon. I suspect that I am suffering from ennui and, as that is a sin (even though only a minor one), I am occupying myself in order to drive it off. I know by now that I am much more prone to such lesser shortcomings as ennui and indolence than to such vulgarities as letting myself be embraced and kissed by a servant. And yet it is not that I feel myself wanting in either energy or passion. It is merely that I lack for anything or anyone worthy of such feelings and refuse to spend them upon what is unworthy. But what a 'merely' is that! How well I understand the universal ennui that possesses our neighbour, Lord Byron! I, a tiny slip of a girl, feel, at least in this particular, at one with the great poet! There might be consolation in the thought, were I capable of consolation. In any case, I am sure that there will be nothing more that is worth record before my eyes close tonight in slumber.

Later. I was wrong! After dinner tonight, it struck me simply to ask the Contessa whether she had ever *met* Lord Byron. I supposed it might not be a thing she would proclaim unsolicited, either when Papa and Mamma were present, or, for reasons of delicacy, on one of the two rare occasions when she and I were alone; but I thought that I might now be sufficiently simpatica to venture a discreet inquiry.

I fear that I managed it very crudely. When Papa and Mamma had become involved in one of their arguments together, I walked across the room and sat down at the end of the sofa on which the Contessa was reclining; and when she smiled at me and said something agreeable, I simply blurted out my question, quite directly. 'Yes, mia cara,' she replied, 'I have met him, but we cannot invite him to our party because he is too political, and many people do not agree with his politics. Indeed, they have already led to several deaths, which some are reluctant to accept at the hands of a straniero, however eminent.' And of course it *was* the wonderful possibility of Lord Byron attending the Contessa's party that *had been* at the back of my thoughts. Not for the first time, the Contessa showed her fascinating insight into the minds of others—or assuredly into my mind.

* * *

7th October. The day of the party! It is quite early in the morning and the sun is shining as I have not seen it shine for some time. Perhaps it regularly shines at this time of the day, when I am still asleep? 'What you girls miss by not getting up!' as Caroline's Mamma always exclaims, though she is the most indulgent of parents. The trouble is that one *always* awakens early just when it is most desirable that one should slumber longest; as today, with the party before us. I am writing this now because I am *quite certain* that I shall be nothing but a tangle of nerves all day and, after everything is over, utterly spent and exhausted. So, for me, it always is with parties! I am glad that the day after tomorrow will be Sunday.

8th October. I met a man at the party, who, I must confess, interested me very much; and, besides that, what matters, as Mrs Fremlinson enquires in 'The Hopeful and the Despairing Heart,' *almost* my favorite of all books, as I truly declare?

Who could believe it? Just now, while I was still asleep, there was a knocking at my door, just loud enough to awaken me, but otherwise so soft and discreet, and there was the Contessa *herself*, in the most beautiful negligee, half rose-colored and half mauve, with a tray on which were things to eat and drink, a complete foreign breakfast, in fact! I must acknowledge that at that moment I could well have devoured a complete English breakfast, but what could have been kinder or more thoughtful on the part of the charming Contessa? Her dark hair (but not so dark as with the majority of the Italians) had not yet been dressed, and hung about her beautiful, though sad, face, but I noticed that all her rings were on her fingers, flashing and sparkling in the sunshine. 'Alas, mia cara,' she said, looking round the room, with its many deficiencies, 'the times that were and the times that are.' Then she actually bent over my face, rested her hand lightly on the top of my nightgown, and kissed me. 'But how pale you look!' she continued. 'You are white as a lily on the altar.' I smiled. 'I am English,' I said, 'and I lack strong coloring.' But the Contessa went on staring at me. Then she said, 'The party has quite fatigued you?' She seemed to express it as a question, so I replied, with vigor: 'Not in the least, I assure you, Contessa. It was the most beautiful evening of my life.' (Which was unquestionably the truth and no more than the truth.) I sat up in the big bed and, so doing, saw myself in the glass. It was true that I did look pale, unusually pale. I was about to remark upon the earliness of the hour, when the Contessa suddenly seemed to draw herself together with a gasp and turn remarkably pale herself, considering the native hue of her skin. She stretched out her hand and pointed. She seemed to be pointing at the pillow behind me. I looked round, disconcerted by her demeanor; and I saw an irregular red mark upon the pillow, not a very large mark, but undoubtedly a mark of blood. I raised my hands to my throat. 'Dio Illustrissimo!' cried out the Contessa. 'Ell' e stregata!' I know enough Italian, from Dante and from elsewhere, to be informed of what that means: 'She is bewitched.' I leapt out of bed and threw my arms round the Contessa before she could flee, as she seemed disposed to do. I besought her to say more, but I was all the time fairly sure that she would not. Italians, even educated ones, still take the idea of 'witchcraft' with a seriousness that to us seems unbelievable, and regularly fear even to speak of it. Here I knew by instinct that Emilia and her mistress would be at one. Indeed, the Contessa seemed most uneasy at my mere embrace, but she soon calmed herself, and left the room saying, quite pleasantly, that she must have a word with my parents about me. She even managed to wish me 'buon appetito' of my little breakfast.

I examined my face and throat in the looking glass, and there, sure enough, was a small scar on my neck which explained everything—except, indeed, how I had come by such a mark, but for that the novelties, the rigors, and the excitements of last night's party would *entirely* suffice. One cannot expect to enter the tournament of love and emerge unscratched: and it is into the tournament that, as I thrill to think, I verily have made my way. I fear it is perfectly typical of the Italian manner of seeing things that a perfectly natural, and very tiny, mishap should have such a disproportionate effect upon the Contessa. For myself, an English girl, the mark upon my pillow does not even disturb me. We must hope that it does not cast into screaming hysterics the girl whose duty it will be to change the linen.

If I look especially pale, it is partly because the very bright sunlight makes a contrast. I returned at once to bed and rapidly consumed every scrap and drop that the Contessa had brought to me. I seemed quite weak from lack of sustenance, and indeed I have but the slenderest recollection of last night's fare, except that, naturally, I drank far more than on most previous days of my short life, probably more than on *any*.

And now I lie here in my pretty nightgown and nothing else, with my pen in my hand and the sun on my face, and think about *him!* I did not believe such people existed in the real world. I thought that such writers as Mrs. Fremlinson and Mrs. Radcliffe *improved* men, in order to reconcile their female readers to their lot, and to put their less numerous male readers in a good conceit of themselves. Caroline's Mamma and Miss Gisborne, in their quite different ways, have both indicated as much most clearly; and my own observation hitherto of the opposite sex has confirmed the opinion. But now I have actually met a man at whom even Mrs. Fremlinson's finest creation does but hint! He is an Adonis! an Apollo! assuredly a god! Where he treads, sprouts asphodel!

The first romantic thing was that he was not properly presented to me—indeed, he was not presented at all. I know this was very incorrect, but it cannot be denied that it was very exciting. Most of the guests were dancing an old-fashioned *minuetto*, but as I did not know the steps, I was sitting at the end of the room with Mamma, when Mamma was suddenly overcome in some way and had to leave. She emphasized that she would be back in only a minute or two, but almost as soon as she had gone, *he* was standing there, quite as if he had emerged from between the faded tapestries that covered the wall or even from the tapestries themselves, except that he looked very far from faded, though later, when more candles were brought in for Supper, I saw that he was older than I had at first supposed, with such a wise and experienced look as I have never seen on any other face.

Of course he had not only to speak to me at once, or I should have risen and moved away, but to *compel* me, with his eyes and words, to remain. He said something pleasant about my being the only rosebud in a garden otherwise autumnal, but I am not such a goose as never to have heard speeches like that before, and it was what he said next that made me fatally hesitate. He said (and never, *never* shall I forget his words): 'As we are both visitants from a world that is not this one, we should know one another.' It was so exactly what I always feel about myself, as this journal (I fancy) makes clear, that I could not but yield a trifle to his apperceptiveness in finding words for my deepest conviction, extremely irregular and dangerous though I well knew my position to be. *And* he spoke in beautiful English; his accent (not, I think, an Italian one) only making his words the more choice-sounding and delightful!

I should remark here that it was not true that *all* the Contessa's guests were 'autumnal,' even though most of them certainly were. Sweet creature that she is, she had invited several cavalieri from the local nobility *expressly* for my sake, and several of them had duly been presented to me, but with small conversation resulting, partly because there was so little available of a common tongue, but more because each single cavaliero seemed to be very much what in

Derbyshire we call a peg-Jack. It was typical of the Contessa's sympathetic nature that she perceived the unsuccess of these recontres, and made no attempt to fan flames that were never so much as faint sparks. How unlike the matrons of Derbyshire, who, when they have set their minds to the task, will work the bellows in such cases not merely for a whole single evening, but for weeks, months, or on occasion, years! But then it would be unthinkable to apply the word 'matron' to the lovely Contessa! As it was, the four cavalieri were left to make what they could of the young Contessina and such other bambine as were on parade.

I pause for a moment seeking words in which to describe him. He is above the average tall, and, while slender and elegant, conveys a wondrous impression of force and strength. His skin is somewhat pallid, his nose aquiline and commanding (though with quivering, sensitive nostrils), his mouth scarlet and (I must apply the word) passionate. Just to look at his mouth made me think of great poetry and wide seas. His fingers are very long and fine, but powerful in their grip: as I learned for myself before the end of the evening. His hair I at first thought quite black, but I saw later that it was delicately laced with grey, perhaps even white. His brow is high, broad, and noble. Am I describing a god or a man? I find it hard to be sure.

As for his conversation I can only say that, indeed, it was not of this world. He proffered none of the empty chatter expected at social gatherings, which, in so far as it has any meaning at all, has a meaning quite different from that which the words of themselves convey—a meaning often odious to me. Everything he said (at least after the first conventional compliment) spoke to something deep within me, and everything I said in reply was what I really wanted to say. I have been able to talk in that way before with no man of any kind, from Papa downwards, and with very few women. And yet I find it difficult to recall what subjects we discussed. I think that may be a *consequence* of the feeling with which we spoke. The feeling I not merely recollect but feel still—all over and through me—deep and warm—transfiguring. The subjects, no. They were life, and beauty, and art, and nature, and myself: in fact, *everything*. Everything, that is, except the very different and very silly things that almost everyone else talks about all the time, chatter and chump without stopping this side of the churchyard. He did once observe that 'words are what prevail with women,' and I could only smile, it was so true.

Fortunately, Mamma *never* reappeared. As for the rest of them, I daresay they were more relieved than otherwise to find the gauche little English girl off their hands, so to speak, and apparently provided for. With Mamma indisposed, the obligation to watch over me would descend upon the Contessa, but her I saw only in the distance. Perhaps she was resolved not to intrude where *I* should not wish it. If so, it would be what I should expect of her. I do not know.

Then came Supper. Much to my surprise (and chagrin), my friend, if so I may call him, excused himself from participating. His explanation, lack of appetite, could hardly be accepted as sufficient or courteous, but the words he employed, succeeded (as always, I feel, with him) in purging the offense. He affirmed most earnestly that I must sustain myself even though he were unable to escort me, and that he would await my return. As he spoke, he gazed at me so movingly that I could but accept the situation, though I daresay I had as little appetite (for the course foods of this world) as he. I perceive that I have so far omitted to refer to the beauty and power of his eyes, which are so dark as to be almost black—at least by the light of candles. Glancing back at him, perhaps a little keenly, it occurred to me that he might be bashful about showing himself in his full years by the bright lights of the Supper tables. It is a vanity *by no means* confined to my own sex. Indeed he seemed almost to be shrinking away from the augmented brightness even at this far end of the room. And this for all the impression of strength which was the most marked thing about him. Tactfully I made to move off. 'You will return?' he asked, so anxiously and compellingly. I remained calm. I merely smiled.

And then Papa caught hold of me. He said that Mamma, having gone upstairs, had succumbed totally, as I might have known in advance she would do, and in fact *did* know; and that, when I had supped, I had 'better come upstairs also.' At that Papa elbowed me through to the tables and started trying to stuff me like a turkey, but, as I have said, I had little gusto for it, so little that I cannot now name a single thing that I ate, or that Papa ate either. Whatever it was, I 'washed it down' (as we say in Derbyshire) with an unusual quantity (for me) of the local wine, which people, including Papa, always say is so 'light,' but which always seems to me no 'lighter' than any other, but noticeably 'heavier' than some I could name. What is more, I had already consumed a certain amount of it earlier in the evening when I was supposed to be flirting with the local peg-Jacks. One curious thing is that Papa, who never fails to demur at my doing almost anything else, seems to have no objection to my drinking wine quite heavily. I do not think I have ever known him even try to impose a limit. That is material, of course, only in the rare absence of Mamma, to whom this observation does not apply. But Mamma herself is frequently unwell after only two or three glasses. At Supper last night, I was in a state of 'trance': eating food was well-nigh impossible, but drinking wine almost fatally facile. Then Papa started trying to push me off to bed again. After all that wine, and with my new friend patiently waiting for me, it was farcical. But I had to dispose of Papa somehow, so I promised him faithfully, and forgot my promise (whatever it was) immediately. Mercifully, I have not so far set eyes upon Papa since that moment.

Or, in reality, upon *anyone* until the Contessa waked me this morning: on anyone but *one*.

There he was quietly awaiting me among the shadows cast by the slightly swaying tapestries and by the flapping bannerets ranged round the walls above us. This time he actually clutched my hand in his eagerness. It was only for a moment, of course, but I felt the firmness of his grip. He said he hoped he was not keeping me from the dance floor, but I replied no, oh, No. In truth, I was barely even capable of dancing at that moment; and I fancy that the measures trod by the musty relics around us were, at the best of times, not for me. Then he said, with a slight smile, that once he had been a great dancer. Oh, I said idly and under the power of the wine; where was that? At Versailles, he replied; and in Petersburg. I must say that, wine or no wine, this surprised me; because surely, as everyone knows, Versailles was burned down by the incendiaries in 1789, a good thirty years ago? I must have glanced at him significantly, because he then said, smiling once more, though faintly: 'Yes, I am very, *very* old.' He said it with such curious emphasis that he did not seem to demand some kind of a denial, as such words normally do. In fact, I could find nothing immediate to say at all. And yet it was nonsense, and denial would have been sincere. I do not know his age, and find even an approximation difficult, but 'very, very old' he most certainly is not, but in all important ways one of the truly youngest people that can be imagined, and one of the most truly ardent. He was wearing the most beautiful black clothes, with a tiny Order of some kind, I am sure *most* distinguished, because so unobtrusive. Papa has often remarked that the flashy display of Honors is no longer correct.

In some ways the most romantic thing of all is that I do not even know his name. As people were beginning to leave the party, not so very late, I suppose, as most of the people were, after all, quite old, he took my hand and this time held it, nor did I even affect to resist. 'We shall meet again,' he said, 'many times,' looking so deeply and steadily into my eyes that I felt he had penetrated my inmost heart and soul. Indeed, there was something so powerful and mysterious about my own feelings at that moment that I could only murmur 'Yes,' in a voice so weak that he could hardly have heard me, and then cover my eyes with my hands, those eyes into which he had been gazing so piercingly. For a moment (it cannot have been longer, or my discomposure would have been observed by others), I sank down into a chair with all about me black and swimming, and when I had recovered myself, he was no longer there, and there was nothing to do but be kissed by the Contessa who said, 'You're looking tired, child,' and he hastened to my big bed, immediately.

And though new emotions are said to deprive us of rest (as I have myself been able to confirm on one or two occasions), I seem to have *slept* immediately too, and very deeply, and for a very long time. I know, too, that I dreamed remarkably, but I cannot at all recollect of what. Perhaps I do not need the aid of memory, for surely I can surmise?

On the first occasion since I have been in Italy, the sun is truly very hot. I do not think I shall write any more today. I have already covered pages in my small, clear handwriting, which owes so much to Miss Gisborne's patience and severity, and to her high standards in all matters touching young girlhood. I am rather surprised that I have been left alone for so long. Though Papa and Mamma do not seem to me to accomplish very much in proportion to the effort they expend, yet they are very inimical to 'lying about and doing nothing,' especially in my case, but in their own cases also, as I must acknowledge. I wonder how Mamma is faring after the excitements of last night? I am sure I should arise, dress, and ascertain; but instead I whisper to myself that once more I feel powerfully drawn towards the embrace of Morpheus.

9th October. Yesterday morning I decided that I had already recorded enough for one single day (though for what wonderful events I had to try, however vainly, to find words!), but there are few private occupations in this world about which I care more than inscribing the thoughts and impressions of my heart in this small, secret journal, which no one else shall ever in this world see (I shall take good care of that), so that I am sure I should again have taken up my pen in the evening, had there been any occurrence sufficiently definite to write about. *That*, I fear, is what Miss Gisborne would call one of my overloaded sentences, but overloaded sentences can be the reflection, I am sure, of overloaded spirits, and even be their only relief and outlet! How well at this moment do I recall Miss Gisborne's moving counsel: Only find the right words for your troubles, and your troubles become half joys. Alas, for me at this hour there can be no right words: in some strange way that I can by no means grasp hold of, I find myself fire and ice in equal parts. I have never before felt so greatly alive and yet I catch in myself an eerie conviction that my days are now closely numbered. It does not frighten me, as one would expect it to do. Indeed, it is very nearly a relief. I have never moved at my ease in this world, despite all the care that has been lavished on me; and if I had never known Caroline, hitherto my dearest friend (and sometimes her Mamma too), by comparison with. . . . Oh, there *are* no words. Also I have not completely recovered from the demands which last night made upon me. This is something I am rather ashamed of and shall admit to no one. But it is true. As well as being torn by emotion, I am worn to a silken thread.

The Contessa, having appeared in my room yesterday morning, then disappeared and was not seen again all day, as on the day we arrived. All the same she seemed to have spoken to Mamma about me, as she had said she would be doing. This soon became clear.

It was already afternoon before I finally rose from my bed and ventured from my sunny room. I was feeling very hungry once more, and I felt that I really must find out whether Mamma was fully recovered. So I went first and knocked at the door of Mamma and Papa's rooms. As there was no answer, I went downstairs, and, though there was no one else around (when it is at all sunny, most Italians simply lie down in the shade), there was Mamma, in full and blooming health, on the terrace overlooking the garden. She had her workbox with her and was sitting in the full sun trying to do two jobs at once, perhaps three, in her usual manner. When Mamma is feeling quite well, she always fidgets terribly. I fear that she lacks what the gentleman we met in Lausanne called 'the gift of repose.' (I have never forgotten that expression.)

Mamma set about me at once. 'Why didn't you dance with even one of those nice young men whom the Contessa had gone to the trouble of inviting simply for your sake? The Contessa is very upset about it. Besides, what have you been doing all the morning? This lovely, sunny day? And what is all this other rubbish the Contessa has been trying to tell me about you? I cannot understand a word of it. Perhaps you can enlighten me? I suppose it is something I ought to know about. No doubt it is a consequence of your Father and Mother agreeing to your going into the town on your own?'

Needless to say, I know by this time how to reply to Mamma when she rants on in terms such as these.

'The Contessa is very upset about it all,' Mamma exclaimed again after I had spoken; as if a band of knaves had stolen all the spoons, and I had been privy to the crime. 'She is plainly hinting at something which courtesy prevents her putting into words, and it is something to do with you. I should be obliged if you would tell me what it is. Tell me at once,' Mamma commanded very fiercely.

Of course I was aware that something had taken place between the Contessa and me that morning, and by now I knew very well what lay behind it: in one way or another the Contessa had divined my recontre of the evening before and had realized something (though how far from the whole!) of the effect it had made upon me. Even to me she had expressed herself in what English people would regard as an overwrought, Italianate way. It was clear that she had said something to Mamma on the subject, but of a veiled character, as she did not wish actually to betray me. She had, indeed, informed me that she was going to do this, and I now wished that I had attempted to dissuade her. The fact is that I had been so somnolent as to be half without my wits.

'Mamma,' I said, with the dignity I have learned to display at these times, 'if the Contessa has anything to complain of in my conduct, I am sure she will complain only when I am present.' And, indeed, I *was* sure of that; though doubtful whether the Contessa would ever consider complaining about me at all. Her addressing herself to Mamma in the present matter was, I could be certain, an attempt to aid me in some way, even though possibly misdirected, as was almost inevitable with someone who did not know Mamma very well.

'You are defying me, child,' Mamma almost screamed. 'You are defying your own Mother.' She had so worked herself up (surely about nothing? even less than usual?) that she managed to prick herself. Mamma is constantly pricking herself when she attempts needlework, mainly, I always think, because she *will* not concentrate upon any one particular task, and she keeps a wad of lint in her box against the next time it occurs. This time, however, the lint seemed to be missing and she appeared to have inflicted quite a gash. Poor Mamma flapped about like a bird beneath a net, while the blood was beginning to flow quite freely. I bent forward and sucked it away with my tongue. It was really strange to have Mamma's blood in my mouth. The strangest part was that it tasted delightful; almost like an exceptionally delicious sweetmeat! I feel my own blood mantling to my cheek as I write the words now.

Mamma then managed to staunch the miniature wound with her pocket handkerchief: one of the pretty ones she had purchased in Besancon. She was looking at me in her usual critical way, but all she said was: 'It is perhaps fortunate that we are leaving here on Monday.'

Though it was our usual routine, nothing had been said on the present occasion, and I was aghast. (Here, I suppose, *was* something definite to record yesterday evening!)

'What!' I cried. 'Leave the sweet Contessa so soon! Leave, within only a week, the town where Dante walked and wrote!' I smile a little as I perceive how, without thinking, I am beginning to follow the flamboyant Italian way of putting things. I am not really sure that Dante did *write* anything much in Ravenna, but to Italians such objections have little influence upon the choice of words. I realize that it is a habit I must guard against.

'Where Dante walked may be not at all a suitable place for you to walk,' rejoined Mamma, uncharitably, but with more sharpness of phrase and thought than is customary with her. She was fondling her injured thumb the while, and had nothing to mollify her acerbity towards me. The blood was beginning to redden the impromptu bandage, and I turned away with what writers call 'very mixed feelings.'

All the same, I did manage to see some more of the wide world before we leave Ravenna; and on the very next day, this day, Sunday, and even though it is a Sunday. Apparently, there is no English church in Ravenna, so that all we could compass was for Papa to read a few prayers this morning and go through the Litany, with Mamma and me making the responses. The Major-Domo showed the three of us to a special room for the purpose. It had nothing in it but an old table with shaky legs and a line of wooden chairs; all dustier and more decrepit even than other things I have seen in the Villa. Of course all this has happened in previous places when it was a Sunday, but never before under such dispiriting conditions—even, as I felt, *unhealthy* conditions. I was *most* disagreeably affected by the entire experience and *entirely* unable to imbibe the Word of God, as I should have done. I have never felt like that before even at the least uplifting of Family Prayers. Positively *irreverent* thoughts raced uncontrolledly through my little head: for example, I found myself wondering how efficacious God's Word could be for Salvation when droned and stumbled over by a mere uncanonized layman such as Papa—no, I mean, of course, *unordained*, but I have let the first word stand because it is so comic when applied to Papa, who is always denouncing 'the Roman

Saints' and all they represent, such as frequent days of public devotion in their honor. English people speak so unkindly of the Roman Catholic priests, but at least they have all, including the most unworthy of them, been touched by hands that go back and back and back to Saint Peter and so to the Spurting Fountain of Grace itself. You can hardly say the same for Papa, and I believe that even Mr. Biggs-Hartley's consecrationary position is a matter of dispute. I feel very strongly that the Blood of the Lamb cannot be mediated unless by the Elect or washed in by hands that are not strong and white.

Oh, how can he fulfill his promise that 'we shall meet again,' if Papa and Mamma drag me, protesting, from the place where we met first? Let alone meet 'many times'? These thoughts distract me, as I need not say; and yet I am quite sure that they distract me less than one might expect. For that the reason is simple enough: deep within me I *know* that some wondrous thing, some special election, has passed between him and me, and that meet again we shall in consequence, and no doubt 'many times.' Distracted about it all though I am, I am simultaneously so sure as to be almost at peace: fire and ice, as I have said. I find I can still sometimes think about other things, which was by no means the case when I fancied, long, long ago, that I was 'in love' (perish the thought!) with Mr. Franklin Stobart. Yes, yes, my wondrous friend has brought to my wild soul a measure of peace at last! I only wish I did not feel so tired. Doubtless it will pass when the events of the night before last are more distant (what sadness, though, when they are! What sadness, happen what may!), and, I suppose, this afternoon's tiring walk also. No, *not* 'tiring.' I refuse to admit the word, and that malapert Emilia returned home 'fresh as a daisy,' to use the expression her kind of person uses where I come from.

But what a walk it proved to be, none the less! We wandered through the *Pineta di Classe:* a perfectly enormous forest between Ravenna and the sea, with pine trees like very thick, dark, bushy umbrellas, and, so they say, either a brigand or a beast hiding behind each one of them! I have never seen such pine trees before; not in France or Switzerland or the Low Countries, let alone in England. They are more like trees in the Thousand Nights and a Night (not that I have read that work), dense enough at the top and stout-trunked enough for rocs to nest in! And such countless numbers of them, all so old! Left without a guide, I should easily have found myself lost within only a few minutes, so many and so vague are the different tracks among the huge conifers; but I have to admit that Emilia, quite shed now of her bien élevée finicking, strode out almost like a boy, and showed a knowledge of the best routes that I could only wonder at and take advantage of. There is now almost an understanding between me and Emilia, and it is mainly from her that I am learning an amount of Italian that is beginning quite to surprise me. All the time I recall, however, that it is a very simple language: the great poet of 'Paradise Lost' (not that I have read that work either) remarked that it was unnecessary to set aside special periods for instruction in Italian, because one could simply pick it up as one went along. So it is proving between me and Emilia.

The forest routes are truly best suited to gentlemen on horseback, and at one place two such emerged from one of the many tracks going off to our left. 'Guardi!' cried out Emilia and clutched my arm as if she were my intimate. 'Milord Byron and Signor Shelley!' (I do not attempt to indicate Emilia's funny approximation to the English names.) What a moment in my life—or in anyone's life! To see at the same time two persons both so great and famous and both so irrevocably doomed! There was not, of course, time enough for any degree of close observation, though Mr. Shelley seemed slightly to acknowledge with his crop our standing back a little to allow him and his friend free passage; but I fear that my main impression was of both giaours looking considerably older than I had expected and Lord Byron considerably more corpulent (as well as being quite grey-headed, though I believe only at the start of his life's fourth decade). Mr. Shelley was remarkably untidy in his dress and Lord Byron most comical: in that respect at least, the reality was in accord with the report. Both were without hats or caps. They cantered away down the track up which we had walked. They were talking in loud voices (Mr. Shelley's noticeably high in pitch), both together, above the thudding of their horses's hoofs. Neither of them really stopped talking even when slowing in order to wheel, so to speak, round the spot where we stood.

And so I have at length set eyes upon the fabled Lord Byron! A wondrous moment indeed; but how much more wondrous for me if it had occurred before that recent most wondrous of all possible moments! But it would be very wrong of me to complain because the red and risen moon has quite dimmed my universal nightlight! Lord Byron, that child of destiny, is for the whole world and, no doubt, for all time, or at least for a great deal of it! My fate is a different one and I draw it to my breast with a young girl's eager arms!

'Come gentili!' exclaimed Emilia, gazing after our two horsemen. It was not perhaps the most appropriate comment upon Lord Byron, or even upon Mr. Shelley, but there was nothing for me to reply (even if I could have found the Italian words), so on went our walk, with Emilia now venturing so far as to sing, in a quite pretty voice, and me lacking heart to chide her, until in the end the pine trees parted and I got my first glimpse of the Adriatic Sea, and, within a few more paces, a whole wide prospect of it. (The Venetian Lagoon I refuse to take seriously.) The Adriatic Sea is linked with the Mediterranean Sea, indeed quite properly a part or portion of it, so that I can now say to myself that I have 'seen the Mediterranean'; which good old Doctor Johnson defined as the true object of all Travel. It was almost as if at long last my own eyes had seen the Holy Grail, with the Redemptive Blood streaming forth in golden splendor; and I stood for whole moments quite lost in my own deep thoughts. The world falls from me once more in a moment as I muse upon that luminous, rapturous flood.

But I can write no more. So unwontedly weary do I feel that the vividness of my vision notwithstanding is something to be marveled at. It is as if my hand were guided as was Isabella's by the distant Traffio in Mrs. Fremlinson's wonderful book; so that Isabella was enabled to leave a record of the strange events that preceded her death—without which record, as it now occurs to me, the book, fiction though it be, could hardly with sense have been written at all. The old moon is drenching my sheets and my nightgown in brightest crimson. In Italy, the moon is always full and always so red.

Oh, when next shall I see my friend, my paragon, my genius!

10th October. I have experienced so sweet and great a dream that I must write down the fact before it is forgotten, and even though I find that already there is almost nothing left that *can* be written. I have dreamed that he was with me; that he induced my neck and breast with kisses that were at once the softest and the sharpest in the world; that he filled my ears with thoughts so strange that they could have come only from a world afar.

And now the Italian dawn is breaking: all the sky is red and purple. The rains have gone, as if forever. The crimson sun calls to me to take flight before it is once more autumn and then winter. Take flight! Today we are leaving for Rimini! Yes, it is but to Rimini that I am to repair. It is farcical.

And in my dawn-red room there is once again blood upon my person. But this time I know. It is at his embrace that my being springs forth, in joy and welcome; his embrace that is at once the softest and sharpest in the world. How strange that I could ever have failed to recall such bliss!

I rose from my bed to look for water, there being, once more, none in my room. I found that I was so weak with happiness that I all but fainted. But after sinking for a moment upon my bed, I somewhat recovered myself and succeeded in gently opening the door. And what should I find there? Or, rather, whom? In the faintly lighted corridor stood silently none other than the little Contessina, whom I cannot recollect having previously beheld since her Mamma's soirée à danse. She was dressed in some kind of loose dark wrapper, and I may only leave between her and her conscience what she can have been doing. No doubt for some good reason allied therewith, she seemed turned to stone by the sight of *me*. Of course I was in déshabillé even more complete than her own. I had omitted even to cover my nightgown. And upon that there was blood—as if I had suffered an injury. When I walked towards her reassuringly (after all, we are but two young girls and I am not her Judge—nor anyone's), she gave a low croaking scream and fled from me as if I had been the Erl Queen herself, but still almost silently, no doubt for her same good reasons. It was foolish of the little Contessina, because all I had in mind to do was to take her in my arms, and then to kiss her in token of our common humanity and the strangeness of our encounter at such an hour.

I was disconcerted by the Contessina's childishness (these Italians manage to be shrinking bambine and hardened women of the world at one and the same time), and, again feeling faint, leaned against the passage wall. When I stood full on my feet once more, I saw by the crimson light coming through one of the dusty windows that I had reached out to stop myself falling and left a scarlet impression of my hand on the painted plaster. It is difficult to excuse and impossible to remove. How I weary of these règles and conventionalities by which I have hitherto been bound! How I long for the measureless liberty that has been promised me and of which I feel so complete a future assurance!

But I managed to find some water (the Contessa's Villa is no longer of the kind that has servitors alert—or supposedly alert—all night in the larger halls), and with this water I did what I could, at least in my own room. Unfortunately I had neither enough water nor enough strength to do all. Besides, I begin to grow reckless.

11th October. No dear dream last night. Considerable crafty unpleasantness, however, attended our departure yesterday from

Ravenna. Mamma disclosed that the Contessa was actually lending us her own carriage. 'It's because she wants to see the last of us,' said Mamma to me, looking at the cornice. 'How can that be Mamma?' I asked. 'Surely, she's hardly seen us at all? She was invisible when we arrived, and now she's been invisible again for days.' 'There's no connection between those two things,' Mamma replied. 'At the time we arrived, the Contessa was feeling unwell, as we Mothers often do, you'll learn that for yourself soon. But for the last few days, she's been very upset by your behavior, and now she wants us to go.' As Mamma was still looking at the wall instead of at me, I put out the tip of my tongue, only the merest scrap of it, but *that* Mamma did manage to see, and had lifted her hand several inches before she recollected that I was now as good as an adult and so not to be corrected by a simple cuff.

And then when we were all about to enter the draggled old carriage, lo and behold, the Contessa did manage to haul herself into the light, and I caught her actually crossing herself behind my back, or what she no doubt thought was behind my back. I had to clench my hands to stop myself spitting at her. I have since begun to speculate whether she did not really *intend* me to see what she did. I was once so fond of the Contessa, so drawn to her—I can still *remember* that quite well—but *all* is now changed. A week, I find, can sometimes surpass a lifetime; and so, for that matter, can one single indelible night. The Contessa took great care to prevent her eyes once meeting mine, though, as soon as I perceived this, I never for a moment ceased glaring at her like a little basilisk. She apologized to Papa and Mamma for the absence of the Contessina, whom she described as being in bed with screaming megrims or the black cramp or some other malady (I truly cared not what! nor care now!) no doubt incident to girlish immaturity in Italy! And Papa and Mamma made response as if they really minded about the silly little child! Another way of expressing their disapproval of *me*, needless to observe. My considered opinion is that the Contessina and her Mamma are simply two of a kind, but that the Contessa has had time to become more skilled in concealment and duplicity. I am sure that all Italian females are alike, when one really knows them. The Contessa had made me dig my fingernails so far into my palms that my hands hurt all the rest of the day and still look as if I had caught a dagger in each of them, as in Sir Walter Scott's tale.

We had a coachman and a footman on the box, neither of them at all young, but more like two old wiseacres; and, when we reached Classe, we stopped in order that Papa, Mamma, and I could go inside the church, which is famous for its Mosaics, going back, as usual, to the Byzantines. The big doors at the western end were open in the quite hot sunshine and indeed the scene inside did look very pretty, all pale azure, the color of Heaven, and shining gold; but I saw no more of it than that, because as I was about to cross the threshold, I was again overcome by my faintness, and sitting down on a bench, bade Papa and Mamma go in without me, which they immediately did, in the sensible English way, instead of trying to make an ado over me, in the silly Italian way. The bench was of marble, with arms in the shape of lions, and though the marble was worn, and cut, and pock-marked, it was a splendid, heavy object, carved, if I mistake not, by the Romans themselves. Seated on it, I soon felt better once more, but then I noticed the two fat old men on the coach doing something or other to the doors and windows. I supposed they were greasing them, which I am sure would have been very much in order, as would have been a considerable application of paint to the entire vehicle. But when Papa and Mamma at last came out of the church, and we all resumed our places, Mamma soon began to complain of a smell, which she said was, or at least resembled, that of the herb, garlic. Of course when one is abroad, the smell of garlic is *everywhere,* so that I quite understood when Papa merely told Mamma not to be fanciful; but then I found that I myself was more and more affected, so that we completed the journey in almost complete silence, none of us, except Papa, having much appetite for the very crude meal set before us en route at Cesenatico. 'You're looking white,' said Papa to me, as we stepped from the coach. Then he added to Mamma, but hardly attempting to prevent my hearing, 'I can see why the Contessa spoke to you as she did.' Mamma merely shrugged her shoulders: something she would never have thought of doing before we came abroad, but which now she does frequently. I nearly said something spiteful. At the end, the Contessa was constantly disparaging my appearance, and indeed I am pale, paler than I once was, though always I have been pale enough, pale as a little phantom; but only I know the reason for the change in me, and no one else shall know it ever, because no one else ever can. It is not so much a 'secret.' Rather it is a revelation.

In Rimini we are but stopping at the inn; and we are almost the only persons to be doing so. I cannot wonder at this: the inn is a gaunt, forbidding place; the Padrona has what in Derbyshire we call a 'harelip'; and the attendance is of the worst. Indeed, no one has so far ventured to come near me. All the rooms, including mine, are very large and all lead into one another, in the style of two hundred years ago. The building resembles a Palazzo that has fallen upon hard times, and perhaps that is what it is. At first I feared that my dear Papa and Mamma were to be ensconced in the apartment adjoining my own, which would have suited me not at all, but, for some reason, it has not happened, so that between my room and the staircase are two dark and empty chambers, which would once have caused me alarm, but which now I welcome. Everything is poor and dusty. Shall I ever repose abroad in such ease and bien-être as one takes for granted in Derbyshire? Why, no, I shall not: and a chill runs down my back as I inscribe the words; but a chill more of excitement than of fear. Very soon now shall I be entirely elsewhere and entirely above such trivia.

I have opened a pair of the big windows, a grimy and, I fear, a noisy task. I flitted out in the moonlight on to the stone balcony, and gazed down into the Piazza. Rimini seems now to be a very poor town, and there is nothing of the nocturnal uproar and riot which are such usual features of Italian existence. At this hour, all is completely silent—even strangely so. It is still very warm, but there is a mist between the Earth and the Moon.

I have crept into another of these enormous Italian beds. He is winging towards me. There is no further need for words. I have but to slumber, and that will be simple, so exhausted I am.

12th, 13th, 14th October. Nothing to relate but him, and of him nothing that can be related. (I am very tired, but it is tiredness that follows exaltation, not the vulgar tiredness of common life; I noticed today that I no longer have either shadow or reflection.) Fortunately Mamma was quite destroyed (as the Irish simpletons express it) by the journey from Ravenna, and has not been seen since. How many, many hours one's elders pass in retirement! How glad I am never to have to experience such bondage! How I rejoice when I think about the new life which spreads before me into infinity, the new ocean which already laps at my feet, the new vessel with the purple sail and the red oars upon which I shall at any moment embark! When one is confronting so tremendous a transformation, how foolish some words, but the habit of them lingers even when I have hardly strength to hold the pen! Soon, soon, new force will be mine, fire that is inconceivable; and the power to assume any night-shape that I may wish, or to fly through the darkness with none. What love is his! How chosen among all women am I; and I am just a little English girl! It is a miracle, and I shall enter the halls of Those Other Women with pride.

Papa is so beset by Mamma that he has failed to notice that I am eating nothing and drinking only water; that at our horrid, odious meals I am but feigning.

Believe it or not, yesterday we visited, Papa and I, the Tempio Malatestiano. Papa went as an English Visitor: I (at least by comparison with Papa) as a Pythoness. It is a beautiful edifice, among the most beautiful in the world, they say. But for me a special splendor lay in the noble and amorous dead it houses, and in the control over them which I feel increase within me. I was so rent and torn with new power that Papa had to help me back to the inn. Poor Papa, burdened, as he supposes, by *two* weak invalid women! I could almost pity him.

I wish I had reached the pretty little Contessina and kissed her throat.

15th October. Last night I opened my pair of windows (the other pair resists me, weak—in terms of this world—as I am) and, without quite venturing forth, stood there in nakedness and raised both my arms. Soon a soft wind began to rustle, where all had previously been still as death. The rustling steadily rose to roaring, and the faint chill of the night turned to heat as when an oven door is opened. A great crying out and weeping, a buzzing and scream-ing and scratching swept in turmoil past the open window, as if invisible (or almost invisible) bodies were turning around and around in the air outside, always lamenting and accusing. My head was split apart by the sad sounds and my body as moist as if I were an ottoman. Then, on an instant, all had passed by. He stood there before me in the dim embrasure of the window. 'That,' he said, 'is Love as the elect of this world know it.' 'The *elect?*' I besought him, in a voice so low that it was hardly a voice at all (but what matter?). 'Why yes,' he seemed to reaffirm. 'Of this world, the elect.'

16th October. The weather in Italy changes constantly. Today once more it is cold and wet.

They have begun to suppose me ill. Mamma, back on her legs for a spell, is fussing like a blowfly round a dying lamb. They even called in a Medico, after discussing at length in my presence whether an Italian physician could be regarded as of any utility. With what voice I have left, I joined in vigorously that he could not. All the same, a creature made his appearance: wearing fusty black, and, believe it or not, a grey *wig*—in all, a veritable Pantalone. What a farce! With my ever sharper fangs, I had him soon despatched, and yelling like the Old Comedy he belonged to. Then I spat forth his enfeebled, senile lymph, cleaned my lips of his skin and smell, and returned, hugging myself, to my couch.

Janua mortis vita, as Mr. Biggs-Hartley says in his funny Dog Latin. And to think that today is Sunday! I wonder why no one has troubled to pray over me?

17th October. I have been left alone all day. Not that it matters.

Last night came the strangest and most beautiful event of my life, a seal laid upon my future.

I was lying here with my double window open, when I noticed that mist was coming in. I opened my arms to it, but my blood began to trickle down my bosom from the wound in my neck, which of course no longer heals—though I seem to have no particular trouble in concealing the mark from the entire human race, not forgetting learned men with certificates from the University of Sciozza.

Outside in the Piazza was a sound of shuffling and nuzzling, as of sheep being folded on one of the farms at home. I climbed out of bed, walked across, and stepped on to the balcony.

The mist was filtering the moonlight into a silver-grey that I have never seen elsewhere.

The entire Piazza, a very big one, was filled with huge, grizzled wolves, all perfectly silent, except for the small sounds I have mentioned, all with their tongues flopping and lolling, black in the silvery light, and all gazing up at my window.

Rimini is near to the Apennine Mountains, where wolves notoriously abound, and commonly devour babies and small children. I suppose that the coming cold is drawing them into the towns.

I smiled at the wolves. Then I crossed my hands on my little bosom and curtsied. They will be prominent among my new people. My blood will be theirs, and theirs mine.

I forgot to say that I have contrived to lock my door. Now, I am assisted in such affairs.

Somehow I have found my way back to bed. It has become exceedingly cold, almost icy. For some reason I think of all the empty rooms in this battered old Palazzo (as I am sure it once was), so fallen from their former stateliness. I doubt if I shall write any more. I do not think I shall have any more to say.

NARAPOIA

Alan Nelson

I don't know exactly how to explain it to you, Doctor,' the young man began. He smoothed back his slick black hair that shone like a phonograph record and blinked his baby blue eyes. 'It seems to be the opposite of a persecution complex.'

Dr. Manly J. Departure was a short severe man who made a point of never exhibiting surprise. 'The opposite of a persecution complex?' he said, permitting one eyebrow to elevate. 'How do you mean—the opposite of a persecution complex, Mr. McFarlane?'

'Well, for one thing, I keep thinking that I'm following someone.' McFarlane sat placidly in the big easy chair, hands folded, pink cheeks glowing, the picture of health and tranquility. Dr. Departure stirred uneasily.

'You mean you think someone is following *you*, don't you?' the doctor corrected.

'No. No, I don't! I mean that while I'm walking along the street, suddenly I have this feeling there is somebody just ahead of me. Somebody I'm after. Someone I'm following. Sometimes I even begin to run to catch up with him! Of course—there's no one there. It's inconvenient. Damned inconvenient. And I hate to run.'

Dr. Departure fiddled with a pencil. 'I see. Is there anything else?'

'Well, yes. I keep having this feeling that people . . . that people . . . well, it's really very silly . . .'

'It's quite all right,' Dr. Departure purred. 'Feel free to tell me anything.'

'Well, I keep having this strange feeling that people are plotting to do me good. That they're trying to be benevolent and kind toward me. I don't know exactly who they are, or why they wish me all this kindness, but . . . it's all very fantastic, isn't it?'

It had been a long hard day for Dr. Departure. Somehow he did not feel up to any more symptoms. He busied himself for the rest of the hour obtaining factual background. McFarlane was 32; happily married; healthy, normal childhood; satisfactory employment as a radio repairman; no physical complaints; no bad dreams; no drinking; no history of parental discord; no financial worries. Nothing.

'Shall we say Thursday at ten, then?' he smiled, ushering McFarlane out.

At ten minutes to ten on Thursday, Dr. Departure looked at his appointment book and frowned. Well, maybe he wouldn't show up. Very often that happened. He certainly hoped that this would be one of the occasions. Opposite of a persecution complex! Delusions of beneficence! Indeed! The man must be . . . he checked himself hastily. He'd almost said 'mad.' At that moment the door buzzer sounded and McFarlane was grinning and shaking his hand.

'Well, well.' Dr. Departure's affability seemed somewhat hollow. 'Any new developments?'

'Seems to me I'm getting worse,' McFarlane beamed. 'This business of following someone, I mean. Yes sir. Yesterday, I must have walked five miles!'

Dr. Departure relaxed into his chair across the desk.

'Well, now, suppose you tell me more about it. *All* about it. Just *anything* that comes to mind.'

McFarlane frowned.

'What do you mean, Doctor, just anything that comes to mind?'

'Just ramble on—about anything—whatever comes into your head.'

'I'm not sure I understand. Could you show me what you mean, Doctor? Just by way of illustration?'

The doctor permitted himself a little chuckle.

'Why, it's very simple . . . Well . . . like right now I'm thinking how one time I stole some money out of Mother's purse . . . and now I'm thinking about my wife, wondering what to get her for our wedding anniversary . . .' The doctor looked up hopefully. 'See? Just anything like that.'

'Anything like what? I still don't quite understand.' But McFarlane's face was not puzzled; it was eager. 'Could you give me just a couple more illustrations? They're very interesting.'

The doctor found himself relating disconnected, half-forgotten images. McFarlane sat back with a strangely contented expression.

At the end of the hour, Dr. Departure was quite exhausted. His voice was hoarse; his collar and tie askew. '. . . and well, my wife—she completely dominates me . . . I always was very sensitive that my eyes are slightly crossed . . . I never will forget—that time in the attic, with the little girl across the street . . . I was only eleven I guess . . .' Reluctantly, he broke off, wiped his eyes and glanced at his watch.

'I feel much better,' he heard McFarlane say. 'Shall we say Tuesday at ten?'

Next Tuesday at ten, Dr. Departure inwardly braced himself.

'There'll be no more nonsense like last Thursday's session,' he assured himself, but he had no cause for concern. McFarlane was strangely silent and preoccupied. He carried a large cardboard box, which he carefully set upon the floor before seating himself in the leather chair. The doctor prodded him with a few preliminary questions.

'I'm afraid I'm beginning to be troubled with hallucinations, Doctor,' McFarlane finally volunteered.

Dr. Departure mentally rubbed his hands. He was back on old familiar territory now. He felt more comfortable.

'Ah, hallucinations!'

'Rather, they're not really hallucinations, Doctor. You might say they were the *opposite* of hallucinations.'

Dr. Departure rested his eyes a moment. The smile disappeared from his face. McFarlane continued:

'Last night, for instance, Doctor, I had a nightmare. Dreamed there was a big ugly bird perched on my short-wave set waiting for me to wake up. It was a hideous thing—a fat bulbous body and a huge beak that turned upward like a sickle. Blood-shot eyes with pouches under them. And ears, Doctor. Ears! Did you ever hear of a bird with ears? Little tiny, floppy ears, something like a cocker spaniel's. Well, I woke up, my heart pounding, and what do you think? There actually *was* an ugly fat bird with ears sitting on the short-wave set.'

Dr. Departure perked up again. A very simple case of confusing the real with the unreal. Traditional. Almost classical.

'A real bird on the short-wave set?' he asked gently. 'With blood-shot eyes?'

'Yes,' McFarlane replied. 'I know it sounds silly. I know it's hard to believe.'

'Oh, not at all. Not at all. That type of visual aberration is a common enough phenomenon.' The doctor smiled soothingly. 'Nothing to . . .'

McFarlane interrupted him by reaching down and hoisting the carton onto the desk. 'You don't understand, Doctor,' he said. 'Go ahead. Open it.'

The doctor looked at McFarlane a moment, then at the brown box which was punctured with air holes and tied with heavy twine. Disconcertedly, the doctor cut the string and folded back the top flaps. He leaned over and peered in—then sucked in his breath. Pouchy, blood-shot eyes leered up at him. Floppy ears. The up-side-down beak. An obscene-looking bird.

'His name is Lafayette,' McFarlane said, tossing a few bread crumbs into the carton which were quickly devoured with a noisy, repulsive gulp. 'He rather grows on you after a while, don't you think?'

After McFarlane left with his hallucination, the doctor sat a few moments meditating. He felt a little dizzy and lightheaded as though he had just emerged from a ride through the Tunnel of Horrors at the beach.

Maybe I *am* witnessing an entirely new psychosis, he told himself. Funny things are happening in the world today. He saw himself before the American Psychiatric Congress delivering a monograph: 'The Emergence of a New Psychosis.' This new disorder apparently had symptoms opposite from Paranoia—he could call it Narapoia. Hopefully, Dr. Departure foresaw the possibility that some of his colleagues would insist on naming it after its discoverer: 'Departureomania.' He would be famous; his name linked with Freud. A sickening thought struck him. Supposing this man McFarlane was a malingerer! A fake! By God, he'd find out! Quickly, he buzzed his secretary, Miss Armstrong, and instructed her to cancel all appointments for the rest of the day. Then he reached for his hat and fled from the building.

Three days later the telephone in Dr. Departure's office rang. Miss Armstrong answered it. It was Mrs. Departure.

'No, he isn't here,' Miss Armstrong said. 'As a matter of fact he hasn't been here for three days except to bounce in and out for his mail.'

'I don't know what's the matter with that man.' Mrs. Departure's exasperated voice rattled the receiver. 'He's gone half the night, too. Comes home utterly exhausted. What do you suppose he's writing in that little notebook?'

'Frankly, I'm worried about him,' Miss Armstrong replied. 'He's so irritable. And in such a frightful rush all the time.'

'You're looking peaked, Doc,' McFarlane said, at his next meeting a week later. It was the first time the doctor had sat behind the desk for many days. His legs ached. Stealthily, beneath the desk, he slipped off both scuffed shoes to relieve the pressure from his blistered feet.

'Never mind about me,' the doctor snapped. 'How are *you*?' The doctor's fingers twitched. He was much thinner and his face was pale and drawn.

'I think I must be getting better,' McFarlane announced. 'I have the feeling lately that someone is following *me*.'

'Nonsense!' Dr. Departure snapped at him irritably. 'It's just your imagination.' He squinted his eyes and gazed at McFarlane. If only he could be sure this McFarlane was not faking. So far there was nothing to indicate he was. After all, his sudden urge on the streets to overtake someone seemed perfectly genuine. McFarlane would raise his head, his pace would quicken, and away he would go. 'Well, I'll just have to watch him a little while longer,' the doctor told himself. He closed his eyes a moment, reviewing his activities for the previous week: the long cross-city jaunts in which he had almost lost McFarlane a dozen times; the long, long waits outside restaurants and bars waiting for McFarlane to emerge. 'I'll just have to keep going until I get all the facts,' he thought. But he was a little concerned with the weight he'd lost, and with the strange ringing noises in his head which had recently developed. . . .

At the end of the hour, McFarlane tiptoed out of the office. Dr. Departure was snoring fuzzily.

On the day of McFarlane's next appointment with the doctor, he was met at the door by Miss Armstrong. 'Doctor isn't here,' she informed him. 'He's taken a leave of absence for three months —possibly a year.'

'Oh, I'm sorry to hear it,' McFarlane said. 'He *was* looking done in, though. Where is he, on vacation?'

'As a matter of fact, he's at Marwood Sanitarium.'

A strange puzzled look suddenly settled over McFarlane's face and he gazed into space a moment. Presently, he smiled at the secretary.

'I just had the funniest feeling,' he said. 'Suddenly I feel like

NARAPOIA

I'm completely cured. All of a sudden. Just when you told me about Dr. Departure.'

The doctors had quite a time with Dr. Departure at the sanitarium.

'Just tell us anything that comes into your mind,' they urged. Departure's eyes were glazed and he was very excited.

'I've got to follow him, I tell you! I can't let him get out of sight. Not for an instant. He's got a bird with baggy eyes and floppy ears.'

'Very interesting. *All* very interesting!' The doctors gloomed among themselves, shaking their heads scientifically:

'Something entirely new!'

'It's rather like a persecution complex—isn't it?—only the opposite!'

'He seems to have the delusion he is following someone. Amazing, isn't it?'

'Probably the emergence of a brand new psychosis. I suggest that we observe him very closely.'

And here one of the doctors went so far as to suggest further that they allow Dr. Departure to move about the city at will—closely watched, of course, by alternately selected members of their staff—so that all his actions could be carefully noted. . . .

BORN OF MAN AND WOMAN

Richard Matheson

X—This day when it had light mother called me a retch. You retch she said. I saw in her eyes the anger. I wonder what it is a retch.

This day it had water falling from upstairs. It fell all around. I saw that. The ground of the back I watched from the little window. The ground it sucked up the water like thirsty lips. It drank too much and it got sick and runny brown. I didn't like it.

Mother is a pretty I know. In my bed place with cold walls around I have a paper thing that was behind the furnace. It says on it SCREEN-STARS. I see in the pictures faces like of mother and father. Father says they are pretty. Once he said it.

And also mother he said. Mother so pretty and me decent enough. Look at you he said and didn't have the nice face. I touched his arm and said it is alright father. He shook and pulled away where I couldn't reach.

Today mother let me off the chain a little so I could look out the little window. That's how I saw the water falling from upstairs.

XX—This day it had goldness in the upstairs. As I know, when I looked at it my eyes hurt. After I look at it the cellar is red.

I think this was church. They leave the upstairs. The big machine swallows them and rolls out past and is gone. In the back part is the *little* mother. She is much small than me. I am big. It is a secret but I have pulled the chain out of the wall. I can see out the little window all I like.

In this day when it got dark I had eat my food and some bugs. I hear laughs upstairs. I like to know why there are laughs for. I took the chain from the wall and wrapped it around me. I walked squish to the stairs. They creak when I walk on them. My legs slip on them because I don't walk on stairs. My feet stick to the wood.

I went up and opened a door. It was a white place. White as white jewels that come from upstairs sometime. I went in and stood quiet. I hear the laughing some more. I walk to the sound and look through to the people. More people than I thought was. I thought I should laugh with them.

Mother came out and pushed the door in. It hit me and hurt. I fell back on the smooth floor and the chain made noise. I cried. She made a hissing noise into her and put her hand on her mouth. Her eyes got big.

She looked at me. I heard father call. What fell he called. She said a iron board. Come help pick it up she said. He came and said now is *that* so heavy you need. He saw me and grew big. The anger came in his eyes. He hit me. I spilled some of the drip on the floor from one arm. It was not nice. It made ugly green on the floor.

Father told me to go to the cellar. I had to go. The light it hurt some now in my eyes. It is not so like that in the cellar.

Father tied my legs and arms up. He put me on my bed. Upstairs I heard laughing while I was quiet there looking on a black spider that was swinging down to me. I thought what father said. Ohgod he said. And only eight.

XXX—This day father hit in the chain again before it had light. I have to try pull it out again. He said I was bad to come upstairs. He said never do that again or he would beat me hard. That hurts.

I hurt. I slept the day and rested my head against the cold wall. I thought of the white place upstairs.

XXXX—I got the chain from the wall out. Mother was upstairs. I heard little laughs very high. I looked out the window. I saw all little people like the little mother and little fathers too. They are pretty.

They were making nice noise and jumping around the ground. Their legs was moving hard. They are like mother and father. Mother says all right people look like they do.

One of the little fathers saw me. He pointed at the window. I let go and slid down the wall in the dark. I curled up as they would not see. I heard their talks by the window and foots running. Upstairs there was a door hitting. I heard the little mother call upstairs. I heard heavy steps and I rushed to my bed place. I hit the chain in the wall and lay down on my front.

I heard mother come down. Have you been at the window she said. I heard the anger. *Stay* away from the window. You have pulled the chain out again.

She took the stick and hit me with it. I didn't cry. I can't do that. But the drip ran all over the bed. She saw it and twisted away and made a noise. Oh mygod mygod she said why have you *done* this to me? I heard the stick go bounce on the stone floor. She ran upstairs. I slept the day.

XXXXX—This day it had water again. When mother was upstairs I heard the little one come slow down the steps. I hidded myself in the coal bin for mother would have anger if the little mother saw me.

She had a little live thing with her. It walked on the arms and had pointy ears. She said things to it.

It was all right except the live thing smelled me. It ran up the coal and looked down at me. The hairs stood up. In the throat it made an angry noise. I hissed but it jumped on me.

I didn't want to hurt it. I got fear because it bit me harder than the rat does. I hurt and the little mother screamed. I grabbed the live thing tight. It made sounds I never heard. I pushed it all together. It was all lumpy and red on the black coal.

I hid there when mother called. I was afraid of the stick. She left. I crept over the coal with the thing. I hid it under my pillow and rested on it. I put the chain in the wall again.

X—This is another times. Father chained me tight. I hurt because he beat me. This time I hit the stick out of his hands and made noise. He went away and his face was white. He ran out of my bed place and locked the door.

I am not so glad. All day it is cold in here. The chain comes slow out of the wall. And I have a bad anger with mother and father. I will show them. I will do what I did that once.

I will screech and laugh loud. I will run on the walls. Last I will hang head down by all my legs and laugh and drip green all over until they are sorry they didn't be nice to me.

If they try to beat me again I'll hurt them. I will.

MYTHAGO WOOD

Robert Holdstock

W hen, in 1944, I was called away to the war, I felt so resentful of my father's barely expressed concern for my safety that, on the eve of my departure, I walked quietly to his desk and tore a page out of his notebook, the diary in which his silent, obsessive work was recorded. The fragment was dated simply 'August 34,' and I read it many times, appalled at its incomprehensibility, but content that I had stolen at least a tiny part of his life with which to support myself through those painful, lonely times.

The entry began with a short and very bitter comment on the distractions in his life—the running of Oak Lodge, our family home, the demands of his two sons and of his wife (by then, I remember, my mother was desperately ill and close to the end of her life)—it ended with a passage quite memorable for its incoherence:

'A letter from Watkins—agrees with me that at certain times of the year the aura around the woodland could reach as far as the house. Must think through the implications of this. He is keen to know the power of the oak vortex that I have measured. What to tell him? Certainly not of the first mythago. Have noticed too that the enrichment of the pre-mythago zone is more persistent, but concomitant with this, am distinctly losing my sense of time.'

I treasured this piece of paper for many reasons, for the moment or two of my father's passionate interest that it represented—and for the way it locked me out of its understanding, as he had locked me out at home. Everything he loved, everything I hated.

I was wounded in early 1945 and when the war finished I managed to stay in France, travelling South to convalesce in a village in the hills behind Marseilles, where I lived with old friends of my father. It was a hot, dry place, very still, very slow; I spent my time sitting in the village square and quickly became a part of the tiny community.

Letters from my brother Christian, the war, arrived every month throughout the long year of 1946. They were chatty, informative letters, but there was an increasing note of tension in them, and it was clear that Christian's relationship with his father was deteriorating rapidly. I never heard a word from the old man himself, but then I never expected to; I had long since resigned myself to the fact that, even at best, he regarded me with total indifference. All his family had been an intrusion in his work, and his guilt at neglecting us, and especially at driving his wife to taking her own life, had blossomed rapidly, during the early years of the war, into an hysterical madness that could be truly frightening. Which is not to say that he was perpetually shouting; on the contrary, most of his life was spent in silent, absorbed contemplation of the oak woodland that bordered our home. At first infuriating, because of the distance it put between him and his family, soon those long periods of quiet became blessed, earnestly welcomed.

He died in November, 1946, of the illness that had afflicted him for years. When I heard the news I was torn between my unwillingness to return to Oak Lodge, at the edge of the Ryhope estate in Herefordshire, and Christian's obvious distress. He was alone, now, in the house where we had lived through our childhood together; I could imagine him prowling through the empty rooms, perhaps sitting in father's dank and unwholesome study and remembering the hours of denial, the smell of wood and compost that the old man had trudged in through the glass-paneled doors after his week-long sorties into the deep woodlands. The forest had spread into that room as if my father could not bear to be away from the rank undergrowth and cool, moist oak glades even when making token acknowledgement of his family. He made that acknowledgement in the only way he knew: by telling us—and mainly telling my brother—stories of the ancient forestlands beyond the house, the primary woodland of oak and ash in whose dark interior (he once said) wild boar could still be heard and smelled and tracked by their spoor.

I doubt if he had ever seen such a creature, but that evening, as I sat in my room overlooking the tiny village in the hills (Christian's letter a crushed ball still held in my hands) I vividly recalled how I had listened to the muffled grunting of some woodland animal and heard the heavy, unhurried crashing of something bulky moving inwards, to the winding pathway that we called Deep Track, a route that led spirally towards the very heartwoods of the forest.

I knew I would have to go home, and yet I delayed my departure for nearly another year. During that time Christian's letters ceased abruptly. In his last letter, dated April 10th, he wrote of Guiwenneth, of his unusual marriage, and hinted that I would be surprised by the lovely girl to whom he had lost his 'heart, mind, soul, reason, cooking ability and just about everything else, Steve.' I wrote to congratulate him, of course, but there was no further communication between us for months.

Eventually I wrote to say I was coming home, that I would stay at Oak Lodge for a few weeks and then find accommodation in one of the nearby towns. I said goodbye to France, and to the community that had become so much a part of my life, and traveled to England by bus and train, by ferry, and then by train again. And on August 20th, hardly able to believe what was happening to me, I arrived by pony and trap at the disused railway line that skirted the edge of the extensive Ryhope estate. Oak Lodge lay on the far side of the grounds, four miles further round the road but accessible via the right of way through the estate's fields and woodlands. I intended to take an intermediate route, and so, lugging my single, crammed suitcase as best I could, I began to walk along the grass-covered railway track, peering, on occasion, over the high red-brick wall that marked the limit of the estate, trying to see through the gloom of the pungent pine woods. Soon this woodland, and the wall, vanished, and the land opened into tight, tree-bordered fields, to which I gained access across a rickety wooden stile, almost lost beneath briar and full-fruited blackberry bushes. I had to trample my way out of the public domain and so onto the south trackway that wound, skirting patchy woodland and the stream called 'sticklebrook,' up to the ivy-covered house that was my home.

It was late morning and very hot as I came in distant sight of Oak Lodge. Somewhere off to my left I could hear the drone of a tractor. I thought of old Alphonse Jeffries, the estate's farm supervisor, and with memory of his weather-tanned, smiling face came images of the millpond and fishing for pike from his tiny rowboat.

Memory of the millpond was as tranquil as its surface, and I moved away from the south track, through waist-high nettles and a tangle of ash and hawthorn scrub until I came out close to the bank of the wide, shadowy pool, its full size hidden by the gloom of the dense stand of oak woodland that began on its far side. Almost hidden among the rushes that crowded the nearer edge of the pond was the shallow boat from which we had fished, years before; its white paint was flaked away almost entirely now, and although the craft looked watertight, I doubted if it would take the weight of a full-grown man. I didn't disturb it but walked around the bank and sat down on the rough concrete steps of the crumbling boathouse; from here I watched the surface of the pool rippling with the darting motions of insects and the occasional passage of a fish, just below.

'A couple of sticks and a bit of string . . . that's all it takes.'

Christian's voice startled me. He must have walked along a beaten track from the lodge, hidden from my view by the shed. Delighted, I jumped to my feet and turned to face him. The shock of his appearance was like a physical blow to me, and I think he noticed the fact, even though I threw my arms about him and gave him a powerful brotherly bear hug.

'I had to see this place again,' I said.

'I know what you mean,' he said, as we broke our embrace. 'I often walk here myself.' There was a moment's awkward silence as we stared at each other. I felt, distinctly, that he was not particularly pleased to see me. 'You're looking brown and drawn, old boy,' he said. 'Healthy and ill together. . . .'

'Mediterranean sun, grape picking, and shrapnel. I'm still not one hundred percent.' I smiled. 'But it *is* good to be back, to see you again.'

'Yes,' he said dully. 'I'm glad you've come, Steve. Very glad. Really. I'm afraid the place . . . well, a bit of a mess. I only got your letter yesterday and I haven't had a chance to do anything. Things have changed quite a bit, you'll find.'

And he more than anything. I could hardly believe that this was the chipper, perky young man who had left with his army unit in 1944. He had aged incredibly, his hair quite streaked with grey, more noticeable for his having allowed it to grow long and untidy on the back and sides. He reminded me very much of father, the same distant, distracted look, the same hollow cheeks and deeply wrinkled face. But it was his whole demeanor that had shocked me. He had always been a stocky, muscular chap; now he was like the proverbial scarecrow, wiry, ungainly, on edge all the time. His eyes darted about but never seemed to focus upon me. And he smelled. Of mothballs, as if the crisp white shirt and grey flannels that he wore had been dragged out of storage; and another smell beyond the naptha . . . the hint of woodland and grass. There was dirt under his fingernails and in his hair, and his teeth were yellowing.

He seemed to relax slightly as the minutes ticked by. We sparred a bit, laughed a bit, and walked around the pond, whacking at the rushes with sticks. I could not shake off the feeling that I had arrived home at a bad time.

'Was it difficult . . . with the old man, I mean? The last days.'

He shook his head. 'There was a nurse here for the final two weeks or so. I can't exactly say that he went peacefully, but she managed to stop him damaging himself . . . or me, for that matter.'

'Your letters certainly suggested a growing hostility. To understate the case.'

Christian smiled quite grimly and glanced at me with a curious expression, somewhere between agreement and suspicion. 'You got that from my letters, did you? Well, yes. He became quite crazed soon after I came back from the war. You should have seen the place, Steve. You should have seen him. I don't think he'd washed for months. I wondered what he'd been eating . . . certainly nothing as simple as eggs and meat. In all honesty I think, for a few months at any rate, he'd been eating wood and leaves. He was in a wretched state. Although he let me help him with his work, he quickly began to resent me. He tried to kill me on several occasions, Steve. And I mean that, really desperate attempts on my life. There was a reason for it, I suppose. . . .'

I was astonished by what Christian was telling me. The image of my father had changed from that of a cold, resentful man into a crazed figure, ranting at Christian and beating at him with his fists.

'I always thought that, for you at least, he had a touch of affection; he always told *you* the stories of the wood; I listened, but it was you who sat on his knee. Why would he try to kill you?'

'I became too involved,' was all Christian said. He was keeping something back, something of critical importance. I could tell from his tone, from his sullen, almost resentful expression. I had never before felt so distant from my own brother. I wondered if his behavior was having an affect on Guiwenneth, the girl he had married. I wondered what sort of atmosphere she was living in up at Oak Lodge.

Tentatively, I broached the subject of the girl.

Christian struck angrily at the rushes by the pond. 'Guiwenneth's gone,' he said simply, and I stopped, startled.

'What does that mean, Chris? Gone where?'

'She's just gone, Steve,' he snapped, angry and cornered. 'She was father's girl, and she's gone, and that's all there is to it.'

'I don't understand what you mean. Where's she gone *to?* In your letter you sounded so happy. . . .'

'I shouldn't have written about her. That was a mistake. Now let it drop, will you?'

After that outburst, my unease with Christian grew stronger by the minute. There was something very wrong with him indeed, and clearly Guiwenneth's leaving had contributed greatly to the terrible change I could see; but I sensed there was something more. Unless he spoke about it, however, there was no way through to him. I could find only the words, 'I'm sorry.'

'Don't be.'

We walked on, almost to the woods, where the ground became marshy and unsafe for a few yards before vanishing into a musty deepness of stone and root and rotting wood. It was cool, here, the sun being behind us now and beyond the thickly foliaged trees. The dense stands of rush moved in the breeze, and I watched the rotting boat as it shifted slightly on its mooring.

Christian followed my gaze, but he was not looking at the boat or the pond; he was lost, somewhere in his own thoughts. For a brief moment I experienced a jarring sadness at the sight of so fine a young man so ruined in appearance and attitude. I wanted desperately to touch his arm, to hug him, and I could hardly bear the knowledge that I was afraid to do so.

Quietly, I asked him, 'What on earth has happened to you, Chris? Are you ill?'

He didn't answer for a moment, then said, 'I'm not ill,' and struck hard at a puffball, which shattered and spread on the breeze. He looked at me, something of resignation in his haunted face. 'I've been going through a few changes, that's all. I've been picking up on the old man's work. Perhaps a bit of his reclusiveness is rubbing off on me, a bit of his detachment.'

'If that's true, then perhaps you should give up for a while. The old man's obsession with the oak forest eventually killed him, and from the look of you, you're going the same way.'

Christian smiled thinly and chucked his reedwhacker out into the pond, where it made a dull splash and floated in a patch of scummy green algae. 'It might even be worth dying to achieve what he tried to achieve . . . and failed.'

I didn't understand the dramatic overtone in Christian's statement. The work that had so obsessed our father had been concerned with mapping the woodland and searching for evidence of old forest settlements. He had clearly invented a whole new jargon for himself and effectively isolated me from any deeper understanding of his work. I said this to Christian and added, 'Which is all very interesting, but hardly *that* interesting.'

'He was doing much more than that, much more than just mapping. But do you remember those maps, Steve? Incredibly detailed. . . .'

I could remember one quite clearly, the largest map, showing carefully marked trackways and easy routes through the tangle of trees and stony outcrops; it showed clearings drawn with almost obsessive precision, each glade numbered and identified, and the whole forest divided into zones and given names. We had made a camp in one of the clearings close to the woodland edge. 'We often tried to get deeper into the heartwoods, remember those expeditions, Chris? But the deep track just ends, and we always managed to get lost, I seem to recall, and very scared.'

'That's true,' Christian said quietly, looking at me quizzically, and added, 'What if I told you the forest had *stopped* us entering? Would you believe me?'

I peered into the tangle of brush, tree and gloom, to where there was a sunlit clearing visible. 'In a way I suppose it did,' I said. 'It stopped us penetrating very deeply because it made us scared, because there are few trackways through and the ground is choked with stone and briar . . . very difficult walking. Is that what you meant? Or did you mean something a little more sinister?'

'Sinister isn't the word I'd use,' said Christian, but added nothing more for the moment; he reached up to pluck a leaf from a small immature oak and rubbed it between thumb and forefinger before crushing it in his palm. All the time he stared into the deep woods. 'This is primary oak woodland, Steve, untouched forest from when all of the country was covered with deciduous forests of oak and ash and elder and rowan and hawthorn. . . .'

'And all the rest,' I said with a smile. 'I remember the old man listing them for us.'

'That's right, he did. And there's more than eight square miles of such forest stretching from here to well beyond Grimley, eight square miles of original, post-Ice Age forestland. Untouched, uninvaded for thousands of years.' He broke off and looked at me hard, before adding, 'Resistant to change.'

I said, 'He always thought there were boars alive in there. I remember hearing something one night, and he convinced me that it was a great big old bull boar, skirting the edge of the woods, looking for a mate.'

Christian led the way back towards the boathouse. 'He was probably right. If boars *had* survived from medieval times, this is just the sort of woodland they'd be found in.'

With my mind opened to those events of years ago, memory

inched back, images of childhood—the burning touch of sun on bramble-grazed skin, fishing trips to the millpond, tree camps, games, explorations . . . and instantly I recalled the Twigling.

As we walked back to the beaten pathway that led up to the lodge, we discussed the sighting. I had been about nine or ten years old. On our way to the sticklebrook to fish we had decided to test out our stick and string rods on the millpond, in the vain hope of snaring one of the predatory fish that lived there. As we crouched by the water (we only ever dared go out in the boat with Alphonse), we saw movement in the trees, across on the other bank. It was a bewildering vision that held us enthralled for the next few moments, and not a little terrified: standing watching us was a man in brown leathery clothes, with a wide, gleaming belt around his waist, and a spiky orange beard that reached to his chest; on his head he wore twigs, held to his crown by the leather band. He watched us for a moment only, before slipping back into the darkness. We heard nothing in all this time, no sound of approach, no sound of departure.

Running back to the house, we had soon calmed down. Christian decided, eventually, that it must have been old Alphonse, playing tricks on us. But when I mentioned what we'd seen to my father, he reacted almost angrily (although Christian recalls him as having been excited, and bellowing for that reason, and not because he was angry with our having been near the forbidden pool). It was father who referred to the vision as 'the Twigling,' and soon after we had spoken to him he vanished into the woodland for nearly two weeks.

'That was when he came back hurt, remember?' We had reached the grounds of Oak Lodge, and Christian held the gate open for me as he spoke.

'The arrow wound. The gypsy arrow. My God, that was a bad day.'

'The first of many.'

I noticed that most of the ivy had been cleared from the walls of the house; it was a grey place now, small, curtainless windows set in the dark brick, the slate roof, with its three tall chimney stacks, partially hidden behind the branches of a big old beech tree. The yard and gardens were untidy and unkempt, the empty chicken coops and animal shelters ramshackle and decaying. Christian had really let the place slip. But when I stepped across the threshold, it was as if I had never been away. The house smelled of stale food and chlorine, and I could almost see the thin figure of my mother, working away at the immense pinewood table in the kitchen, cats stretched out around her on the red-brick floor.

Christian had grown tense again, staring at me in that fidgety way that marked his unease. I imagined he was still unsure whether to be glad or angry that I had come home like this. For a moment I felt like an intruder. He said. 'Why don't you unpack and freshen up. You can use your old room. It's a bit stuffy, I expect, but it'll soon air. Then come down and we'll have some late lunch. We've got all the time in the world to chat, as long as we're finished by tea.' He smiled, and I thought this was some slight attempt at humor. But he went on quickly, staring at me in a cold, hard way, 'Because if you're going to stay at home for a while, then you'd better know what's going on here. I don't want you interfering with it, Steve, or with what I'm doing.'

'I wouldn't interfere with your life, Chris—'

'Wouldn't you? We'll see. I'm not going to deny that I'm nervous of you being here. But since you are. . . .' he trailed off, and for a second looked almost embarrassed. 'Well, we'll have a chat later on.'

Intrigued by what Christian had said, and worried by his apprehension of me, I nonetheless restrained my curiosity and spent an hour exploring the house again, from top to bottom, inside and out, everywhere save father's study, the contemplation of which chilled me more than Christian's behavior had done. Nothing had changed, except that it was untidy and untenanted. Christian had employed a part-time cleaner and cook, a good soul from a nearby village who cycled to the Lodge every week and prepared a pie or stew that would last the man three days. Christian did not go short of farm produce, so much so that he rarely bothered to use his ration book. He seemed to get all he needed, including sugar and tea, from the Ryhope estate, which had always been good to my family.

My own room was dust free but quite stale. I opened the window wide and lay down on the bed for a few minutes, staring out and up into the hazy late-summer sky, past the waving branches of the gigantic beech that grew so close to the lodge. Several times, in the years before my teens, I had climbed from window to tree and made a secret camp among the thick branches; by moonlight I had shivered in my underpants, crouched in that private place, imagining the dark doings of night creatures below.

Lunch, in midafternoon, was a substantial feast of cold pork, chicken and hard-boiled eggs, in quantities that, after two years in France on strict rations, I had never thought to see again. We were, of course, eating his food supply for several days, but the fact seemed irrelevant to Christian, who at any rate only picked at his meal.

Afterwards we talked for a couple of hours, and Christian relaxed quite noticeably, although he never referred to Guiwenneth or to father's work, and I never broached either subject. We were sprawled in the uncomfortable armchairs that had belonged to my grandparents, surrounded by the time-faded mementos of our family . . . photographs, a noisy rose-wood clock, horrible pictures of exotic Spain, all framed in cracked mock-gilded wood, and all pressed hard against the same floral wallpaper that had hugged the walls of the sitting room since a time before my birth. But it was home, and Christian was home, and the smell, and the faded surrounds, all were home to me. I knew, within two hours of arriving, that I would have to stay. It was not so much that I belonged here—although I certainly felt that—but simply that the place belonged to me, not in any mercenary sense of ownership, more in the way that the house and the land around the house shared a common life with me; we were part of the same evolution; even in France, even as far as Greece, where I had been in action, I had not been separated from that evolution, merely stretched to an extreme.

As the heavy old rose-wood clock began to whirr and click, preceding its labored chiming of the hour of five, Christian abruptly rose from his chair and tossed his half-smoked cigarette into the empty fire grate.

'Let's go to the study,' he said, and I rose without speaking and followed him through the house to the small room where our father had worked. 'You're scared of this room, aren't you?' he said as he opened the door and walked inside, crossing to the heavy oak desk and pulling out a large leather-bound book from one of the drawers.

I hesitated outside the study, watching Christian, almost unable to move my legs to carry myself into the room. I recognized the book he held, my father's notebook. I touched my back pocket, the wallet I carried there, and thought of the fragment of that notebook that was hidden inside the thin leather. I wondered if anyone, my father or Christian, had ever noticed that a page was missing. Christian was watching me, his eyes bright with excitement, now, his hands trembling as he placed the book on the desk top.

'He's dead, Steve. He's gone from this room, from the house. There's no need to be afraid any more.'

'Isn't there?'

But I found the sudden strength to move and stepped across the threshold. The moment I entered the musty room I felt totally subdued, deeply affected by the coolness of the place, the stark, haunted atmosphere that hugged the walls and carpets and windows. It smelled slightly of leather, here, and dust too, with just a distant hint of polish, as if Christian made a token effort to keep this stifling room clean. It was not a crowded room, not a library as my father would have perhaps liked it to be. There were books on zoology and botany, on history and archaeology, but these were not rare copies, merely the cheapest copies he could find at the time. There were more paperbacks than stiff-covered books, and the exquisite binding of his notes, and the deeply varnished desk, had an air of Victorian elegance about them that belied the otherwise shabby studio.

On the walls, between the cases of books, were his glass-framed specimens, pieces of wood, collections of leaves, crude sketches of animal and plant life made during the first years of his fascination with the forest. And almost hidden away among the cases and the shelves was the patterned shaft of the arrow that had struck him fifteen years before, its flights twisted and useless, the broken shaft glued together, the iron head dulled with corrosion, but a lethal-looking weapon nonetheless.

I stared at that arrow for several seconds, reliving the man's agony, and the tears that Christian and I had wept for him as we had helped him back from the woodlands, that cold autumn afternoon, convinced that he would die.

How quickly things had changed after that strange and never fully explained incident. If the arrow linked me with an earlier day, when some semblance of concern and love had remained in my father's mind, the rest of the study radiated only coldness.

I could still see the greying figure, bent over his desk, writing furiously. I could hear the troubled breathing, the lung disorder that finally killed him; I could hear his caught breath, the vocalized sound of irritation as he grew aware of my presence and waved me away with a half-irritated gesture, as if he begrudged even that split second of acknowledgement.

How like him Christian looked now, standing there all disheveled and sickly looking, and yet with the mark of absolute confidence about him, his hands in the pockets of his flannels, shoulders drooped, his whole body visibly shaking.

He had waited quietly as I adjusted to the room and let the memories and atmosphere play through me. As I stepped up to the desk, my mind back on the moment at hand, he said, 'Steve, you should read the notes. They'll make a lot of things clear to you and help you understand what it is I'm doing as well.'

I turned the notebook towards me, scanning the sprawling untidy handwriting, picking out words and phrases, reading through the years of my father's life in a few scant seconds. The words were as meaningless, on the whole, as those on my purloined sheet. To read them brought back a memory of anger and of danger, and of fear. The life in the notes had sustained me through nearly a year of war and had come to mean something outside of their proper context. I felt reluctant to dispel that powerful association with the past.

'I intend to read them, Chris. From beginning to end, and that's a promise. But not for the moment.'

I closed the book, noticing as I did that my hands were clammy and trembling. I was not yet ready to be so close to my father again, and Christian saw this and accepted it.

Conversation died quite early that night, as my energy expired, and the tensions of the long journey finally made themselves known to me. Christian came up with me and stood in the doorway of my room, watching as I turned back the sheets and pottered about, picking up bits and pieces of my past life, laughing, shaking my head and trying to evoke a last moment's tired nostalgia. 'Remember making camp out in the beech?' I said, watching the grey of branch and leaf against the still-bright evening sky. 'Yes,' said Christian with a smile. 'Yes, I remember very clearly.'

But it was as fatigued as that, and Christian took the hint and said, 'Sleep well, old chap. I'll see you in the morning.'

If I slept at all, it was for the first two or three hours after putting head to pillow. I woke sharply, and brightly, in the dead of night, one or two o'clock, perhaps; the sky was very dark now, and it was quite windy outside. I lay and stared at the window, wondering how my body could feel so fresh, so alert. There was movement downstairs, and I guessed that Christian was doing some tidying, restlessly walking through the house, trying to adjust to the idea of me moving in.

The sheets smelled of mothballs and old cotton; the bed creaked in a metallic way when I shifted on it, and when I lay still, the whole room clicked and shuffled, as if adapting itself to its first company in so many years. I lay awake for ages but must have drifted to sleep again before first light, because suddenly Christian was bending over me, shaking my shoulder gently.

I started with surprise, awake at once, and propped up on my elbows, looking around. It was dawn. 'What is it, Chris?'

'I've got to go, old boy. I'm sorry, but I have to.'

I realized he was wearing a heavy oilskin cape and thick-soled walking boots on his feet. 'Go? What d'you mean, go?'

'I'm sorry, Steve. There's nothing I can do about it.' He spoke softly, as if there were someone else in the house who might be woken by raised voices. He looked more drawn than ever in this pale light, and his eyes were narrowed, I thought with pain or anxiety. 'I have to go away for a few days. You'll be all right. I've left a list of instructions downstairs, where to get bread, eggs, all that sort of thing. I'm sure you'll be able to use my ration book until yours comes. I shan't be long, just a few days. That's a promise. . . .'

He rose from his crouch and walked out the door. 'For God's sake, Chris, where are you going?'

'Inwards,' was all he said, before I heard him clump heavily down the stairs. I remained motionless for a moment or two, trying to clear my thoughts, then rose, put on my dressing gown and followed him down to the kitchen. He had already left the house. I went back up to the landing window and saw him skirting the edge of the yard and walking swiftly down towards the south track. He was wearing a wide-brimmed hat and carrying a long black staff; on his back he had a small rucksack, slung uncomfortably over one shoulder.

'Where's inwards, Chris?' I said to his vanishing figure, and watched long after he had disappeared from view. 'What's going on inside your head?' I asked of his empty bedroom as I wandered restlessly through the house; Guiwenneth, I decided in my wisdom, her loss, her leaving . . . how little one could interpret from the words 'she's gone.' And in all our chat of the evening before he had never alluded to the girl again. I had come home to England expecting to find a cheerful young couple and instead had found a haunted, wasting brother living in the derelict shadow of our family home.

By the afternoon I had resigned myself to a period of solitary living, for wherever Christian had gone (and I had a fairly good idea), he had hinted clearly that he would be gone for some time. There was a lot to do about the house and the yard, and there seemed no better way to spend my time than in beginning to rebuild the personality of the house. I made a list of essential repairs and the following day walked into the nearest town to order what materials I could, mostly wood and paint, which I found in reasonable supply.

I renewed my acquaintance with the Ryhope family and with many of the local families with whom I had once been friendly. I terminated the services of the part-time cook; I could look after myself quite well enough. And I visited the cemetery, a single, brief visit, coldly accomplished.

The month of August turned to September, and I noticed a definite crispness in the air by evening and early in the morning. It was a season I loved, the turn from summer to autumn, although it bore with it associations of return to school after the long vacation, and that was a memory I didn't cherish. I soon grew used to being on my own in the house, and although I took long walks around the deep woodlands, watching the road and the railway track for Christian's return, I had ceased to feel anxious about him by the end of my first week home and had settled comfortably into a daily routine of building in the yard, painting the exterior woodwork of the house ready for the onslaught of winter, and digging over the large untended garden.

It was during the evening of my eleventh day at home that this domestic routine was disturbed by a circumstance of such peculiarity that afterwards I could not sleep for thinking about it.

I had been in the town of Hobbhurst for most of the afternoon and after a light evening meal was sitting reading the newspaper; towards nine o'clock, as I began to feel ready for an evening stroll, I thought I heard a dog, not so much barking as howling. My first thought was that Christian was coming back; my second that there were no dogs in this immediate area at all.

I went out into the yard; it was after dusk but still quite bright, although the oak woods were melded together into a grey-green blur. I called for Christian, but there was no response. I was about to return to my paper when a man stepped out of the distant woodland and began to trot towards me; on a short leather leash he was holding the most enormous hound I have ever seen.

At the gate to our private grounds he stopped, and the dog began to growl; it placed its forepaws on the fence and, in so doing, rose almost to the height of its master. I felt nervous at once, keeping my attention balanced between the gaping, panting mouth of that dark beast and the strange man who held it in check.

It was difficult to make him out clearly, for his face was painted with dark patterns and his mustaches drooped to well below his chin; his hair was plastered thickly about his scalp; he wore a dark woollen shirt, with a leather jerkin over the top, and tight, check-patterned breeches that reached to just below his knees. When he stepped cautiously through the gate, I could see his rough and ready sandals. Across his shoulder he carried a crude-looking bow, and a bundle of arrows, held together with a simple thong and tied to his belt. He, like Christian, carried a staff.

Inside the gate he hesitated, watching me. The hound was restless beside him, licking its mouth and growling softly. I had never seen a dog such as this, shaggy and dark-furred, with the narrow pointed face of an Alsatian, but the body, it seemed to me, of a bear; except that its legs were long and thin, an animal made for chasing, for hunting.

The man spoke to me, and although I felt familiar with the words, they meant nothing. I didn't know what to do. So I shook my head and said that I didn't understand. The man hesitated just a moment before repeating what he had said, this time with a distinct edge of anger in his voice. And he started to walk towards me, tugging at the hound to prevent it straining at the leash. The light was draining from the sky, and he seemed to grow in stature in the greyness as he approached. The beast watched me, hungrily.

'What do you want?' I called, and tried to sound firm when I would rather have run inside the house. The man was ten paces away from me. He stopped, spoke again and this time made eating motions with the hand that held his staff. *Now* I understood. I nodded vigorously. 'Wait here,' I said, and went back to the house to fetch the cold joint of pork that was to last me four more days. It was not large, but it seemed an hospitable thing to do. I took this, half a granary loaf, and a jug of bottled beer out into the yard. The stranger was crouched now, the hound lying down beside him, rather reluctantly, it seemed to me. As I tried to approach them, the dog roared in a way that set my heart racing and nearly made me drop my gifts. The man shouted at the beast and said something to me. I placed the food where I stood and backed away. The gruesome pair approached and again squatted down to eat.

As he picked up the joint, I saw the scars on his arm, running down and across the bunched muscles. I also smelled him, a raw, rancid odor, sweat and urine mixed with the fetid aroma of rotting meat. I nearly gagged but held my ground, watching as the stranger tore at the pork with his teeth, swallowing hard and fast. The hound watched me.

After a few minutes the man stopped eating, looked at me, and with his gaze fixed on mine, almost challenging me to react, passed the rest of the meat to the dog, which growled loudly and snappped at the joint. The hound chewed, cracked and gulped the entire piece of pork in less than four minutes, while the stranger cautiously—and without much apparent pleasure—drank beer and chewed on a large mouthful of bread.

Finally this bizarre feast was over. The man rose to his feet and jerked the hound away from where it was licking the ground noisily. He said a word I intuitively recognized as 'thankyou.' He was about to turn when the hound scented something; it uttered a high-pitched keen, followed by a raucous bark, and snatched itself away from its master's restraining grip, racing across the yard to a spot between the ramshackle chicken houses. Here it sniffed and scratched until its master reached it, grabbed the leather leash, and shouted angrily and lengthily at his charge. The hound moved with him, padding silently and monstrously into the gloom beyond the yard. The last I saw of them they were running at full speed, around the edge of the woodland, towards the farmlands around the village of Grimley.

In the morning the place where man and beast had rested *still* smelled rank. I skirted the area quickly as I walked to the woods and found the place where my strange visitors had exited from the trees; it was trampled and broken, and I followed the line of their passage for some yards into the shade before stopping and turning back.

Where on earth had they come from? Had the war had such an effect on men in England that some had returned to the wild, using bow and arrow and hunting dog for survival?

Not until midday did I think to look between the chicken huts, at the ground so deeply scored by that brief moment's digging. What had the beast scented, I wondered, and a sudden chill clawed at my heart. I left the place at a run, unwilling, for the moment, to confirm my worst fears.

How I knew I cannot say; intuition, or perhaps something that my subconsicous had detected in Christian's words and mannerisms the week or so before, during our brief encounter. In any event, late in the afternoon that same day I took a spade to the chicken huts and within a few minutes of digging had proved my instinct right.

It took me half an hour of sitting on the back doorstep of the house, staring across the yard at the grave, to find the courage to uncover the woman's body totally. I was dizzy, slightly sick, but most of all I was shaking; an uncontrollable, unwelcome shaking of arms and legs so pronounced that I could hardly pull on a pair of gloves. But eventually I knelt by the hole and brushed the rest of the dirt from the girl's body.

Christian had buried her three feet deep, face down; her hair was long and red; her body was still clad in a strange green garment, a patterned tunic that was laced at the sides and, though it was crushed up almost to her waist now, would have reached her calves. A staff was buried with her. I turned the head, holding my breath against the almost intolerable smell of putrefaction, and with a little effort could gaze upon the withering face. I saw then how she had died, for the head and stump of the arrow were still embedded in her eye. Had Christian tried to withdraw the weapon and succeeded only in breaking it? There was enough of the shaft left for me to notice that it had the same carved markings as the arrow in my father's study.

Poor Guiwenneth, I thought, and let the corpse drop back to its resting place. I filled in the dirt again. When I reached the house I was cold with sweat and in no doubt that I was about to be violently sick.

Two days later, when I came down in the morning, I found the kitchen littered with Christian's clothes and effects, the floor covered with mud and leaf litter, the whole place smelling unpleasant. I crept upstairs to his room and stared at his semi-naked body; he was belly down on the bed, face turned towards me, sleeping soundly and noisily, and I imagined that he was sleeping enough for a week. The state of his body, though, gave me cause for concern. He was scratched and scarred from neck to ankle, and filthy, and malodorous to an extreme. His hair was matted with dirt. And yet, about him there was something hardened and strong, a tangible physical change from the hollow-faced, rather skeletal young man who had greeted me nearly two weeks before.

He slept for most of the day, emerging at six in the evening wearing a loose-fitting grey shirt and flannels, torn off just above the knee. He had half-heartedly washed his face, but still reeked of sweat and vegetation, as if he had spent the days away buried in compost.

I fed him, and he drank the entire contents of a pot of tea as I sat watching him; he kept darting glances at me, suspicious little looks as if he were nervous of some sudden move or surprise attack upon him. The muscles of his arms and wrists were pronounced. This was almost a different man.

'Where have you been, Chris?' I asked after a while, and was not at all surprised when he answered, 'In the woods, old boy. Deep in the woods.' He stuffed more meat into his mouth and chewed noisily. As he swallowed he found a moment to say, 'I'm quite fit. Bruised and scratched by the damned brambles, but quite fit.'

In the woods. Deep in the woods. What in heavens name could

he have been doing there? As I watched him wolf down his food, I saw again the stranger, crouching like an animal in my yard, chewing on meat as if he were some wild beast. Christian reminded me of that man. There was the same air of the primitive about him.

'You need a bath rather badly,' I said, and he grinned and made a sound of affirmation. 'What have you been doing, Chris? In the woods. Have you been camping?'

He swallowed noisily and drank half a cup of tea before shaking his head. 'I have a camp there, but I've been searching, walking as deep as I could get. But I still can't get beyond. . . .' He broke off and glanced at me, a questioning look in his eyes. 'Did you read the old man's notebook?'

I said that I hadn't. In truth, I had been so surprised by his abrupt departure and so committed to getting the house back into some sort of shape that I had forgotten all about father's notes on his work. And even as I said this, I wondered if the truth of the matter was that I had put father, his work and his notes, as far from my mind as possible, as if they were specters whose haunting would reduce my resolve to go forward.

Christian wiped his hand across his mouth and stared at his empty plate. He suddenly sniffed himself and laughed. 'By the Gods, I do stink. You'd better boil me up some water, Steve. I'll wash right now.'

But I didn't move. Instead I stared across the wooden table at him; he caught my gaze and frowned. 'What is it? What's on your mind?'

'I found her, Chris. I found her body. Guiwenneth. I found where you buried her.'

I don't know what reaction I expected from Christian. Anger, perhaps, or panic, or a sudden babbling burst of explanation. I half hoped he would react with puzzlement, that the corpse in the yard would turn out not to be the remains of his wife and that he had had no involvement with its burial. But Christian knew about the body. He stared at me blankly, and a heavy, sweaty silence made me grow uncomfortable.

Suddenly I realized that Christian was crying, his gaze unwavering from my own, but moistened, now, by the great flood of tears through the remaining grime on his face. And yet he made no sound, and his face never changed its expression from that of bland, almost blind contemplation.

'Who shot her, Chris?' I asked quietly. 'Did you?'

'Not me,' he said, and with the words his tears stopped, and his gaze dropped to the table. 'She was shot by a mythago. There was nothing I could do about it.'

Mythago? The meaning was alien to me, although I recognized the word from the scrap of my father's notebook that I carried. I queried it, and Chris rose from the table but rested his hands upon it as he watched me. 'A mythago,' he repeated. 'It's still in the woods . . . they all are. That's where I've been, seeking among them. I tried to save her, Steve. She was alive when I found her, and she might have stayed alive, but I brought her out of the woods . . . in a way, I did kill her. I took her away from the vortex, and she died quite quickly. I panicked, then. I didn't know what to do. I buried her because it seemed the easiest way out. . . .'

'Did you tell the police? Did you report her death?'

Christian grinned, but it was not with any morbid humor. It was a knowing grin, a response to some secret that he had not yet shared; and yet the grin was merely a defense, for it faded rapidly. 'Not necessary Steve. . . . The police would not have been interested.'

I rose angrily from the table. It seemed to me that Christian was behaving, and had behaved, with appalling irresponsibility. 'Her family, Chris . . . her parents! They have a right to know.'

And Christian laughed.

I felt the blood rise in my face. 'I don't see anything to laugh at.'

He sobered instantly, looked at me almost abashed. 'You're right. I'm sorry. You don't understand, and it's time you did. Steve, she had no parents because she had no life, no real life. She's lived a thousand times, and she's never lived at all. But I still fell in love with her . . . and I shall find her again in the woods; she's in there somewhere. . . .'

Had he gone mad? His words were the unreasoned babblings of one insane, and yet something about his eyes, something about his demeanor, told me that it was not so much insanity as obsession. But obsession with what?

'You *must* read the old man's notes, Steve. Don't put it off any longer. They will tell you about the wood, about what's going on in there. I mean it. I'm neither mad nor callous. I'm just trapped, and before I go away again, I'd like you to know why, and how, and where I'm going. Perhaps you'll be able to help me. Who knows? Read the book. And then we'll talk. And when you know what our dear departed father managed to do, then I'm afraid I have to take my leave of you again.'

* * *

There is one entry in my father's notebook that seems to mark a turning point in his research, and in his life. It is a longer entry than the rest of that particular time and follows an absence of seven months from the pages. While his entries are detailed, he could not be described as having been a dedicated diarist, and the style varies from clipped notes to fluent description. (I discovered, too, that he himself had torn many pages from the thick book, thus concealing my minor crime quite effectively. Christian had never noticed the missing page.) On the whole, he seems to have used the notebook and the quiet hours of recording as a way of conversing with himself—a means of clarification of his own thoughts.

The entry in question is dated September, 1933, and was written shortly after our encounter with the Twigling. After reading the entry for the first time, I thought back to that year and realized I had been just nine years old.

'Wynne-Jones arrived after dawn. Walked together along the south track, checking the flux-drains for sign of mythago activity. Back to the house quite shortly after—no one about, which suited my mood. A crisp, dry autumn day. Like last year, images of the Urscumug are strongest as the season changes. Perhaps he senses autumn, the dying of the green. He comes forward, and the oak woods whisper to him. He must be close to genesis. Wynne-Jones thinks a further time of isolation needed, and it must be done. Jennifer already concerned and distraught by my absences. I feel helpless—can't speak to her. Must do what is needed.

'Yesterday the boys glimpsed the Twigling. I had thought him resorbed—clearly the resonance stronger than we had believed. He seems to frequent woodland edge, which is to be expected. I have seen him along the track several times, but not for a year or so. The persistence is worrying. Both boys clearly disturbed by the sighting; Christian less emotional. I suspect it meant little to him, a poacher perhaps, or local man taking short cut to Grimley. Wynne-Jones suggests we go back into woods and call the Twigling deep, perhaps to the hogback glade where he might remain in strong oak-vortex and eventually fade. But I know that penetrating into deep woodland will involve more than a week's absence, and poor Jennifer already deeply depressed by my behavior. Cannot explain it to her, though I dearly want to. Do not want the children involved in this, and it worries me that they have now twice seen a mythago. I have invented magic forest creatures—stories for them. Hope they will associate what they see with products of their own imaginations. But must be careful. Until it is resolved, until the Urscumug mythago forms must not let any but Wynne-Jones know of what I have discovered. The completeness of the resurrection essential. The Urscumug is the most powerful because he is the primary. I know for certain that the oak woods will contain him, but others might be frightened of the power they would certainly be able to feel, and end it for everyone. Dread to think what would happen if these forests were destroyed, and yet they cannot survive forever.

'Today's training with Wynne-Jones: test pattern 26:iii, shallow hypnosis, green light environment. As the frontal bridge reached sixty volts, despite the pain the flow across my skull was the most powerful I have ever known. Am now totally convinced that each half of the brain functions in a slightly different way and that the hidden awareness is located on the right-hand side. It has been lost for so long! The Wynne-Jones bridge enables a superficial communion between the fields around each hemisphere, and the zone of the pre-mythago is excited accordingly. If only there were some way of exploring the living brain to find exactly where the site of this occult presence lies.

'The forms of the mythagos cluster in my peripheral vision, still. Why never in fore-vision? These unreal images are mere reflections, after all. The form of Hood was subtly different—more brown than green, the face less friendly, more haunted, drawn. This is certainly because earlier images (even the Hood mythago that actually formed in the woodland, two years ago) were affected by my own confused childhood images of the greenwood and the merry band. But now, evocation of the pre-mythago is more powerful, reaches to the basic form, without interference. The Arthur form was more real as well, and I glimpsed the various marshland forms from the latter part of the first millennium AD. Wynne-Jones would love me to explore these folk heroes, unrecorded and unknown, but I am anxious to find the primary image.

'The Urscumug formed in my mind in the clearest form I have ever seen him. Hints of the Twigling in form, but he is much more ancient, far bigger. Decks himself with wood and leaves, on top of animal hides. Face seems smeared with white clay, forming a mask upon the exaggerated features below; but it is hard to see the face clearly. A mask upon a mask? The hair a mass of stiff and spiky points; gnarled hawthorn branches are driven up through the matted hair, giving a most bizarre appearance. I believe he carries a spear, with a wide stone blade . . . an angry looking weapon, but again, hard to see, always just out of focus. He is so old, this primary image, that he is fading from the human mind, and in any event is touched with confusion, the overassertion of later cultural

Urscumug was powerful enough to carry through all the neolithic and on into the second millennium BC, perhaps even later. Wynne-Jones thinks the Urscumug may pre-date even the neolithic.

'Essential, now, to spend time in the forest, to allow the vortex to interact with me and form the mythago. I intend to leave the house within the next week.'

Without commenting on the strange, confusing passage that I had read, I turned the pages of the diary and read entries here and there. I could clearly recall that autumn in 1933, the time when my father had packed a large rucksack and wandered into the woods, walking swiftly away from my mother's hysterical shouting, and flanked by his diminutive scientist friend (a sour-faced man who never acknowledged anyone but my father and who seemed embarrassed to be in the house when he came to visit). Mother had not spoken for the rest of the day, and she did nothing but sit in her bedroom and occasionally weep. Christian and I had become so distraught by her behavior that in the late afternoon we had penetrated the oakwoods as deeply as we dared, calling for our father, and finally panicking at the gloomy silence and the loud, sudden sounds that disturbed it. He had returned weeks later, disheveled and stinking like a tramp. The entry in his notebook, a few days later, is a short and bitter account of failure. Nothing had happened. A single, rather rambling paragraph caught my attention.

'The mythogenetic process is not only complex, it is reluctant. My mind is not at rest and, as Wynne-Jones has explained, it is likely that my human considerations, my worries, form an effective barrier between the two mythopoetic energy flows in my cortex —the *form* from the right brain, the *reality* from the left. The pre-mythago zone is not sufficiently enriched by my own life force for it to interact in the oak vortex. I fear too that the natural disappearance of so much life from the forest is affecting the interface. The boars are there, I'm sure. But perhaps the life number is critical. I estimate no more than forty, moving within the spiral vortex bounded by the ashwood intrusions into the oak circle. There are no deer, no wolves, although the most important animal, the hare, frequents the woodland edge in profusion. But perhaps the absence of so much that had once lived here has thrown the balance of the formula. And yet, through the primary existence of these woods, life was changing. By the thirteenth century there was much botanical life that was alien to the 'ley matrix' in places where the mythagos still formed. The form of the myth-men changes, adapts, and it is the later forms that generate easiest. Hood is back—like all the Jack in the Greens, is a nuisance, and several times moved into the ridge zone around the hogback glade. He shot at me, and this is becoming a cause of great concern! But I cannot enrich the oak vortex sufficiently with the pre-mythago of the Urscumug. What is the answer? Perhaps the memory is too far gone, too deep in the silent zones of the brain, now, to touch the trees.'

Christian saw me frown as I read through this tumble of words and images. Hood? Robin Hood? And someone—this Hood —shooting at my father in the woods? I glanced around the study and saw the iron-tipped arrow in its long, narrow glass case, mounted above the display of woodland butterflies. Christian was turning the pages of the notebook, having watched me read in silence for the better part of an hour. He was perched on the desk; I sat in father's chair.

'What's all this about, Chris? It reads as if he were actually trying to create copies of storybook heroes.'

'Not copies, Steve. The real thing. There. Last bit of reading for the moment, then I'll go through it with you in layman's terms.'

It was an earlier entry, not dated by year, only by day and month, although it was clearly from some years before the 1933 recording.

'I call those particular times 'cultural interfaces'; they form zones, bounded in space, of course, by the limits of the country, but bounded also in time, a few years, a decade or so, when the two cultures—that of the invaded and the invader—are in a highly anguished state. The mythagos grow from the power of hate, and fear, and form in the natural woodlands from which they can either emerge—such as the Arthur, or Artorius form, the bear-like man with his charismatic leadership—or remain in the natural land-scape, establishing a hidden focus of hope—the Robin Hood form, perhaps Hereward, and of course the hero-form I call the Twigling, harassing the Romans in so many parts of the country. I imagine that it is the combined emotion of the two races that draws out the mythago, but it clearly sides with that culture whose roots are longest established in what I agree could be a sort of *ley matrix;* thus, Arthur forms and helps the Britons against the Saxons, but later Hood is created to help the Saxons against the Norman invader.'

I drew back from the book, shaking my head. The expressions were confusing, bemusing. Christian grinned as he took the notebook and weighed it in his hands. 'Years of his life, Steve, but his concern with keeping detailed records was not everything it might have been. He records nothing for years, then writes every day for a month.'

'I need a drink of something. And a few definitions.'

We walked from the study, Christian carrying the notebook. As we passed the framed arrow, I peered closely at it. 'Is he saying that the real Robin Hood shot that into him? And killed Guiwenneth too?'

'It depends,' said Christian thoughtfully, 'on what you mean by real. Hood came to that oak forest and may still be there. I think he is. As you have obviously noticed, he was there four months ago when he shot Guiwenneth. But there were many Robin Hoods, and all were as real or unreal as each other, created by the Saxon peasants during their time of repression by the Norman invader.'

'I don't comprehend this at all, Chris—but what's a "ley matrix"? What's an "oak vortex"? Does it mean anything?'

As we sipped scotch and water in the sitting room, watching the dusk draw closer, the yard beyond the window greying into a place of featureless shapes, Christian explained how a man called Alfred Watkins had visited our father on several occasions and shown him on a map of the country how straight lines connected places of spiritual or ancient power—the barrows, stones and churches of three different cultures. These lines he called leys and believed that they existed as a form of earth energy running below the ground, but influencing that which stood upon it. My father had thought about leys, and apparently tried to measure the energy in the ground below the forest, but without success. And yet he had measured *something* in the oak woods—an energy associated with all the life that grew there. He had found a spiral vortex around each tree, a sort of aura, and those spirals bounded not just trees, but whole stands of trees and glades. Over the years he had mapped the forest. Christian brought out that map of the woodland area, and I looked at it again, but from a different point of view, beginning to understand the marks made upon it by the man who had spent so much time within the territories it depicted. Circles within circles were marked, crossed and skirted by straight lines, some of which were associated with the two pathways we called south and deep track. The letters HB in the middle of the vast acreage of forest were clearly meant to refer to the 'Hogback' glade that existed there, a clearing that neither Christian nor I had ever been able to find. There were zones marked out as 'spiral oak,' 'dead ash zone' and 'oscillating traverse.'

'The old man believed that all life is surrounded by an energetic aura—you can see the human aura as a faint glow in certain light. In these ancient woodlands, *primary* woodlands, the combined aura forms something far more powerful, a sort of creative field that can interact with our unconscious. And it's in that unconscious that we carry what he calls the pre-mythago—that's *myth imago*, the image of the idealized form of a myth creature. This takes on substance in a natural environment, solid flesh, blood, clothing, and—as you saw—weaponry. The form of the idealized myth, the hero figure, alters with cultural changes, assuming the identity and technology of the time. When one culture invades another—according to father's theory—the heroes are made manifest, and not just in one location! Historians and legend seekers argue about where Arthur of the Britons, and Robin Hood *really* lived and fought and don't realize that they lived in *many* sites. And another important fact to remember is that when the pre-mythago forms, it forms in the *whole* population . . . and when it is no longer needed, it remains in our collective unconscious and is transmitted through the generations.'

'And the changing form of the mythago,' I said, to see if I had understood my sketchy reading of father's notes, 'is based on an archetype, an archaic primary image which father called the Urscumug and from which all later forms come. And he tried to raise the Urscumug from his own unconscious mind. . . .'

'And failed to do so,' said Christian, 'although not for want of trying. The effort killed him. It weakened him so much that his body couldn't take the pace. But he certainly seems to have created several of the more recent adaptations of the Urscumug.'

There were so many questions, so many areas that begged for clarification. One above all: 'But a thousand years ago, if I understand the notes correctly, there was a country-wide *need* of the hero, the legendary figure, acting for the side of Right. How can one man capture such a passionate mood? How did he *power* the interaction? Surely not from the simple family anguish he caused among us, and in his own head. As he said, that created an unsettled mind and he couldn't function properly.'

'If there's an answer,' said Christian calmly, 'it's to be found in the woodland area, perhaps in the hogback glade. The old man wrote in his notes of the need for a period of solitary existence, a period of meditation. For a year, now, I've been following his example directly. He invented a sort of electrical bridge which seems to *fuse* elements from each half of the brain. I've used his equipment a great deal, with and without him. But I already find images—the pre-mythagos—forming in my peripheral vision *with-*

out the complicated program that he used. He was the pioneer; his own interaction with the wood has made it easier for those who come after. He achieved a certain success; I intend to complete his work, eventually. I shall raise the Urscumug, this hero of the first men.'

'To what end, Chris?' I asked quietly, and in all truth could not see a reason for so tampering with the ancient forces that inhabited both woodland and human spirit. Christian was clearly obsessed with the idea of raising these dead forms, of finishing something the old man had begun. But in reading his notebook, and in my conversation with Christian, I had not heard a single word that explained *why* so bizarre a state of nature should be so important to the ones who studied it.

Christian had an answer. And as he spoke to me his voice was hollow, the mark of his uncertainty, the stigma of his lacking conviction in the truth of what he said. 'Why, to study the earliest times of man, Steve. From these mythagos we can learn so much of how it was and how it was hoped to be. The aspirations, the visions, the cultural identity of a time so far gone that even its stone monuments are incomprehensible to us. To learn. To communicate through those persistent images of our past that are locked in each and every one of us.'

He stopped speaking, and there was the briefest of silence, interrupted only by the heavy rhythmic sound of the clock. I said, 'I'm not convinced, Chris.' For a moment I thought he would shout his anger; his face flushed, his whole body tensed up, furious with my calm dismissal of his script. But the fire softened, and he frowned, staring at me almost helplessly. 'What does that mean?'

'Nice sounding words; no conviction.'

After a second he seemed to acknowledge some truth in what I said. 'Perhaps my conviction has gone, then, buried beneath . . . beneath the other thing. Guiwenneth. She's become my main reason for going back now.'

I remembered his callous words of a while ago, about how she had no life yet a thousand lives. I understood instantly and wondered how so obvious a fact could have remained so doggedly elusive to me. 'She was a mythago herself,' I said. 'I understand now.'

'She was my father's mythago, a girl from Roman times, a manifestation of the Earth Goddess, the young warrior princess who can unite the tribes. I can find no recorded legends about her, but she is associated with the oral tradition, with the Celtic tradition of keeping a name silent. She was a powerful woman, and led—in all her appearances—a powerful resistance to the Romans. . . .'

'Like Queen Boadicea.'

'Before and after that uprising. Legends of Guiwenneth inspired many tribes to take offensive action against the invader.' His gaze became distant for a moment. 'And then she was formed in this wood, and I found her and came to love her. She was not violent, perhaps because the old man himself could not think of a woman being violent. He imposed a structure on her, disarming her, leaving her quite helpless in the forest.'

'How long did you know her?' I asked, and he shrugged.

'I can't tell, Steve. How long have I been away?'

'Twelve days or so.'

'As long as that?' He seemed surprised. 'I thought no more than three. Perhaps I knew her for many months, then, but it seems no time at all. I lived in the forest with her, trying to understand her language, trying to teach her mine, speaking with signs and yet always able to talk quite deeply. But the old man pursued us right to the heartwoods, right to the end. He wouldn't let up—she was *his* girl, and he had been as struck by her as had I. I found him, one day, exhausted and terrified, half buried by leaves at the forest edge. I took him home and he was dead within the month. That's what I meant by his having had a reason for attacking me. I took Guiwenneth from him.'

'And then she was taken from you. Shot dead.'

'A few months later, yes. I became a little too happy, a little too content. I wrote to you because I had to tell *someone* about her . . . clearly that was too much for fate. Two days later I found her in a glade, dying. She might have lived if I could have got help to her in the forest, and left her there. I carried her out of the wood, though, and she died.' He stared at me and the expression of sadness hardened to one of resolve. 'But when I'm back in the wood, her myth image in my own subconscious has a chance of being formed . . . she might be a little tougher than my father's version, but I can find her again, Steve, if I look hard, if I can find that energy you asked about, if I can get into the deepest part of the wood, to that central vortex. . . .'

I looked at the map again, at the spiral field around the hogback glade. 'What's the problem? Can't you find it?'

'It's well defended. I get near it, but I can't ever get beyond the field that's about two hundred yards around it. I find myself walking in elaborate circles even though I'm convinced I've walked straight. I can't get in, and whatever's in there can't get out. All the mythagos are tied to their genesis zones, although the Twigling, and Guiwenneth too, could get to the very edge of the forest, down by the pool.'

But that wasn't true! And I'd spent a shaky night to prove it. I said, 'One of the mythagos has come out of the wood . . . a tall man with the most unbelievably terrifying hound. He came into the yard and ate a leg of pork.'

Christian looked stunned. 'A mythago? Are you sure?'

'Well, no. I had no idea at all what he was until now. But he stank, was filthy, had obviously lived in the woods for months, spoke a strange language, carried a bow and arrows. . . .'

'And ran with a hunting dog. Yes, of course. It's a late Bronze Age, early Iron Age image, very widespread. The Irish have taken him to their own with Cuchulainn, made a big hero out of him, but he's one of the most powerful of the myth images, recognizable all across Europe.' Christian frowned then. 'I don't understand . . . a year ago I saw him and avoided him, but he was fading fast, decaying . . . it happens to them after a while. Something must have fed the mythago, strengthened it. . . .'

'Some *one*, Chris.'

'But who?' It dawned on him then, and his eyes widened slightly. 'My God. Me. From my own mind. It took the old man years, and I thought it would take me a lot longer, many more months in the woodlands, much more isolation. But it's started already, my own interaction with the vortex. . . .'

He had gone quite pale, and he walked to where his staff was propped against the wall, picked it up and weighed it in his hands. He stared at it, touched the markings upon it.

'You know what this means,' he said quietly, and, before I could answer, went on, 'She'll form. She'll come back, my Guiwenneth. She may be back already.'

'Don't go rushing off again, Chris. Wait a while; rest.'

He placed his staff against the wall again. 'I don't care. If she has formed by now, she's in danger. I have to go back.' He looked at me and smiled thinly, apologetically. 'Sorry brother. Not much of a homecoming for you.'

As quickly as this, after the briefest of reunions, I had lost Christian again. He was in no mood to talk, too distracted by the thought of Guiwenneth alone and trapped in the forest to allow me much of an insight into his plans and into his hopes and fears for some resolution to their impossible love affair.

I wandered through the kitchen and the rest of the house as he gathered his provisions together. Again and again he assured me that he would be gone for no more than a week, perhaps two. If she was in the wood, he would have found her by that time; if not, then he would return and wait awhile before going back to the deep zones and trying to form her mythago. In a year, he said, many of the more hostile mythagos would have faded into non-existence, and she would be safer. His thoughts were confused, his plan that he would strengthen her to allow her the same freedom as the man and the hound did not seem supportable on the evidence from our father's notes; but Christian was a determined man. If one mythago could escape, then so could the one he loved.

One idea that appealed to him was that I should come with him as far as the glade where we had made camp as children, and pitch a tent there. This could be a regular rendezvous for us, he said, and it would keep his time-sense on the right track. And if I spent time in the forest, I might encounter other mythagos and could report on their state. The glade he had in mind was at the edge of the wood, and quite safe.

When I expressed concern that my own mind would begin to produce mythagos, he assured me that it would take months for the first pre-mythago activity to show up as a haunting presence at the edge of my vision. He was equally blunt in saying that, if I stayed in the area for too long, I would certainly start to relate to the woodland, whose aura—he thought—had spread more towards the house in the last few years.

Late the following morning we set off along the south track. A pale yellow sun hung high above the forest. It was a cool, bright day, the air full of the scent of smoke, drifting from the distant farm where the stubbly remains of the summer harvest were being burned. We walked in silence until we came to the millpond; I had assumed Christian would enter the oak woodland here, but wisely he decided against it; not so much because of the strange movements we had seen there as children, but because of the marshy conditions. Instead, we walked on until the woodland bordering the track thinned. Here Christian turned off the path.

I followed him inwards, seeking the easiest route between tangles of bracken and nettles, enjoying the heavy stillness. The trees were small, here at the edge, but within a hundred yards they began to show their real age, great gnarled oakwood trunks, hollow and half-dead, twisting up from the ground, almost groaning beneath the weight of their branches. The ground rose slightly, and the tangled undergrowth was broken by weathered, lichen-covered stubs of grey limestone; we passed over the crest, and the earth dipped sharply down, and a subtle change came over the woodland; it seemed darker, somehow, more alive, and I noticed that the shrill September bird-sound of the forest edge was replaced here by a more sporadic, mournful song.

Christian beat his way through bramble thickets, and I trudged wearily after, and we soon came to the large glade where, years before, we had made our camp. One particularly large oak tree dominated the surrounds, and we laughed as we traced the faded initials we had once carved there. In its branches we had made our lookout tower, but we had seen very little from that leafy vantage point.

'Do I look the part?' asked Christian, holding his arms out, and I grinned as I surveyed his caped figure, the rune-inscribed staff looking less odd now, more functional.

'You look like something. Quite what, I don't know.'

He glanced around the clearing. 'I'll do my best to get back here as often as I can. If anything goes wrong, I'll try and leave a message if I can't find you, some mark to let you know. . . .'

'Nothing's going to go wrong,' I said with a smile. It was clear that he didn't wish me to accompany him beyond this glade, and that suited me. I felt a chill, an odd tingle, a sense of being watched. Christian noticed my discomfort and admitted that he felt it too, the presence of the wood, the gentle breathing of the trees.

We shook hands, then embraced awkwardly, and he turned on his heels and paced off into the gloom. I watched him go, then listened, and only when all sound had gone did I set about pitching the small tent.

For most of September the weather remained cool and dry, a dull sort of month, that enabled me to drift through the days in a very low-key state. I worked on the house, read some more of father's notebook (but quickly tired of the repetitive images and thoughts) and with decreasing frequency walked into the woodlands and sat near, or in the tent, listening for Christian, cursing the midges that haunted the place, and watching for any hint of movement.

With October came rain and the abrupt, almost startling realization that Christian had been gone for nearly a month. The time had slipped by, and instead of feeling concerned for him I had merely assumed that he knew what he was doing and would return when he was quite ready. But he had been absent for weeks without even the slightest sign! He could surely have come back to the glade once and left some mark of his passing.

Now I began to feel more concern for his safety than perhaps was warranted. As soon as the rain stopped, I trudged back through the forest and waited out the rest of the day in the miserable, leaking canvas shelter. I saw hares and a wood owl and heard distant movements that did not respond to my cries of 'Christian? Is that you?'

It got colder. I spent more time in the tent, creating a sleeping bag out of blankets and some tattered oilskins I found in the cellar of Oak Lodge. I repaired the splits in the tent and stocked it with food and beer and dry wood for fires. By the middle of October I noticed that I could not spend more than an hour at the house before becoming restless, an unease that could only be dispelled by returning to the glade and taking up my watching post, seated cross-legged just inside the tent, watching the gloom a few yards away. On several occasions I took long, rather nervous sorties further into the forest, but I disliked the sensation of stillness and the tingling of my skin that seemed to repeatedly say that I was being watched. All imagination, of course, or an extremely sensitive response to woodland animals, for on one occasion, when I ran screaming and yelling at the thicket wherein I imagined the voyeur was crouched, I saw nothing but a red squirrel go scampering in a panic up into the crossed and confused branches of its home oak.

Where *was* Christian? I tacked paper messages as deep in the woods and in as many locations, as I could. But I found that whenever I walked too far into the great dip that seemed to be swallowing the forest down, I would, at some point within the span of a few hours, find myself approaching the glade and the tent again. Uncanny, yes, and infuriating too, but I began to get an idea of Christian's own frustration at not being able to maintain a straight line in the dense oakwood. Perhaps, after all, there *was* some sort of field of force, complex and convoluted, that channeled intruders back onto an outward track.

And November came, and it was very cold indeed. The rain was sporadic and icy, but the wind reached down through the dense, browning foliage of the forest and seemed to find its way through clothes and oilskin and flesh to the cooling bones beneath. I was miserable, and my searches for Christian grew more angry, more frustrated. My voice was often hoarse with shouting, my skin blistered and scratched from climbing trees. I lost track of time, realizing on more than one occasion, and with some shock, that I had been two, or perhaps three days in the forest without returning to the house. Oak Lodge grew stale and deserted. I used it to wash, to feed, to rest, but as soon as the worst ravages to my body were corrected, thoughts of Christian, anxiety about him, grew in my mind and pulled me back to the glade, as surely as if I were a metal filing tugged to a magnet.

I began to suspect that something terrible had happened to him, or perhaps not terrible, just natural: if there really were boars in the wood, he might have been gored by one and be either dead or dragging himself from the heartwoods to the edge, unable to cry for help. Or perhaps he had fallen from a tree or quite simply gone to sleep in the cold and wet and failed to revive in the morning.

I searched for any sign of his body or his having passed by, and I found absolutely nothing, although I discovered the spoor of some large beast and marks on the lower trunks of several oaks that looked like nothing else than the scratchings of a tusked animal.

But my mood of depression passed, and by mid-November I was quite confident again that Christian was alive. My feelings, now, were that he had somehow become trapped in this autumnal forest.

For the first time in two weeks I went into the village, and after obtaining food supplies, I picked up the papers that had been accumulating at the tiny newsagents. Skimming the front pages of the weekly local, I noticed an item concerning the decaying bodies of a man and an Irish wolfhound, discovered in a ditch on a farmland near Grimley. Foul play was not suspected. I felt no emotion, apart from a curious coldness, a sense of sympathy for Christian, whose dream of freedom for Guiwenneth was surely no more than that, a fervent hope, a desire doomed to frustration.

As for mythagos, I had only two encounters, neither of them of much note; the first was with a shadowy man-form that skirted the clearing, watching me, and finally ran into the darkness, striking at the trunks of trees with a short wooden stick. The second meeting was with the Twigling, whose shape I followed stealthily as he walked to the millpond and stood in the trees, staring across at the boathouse. I felt no real fear of these manifestations, merely a slight apprehension. But it was only after the second meeting that I began to realize how alien was the wood to the mythagos, and how alien were the mythagos to the wood. These were creatures created far away from their natural age, echoes of the past given substance, equipped with a life, a language and a certain ferocity that was quite inappropriate to the war-scarred world of 1947. No wonder the aura of the woodland was so charged with a sense of solitude, an infectious loneliness that had come to inhabit the body of my father, and then Christian, and which was even now crawling through my own tissues and would trap me if I allowed it.

It was at this time, too, that I began to hallucinate. Notably at dusk, as I stared into the woodlands, I saw movement at the edge of my vision. At first I put this down to tiredness or imagination, but I remembered clearly the passage from my father's notebook in which he described how the pre-mythagos, the initial images, always appeared at his peripheral vision. I was frightened at first, unwilling to acknowledge that such creatures could be resident in my own mind and that my own interaction with the woodland had begun far earlier than Christian had thought; but after a while I sat and tried to see details of them. I failed to do so. I could sense movement and the occasional manlike shape, but whatever field was inducing their appearance was not yet strong enough to pull them into full view; either that, or my mind could not yet control their emergence.

On the 24th of November I went back to the house and spent a few hours resting and listening to the radio. A thunderstorm passed overhead, and I watched the rain and the darkness, feeling quite wretched and cold. But as soon as the air cleared and the clouds brightened, I draped my oilskin about my shoulders and headed back to the glade. I had not expected to find anything different, and so what should have been a surprise was more of a shock.

The tent had been demolished, its contents strewn and trampled into the sodden turf of the clearing. Part of the guy rope dangled from the higher branches of the large oak, and the ground hereabouts was churned as if there had been a fight. As I walked into the space, I noticed that the ground was pitted by strange footprints, round and cleft, like hooves, I thought. Whatever the beast had been, it had quite effectively torn the canvas shelter to tatters.

I noticed then how silent the forest was, as if holding its breath and watching. Every hair on my body stood on end, and my heartbeat was so powerful that I thought my chest would burst. I stood by the ruined tent for just a second or two and the panic hit me, making my head spin and the forest seem to lean towards me. I fled from the glade, crashing into the sopping undergrowth between two thick oak trunks. I ran through the gloom for several yards before realizing I was running *away* from the woodland edge. I think I cried out, and I turned and began to run back.

A spear thudded heavily into the tree beside me, and I had run into the black wood shaft before I could stop; a hand gripped my shoulder and flung me against the tree. I shouted out in fear, staring into the mud-smeared, gnarled face of my attacker. He shouted back at me:

'Shut up, Steve! For God's sake, shut up!'

My panic quietened, my voice dropped to a whimper, and I

peered hard at the angry man who held me. It was Christian, I realized, and my relief was so intense that I laughed and for long moments failed to notice what a total change had come about him.

He was looking back towards the glade. 'You've got to get out of here,' he said, and before I could respond, he had wrenched me into a run and was practically dragging me back to the tent.

In the clearing he hesitated and looked at me. There was no smile from behind the mask of mud and browning leaves. His eyes shone, but they were narrowed and lined. His hair was slick and spiky. He was naked but for a breechclout and a ragged skin jacket that could not have supplied much warmth. He carried three viciously pointed spears. Gone was the skeletal thinness of summer. He was muscular and hard, deep-chested and heavy-limbed. He was a man made for fighting.

'You've got to get out of the wood, Steve, and for God's sake don't come back.'

'What's happened to you, Chris . . . ?' I stuttered, but he shook his head and pulled me across the clearing and into the woods again, towards the south track.

Immediately he stopped, staring into gloom, holding me back. 'What is it, Chris?' And then I heard it too, a heavy crashing sound, something picking its way through the bracken and the trees towards us. Following Christian's gaze, I saw a monstrous shape, twice as high as a man, but man-shaped and stooped, black as night save for the great white splash of its face, still indistinct in the distance and greyness.

'God, it's broken out!' said Chris. 'It's got between us and the edge.'

'What is it? A mythago?'

'*The* mythago,' said Chris quickly, and turned and fled back across the clearing. I followed, all tiredness suddenly gone from my body.

'The Urscumug? That's *it*? But it's not human . . . it's animal. No human was ever that tall.'

Looking back as I ran, I saw it enter the glade and move across the open space so fast I thought I was watching a speeded up film. It plunged into the wood behind us and was lost in darkness again, but it was running now, weaving between trees as it pursued us, closing the distance with incredible speed.

Quite suddenly the ground went out from under me. I fell heavily into a depression in the ground, to be steadied, as I tumbled, by Christian, who moved a bramble covering across us and put a finger to his lips. I could barely make him out in this dark hidey hole, but I heard the sound of the Urscumug die away. I queried what was happening.

'Has it moved off?'

'Almost certainly not,' said Christian. 'It's waiting, listening. It's been pursuing me for two days, out of the deep zones of the forest. It won't let up until I'm gone.'

'But why, Chris? Why is it trying to kill you?'

'It's the old man's mythago,' he said. 'He brought it into being in the heartwoods, but it was weak and trapped until I came along and gave it more power to draw on. But it was the old man's mythago, and he shaped it slightly from his own mind, his own ego. Oh God, Steve, how he must have hated, and hated *us,* to have imposed such terror onto the thing.'

'And Guiwenneth . . .' I said.

'Yes . . . Guiwenneth . . .' Christian echoed, speaking softly now. 'He'll revenge himself on me for that. If I give him half a chance.'

He stretched up to peer through the bramble covering. I could hear a distant restless movement, and thought I caught the sound of some animal grumbling deep in its throat.

'I thought he'd failed to create the primary mythago.'

Christian said, 'He died believing that. What would he have done, I wonder, if he'd seen how successful he'd been.' He crouched back down in the ditch. 'It's like a boar. Half boar, half man; it walks upright, but can run like the wind. It paints its face white in the semblance of a human face. Whatever age it lived in, one thing's for sure, it lived a long time before man as *we* understand 'man' existed; this thing comes from a time when man and nature were so close that they were indistinguishable.'

He touched me then, on the arm, a hesitant touch, as if he were half afraid to make this contact with one from whom he had grown so distant.

'When you run,' he said, 'run for the edge. Don't stop. And when you get out of the wood, don't come back. There is no way out for me now. I'm trapped in this wood by something in my own mind as surely as if I were a mythago myself. Don't come back here, Steve. Not for a long, long time.'

'Chris—' I began, but too late. He had thrown back the covering of the hole and was running from me. Moments later the most enormous shape passed overhead, one huge black foot landing just inches from my frozen body. It passed by in a split second, but as I scrambled from the hole and began to run, I glanced back, and the creature, hearing me, glanced back too, and for that instant of mutual contemplation, as we both moved apart in the forest, I saw the face that had been painted across the blackened features of the boar.

The Urscumug opened its mouth to roar, and my father seemed to leer at me.

CODA

One morning, in early spring, I found a brace of hare hanging from one of the pothooks in the kitchen; below them, scratched in the yellow paintwork on the wall, was the letter C. The gift was repeated about two months later, but then nothing, and a year has passed.

I have not been back to the wood.

I have read my father's diary ten times if I have read it once, steeping myself in the mystery of his life as much as he had steeped himself in the mystery of his own unconscious links with the primeval woodland. I find, in his erratic recordings, much that tells of his sense of danger, of what—just once—he calls 'ego's mythological ideal,' the involvement of the creator's mind which he feared would influence the shape and behavior of the mythago forms. He had known of the danger, then, but I wonder if Christian had fully comprehended this most subtle of the occult processes occuring in the forest. From the darkness and pain of my father's mind a single thread of gentleness and love had emerged in the fashioning of a girl in a green tunic, dooming her to a helplessness in the forest that was contrary to her natural form. But if she were to emerge again, it would be with Christian's mind controlling her, and Christian had no such preconceived ideas about a woman's strength or weakness. It would not be the same encounter.

It is summer now. The trees are full-leaved, the forest at its most impenetrable. I stay in the house, out of range, although I've noticed that, at dusk especially, shapes and figures begin to cluster in my peripheral vision. The aura of the woodland has reached the front of the house. Only in the back room, among the books and specimens, can I find a temporary escape from the encroaching dark.

A revised and expanded version of this story forms the first part of the novel *Mythago Wood*.

HARRISON BERGERON

Kurt Vonnegut, Jr.

*T*he year was 2081, and everybody was finally equal. They weren't only equal before God and the law, they were equal every which way. Nobody was smarter than anybody else; nobody was better looking than anybody else; nobody was stronger or quicker than anybody else. All this equality was due to the 211th, 212th, and 213th Amendments to the Constitution, and to the unceasing vigilance of agents of the United States Handicapper General.

Some things about living still weren't quite right, though. April, for instance, still drove people crazy by not being springtime. And it was in that clammy month that the H-G men took George and Hazel Bergeron's fourteen-year-old son, Harrison, away.

It was tragic, all right, but George and Hazel couldn't think about it very hard. Hazel had a perfectly average intelligence, which meant she couldn't think about anything except in short bursts. And George, while his intelligence was way above normal, had a little mental handicap radio in his ear—he was required by law to wear it at all times. It was tuned to a government transmitter, and every twenty seconds or so, the transmitter would send out some sharp noise to keep people like George from taking unfair advantage of their brains.

George and Hazel were watching television. There were tears on Hazel's cheeks, but she'd forgotten for the moment what they were about, as the ballerinas came to the end of a dance.

A buzzer sounded in George's head. His thoughts fled in panic, like bandits from a burglar alarm.

'That was a real pretty dance, that dance they just did,' said Hazel.

'Huh?' said George.

'That dance—it was nice,' said Hazel.

'Yup,' said George. He tried to think a little about the ballerinas. They weren't really very good—no better than anybody else would have been, anyway. They were burdened with sashweights and bags of birdshot, and their faces were masked, so that no one, seeing a free and graceful gesture or a pretty face, would feel like something the cat dragged in. George was toying with the vague notion that maybe dancers shouldn't be handicapped. But he didn't get very far with it before another noise in his ear radio scattered his thoughts.

George winced. So did two out of the eight ballerinas.

Hazel saw him wince. Having no mental handicap herself, she had to ask George what the latest sound had been.

'Sounded like somebody hitting a milk bottle with a ball-peen hammer,' said George.

'I'd think it would be real interesting, hearing all the different sounds,' said Hazel, a little envious. 'The things they think up.'

'Um,' said George.

'Only, if I was Handicapper General, you know what I would do?' said Hazel. Hazel, as a matter of fact, bore a strong resemblance to the Handicapper General, a woman named Diana Moon Glampers. 'If I was Diana Moon Glampers,' said Hazel, 'I'd have chimes on Sunday—just chimes. Kind of in honor of religion.'

'I could think, if it was just chimes,' said George.

'Well—maybe make 'em real loud,' said Hazel. 'I think I'd make a good Handicapper General.'

'Good as anybody else,' said George.

'Who knows better'n I do what normal is?' said Hazel.

'Right,' said George. He began to think glimmeringly about his abnormal son who was now in jail, about Harrison, but a twenty-one gun salute in his head stopped that.

'Boy!' said Hazel, 'that was a doozy, wasn't it?'

It was such a doozy that George was white and trembling, and tears stood on the rims of his red eyes. Two of the eight ballerinas had collapsed to the studio floor, were holding their temples.

'All of a sudden you look so tired,' said Hazel. 'Why don't you stretch out on the sofa, so's you can rest your handicap bag on the pillows, honeybunch.' She was referring to the forty-seven pounds of birdshot in a canvas bag, which was padlocked around George's neck. 'Go on and rest the bag for a little while,' she said. 'I don't care if you're not equal to me for a while.'

George weighed the bag with his hands. 'I don't mind it,' he said. 'I don't notice it any more. It's just a part of me.'

'You been so tired lately—kind of wore out,' said Hazel. 'If there was just some way we could make a little hole in the bottom of the bag, and just take out a few of them lead balls. Just a few.'

'Two years in prison and two-thousand dollars fine for every ball I took out,' said George. 'I don't call that a bargain.'

'If you could just take a few out when you came home from work,' said Hazel. 'I mean—you don't compete with anybody around here. You just set around.'

'If I tried to get away with it,' said George, 'then other people'd get away with it—and pretty soon we'd be right back to the dark ages again, with everybody competing against everybody else. You wouldn't like that, would you?'

'I'd hate it,' said Hazel.

'There you are,' said George. 'The minute people start cheating on laws, what do you think happens to society?'

If Hazel hadn't been able to come up with an answer to this question, George couldn't have supplied one. A siren was going off in his head.

'Reckon it'd fall all apart,' said Hazel.

'What would?' said George blankly.

'Society,' said Hazel uncertainly. 'Wasn't that what you just said?'

'Who knows?' said George.

The television program was suddenly interrupted for a news bulletin. It wasn't clear at first as to what the bulletin was about, since the announcer, like all announcers, had a serious speech impediment. For about half a minute, and in a state of high excitement, the announcer tried to say, 'Ladies and gentlemen—'

He finally gave up, handed the bulletin to a ballerina to read.

'That's all right,' Hazel said of the announcer, 'he tried. That's the big thing. He tried to do the best he could with what God gave him. He should get a nice raise for trying so hard.'

'Ladies and gentlemen—' said the ballerina, reading the bulletin. She must have been extraordinarily beautiful, becasue the mask she wore was hideous. And it was easy to see that she was the strongest and most graceful of all the dancers, for her handicap bags were as big as those worn by two-hundred-pound men.

And she had to apologize at once for her voice, which was a very unfair voice for a woman to use. Her voice was a warm, luminous, timeless melody. 'Excuse me—' she said, and she began again, making her voice absolutely uncompetitive.

'Harrison Bergeron, age fourteen,' she said in a grackle squawk, 'has just escaped from jail, where he was held on suspicion of plotting to overthrow the government. He is a genius and an athlete, is under-handicapped, and is extremely dangerous.'

A police photograph of Harrison Bergeron was flashed on the screen—upside down, then sideways, upside down again, then right-side up. The picture showed the full length of Harrison against a background calibrated in feet and inches. He was exactly seven feet tall.

The rest of Harrison's appearance was Halloween and hardware. Nobody had ever borne heavier handicaps. He had outgrown hindrances faster than the H-G men could think them up. Instead of a little ear radio for a mental handicap, he wore a tremendous pair of earphones, and spectacles with thick, wavy lenses besides. The spectacles were intended not only to make him half blind, but to give him whanging headaches besides.

Scrap metal was hung all over him. Ordinarily, there was a certain symmetry, a military neatness to the handicaps issued to strong people, but Harrison looked like a walking junkyard. In the race of life, Harrison carried three-hundred pounds.

And to offset his good looks, the H-G men required that he wear at all times a red rubber ball for a nose, keep his eyebrows shaved off, and cover his even white teeth with black caps at snaggle-tooth random.

'If you see this boy,' said the ballerina, 'do not—I repeat, do not—try to reason with him.'

There was the shriek of a door being torn from its hinges.

Screams and barking cries of consternation came from the television set. The photograph of Harrison Bergeron on the screen jumped again and again, as though dancing to the tune of an earthquake.

George Bergeron correctly identified the earthquake, and well he might have—for many was the time his own home had danced to the same crashing tune. 'My God!' said George. 'That must be Harrison!'

The realization was blasted from his mind instantly by the sound of an automobile collision in his head.

When George could open his eyes again, the photograph of Harrison was gone. A living, breathing Harrison filled the screen.

Clanking, clownish, and huge, Harrison stood in the center of the studio. The knob of the uprooted studio door was still in his hand. Ballerinas, technicians, musicians and announcers cowered on their knees before him, expecting to die.

'I am the Emperor!' cried Harrison. 'Do you hear? I am the

Emperor! Everybody must do what I say at once!' He stamped his foot and the studio shook.

'Even as I stand here,' he bellowed, 'crippled, hobbled, sickened —I am a greater ruler than any man who ever lived! Now watch me become what I *can* become!'

Harrison tore the straps of his handicap harness like wet tissue paper, tore straps guaranteed to support five thousand pounds.

Harrison's scrap-iron handicaps crashed to the floor.

Harrison thrust his thumbs under the bar of the padlock that secured his head harness. The bar snapped like celery. Harrison smashed his headphones and spectacles against the wall.

He flung away his rubber-ball nose, revealed a man that would have awed Thor, the god of thunder.

'I shall now select my Empress!' he said, looking down on the cowering people. 'Let the first woman who dares rise to her feet claim her mate and her throne!'

A moment passed, and then a ballerina arose, swaying like a willow.

Harrison plucked the mental handicap from her ear, snapped off her physical handicaps with marvelous delicacy. Last of all, he removed her mask.

She was blindingly beautiful.

'Now—' said Harrison, taking her hand. 'Shall we show the people the meaning of the word dance? Music!' he commanded.

The musicians scrambled back into their chairs, and Harrison stripped them of their handicaps, too. 'Play your best,' he told them, 'and I'll make you barons and dukes and earls.'

The music began. It was normal at first—cheap, silly, false. But Harrison snatched two musicians from their chairs, waved them like batons as he sang the music as he wanted it played. He slammed them back into their chairs.

The music began again, and was much improved.

Harrison and his Empress merely listened to the music for a while—listened gravely, as though synchronizing their heart-beats with it.

They shifted their weight to their toes.

Harrison placed his big hands on the girl's tiny waist, letting her sense the weightlessness that would soon be hers.

And then, in an explosion of joy and grace, into the air they sprang!

Not only were the laws of the land abandoned, but the law of gravity and the laws of motion as well.

They reeled, whirled, swiveled, flounced, capered, gamboled and spun.

They leaped like deer on the moon.

The studio ceiling was thirty feet high, but each leap brought the dancers nearer to it.

It became their obvious intention to kiss the ceiling.

They kissed it.

And then, neutralizing gravity with love and pure will, they remained suspended in air inches below the ceiling, and they kissed each other for a long, long time.

It was then that Diana Moon Glampers, the Handicapper General, came into the studio with a double-barreled ten-gauge shot-gun. She fired twice, and the Emperor and the Empress were dead before they hit the floor.

Diana Moon Glampers loaded the gun again. She aimed it at the musicians and told them they had ten seconds to get their handicaps back on.

It was then that the Bergerons' television tube burned out.

Hazel turned to comment about the blackout to George. But George had gone out into the kitchen for a can of beer.

George came back in with the beer, paused while a handicap signal shook him up. And then he sat down again. 'You been crying?' he said to Hazel, watching her wipe her tears.

'Yup,' she said.

'What about?' he said.

'I forget,' she said. 'Something real sad on television.'

'What was it?' he said.

'It's all kind of mixed up in my mind,' said Hazel.

'Forget sad things,' said George.

'I always do,' said Hazel.

'That's my girl,' said George. He winced. There was the sound of a riveting gun in his head.

'Gee—I could tell that one was a doozy,' said Hazel.

'You can say that again,' said George.

'Gee—' said Hazel—'I could tell that one was a doozy.'

FOUR GHOSTS IN HAMLET

Fritz Leiber

Actors are a superstitious lot, probably because chance plays a big part in the success of a production of a company or merely an actor—and because we're still a little closer than other people to the gypsies in the way we live and think. For instance, it's bad luck to have peacock feathers on stage or say the last line of a play at rehearsals or whistle in the dressing room (the one nearest the door gets fired) or sing God Save the Sovereign on a railway train. (A Canadian company got wrecked that way.)

Shakespearean actors are no exceptions. They simply travel a few extra superstitions, such as the one which forbids reciting the lines of the Three Witches, or anything from *Macbeth*, for that matter, except at performances, rehearsals, and on other legitimate occasions. This might be a good rule for outsiders too—then there wouldn't be the endless flood of books with titles taken from the text of *Macbeth*—you know, *Brief Candle, Tomorrow and Tomorrow, The Sound and the Fury, A Poor Player, All Our Yesterdays*, and those are all just from one brief soliloquy.

And our company, the Governor's company, has a rule against the Ghost in *Hamlet* dropping his greenish cheesecloth veil over his helmet-framed face until the very moment he makes each of his entrances. Hamlet's dead father mustn't stand veiled in the darkness of the wings.

This last superstition commemorates something which happened not too long ago, an actual ghost story. Sometimes I think its the greatest ghost story in the world—though certainly not from my way of telling it, which is gossipy and poor, but from the wonder blazing at its core.

It's not only a true tale of the supernatural, but also very much a story about people, for after all—and before everything else —ghosts are people.

The ghostly part of the story first showed itself in the tritest way imaginable: three of our actresses (meaning practically all the ladies in a Shakespearean company) took to having sessions with a Ouija board in the hour before curtain time and sometimes even during a performance when they had long offstage waits, and they became so wrapped up in it and conceited about it and they squeaked so excitedly at the revelations which the planchette spelled out—and three or four times almost missed entrances because of it—that if the Governor weren't such a tolerant commander-in-chief, he would have forbidden them to bring the board to the theater. I'm sure he was tempted to and might have, except that Props pointed out to him that our three ladies probably wouldn't enjoy Ouija sessions one bit in the privacy of a hotel room, that much of the fun in operating a Ouija board is in having a half exasperated, half intrigued floating audience, and that when all's done the basic business of all ladies is glamour, whether of personal charm or of actual witchcraft, since the word means both.

Props—that is, our property man, Billy Simpson—was fascinated by their obsession, as he is by any new thing that comes along, and might very well have broken our Shakespearean taboo by quoting the Three Witches about them, except that Props has no flair for Shakespearean speech at all, no dramatic ability whatsoever, in fact he's the one person in our company who never acts even a bit part or carries a mute spear on stage, though he has other talents which make up for this deficiency—he can throw together a papier mache bust of Pompey in two hours, or turn out a wooden prop dagger all silvery-bladed and hilt-gilded, or fix a zipper, and that's not all.

As for myself, I was very irked at the ridiculous alphabet board, since it seemed to occupy most of Monica Singleton's spare time and satisfy all her hunger for thrills. I'd been trying to promote a romance with her—a long touring season becomes deadly and cold without some sort of heart-tickle—and for a while I'd made progress. But after Ouija came along, I became a ridiculous Guildenstern mooning after an unattainable unseeing Ophelia —which were the parts I and she actually played in *Hamlet*.

I cursed the idiot board with its childish corner-pictures of grinning suns and smirking moons and windblown spirits, and I further alienated Monica by asking her why wasn't it called a Nenein or No-No board (Ninny board!) instead of a Yes-Yes board? Was that, I inquired, because all spiritualists are forever accentuat-

ing the positive and behaving like a pack of fawning yes-men?
—yes, we're here; yes, we're your uncle Harry; yes, we're happy on
this plane; yes, we have a doctor among us who'll diagnose that pain
in your chest; and so on.

Monica wouldn't speak to me for a week after that.

I would have been even more depressed except that Props
pointed out to me that no flesh-and-blood man can compete with
ghosts in a girl's affections, since ghosts being imaginary have all
the charms and perfections a girl can dream of, but that all girls
eventually tire of ghosts, or if their minds don't, their bodies do.
This eventually did happen, thank goodness, in the case of myself
and Monica, though not until we'd had a grisly, mind-wrenching
experience—a night of terrors before the nights of love.

So Ouija flourished and the Governor and the rest of us put up
with it one way or another, until there came that three-night-stand
in Wolverton, when its dismal uncanny old theater tempted our
three Ouija-women to ask the board who was the ghost haunting
the spooky place and the swooping planchette spelled out the name
S-H-A-K-E-S-P-E-A-R-E . . .

But I am getting ahead of my story. I haven't introduced our
company except for Monica, Props, and the Governor—and I
haven't identified the last of those three.

We call Gilbert Usher the Governor out of sheer respect and
affection. He's about the last of the old actor-managers. He hasn't
the name of Gielgud or Olivier or Evans or Richardson, but he's
spent most of a lifetime keeping Shakespeare alive, spreading that
magical a-religious gospel in the more remote counties and the
Dominions and the United States, like Benson once did. Our other
actors aren't names at all—I refuse to tell you mine!—but with the
exception of myself they're good troupers, or if they don't become
that the first season, they drop out. Gruelingly long seasons, much
uncomfortable traveling, and small profits are our destiny.

This particular season had got to that familiar point where the
plays are playing smoothly and everyone's a bit tireder than he
realizes and the restlessness sets in. Robert Dennis, our juvenile,
was writing a novel of theatrical life (he said) mornings at the
hotel—up at seven to slave at it, our Robert claimed. Poor old
Guthrie Boyd had started to drink again, and drink quite too much,
after an abstemious two months which had astonished everyone.

Francis Farley Scott, our leading man, had started to drop hints
that he was going to organize a Shakespearean repertory company
of his own next year and he began to have conspiratorial conversations with Gertrude Grainger, our leading lady, and to draw us

furtively aside one by one to make us hypothetical offers, no exact salary named. F. F. is as old as the Governor—who is our star, of course—and he has no talents at all except for self-infatuation and a somewhat grandiose yet impressive fashion of acting. He's portly like an opera tenor and quite bald and he travels an assortment of thirty toupees, ranging from red to black shot with silver, which he alternates with shameless abandon—they're for wear offstage, not on. It doesn't matter to him that the company knows all about his multi-colored artificial toppings, for we're part of his world of illusion, and he's firmly convinced that the stage-struck local ladies he squires about never notice, or at any rate mind the deception. He once gave me a lecture on the subtleties of suiting the color of your hair to the lady you're trying to fascinate—her own age, hair color, and so on.

Every year F. F. plots to start a company of his own—it's a regular midseason routine with him—and every year it comes to nothing, for he's as lazy and impractical as he is vain. Yet F. F. believes he could play any part in Shakespeare or all of them at once in a pinch; perhaps the only F. F. Scott Company which would really satisfy him would be one in which he would be the only actor—a Shakespearean monologue; in fact, the one respect in which F. F. is not lazy is in his eagerness to double as many parts as possible in any single play.

F. F.'s yearly plots never bother the Governor a bit—he keeps waiting wistfully for F. F. to fix him with an hypnotic eye and in a hoarse whisper ask *him* to join the Scott company.

And I of course was hoping that now at last Monica Singleton would stop trying to be the most exquisite ingenue that ever came tripping Shakespeare's way (rehearsing her parts even in her sleep, I guessed, though I was miles from being in a position to know that for certain) and begin to take note and not just advantage of my devoted attentions.

But then old Sybil Jameson bought the Ouija board and Gertrude Grainger dragooned an unwilling Monica into placing her fingertips on the planchette along with theirs 'just for a lark.' Next day Gertrude announced to several of us in a hushed voice that Monica had the most amazing undeveloped mediumistic talent she'd ever encountered, and from then on the girl was a Ouija-addict. Poor tight-drawn Monica, I suppose she had to explode out of her self-imposed Shakespearean discipline somehow, and it was just too bad it had to be the board instead of me. Though come to think of it, I shouldn't have felt quite so resentful of the board, for she might have exploded with Robert Dennis, which would have been infinitely worse, though we were never quite sure of Robert's sex. For that matter I wasn't sure of Gertrude's and suffered agonies of uncertain jealousy when she captured my beloved. I was obsessed with the vision of Gertrude's bold knees pressing Monica's under the Ouija board, though with Sybil's bony ones for chaperones, fortunately.

Francis Farley Scott, who was jealous too because this new toy had taken Gertrude's mind off their annual plottings, said rather spitefully that Monica must be one of those grabby girls who have to take command of whatever they get their fingers on, whether it's a man or a planchette, but Props told me he'd bet anything that Gertrude and Sybil had 'followed' Monica's first random finger movements like the skillfulest dancers guiding a partner while seeming to yield, in order to coax her into the business and make sure of their third.

Sometimes I thought that F. F. was right and sometimes Props and sometimes I thought that Monica had a genuine supernatural talent, though I don't ordinarily believe in such things, and that last really frightened me, for such a person might give up live men for ghosts forever. She was such a sensitive, subtle, wraith-cheeked girl and she could get so keyed up and when she touched the planchette her eyes got such an empty look, as if her mind had traveled down into her fingertips or out to the ends of time and space. And once the three of them gave me a character reading from the board which embarrassed me with its accuracy. The same thing happened to several other people in the company. Of course, as Props pointed out, actors can be pretty good character analysts whenever they stop being egomaniacs.

After reading characters and foretelling the future for several weeks, our Three Weird Sisters got interested in reincarnation and began asking the board and then telling us what famous or infamous people we'd been in past lives. Gertrude Grainger had been Queen Boadicea, I wasn't surprised to hear. Sybil Jameson had been Cassandra. While Monica was once mad Queen Joanna of Castile and more recently a prize hysterical patient of Janet at the Salpetriere—touches which irritated and frightened me more than they should have. Billy Simpson—Props—had been an Egyptian silversmith under Queen Hatshepsut and later a servant of Samuel Pepys; he heard this with a delighted chuckle. Guthrie Boyd had been the Emperor Claudius and Robert Dennis had been Caligula. For some reason I had been both John Wilkes Booth and Lambert Simnel, which irritated me considerably, for I saw no romance but only neurosis in assassinating an American president and dying in a burning barn, or impersonating the Earl of Warwick, pretending unsuccessfully to the British throne, being pardoned for it—of all things!—and spending the rest of my life as a scullion in the kitchen of Henry VII and his son. The fact that both Booth and Simnel had been actors of a sort—a poor sort—naturally irritated me the more. Only much later did Monica confess to me that the board had probably made those decisions because I had had such a 'tragic, dangerous, defeated look'—a revelation which surprised and flattered me.

Francis Farley Scott was flattered too, to hear he'd once been Henry VIII—he fancied all those wives and he wore his golden blond toupe after the show that night—until Gertrude and Sybil and Monica announced that the Governor was a reincarnation of no less than William Shakespeare himself. That made F. F. so jealous that he instantly sat down at the prop table, grabbed up a quill pen, and did an impromptu rendering of Shakespeare composing Hamlet's 'To be or not to be' soliloquy. It was an effective performance, though with considerably more frowning and eye-rolling and trying of lines for sound than I imagine Willy S. himself used originally, and when F. F. finished, even the Governor, who'd been standing unobserved in the shadows beside Props, applauded with the latter.

Governor kidded the pants off the idea of himself as Shakespeare. He said that if Willy S. were ever reincarnated it ought to be as a world-famous dramatist who was secretly in his spare time the world's greatest scientist and philosopher and left clues to his identity in his mathematical equations—that way he'd get his own back at Bacon, or rather the Baconians.

Yet I suppose if you had to pick someone for a reincarnation of Shakespeare, Gilbert Usher wouldn't be a bad choice. Insofar as a star and director ever can be, the Governor is gentle and self-effacing—as Shakespeare himself must have been, or else there would never have arisen that ridiculous Bacon-Oxford-Marlowe-Elizabeth-take-your-pick-who-wrote-Shakespeare-controversy. And the Governor has a sweet melancholy about him, though he's handsomer and despite his years more athletic than one imagines Shakespeare being. And he's generous to a fault, especially where old actors who've done brave fine things in the past are concerned.

This season his mistake in that last direction had been in hiring Guthrie Boyd to play some of the more difficult older leading roles, including a couple F. F. usually handles: Brutus, Othello, and besides those Duncan in *Macbeth*, Kent in *King Lear*, and the Ghost in *Hamlet*.

Guthrie was a bellowing hard-drinking bear of an actor, who'd been a Shakespearean star in Australia and successfully smuggled some of his reputation west—he learned to moderate his bellowing, while his emotions were always simple and sincere, though explosive—and finally even spent some years in Hollywood. But there his drinking caught up with him, probably because of the stupid film parts he got, and he failed six times over. His wife divorced him. His children cut themselves off. He married a starlet and she divorced him. He dropped out of sight.

Then after several years the Governor ran into him. He'd been rusticating in Canada with a stubborn teetotal admirer. He was only a shadow of his former self, but there was some substance to the shadow—and he wasn't drinking. The Governor decided to take a chance on him—although the company manager Harry Grossman was dead set against it—and during rehearsals and the first month or so of performances it was wonderful to see how old Guthrie Boyd came back, exactly as if Shakespeare were a restorative medicine.

It may be stuffy or sentimental of me to say so, but you know, I think Shakespeare's good for people. I don't know of an actor, except myself, whose character hasn't been strengthened and his vision widened and charity quickened by working in the plays. I've heard that before Gilbert Usher became a Shakespearean, he was a more ruthlessly ambitious and critical man, not without malice, but the plays mellowed him, as they've mellowed Props's philosophy and given him a zest for life.

Because of his contact with Shakespeare, Robert Dennis is a less strident and pettish swish (if he is one), Gertrude Grainger's outbursts of cold rage have an undercurrent of queenly make-believe, and even Francis Farley Scott's grubby little seductions are probably kinder and less insultingly illusionary.

In fact I sometimes think that what civilized serenity the British people possess, and small but real ability to smile at themselves, is chiefly due to their good luck in having had William Shakespeare born one of their company.

But I was telling how Guthrie Boyd performed very capably those first weeks, against the expectations of most of us, so that we almost quit holding our breaths—or sniffing at his. His Brutus was workmanlike, his Kent quite fine—that bluff rough honest part suited him well—and he regularly got admiring notices for his Ghost in *Hamlet*. I think his years of living death as a drinking alcoholic had given him an understanding of loneliness and frozen abilities and despair that he put to good use—probably unconsciously—in interpreting that small role.

He was really a most impressive figure in the part, even just visually. The Ghost's basic costume is simple enough—a big all-enveloping cloak that brushes the ground-cloth, a big dull helmet with the tiniest battery light inside its peak to throw a faint green glow on the Ghost's features, and over the helmet a veil of greenish cheesecloth that registers as mist to the audience. He wears a suit of stage armor under the cloak, but that's not important and at a pinch he can do without it, for his cloak can cover his entire body.

The Ghost doesn't switch on his helmet-light until he makes his entrance, for fear of it being glimpsed by an edge of the audience, and nowadays because of that superstition or rule I told you about, he doesn't drop the cheesecloth veil until the last second either, but when Guthrie Boyd was playing the part that rule didn't exist and I have a vivid recollection of him standing in the wings, waiting to go on, a big bearish inscrutable figure about as solid and un- supernatural as a bushy seven-foot evergreen covered by a gray tarpaulin. But then when Guthrie would switch on the tiny light and stride smoothly and silently on stage and his hollow distant tormented voice boom out, there'd be a terrific shivery thrill, even for us backstage, as if we were listening to words that really had traveled across black windy infinite gulfs from the Afterworld or the Other Side.

At any rate Guthrie was a great Ghost, and adequate or a bit better than that in most of his other parts—for those first nondrink- ing weeks. He seemed very cheerful on the whole, modestly buoyed up by his comeback, though sometimes something empty and dead would stare for a moment out of his eyes—the old drinking alcoholic wondering what all this fatiguing sober nonsense was about. He was especially looking forward to our three-night-stand at Wolverton, although that was still two months in the future then. The reason was that both his children—married and with families now, of course—lived and worked at Wolverton and I'm sure he set great store on proving to them in person his rehabilitation, figuring it would lead to a reconciliation and so on.

But then came his first performance as Othello. (The Governor, although the star, always played Iago—an equal role, though not the title one.) Guthrie was almost too old for Othello, of course, and besides that, his health wasn't good—the drinking years had taken their toll of his stamina and the work of rehearsals and of first nights in eight different plays after years away from the theater had exhausted him. But somehow the old volcano inside him got seething again and he gave a magnificent performance. Next morning the papers raved about him and one review rated him even better than the Governor.

That did it, unfortunately. The glory of his triumph was too much for him. The next night—*Othello* again—he was drunk as a skunk. He remembered most of his lines—though the Governor had to throw him about every sixth one out of the side of his mouth—but he weaved and wobbled, he planked a big hand on the shoulder of every other character he addressed to keep from falling over, and he even forgot to put in his false teeth the first two acts, so that his voice was mushy. To cap that, he started really to strangle Gertrude Grainger in the last scene, until that rather brawny Desdemona, unseen by the audience, gave him a knee in the gut; then, after stabbing himself, he flung the prop dagger high in the flies so that it came down with two lazy twists and piercing the groundcloth buried its blunt point deep in the soft wood of the stage floor not three feet from Monica, who plays Iago's wife Emilia and so was lying dead on the stage at that point in the drama, murdered by her villainous husband—and might have been dead for real if the dagger had followed a slightly different trajectory.

Since a third performance of *Othello* was billed for the following night, the Governor had no choice but to replace Guthrie with Francis Farley Scott, who did a good job (for him) of covering up his satisfaction at getting his old role back. F. F., always a plushy and lascivious-eyed Moor, also did a good job with the part, coming in that way without even a brush-up rehearsal, so that one critic, catching the first and third shows, marveled how we could change big roles at will, thinking we'd done it solely to demonstrate our virtuosity.

Of course the Governor read the riot act to Guthrie and carried him off to a doctor, who without being prompted threw a big scare into him about his drinking and his heart, so that he just might have recovered from his lapse, except that two nights later we did *Julius Caesar* and Guthrie, instead of being satisfied with being workman-like, decided to recoup himself with a really rousing performance. So he bellowed and groaned and bugged his eyes as I suppose he had done in his palmiest Australian days. His optimistic self-satisfaction between scenes was frightening to behold. Not too terrible a performance, truly, but the critics all panned him and one of them said, 'Guthrie Boyd played Brutus—a bunch of vocal cords wrapped up in a toga.'

That tied up the package and knotted it tight. Thereafter Guthrie was medium pie-eyed from morning to night—and often more than medium. The Governor had to yank him out of Brutus too (F. F. again replacing), but being the Governor he didn't sack him. He put him into a couple of bit parts—Montano and the Soothsayer —in *Othello* and *Caesar* and let him keep on at the others and he gave me and Joe Rubens and sometimes Props the job of keeping an eye on the poor old sot and making sure he got to the theater by the half hour and if possible not too plastered. Often he played the Ghost or the Doge of Venice in his street clothes under cloak or scarlet robe, but he played them. And many were the nights Joe and I made the rounds of half the local bars before we corraled him. The Governor sometimes refers to Joe Rubens and me in mild derision as 'the American element' in his company, but just the same he depends on us quite a bit; and I certainly don't mind being one of his trouble-shooters—it's a joy to serve him.

All this may seem to contradict my statement about our getting to the point, about this time, where the plays were playing smoothly and the monotony setting in. But it doesn't really. There's always something going wrong in a theatrical company—anything else would be abnormal; just as the Samoans say no party is a success until somebody's dropped a plate or spilled a drink or tickled the wrong woman.

Besides, once Guthrie had got Othello and Brutus off his neck, he didn't do too badly. The little parts and even Kent he could play passably whether drunk or sober. King Duncan, for instance, and the Doge in *The Merchant* are easy to play drunk because the actor always has a couple of attendants to either side of him, who can guide his steps if he weaves and even hold him up if necessary —which can turn out to be an effective dramatic touch, registering as the infirmity of extreme age.

And somehow Guthrie continued to give that same masterful performance as the Ghost and get occasional notices for it. In fact Sybil Jameson insisted he was a shade better in the Ghost now that he was invariably drunk; which could have been true. And he still talked about the three-night-stand coming up in Wolverton, though now as often with gloomy apprehension as with proud fatherly anticipation.

Well, the three-night-stand eventually came. We arrived at Wolverton on a non-playing evening. To the surprise of most of us, but especially Guthrie, his son and daughter were there at the station to welcome him with their respective spouses and all their kids and numerous in-laws and a great gaggle of friends. Their cries of greeting when they spotted him were almost an organized cheer and I looked around for a brass band to strike up.

I found out later that Sybil Jameson, who knew them, had been sending them all his favorable notices, so that they were eager as weasels to be reconciled with him and show him off as blatantly as possible.

When he saw his childrens' and grandchildrens' faces and realized the cries were for him, old Guthrie got red in the face and beamed like the sun, and they closed in around him and carried him off in triumph for an evening of celebrations.

Next day I heard from Sybil, whom they'd carried off with him, that everything had gone beautifully. He'd drunk like a fish, but kept marvellous control, so that no one but she noticed, and the warmth of the reconciliation of Guthrie to everyone, complete strangers included, had been wonderful to behold. Guthrie's son-in-law, a pugnacious chap, had got angry when he'd heard Guthrie wasn't to play Brutus the third night, and he declared that Gilbert Usher must be jealous of his magnificent father-in-law. Everything was forgiven twenty times over. They'd even tried to put old Sybil to bed with Guthrie, figuring romantically, as people will about actors, that she must be his mistress. All this was very fine, and of course wonderful for Guthrie, and for Sybil too in a fashion, yet I suppose the unconstrained night-long bash, after two months of uninterrupted semi-controlled drunkenness, was just about the worst thing anybody could have done to the old boy's sodden body and laboring heart.

Meanwhile on that first evening I accompanied Joe Rubens and Props to the theater we were playing at Wolverton to make sure the scenery got stacked right and the costume trunks were all safely arrived and stowed. Joe is our stage manager besides doing rough or Hebraic parts like Caliban and Tubal—he was a professional boxer in his youth and got his nose smashed crooked. Once I started to take boxing lessons from him, figuring an actor should know everything, but during the third lesson I walked into a gentle right cross and although it didn't exactly stun me there were bells ringing faintly in my head for six hours afterwards and I lived in a world of faery and that was the end of my fistic career. Joe is actually a most versatile actor—for instance, he understudies the Governor in Macbeth, Lear, Iago, and of course Shylock—though his brutal moon-face is against him, especially when his make-up doesn't include a beard. But he dotes on being genial and in the States he often gets a job by day playing Santa Claus in big department stores during the month before Christmas.

The Monarch was a cavernous old place, very grimy backstage, but with a great warren of dirty little dressing rooms and even a property room shaped like an L stage left. Its empty shelves were thick with dust.

There hadn't been a show in the Monarch for over a year, I saw from the yellowing sheets thumbtacked to the callboard as I tore them off and replaced them with a simple black-crayoned HAMLET: TONIGHT AT 8:30.

Then I noticed, by the cold inadequate working lights, a couple of tiny dark shapes dropping down from the flies and gliding around in wide swift circles—out into the house too, since the curtain was up. Bats, I realized with a little start—the Monarch was really halfway through the lich gate. The bats would fit very nicely with *Macbeth*, I told myself, but not so well with *The Merchant of Venice*, while with Hamlet they should neither help nor hinder, provided they didn't descend in nightfighter squadrons; it would be nice if they stuck to the Ghost scenes.

I'm sure the Governor had decided we'd open at Wolverton with *Hamlet* so that Guthrie would have the best chance of being a hit in his children's home city.

Billy Simpson, shoving his properties table into place just in front of the dismal L of the prop room, observed cheerfully, 'It's a proper haunted house. The girls'll find some rare ghosts here, I'll wager, if they work their board.'

Which turned out to be far truer than he realized at the time—I think.

'Bruce!' Joe Rubens called to me. 'We better buy a couple of rat traps and set them out. There's something scuttling back of the drops.'

But when I entered the Monarch next night, well before the hour, by the creaky thick metal stage door, the place had been swept and tidied a bit. With the groundcloth down and the *Hamlet* set up, it didn't look too terrible, even though the curtain was still unlowered, dimly showing the house and its curves of empty seats and the two faint green exit lights with no one but myself to look at them.

There was a little pool of light around the callboard stage right, and another glow the other side of the stage beyond the wings, and lines of light showing around the edges of the door of the second dressing room, next to the star's.

I started across the dark stage, sliding my shoes softly so as not to trip over a cable or stage-screw and brace, and right away I got the magic electric feeling I often do in an empty theater the night of a show. Only this time there was something additional, something that started a shiver crawling down my neck. It wasn't, I think, the thought of the bats which might now be swooping around me unseen, skirling their inaudibly shrill trumpet calls, or even of the rats which *might* be watching sequin-eyed from behind trunks and flats, although not an hour ago Joe had told me that the traps he'd actually procured and set last night had been empty today.

No, it was more as if all of Shakespeare's characters were invisibly there around me—all the infinite possibilities of the theater. I imagined Rosalind and Falstaff and Prospero standing arm-in-arm watching me with different smiles. And Caliban grinning down from where he silently swung in the flies. And side by side, but unsmiling and not arm-in-arm: Macbeth and Iago and Dick the Three Eyes—Richard III. And all the rest of Shakespeare's myriad-minded good-evil crew.

I passed through the wings opposite and there in the second pool of light Billy Simpson sat behind his table with the properties for *Hamlet* set out on it: the skulls, the foils, the lantern, the purses, the parchmenty letters, Ophelia's flowers, and all the rest. It was odd Props having everything ready quite so early and a bit odd too that he should be alone, for Props has the un-actorish habit of making friends with all sorts of locals, such as policemen and porters and flower women and newsboys and shopkeepers and tramps who claim they're indigent actors, and even inviting them backstage with him—a fracture of rules which the Governor allows since Props is such a sensible chap. He has a great liking for people, especially low people, Props has, and for all the humble details of life. He'd make a good writer, I'd think, except for his utter lack of dramatic flair and story-skill—a sort of prosiness that goes with his profession.

And now he was sitting at his table, his stooped shoulders almost inside the doorless entry to the empty-shelfed prop room—no point in using it for a three-night-stand—and he was gazing at me quizzically. He has a big forehead—the light was on that—and a tapering chin—that was in shadow—and rather large eyes, which were betwixt the light and the dark. Sitting there like that, he seemed to me for a moment (mostly because of the outspread props, I guess) like the midnight Master of the Show in *The Rubaiyat* round whom all the rest of us move like shadow shapes.

Usually he has a quick greeting for anyone, but tonight he was silent, and that added to the illusion.

'Props,' I said, 'this theater's got a supernatural smell.'

His expression didn't change at that, but he solemnly sniffed the air in several little whiffles adding up to one big inhalation, and as he did so he threw his head back, bringing his weakish chin into the light and shattering the illusion.

'Dust,' he said after a moment. 'Dust and old plush and scenery water-paint and sweat and drains and gelatin and greasepaint and powder and a breath of whisky. But the supernatural . . . no, I can't smell that. Unless . . .' And he sniffed again, but shook his head.

I chuckled at his materialism—although that rough about whisky did seem fanciful, since I hadn't been drinking and Props never does and Guthrie Boyd was nowhere in evidence. Props has a mind like a notebook for sensory details—and for the minutia of human habits too. It was Props, for instance, who told me about the actual notebook in which John McCarthy (who would be playing Fortinbras and the Player King in a couple of hours) jots down the exact number of hours he sleeps each night and keeps totting them up, so he knows when he'll have to start sleeping extra hours to average the full nine he thinks he must get each night to keep from dying.

It was also Props who pointed out to me that F. F. is much more careless gumming his offstage toupees to his head than his theater wigs—a studied carelessness, like that in tying a bowtie, he assured me; it indicated, he said, a touch of contempt for the whole offstage world.

Props isn't *only* a detail-worm, but it's perhaps because he is one that he has sympathy for all human hopes and frailties, even the most trivial, like my selfish infatuation with Monica.

Now I said to him, 'I didn't mean an actual smell, Billy. But back there just now I got the feeling anything might happen tonight.'

He nodded slowly and solemnly. With anyone but Props I'd have wondered if he weren't a little drunk. Then he said, 'You were on a stage. You know, the science-fiction writers are missing a bet there. We've got time machines right now. Theaters. Theaters are time machines and spaceships too. They take people on trips through the future and the past and the elsewhere and the might-have-been —yes, and if it's done well enough, give them glimpses of Heaven and Hell.'

I nodded back at him. Such grotesque fancies are the closest Props ever comes to escaping from prosiness.

I said, 'Well, let's hope Guthrie gets aboard the spaceship before the curtain up-jets. Tonight we're depending on his children having the sense to deliver him here intact. Which from what Sybil says about them is not to be taken for granted.'

Props stared at me owlishly and slowly shook his head. 'Guthrie got here about ten minutes ago,' he said, 'and looking no drunker than usual.'

'That's a relief,' I told him, meaning it.

'The girls are having a Ouija session,' he went on, as if he were determined to account for all of us from moment to moment. 'They smelt the supernatural here, just as you did, and they're asking the board to name the culprit.' Then he stopped so that he looked almost hunchbacked and he felt for something under the table.

I nodded. I'd guessed the Ouija-part from the lines of light showing around the door of Gertrude Grainger's dressing room.

Props straightened up and he had a pint bottle of whisky in his hand. I don't think a loaded revolver would have dumbfounded me as much. He unscrewed the top.

'There's the Governor coming in,' he said tranquilly, hearing the stage door creak and evidently some footsteps my own ears missed. 'That's seven of us in the theater before the hour.'

He took a big slow swallow of whisky and recapped the bottle, as naturally as if it were a nightly action. I goggled at him without comment. What he was doing was simply unheard of—for Billy Simpson.

At that moment there was a sharp scream and a clatter of thin wood and something twangy and metallic falling and a scurry of footsteps. Our previous words must have cocked a trigger in me, for I was at Gertrude Grainger's dressing-room door as fast as I could sprint—no worry this time about tripping over cables or braces in the dark.

I yanked the door open and there by the bright light of the bulbs framing the mirror were Gertrude and Sybil sitting close together with the Ouija board face down on the floor in front of them along with a flimsy wire-backed chair, overturned. While pressing back into Gertrude's costumes hanging on the rack across the little room, almost as if she wanted to hide behind them like bedclothes, was Monica pale and staring-eyed. She didn't seem to recognize me. The dark-green heavily brocaded costume Gertrude wears as the Queen in *Hamlet*, into which Monica was chiefly pressing herself, accentuated her pallor. All three of them were in their street-clothes.

I went to Monica and put an arm around her and gripped her hand. It was cold as ice. She was standing rigidly.

While I was doing that Gertrude stood up and explained in rather haughty tones what I told you earlier: about them asking the board

who the ghost was haunting the Monarch tonight and the planchette spelling out S-H-A-K-E-S-P-E-A-R-E . . .

'I don't know why it startled you so, dear,' she ended crossly,
speaking to Monica. 'It's very natural his spirit should attend
performances of his plays.'

I felt the slim body I clasped relax a little. That relieved me. I was
selfishly pleased at having got an arm around it, even under such
public and unamorous circumstances, while at the same time my
silly mind was thinking that if Props had been lying to me about
Guthrie Boyd having come in no more drunken than usual (this
new Props who drank straight whisky in the theater could lie too, I
supposed) why then we could certainly use William Shakespeare
tonight, since the Ghost in *Hamlet* is the one part in all his plays
Shakespeare himself is supposed to have acted on the stage.

'I don't know why myself now,' Monica suddenly answered from
beside me, shaking her head as if to clear it. She became aware of
me at last, started to pull away, then let my arm stay around her.

The next voice that spoke was the Governor's. He was standing
in the doorway, smiling faintly, with Props peering around his
shoulder. Props would be as tall as the Governor if he ever
straightened up, but his stoop takes almost a foot off his height.

The Governor said softly, a comic light in his eyes, 'I think we
should be content to bring Shakespeare's plays to life, without
trying for their author. It's hard enough on the nerves just to *act*
Shakespeare.'

He stepped forward with one of his swift, naturally graceful
movements and kneeling on one knee he picked up the fallen board
and planchette. 'At all events I'll take these in charge for tonight.
Feeling better now, Miss Singleton?' he asked as he straightened
and stepped back.

'Yes, quite all right,' she answered flusteredly, disengaging my
arm and pulling away from me rather too quickly.

He nodded. Gertrude Grainger was staring at him coldly, as if
about to say something scathing, but she didn't. Sybil Jameson was
looking at the floor. She seemed embarrassed, yet puzzled too.

I followed the Governor out of the dressing room and told him, in
case Props hadn't, about Guthrie Boyd coming to the theater early.
My momentary doubt of Props's honesty seemed plain silly to me
now, although his taking that drink remained an astonishing riddle.

Props confirmed me about Guthrie coming in, though his
manner was a touch abstracted.

The Governor nodded his thanks for the news, then twitched a
nostril and frowned. I was sure he'd caught a whiff of alcohol and

didn't know to which of us two to attribute it—or perhaps even to one of the ladies, or to an earlier passage of Guthrie this way.

He said to me, 'Would you come into my dressing room for a bit, Bruce?'

I followed him, thinking he'd picked me for the drinker and wondering how to answer—best perhaps simply silently accept the fatherly lecture—but when he'd turned on the lights and I'd shut the door, his first question was, 'You're attracted to Miss Singleton, aren't you, Bruce?'

When I nodded abruptly, swallowing my morsel of surprise, he went on softly but emphatically, 'Then why don't you quit hovering and playing Galahad and really go after her? Ordinarily I must appear to frown on affairs in the company, but in this case it would be the best way I know of to break up those Ouija sessions, which are obviously harming the girl.'

I managed to grin and tell him I'd be happy to obey his instructions—and do it entirely on my own initiative too.

He grinned back as I started to toss the Ouija board on his couch, but instead put it and the planchette carefully down on the end of his long dressing table and put a second question to me.

'What do you think of some of this stuff they're getting over the board, Bruce?'

I said, 'Well, that last one gave me a shiver, all right—I suppose because . . .' and I told him about sensing the presence of Shakespeare's characters in the dark. I finished, 'But of course the whole idea is nonsense,' and I grinned.

He didn't grin back.

I continued impulsively, 'There was one idea they had a few weeks back that impressed me, though it didn't seem to impress you. I hope you won't think I'm trying to butter you up, Mr. Usher. I mean the idea of you being a reincarnation of William Shakespeare.'

He laughed delightedly and said, 'Clearly you don't yet know the difference between a player and a playwright, Bruce. Shakespeare striding about romantically with head thrown back?—and twirling a sword and shaping his body and voice to every feeling handed him? Oh no! I'll grant he might have played the Ghost—it's a part within the scope of an average writer's talents, requiring nothing more than that he stand still and sound off sepulchrally.'

He paused and smiled and went on. 'No, there's only one person in this company who might be Shakespeare come again, and that's Billy Simpson. Yes, I mean Props. He's a great listener and he knows how to put himself in touch with everyone and then he's got that rat-trap mind for every hue and scent and sound of life, inside or out the mind. And he's very analytic. Oh, I know he's got no poetic talent, but surely Shakespeare wouldn't have that in *every* reincarnation. I'd think he'd need about a dozen lives in which to gather material for every one in which he gave it dramatic form. Don't you find something very poignant in the idea of a mute inglorious Shakespeare spending whole humble lifetimes collecting the necessary stuff for one great dramatic burst? Think about it some day.'

I was doing that already and finding it a fascinating fantasy. It crystalized so perfectly the feeling I'd got seeing Billy Simpson behind his property table. And then Props did have a high-foreheaded poet-schoolmaster's face like that given Shakespeare in the posthumous engravings and woodcuts and portraits. Why, even their initials were the same. It made me feel strange.

Then the Governor put his third question to me.

'He's drinking tonight, isn't he? I mean Props, not Guthrie.'

I didn't say anything, but my face must have answered for me—at least to such a student of expressions as the Governor—for he smiled and said, 'You needn't worry. I wouldn't be angry with him. In fact, the only other time I know of that Props drank spirits by himself in the theater, I had a great deal to thank him for.' His lean face grew thoughtful. 'It was long before your time, in fact it was the first season I took out a company of my own. I had barely enough money to pay the printer for the three-sheets and get the first-night curtain up. After that it was touch and go for months. Then in mid-season we had a run of bad luck—a two-night heavy fog in one city, an influenza scare in another, Harvey Wilkins' Shakespearean troupe two weeks ahead of us in a third. And when in the next town we played it turned out the advance sale was very light—because my name was unknown there and the theater an unpopular one—I realized I'd have to pay off the company while there was still money enough to get them home, if not the scenery.

'That night I caught Props swigging, but I hadn't the heart to chide him for it—in fact I don't think I'd have blamed anyone, except perhaps myself, for getting drunk that night. But then during the performance the actors and even the union stagehands we travel began coming to my dressing room by ones and twos and telling me they'd be happy to work without salary for another three weeks, if I thought that might give us a chance of recouping. Well, of course I grabbed at their offers and we got a spell of brisk pleasant weather and we hit a couple of places starved for Shakespeare, and things worked out, even to paying all the back salary owed before the season was ended.

'Later on I discovered it was Props who had put them all up to doing it.'

Gilbert Usher looked up at me and one of his eyes was wet and his lips were working just a little. 'I couldn't have done it myself,' he said, 'for I wasn't a popular man with my company that first season—I'd been riding everyone much too hard and with nasty sarcasms—and I hadn't yet learned how to ask anyone for help when I really needed it. But Billy Simpson did what I couldn't, though he had to nerve himself for it with spirits. He's quick enough with his tongue in ordinary circumstances, as you know, particularly when he's being the friendly listener, but apparently when something very special is required of him, he must drink himself to the proper pitch. I'm wondering . . .'

His voice trailed off and then he straightened up before his mirror and started to unknot his tie and he said to me briskly, 'Better get dressed now, Bruce. And then look in on Guthrie, will you?'

My mind was churning some rather strange thoughts as I hurried up the iron stairs to the dressing room I shared with Robert Dennis. I got on my Guildenstern make-up and costume, finishing just as Robert arrived; as Laertes, Robert makes a late entrance and so needn't hurry to the theater on *Hamlet* nights. Also, although we don't make a point of it, he and I spend as little time together in the dressing room as we can.

Before going down I looked into Guthrie Boyd's. He wasn't there, but the lights were on and the essentials of the Ghost's costume weren't in sight—impossible to miss that big helmet!—so I assumed he'd gone down ahead of me.

It was almost the half hour. The house lights were on, the curtain down, more stage lights on too, and quite a few of us about. I noticed that Props was back in the chair behind his table and not looking particularly different from any other night—perhaps the drink had been a once-only aberration and not some symptom of a crisis in the company.

I didn't make a point of hunting for Guthrie. When he gets costumed early he generally stands back in a dark corner somewhere, wanting to be alone—perchance to sip, aye, there's the rub!—or visits with Sybil in her dressing room.

I spotted Monica sitting on a trunk by the switchboard, where backstage was brightest lit at the moment. She looked ethereal yet springlike in her blonde Ophelia wig and first costume, a pale green one. Recalling my happy promise to the Governor, I bounced up beside her and asked her straight out about the Ouija business, pleased to have something to the point besides the plays to talk with her about—and really not worrying as much about her nerves as I suppose I should have.

She was in a very odd mood, both agitated and abstracted, her gaze going back and forth between distant and near and very distant. My questions didn't disturb her at all, in fact I got the feeling she welcomed them, yet she genuinely didn't seem able to tell me much about why she'd been so frightened at the last name the board had spelled. She told me that she actually did get into a sort of dream state when she worked the board and that she'd screamed before she'd quite comprehended what had shocked her so; then her mind had blacked out for a few seconds, she thought.

'One thing though, Bruce,' she said. 'I'm not going to work the board any more, at least when the three of us are alone like that.'

'That sounds like a wise idea,' I agreed, trying not to let the extreme heartiness of my agreement show through.

She stopped peering around as if for some figure to appear that wasn't in the play and didn't belong backstage, and she laid her hand on mine and said, 'Thanks for coming so quickly when I went idiot and screamed.'

I was about to improve this opportunity by telling her that the reason I'd come so quickly was that she was so much in my mind, but just then Joe Rubens came hurrying up with the Governor behind him in his Hamlet black to tell me that neither Guthrie Boyd nor his Ghost costume was to be found anywhere in the theater.

What's more, Joe had got the phone numbers of Guthrie's son and daughter from Sybil and rung them up. The one phone hadn't answered, while on the other a female voice—presumably a maid's—had informed him that everyone had gone to see Guthrie Boyd in *Hamlet*.

Joe was already wearing his cumbrous chain-mail armor for Marcellus—woven cord silvered—so I knew I was elected. I ran upstairs and in the space of time it took Robert Dennis to guess my mission and advise me to try the dingiest bars first and have a drink or two myself in them, I'd put on my hat, overcoat, and wristwatch and left him.

So garbed and as usual nervous about people looking at my ankles, I sallied forth to comb the nearby bars of Wolverton. I consoled myself with the thought that if I found Hamlet's father's ghost drinking his way through them, no one would ever spare a glance for my own costume.

Almost on the stroke of curtain I returned, no longer giving a damn what anyone thought about my ankles. I hadn't found Guthrie or spoken to a soul who'd seen a large male imbiber—most likely of Irish whisky—in great-cloak and antique armor, with perhaps some ghostly green light cascading down his face.

Beyond the curtain the overture was fading to its sinister close and the backstage lights were all down, but there was an angry hushed voice dispute going on stage left, where the Ghost makes all his entrances and exits. Skipping across the dim stage in front of the blue-lit battlements of Elsinore—I still in my hat and overcoat—I found the Governor and Joe Rubens and with them John McCarthy all ready to go on as the Ghost in his Fortinbras armor with a dark cloak and some green gauze over it.

But alongside them was Francis Farley Scott in a very similar get-up—no armor, but a big enough cloak to hide his King costume and a rather more impressive helmet than John's.

They were all very dim in the midnight glow leaking back from the dimmed-down blue floods. The five of us were the only people I could see on this side of the stage.

F. F. was arguing vehemently that he must be allowed to double the Ghost with King Claudius because he knew the part better than John and because—this was the important thing—he could imitate Guthrie's voice perfectly enough to deceive his children and perhaps save their illusions about him. Sybil had looked through the curtain hole and seen them and all of their yesterday crowd, with new recruits besides, occupying all of the second, third, and fourth rows center, chattering with excitement and beaming with anticipation. Harry Grossman had confirmed this from the front of the house.

I could tell that the Governor was vastly irked at F. F. and at the same time touched by the last part of his argument. It was exactly the sort of sentimental heroic rationalization with which F. F. cloaked his insatiable yearnings for personal glory. Very likely he believed it himself.

John McCarthy was simply ready to do what the Governor asked him. He's an actor untroubled by inward urgencies—except things like keeping a record of the hours he sleeps and each penny he spends—though with a natural facility for portraying on stage emotions which he doesn't feel one iota.

The Governor shut up F. F. with a gesture and got ready to make his decision, but just then I saw that there was a sixth person on this side of the stage.

Standing in the second wings beyond our group was a dark figure like a tarpaulined Christmas tree topped by a big helmet of unmistakable general shape despite its veiling. I grabbed the Governor's arm and pointed at it silently. He smothered a large curse and strode up to it and rasped, 'Guthrie, you old Son of a B! Can you go on?' The figure gave an affirmative grunt.

Joe Rubens grimaced at me as if to say 'Show business!' and grabbed a spear from the prop table and hurried back across the stage for his entrance as Marcellus just before the curtain lifted and the first nervous, superbly atmospheric lines of the play rang out, loud at first, but then going low with unspoken apprehension.

'Who's there?'

'Nay, answer me; stand, and unfold yourself.'

'Long live the king!'

'Bernardo?'

'He.'

'You come most carefully upon your hour.'

' 'Tis now struck twelve; get thee to bed, Francisco.'

'For this relief much thanks; 'tis bitter cold and I am sick at heart.'

'Have you had quiet guard?'

'Not a mouse stirring.'

With a resigned shrug, John McCarthy simply sat down. F. F. did the same, though *his* gesture was clench-fisted and exasperated. For a moment it seemed to me very comic that two Ghosts in *Hamlet* should be sitting in the wings, watching a third perform. I unbuttoned my overcoat and slung it over my left arm.

The Ghost's first two appearances are entirely silent ones. He merely goes on stage, shows himself to the soldiers, and comes off again. Nevertheless there was a determined little ripple of hand-clapping from the audience—the second, third, and fourth rows center greeting their patriarchal hero, it seemed likely. Guthrie didn't fall down at any rate and he walked reasonably straight—an achievement perhaps rating applause, if anyone out there knew the degree of intoxication Guthrie was probably burdened with at this moment—a cask-bellied Old Man of the Sea on his back.

The only thing out of normal was that he had forgot to turn on the little green light in the peak of his helmet—an omission which hardly mattered, certainly not on this first appearance. I hurried up to him when he came off and told him about it in a whisper as he moved off toward a dark back-stage corner. I got in reply, through the inscrutable green veil, an exhalation of whisky and three affirmative grunts: one, that he knew it; two, that the light was working; three, that he'd remember to turn it on next time.

Then the scene had ended and I darted across the stage as they changed to the room-of-state set. I wanted to get rid of my overcoat. Joe Rubens grabbed me and told me about Guthrie's green light not being on and I told him that was all taken care of.

'Where the hell was he all the time we were hunting for him?' Joe asked me.

'I don't know,' I answered.

By that time the second scene was playing, with F. F., his Ghost-coverings shed, playing the King as well as he always does (it's about his best part) and Gertrude Grainger looking very regal beside him as the Queen, her namesake, while there was another flurry of applause, more scattered this time, for the Governor in his black doublet and tights beginning about his seven hundredth performance of Shakespeare's longest and meatiest role.

Monica was still sitting on the trunk by the switchboard, looking paler than ever under her makeup, it seemed to me, and I folded my overcoat and silently persuaded her to use it as a cushion. I sat beside her and she took my hand and we watched the play from the wings.

After a while I whispered to her, giving her hand a little squeeze, 'Feeling better now?'

She shook her head. Then leaning toward me, her mouth close to my ear, she whispered rapidly and unevenly, as if she just had to tell someone, 'Bruce, I'm frightened. There's something in the theater. I don't think that was Guthrie playing the Ghost.'

I whispered back, 'Sure it was. I talked with him.'

'Did you see his face?' she asked.

'No, but I smelled his breath,' I told her and explained to her about him forgetting to turn on the green light. I continued, 'Francis and John were both ready to go on as the Ghost, though, until Guthrie turned up. Maybe you glimpsed one of them before the play started and that gave you the idea it wasn't Guthrie.'

Sybil Jameson in her Player costume looked around at me warningly. I was letting my whispering get too loud.

Monica put her mouth so close that her lips for an instant brushed my ear and she mouse-whispered, 'I don't mean another *person* playing the Ghost—not that exactly. Bruce, there's *something* in the theater.'

'You've got to forget that Ouija nonsense,' I told her sharply.

'And buck up now,' I added, for the curtain had just gone down on Scene Two and it was time for her to get on stage for her scene with Laertes and Polonius.

I waited until she was launched into it, speaking her lines brightly enough, and then I carefully crossed the stage behind the backdrop. I was sure there was no more than nerves and imagination to her notions, though they'd raised shivers on me, but just the same I wanted to speak to Guthrie again and see his face.

When I'd completed my slow trip (you have to move rather slowly, so the drop won't ripple or bulge), I was dumbfounded to find myself witnessing the identical backstage scene that had been going on when I'd got back from my tour of the bars. Only now there was a lot more light because the scene being played on stage was a bright one. And Props was there behind his table, watching everything like the spectator he basically is. But beyond him were Francis Farley Scott and John McCarthy in their improvised Ghost costumes again, and the Governor and Joe with them, and all of them carrying on that furious lip-reader's argument, now doubly hushed.

I didn't have to wait to get close to them to know that Guthrie must have disappeared again. As I made my way toward them, watching their silent antics, my silly mind became almost hysterical with the thought that Guthrie had at last discovered that invisible hole every genuine alcoholic wishes he had, into which he could decorously disappear and drink during the times between his absolutely necessary appearances in the real world.

As I neared them, Donald Fryer (our Horatio) came from behind me, having made the trip behind the backdrop faster than I had, to tell the Governor in hushed gasps that Guthrie wasn't in any of the dressing rooms or anywhere else stage right.

Just at that moment the bright scene ended, the curtain came down, the drapes before which Ophelia and the others had been playing swung back to reveal again the battlements of Elsinore, and the lighting shifted back to the midnight blue of the first scene, so that for the moment it was hard to see at all. I heard the Governor say decisively, '*You* play the Ghost,' his voice receding as he and Joe and Don hurried across the stage to be in place for their proper entrance. Seconds later there came the dull soft hiss of the main curtain opening and I heard the Governor's taut resonant voice saying, 'The air bites shrewdly; it is very cold,' and Don responding as Horatio with, 'It is a nipping and an eager air.'

By that time I could see again well enough—see Francis Farley

Scott and John McCarthy moving side by side toward the back wing through which the Ghost enters. They were still arguing in whispers. The explanation was clear enough: each thought the Governor had pointed at him in the sudden darkness—or possibly in F. F.'s case was pretending he so thought. For a moment the comic side of my mind, grown a bit hysterical by now, almost collapsed me with the thought of twin Ghosts entering the stage side by side. Then once again, history still repeating itself, I saw beyond them that other bulkier figure with the unmistakable shrouded helmet. They must have seen it too for they stopped dead just before my hands touched a shoulder of each of them. I circled quickly past them and reached out my hands to put them lightly on the third figure's shoulders, intending to whisper, 'Guthrie, are you okay?' It was a very stupid thing for one actor to do to another —startling him just before his entrance—but I was made thoughtless by the memory of Monica's fears and by the rather frantic riddle of where Guthrie could possibly have been hiding.

But just then Horatio gasped, 'Look, my lord, it comes,' and Guthrie moved out of my light grasp onto the stage without so much as turning his head—and leaving me shaking because where I'd touched the rough buckram-braced fabric of the Ghost's cloak I'd felt only a kind of insubstantiality beneath instead of Guthrie's broad shoulders.

I quickly told myself that was because Guthrie's cloak had stood out from his shoulders and his back as he had moved. I had to tell myself something like that. I turned around. John McCarthy and F. F. were standing in front of the dark prop table and by now my nerves were in such a state that their paired forms gave me another start. But I tiptoed after them into the downstage wings and watched the scene from there.

The Governor was still on his knees with his sword held hilt up like a cross doing the long speech that begins, 'Angels and ministers of grace defend us!' And of course the Ghost had his cloak drawn around him so you couldn't see what was under it—and the little green light still wasn't lit in his helmet. Tonight the absence of that theatric touch made him a more frightening figure—certainly to me, who wanted so much to see Guthrie's ravaged old face and be reassured by it. Though there was still enough comedy left in the ragged edges of my thoughts that I could imagine Guthrie's pugnacious son-in-law whispering angrily to those around him that Gilbert Usher was so jealous of his great father-in-law that he wouldn't let him show his face on the stage.

Then came the transition to the following scene where the Ghost has led Hamlet off alone with him—just a five-second complete darkening of the stage while a scrim is dropped—and at last the Ghost spoke those first lines of 'Mark me' and 'My hour is almost come, When I to sulphurous and tormenting flames Must render up myself.'

If any of us had any worries about the Ghost blowing up on his lines or slurring them drunkenly, they were taken care of now. Those lines were delivered with the greatest authority and effect. And I was almost certain that it was Guthrie's rightful voice—at least I was at first—but doing an even better job than the good one he had always done of getting the effect of distance and otherworldliness and hopeless alienation from all life on Earth. The theater became silent as death, yet at the same time I could imagine the soft pounding of a thousand hearts, thousands of shivers crawling—and I *knew* that Francis Farley Scott, whose shoulder was pressed against mine, was trembling.

Each word the Ghost spoke was like a ghost itself, mounting the air and hanging poised for an impossible extra instant before it faded towards eternity.

Those great lines came: 'I am thy father's spirit; Doomed for a certain term to walk the night . . .' and just at that moment the idea came to me that Guthrie Boyd might be dead, that he might have died and be lying unnoticed somewhere between his children's home and the theater—no matter what Props had said or the rest of us had seen—and that his ghost might have come to give a last performance. And on the heels of that shivery impossibility came the thought that similar and perhaps even eerier ideas must be frightening Monica. I knew I had to go to her.

So while the Ghost's words swooped and soared in the dark —marvellous black-plumed birds—I again made that nervous cross behind the back drop.

Everyone stage right was standing as frozen and absorbed —motionless loomings—as I'd left John and F. F. I spotted Monica at once. She'd moved forward from the switchboard and was standing, crouched a little, by the big floodlight that throws some dimmed blue on the backdrop and across the back of the stage. I went to her just as the Ghost was beginning his exit stage left, moving backward along the edge of the light from the flood, but not quite in it, and reciting more lonelily and eerily than I'd ever heard them before those memorable last lines:

'Fare thee well at once!'
'The glow-worm shows the
        matin to be near,
'And 'gins to pale his unef-
        fectual fire;
'Adieu, adieu! Hamlet, re-
        member me.'

One second passed, then another, and then there came two
unexpected bursts of sound at the same identical instant: Monica
screamed and a thunderous applause started out front, touched off
by Guthrie's people, of course, but this time swiftly spreading to all
the rest of the audience.

I imagine it was the biggest hand the Ghost ever got in the history
of the theater. In fact, I never heard of him getting a hand before. It
certainly was a most inappropriate place to clap, however much the
performance deserved it. It broke the atmosphere and the thread of
the scene.

Also, it drowned out Monica's scream, so that only I and a few of
those behind me heard it.

At first I thought I'd made her scream, by touching her as I had
Guthrie, suddenly, like an idiot, from behind. But instead of
shrinking or dodging away she turned and clung to me, and kept
clinging too even after I'd drawn her back and Gertrude Grainger
and Sybil Jameson had closed in to comfort her and hush her
gasping sobs and try to draw her away from me.

By this time the applause was through and Governor and
Don and Joe were taking up the broken scene and knitting together its finish as best they could, while the floods came up little
by little, changing to rosy, to indicate dawn breaking over Elsinore.

Then Monica mastered herself and told us in quick whispers
what had made her scream. The Ghost, she said, had moved for a
moment into the edge of the blue floodlight, and she had seen for a
moment through his veil, and what she had seen had been a face
like Shakespeare's. Just that and no more. Except that at the
moment when she told us—later she became less certain—she was
sure it was Shakespeare himself and no one else.

I discovered then that when you hear something like that you
don't exclaim or get outwardly excited. Or even inwardly, exactly.
It rather shuts you up. I know I felt at the same time extreme awe
and a renewed irritation at the Ouija board. I was deeply moved,
yet at the same time pettishly irked, as if some vast adult creature
had disordered the toy world of my universe.

It seemed to hit Sybil and even Gertrude the same way. For the moment we were shy about the whole thing, and so, in her way, was Monica, and so were the few others who had overheard in part or all what Monica had said.

I knew we were going to cross the stage in a few more seconds when the curtain came down on that scene, ending the first act, and stagelights came up. At least I knew that I was going across. Yet I wasn't looking forward to it.

When the curtain did come down—with another round of applause from out front—and we started across, Monica beside me with my arm still tight around her, there came a choked-off male cry of horror from ahead to shock and hurry us. I think about a dozen of us got stage left about the same time, including of course the Governor and the others who had been on stage.

F. F. and Props were standing inside the doorway to the empty prop room and looking down into the hidden part of the L. Even from the side, they both looked pretty sick. Then F. F. knelt down and almost went out of view, while Props hunched over him with his natural stoop.

As we craned around Props for a look—myself among the first, just beside the Governor, we saw something that told us right away that this Ghost wasn't ever going to be able to answer that curtain call they were still fitfully clapping for out front, although the house lights must be up by now for the first intermission.

Guthrie Boyd was lying on his back in his street clothes. His face looked gray, the eyes staring straight up. While swirled beside him lay the Ghost's cloak and veil and the helmet and an empty fifth of whiskey.

Between the two conflicting shocks of Monica's revelation and the body in the prop room, my mind was in a useless state. And from her helpless incredulous expression I knew Monica felt the same. I tried to put things together and they wouldn't fit anywhere.

F. F. looked up at us over his shoulder. 'He's not breathing,' he said. 'I think he's gone.' Just the same he started loosing Boyd's tie and shirt and pillowing his head on the cloak. He handed the whisky bottle back to us through several hands and Joe Rubens got rid of it.

The Governor sent out front for a doctor and within two minutes Harry Grossman was bringing us one from the audience who'd left his seat number and bag at the box office. He was a small man—Guthrie would have made two of him—and a bit awestruck, I could see, though holding himself with greater professional dignity because of that, as we made way for him and then crowded in behind.

He confirmed F. F.'s diagnosis by standing up quickly after kneeling only for a few seconds where F. F. had. Then he said hurriedly to the Governor, as if the words were being surprised out of him against his professional caution, 'Mr. Usher, if I hadn't heard this man giving that great performance just now, I'd think he'd been dead for an hour or more.'

He spoke low and not all of us heard him, but I did and so did Monica, and there was Shock Three to go along with the other two, raising in my mind for an instant the grisly picture of Guthrie Boyd's spirit, or some other entity, willing his dead body to go through with that last performance. Once again I unsuccessfully tried to fumble together the parts of this night's mystery.

The little doctor looked around at us slowly and puzzledly. He said, 'I take it he just wore the cloak over his street clothes?' He paused. Then, 'He *did* play the Ghost?' he asked us.

The Governor and several others nodded, but some of us didn't at once and I think F. F. gave him a rather peculiar look, for the doctor cleared his throat and said, 'I'll have to examine this man as quickly as possible in a better place and light. Is there—?' The Governor suggested the couch in his dressing room and the doctor designated Joe Rubens and John McCarthy and Francis Farley Scott to carry the body. He passed over the Governor, perhaps out of awe, but Hamlet helped just the same his black garb most fitting.

It was odd the doctor picked the older men—I think he did it for dignity. And it was odder still that he should have picked two ghosts to help carry a third, though he couldn't have known that.

As the designated ones moved forward, the doctor said, 'Please stand back, the rest of you.'

It was then that the very little thing happened which made all the pieces of this night's mystery fall into place—for me, that is, and for Monica too, judging from the way her hand trembled in and then tightened around mine. We'd been given the key to what had happened. I won't tell you what it was until I've knit together the ends of this story.

The second act was delayed perhaps a minute, but after that we kept to schedule, giving a better performance than usual—I never knew the Graveyard Scene to carry so much feeling, or the bit with Yorick's skull to be so poignant.

Just before I made my own first entrance, Joe Rubens snatched off my street hat—I'd had it on all this while—and I played all of

Guildenstern wearing a wrist-watch, though I don't imagine anyone noticed.

F. F. played the Ghost as an off-stage voice when he makes his final brief appearance in the Closet Scene. He used Guthrie's voice to do it, imitating him very well. It struck me afterwards as ghoulish—but right.

Well before the play ended, the doctor had decided he could say that Guthrie had died of a heart seizure, not mentioning the alcoholism. The minute the curtain came down on the last act, Harry Grossman informed Guthrie's son and daughter and brought them backstage. They were much moved, though hardly deeply smitten, seeing they'd been out of touch with the old boy for a decade. However, they quickly saw it was a Grand and Solemn Occasion and behaved accordingly, especially Guthrie's pugnacious son-in-law.

Next morning the two Wolverton papers had headlines about it and Guthrie got his biggest notices ever in the Ghost. The strangeness of the event carried the item around the world—a six-line filler, capturing the mind for a second or two, about how a once-famous actor had died immediately after giving a performance as the Ghost in *Hamlet*, though in some versions, of course, it became Hamlet's Ghost.

The funeral came on the afternoon of the third day, just before our last performance in Wolverton, and the whole company attended along with Guthrie's children's crowd and many other Wolvertonians. Old Sybil broke down and sobbed.

Yet to be a bit callous, it was a neat thing that Guthrie died where he did, for it saved us the trouble of having to send for relatives and probably take care of the funeral ourselves. And it did give old Guthrie a grand finish, with everyone outside the company thinking him a hero-martyr to the motto The Show Must Go On. And of course we knew too that in a deeper sense he'd really been that.

We shifted around in our parts and doubled some to fill the little gaps Guthrie had left in the plays, so that the Governor didn't have to hire another actor at once. For me, and I think for Monica, the rest of the season was very sweet. Gertrude and Sybil carried on with the Ouija sessions alone.

And now I must tell you about the very little thing which gave myself and Monica a satisfying solution to the mystery of what had happened that night.

You'll have realized that it involved Props. Afterwards I asked him straight out about it and he shyly told me that he really couldn't help me there. He'd had this unaccountable devilish compulsion to get drunk and his mind had blanked out entirely from well before the performance until he found himself standing with F. F. over Guthrie's body at the end of the first act. He didn't remember the Ouija-scare or a word of what he'd said to me about theaters and time machines—or so he always insisted.

F. F. told us that after the Ghost's last exit he'd seen him—very vaguely in the dimness—lurch across backstage into the empty prop room and that he and Props had found Guthrie lying there at the end of the scene. I think the queer look F. F.—the old reality-fuddling rogue!—gave the doctor was to hint to him that *he* had played the Ghost, though that wasn't something I could ask him about.

But the very little thing—When they were picking up Guthrie's body and the doctor told the rest of us to stand back, Props turned as he obeyed and straightened his shoulders and looked directly at Monica and myself, or rather a little over our heads. He appeared compassionate yet smilingly serene as always and for a moment transfigured, as if he were the eternal observer of the stage of life and this little tragedy were only part of an infinitely vaster, endlessly interesting pattern.

I realized at that instant that Props could have done it, that he'd very effectively guarded the doorway to the empty prop room during our searches, that the Ghost's costume could be put on or off in seconds (though Props's shoulders wouldn't fill the cloak like Guthrie's), and that I'd never once before or during the play seen him and the Ghost at the same time. Yes, Guthrie had arrived a few minutes before me . . . and died . . . and Props, nerved to it by drink, had covered for him.

While Monica, as she told me later, knew at once that here was the great-browed face she'd glimpsed for a moment through the greenish gauze.

Clearly there had been four ghosts in *Hamlet* that night—John McCarthy, Francis Farley Scott, Guthrie Boyd, and the fourth who had really played the role. Mentally blacked out or not, knowing the lines from the many times he'd listened to *Hamlet* performed in this life, or from buried memories of times he'd taken the role in the days of Queen Elizabeth the First, Billy (or Willy) Simpson, or simply Willy S., had played the Ghost, a good trouper responding automatically to an emergency.

GORILLA SUIT

John Shepley

Man with gorilla suit or gorilla to help publicize newest Bing Crosby—Bob Hope—Dorothy Lamour Technicolor comedy 'Road to Bali.' 1 day's employment. Apply Bali-Bally Dept, Paramount Pictures, 11th floor, 1501 Broadway, Monday AM.

> —Classified Advertisement
> in the New York *Times*
> Sunday, January 25, 1953.

Toto judged it a very dull issue of the Sunday *Times*. He had read the theater section, admitting himself reluctantly in agreement with the critics: Broadway was having another disappointing season. He had not been impressed by any of the book reviews; the news was the usual alternating succession of horrors and trivia; the articles in the magazine section had left him cold. Finally, glumly, he had begun the crossword puzzle, much to the amusement of the crowd on the other side of the bars. They always distracted and irritated him particularly, these familial Sunday crowds, the mournful dutiful fathers, the stout women in hats, the noisy children with candy-smeared faces and sticky pointing fingers, but nevertheless he had become fairly absorbed . . . until he came to 143 Across: '*U.S. experimental $4 gold pieces, 1879—80.*' A seven-letter word, the sixth 'A.' But who but a financial historian could be expected to know what it was? Specialization was creeping even into the simplest Sunday pastimes—it was unfair. Standing to the front of the crowd and holding the string of a pink balloon was a kind-looking lady with dim blue eyes. Perhaps *she* was a financial historian—Toto earnestly approached her. She shrieked, letting go of the balloon, and as it floated upwards, the children twittered in chorus and some cried. Toto gave up, threw down pencil and puzzle, and took refuge on the topmost perch of the cage, where he clung sulkily until the crowd, bored by his inactivity, moved away. Then he dropped back to the floor, and, consumed by a sense of futility, began leafing through the Classified Advertisements.

And there he came across it. Incredulous, he blinked his eyes, scratched his head and sides, read it through a second, then a third, time . . . but no, it was no mistake: there in cold print was a job opening for a man with a gorilla suit *or a gorilla* to help publicize Dorothy Lamour's latest picture. Toto pulled himself up, reflecting that he didn't need a job, that in a sense he had one already, but the implications contained in the little boxed announcement would not be silenced, the fun it would be, the glory (he might even be photographed with Dorothy Lamour!), though only for one day. He found himself skipping and swinging all over the cage.

But when, with a certain critical caution, he returned to peruse the ad for a fourth time, subtle qualms began to arise in his mind. Perhaps what they wanted was a man with a gorilla suit or *a man with* a gorilla—in which case, there was no point in *his* applying. It was really rather obscure, just what they thought they wanted, and Toto, trying to figure it out, scratched himself for a long time. Yet, if the idea was to have a gorilla, simulated or otherwise, why shouldn't one apply? And indeed, there was a simple solution: if they insisted that the gorilla be humanly escorted, why not show the ad to his keeper, Mr. McCready, while pointing with especial emphasis to '*11th floor, 1501 Broadway, Monday AM*'?

But no, that wouldn't do, he immediately recognized the impracticality of it. It wasn't that Mr. McCready would refuse—he wouldn't—but he wouldn't agree either. He would be doubtful; he would give a pompous little laugh, a nervous cough; he would look puzzled and hurt; until Toto, feeling guilty, would withdraw his request altogether. Or, on the off-chance that Mr. McCready did agree, it would be only with the understanding that he must first ask the directors, and he would so procrastinate in doing so that (even assuming that the directors ultimately gave their approval) it would then be too late to apply for the job. Someone else would already have enjoyed the brief, glorious limelight with Dorothy Lamour. No, the only thing to do, Toto decided, was to present Mr. McCready and the zoo authorities with a *fait accompli*.

He could hardly wait for closing time, when the visitors would vanish and the doors be locked, so that he might have a little quiet in which to think out a plan. Surely, he reasoned, as he watched the attendants sweeping up the trash left by the departed crowd, surely he would be hired in preference to any man dressed up like a gorilla. It shouldn't be difficult to beat out *that* kind of competition. But suppose *other gorillas* applied, ones with previous experience in the theater or public relations? This prospect so frightened him that he decided to abandon the whole idea. He curled himself up in a fetid darkness, sadly caressing his toes and listening to familiar noises, metal somewhere scraping against cement, mechanical rumblings in an underground distance, the nightly asthmatic wheezing of his neighbor, an old prowling mandrill. Toto closed his eyes, covered his ears, went on arguing to himself . . . what was there to lose? Nothing, really. It wasn't even as though he were risking anything, for the worst that could happen was that he simply wouldn't get the job. All the same, it wouldn't be easy to get out of the cage.

Nothing ventured, nothing gained. It was tiresome having to bolster oneself with truisms—still, cheerfully enough, he set about testing the bars, one by one. He went all over the cage, without finding a single loose bar. He groaned, realizing how much time he had already wasted, for not only must he be out of the cage and away from the zoo before Mr. McCready arrived in the morning, but he must be at 1501 Broadway in time to be among the first in line. Now, painfully, he tried to squeeze himself between the bars, aware that the mandrill had stopped his prowling, was crouching there on his haunches, his eyes a phosphorescent green, watching it all with the bemused curiosity of the senile. Toto went on pushing and lunging, but all he succeeded in doing was to scrape some patches of fur from his forearms and sides. And it was so important to look his best!

It was useless, the space between the bars was too small. In a final, despairing, almost whimsical gesture, he tried the door—it opened easily. But that showed that they *trusted* him! Astonished, he could only stand there holding the catch of the door, wondering if it would not be ungrateful to take advantage of such trust. Ah, but if he got the job, how proud Mr. McCready would be! Or would he? Toto wavered . . . the mandrill resumed wheezing . . . familiar sounds. And then he heard an unfamiliar sound, a rustling of jungle leaves, and the bright image of Dorothy Lamour stepped out into the sunlight. Toto leapt confidently out of the cage.

But he had forgotten that the door of the building itself would be locked. He kicked it, pulled it, beat on it with his fists, which only awoke the spider monkeys, spiteful little creatures who tumbled and gibbered and pointed their fingers at him. Then the most fearful racket broke out—the chimpanzees woke up and began screaming, a chorus of baboons howled, even the mandrill joined in. *'What's going on in there?'*—and the door opened, pressing Toto behind it, as the night guard came in, cursing softly and flashing his light about the cages. Everybody, blinking, became silent, and Toto had just enough time to slip around the door and hide himself behind a low cement wall before the guard re-emerged and turned the lock. Toto held his breath, but the guard merely went away whistling, swinging his extinguished light.

He rested, until the pounding of his heart subsided and the guard was out of sight. Then, happily, cutting a little caper, he set out across the park.

It was quarter to nine when he took the elevator to the eleventh floor at 1501 Broadway. Again he was feeling worried and uncomfortable. For one thing, he was hungry, and he was afraid he had caught cold during two hours of furtive slumber in some bushes near the skating rink. And all the way from the park, down Broadway to 44th Street, he had reproached himself for forgetting to bring along the Classified Advertisements Section of the *Times*. It would have been most helpful in explaining his presence on the streets had a policeman or anyone else stopped him. But fortunately no one had stopped him. The people in the street had all passed him by with Monday-morning expressions on their faces.

In the crowded elevator, he tried to spruce himself up, brushing from his shoulders and legs the bits of dried grass that clung there from his sleeping in the park. But a murmur of protest arose —'Hey, quit y'r shovin', Mac,' said a man on his right, who, Toto suddenly saw, had a rolled-up gorilla suit under his arm. He resigned himself to standing quietly, fervently hoping that he had got rid of most of the grass.

The elevator emptied itself at the eleventh floor, they all streamed out together, and to Toto's amazement, each of his fellow passengers was carrying a gorilla suit—some in a neat bundle with the jaws gaping out from under the owner's arm, some draped across human shoulders with a gorilla head bobbing along ludicrously a few inches from the floor, some apparent only by the patches of fur sticking out from the apertures of shabby cardboard suitcases or corrugated boxes. He had not expected so much competition, but there was at least one cause for relief—neither getting out of the elevator nor in the crowd already waiting at the door of the Bali-Bally Department was there a single other real gorilla. He joined the increasing throng milling about the unopened office.

Although he knew it was not quite fair to do so, he could not help feeling a little contemptuous. Not only were they not gorillas, they were a sorry lot of men—wan, and thin, and old. He overheard a bit of conversation, one man saying to another, 'Hey, I seen you before! Wasn't you a Santa Claus in Herald Square last Christmas?'

'Yeah. But I don't remember seein' you.'

'I was there awright, Mac, you shoulda looked. I tried to get into Macy's, Gimbel's, anyplace warm, but the best I could get was one of them street jobs. It's a tough racket.'

'Sure is,' the other agreed. 'I got an Easter Bunny job lined up maybe, but I don't know what I'll do till then if I don't get this thing.' And he patted his gorilla suit, while the first man eyed him jealously. 'Even if it *is* just one day.'

And now Toto began to feel sorry for them, wondering if it was not grasping and presumptuous of him to be there at all. He, for whom food and shelter had been generously provided, who had even a recognized social function, had descended to trying to take work away from individuals who really needed it. Perhaps he should turn back . . . but at that point the elevator opened again, another mob of men with gorilla suits poured out, and they were followed by a young woman, who, after fumbling in her purse, produced a key and unlocked the door of the Bali-Bally Department.

'Come in, all of you,' she said. 'Take seats along the wall. Mr. Phineas will be here any minute to conduct the interviews.'

Toto thought her very attractive, in her hard blond way, though by no means so beautiful as Dorothy Lamour. Even so, it occurred to him, it might be fun to whisk her away for a weekend atop the Empire State Building while crowds gathered and the police hovered in helicopters; but he quickly suppressed this whimsical idea, and filed respectfully into the office along with the other applicants.

There were not enough chairs for all of them. Toto joined a nervous little group standing by the wall, while the blond secretary busied herself at her desk. 'I might as well start the ball rolling,' she announced, 'while we're waiting for Mr. Phineas. I certainly didn't expect so many. Let me make it clear at the beginning that we want somebody experienced and responsible, preferably with references. There's every chance that Miss Lamour will ask to be photographed with the successful applicant.'

Toto's heart trembled, beat faster. He had no experience to offer, and no references, but he took pride in thinking he was responsible. And how could they possibly not prefer *him* over these wretched fakes? And to be photographed with . . . with . . . 'I'll take your names,' he heard the secretary saying. 'You first.' The man next to him started forward. 'No, no, the other one. The one that's already got his suit on.' Slowly, fearfully, Toto approached the desk.

'Name?' she said, pencil poised.

. . .

'Speak up. Don't mumble so. What is it?'

. . .

She threw down the pencil. 'Oh, never mind! I can't take everybody's name anyway—there are too many. Why the hell didn't that stupid Phineas do all this through an employment agency?'

Toto, ashamed of his failure to communicate with her, desperately racked his brain. He might, of course, establish for her his authenticity by performing some of the indelicate little antics that so unfailingly delighted visitors to the zoo . . . But no, that would probably do more harm than good, would, in fact, quite ruin his chances of being thought responsible. It was better to retire and wait for Mr. Phineas.

'I can't say your costume is very convincing,' she called after him as he backed away from the desk. 'Still, it's up to Phineas to decide——Oh, *Mr. Phineas!*'

A little bowlegged man had bounded in, breathlessly throwing off his hat and overcoat. 'I'm terribly sorry, Eloise honey,' he cried, 'to have dumped all this on you. Honestly, I didn't *realize*. Next time, sweetie, I'll do it all through an employment agency and let *them* screen people first.'

'Oh, I don't mind, Mr. Phineas,' she said, with a brave smile.

'That's the spirit, girl!' He patted her on the shoulder. 'All right, all you Tarzans, let's have a look at you! Into the monkey suits and make it snappy!' And glancing at Toto, he added aside to Eloise, 'A-ha, a real eager beaver!'

A real eager *gorilla*. But he stood patiently, waiting while all the men clambered into their suits. 'Line up!' commanded Mr. Phineas, and they all took their places, as he walked along examining them with a shrewd, suspicious eye.

'Just look at *this* one!' he shrieked, pointing to an especially seedy individual standing next to Toto. 'The *buttons* even show. He might as well have turned up in his long winter underwear! I'll bet there's not a *zipper* in the whole crowd.' Toto was on the point of stepping forward to demonstrate that he had neither buttons nor zippers—most important of all, didn't need them—but before he could think of a decorous approach, Mr. Phineas had moved on.

'*Honest*, Eloise,' he was saying, sauntering up and down with his hands on his hips, 'did you *ever* in your life see such a bunch of mangy, moth-eaten gorillas? That one there'—he flipped a hand in Toto's direction—'isn't *too* bad, I suppose. What do *you* think, honey?'

'Gee, Mr. Phineas, I *just* don't know,' she said, gazing at them all in bewildered disappointment. 'Would you like me to call up one of the employment agencies after all?'

'No, we haven't got time. It'll have to be one of these.' And he gave Toto a long critical look.

Toto's heart was bursting with hope and joy, but he made every effort to contain himself. And then it happened, in all its horror —the door opened, and in came another *real gorilla*, an arrogant creature carrying a shining aluminum suitcase.

'I'm sorry, sir, I think we have *enough* applicants already——' Eloise began, but the newcomer, grinning, merely slavered at her lecherously. He set down his suitcase, opened it, and—to Toto's stunned mortification—took out a lustrous gorilla suit, into which he deftly proceeded to zipper himself. This process completed, he made a little bow to Mr. Phineas and Eloise, offering his arm for their inspection.

'Why, it's not gorilla fur at all,' said Mr. Phineas, feeling the suit. 'It's *genuine*, fine-spun, combed, nylon-acetate!'

'It's beautiful,' breathed the secretary. 'It's perfectly divine.'

'And so *chic*,' marveled Mr. Phineas. 'Well, that settles it. He's definitely hired. All the rest of you can go now. Leave by the side door, please.'

The men, grumbling and disconsolate, took off their gorilla suits and trooped out. Toto heard Eloise saying to the successful applicant, 'It's just for one day, but you'll still have to fill out a withholding statement. What's your social security——' And then he was in the hallway, shuffling sadly towards the elevator. 'Too bad, eh, Mac?' said the man next to him. 'That's what always happens.' But Toto had no idea whom he might be addressing.

He reached the street and began walking dejectedly up Broadway. Hurrying pedestrians brushed against him, but he hardly noticed them. He tried to take comfort in the knowledge that he hadn't really needed a job, and he only hoped that Mr. McCready wouldn't be too angry when he presented himself back at the zoo.

At a corner newsstand he suddenly stopped, his attention caught by a screaming headline in the *Daily News:*

DRAGNET OUT FOR ESCAPED GORILLA

And the *Journal-American* announced in bold red letters:

TERROR GRIPS CITY AS KILLER
APE PROWLS!

while underneath was a photograph, *his*, Toto's, with the caption, 'Have You Seen This Gorilla?' and the telephone number to call in case you had. People milled about the newsstand trying to get a look at the picture, a few women clutched their bosoms, and one of them stepped on Toto's foot. 'Oh, excuse me,' she said, looking him right in the face.

Still, someone soon would recognize him—it was only a matter of time. He wondered whether to strike out boldly along Broadway or try to hide in some side-street, and as he stood, hesitating on the corner, a squad car stopped, and a policeman got out and tapped him on the shoulder.

GREEN MAGIC

Jack Vance

Howard Fair, looking over the relics of his great uncle Gerald McIntyre, found a large ledger entitled:

WORKBOOK & JOURNAL
Open at Peril!

Fair read the journal with interest, although his own work went far beyond ideas treated only gingerly by Gerald McIntyre.

'The existence of disciplines concentric to the elementary magics must now be admitted without further controversy,' wrote McIntyre. 'Guided by a set of analogies from the white and black magics (to be detailed in due course), I have delineated the basic extension of purple magic, as well as its corollary, Dynamic Nomism.'

Fair read on, remarking the careful charts, the projections and expansions, the transpolations and transformations by which Gerald McIntyre had conceived his systemology. So swiftly had the technical arts advanced that McIntyre's expositions, highly controversial sixty years before, now seemed pedantic and overly rigorous.

'Whereas benign creatures: angels, white sprites, merrihews, sandestins—are typical of the white cycle; whereas demons, magners, trolls and warlocks are evinced by black magic; so do the purple and green cycles sponsor their own particulars, but these are neither good nor evil, bearing, rather, the same relation to the black and white provinces that these latter do to our own basic realm.'

Fair re-read the passage. The 'green cycle?' Had Gerald McIntyre wandered into regions overlooked by modern workers?

He reviewed the journal in the light of this suspicion, and discovered additional hints and references. Especially provocative was a bit of scribbled marginalia: 'More concerning my latest researches I may not state, having been promised an infinite reward for this forbearance.'

The passage was dated a day before Gerald McIntyre's death, which had occurred on March 21, 1898, the first day of spring. McIntyre had enjoyed very little of his 'infinite reward,' whatever had been its nature . . . Fair returned to a consideration of the journal, which, in a sentence or two, had opened a chink on an entire new panorama. McIntyre provided no further illumination, and Fair set out to make a fuller investigation.

His first steps were routine. He performed two divinations, searched the standard indexes, concordances, handbooks and formularies, evoked a demon whom he had previously found knowledgeable: all without success. He found no direct reference to cycles beyond the purple; the demon refused even to speculate.

Fair was by no means discouraged; if anything, the intensity of his interest increased. He re-read the journal, with particular care to the justification for purple magic, reasoning that McIntyre, groping for a lore beyond the purple, might well have used the methods which had yielded results before. Applying stains and ultraviolet light to the pages, Fair made legible a number of notes McIntyre had jotted down, then erased.

Fair was immensely stimulated. The notes assured him that he was on the right track, and further indicated a number of blind alleys which Fair profited by avoiding. He applied himself so successfully that before the week was out he had evoked a sprite of the green cycle.

It appeared in the semblance of a man with green glass eyes and a thatch of young eucalyptus leaves in the place of hair. It greeted Fair with cool courtesy, would not seat itself, and ignored Fair's proffer of coffee.

After wandering around the apartment inspecting Fair's books and curios with an air of negligent amusement, it agreed to respond to Fair's questions.

Fair asked permission to use his tape-recorder, which the sprite allowed, and Fair set the apparatus in motion. (When subsequently he replayed the interview, no sound could be heard.)

'What realms of magic lie beyond the green?' asked Fair.

'I can't give you an exact answer,' replied the sprite, 'because I don't know. There are at least two more, corresponding to the colors we call rawn and pallow, and very likely others.'

Fair arranged the microphone where it would more directly intercept the voice of the sprite.

'What,' he asked, 'is the green cycle like? What is its physical semblance?'

The sprite paused to consider. Glistening mother-of-pearl films wandered across its face, reflecting the tinge of its thoughts. 'I'm rather severely restricted by your use of the word "physical." And "semblance" involves a subjective interpretation, which changes with the rise and fall of the seconds.'

'By all means,' Fair said hastily, 'describe it in your own words.'

'Well—we have four different regions, two of which floresce from the basic skeleton of the universe, and so subsede the others. The first of these is compressed and isthiated, but is notable for its wide pools of mottle which we use sometimes for deranging stations. We've transplanted clubmosses from Earth's Devonian and a few ice-fires from Perdition. They climb among the rods which we call devil-hair—' he went on for several minutes but the meaning almost entirely escaped Fair. And it seemed as if the question by which he had hoped to break the ice might run away with the entire interview. He introduced another idea.

' "Can we freely manipulate the physical extensions of Earth?" ' The sprite seemed amused. 'You refer, so I assume, to the various aspects of space, time, mass, energy, life, thought and recollection.'

'Exactly.'

The sprite raised its green cornsilk eyebrows. 'I might as sensibly ask can you break an egg by striking it with a club? The response is on a similar level of seriousness.'

Fair had expected a certain amount of condescension and impatience, and was not abashed. 'How may I learn these techniques?'

'In the usual manner: through diligent study.'

'Ah, indeed—but where could I study? Who would teach me?'

The sprite made an easy gesture, and whorls of green smoke trailed from his fingers to spin through the air. 'I could arrange the matter, but since I bear you no particular animosity, I'll do nothing of the sort. And now, I must be gone.'

'Where do you go?' Fair asked in wonder and longing. 'May I go with you?'

The sprite, swirling a drape of bright green dust over its shoulders, shook his head. 'You would be less than comfortable.'

'Other men have explored the worlds of magic!'

'True: your uncle Gerald McIntyre, for instance.'

'My uncle Gerald learned green magic?'

'To the limit of his capabilities. He found no pleasure in his learning. You would do well to profit by his experience and modify your ambitions.' The sprite turned and walked away.

Fair watched it depart. The sprite receded in space and dimension, but never reached the wall of Fair's room. At a distance which might have been fifty yards, the sprite glanced back, as if to make sure that Fair was not following, then stepped off at another angle and disappeared.

Fair's first impulse was to take heed and limit his explorations. He was an adept in white magic, and had mastered the black art—occasionally he evoked a demon to liven a social gathering which otherwise threatened to become dull—but he had by no means illuminated every mystery of purple magic, which is the realm of Incarnate Symbols.

Howard Fair might have turned away from the green cycle except for three factors.

First was his physical appearance. He stood rather under medium height, with a swarthy face, sparse black hair, a gnarled nose, a small heavy mouth. He felt no great sensitivity about his appearance, but realized that it might be improved. In his mind's eye he pictured the personified ideal of himself: he was taller by six inches, his nose thin and keen, his skin cleared of its muddy undertone. A striking figure, but still recognizable as Howard Fair. He wanted the love of women, but he wanted it without the interposition of his craft. Many times he had brought beautiful girls to his bed, lips wet and eyes shining; but purple magic had seduced them rather than Howard Fair, and he took limited satisfaction in such conquests.

Here was the first factor which drew Howard Fair back to the green lore; the second was his yearning for extended, perhaps eternal, life; the third was simple thirst for knowledge.

The fact of Gerald McIntyre's death, or dissolution, or disappearance—whatever had happened to him—was naturally a matter of concern. If he had won to a goal so precious, why had he died so quickly? Was the 'infinite reward' so miraculous, so exquisite, that the mind failed under its possession? (If such were the case, the reward was hardly a reward.)

Fair could not restrain himself, and by degrees returned to a study of green magic. Rather than again invoke the sprite whose air of indulgent contempt he had found exasperating, he decided to seek knowledge by an indirect method, employing the most advanced concepts of technical and cabalistic science.

He obtained a portable television transmitter which he loaded into his panel truck along with a receiver. On a Monday night in early May, he drove to an abandoned graveyard far out in the wooded hills, and there, by the light of a waning moon, he buried the television camera in graveyard clay until only the lense protruded from the soil.

With a sharp alder twig he scratched on the ground a monstrous outline. The television lens served for one eye, a beer bottle pushed neck-first into the soil the other.

During the middle hours, while the moon died behind wisps of pale cloud, he carved a word on the dark forehead; then recited the activating incantation.

The ground rumbled and moaned, the golem heaved up to blot out the stars.

The glass eyes stared down at Fair, secure in his pentagon.

'Speak!' called out Fair. '*Enteresthes, Akmai Adonai Bidemgirl! Elohim, pa rahulli! Enteresthes, HVOI!* Speak!'

'Return me to earth, return my clay to the quiet clay from whence you roused me.'

'First you must serve.'

The golem stumbled forward to crush Fair, but was halted by the pang of protective magic.

'Serve you I will, if serve you I must.'

Fair stepped boldly forth from the pentagon, strung forty yards of green ribbon down the road in the shape of a narrow V. 'Go forth into the realm of green magic,' he told the monster. 'The ribbons reach forty miles, walk to the end, turn about, return, and then fall back, return to the earth from which you rose.'

The golem turned, shuffled into the V of green ribbon, shaking off clods of mold, jarring the ground with its ponderous tread.

Fair watched the squat shape dwindle, recede, yet never reach the angle of the magic V. He returned to his panel truck, tuned the television receiver to the golem's eye, and surveyed the fantastic vistas of the green realm.

Two elementals of the green realm met on a spun-silver landscape. They were Jaadian and Misthemar, and they fell to discussing the earthen monster which had stalked forty miles through the region known as Cil; which then, turning in its tracks, had retraced its steps, gradually increasing its pace until at the end it moved in a shambling rush, leaving a trail of clods on the fragile moth-wing mosaics.

'Events, events, events,' Misthemar fretted, 'they crowd the chute of time till the bounds bulge. Or then again, the course is as lean and spare as a stretched tendon . . . But in regard to this incursion . . .' He paused for a period of reflection, and silver clouds moved over his head and under his feet.

Jaadian remarked, 'You are aware that I conversed with Howard Fair; he is so obsessed to escape the squalor of his world that he acts with recklessness.'

'The man Gerald McIntyre was his uncle,' mused Misthemar. 'McIntyre besought, we yielded; as perhaps now we must yield to Howard Fair.'

Jaadian uneasily opened his hand, shook off a spray of emerald fire. 'Events press, both in and out. I find myself unable to act in this regard.'

'I likewise do not care to be the agent of tragedy.'

A Meaning came fluttering up from below: 'A disturbance among the spiral towers! A caterpillar of glass and metal has come clanking; it has thrust electric eyes into the Portinone and broke open the Egg of Innocence. Howard Fair is the fault.'

Jaadian and Misthemar consulted each other with wry disinclination. 'Very well, both of us will go; such a duty needs two souls in support.'

They impinged upon Earth and found Howard Fair in a wall booth at a cocktail bar. He looked up at the two strangers and one of them asked, 'May we join you?'

Fair examined the two men. Both wore conservative suits and carried cashmere topcoats over their arms. Fair noticed that the left thumb-nail of each man glistened green.

Fair rose politely to his feet. 'Will you sit down?'

The green sprites hung up their overcoats and slid into the booth. Fair looked from one to the other. He addressed Jaadian. 'Aren't you he whom I interviewed several weeks ago?'

Jaadian assented. 'You have not accepted my advice.'

Fair shrugged. 'You asked me to remain ignorant, to accept my stupidity and ineptitude.'

'And why should you not?' asked Jaadian gently. 'You are a primitive in a primitive realm; nevertheless not one man in a thousand can match your achievements.'

Fair agreed, smiling faintly. 'But knowledge creates a craving for further knowledge. Where is the harm in knowledge?'

Mithemar, the more mercurial of the sprites, spoke angrily. 'Where is the harm? Consider your earthen monster! It befouled forty miles of delicacy, the record of ten million years. Consider your caterpillar! It trampled our pillars of carved milk, our dreaming towers, damaged the nerve-skeins which extrude and waft us our Meanings.'

'I'm dreadfully sorry,' said Fair. 'I meant no destruction.'

The sprites nodded. 'But your apology conveys no guarantee of restraint.'

Fair toyed with his glass. A waiter approached the table, addressed the two sprites. 'Something for you two gentlemen?'

Jaadian ordered a glass of charged water, as did Misthemar. Fair called for another highball.

'What do you hope to gain from this activity?' inquired Misthemar. 'Destructive forays teach you nothing!'

Fair agreed. 'I have learned little. But I have seen miraculous sights. I am more than ever anxious to learn.'

The green sprites glumly watched the bubbles rising in their glasses. Jaadian at last drew a deep sigh. 'Perhaps we can obviate toil on your part and disturbance on ours. Explicitly, what gains or advantages do you hope to derive from green magic?'

Fair, smiling, leaned back into the red imitation-leather cushions. 'I want many things. Extended life—mobility in time —comprehensive memory—augmented perception, with vision across the whole spectrum. I want physical charm and magnetism, the semblance of youth, muscular endurance . . . Then there are qualities more or less speculative, such as—'

Jaadian interrupted. 'These qualities and characteristics we will confer upon you. In return you will undertake never again to disturb the green realm. You will evade centuries of toil; we will be spared the nuisance of your presence, and the inevitable tragedy.'

'Tragedy?' inquired Fair in wonder. 'Why tragedy?'

Jaadian spoke in a deep reverberating voice. 'You are a man of Earth. Your goals are not our goals. Green magic makes you aware of our goals.'

Fair thoughtfully sipped his highball. 'I can't see that this is a disadvantage. I am willing to submit to the discipline of instruction. Surely a knowledge of green magic will not change me into a different entity?'

'No. And this is the basic tragedy!'

Misthemar spoke in exasperation. 'We are forbidden to harm lesser creatures, and so you are fortunate; for to dissolve you into air would end all the annoyance.'

Fair laughed. 'I apologize again for making such a nuisance of myself. But surely you understand how important this is to me?'

Jaadian asked hopefully, 'Then you agree to our offer?'

Fair shook his head. 'How could I live, forever young, capable of extended learning, but limited to knowledge which I already see bounds to? I would be bored, restless, miserable.'

'That well may be,' said Jaadian. 'But not so bored, restless and miserable as if you were learned in green magic.'

Fair drew himself erect. 'I must learn green magic. It is an opportunity which only a person both torpid and stupid could refuse.'

Jaadian sighed. 'In your place I would make the same response.' The sprites rose to their feet. 'Come then, we will teach you.'

'Don't say we didn't warn you,' said Misthemar.

Time passed. Sunset waned and twilight darkened. A man walked up the stairs, entered Howard Fair's apartment. He was tall, unobtrusively muscular. His face was sensitive, keen, humorous; his left thumb-nail glistened green.

Time is a function of vital processes. The people of Earth had perceived the motion of their clocks. On this understanding, two hours had elapsed since Howard Fair had followed the green sprites from the bar.

Howard Fair had perceived other criteria. For him the interval had been seven hundred years, during which he had lived in the green realm, learning to the utmost capacity of his brain.

He had occupied two years training his senses to the new conditions. Gradually he learned to walk in the six basic three-dimensional directions, and accustomed himself to the fourth-dimensional short-cuts. By easy stages the blinds over his eyes were removed, so that the dazzling over-human intricacy of the land-scape never completely confounded him.

Another year was spent training him to the use of a code-language—an intermediate step between the vocalizations of Earth and the meaning-patterns of the green realm, where a hundred symbol-flakes (each a flitting spot of delicate iridescence) might be displayed in a single swirl of import. During this time Howard Fair's eyes and brain were altered, to allow him the use of the many new colors, without which the meaning-flakes could not be recognized.

These were preliminary steps. For forty years he studied the flakes, of which there were almost a million. Another forty years was given to elementary permutations and shifts, and another forty to parallels, attenuation, diminishments and extensions; and during this time he was introduced to flake patterns, and certain of the more obvious displays.

Now he was able to study without recourse to the code-language, and his progress became more marked. Another twenty years found him able to recognize more complicated Meanings, and he was

introduced to a more varied program. He floated over the field of
moth-wing mosaics, which still showed the footprints of the golem.
He sweated in embarrassment, the extent of his wicked willfulness
now clear to him.

So passed the years. Howard Fair learned as much green magic as
his brain could encompass.

He explored much of the green realm, finding so much beauty
that he feared his brain might burst. He tasted, he heard, he felt, he
sensed, and each one of his senses was a hundred times more
discriminating than before. Nourishment came in a thousand
different forms: from pink eggs which burst into a hot sweet gas,
suffusing his entire body; from passing through a rain of stinging
metal crystals; from simple contemplation of the proper symbol.

Homesickness for Earth waxed and waned. Sometimes it was
insupportable and he was ready to forsake all he had learned and
abandon his hopes for the future. At other times the magnificence
of the green realm permeated him, and the thought of departure
seemed like the threat of death itself.

By stages so gradual he never realized them he learned green
magic.

But the new faculty gave him no pride: between his crude
ineptitudes and the poetic elegance of the sprites remained a
tremendous gap—and he felt his innate inferiority much more
keenly than he ever had in his old state. Worse, his most earnest
efforts failed to improve his technique, and sometimes, observing
the singing joy of an improvised manifestation by one of the sprites,
and contrasting it to his own labored constructions, he felt futility
and shame.

The longer he remained in the green realm, the stronger grew the
sense of his own maladroitness, and he began to long for the easy
environment of Earth, where each of his acts would not shout aloud
of vulgarity and crassness. At times he would watch the sprites (in
the gossamer forms natural to them) at play among the pearl-petals,
or twining like quick flashes of music through the forest of pink
spirals. The contrast between their verve and his brutish fumbling
could not be borne and he would turn away. His self-respect
dwindled with each passing hour, and instead of pride in his
learning, he felt a sullen ache for what he was not and could never
become. The first few hundred years he worked with the enthusiasm of ignorance, for the next few he was buoyed by hope. During
the last part of his time, only dogged obstinacy kept him plodding
through what now he knew for infantile exercises.

In one terrible bitter-sweet spasm, he gave up. He found Jaadian weaving tinkling fragments of various magics into a warp of shining long splines. With grave courtesy, Jaadian gave Fair his attention, and Fair laboriously set forth his meaning.

Jaadian returned a message. 'I recognize your discomfort, and extend my sympathy. It is best that you now return to your native home.'

He put aside his weaving and conveyed Fair down through the requisite vortices. Along the way they passed Misthemar. No flicker of meaning was expressed or exchanged, but Howard Fair thought to feel a tinge of faintly malicious amusement.

Howard Fair sat in his apartment. His perceptions, augmented and sharpened by his sojourn in the green realm, took note of the surroundings. Only two hours before, by the clocks of Earth, he had found them both restful and stimulating; now they were neither. His books: superstition, spuriousness, earnest nonsense. His private journals and workbooks: a pathetic scrawl of infantilisms. Gravity tugged at his feet, held him rigid. The shoddy construction of the house, which heretofore he never had noticed, oppressed him. Everywhere he looked he saw slipshod disorder, primitive filth. The thought of the food he must now eat revolted him.

He went out on his little balcony which overlooked the street. The air was impregnated with organic smells. Across the street he could look into windows where his fellow humans lived in stupid squalor.

Fair smiled sadly. He had tried to prepare himself for these reactions, but now was surprised by their intensity. He returned into his apartment. He must accustom himself to the old environment. And after all there were compensations. The most desirable commodities of the world were now his to enjoy.

Howard Fair plunged into the enjoyment of these pleasures. He forced himself to drink quantities of expensive wines, brandies, liqueurs, even though they offended his palate. Hunger overcame his nausea, he forced himself to the consumption of what he thought of as fried animal tissue, the hypertrophied sexual organs of plants. He experimented with erotic sensations, but found that beautiful women no longer seemed different from the plain ones, and that he could barely steel himself to the untidy contacts. He bought libraries of erudite books, glanced through them with contempt. He tried to amuse himself with his old magics; they seemed ridiculous.

He forced himself to enjoy these pleasures for a month; then he fled the city and established a crystal bubble on a crag in the Andes. To nourish himself, he contrived a thick liquid, which, while by no means as exhilarating as the substances of the green realm, was innocent of organic contamination.

After a certain degree of improvisation and make-shift, he arranged his life to its minimum discomfort. The view was one of austere grandeur; not even the condors came to disturb him. He sat back to ponder the chain of events which had started with his discovery of Gerald McIntyre's workbook. He frowned. Gerald McIntyre? He jumped to his feet, looked far off over the crags.

He found Gerald McIntyre at a wayside service station in the heart of the South Dakota prairie. McIntyre was sitting in an old wooden chair, tilted back against the peeling yellow paint of the service station, a straw hat shading his eyes from the sun.

He was a magnetically handsome man, blond of hair, brown of skin, with blue eyes whose gaze stung like the touch of icicle. His left thumb-nail glistened green.

Fair greeted him casually; the two men surveyed each other with wry curiosity.

'I see you have adapted yourself,' said Howard Fair.

McIntyre shrugged. 'As well as possible. I try to maintain a balance between solitude and the pressure of humanity.' He looked into the bright blue sky where crows flapped and called. 'For many years I lived in isolation. I began to detest the sound of my own breathing.'

Along the highway came a glittering automobile, rococo as a hybrid goldfish. With the perceptions now available to them, Fair and McIntyre could see the driver to be red-faced and truculent, his companion a peevish woman in expensive clothes.

'There are other advantages to residence here,' said McIntyre. 'For instance, I am able to enrich the lives of passers-by with trifles of novel adventure.' He made a small gesture; two dozen crows swooped down and flew beside the automobile. They settled on the fenders, strutted back and forth along the hood, fouled the windshield.

The automobile squealed to a halt, the driver jumped out, put the birds to flight. He threw an ineffectual rock, waved his arms in outrage, returned to his car, proceeded.

'A paltry affair,' said McIntyre with a sigh. 'The truth of the matter is that I am bored.' He pursed his mouth and blew forth three bright puffs of smoke: first red, then yellow, then blazing blue. 'I have arrived at the estate of foolishness, as you can see.'

Fair surveyed his great-uncle with a trace of uneasiness. McIntyre laughed. 'No more pranks. I predict, however, that you will presently share my malaise.'

'I share it already,' said Fair. 'Sometimes I wish I could abandon all my magic and return to my former innocence.'

'I have toyed with the idea,' McIntyre replied thoughtfully. 'In fact I have made all the necessary arrangements. It is really a simple matter.' He led Fair to a small room behind the station. Although the door was open, the interior showed a thick darkness.

McIntyre, standing well back, surveyed the darkness with a quizzical curl to his lip. 'You need only enter. All your magic, all your recollections of the green realm will depart. You will be no wiser than the next man you meet. And with your knowledge will go your boredom, your melancholy, your dissatisfaction.'

Fair contemplated the dark doorway. A single step would resolve his discomfort.

He glanced at McIntyre; the two surveyed each other with sardonic amusement. They returned to the front of the building.

'Sometimes I stand by the door and look into the darkness,' said McIntyre. 'Then I am reminded how dearly I cherish my boredom, and what a precious commodity is so much misery.'

Fair made himself ready for departure. 'I thank you for this new wisdom, which a hundred more years in the green realm would not have taught me. And now—for a time, at least—I go back to my crag in the Andes.'

McIntyre tilted his chair against the wall of the service station. 'And I—for a time, at least—will wait for the next passer-by.'

'Goodby then, Uncle Gerald.'

'Goodby, Howard.'

BLACK AIR

Kim Stanley Robinson

They sailed out of Lisbon harbor with the flags snapping and the brass culverins gleaming under a high white sun—priests proclaiming in sonorous Latin the blessing of the Pope, soldiers in armor jammed on the castles fore and aft, and sailors spider-like in the rigging, waving at the citizens of the town who had left their work to come out on the hills and watch the ships crowd out the sunbeaten roads—for this was the Armada, the Most Fortunate Invincible Armada, off to subjugate the heretic English to the will of God. There would never be another departure like it.

Unfortunately, the wind blew out of the northeast for a month after they left without shifting even a point on the compass, and at the end of that month the Armada was no closer to England than Iberia itself. Not only that, but the hard-pressed coopers of Portugal had made many of the Armada's casks of green wood, and when the ship's cooks opened them the meat was rotten and the water stank. So they trailed into the port of Corunna, where several hundred soldiers and sailors swam to the shores of Spain and were never seen again. A few hundred more had already died of disease, so from his sickbed on the flagship Don Alonso Perez de Guzman el Bueno, seventh Duke of Medina Sidonia and Admiral of the Armada, interrupted the composition of his daily complaint to Phillip II, and instructed his soldiers to go out into the countryside and collect peasants to help man the ships.

One of the squads of these soldiers stopped at a Franciscan monastery on the outskirts of Corunna, to impress all the boys who lived there and helped the monks, waiting to join the order themselves. Although they did not like it the monks could not object to the proposal, and off the boys went to join the fleet.

Among these boys, who were each taken to a different ship, was

Manuel Carlos Agadir Tetuán. He was seventeen years old; he had been born in Morocco, the son of West Africans who had been captured and enslaved by Arabs. In his short life he had already lived in the Moroccan coastal town of Tetuán, in Gibraltar, the Balearics, Sicily, and Lisbon. He had worked in fields and cleaned stables, he had helped make rope and later cloth, and he had served food in inns. After his mother died of the pox and his father drowned, he begged in the streets and alleys of Corunna, the last port his father had sailed out of, until in his fifteenth year a Franciscan had tripped over him sleeping in an alley, inquired after him, and taken him to the refuge of the monastery.

Manuel was still weeping when the soldiers took him aboard *La Lavia*, a Levantine galleon of nearly a thousand tons. The sailing master of the ship, one Laeghr, took him in charge and led him below decks. Laeghr was an Irishman, who had left his country principally to practice his trade, but also out of hatred of the English who ruled Ireland. He was a huge man with a torso like a boar's, and arms as thick as the yardarms of their ship. When he saw Manuel's distress he showed that he was not without kindness; clapping a calloused hand to the back of Manuel's neck he said, in accented but fluent Spanish, 'Stop your sniveling boy, we're off to conquer the damned English, and when we do your fathers at the monastery will make you their abbot. And before that happens a dozen English girls will fall at your feet and ask for the touch of those black hands, no doubt. Come on, stop it. I'll show you your berth first, and wait till we're at sea to show you your station. I'm going to put you in the maintop; all our blacks are good topmen.'

Laeghr slipped through a door half his height with the ease of a weasel ducking into one of its tiny holes in the earth. A hand half as wide as the doorway re-emerged and pulled Manuel into the gloom. The terrified boy nearly fell down a broad-stepped ladder, but caught himself before falling onto Laeghr. Far below several soldiers laughed at him. Manuel had never been on anything larger than a Sicilian pataches, and most of his fairly extensive seagoing experience was of coastal carracks; so the broad deck under him, cut by bands of yellow sunlight that flowed in at open ports big as church windows, crowded with barrels and bales of hay and tubs of rope, and a hundred busy men, was a marvel. 'Saint Anna, save me,' he said, scarcely able to believe he was on a ship. Why, the monastery itself had no room as large as the one he descended into now. 'Get down here,' Laeghr said in an encourging way.

Once on the deck of that giant room they descended again, to a stuffy chamber a quarter the size, illuminated by narrow fans of sunlight that were let in by ports that were mere slits in the hull. 'Here's where you sleep,' Laeghr said, pointing at a dark corner of the deck, against one massive oak wall of the ship. Forms there shifted; eyes appeared as lids lifted; a dull voice said: 'Another one you'll never find again in this dark, eh, master?'

'Shut up, Juan. See boy, there are beams dividing your berth from the rest, that will keep you from rolling around when we get to sea.'

'Just like a coffin, with the lid up there.'

'Shut up, Juan.'

After the sailing master had made clear which slot in particular was Manuel's, Manuel collapsed in it and began to cry again. The slot was shorter than he was, and the dividing boards set in the deck were cracked and splintered. The men around him slept, or talked among themselves, ignoring Manuel's presence. His medallion chord choked him, and he shifted it on his neck and remembered to pray.

His guardian saint, the monks had decided, was Anne, mother of the Virgin Mary and grandmother of Jesus. Manuel owned a small wooden medallion with her face painted on it, which Abbot Alonso had given him. Now he took the medallion between his fingers, and looked in the tiny brown dots that were the face's eyes. 'Please, Mother Anna,' he prayed silently, 'take me from this ship to my home. Take me home.' He clenched the tag in his fist so tightly that the back of it, carved so that a cross of wood stood out from its surface, left an imprinted red cross in his palm. Many hours passed before he fell asleep.

Two days later the Most Fortunate Invincible Armada left Corunna, this time without the flags, or the crowds of spectators, or the clouds of priestly incense trailing downwind. This time God favored them with a westerly wind, and they sailed north at good speed. The ships were arranged in a formation devised by the soldiers, orderly phalanxes rising and falling on the swells: the galleasses in front, the supply hulks in the center, and the big galleons on either flank. The thousands of sails stacked on hundreds of masts made a grand and startling sight, like a copse of white trees on a broad blue plain.

Manuel was as impressed by the sight as the rest of the men. There were four hundred men on *La Lavia*, and only thirty were needed at any one time to sail the ship, so all of the three hundred soldiers stood on the sterncastle observing the fleet, and the sailors

who were not on duty or sleeping did the same on the slightly lower
forecastle.

Manuel's duties as a sailor were simple. He was stationed at the
port midships taffrail, to which were tied the sheets for the port side
of the mainmast's sails, and the sheets for the big lateen-rigged sail
of the foremast. Manuel helped five other men pull these ropes in or
let them out, following Laeghr's instructions; the other men took
care of the belaying knots, so Manuel's job came down to pulling a
rope when told to. It could have been more difficult, but Laeghr's
plan to make him a topman like the other Africans aboard had come
to grief. Not that Laeghr hadn't tried. 'God made you Africans with
a better head for heights, so you can climb trees to keep from being
eaten by lions, isn't that right?' But when Manuel had followed a
Moroccan named Habedeen up the halyard ladder to the maintop,
he found himself plunging about space, nearly scraping low foggy
clouds, and the sea, embroidered with the wakes of the ship ahead,
was more often than not *directly below him*. He had clamped arms
and legs around a stanchion of the maintop, and it had taken
fivemen, laughing and cursing, to pry him loose and pull him
down.

With rich disgust, but no real physical force, Laeghr had
pounded him with his cane and shoved him to the port taffrail. 'You
must be a Sicilian with a sunburn.' And so Manuel had been
assigned his station.

Despite this incident he got on well with the rest of the crew. Not
with the soldiers; they were rude and arrogant to the sailors, who
stayed out of their way to avoid a curse or a blow. So three-quarters
of the men aboard were of a different class, and remained strangers.
The sailors therefore hung together. They were a mongrel lot,
drawn from all over the Mediterranean, and Manuel was not
unusual because of his recent arrival. They were united only in
their dislike and resentment of the soldiers. 'Those heroes wouldn't
be able to conquer the Isle of Wight if we didn't sail them there,'
Juan said.

Manuel became acquainted first with the men at his post, and
then with the men in his berth. As he spoke Spanish and
Portuguese, and fair amounts of Arabic, Sicilian, Latin, and a
Moroccan dialect, he could converse with everyone in his corner of
the lower foredeck. Occasionally he was asked to translate for the
Morocans; more than once this meant he was the arbiter of a
dispute, and he thought fast and mistranslated when it would help
make peace.

Juan, the one who made the bitter comments to Laeghr on Manuel's arrival, was the only pure Spaniard in the berth. He loved to talk, and complained to Manuel and the others continuously. 'I've fought El Draco before, in the Indies,' he boasted. 'We'll be lucky to get past that devil. You mark my words, we'll never do it.'

Manuel's mates at the main taffrail were more cheerful, and he enjoyed his watches with them and the drills under Laeghr's demanding instruction. These men called him Topman or Climber, and made jokes about his knots around the belaying pins, which defied quick untying. This inability earned Manuel quite a few swats from Laeghr's cane, but there were worse sailors aboard, and the sailing master seemed to bear him no ill will.

A life of perpetual change had made Manuel adaptable, and shipboard routine became for him the natural course of existence. Laeghr or Pietro, the leader at Manuel's station, would wake him with a shout. Up to the gun deck, which was the domain of the soldiers, and from there up the big ladder that led to fresh air. Only then could Manuel be sure of the time of day. For the first few weeks it was an inexpressible delight to get out of the gloom of the lower decks and under the sky, in the wind and clean salt air; but as they proceeded north, it began to get too cold for comfort.

After their watches were over, Manuel and his mates would retire to the galley and be given their biscuits, water, and wine. Sometimes the cooks would have killed some of the goats and chickens and made soup. Usually, though, it was just biscuits, biscuits that had not yet hardened in their barrels. The men complained grievously about this.

'The biscuits are best when they're hard as wood, and bored through by worms,' Habedeen told Manuel.

'How do you eat it, then?' Manuel asked.

'You bang pieces of biscuit against the table until the worms fall out. You can eat the worms if you want.' The men laughed, and Manuel assumed Habedeen was joking, but he wasn't certain.

'I despise this doughy shit,' Pietro said in Portuguese. Manuel translated into Moroccan Arabic for the two silent Africans, and agreed in Spanish that it was hard to stomach. 'The worst part,' he offered, 'is that some parts are stale while others are still fresh.'

'The fresh part was never cooked.'

'No, that's the worms.'

As the voyage progressed, Manuel's berthmates became more intimate. Farther north the Moroccans suffered terribly from the cold. They came belowdecks after a watch with their dark skins completely goosepimpled, like little fields of stubble after a harvest.

Their lips and fingernails were blue, and they shivered an hour before falling asleep, teeth chattering like the castanets in a fiesta band. Not only that, but the swells of the Atlantic were getting bigger, and the men, since they were forced to wear every scrap of clothing they owned, rolled in their wooden berths unpadded and unprotected.

So the Moroccans, and then everyone in the lower foredeck, slept three to a berth, taking turns in the middle, huddling together like spoons. Crowded together like that the pitching of the ship could press them against the beams, but it couldn't roll them around. Manuel's willingness to join these bundlings, and to lie against the beams, made him well-liked. Everyone agreed he made a good cushion.

Perhaps it was because of his hands that he fell ill. Though his spirit had been reconciled to the crusade north, his flesh was slower. Hauling on the coarse hemp ropes every day had ripped the skin from his palms, and salt, splinters, belaying pins, and the odd boot had all left their marks as well, so that after the first week he had wrapped his hands in strips of cloth torn from the bottom of his shirt. When he became feverish, his hands pulsed painfully at every nudge from his heart, and he assumed that the fever had entered him through the wounds in his palms.

Then his stomach rebelled, and he could keep nothing down. The sight of biscuits or soup revolted him; his fever worsened, and he became parched and weak; he spent a lot of time in the head, racked by dysentery.

'You've been poisoned by the biscuits,' Juan told him. 'Just like I was in the Indies. That's what comes of boxing fresh biscuits. They might as well have put fresh dough in those barrels.'

Manuel's berthmates told Laeghr of his condition, and Laeghr had him moved to the hospital, which was at the stern of the ship on a lower deck, in a wide room that the sick shared with the rudder post, a large smoothed tree trunk thrusting through floor and ceiling. All of the other men were gravely ill. Manuel was miserable as they laid him down on his pallet, wretched with nausea and in great fear of the hospital, which smelled of putrefaction. The man on the pallet next to his was insensible, and rolled with the sway of the ship. Three candle-lanterns lit the low chamber and filled it with shadows.

One of the Dominican friars, a Friar Lucien, gave him hot water and wiped his face. They talked for a while, and the friar heard Manuel's confession, which only a proper priest should have done.

Neither of them cared. The priests on board avoided the hospital, and tended to serve only the officers and the soldiers. Friar Lucien was known to be willing to minister to the sailors, and he was popular among them.

Manuel's fever got worse, and he could not eat. Days passed, and when he woke up the men around him were not the same men who had been there when he fell asleep. He became convinced he was going to die, and once again he felt despair that he had been made a member of the Most Fortunate Invincible Armada.

'Why are we here?' he demanded of the friar in a cracked voice. 'Why shouldn't we let the English go to hell if they please?'

'The purpose of the Armada is not only to smite the heretic English,' said Lucien. He held a candle closer to his book, which was not the Bible, but a slender little thing which he kept hidden in his robes. Shadows leaped on the blackened beams and planks over them, and the rudder post squeaked as it turned against the leather collar in the floor. 'God also sent us as a test. Listen:

' "I assume the appearance of a refiner's fire, purging the dross of forms outworn. This is mine aspect of severity; I am as one who testeth gold in a furnace. Yet when thou hast been tried as by fire, the gold of thy soul shall be cleansed, and visible as fire: then the vision of the Lord shall be granted unto thee, and seeing Him shall thou behold the shining one, who is thine own true self." '

'Remember that, and be strong. Drink this water here—come on, do you want to fail your God? This is part of the test.'

Manuel drank, threw up. His body was no more than a tongue of flame contained by his skin, except where it burst out of his palms. He lost track of the days, and forgot the existence of anyone beyond himself and Friar Lucien. 'I never wanted to leave the monastery,' he told the friar, 'yet I never thought I would stay there long. I've never stayed long anyplace yet. It was my home but I knew it wasn't. I haven't found my home yet. They say there is ice in England—I saw the snow in the Catalonian mountains once. Father, will we go home? I only want to return to the monastery and be a father like you.'

'We will go home. What you will become, only God knows. He has a place for you. Sleep now. Sleep now.'

By the time his fever broke his ribs stood out from his chest as clearly as the fingers of a fist. He could barely walk. Lucien's narrow face appeared out of the gloom clear as a memory.

'Try this soup. Apparently God has seen fit to keep you here.'

'Thank you, Saint Anne, for your intercession,' Manuel croaked. He drank the soup eagerly. 'I want to return to my berth.'

'Soon.'

They took him up to the deck. Walking was like floating, as long as he held on to railings and stanchions. Laeghr greeted him with pleasure, as did his station mates. The world was a riot of blues; waves hissed past, low clouds jostled together in their rush east, tumbling between them shafts of sunlight that spilled onto the water. He was excused from active duty, but he spent as many hours as he could at his station. He found it hard to believe that he had survived his illness.

Of course, he was not entirely recovered; he could not yet eat any solids, particularly biscuit, so that his diet consisted of soup and wine. He felt weak, and perpetually light-headed. But when he was on deck in the wind he was sure that he was getting better, so he stayed there as much as possible. He was on deck, in fact, when they first caught sight of England. The soldiers pointed and shouted in great excitement, as the point Laeghr called the Lizard bounced over the horizon. Manuel had grown so used to the sea that the low headland rising off their port bow seemed unnatural, an intrusion into a marine world, as if the deluge were just now receding and these drowned hillsides were just now shouldering up out of the waves, soaking wet and covered by green seaweed that had not yet died. And that was England.

A few days after that they met the first English ships—faster than the Spanish galleons, but much smaller. They could no more impede the progress of the Armada than flies could slow a herd of cows. The swells became steeper and followed each other more closely, and the changed pitching of La Lavia made it difficult for Manuel to stand. He banged his head once, and another time ripped away a palmful of scabs, trying to keep his balance in the violent yawing caused by the chop. Unable to stand one morning, he lay in the dark of his berth, and his mates brought him cups of soup. That went on for a long time. Again he worried that he was going to die. Finally Laeghr and Lucien came below together.

'You must get up now,' Laeghr declared. 'We fight within the hour, and you're needed. We've arranged easy work for you.'

'You have only to provide the gunners with slow match,' said Friar Lucien as he helped Manuel to his feet. 'God will help you.'

'God will have to help me,' Manuel said. He could see the two men's souls flickering above their heads: little triple knots of transparent flame, that flew up out of their hair and lit the features of their faces. 'The gold of thy soul shall be cleansed, and visible as fire,' Manuel recalled.

'Hush,' said Lucien with a frown, and Manuel realized that what Lucien had read to him was a secret.

Amidships, Manuel noticed that now he was also able to see the air, which was tinged red. They were on the bottom of an ocean of red air, just as they were on top of an ocean of blue water. When they breathed they turned the air a darker red; men expelled plumes of air like horses breathing out clouds of steam on a frosty morning, only the steam was red. Manuel stared and stared, marveling at the new abilities God had given his sight.

'Here,' Laeghr said, roughly directing him across the deck. 'This tub of punk is yours. This is slow match, understand?' Against the bulkhead was a tub full of coils of closely braided cord. One end of the cord was hanging over the edge of the tub burning, fizzing the air around it to deep crimson.

Manuel nodded: 'Slow match.'

'Here's your knife. Cut sections about this long, and light them with a piece of it that you keep beside you. Then give sections of it to the gunners who come by, or take it to them if they call for it. But don't give away all your lit pieces. Understand?'

Manuel nodded that he understood and sat down dizzily beside the tub. One of the largest cannons poked through a port in the bulwarks just a few feet from him. Its crew greeted him. Across the deck his stationmates stood at their taffrail. The soldiers were ranked on the fore- and stern-castles, shouting with excitement, gleaming like shellfish in the sun. Through the port Manuel could see some of the English coast.

Laeghr came over to see how he was doing. 'Hey, don't you lop your fingers off there, boy. See out there? That's the Isle of Wight. We're going to circle and conquer it, I've no doubt, and use it as our base for our attack on the mainland. With these soldiers and ships they'll *never* get us off that island. It's a good plan.'

But things did not progress according to Laeghr's plan. The Armada swung around the east shore of the Isle of Wight, in a large crescent made of five distinct phalanxes of ships. Rounding the island, however, the forward galleasses encountered the stiffest English resistence they had met so far. White puffs of smoke appeared out of the ships and were quickly stained red, and the noise was tremendous.

Then the ships of El Draco swept around the southern point of the island onto their flank, and suddenly *La Lavia* was in the action. The soldiers roared and shot off their arquebuses, and the big cannon beside Manuel leaped back in its truck with a bang that knocked him into the bulkhead. After that he could barely hear. His slow match was suddenly in demand; he cut the cord and held the lit tip to unlit tips, igniting them with his red breath. Cannonballs passing overhead left rippling wakes in the blood air. Grimy men snatched the slow match and dashed to their guns, dodging tackle blocks that thumped to the deck. Manuel could see the cannonballs, big as grapefruit, flying at them from the English ships and passing with a whistle. And he could see the transparent knots of flame, swirling higher than ever about men's heads.

Then a cannonball burst through the porthole and knocked the cannon off its truck, the men to the deck. Manuel rose to his feet and noticed with horror that the knots of flame on the scattered gunners were gone; he could see their heads clearly now, and they were just men, just broken flesh draped over the plowed surface of the deck. He tried, sobbing, to lift a gunner who was bleeding only from the ears. Laeghr's cane lashed across his shoulders: 'Keep cutting match! There's others to tend to these men!' So Manuel cut lengths of cord and lit them with desperate puffs and shaking hands, while the guns roared, and the exposed soldiers on the castles shrieked under a hail of iron, and the red air was ripped by passing shot.

The next few days saw several battles like that, as the Armada was forced past the Isle of Wight and up the Channel. His fever kept him from sleeping, and at night, Manuel helped the wounded on his deck, holding them down and wiping sweat from their faces, nearly as delirious as they were. At dawn he ate biscuits and drank from his cup of wine, and went to his tub of slow match to await the next engagement. *La Lavia*, being the largest ship on the left flank, always took the brunt of the English attack.

It was on the third day that *La Lavia's* mainmast topgallant yard fell on his old taffrail crew, crushing Hanan and Pietro. Manuel rushed across the deck to help them, shouting his anguish. He got a dazed Juan down to their berth and returned amidships. Around him men were being dashed to the decks but he didn't care. He hopped through red mist that nearly obscured his sight, carrying lengths of match to the gun crews, who were now so depleted that they couldn't afford to send men to him. He helped the wounded below to the hospital, which had truly become an antechamber of hell; he helped toss the dead over the side, croaking a short prayer in every case; he ministered to the soldiers hiding behind the bulwarks, waiting vainly for the English to get within range of their arquebuses.

Now the cry amidships was 'Manuel, match here! Manuel, some water! Help, Manuel!' In a dry fever of energy Manuel hurried to their aid.

He was in such perpetual haste that in the middle of a furious engagement he nearly ran into his patroness, Saint Anne, who was suddenly standing there in the corner by his tub. He was startled to see her.

'Grandmother!' he cried. 'You shouldn't be here, it's dangerous.'

'As you have helped others, I am here to help you,' she replied. She pointed across the purplish chop to one of the English ships. Manuel saw a puff of smoke appear from its side, and out of the puff came a cannonball, floating in an arc over the water. He could see it as clearly as he could have seen an olive tossed at him from across a room: a round black ball, spinning lazily, growing bigger as it got closer. Now Manuel could tell that it was coming at him, *directly* at him, so that its trajectory would intersect his heart. 'Um, blessed Anna,' he said, hoping to bring this to his saint's attention. But she had already seen it, and with a brief touch to his forehead she floated up into the maintop, among the unseeing soldiers. Manuel watched her, eyeing the approaching cannonball's flight, knocking the ball downward into the hull where it stuck, half-embedded in the thick wood. Manuel stared at the black half-sphere, mouth open. He waved up at Saint Anna, who waved back and flew up into the red clouds towards heaven. Manuel kneeled and said a prayer of thanks to her, and to Jesus for sending her, and went back to cutting match.

A night or two later—Manuel himself was not sure, as the passage of time had become for him something pliable and elusive and, more than anything else, meaningless—the Armada anchored at Calais Roads, just off the Flemish coast. For the first time since they had left Corunna, *La Lavia* lay still, and listening at night Manuel realized how much the constant chorus of wooden squeaks and groans was the voice of the crew, and not the ship. He drank his ration of wine and water quickly, and walked the length of the lower deck, talking with the wounded and helping when he could to remove splinters. Many of the men wanted him to touch them, for his safe passage through some of the worst scenes of carnage had not gone unnoticed. He touched them and, when they wanted, said a prayer.

Afterwards he went up on deck. There was a fair breeze from the southwest, and the ship rocked ever so gently on the tide. For the first time in a week the air was not suffused red: Manuel could see stars, and distant bonfires on the Flemish shore, like stars that had fallen and now burnt out their life on the land.

Laeghr was limping up and down amidship, detouring from his usual path to avoid a bit of shattered decking.

'Are you hurt, Laeghr?' Manuel inquired.

For answer Laeghr growled. Manuel walked beside him. After a bit Laeghr stopped and said, 'They're saying you're a holy man now because you were running all over the deck these last few days, acting like the shot we were taking was hail and never getting hit for it. But I say you're just too foolish to know any better. Fools dance where angels would hide. It's part of the curse laid on us. Those who learn the rules and play things right end up getting hurt —sometimes from doing just the things that will protect them the most. While the blind fools who wander right into the thick of things are never touched.'

Manuel watched Laeghr's stride. 'Your foot?'

Laeghr shrugged. 'I don't know what will happen to it.'

Under a lantern Manuel stopped and looked Laeghr in the eye. 'Saint Anna appeared and plucked a cannonball that was heading for me right out of the sky. She saved my life for a purpose.'

'No.' Laeghr thumped his cane on the deck. 'Your fever has made you mad, boy.'

'I can show you the shot!' Manuel said. 'It stuck in the hull!' Laeghr stumped away.

Manuel looked across the water at Flanders, distressed by Laeghr's words, and by his hobbled walk. He saw something he didn't comprehend.

'Laeghr?'

'What?' came Laeghr's voice from across midships.

'Something bright . . . the souls of all the English at once, maybe. . . .' his voice shook.

'*What?*'

'Something coming at us. Come here, master.'

Thump, thump, thump. Manuel heard the hiss of Laeghr's indrawn breath, the muttered curse.

'*Fireships,*' Laeghr bellowed at the top of his lungs. 'Fireships! Awake!'

In a minute the ship was bedlam, soldiers running everywhere. 'Come with me,' Laeghr told Manuel, who followed the sailing master to the forecastle, where the anchor hawser descended into the water. Somewhere along the way Laeghr had gotten a halberd, and he gave it to Manuel. 'Cut the line.'

'But master, we'll lose the anchor.'

'Those fireships are too big to stop, and if they're hellburners they explode and kill us all. Cut it.'

Manuel began chopping at the thick hawser, which was very like the trunk of a small tree. He chopped and chopped, but only one strand of the huge rope was cut when Laeghr seized the halberd and began chopping himself, awkwardly to avoid putting his weight on his bad foot. They heard the voice of the ship's captain—'Cut the anchor cable!'—and Laeghr laughed.

The rope snapped, and they were floating free. But the fireships were right behind them. In the hellish light Manuel could see English sailors walking on their burning decks, passing through the flames like salamanders or demons. No doubt they were devils. The fires towering above the eight fireships shared the demonic life of the English; each tongue of yellow flame contained an English demon eye looking for the Armada, and some of these leaped free of the blaze that twisted above the fireships, in vain attempts to float onto *La Lavia* and incinerate it.

Manuel held off these embers with his wooden medallion, and the gesture that in his boyhood in Sicily had warded off the evil eye. Meanwhile the ships of the fleet were cut loose and drifting on the tide, colliding in the rush to avoid the fireships. Captains and officers screamed furiously at their colleagues on other ships, but to no avail. In the dark and without anchors, the ships could not be regathered, and as the night progressed most were blown out into the North Sea. For the first time the neat phalanxes of the Armada were broken, and they were never to be reformed again.

When it was all over *La Lavia* held its position in the North Sea by sail, while the officers attempted to identify the ships around them, and to find out what Medina Sidonia's orders were. Manuel and Juan stood amidships with the rest of their berthmates. Juan shook his head. 'I used to make corks in Portugal. We were like a cork back there in the Channel, being pushed into the neck of a bottle. As long as we were stuck in the neck we were all right—the neck got narrower and narrower, and they might never have gotten us out. Now the English have pushed us right down into the bottle itself. We're floating about in our own dregs. And we'll never get out of the bottle again.'

'Not through the neck, anyway,' one of the others agreed.

'Not any way.'

'God will see us home,' Manuel said.
Juan shook his head.

Rather than try to force the Channel, Admiral Medina Sidonia decided that the Armada should sail around Scotland, and then home. Laeghr was taken to the flagship for a day to help chart a course, for he was familiar with the north as none of the Spanish pilots were.

The battered fleet headed away from the sun, ever higher into the cold North Sea. After the night of the fireships Medina Sidonia had restored discipline with a vengeance. One day the survivors of the many Channel battles were witness to the hanging from the yardarm of a captain who let his ship get ahead of the admiral's flagship, a position which was now forbidden. A carrack sailed through the fleet again and again so every crew could see the corpse of the disobedient captain, swinging freely from its spar.

Manuel observed the sight with distaste. Once dead, a man was only a bag of bones; nowhere in the clouds overhead could he spot the captain's soul. Perhaps it had plummeted into the sea, on its way to hell. It was an odd transition, death. Curious that God did not make more explicit the aftermath.

So *La Lavia* faithfully trailed the admiral's flagship, as did the rest of the fleet. They were led farther and farther north, into the domain of cold. Some mornings when they came on deck in the raw yellow of dawn the riggings would be rimed with icicles, so that they seemed strings of diamonds. Some days it seemed they sailed across a sea of milk, under a silver sky. Other days the ocean was the color of a bruise, and the sky a fresh pale blue so clear that Manuel gasped with the desire to survive this voyage and live. Yet he was as cold as death. He remembered the burning nights of his fever as fondly as if he were remembering his first home on the coast of North Africa.

All the men were suffering from the cold. The livestock was dead, so the galley closed down: no hot soup. The admiral imposed rationing on everyone, including himself; the deprivation kept him in his bed for the rest of the voyage. For the sailors, who had to haul wet or frozen rope, it was worse. Manuel watched the grim faces, in line for their two biscuits and one large cup of wine and water —their daily ration—and concluded that they would continue sailing north until the sun was under the horizon and they were in the icy realm of death, the north pole where God's dominion was weak, and there they would give up and die all at once. Indeed, the winds drove them nearly to Norway, and it was with great difficulty that they brought the shot-peppered hulks around to a westerly heading.

When they did, they discovered a score of new leaks in *La Lavia's* hull, and the men, already exhausted by the effort of bringing the ship about, were forced to man the pumps around the clock. A pint of wine and a pint of water a day were not enough. Men died. Dysentery, colds, the slightest injury: all were quickly fatal.

Once again Manuel could see the air. Now it was a thick blue, distinctly darker when men breathed it out, so that they all were shrouded in dark blue air that obscured the burning crowns of their souls. All of the wounded men in the hospital had died. Many of them had called for Manuel in their last moments; he held their hands or touched their heads, and as their souls had flickered away from their heads like the last pops of flame out of coals of a dying fire, he had prayed for them. Now other men too weak to leave their berths called for him, and he went and stood by them in their distress. Two of these men recovered from dysentery, so his presence was requested even more frequently. The captain himself asked for Manuel's touch when he fell sick; but he died anyway, like most of the rest.

One morning Manuel was standing with Laeghr at the midships bulkhead. It was chill and cloudy, the sea the color of flint. The soldiers were bringing their horses up and forcing them over the side, to save water.

'That should have been done as soon as we were forced out of the Sleeve,' Laeghr said. 'Waste of water.'

'I didn't even know we had horses aboard,' Manuel said.

Laeghr laughed briefly. 'Boy, you are a prize of a fool. One surprise after another.'

They watched the horses' awkward falls, their rolling eyes, their flared nostrils expelling clouds of blue air. Their brief attempts to swim.

'On the other hand, we should probably be eating some of those,' Laeghr said.

'Horsemeat?'

'It can't be that bad.'

The horses all disappeared, exchanging blue air for flint water. 'It's cruel,' Manuel said.

'In the horse latitudes they swim for an hour,' Laeghr said. 'This is better.' He pointed to the west. 'See those tall clouds?'

'Yes.'

'They stand over the Orkneys. The Orkneys or the Shetlands, I can't be sure any more. It will be interesting to see if these fools can get this wreck through the islands safely.' Looking around, Manuel could spot only a dozen or so ships; presumably, the rest of the Armada lay over the horizon ahead of them. He stopped to wonder about what Laeghr had just said, for it would naturally be Laeghr's task to navigate them through the northernmost of the British Isles; at that very moment Laeghr's eyes rolled like the horses' had, and he collapsed on the deck. Manuel and some other sailors carried him down to the hospital.

'It's his foot,' said Friar Lucien. 'His foot is crushed and his leg has putrefied. He should have let me amputate.'

Around noon Laeghr regained consciousness. Manuel, who had not left his side, held his hand, but Laeghr frowned and pulled it away.

'Listen,' Laeghr said with difficulty. His soul was no more than a blue cap covering his tangled salt-and-pepper hair. 'I'm going to teach you some words that may be useful to you later.' Slowly he said, *'Tor conaloc an dhia,'* and Manuel repeated it. 'Say it again.' Manuel repeated the syllables over and over, like a Latin prayer. Laeghr nodded. *'Tor conaloc an naom dhia.* Good. Remember the words always.' After that he stared at the deckbeams above, and would answer none of Manuel's questions. Emotions played over his face like shadows, one after another. Finally he took his gaze from the infinite and looked at Manuel. 'Touch me, boy.'

Manuel touched his forehead, and with a sardonic smile Laeghr closed his eyes: his blue crown of flames flickered up through the deck above and disappeared.

They buried him that evening, in a smoky, hellish brown sunset. Friar Lucien said the shortened Mass, mumbling in a voice that no one could hear, and Manuel pressed the back of his medallion against the cold flesh of Laeghr's arm, until the impression of the cross remained. Then they tossed him overboard. Manuel watched with a serenity that surprised him. Just weeks ago he had shouted with rage and pain as his companions had been torn apart; now he watched with a peace he did not understand as the man who had taught him and protected him sank into the iron water and disappeared.

A couple of nights after that Manuel sat apart from his remaining berthmates, who slept in one pile like a litter of kittens. He watched the blue flames wandering over the exhausted flesh, watched without reason or feeling. He was tired.

Friar Lucien looked in the narrow doorway and hissed. 'Manuel! Are you there?'

'I'm here.'

'Come with me.'

Manuel got up and followed him. 'Where are we going?'

Friar Lucien shook his head. 'It's time.' Everything else he said was in Greek. He had a little candle lantern with three sides shuttered, and by its illumination they made their way to the hatch that led to the lower decks.

Manuel's berth, though it was below the gun deck, was not on the lowest deck of the ship. *La Lavia* was very much bigger than that. Below the berth deck were three more decks that had no ports, as they were beneath the waterline. Here in perpetual gloom were stored the barrels of water and biscuit, the cannonballs and rope and other supplies. They passed by the powder room, where the armorer wore felt slippers so that a spark from his boots might not blow up the ship. They found a hatchway that held a ladder leading to an even lower deck. At each level the passages became narrower, and they were forced to stoop.

Manuel was astounded when they descended yet again, for he would have imagined them already on the keel, or in some strange chamber suspended beneath it; but Lucien knew better. Down they went, through a labyrinth of dank black wooden passageways. Manuel was long lost, and held Lucien's arm for fear of being separated from him, and becoming hopelessly trapped in the bowels of the ship. Finally they came to a door that made their narrow hallway a dead end. Lucien rapped on the door and hissed something, and the door opened, letting out enough light to dazzle Manuel.

After the passageways, the chamber they entered seemed very large. It was the cable tier, located in the bow of the ship just over the keel. Since the encounter with the fireships, *La Lavia* had little cable, and what was left lay in the corners of the room. Now it was lit by candles, set in small iron candelabra that had been nailed to the side beams. The floor was covered by an inch of water, which reflected each of the candle flames as a small spot of white light. The curving walls dripped and gleamed. In the center of the room a box had been set on end, and covered with a bit of cloth. Around the box stood several men: a soldier, one of the petty officers, and some sailors Manuel knew only by sight. The transparent knots of cobalt flame on their heads added a bluish cast to the light in the room.

'We're ready, Father,' one of the men said to Lucien. The friar led Manuel to a spot near the upturned box, and the others arranged themselves in a circle around him. Against the aft wall, near gaps where floor met wall imperfectly, Manuel spotted two big rats with shiny brown fur, all ablink and twitch-whiskered at the unusual activity. Manuel frowned and one of the rats plopped into the water covering the floor and swam under the wall, its tail swishing back and forth like a small snake, revealing to Manuel its true nature. The other rat stood its ground and blinked its bright little round eyes as it brazenly returned Manuel's unwelcoming gaze.

From behind the box Lucien looked at each man in turn, and read in Latin. Manuel understood the first part: 'I believe in God the Father Almighty, maker of heaven and earth, and of all things visible and invisible. . . .' From there Lucien read on, in a voice powerful yet soothing, entreatful yet proud. After finishing the creed he took up another book, the little one he always carried with him, and read in Spanish:

' "Know ye, O Israel, that what men call life and death are as beads of white and black strung upon a thread; and this thread of perpetual change is mine own changeless life, which bindeth together the unending string of little lives and little deaths.

' "The wind turns a ship from its course upon the deep: the wandering winds of the senses cast man's mind adrift on the deep.

' "But lo! That day shall come when the light that *is* shall still all winds, and bind every hideous liquid darkness; and all thy habitations shall be blest by the white brilliance which descendeth from the crown." '

While Lucien read this, the soldier moved slowly about the chamber. First he set on the top of the box a plate of sliced biscuit; the bread was hard, as it became after months at sea, and someone had taken the trouble to cut slices, and then polish them into wafers so thin that they were translucent, and the color of honey. Occasional wormholes gave them the look of old coins that had been beaten flat and holed for use as jewelry.

Next the soldier brought forth from behind the box an empty glass bottle, with its top cut off so that it was a sort of bowl. Taking the flask in his other hand, he filled the bowl to the midway point with *La Lavia's* awful wine. Putting the flask down, he circled the group while the friar finished reading. Every man there had cuts on his hands that more or less continuously leaked blood, and each man pulled a cut open over the bottle held to him, allowing a drop to splash in, until the wine was so dark that to Manuel, aware of the blue light, it was a deep violet.

The soldier replaced the bottle beside the plate of wafers on the box. Friar Lucien finished his reading, looked at the box, and recited one final sentence: 'O, lamps of fire! make bright the deep caverns of sense; with strange brightness give heat and light together to your beloved, that we may be one with you.' Taking the plate in hand, he circled the chamber, putting a wafer in the mouths of the men. 'The body of Christ, given for you. The body of Christ, given for you.'

Manuel snapped the wafer of biscuit between his teeth and chewed it. At last he understood what they were doing. This was a communion for the dead: a service for Laeghr, a service for all of them, for they were all doomed. Beyond the damp curved wall of their chamber was the deep sea, pressing against the timbers, pressing in on them. Eventually they would all be swallowed, and would sink down to become food for the fishes, after which their bones would decorate the floor of the ocean, where God seldom visited. Manuel could scarcely get the chewed biscuit past the lump in his throat. When Friar Lucien lifted the half-bottle and put it to his lips, saying first, 'The blood of Christ, shed for you,' Manuel stopped him. He took the friar's hand. The soldier stepped forward, but Lucien waved him away. The friar kneeled before Manuel and crossed himself, but backwards as Greeks did, left to right rather than the proper way.

Manuel said, 'You are the blood of Christ,' and held the half-bottle to Lucien's lips, tilting it so he could drink.

He did the same for each of the men, the soldier included. 'You are the Christ.' This was the first time any of them had partaken of this part of the communion, and some of them could barely swallow. When they had all drunk, Manuel put the bottle to his lips and drained it to the dregs. 'Friar Lucien's book says, all they habitations shall be blest by the white brilliance that is the crown of fire, and we shall all be made the Christ. And so it is. We drank, and now we are the Christ. See'—he pointed at the remaining rat, which was now on its hind legs, washing its forepaws so that it appeared to pray, its bright round eyes fixed on Manuel—'even the beasts know it.' He broke off a piece of biscuit wafer, and leaned down to offer it to the rat. The rat accepted the fragment in its paws, and ate it. It submitted to Manuel's touch.

Standing back up, Manuel felt the blood rush to his head. The crowns of fire blazed on every head, reaching far above them to lick the beams of the ceiling, filling the room with light—'He is here!' Manuel cried, 'He has touched us with light, see it!' He touched each of their foreheads in turn, and saw their eyes widen as they perceived the others' burning souls in wonder, pointing at each other's heads; then they were all embracing in the clear white light, hugging one another with the tears running down their cheeks and giant grins splitting their beards. Reflected candlelight danced in a thousand parts on the watery floor. The rat, startled, splashed under the gap in the wall, and they laughed and laughed and laughed.

Manuel put his arm around the friar, whose eyes shone with joy. 'It is good,' Manuel said when they were all quiet again. 'God will see us home.'

They made their way back to the upper decks like boys playing in a cave they know very well.

The Armada made it through the Orkneys without Laeghr, though it was a close thing for some ships. Then they were out in the North Atlantic, where the swells were broader, their troughs deeper, and their tops as high as the castles of *La Lavia*, and then higher than that.

Winds came out of the southwest, bitter gales that never ceased, and three weeks later they were no closer to Spain than they had been when they slipped through the Orkneys. The situation on *La Lavia* was desperate, as it was all through the fleet. Men on *La Lavia* died every day, and were thrown overboard with no ceremony except the impression of Manuel's medallion into their arms. The deaths made the food and water shortage less acute, but it was still serious. *La Lavia* was now manned by a ghost crew, composed mostly of soldiers. There weren't enough of them to properly man the pumps, and the Atlantic was springing new leaks every day in the already broken hull. The ship began taking on water in such quantities that the acting captain of the ship—who had started the voyage as third mate—decided that they must make straight for Spain, making no spare leeway for the imperfectly known west coast of Ireland.

This decision was shared by the captains of several other damaged ships, and they conveyed their decision to the main body of the fleet, which was reaching farther west before turning south to Spain. From his sickbed Medina Sidonia gave his consent, and *La Lavia* sailed due south.

Unfortunately, a storm struck from just north of west soon after they had turned homeward. They were helpless before it. *La Lavia* wallowed in the troughs and was slammed by crest after crest, until the poor hulk lay just off the lee shore, Ireland.

It was the end, and everyone knew it. Manuel knew it because the air had turned black. The clouds were like thousands of black English cannonballs, rolling ten deep over a clear floor set just above the masts, and spitting lightning into the sea whenever two of them banged together hard enough. The air beneath them was black as well, just less thick: the wind as tangible as the waves, and swirling around the masts with smoky fury. Other men caught glimpses of the lee shore, but Manuel couldn't see it for the blackness. These men called out in fear; apparently the western coast of Ireland was sheer cliff. It was the end.

Manuel had nothing but admiration for the third-mate-now-captain, who took the helm and shouted to the lookout in the top to find a bay in the cliffs they were drifting towards. But Manuel, like many of the men, ignored the mate's commands to stay at post, as they were clearly pointless. Men embraced each other on the castles, saying their farewells; others cowered in fear against the bulkheads. Many of them approached Manuel and asked for a touch, and Manuel brushed their foreheads as he angrily marched about the forecastle. As soon as Manuel touched them, some of the men flew directly up toward heaven while others dove over the side of the ship and became porpoises the moment they struck the water. But Manuel scarcely noticed these occurrences, as he was busy praying, praying at the top of his lungs.

'*Why* this storm, Lord, *why?* First there were winds from the north holding us back, which is the only reason I'm here in the first place. So you wanted me here, but why why why? Juan is dead and Laeghr is dead and Pietro is dead and Habedeen is dead and soon we will all be dead, and why? It isn't just. You promised you would take us home.' In a fury, he took his slowmatch knife, climbed down to the swamped midships, and went to the mainmast. He thrust the knife deep into the wood, stabbing with the grain. 'There! I say *that* to your storm!'

'Now, that's blasphemy,' Laeghr said as he pulled the knife from the mast and threw it over the side. 'You know what stabbing the mast means. To do it in a storm like this—you'll offend gods a lot older than Jesus, and more powerful, too.'

'Talk about blasphemy,' Manuel replied. 'And you wonder why you're still wandering the seas a ghost, when you say things like that. You should take more care.' He looked up and saw Saint Anne, in the maintop giving directions to the third mate. 'Did you hear what Laeghr said?' he shouted up to her. She didn't hear him.

'Do you remember the words I taught you?' Laeghr inquired.

'Of course. Don't bother me now. Laeghr; I'll be a ghost with you soon enough.' Laeghr stepped back, but Manuel changed his mind, and said, 'Laeghr, why are we being punished like this? We were on a crusade for God, weren't we? I don't understand.'

Laeghr smiled and turned around, and Manuel saw then that he had wings, wings with feathers intensely white in the black murk of the air. He clasped Manuel's arm. 'You know all that I know.' With some hard flaps he was off, tumbling east swiftly in the black air, like a gull.

With the help of Saint Anne the third mate had actually found a break in the cliffs, a quite considerable bay. Other ships of the Armada had found it as well, and they were already cracking up on a wide beach as *La Lavia* limped near shore. The keel grounded and immediately things began breaking. Soupy waves crashed over the canted midships, and Manuel leaped up the ladder to the forecastle, which was now under a tangle of rigging from the broken foremast. The mainmast went over the side, and the lee flank of the ship splintered like a match tub and flooded, right before their eyes.

Among the floating timbers Manuel saw one that held a black cannonball embedded in it, undoubtedly the very one that Saint Anne had deflected from its course toward him. Reminded that she had saved his life before, Manuel grew calmer and waited for her to appear. The beach was only a few ship-lengths away, scarcely visible in the thick air; like most of the men, Manuel could not swim, and he was searching with some urgency for a sight of Saint Anne when Friar Lucien appeared at his side, in his black robes. Over the shriek of the dark wind Lucien shouted, 'If we hold on to a plank we'll float ashore.'

'You go ahead,' Manuel shouted back. 'I'm waiting for Saint Anna.' The friar shrugged. The wind caught his robes and Manuel saw that Lucien was attempting to save the ship's liturgical gold, which was in the form of chains that were now wrapped around the friar's middle. Lucien made his way to the rail and jumped over it, onto a spar that a wave was carrying away from the ship. He missed his hold on the rounded spar, however, and sank instantly.

The forecastle was now awash, and soon the foaming breakers would tear it loose from the keel. Most of the men had already left the wreck, trusting to one bit of flotsam or other. But Manuel still waited. Just as he was beginning to worry he saw the blessed grandmother of God, standing among figures on the beach that he perceived but dimly, gesturing to him. She walked out onto the white water, and he understood. 'We are the Christ, of course! I will walk to shore as He once did.' He tested the surface with one shoe; it seemed a little, well, infirm, but surely it would serve—it would be like the floor of their now-demolished chapel, a sheet of water covering one of God's good solids. So Manuel walked out onto the next wave that passed at the level of the forecastle, and plunged deep into the brine.

'Hey!' he spluttered as he struggled back to the surface. 'Hey!' No answer from Saint Anne this time; just cold salt water. He began the laborious process of drowning, remembering as he struggled a time when he was a child, and his father had taken him down to the beach in Morocco, to see the galley of the pilgrims to Mecca rowing away. Nothing could have been less like the Irish coast than that serene, hot, tawny beach, and he and his father had gone out into the shallows to splash around in the warm water, chasing lemons. His father would toss the lemons out into the deeper water, where they bobbed just under the surface, and then Manuel would paddle out to retrieve them, laughing and choking on water.

Manuel could picture those lemons perfectly, as he snorted and coughed and thrashed to get his head back above the freezing soup one more time. Lemons bobbing in the green sea, lemons oblong and bumpy, the color of the sun when the sun is its own width above the horizon at dawn . . . bobbing gently just under the surface, with a knob showing here and there. Manuel pretended he was a lemon, at the same time that he tried to remember the primitive dogpaddle that had gotten him around the shallows. Arms, pushing downward. It wasn't working. Waves tumbled him, lemonlike, in towards the strand. He bumped on the bottom and stood up. The water was only waist deep. Another wave smashed him from behind and he couldn't find the bottom again. Not fair! he thought. His elbow ran into sand, and he twisted around and stood. Knee deep, this time. He kept an eye on the treacherous waves as they came out of the black, and trudged through them up to a beach made of coarse sand, covered by a mat of loose seaweed.

Down on the beach a distance were sailors, companions, survivors of the wrecks offshore. But there among them—soldiers on horses. English soldiers, on horses and on foot—Manuel groaned to see it—wielding swords and clubs on exhausted men strewn across the seaweed. 'No!' Manuel cried, 'No!' But it was true. 'Ah, God,' he said, and sank till he was sitting. Down the strand soldiers clubbed his brothers, splitting their fragile eggshell skulls so that the yolk of their brains ran into the kelp.

Manuel beat his insensible fists against the sand. Filled with horror at the sight, he watched horses rear in the murk, giant and shadowy. They were coming down the beach towards him. 'I'll make myself invisible,' he decided. 'Saint Anna will make me invisible.' But remembering his plan to walk on the water, he determined to help the miracle, by staggering up the beach and burrowing under a particularly tall pile of seaweed. He was invisible without it, of course, but the cover of kelp would help keep him warm. Thinking such thoughts, he shivered and shivered and on the still land fell insensible as his hands.

When he woke up, the soldiers were gone. His fellows lay up and down the beach like white driftwood; ravens and wolves already converged on them. He couldn't move very well. It took him half an hour to move his head to survey the beach, and another half hour to free himself from his pile of seaweed. And then he had to lie down again.

When he regained consciousness, he found himself behind a large log, an old piece of driftwood that had been polished silver by its years of rolling in the sand. The air was clear again. He could feel it filling him and leaving him, but he could no longer see it. The sun was out; it was morning, and the storm was over. Each movement of Manuel's body was a complete effort, a complete experience. He could see quite deeply into his skin, which appeared pickled. He had lost all of his clothes, except for a tattered shred of trousers around his middle. With all his will he made his arm move his hand, and with his stiff forefinger he touched the driftwood. He could feel it. He was still alive.

His hand fell away in the sand. The wood touched by his finger was changing, becoming a bright green spot in the surrounding silver. A thin green sprig bulged from the spot, and grew up toward the sun; leaves unfolded from this sprout as it thickened, and beneath Manuel's fascinated gaze a bud appeared and burst open: a white rose, gleaming wetly in the white morning light.

He had managed to stand, and cover himself with kelp, and walk a full quarter of a mile inland, when he came upon people. Three of them, to be exact, two men and a woman. Wilder-looking people Manuel couldn't imagine: the men had beards that had never been cut, and arms like Laeghr's. The woman looked exactly like his miniature portrait of Saint Anne, until she got closer and he saw that she was dirty and her teeth were broken and her skin was brindled like a dog's belly. He had never seen such freckling before, and he stared at it, and her, every bit as much as she and her companions stared at him. He was afraid of them.

'Hide me from the English, please,' he said. At the word *English* the men frowned and cocked their heads. They jabbered at him in a tongue he did not know. 'Help me,' he said. 'I don't know what you're saying. Help me.' He tried Spanish and Portuguese and Sicilian and Arabic. The men were looking angry. He tried Latin, and they stepped back. 'I believe in God the Father Almighty, Maker of Heaven and Earth, and in all things visible and invisible.' He laughed, a bit hysterically. 'Especially invisible.' He grabbed his medallion and showed them the cross. They studied him, clearly at a loss.

'*Tor conaloc an dhia*,' he said without thinking. All four of them jumped. Then the two men moved to his sides to hold him steady. They chattered at him, waving their free arms. The woman smiled, and Manuel saw that she was young. He said the syllables again, and they chattered some more. 'Thank you, Laeghr,' he said. 'Thank you, Anna. Anna,' he said to the girl, and reached for her. She squealed and stepped back. He said the phrase again. The men lifted him, for he could no longer walk, and carried him across the heather. He smiled and kissed both men on the cheek, which made them laugh, and he said the magic phrase again and started to fall asleep and said the phrase. *Tor conaloc an dhia.* The girl brushed his wet hair out of his eyes; Manuel recognized the touch, and he could feel the flowering begin inside him.

Give mercy for God's sake.

ACKNOWLEDGMENTS

The publishers would like to thank the following authors, publishers and others for their permission to reproduce the copyright material included in this volume:

FAR FROM HOME by Walter S. Trevis. Copyright © 1958 by Mercury Press, Inc. Copyright renewed 1985 by The Walter Tevis Copyright Trust. By permission of The Walter Tevis Copyright Trust. MY DEAR EMILY by Joanna Russ. Copyright © 1962 by Mercury Press, Inc. By permission of the author. THE MAN WHO PAINTED THE DRAGON GRIAULE by Lucius Shepard. Copyright © 1984 by Mercury Press, Inc. By permission of the author. THE VANISHING AMERICAN by Charles Beaumont. Copyright © 1955 by Fantasy House, Inc. Copyright renewed 1983 by Mercury Press, Inc. By permission of Don Congdon Associates. THE CLOUD-SCULPTORS OF CORAL D by J.G. Ballard. Copyright ©1967 by Mercury Press, Inc. By permission of the author. INVASION OF THE CHURCH OF THE HOLY GHOST by Russell Kirk. Copyright ©1983 by Mercury Press, Inc. By permission of the author and his agent, Kirby McCauley. THE ACCOUNTANT by Robert Sheckley. Copyright © 1954 by Fantasy House, Inc. Copyright renewed 1982 by Mercury Press, Inc. By permission of the author. THE FIRE WHEN IT COMES by Parke Godwin. Copyright © 1981 by Mercury Press, Inc. By permission of the author. MY BOY FRIEND'S NAME IS JELLO by Avram Davidson. Copyright © 1954 by Fantasy House Inc. Copyright renewed 1982 by Mercury Press, Inc. By permission of the author. SAN DIEGO LIGHTFOOT SUE by Tom Reamy. Copyright © 1975 by Mercury Press Inc. By permission of Virginia Kidd. SOONER OR LATER OR NEVER, NEVER by Gary Jennings. Copyright © 1972 by Mercury Press, Inc. By permission of the author. JEFFTY IS FIVE by Harlan Ellison. Copyright © 1977 by Harlan Ellison. By permission of the author. THE THIRD LEVEL by Jack Finney. Copyright © 1950 by Jack Finney. Copyright renewed 1977. By permission of the author's agent, Don Congdon Associates. THE SILKEN SWIFT by Theodore Sturgeon. Copyright © 1953 by Fantasy House, Inc. Copyright renewed 1981 by Mercury Press, Inc. By permission of the author. ANOTHER ORPHAN by John Kessel. Copyright © 1982 by Mercury Press, Inc. By permission of the author. THE MANOR OF ROSES by Thomas Burnett Swann. Copyright ©